THE INFERNAL BATTALION

ALSO BY DJANGO WEXLER

THE SHADOW CAMPAIGNS

THE FORBIDDEN LIBRARY NOVELS

The Infernal Battalion

BOOK FIVE OF THE SHADOW CAMPAIGNS

Django Wexler

ACE
NEW YORK

ACE
Published by Berkley
An imprint of Penguin Random House LLC
375 Hudson Street, New York, New York 10014

Copyright © 2018 by Django Wexler
Penguin Random House supports copyright. Copyright fuels creativity, encourages diverse
voices, promotes free speech, and creates a vibrant culture. Thank you for buying an authorized
edition of this book and for complying with copyright laws by not reproducing, scanning, or
distributing any part of it in any form without permission. You are supporting writers and
allowing Penguin Random House to continue to publish books for every reader.

ACE is a registered trademark and the A colophon is a trademark of
Penguin Random House LLC.

Library of Congress Cataloging-in-Publication Data

Names: Wexler, Django, author.
Title: The infernal battalion/Django Wexler.
Description: First Edition. | New York: Ace, 2018. | Series: Shadow campaigns; book 5
Identifiers: LCCN 2017030626 (print) | LCCN 2017033326 (ebook) | ISBN 9780698409477
(ebook) | ISBN 9780451477347 (hardback)
Subjects: LCSH: Imaginary wars and battles—Fiction. | BISAC: FICTION/Fantasy/Epic. |
FICTION/Fantasy/Historical. | GSAFD: Fantasy fiction. | War stories.
Classification: LCC PS3623.E94 (ebook) | LCC PS3623.E94 I54 2018 (print) |
DDC 813/.6—dc23
LC record available at https://lccn.loc.gov/2017030626

First Edition: January 2018

Printed in the United States of America
1   3   5   7   9   10   8   6   4   2

Jacket illustration by Paul Youll
Jacket design by Adam Auerbach
Map illustration by Cortney Skinner

Once again,
for Mom and Dad

ACKNOWLEDGMENTS

Sometime around the end of 2011, I wrote the outline for The Shadow Campaigns, although it had not yet acquired that title. Looking back at it, I'm actually surprised how little has changed. A few plot points got dropped or altered, a few characters added or combined, but overall we've arrived, after five books and a million words, at roughly the place I envisioned when we started. This feels incomparably strange to me; I have never done anything remotely like it before. (Though, gods and publishers willing, I certainly hope to again.)

To list everyone I owe thanks to for this series would require (as a wit on Twitter suggested) *a thousand names*, so this will have to be something of an abridged version. For the original inspiration, there's George R. R. Martin's *A Song of Ice and Fire*, S. M. Stirling and David Drake's *The General*, David Chandler's *The Campaigns of Napoleon*, and Simon Schama's *Citizens*. For introducing me to good history writing in general and the latter two in particular, Neal Altman, Jim Naughton, and the rest of my Pittsburgh war-gaming crew.

My agent, Seth Fishman, I can never thank enough. While he's done (and continues to do) a fantastic job with all my books, *this* was the series he plucked out of the slush pile, helped me polish, and sold when I had no credits to my name. That is, quite literally, a once-in-a-lifetime service. My thanks as well to everyone at the Gernert Company: Will Roberts, Rebecca Gardner, and Jack Gernert, as well as Caspian Dennis in the UK.

My editor Jess Wade has been a joy to work with throughout. Many wonderful touches in the books can be credited to her, and many plot problems and awkward moments were slain by her intervention. Thanks as well to editorial director Claire Zion and editorial assistant Miranda Hill. For the first three books, Jess was joined by the excellent Michael Rowley in the UK, who in addition to his sterling editorial work played tour guide to this clueless American tourist in London.

For this volume, my beta readers were Rhiannon Held and M. L. Brennan, who have my eternal gratitude. Casey Blair, as always, provided invaluable assistance working through thorny plot and character problems. All three are wonderful writers, and you should go and read their work at once.

As always, I want to thank everyone at Ace. There's so much work involved in turning my Word file full of red squiggles into the book you're holding, and the people who do it never get enough credit.

Finally, of course, my thanks to the readers across the world. None of this would exist without you.

THE INFERNAL BATTALION

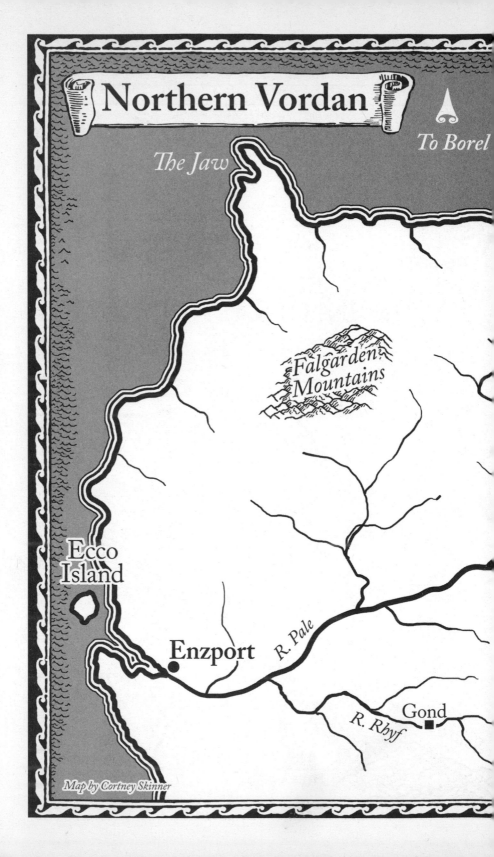

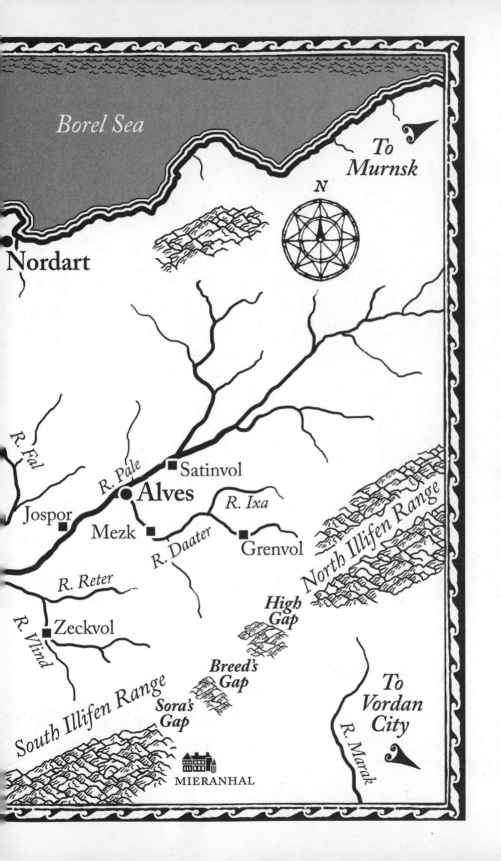

PROLOGUE

THE BEAST

How to describe a mind seen from the inside? Metaphor is a weak reed, but metaphor is all we have. And so—

The mind of the Beast was a hurricane.

In the center was the Beast's core, a pulsing, writhing mass of tightly webbed darkness. It was surrounded by a wind that screamed through the non-space, smearing out streamers and tendrils of darkness into a ragged accretion disk. These were the shredded, broken shards of minds absorbed by the Beast, moments torn from lives and thoughts ripped into a tangle, whirling around and around the core in a terminal spiral. When they finally impacted, reduced to their most elemental pieces, the Beast absorbed them into its bulk and so grew ever larger.

Beyond the frenetic violence of the center was a calmer interval, where the winds were not quite as strong. Here the minds were left in larger fragments— a child wailing in terror, a soldier cowering during a cannonade, a young woman embracing her lover. Memories repeating over and over, echoes of the people they'd once been. A few even larger pieces were aware enough to perceive their surroundings, shouting desperate questions or threats into the uncaring mindscape.

New minds popped into being at the periphery, as in the real world the Beast continued to spread, taking body after body. They were tiny hurricanes in their own right, dust devils spinning inside the greater gale. For the most part, they didn't last long. Few minds had the necessary strength of will to adapt to this strange environment, to hold themselves together against the pull of the Beast. Eventually, they lost their sense of self and tore apart, to be drawn into the core and devoured.

Far below—if that term had any meaning here—was an unfathomably complex network of silver lines, shimmering with coruscating bolts of lightning. These were the bodies of the Beast, viewed from the inside. Separated, but always connected *here*, laid bare before the demon's controlling intelligence.

It would not be correct to say that the Beast moved through the mindscape, because the mindscape *was* the Beast. But its focus of attention could flit at will from the core to the periphery, down to the network of bodies and out through their senses into the real world. The demon reveled in the freedom, the sense of *scale*. It had spent a thousand years crammed into a single body, packed into a space barely big enough for a human mind. Now it blossomed outward like a flower, fueled by the never-ceasing torrent of fresh victims.

Its first flowering, so long ago, had been stunted, incomplete, and ultimately disastrous. But it had been young and foolish then, newly born, ignorant of the human world and its complexities. A thousand years of digesting new minds—even the trickle the Black Priests had allowed it, a fresh one only when the old body died—had made it canny, and it had planned deep. Last time, it had kept its bodies together, and they had all been hunted down. It would not make the same mistake again. Bodies were already being squirreled away, hidden against disaster, so that if worse came to worst, it could always begin anew.

I will not be banished again.

In the process it had, annoyingly, discovered its own limitations. It could ingest new minds only so fast, for example. And its ability to control its bodies was limited by physical distance—too far from the core and they no longer had enough strength to convert fresh bodies, and after a few hundred miles it lost its hold on them entirely, leaving them empty husks. But the larger it grew, the faster it could eat and the farther it could reach. Eventually, every human in the world would be a part of it. It would breed new children, consume them as well, and continue on forever.

I will not be stopped.

Its attention was drawn back to the mindscape, where one of the little hurricanes seemed to be maintaining its shape against the steady pull of the core. That took uncommon determination, and the Beast examined the mind more closely. Its flavor was familiar.

Janus bet Vhalnich. The name sparked a hint of disgust deep in the Beast's center. It felt a brief irritation. That was Jane Verity's emotion, and it had grown far beyond the template her meager mind had imprinted, sloughed her off like a butterfly shedding a cocoon. It wondered how much Jane had influenced the decision to capture Vhalnich in the first place. *He brought knowledge I need, in any event. And a potentially useful body.*

"I'm flattered by the attention." It wasn't speech, as such, but a close equivalent. Janus was addressing the Beast, which would have made it raise an eyebrow, had it possessed one. "Can you understand me?"

"I can." The Beast's voice was like thunder. "I am impressed. Not many can hold on to their sense of self without a body as an anchor."

"I do the best I can," Janus said. The hurricane of his mind wobbled slightly, then settled down again. "It may help that I spent a great deal of time in my own head in any case."

"But I am curious why you persist," the Beast said. "It must be such an effort. Better to let go, dissolve into me, and be done. You cannot put it off forever."

"I can put it off for a little while longer. That's all humans can ever manage, isn't it?"

"I could, of course, destroy you," the Beast said idly. "Tear you to shreds. It would be as easy as dragging a finger through the soap scum in a bath."

"I would rather you did not. You have my body and my knowledge. Perhaps my mind can be useful as well. I am—I was—a general, and you may have need of one."

The Beast laughed, a crackle of warring lightning. "Need, little mind? Do not speak to me of need."

"You must need something," Janus said.

"I will grow," the Beast said. "I will consume. Forever."

"But you have enemies," Janus said. "What can threaten you?"

The Beast's voice dropped to a growl. "The devourer. Infernivore. It must be destroyed." The Beast searched the memories it had accumulated, including Janus' own. "Winter Ihernglass bears it for the moment. She must be killed. And the Thousand Names, where its summoning is recorded, must be destroyed. Then I will be secure."

There was a moment of silence, aside from the ever-present howl of the wind.

"That should be straightforward," Janus said. "Would you care to hear my plan?"

Another flaring, actinic laugh. "You amuse me, little mind. Go on."

"I think," Janus said, "this is where I—that is, my body—may be useful . . ."

PART ONE

CHAPTER ONE

RAESINIA

"Is that all?" Raesinia said.

"Nearly, Your Highness," said the royal dressmaker, a plump, red-faced woman who towered over her diminutive monarch. "One more, if you please. Take a breath and hold it."

Raesinia complied, and the dressmaker whipped a knotted cord around her middle with expert speed. She muttered to herself and tugged it a bit tighter, then looked.

"Wonderful. Thank you, Your Highness. I must say you are very lucky to have such a slender frame. And such beautiful skin! You will look magnificent."

Raesinia caught her own gaze in the mirror over the dressmaker's shoulder and rolled her eyes. Stripped down to her underthings, she could see the truth clearly enough. *I look like a child.* And she always would.

Her unaging state could be inconvenient, but her actual appearance had never really bothered her. It could be useful even—with the right outfit, she could pass for a boy, and political opponents had a persistent tendency to underestimate her. She'd never particularly wanted male attention, though it had occasionally come her way regardless. *Poor Ben, who tried to protect me and died for it.* Now, though . . .

"One in sea green, I think," the dressmaker was saying. "And one in that lovely Hamveltai crimson. I know just the supplier. And then—"

"I leave it entirely in your hands," Raesinia said. "But you must excuse me. There's a great deal of business to attend to."

That was wrong, she realized at once. A queen didn't ask a servant to excuse her. *I should tell her to go.* But politeness had been ground into Raesinia since her earliest education, and now that she was back in the palace, all the old lessons had resurfaced.

"Of course." The dressmaker bowed deeply. "I am honored by your custom, Your Highness."

Joanna opened the door. The large, silent woman and her slim, more talkative partner, Barely, were on permanent detachment from the Girls' Own as Raesinia's personal guards. Their presence had already become a comforting part of her landscape, and it was hard to imagine that she'd once been without them. They'd been part of the group that rescued her from the Penitent Damned and Maurisk's Directory, and they'd stayed at her side through the horrors of the Murnskai campaign. While Joanna was resplendent in a well-tailored blue-and-silver dress uniform, Raesinia had no doubt that the sword and pistol on her belt were extremely functional. Even with Vordan more or less at peace, it was a comforting thought.

"Tell Barely to send the girls in, please," Raesinia said.

Joanna nodded and leaned out the door. She never spoke, but she and her partner had a private language of hand signals that let her make herself understood. Raesinia was resolved to learn it herself someday. *When I have time.*

Someday I'll have all the time in the world.

Two young women in palace livery swept in and went to work, silent and efficient. Raesinia stood stock-still, raising or lowering her arms as required, feeling a bit like an articulated dummy. On campaign with the army, she'd mostly gotten away with reasonably practical riding outfits, and before that she'd still been in official mourning for her father. Now, though, with the echoes of the victory celebrations still fading from the palace and life returning to something like normal, standards had to be maintained. Or so said Mistress Lagovil, the intimidating head of the palace staff, and Raesinia hadn't yet worked up the nerve to argue with her.

One of those standards, apparently, was that the queen couldn't be seen in any outfit that she could possibly don under her own power. Raesinia had pushed for a *little* practicality—she did have work to do, whatever Mistress Lagovil might say—but that still meant yards of lace and silk, carefully matched with rings, bracelets, combs, necklaces, and whatever else could be scrounged from the Royal Jewelhouse. To Raesinia's eyes the final effect was, at best, "sparkly." She'd been raised to appreciate palace fashion, but the lessons had never really sunk in.

Mistress Lagovil had apologized for the sorry state of the wardrobe, and indeed the rest of Ohnlei. The palace had been sacked once by the revolution and again when Janus' army had been quartered there. Furniture had been broken up for firewood and drapes torn apart for uniforms and bandages. Much of the staff was gone, fled or drafted into the army, and only a handful had returned despite the end of the war. The nobles who'd once lent their splendor to the court were still mostly hunkered down at their country estates, waiting to be sure the storm had well and truly passed, and Raesinia couldn't say she blamed them.

At least some of the more tedious rituals had been temporarily suspended. Raesinia could take her meals in her quarters—the Grand Hall had been used to stable cavalry mounts and was still being cleaned out—and there were few dignitaries who required official receptions. No one suggested going hunting. Privately, Raesinia dreaded the day the full splendor of the palace was restored. Before her father's death, her days had been as tightly regulated as a clockmaker's apprentice, jammed with lessons, formal dinners, court outings, and other official occasions.

Once she was dressed, Raesinia took a few tentative steps in front of the mirror, to confirm that she could walk without anything falling off. It wasn't a *bad* dress, really, a deep Vordanai blue accented with silver, flattering to a figure that didn't have much to flatter. Raesinia rolled her eyes at herself again, signaled her approval to the maids, and followed them out into her private chambers.

Eric was waiting for her, practically vibrating with nerves, and Raesinia stifled a sigh. It really wasn't his fault, as he'd been thrust into a job he'd had no preparation for—he'd been a clerk doing the palace accounts until Raesinia had asked Mistress Lagovil for an assistant, and he was still overawed by the royal presence. He was competent enough, but . . .

No but. It's not his fault that he's not Sothe. Every time she saw Eric's tooserious face, struggling to maintain the constipated expression he associated with proper dignity, Raesinia missed her old maidservant. *Maidservant, bodyguard, spy, assassin. Friend.* She'd left, after thwarting Orlanko's assassins on the final night of the Murnskai campaign. *Where are you, Sothe?*

"Your Highness," Eric said. "You look lovely. And the dressmaker has given me her assurances that everything will be ready before—"

Raesinia waved a hand. "I'm sure she'll do fine. What do we have today?"

Eric looked down at the leather notebook he always carried. "The Duke of Brookspring is expecting you in twenty minutes, Your Highness. Then lunch with Mistress Cora, and you agreed to grant an audience to Deputy d'Andorre."

See? I do *have work to do.* Even if it sometimes seemed like everyone wanted her to sit back and ignore it. "We'd better get started, then."

The old Borelgai embassy, a rambling, ancient stone pile at the edge of the palace grounds, had been burned by a mob during the revolution. For now the Borelgai ambassador and his staff had been assigned to a suite in the palace itself. Eric led the way there, through corridors largely deserted except for guards at regular intervals. The soldiers—part of the First Division had the honor today, Raesinia saw—came smartly to attention as she passed. Joanna and Barely, her constant shadows, followed a few steps behind her.

"Did Dorsay say why he wanted to see me?" Raesinia said.

"His Grace did not mention a specific reason," Eric said. "As far as I'm aware, the treaty is progressing well, if slowly."

That was Dorsay's ostensible reason for being in Vordan, the peace treaty that would officially end the war between their two countries. There were a great many details to be ironed out, and in practice the negotiations were conducted between a swarm of bureaucrats from both sides. Trying to understand the actual points of contention made Raesinia's head hurt, but she did her best to keep abreast of the general shape of things. Dorsay didn't even seem to do that, happy to let his underlings do the work. Raesinia suspected he was here more as a reminder than anything else, Borel's greatest living soldier showing the flag to underline the fact that—unlike all her other opponents—Vordan hadn't beaten the Borelgai in open battle.

Two Borelgai Life Guards, their shakos lined with their trademark white fur, stood guard outside the door to the embassy suite. They came to attention as well, and the door opened to reveal the perpetual smile of Ihannes Pulwer-Monsangton, Borel's ambassador to Vordan. If Dorsay was all bluff informality, which Raesinia had come to respect during their time in Murnsk, Ihannes was the opposite, with the oily charm of the professional diplomat. Raesinia presented him with her own best smile and acknowledged his slight bow with a nod.

"Your Highness," he said. "You honor us."

"Ambassador." Raesinia paused when Ihannes didn't move aside.

His smile turned apologetic. "His Grace has asked that this be a *private* meeting."

"Of course." Raesinia gestured for Joanna and Barely to wait. "Eric, find me after my meeting with Mistress Cora."

Ihannes stepped aside, and Raesinia swept past him. The Borelgai suite was elaborately furnished, by the standards of the depleted palace, with furniture and decorations in the severe Borelgai style. More diplomatic posturing, she assumed.

Attua Dorsay, the Duke of Brookspring, was seated at the head of the long table, vigorously applying butter and jam to several slices of toast. Ihannes cleared his throat theatrically, and Dorsay looked up.

"You getting a cough, Ihannes?" he said. The twinkle in his eye made Raesinia certain he was needling the ambassador.

"No, Your Grace." Ihannes stepped aside. "The queen is here."

"I can see that," Dorsay said. He gestured at his plate. "Care for any breakfast, Your Highness?"

"No, thank you," Raesinia said, barely restraining a smile at Ihannes' pained expression.

"Sit down, then. That'll be all, Ihannes."

"Your Grace?" The ambassador's brow furrowed.

"I mean take yourself somewhere else," Dorsay said. "I told you I wanted this to be a private meeting."

Ihannes' expression went even frostier, but he bowed silently and left through an inner door. Dorsay resumed buttering his toast, which was already dripping.

"Butter," he said without much preamble. "You people have always been good at it."

"Thank you, Your Grace," Raesinia said cautiously.

"Butter, cream, cheese, and so on. All in short supply back home, since the war started. Do you know how much of our cheese comes from Vordan?" Before she could answer, he waved a hand. "I didn't, and neither did Georg. Nobody thinks about these things before they start a war."

Georg referred to Georg Pulwer, the King of Borel, with whom Dorsay was apparently on a first-name basis. Raesinia wasn't sure how much of that was bluster and how much was truth. It was always hard to tell with Dorsay.

"It was you who put us under blockade," Raesinia said, keeping her tone light. "If it were up to me, His Majesty could have all the cheese he could eat."

"Which is a shockingly large amount, I can attest." Dorsay crunched into the toast, getting flecks of butter in his bristly mustache. He sat back and sighed with pleasure. "Hells. No beating the real stuff. Back home they try to make something with goat's milk, if you can believe that. Goat's milk! Ha."

"Once the treaty is finished, I'll send a few casks with you, as a going-away present."

"A small price to pay to be rid of me!" Dorsay cackled. "No doubt you'll throw a party to celebrate."

"You'll always be welcome at my court," Raesinia said. "You helped me keep the peace when we might as easily have been at each other's throats."

"And your man d'Ivoire saved my neck from that snake Orlanko," Dorsay said. "I won't forget it, believe me." He finished the toast, wiped his face on a napkin, and turned to look up at her. His famous nose, long and curved, stuck out like the prow of a ship. "That's the spirit in which I asked you here, in fact. Nothing to do with the treaty. Wanted to pass on a bit of private information."

"Oh?" Raesinia hesitated for moment, then pulled a heavy wooden chair from the table and settled herself facing Dorsay. "Information is always appreciated."

"How much are you hearing out of Murnsk?"

"Not a great deal," Raesinia admitted. "They withdrew their ambassador when the war started, and we haven't received any official response to our inquiries since. The Army of the North has pulled back over the border into Vordan."

"I suspected as much. Our forces have pulled out as well, but Borel has significant commercial interest in western Murnsk, and sometimes they pass tidbits along."

Raesinia nodded. Once again, she missed Sothe. Vordan's intelligence service had been largely dismantled in the wake of Orlanko's rebellion, but Sothe had a knack for acquiring information. Raesinia had tasked Alek Giforte with creating something to fill the void left by the Concordat, but that project was still in its infancy.

"Western Murnsk is in chaos," Dorsay went on. "To put it mildly. The bizarre weather has wreaked havoc, and to make matters worse, the northern savages have crossed the Bataria in strength, raiding and burning as they go. I imagine you saw some of that for yourself."

"I did indeed," Raesinia said. Dorsay didn't know that neither event was a coincidence—the summer had turned freezing under the magical influence of the Black Priests, and the Trans-Batariai tribes had come in response to Elysium's call to defeat the approaching Vordanai army. "What is the emperor doing about it?"

"Not a great deal, and that's the part that's odd. There are some strange rumors coming out of Mohkba. Some people are saying the emperor's dead, and others insist that Prince Cesha Dzurk is a traitor and is lying about it to seize the throne."

"Janus smashed at least two sizable Murnskai armies on his way north," Raesinia said. "We heard that the crown prince was killed in the fighting. It wouldn't be a surprise if all that caused some upheaval." She shook her head. "If the harvest was ruined, the whole region must be facing famine. Perhaps we should organize some kind of aid."

"It's not usually the winners of a war who offer help to the losers," Dorsay said, eyes twinkling.

"We were never at war with the people of Murnsk," Raesinia said. "Our quarrel was with Elysium. And the emperor, once he set himself against us."

"Elysium is the crux of it," Dorsay said. "Something very strange has happened there. As best we can tell, much of the Church administration has decamped, legging it for Mohkba and points east as fast as their mules will carry them. No one has gotten close enough to Elysium to find out what's happening there in weeks. People who try just . . ." He waved his hands. "Vanish."

"Has it been sacked by the barbarians?" Raesinia said.

"That's what everyone seems to think, but I haven't seen any real information. You'd think the savages would loot and then run home, not hang about picking off scouts. For that matter, it would take a hell of an army to sack Elysium, even with modern guns. I have a hard time imagining a bunch of primitives managing it with bows and spears."

Destroying Elysium had been Janus' goal, his reason for marching north. He'd been turned back by the weather, the efforts of the Black Priests, and his own officers, who'd sided with Raesinia and refused to waste more lives on his crusade. Now, it seemed, someone might have accomplished the task for him.

And it mattered more than Dorsay knew. Elysium was, publicly, the seat of the Sworn Church, revered by millions as the holiest place on the continent. Only a few knew it was also home to the Priests of the Black, the secret order dedicated to rooting out and destroying sorcery, architects of the war intended to remove Raesinia from the throne. Anything that had damaged *them* had to be good news, but Raesinia felt strangely unsettled. *We need to know what's happening.*

"Very interesting," she said aloud. "May I ask, though, why you wanted to share this with me?"

"Partly because I thought you might have something to add," Dorsay said.

"I would if I did," Raesinia said, wincing internally at the lie. Dorsay seemed sincere, but she was hardly going to talk to him about magic and demons, not least because it might lead to questions about her own condition. "You seem to be considerably better informed than I am."

"Fair enough. But I also wanted to ask a favor. Do you have any news of Vhalnich?"

"He's on his way to his old estate, in Mieran County." Raesinia frowned. "Why? You think *he* could be behind this business at Elysium?"

"More rumors. Nothing solid. But . . . troubling." Dorsay shrugged. "It would . . . ease my mind, let's say, if we could confirm that Vhalnich is settling down to country life and not causing trouble."

"I understand," Raesinia said. "I'll send a courier to check on him. We have people there, and I'll get you a full report."

"Thank you." Dorsay extended a hand. "It's been such a bear getting the peace talks this far, I'd hate for anything to cause problems now."

From another man, those words might have been a veiled threat, but Dorsay meant them honestly. Raesinia shook his hand and nodded.

Count Albrecht Strav was seventy years old if he was a day, with a long queue of bone white hair and wild, bushy eyebrows. He laughed frequently and without modesty, the full-throated cackles of someone who is long past caring what other people think of him. His desk, a massive slab of a thing polished to a fine sheen, was clear of everything but a daggerlike letter opener. One side of his office was occupied by a hearth, and he'd built the fire up to massive proportions, hot enough to make Raesinia sweat.

"Sorry for that," he said when she arrived. "Always cold these days, even at midsummer. Don't get old, m'girl, if you can avoid it."

"I'll try my best," Raesinia said, unable to keep a hint of wry humor out of her voice.

"Expect you want an update," Strav went on. "Commendable, commendable. Your father never took an interest. Didn't have much of a head for figures." Strav guffawed. "Neither do I, tell the truth, but I make do."

Strav had been Deputy Minister of the Treasury nearly thirty years ago, well before Raesinia was born. Not having a head for figures was probably one reason he'd never gotten the top job, though he was right that King Farus VIII hadn't paid much attention to financial matters. Orlanko had given the job to

Rackhil Grieg, whose blatant profiteering and sale of "tax farm" franchises had brought the Vordanai economy to the brink of ruin before the revolution had intervened.

Now Raesinia had brought in her own expert to set things right. And she'd brought in Strav to, more or less, occupy a chair and provide the weight of his noble pedigree. As best she could tell, he was accomplishing both tasks nicely.

"So," she said, out of politeness. "How are things progressing?"

"Splendidly!" Strav laughed. "Just splendidly. All the lads are doing splendid work. And the lass, of course. Mustn't forget her. She seems to work as hard as the rest of 'em put together. She's a good girl, that one. Reminds me of my granddaughter, Vincent's girl." He paused. "Or was it Jaten's? I lose track after I can't count 'em on my fingers anymore, ha!"

"Wonderful," Raesinia said smoothly. "I'll just have a word with her about the figures, then."

"Of course! She can come up with any figures you need. She's a demon for 'em. Never known a girl who liked figurin' so much."

"Thank you, Count Strav." Raesinia beckoned to her guards, and they escaped from the sweltering heat of the office. Their true destination was down the hall, but it wouldn't have been polite to pay a call on the Treasury without at least a token visit to the minister.

The real heart of the ministry was a large, airy room that had once been a servants' dining hall. It had been taken over to be the financial equivalent of a workshop. The walls were lined with bookshelves, piled high with thick, leather-bound volumes and scrolls tied with colored ribbons. Several tables were set side by side, flanked by benches and almost completely covered with paper. The occupants of the room were nearly lost amid the clutter, a half dozen young men and women who looked like they'd had about a day of sleep in the last week among them. At the center was a girl of fifteen, her straw-colored hair tied back into an unruly tail, her face a mass of freckles.

"Raes!" Cora squeaked, bounding to her feet. Then, seeing the looks she got from the other clerks, she cleared her throat and said, in more ordinary tones, "Your Highness, I mean. It's an honor."

Cora bowed, and the rest bowed with her. Raesinia nodded to them and grinned at Cora.

"I appreciate your hard work, all of you," she said. "Cora, I wonder if we could speak privately?"

"Of course!" Cora extracted herself from her spot at the table, while the young woman next to her grabbed a stack of papers to keep it from toppling. Oblivious, Cora opened a door in the corner. "There's room in here."

The private space proved to be an old servant's bedroom, with a cot in one corner and a desk in the other. More books were stacked in untidy piles on the floor.

Raesinia's guards waited outside, and as soon as the door was closed she wrapped Cora in a hug.

"Sorry," Cora said. "I'm still not good at remembering—you know." *You know* apparently meant the fact that her friend was now the Queen of Vordan.

"You're improving," Raesinia said. "And it's only for everyone else's benefit. In private you can always call me Raes."

Of the original cabal—the conspiracy that Raesinia had started against her own government and Duke Orlanko, which had helped to spark the revolution—Cora was the only one who hadn't died or betrayed her. Apart from Sothe, she was Raesinia's oldest friend and one of the few who knew all her secrets.

She was also a financial genius. It had been Cora who'd parlayed the information Raesinia had brought from the palace into a fortune in the markets, then used that fortune to support the revolution. She'd engineered the run on the Second Pennysworth Bank that had given the supernatural orator Danton his first push, and later she'd helped Raesinia and Marcus expose Maurisk's conspiracy by following the paper trail of missing flash powder.

As soon as she'd had the chance, Raesinia had installed her here, in the Ministry of Finance. She would have made Cora minister, but it seemed unlikely that the Deputies-General would accept a fifteen-year-old girl, however brilliant, at the head of the nation's finances. Count Strav was amiable, unambitious, and unlikely to interfere, so he made an acceptable figurehead, while Cora and a contingent recruited from the University did the actual business of righting the listing Vordanai ship.

"Raes." Cora squeezed her again. "God. The back room of the Blue Mask feels like a hundred years ago, doesn't it?"

"Longer," Raesinia said.

She pulled away far enough to study Cora's face. The girl had grown—taller than Raesinia now and not quite as ravaged by acne as before—but it was more than that. She'd been innocent when Raesinia had recruited her, and none of them were innocent now. There was a sadness in her dark green eyes that hadn't been there before.

A moment of silence stretched, uncomfortably, until Raesinia cleared her throat.

"I'm sorry I haven't come to see you more often," she said. "It's been . . . chaotic since we got back."

"You're the *queen*, Raes. Of course you're going to be busy." Cora grinned, and just like that she was once again the bright, cocky girl Raesinia had first met. "How's . . . ?" She waved a hand vaguely. "The country, I guess?"

"I was hoping you could tell me," Raesinia said. "Is your team working all right?"

Cora nodded enthusiastically. "They're great. Especially Annabel. She's terrifyingly bright. She's from Murnsk—did you know her parents didn't even want her to learn to *read*? She had to run away from a caravan to get here. And—" Cora paused and coughed. "Sorry. I can introduce you later, if you'd like."

"I would." Raesinia couldn't help but smile. Cora's enthusiasm was infectious. "And Strav isn't giving you any trouble?"

"As long as he gets to sign his name to the reports, he seems happy. And we send him around to the other ministries when they won't listen to me." Cora frowned. "It would help if we had a Minister of War. Someone needs to get the spending there under control."

Raesinia sighed. "Tell that to the Deputies. God knows I have."

"Anyway, we're making some progress on taxes. Orlanko left us a mess, and I figured trying to go back to the old system right away would just cause more problems. So we've been working at the local level to try to get something people can live with. It's slow work, but—" Cora stopped herself again. She really was getting better. "The details are all in my reports. We're getting there."

"So what's the problem?" *There's always a problem.*

"Debt, piled on more debt." Cora made a face. "The old Crown had debts to everyone—the nobles, the Borels, the League cities, even the churches. The first Deputies-General declared all of that void, but then we started issuing scrip, especially when Janus' armies were fighting the League. Now nobody knows what the status of all of that is, and the people who held the *old* debt are petitioning for some kind of settlement, which we definitely can't afford."

"Anything I can do to help?"

"Get the Deputies to reaffirm their commitment to honor the scrip we paid to Desland and the other League cities," Cora said.

"If we have too much debt, wouldn't it be better *not* to pay them?"

"No, because if we can convince them we *will* honor the scrip, then I can borrow in the Hamvelt market, and the rates there are better than anything we can get internally. And then I can use *that* to pay off some of the most expensive liabilities, and that will give us more room to—" She stopped again. "It would help, basically."

"I'll take your word for it." Raesinia smiled. "I'll do what I can, though trying to get the Deputies to do *anything* is like wrestling a sack of cats."

"I know." Cora leaned back against the desk, studying Raesinia more closely. "You look tired."

"I am," Raesinia admitted. Not physically—she couldn't *sleep*, much less get tired—but there were other kinds of weariness. She sat down heavily on the bed, which creaked. "It's just . . . it never ends, you know? While we were fighting a war it was hard for everyone, but it felt . . . worthwhile, I guess. If we could get to peace. Now we're there, almost, and . . ." *And I can see the rest of my life stretching out in front of me, formal dresses and balls and arguing with the Deputies. Until I have to fake my own death and leave forever.*

"I wish I could help." Cora looked haunted.

"You *are* helping," Raesinia said. "This place would have fallen apart without you. Honestly. You're a hero, Cora."

"I'm . . ." Cora flushed, pale face turning a brilliant scarlet. She changed the subject, her smile turning wicked. "Speaking of heroes. Have you seen Marcus?"

"We're having dinner tonight. Assuming nothing comes up."

"You sound worried. What happened?"

"Nothing." Raesinia sighed. "That's the problem, really."

Cora was the only one Raesinia had thus far told about what she and Marcus had shared. For Cora, it was storybook romance, plain and simple, the queen and heroic general and a love for the ages. Sometimes Raesinia agreed with her. When she looked back on that night, the horrible moment when she'd thought he'd turned her down, the first, tentative kiss, it made her feel warm and giddy both at once. *The feeling of having done something unspeakably dangerous and survived.* And there were times, looking at Marcus, when she wanted to grab hold of him and never let go.

Somehow, when they actually *met*, things were always more complicated. Marcus was . . . polite. Always polite, always courteous, and always just the slightest bit distant. Even when they managed to get out of sight for a few moments to steal a kiss, it was so *careful*. It was as though, having admitted their love for each other, they were each waiting for the other to make the next move.

"It's Ohnlei," Raesinia said. "Something about this place. I grew up here, and being back makes me . . . remember who I am. And I think it reminds Marcus of the same thing."

"You need to tell everyone," Cora said. "You don't have to sneak around behind your parents' backs. You're the *queen*."

"It's not that simple," Raesinia said. "Things are fragile right now. Marcus is a hero, and he's the highest-ranking officer in the army. If I announce that we're—engaged, the Deputies-General might think I'm trying to secure my authority and displace them."

"You love him, and you're worried about what the *Deputies* will think?"

"And the people. The press. Other countries." Raesinia gave a wan smile. "That's what it means, being queen."

Besides, she thought, *it isn't like* he's *pushing to take things further.* It wasn't as though she wanted Marcus to toss her on the bed and tear her dress off—*not really, I suppose*—but she had to admit she would have appreciated a little more evidence of . . . interest. *Maybe it's that I look closer to Cora's age than his.* She always pushed that thought away, but it came back every time she saw herself in the mirror.

Cora flopped down next to her on the narrow bed and put an arm around her shoulders. Raesinia felt faintly ridiculous—*here's the Queen of Vordan, weighed down with boy troubles, being comforted by the Deputy Minister of Finance*—but she leaned against Cora's shoulder nonetheless.

"It'll be all right," Cora said. "Things will calm down eventually."

"How long do I have, though?" Raesinia's voice was a whisper. "Before someone starts asking questions. Five years? Ten?"

"You'll deal with it when they do," Cora said. "I'll help, and so will Marcus."

"Thanks." Raesinia took a deep breath. "And you're right. Once the treaty is signed, Marcus and I will have to . . . move forward."

"Or," Cora said, "when he comes over tonight, you could—"

She whispered the rest, like a guilty schoolgirl, and Raesinia laughed out loud. "Can you imagine the look on his face?"

"All too easily," Cora said. She puffed out her cheeks and lowered her voice. "Hum, hum. I *hardly* think that's appropriate, Your Highness."

"He's not *that* bad," Raesinia said, still laughing. "He's just . . . cautious."

There was a knock at the door, and Eric's voice came from outside. "Your Highness?"

"Damn." Raesinia gave Cora a squeeze. "Thanks. Really. Being queen is a little suffocating sometimes."

"We could always sneak out, like in the old days. I hear they've rebuilt the Blue Mask."

"Are you sure you're old enough for that?"

They dissolved into laughter again, ignoring Eric's plaintive voice for a few moments longer.

Thank God for Cora. With Sothe gone, there was no one else Raesinia could talk to honestly. It felt like a clean breath after a smoke-shrouded room.

"Deputy d'Andorre will be waiting," Eric complained as they walked quickly through the corridors of the palace.

"It won't kill him to wait for the queen," Raesinia said.

"It might annoy him," Eric said. "And we need his help. While the Liberals hold the balance of the Deputies, d'Andorre is in charge."

"As much as anyone is." The Liberals were less a political party than a menagerie of tiny factions, united only by their dislike of the old, entrenched structures of power. They had emerged as the leading force mostly by default—the Conservatives had been broken with the fall of the Directory, and the Radicals, opposed to the war, had seen their support wither as the tide turned in Vordan's favor. "D'Andorre can't keep his own people in line, much less unite the rest."

"He's still very influential."

"I know." Raesinia sighed. "I'll apologize, all right?"

There were a variety of royal receiving rooms, where the monarch could meet anyone from a peasant to a full delegation from a foreign court. This was one of the less ostentatious ones, the furniture expensive but not gilded, the walls hung with portraits of kings past. Raesinia spent a moment in the small anteroom making sure she still looked presentable, then bustled in with Joanna and Barely in her wake.

"Deputy d'Andorre!"

He stood smoothly from the sofa and gave her a deep bow. Fashion among the Liberals had tended toward the patriotic of late, and d'Andorre was dressed accordingly in a sober, dark blue suit with silver piping and an almost military cut. He was a short, solidly built man with wings of gray in his hair and a fashionable queue. By the standards of the new Vordanai politics, Chrest d'Andorre was an elder statesman, having survived the rough-and-tumble of the Deputies since the very beginning, mostly by not being important enough to notice. The Liberals had a reputation for being more interested in abstract political philosophy than in taking power, which had kept them safely out of the fray during the revolution and the Directory's attempted coup. Now that the wheel of politics had come full circle, Raesinia wondered what d'Andorre would do with his newfound authority.

"Your Highness."

"I apologize if you were kept waiting." The passive non-apology, an ever-useful tool of statecraft. *My old tutors would be proud.* "Please, sit."

She took a chair opposite the sofa, and d'Andorre sat stiffly across from her.

"I don't intend to take up much of your time, Your Highness," he said. "I'll be frank. My constituents—and many of my colleagues in the Deputies—have urged me to come and ask certain questions directly. I have enormous respect for the Crown, so I have been hesitant, but our deliberations have reached a point where your position must be made clear."

"I see," Raesinia said, keeping her expression carefully bland. She wasn't sure if he was beating around the bush for a reason, or if d'Andorre was one of those politicians constitutionally incapable of coming directly to a point. "By all means, then, ask your questions."

"They concern the nature of the authority of the Ministry of War. I understand that in the late campaign you undertook to issue orders directly to the commanders of the Grand Army?"

"In an emergency," Raesinia said. "The army was on the point of starvation, and both the First Consul and Column-General d'Ivoire were missing."

"The army has a chain of command for a reason," d'Andorre said. "We—my colleagues and I—feel that this sets a dangerous precedent. Do you, at the present moment, consider yourself still in command of the Grand Army?"

"Of course not," Raesinia said. "And I'd be happy to say so officially to the Minister of War, but as I understand it, you still haven't managed to decide on one."

"Negotiations on that point are proceeding," d'Andorre said. "But I'm glad to hear your answer. Some of my colleagues intend to propose legislation more precisely defining the monarch's role with respect to the army, and strengthening the principle of civil control over the military. Soldiers must, in the end, answer to the people, as embodied in the Deputies-General. Would you oppose such legislation?"

Raesinia, who'd been waiting patiently for the actual question, decided that d'Andorre couldn't be putting her on—he was just intrinsically boring. "I'd have to read it, of course," she said carefully. "But not in principle, no."

"And where do you stand on a reduction in the size of the army, now that the war has been concluded? I believe it has become a considerable drain on the public purse."

"I think it may be a little premature," Raesinia said. "Once the final peace with Borel is signed, it might be worth investigating."

"Thank you, Your Highness." D'Andorre got to his feet. "It's been an honor to meet with you."

That's it? Raesinia suppressed a sigh. *This is going to be my life, isn't it? Listening to d'Andorre or someone like him blather on.* Until it wasn't her life anymore, of course. *And maybe that won't be such a bad thing after all.*

"Thank you, Deputy d'Andorre," she said, standing to acknowledge his bow. "I am eager to work with the Deputies, now that we have peace."

When the deputy was gone, Raesinia turned to Eric. "Is he always such a bore?"

Her assistant swallowed, looking uncomfortable. "He's considered an excellent speaker in the Deputies. His most famous speech kept the chamber spellbound for nearly four hours."

"I bet it did." Raesinia shook her head. "I need to change before Marcus arrives. Is there anything else?"

To her surprise, Barely spoke up from the doorway. She had a lilting Deslandai accent, which gave her a musical tone at odds with her hard-edged attitude.

"There's a Colonel Giforte who wants to see you, Your Highness," she said. "He's waiting in the hall. Says it can't wait."

"Alek?" Raesinia frowned. "Bring him in."

Alek Giforte had been Vice Captain of Armsmen before the revolution. He'd served in various capacities since then, most recently as chief of staff for Marcus during the Murnskai campaign. Now that they were settled back in Vordan, Raesinia had put him in charge of the Armsmen again and unofficially given him the task of rebuilding the intelligence apparatus that the revolution had smashed.

The Murnskai campaign had aged him, Raesinia thought as he came in.

His salt-and-pepper beard had gone fully white, and his hairline was receding. At the moment he looked as serious as she'd ever seen him, even when they'd been surrounded by hostile armies. *Something is very wrong.*

"Colonel?" Raesinia said.

"You need to see this," he said, gesturing with a single sheet of folded paper. "Alone."

Raesinia hesitated, then nodded at Eric and her guards. They filed out, and she took the page from Giforte. It was only a few lines, but she read it three times over, just to be certain.

"This is reliable?" she said, her voice carefully controlled.

"We've gotten it from three different sources," Giforte said.

"Find Marcus." She handed the note back to him. "Tell him I want to see him in my apartments. *Now.*"

Chapter Two

MARCUS

Marcus stared at the page, written in a neat, dispassionate hand. He wondered what clerk had copied it somewhere and whether he'd known what it portended.

> Janus bet Vhalnich is in Yatterny, with one division of the Grand Army and several battalions of Murnskai soldiers. He has given a speech announcing that the Queen of Vordan has betrayed him and in so doing she has forfeited her right to rule, as he is the true embodiment of the people's will. Prince Cesha Dzurk is with him, and says that his father the emperor is dead, leaving Murnsk in chaos. Janus claims he has no choice, at the urging of those around him, but to assume the title of Emperor of Vordan and Murnsk. He calls on all loyal citizens of both countries to support him and all true soldiers of either crown to follow his orders.
>
> He appears to have the complete support of the forces here and considerable popularity among the Murnskai civilians. He is already preparing to march on Talbonn, and from there declares his intention to move south.

"Madness," Marcus said. "Utter nonsense."

"It's been confirmed in every way we can think of," Raesinia said. "And rumors are already spreading. In six hours everyone in the city will know."

"Then there has to be some kind of mistake."

"Why?"

"Because Janus would never do such a thing!"

Raesinia squared her shoulders and faced him. "Are you certain? Absolutely certain?"

Just for a moment Marcus was back in the barn that had been Janus' makeshift prison, watching the rage grow in those huge gray eyes when the general realized that Marcus, too, had turned away from him. It had been one of the hardest moments of Marcus' life. But Janus had calmed quickly, as he always did. *Too quickly? Could he have already been planning this?*

"I'm certain," Marcus grated, "because it doesn't make any *sense*. What can he possibly gain?"

"Aside from the throne? The mob still considers him a hero, and the soldiers worship him. If he walked in here tomorrow, could we stop him?"

"We could stop him," Marcus said, more confidently than he felt. "And why would he call himself Emperor of *Murnsk* as well?"

"Cesha Dzurk has obviously thrown in his lot with Janus. Maybe he's popular enough to make that stick." Raesinia tapped the note. "It seems to be working so far."

Marcus sat down. They were in Raesinia's private apartments, not yet restored to the lavishness of the prerevolution royal chambers but still comfortably furnished. The crushed-velvet sofa was absurdly soft and enveloping, but he hardly noticed. Raesinia stood by the table. Her expression was the forced calm she wore when she would rather be screaming.

"I still don't believe it," Marcus said. "Janus doesn't *want* the throne. He told me himself."

"Maybe he used you like he uses everyone else," Raesinia said. "Or maybe his plans have changed."

"Or maybe something's happened to him." Marcus bounced to his feet again. "Last we saw him, he was on his way back to Mieran County. Maybe someone got to him, and now he's got a gun to his head. Hell, Orlanko could be using him to try to get to you—"

"Do you really think Janus would do this for Orlanko, even *with* a gun to his head?"

"Either way, we need to know for certain," Marcus said. "I'll leave tonight. If I use the courier posts, I can be in Talbonn—"

"*No.*"

There was enough emotion in the word that it brought Marcus up short.

He turned back to look at Raesinia, and found that her calm had cracked. Her eyes were shimmering.

"Marcus, please," she said. "You have to think."

"Think about what? If Janus is a captive—"

"You don't know he's a captive. What happens if you get there and he's sincere?"

"Then I'll try to talk some sense into him." But Marcus' conviction was already fading.

"And if that doesn't work?"

"Then I'd . . ." He shook his head. "I'd come back here, of course. I made my choice, Raes. You know that."

She took a deep breath, blew it out, and nodded. "I know. But what about everyone else?"

"I'm not sure what you mean."

"Janus declares himself emperor. As soon as the news breaks, Marcus d'Ivoire, Janus' closest ally and right-hand man, immediately decamps to go to his old friend's side. Surely you see how that's going to look?"

"Ah." Marcus had the distinct feeling of an unexpected pit opening beneath his feet. All the strength seemed to go out of him, and he sat back down abruptly. "Oh. I . . ."

"I know this is hard," Raesinia said. "He's your friend."

"It's more than that," Marcus said. "He's . . . Janus." He paused, then looked up at Raesinia. "You don't trust me."

"I do." She grabbed his hand in both of hers. "*Please*, Marcus. Believe that if you believe nothing else. I have always trusted you with my life, and I always will."

He squeezed her fingers, tentatively, and she squeezed back. Marcus swallowed.

"Sorry. I'm just . . . a little off-balance."

"I know," Raesinia said. "Shove over."

Marcus obligingly slid sideways, and Raesinia sat down next to him. She bent her head, looking at her hands.

"The thing is," she said, "it's not my trust you need to worry about. The Deputies-General is going to suspect you on principle, along with anyone else who worked closely with Janus. You can't do anything that would give them ammunition."

"Right." Marcus' hand clenched tight around his knee. Raesinia was next to him, distractingly close, practically leaning against him. "So what *are* we going to do?"

"We need more information, obviously. Alek is doing everything he can." She shook her head. "Until we get it, we have to assume that Janus honestly intends to take the throne. What will the army do when the news gets out?"

Marcus frowned. "The soldiers will watch their commanders to see which way they jump."

"And the commanders?"

"I'm sure of a few. We'll have to ride herd on the rest until we know more."

Raesinia nodded. "That's the most important first step, then. I don't want any violence, but we can't afford to have troops marching away to join Janus. Not if we're going to have to fight him."

Fight him. Fight Janus. An involuntary shiver went through Marcus at the prospect. "Hell. Saints and *fucking* martyrs. I thought we'd finally—"

"I know." She closed her eyes. "Believe me, I know."

"I should go. If all hell is going to break loose, at the very least everyone needs to know where to find me."

He got to his feet, then paused when Raesinia took his hand again.

"Marcus . . ."

He looked down at her, slim and beautiful, pale in the flickering light of the lamps. At that moment he wanted nothing more than to kiss her, the way he had in Murnsk. They'd dallied all through the return trip, snatching brief moments from official business. But she'd made it clear that she didn't want them to be seen together. And here in Ohnlei someone was always watching.

In his worst moments Marcus wondered if Raesinia wasn't rethinking what she'd said, the offer she'd made him. It was one thing to talk about love when battle was looming. It was another to do it in the cold light of day, with the court and the Deputies-General looking over your shoulder. She'd certainly been more reserved since they'd returned, and Marcus had told himself that he wouldn't blame her if she wanted to pretend none of it had ever happened.

I should have just talked to her ages ago. But that meant facing the possibility that she'd say it out loud and make it real.

"Is something wrong?" he said.

"No." Raesinia let her gaze fall. "Just . . . be careful. A lot might change in the next few hours. Make sure you stick close to people you trust."

"You too. I'll send a report when I know the situation."

She nodded, looking away.

The Grand Army—most of it, anyway—was encamped on the rolling countryside north of Ohnlei, busily ruining the well-kept meadows and scenic little.
They'd constructed their camp with more care than usual, since it seemed likely
they were going to be there through the winter, and while the soldiers had
started under canvas, they'd set to improving their situation with the typical
ingenuity of veterans. Now the camp resembled a small town, with two main
roads crossing at a central square and smaller streets marking off a well-defined
grid, while the tents had mostly been replaced with wooden lean-tos and even
small log cabins. Hawkers drove carts up from the city every day and set up
shop in designated spaces, eager to relieve the soldiers of their surplus pay.
There was even a section designated for brothel tents, well patrolled by trusted
men and women.

Marcus was proud of the camp, though he had to admit that Fitz Warus
had done most of the actual administrative work. He'd hoped that the army
could turn it into their winter quarters, and spend their time on making good
the damage of the brutal Murnskai campaign. Now—

Let's not jump to conclusions yet.

Only roughly two-thirds of the army had made the journey south to Vordan City—specifically the First, Second, Third, Fourth, Sixth, and Eighth
Divisions, leaving the Fifth, Seventh, Ninth, and Tenth on the frontier. The
split had seemed like the right idea at the time, with the units that had seen the
least fighting remaining in the north to keep an eye on the Murnskai border,
while the battered divisions that had borne the brunt of the campaign went
back to Vordan for reinforcement and training. Now, though, Marcus was
acutely aware that he'd left four nearly fresh divisions, some thirty-six thousand
men, far beyond his immediate reach, while the six that he had to hand were
either well below strength or had a high proportion of raw recruits.

On the positive side, apart from divisional batteries, the bulk of the artillery
had come south with the army. The same was true of Give-Em-Hell's cavalry,
although casualties in that arm had been particularly appalling. *Still. We'd better
hope that Alek's spies are wrong, or at least that not everyone in the north goes over to
Janus. The odds are way too close for my liking.*

The news was already loose. Marcus could *feel* it as he rode through the
camp. The normal raucous chatter of the evening was gone, replaced with
hundreds of furtive, whispered conversations. Messengers rode to and fro. Even
if Raesinia hadn't warned him, Marcus' instinctive sense for camp life would

have told him that something was badly wrong. As it was, he had to restrain himself from kicking his horse into a gallop.

His own dwelling was a tent, albeit a large and comfortable one. He'd refused Fitz' offer to build him a more permanent shelter, wanting to set a virtuous example; now he looked at it and saw only how indefensible it was, how easy it would be for any attackers to get inside. *Stop. It won't come to that. It had better not.*

A sentry outside held two horses, and saluted as Marcus dismounted.

"Division-Generals Warus and Solwen to see you, sir! They're waiting inside."

"Thanks." Marcus slid from his saddle and handed the man his reins. "Send someone for coffee, would you? I think it's going to be a late night."

Inside, much of the tent was taken up with a folding table, adrift in maps and paperwork. Marcus' humble camp-bed was concealed behind a thin curtain, leaving the rest of the space for interviews and planning. He still had most of Giforte's old staff to help him, though he badly missed the man himself. But Raesinia had greater need of him, and until tonight it had seemed like there wasn't any chance of action soon. *Damn, damn, damn.*

The two men waiting for him were some of the longest-serving soldiers in the army, Old Colonials both. Valiant Solwen—"Val" to nearly everyone—was a short, wide-shouldered man with a ruddy face and a pencil mustache. He and Marcus had each commanded a battalion in Khandar, back when they'd been captains at the edge of the world. Marcus had gone there voluntarily, running from everything after he'd heard about the fire that had killed his family. Val had been banished for some slight, terrifyingly important at the time, which had long since been forgotten in the uproar that had followed.

Fitz Warus hadn't even been a captain in those days, just a staff lieutenant serving under his older brother, Colonel Ben Warus. He'd changed very little since then, outwardly. A decade younger than Marcus and Val, he was as slender as a blade, always impeccably uniformed even in the harshest conditions. Looking at him now, though, Marcus was struck by the thought that even dependable Fitz *had* changed in the last year. He'd not grown *up* exactly—he'd always been the responsible one—but grown *out*, taking responsibility on his own instead of serving as Marcus' right hand. Something in the way he carried himself exuded competence. There was a good reason Janus had made him commander of the First Division.

"You've heard?" Marcus said, as he let the tent flap fall closed behind him. No need to specify what.

They both nodded.

"I think everyone knows by now," Val said. "Or will shortly. Rumors are the damnedest thing."

"Some of the carters have admitted they were tipped to spread the story," Fitz said. "Someone wants all of Vordan to know about this."

"Right. So no point trying to keep things under wraps." Marcus eased himself into one of the camp chairs. "Have you talked to your colonels?"

Fitz nodded, but Val shook his head, staring fixedly at Marcus.

"I wanted to come here first," he said slowly. "Just to . . . check on things."

"To check . . ." Marcus raised his eyebrows. "Ah. To make sure I wasn't about to declare for Janus, you mean?"

"Not that I really thought you'd do it," Val said hastily. He gave a *harrumph*. "I just didn't want you to say anything you'd regret later."

Or else you wanted to make sure to be on my side, whatever I did, Marcus thought ruefully. Val was a good man and a respectable commander, but he had no head for politics—witness his getting banished to Khandar in the first place. He'd negotiated the tricky waters of the revolution and subsequent wars by sticking close to Marcus, whatever happened.

There are a lot of soldiers in that position. Without a particular ideology, or at least not one they'd bet their lives on, but with a great deal of trust in their commanders. *It's like I told Raesinia. The army will obey the generals.* He took a deep breath. *We just need to make sure of the generals, then.*

"I'm not sure of anything at this point," Marcus said. "I'm not convinced that this really came from Janus, or that he's acting of his own free will. But whatever happens, my loyalty is with the people of Vordan, and that means Raesinia and the Deputies. Is that clear?" *I made that choice once already.*

"Of course, of course," Val said. "I just thought . . . heat of the moment, you understand . . ."

"Thank you, Val," Marcus said. "I must admit that my first instinct was to ride north to see what was going on for myself. Thankfully, Raesinia was there to point out that it might have looked . . . politically dubious, under the circumstances." He looked down at the table, with its burden of paperwork, and frowned. "What's our first priority?"

"So far the men are under control," Fitz said. "There's been a lot of whispering, but no action. I've warned my colonels to be on the lookout for spontaneous demonstrations. We may want to institute a curfew."

Val nodded vigorous agreement. "I told Lieutenant Fylar to make sure everyone stayed put. He'll keep my division in line."

"That accounts for the First and the Third," Marcus said. "What about the rest?"

"The Fourth is temporarily under my command," Fitz said. "Pending the trial of General Kaanos."

Morwen Kaanos—Mor—had been, along with Adrecht Roston, the other half of the commanders of the original Colonials. Adrecht had led a mutiny against Janus, and nearly killed Marcus himself; he'd been left to die in the desert with his coconspirators. Mor had served in the revolutionary army until the Murnskai campaign, but he'd made no secret of his distaste for Janus and Raesinia, and it had come to a head just before Marcus' return, when he'd tried to assume command. Raesinia had outmaneuvered him, and he'd been arrested, but his trial had been postponed until the appointment of a new Minister of War.

"Given Kaanos' attitude toward Janus," Fitz went on, "I doubt any of his officers are likely to be leading their men in that direction."

"And we can be sure of the Second," Val said. "They may still be in mourning for Ihernglass, but Abby Giforte would never turn on you."

Not to mention, Marcus thought, *that her father now works directly for the queen.* That was unfair—Abby would stay loyal, regardless of what Alek did. She'd proved that in the revolution, and again when she took command of the Second Division's First Regiment—widely known as the Girls' Own, the only female regiment in the Vordanai army.

Certain as he was of Abby, though, Marcus would have felt better if Winter Ihernglass had been here. He was another Colonial, a man of extraordinary talent who'd been bumped up to sergeant by chance and climbed the ranks from there to become one of Janus' most trusted officers. While Marcus continued to feel uncomfortable letting the women of the Second Division put themselves in danger, he couldn't dispute that the Girls' Own had performed wonders under Ihernglass' command, from the campaign on the Velt through the worst of the fighting in Murnsk.

But Ihernglass was gone, in pursuit of the Penitent Damned who'd poisoned Janus with some foul magic. Since Janus had recovered, Marcus assumed that Ihernglass had successfully completed his mission, but no reports of his party had ever come back. Given the chaos in northern Murnsk, the freak blizzards and wild tribesmen roaming the country, Ihernglass was presumed dead by almost everyone. *If it's true, it's a damn shame.*

"The Eighth is de Manzet," Marcus said. "He'll play it safe, whatever happens."

"That leaves the Sixth. New fellow there. Quord, isn't it?"

Fitz nodded. "Herran Quord. Janus appointed him after General Ibsly was killed at Gilphaite. I've only met him briefly."

"Likewise," Marcus said. "All right. Fitz, do you have a few men you trust for quiet work?"

"Of course," Fitz said.

"Have them walk around the camp, see if there's any unusual activity, especially from the Sixth. I want to hear as soon as you have anything."

"Yes, sir." Fitz saluted and got to his feet. "If you'll excuse me."

"Val, once you're sure your own people are in order, go and find Give-Em-Hell. Tell him to make sure his men are ready, but *quietly*. If we need to put down a riot, I want him on hand." The moral impact of a squadron of advancing cavalry was the best chance of dispersing a crowd without real bloodshed. And Marcus had no doubts at all about the loyalty of Give-Em-Hell's men, who felt a nearly religious awe toward their diminutive commander.

"Understood." Val hesitated. "Then what? Do you really think it'll come to fighting?"

Val looked stricken, and Marcus wanted to give him some reassurance, but all he could offer was a shrug. "I don't know, and neither does anyone else. We're at least four days' ride from Yatterny, even by military courier. The whole thing could be over already, and we might not find out until tomorrow."

"Or Janus could already be on the march," Val said glumly. "I'll tell Give-Em-Hell to be ready."

"They're trying to keep quiet about it," Fitz said, an hour later. "But the Sixth is definitely up to something."

Marcus sat at his desk, massaging his temples to fight off an incipient headache. "You're certain?"

"Nearly. There's activity at their supply depot, and the divisional artillery is restocking their caissons. Lots of men suddenly cooking or trying to trade for extra food, like they're expecting to march."

"Any chance its spontaneous?"

"No, sir. I visited the quartermaster myself, and there's a half dozen fresh requisitions over Division-General Quord's signature. Either he's behind this, or someone's framing him fairly competently."

Marcus felt his teeth grinding. *It's better than a mass uprising,* he told himself. But his experiences in Khandar and the revolution had left him with a pronounced dislike of mutiny.

"Send a message to all commanders that I'm calling a council here in half an hour," Marcus said. "That shouldn't push Quord into anything rash; he knows I have to do *something.* Get a few of your men to go after the messengers and let everyone *but* Quord know they should wait another hour. I want him here alone." Marcus sighed. "And have a dozen muskets you can count on waiting when he arrives. In case he decides to be *really* rash."

Fitz saluted and stepped outside to give the necessary orders. Marcus leaned back in his chair and scratched his beard.

Then what? Val had asked the question, but it was what everyone was thinking. *Secure the army. Then what? Will any troops rally to Janus? If they do, where will he march?* It had to be south. *He'll come for Vordan City. His best chance at legitimacy is to take the palace and the Deputies quickly.* No doubt the Deputies could be persuaded to ratify Janus' ascension at bayonet point. *So that means he can either descend the Pale, or try for the high passes—*

Marcus reached for a leather-bound stack of maps, then stopped himself. *Not* yet, *damn it. As soon as we start thinking of this as a war, it becomes one. If there's any chance of stopping it, we have to take it.*

Fitz reentered, with two soldiers behind him. Both wore the scorpion badge of the Old Colonials. Some of the Khandarai veterans were deeply loyal to Janus after his near-miraculous performance there, while others—mostly those who'd served under Ben Warus before the Redeemer revolt—were more divided. Marcus could only trust that Fitz knew his men.

"You can wait there," Marcus said, pointing at the curtained-off nook that held his bed. "Stay out of sight until I call."

"The others are outside," Fitz said. "I told them to watch for Quord and come in just behind him."

"Good." Marcus pursed his lips. "What do you know about Quord?"

"Not much. He's my age, promoted up from lieutenant for service under the Directory. Janus made him a colonel after the coup, and then a general."

"Which means he's smart." Janus was a good judge of ability, and the men he'd promoted to fill the decimated ranks of the post-revolution army had usually been competent and intelligent. Unfortunately, his eye for character hadn't always been as keen. "Has he seen any fighting since then?"

"Not that I'm aware of."

We'll see, then. Marcus was holding out hope that there was some kind of misunderstanding, though it seemed unlikely. *It's never pleasant to accuse a fellow officer of treachery.*

There was a scratch at the tent flap a few minutes later, and a young man's voice. "Column-General d'Ivoire?"

"Come in," Marcus said.

Quord was pale, clean-shaven, and nearly as neat in appearance as Fitz, with a pair of narrow, square spectacles and close-cropped hair. He held himself as straight as a ranker under inspection, and snapped a crisp salute.

"Sir! Reporting as ordered for the council."

"Division-General," Marcus said. "Good to see you. Please, have a seat."

Quord's eyes went to Fitz, then to the empty chairs around the table. "Are we expecting the others, sir? I—"

The tent flap rustled, and four soldiers filed in, muskets at the ready. At the same time the two men behind the curtain stepped out and took their places flanking Marcus. Marcus kept his eyes on Quord, and the expressions on his face were unmistakable—a brief, animal panic, followed by a mixture of rage and resignation. *No misunderstanding, then.*

"I see," Quord said, looking over his shoulder and then back at Marcus. He slumped. "If it's all the same, sir, I prefer to stand."

"As you wish," Marcus said. "You've given orders to the Sixth to prepare to march, have you not?"

"Yes," Quord said, a slight hitch in his voice.

"And is there a specific time those instructions become operative?"

"No, sir," Quord said. "They're waiting on my word."

"I would like you to write an order for them to stand down, please. Fitz?"

Fitz offered Quord a pen and paper. The general bent, stiffly, and scribbled a few lines. Fitz examined the note, then nodded.

"It doesn't seem to be any sort of code, sir," Fitz said.

"Take precautions in any case."

Fitz gave a slight smile, as if to say, *You hardly need to tell me that.* That made Marcus smile himself—he and Fitz had spent so long together that at one point they'd scarcely needed words to understand each other. It was good to know they hadn't lost the knack entirely. Then his eyes went back to Quord, and his expression soured.

"Go."

As Fitz left, Quord said, "Everything that was done was done on my direct orders, sir. None of my officers or men should be blamed."

"I'm sure." Marcus shifted uncomfortably. "I assume your intention was to take your men to the aid of the former First Consul."

"Yes." Quord stood a little straighter.

"Would you care to offer an explanation for your treason?"

"With all due respect, sir, you're the traitor here."

"Oh?" Marcus said. "I believe I swore to defend the Queen of Vordan and obey orders."

"We have to defend the *people* of Vordan," Quord said. "No one has *ever* had the chance you have right now. This country cannot afford another civil war."

"I agree. I'm in the process of trying to prevent one."

"Don't act stupid," Quord said. "The people will follow Janus over some little girl. He's proven himself again and again, while she sat in the palace and let him win her battles."

"I suggest," Marcus grated, "you don't speak of matters you don't understand. *I* was there for some of those battles."

"Then you know that Janus will win in the end. He *always* wins. The only question is how many have to die before that happens." Quord leaned forward, military decorum forgotten in his excitement. "It doesn't have to come to that, General d'Ivoire. The army respects you, the people think you're a hero, and there's no one else with comparable authority. If you were to declare for Janus, the war would be over *tonight*. Raesinia would have no choice but to surrender!"

"And I'd be a traitor."

"To the queen, not to the Deputies. How can it be treason to save lives?" Quord waved a hand. "How many of these men will die if you lead them against Janus? How many civilians, if the war goes on? If you act now history will call you a peacemaker. Do nothing and you're just another general on the losing side."

There was a moment of silence. Quord had become quite heated, and the soldiers behind him had drawn close, ready to grab him if he made a lunge across the table. Now he regained his hold on himself and straightened up. Marcus, stomach churning, kept his expression flat.

"I was hoping," he said eventually, "that you might know something I didn't. That you were part of some conspiracy."

Quord shook his head. "There's no conspiracy. There's just—"

"One general who wanted to be on the winning side. Not even a matter of high principle." Marcus sighed. "Fair enough, I suppose."

"You really think you can beat him?" Quord's face twisted. "You think you can take the field against *Janus*?"

"With any luck I won't have to," Marcus said. "But if it comes to it, I'm going to damned well try." He nodded at the soldiers. "Take him to the palace. The Minister of War will decide what to do with him." *Assuming they eventually pick one.*

"We appear to have passed the crisis," Fitz said, when the real council convened an hour later. "The Sixth Division has ceased its preparations, and guards have been posted."

"Quord couldn't have acted alone," de Manzet said. He was a polite, balding man in his forties, an old-line royal officer who'd maintained his position by quiet competence and keeping his head down. "At the very least, his colonels *should* have informed the column-general what was going on."

"Let's say that I'm choosing to believe it was just Quord. His men might have thought his plans were authorized," Marcus said. "Regardless, I'm not going to convict anyone for following reasonable orders from their superior. In the end there was no harm done."

"Except to morale," grumbled Give-Em-Hell. As always, the cavalry commander looked out of place when not on horseback. More properly Division-General Henry Stokes, he had a slight frame and wispy hair that belied a fiery temper and a boundless appetite for action that had made his nickname nearly universal. "This kind of finger-pointing always brings everyone down. They're looking over their shoulders when they should be facing toward the enemy."

"We haven't got an enemy yet." This was from Colonel Vahkerson, the Preacher, who'd gotten *his* nickname from his conspicuous faith. In Khandar, he'd inscribed every one of his cannon with verses from the *Wisdoms*, insisting that it improved their accuracy. "And I pray to God that we still won't. Bad enough that good Karisai fight one another, but Vordanai fighting among themselves is an even greater tragedy."

"Agreed," Marcus said.

"Then you don't plan to march?" Val said, a touch too eagerly.

"I plan," Marcus said, "to do whatever the queen and the Deputies-General ask me to do. As should all of you. That's what being loyal *means*. We don't decide for ourselves what's best for the country."

"How many of these men will die if you lead them against Janus?" Quord's question rattled through his mind, no matter how he tried to ignore it. So many of his friends were gone already. Adrecht and Jen Alhundt, twin betrayals that had shaken him to the core. Andy and Hayver, his eager young assistants. Stalwart, dependable Ihernglass. Mor, buried in some military prison.

And further back. His parents, burned in their home on the orders of the arch-traitor Duke Orlanko. And his sister, Ellie, who Sothe had told him could be still alive, somewhere—

No. Marcus pulled up short, as though at the edge of an abyss. *I'm not thinking about Ellie.*

He'd been quiet too long. They were all looking at him: a guarded, curious stare from de Manzet, worry from Val, genuine sympathy from the Preacher, Fitz as straight-faced as ever. *Every one of them could have done what Quord did. But they've put their faith in me, as always. Better not to let them wonder if that was a bad idea.*

He cleared his throat. "For the moment, we need to wait on events. I want order kept in the camps, no matter what news trickles in. Keep things as normal as possible, but no large meetings and no passes to the city. Curfew is sundown, and spread the word that I'm taking it *seriously*. The days when we could afford to go easy on people who skirt the rules just ended." Marcus looked at Give-Em-Hell. "I'm going to be leaning on you for a lot of this. Are your troopers up for stopping fights instead of starting them?"

"It's not our preferred trade," Give-Em-Hell said with a grin, "but we can manage."

"If I might make a request," Fitz said, "I think special care should be taken with the men of my First Regiment. The Old Colonials are . . . stubborn. I don't think they'd go as far as treason, but brawling is a distinct possibility if there's a disagreement. It'd be better if there were outsiders around to keep the peace."

"Noted. Anything else?"

"The Second," de Manzet said. "They still don't have a commander."

"Ihernglass is officially only missing."

De Manzet shrugged. "Be that as it may, someone is going to have to take charge."

"Right now, Colonel Cytomandiclea is in acting command, with the assistance of Colonel Giforte," Fitz said. "But it's an informal arrangement."

"That's tricky," Val said. "You can't just put someone new in charge. Not with their . . . special circumstances."

"I'm sure the Second Division would obey whichever commander the Ministry sees fit to appoint," Marcus said loudly. "But yes, I agree that there might be complications for morale. I'll speak to the queen about it."

"While you're at it," de Manzet said, "try to find out if we're at war or not."

CHAPTER THREE

WINTER

*T*hok. *Scrape.* Tug. *Thok. Scrape.* Tug.

The sky overhead was a brilliant, crystalline blue, unmarred by clouds. The mountain peaks in every direction were capped with snow, but the sun beat down on her back with a pleasant warmth.

Thok. Scrape. Tug.

Her shoulders burned. One arm ached, as though it knew deep in the bone that it still *ought* to be broken.

Thok. Scrape. Tug.

She had a . . . thing, like a pick but a little bit wider. She brought it down with both hands, to bite deep into the earth. *Thok.* Then she twisted it, with a scratchy sound of soil on metal. *Scrape.* Then she tugged and pulled, one boot braced against the earth, until it came free. One stride forward, and start again.

Thok. Scrape. Tug.

Winter had no idea why she was doing this. It had something to do with potatoes, and a fall harvest, but beyond that she was lost. Mrs. Wilmore's long-ago lessons on running a farm hadn't covered potatoes, and in any case she'd forgotten almost everything. But Snowfox had told her this was how she could help, and so here she was, helping. It had been some time, but she figured sooner or later either she'd run out of field or someone would tell her to stop.

She liked the work. The Eldest had made it clear she was an honored guest at the Mountain and she wasn't obligated to lend a hand, but Winter found herself dreading the quiet of her empty chamber. The honest simplicity of swinging a pointy stick into the ground, over and over, brought her a kind of peace. She suspected her untrained efforts weren't really all that helpful, but at least it was something.

Something other than—

—*red eyes, a sea of red eyes—*

—*the flawless face of a crystal statue—*

—*the roar of cannon and the howl of the killing wind—*

—bad dreams.

Thok. Scrape. Tug.

One of the Mountain people was waving to her. Winter stopped and waited while the young woman trudged across the field. She hadn't learned any of their names.

Better for them if I don't. Better for them if they stay away. On some level she knew this was nonsense, but she couldn't banish the chains of guilt. *Jane. Bobby.* Dozens of soldiers whose names and faces were fading shamefully from her mind, merging into a single broken figure. *People who get close to me end up dead.*

"Winter! They are asking for you," the woman called. She spoke in Murnskai, which Winter still didn't understand perfectly, but the Mountain people were used to talking slowly for her benefit. "Eldest requests your presence in the high chamber."

She'd known this was coming. The world was calling, dragging her back to the place where bad dreams were forged. For just a moment, she wondered if she could say no. Stay here in the fields forever, learning to plant potatoes.

The demon in the pit of her soul gave a restless twitch. It sensed the presence of its kin.

There's no escape from dreams.

"He has returned," the Mountain woman said. "The masked one."

The Steel Ghost.

Winter straightened up with a sigh and dropped her potato pick. She could feel her life, her responsibilities, settling back onto her, like a cloak lined with lead weights. Her voice was a croak after days of disuse.

"Show me the way," she said.

The Mountain referred to both the hidden valley—preserved from the weather and the vengeance of the Church by precarious threads of magic—and the enormous fortress that occupied one end of it. Naturally occurring caves and cracks had been expanded into a warren of rooms and tunnels, with arrow-slit windows and well-stocked storerooms. It was far too large for the few people who lived there, being designed to house the entire population of the valley in case of invasion, and so the corridors the young woman led Winter down were mostly empty. Here and there, young men and women in long priestly robes gave her a respectful nod as they hurried about their errands.

They followed a spiral staircase through several turns, until they were well above the valley floor. Here the rooms had larger openings, lips of rock carved into balconies, many overrun with the birds' nests and guano. The highest chamber was completely open on one side, like a house with one wall missing, and a massive fire burned there day and night. Winter had seen it from the valley floor, like a glowing, unblinking eye.

Thin cushions were laid on the rock in a rough circle. On one of them sat the Eldest, who ruled—if that was the appropriate word—the Mountain and its people. He was an old man, with a bare skull and a wispy beard, gleaming, intelligent eyes set deep in a heavily lined face. Nothing distinguished him from the other priests except age, but it was impossible to miss the deference everyone else gave him.

The other figure present was a tall man, but aside from his height almost nothing about him was visible. His body was swathed in loose cloth, drawn tight at the wrists, waist, and ankles—an alien style of dress, suited to a desert half the world away. He wore gloves, thick leather boots, and a wrap of black cloth over his hair, so no inch of skin was visible. His face was concealed by an oval mask, smooth and featureless except for three rectangular slits for the eyes and mouth.

This was the *Malik-dan-Belial*, the Steel Ghost of Khandar, leader of the desert-dwelling Desoltai. Rumor had imbued him with fearsome powers, but the original Ghost had been little more than a conjuror's trick. *One man took off a mask, another put it on, and together they're a hero who can step across leagues in an instant.* Janus had figured it out, broken the Desoltai, and captured their ancient temple. *Where all of this began.*

This Ghost was something else. Infernivore pressed against Winter's control, straining for him. He carried his own demon, a thing that let him dissolve into flowing desert sand. By his own admission, he was the last survivor of the cult Winter, Bobby, and Feor had fought in Khandar, the original protectors of the Thousand Names.

And he saved my life. It had taken her some time to realize that. Bobby had flown her away from Elysium and the Beast, but she'd been left alone in the mountains, no food or water, one arm broken. The Ghost had found her and led her back here. At the time, she'd been too wrapped in grief to do more than put one foot in front of the other, but her stint in the potato fields had cleared her head. *If he hadn't found me, I'd have frozen or starved.* She wasn't entirely sure whether she was grateful.

"Thank you for coming," the Eldest said. "Antov, tea for Winter, please."

A young boy, sitting so still near the entrance that Winter had barely noticed him, sprang to life and scurried away. Winter took her place on the cushion equidistant from the two men. The Ghost inclined his masked head, firelight gleaming off brushed steel.

"You're back," Winter said. The Ghost had left again as soon as she'd been safely delivered to the Mountain. "Did you find anything?"

"A great deal," the Ghost said, in his Khandarai-accented Vordanai. "None of it good."

"Elysium?" the Eldest said.

"Nearly abandoned. The Beast is on the move."

Winter shuddered. She and her friends had broken into the stronghold of the Church, expecting to face the Priests of the Black, only to find that their thirteen-hundred-year watch had finally ended. The Beast, brought into the body of Winter's old lover Jane, had slipped its bonds. It spread from mind to mind, converting all of Elysium into its thralls.

"Where?" Winter said. Her throat was dry, and when Antov returned she gladly accepted the steaming mug of tea.

"Hard to say. It does not keep its bodies together. As we feared, it has learned. It will not allow itself to be wiped out again."

The Eldest gave a little sigh. *Not much of a reaction,* Winter thought, *to the news that the world is doomed.*

"There's more," the Ghost went on. "Janus bet Vhalnich has crowned himself Emperor of Vordan and Murnsk and declared the queen deposed."

"What?" Winter said, her numb detachment suddenly broken. There was a crash, and it took her a moment to realize she'd jumped to her feet, her forgotten mug of tea now smashed in a puddle on the rock.

The Eldest sipped from his own tea. "Another mug, I think, Antov. With perhaps a dash of something stronger."

"You can't be serious," Winter said to the Ghost.

"I have not seen Vhalnich myself, but the news is everywhere. If it is a lie, it is an exceedingly widespread and consistent one."

"But . . ." Winter paused, trying to get her racing heart under control. *Emperor?* She sat down, legs crossed underneath her. Her mind felt rusty from disuse. "That doesn't make any *sense.* If Janus wanted the throne of Vordan, he could have taken it after Maurisk's coup. I'm certain that Elysium was his real objective." She shook her head. "And anyway, how can he be Emperor of *Murnsk*? They've already got one."

"There are rumors that he is dead," the Ghost said. "Others say he has fled to the east. Either way, Vhalnich has the support of Cesha Dzurk, who claims to be heir to the Murnskai throne."

"It's still insane," Winter said. "The people of Murnsk will never accept a foreigner on the throne—I know that better than anyone." That was a scene from one of her recurring nightmares, the desperate Murnskai peasants-turned-partisans hurling themselves onto the bayonets of the Girls' Own, slaughtering their own children to keep them out of the hands of the invaders. "Janus isn't that stupid."

"It does seem out of character," the Eldest said mildly. "Though I have never met the man."

Antov returned with another mug. Winter drank deep, and tasted the faint bite of liquor under the astringent tea.

"I agree," the Ghost said. "The explanation seems obvious."

"You think he's been taken," the Eldest said.

The Ghost nodded.

"Taken?" For a moment Winter's brain refused to process that. "Taken by the *Beast*?"

"The Beast is not a mindless plague," the Ghost said. "It is *intelligent*, and it has had thirteen hundred years to learn the ways of men. Its knowledge grows with each mind it conquers. It must know that having Janus as a figurehead will help it immeasurably."

"Why would it need him?" Winter said. "I thought it was just converting everyone in its path."

"We believe its power is not sufficient for that," the Eldest said. "Not yet. We have studies from Karis' time, and extrapolations based on other demons. Our guess is that there is an upper limit on the number of individuals the Beast can convert in a day, probably fewer than a thousand to begin with. It also cannot spread itself an unlimited distance, though it can certainly cover hundreds of miles."

"Which is fortunate," the Ghost said. "If the Beast could truly double in size every day, the world would be submerged by now."

"But the more it grows, the more power it gains. And the more power it gains, the faster it can grow." The Eldest shook his head. "We do not have much time."

"But that *would* make sense," Winter said, feeling like she was finally getting a handle on the conversation. She took another sip of tea and savored the burn as it went down. "If it can't just convert everyone, installing Janus as a figurehead would save a lot of trouble."

"And it gains access to all his knowledge and talent," the Eldest said. "Which, from your description, is considerable."

"In that case, the Murnskai prince is probably taken as well," the Ghost said. "And presumably enough officers and officials to ensure that Janus' rule is respected."

"Damn." Winter put the empty mug down and took a deep, clean breath. "You weren't kidding when you said it was smart."

"It is also looking for you," the Ghost said. "I could sense it, faintly. Most of its forces have departed, but it has not abandoned the hunt."

"Nor will it," the Eldest said. His voice was quiet. "You hold the Infernivore. The tool our order"—he glanced sidelong at the Ghost—"has sought for a millennium, capable of destroying the Beast once and for all. It cannot afford to let you live." He paused for a moment to sip his tea, his ancient eyes finding Winter's. "What will you do?"

"Isn't that obvious?" the Ghost said. "She *must* destroy it. Nothing else matters."

Winter opened her mouth to speak, looking from the Ghost to the Eldest, and stopped. Her fists went tight, and there was a long silence.

"I think," the Eldest said, "that it would be best if I spoke to Winter alone for a moment."

He glanced at Antov, who obediently scurried out of the chamber. The Ghost sat silently for a few seconds longer, his expression invisible behind his steel mask, but in the end he nodded and rose. When he was gone, the Eldest let out a heavy sigh.

"They have been interesting, my conversations with our friend," he said, indicating the direction the Ghost had gone. "I wish I had more time to question him about the history of his order, although he admits his knowledge is limited. They are surely the descendants of the Mages who fled to Khandar—intellectually, if not physically—but his conception of our mission is somewhat different from my own. At another time, it would make for an interesting debate."

"You think he's right?" Winter said. "That I should go after the Beast?"

"I would not presume to make such a decision for you. The primacy of an individual's will is paramount in *our* philosophy. It is part of why we find the

Priests of the Black and their Penitent Damned so abhorrent, this notion of sacrificing oneself completely being the highest virtue." The Eldest leaned closer. "What do *you* want to do, Winter Ihernglass?"

"I . . . don't know." She shook her head. "If you'd asked me an hour ago, I would have said I was happy to stay here and plant potatoes."

"Unfortunately, that cannot be." The Eldest sighed. "The longer you stay at the Mountain, the more likely it is that the Beast finds its way here in search of you. I must think first of those who are in my charge."

"I know." Winter's arm was aching again where Abraham had repaired the break. He'd assured her the pain was only in her mind, but it was no less real for that. She clutched the spot tightly with her other hand. "What I *want* is to go home."

Home. What did that mean, anymore? Surely not Mrs. Wilmore's, where her real memories began. Not Khandar, for all that she'd felt comfortable there. For a moment she'd thought she'd found her home with Jane, in Vordan, but that was gone, too.

Home meant her tent, her soldiers. The Second Division, the Girls' Own. Abby, Graff, Folsom, all the rest. The routine of marching, cooking, laughter and tears, new recruits and battlefield burials. *Is that my home?*

It meant Cyte. Her bright eyes, her razor wit. The softness of her lips, the swell of her breasts, the delicate touch of her fingers. *Oh, Cyte.* Winter swallowed through a sudden knot in her throat.

The Eldest waited for a moment in silence.

"If the Beast is using Janus as a figurehead," Winter said, voice husky, "it will move on Vordan next."

"Not the rest of Murnsk?" the Eldest said, cocking his head.

"In Vordan it can kill two birds with one stone," Winter said. "It can gather all the bodies it wants, and it can find the Thousand Names. Janus brought the archive to the city." She took a deep breath. "If it kills me, that's the last thing it needs, isn't it? To destroy the name of Infernivore, so there's no chance it can be resummoned."

"And if it has indeed taken Vhalnich, the Beast will know where the archive has been hidden." The Eldest nodded. "It does seem logical."

Raesinia will fight. She might not know it was the Beast she was up against, but she'd never simply yield the throne to Janus. *That means the Second Division will be stuck in the war, on one side or the other.* Her guess was that they'd stand by the queen, especially if Marcus d'Ivoire was in command.

In a way, it made things simpler. Whatever home was, whatever it meant, all of it was standing directly in the path of the Beast. *If there's a chance I can help them, I have to take it.*

Winter looked at the Eldest. "You know what I'm going to say, don't you?"

The old man smiled. "I fancy myself a good judge of character. Under the circumstances, I could probably hazard a guess."

"So much for the primacy of the individual will."

"*Will* is just another word for who we are," the Eldest said. "Sometimes a choice may be so finely balanced that we waver between the alternatives. Other times, our basic nature drives us in one direction whether we like it or not." The Eldest spread his hands. "Philosophers have debated for centuries on the question of whether this means we are not truly free. Personally, I don't think there's a lot of point to the argument."

"So what's my basic nature?"

"A question I wouldn't attempt to answer, Winter Ihernglass." The Eldest's smile widened. "But I can say this much: you are not someone who would abandon her friends, no matter the cost."

"No," Winter said, looking into her empty mug. "I suppose I'm not."

The Ghost, waiting outside the high chamber, bowed deeply when Winter emerged.

"My apologies," he said. "I was inconsiderate of your feelings."

"I understand," Winter said. "And you're right. There's really only one choice."

"So I believe."

Winter looked at the impassive mask and frowned. "What, exactly, do I need to do? I tried to use Infernivore on the Beast at least twice. The second time, it just abandoned the body before I could get a hold on it. The first time, though . . ." She thought back to that moment, when she and Jane had gripped each other, two demons thrashing in invisible coruscations of power. "It felt as though the Beast was devouring Infernivore as fast as Infernivore was absorbing the Beast. Like two snakes eating each other's tails. I don't know if Infernivore is strong enough."

The Ghost nodded. "The Beast has a . . . core, one might say. The body into which it was first summoned. That is the center of its power. If that body is killed, another will take on the role, but the process would be inconvenient, so the Beast will keep the core safe as long as it can."

"That's Jane," Winter said. The woman she'd loved, and who had betrayed her. "The Priests of the Black made her read the name of the Beast."

"You must use Infernivore on her," the Ghost said. "And at the same time, you must invite the Beast into your own body."

"Invite it?" She remembered Jane's glowing red eyes, the feeling of the Beast pressing at the gates of her soul, and shivered. "And that will help?"

"It will entangle it too deeply for it to pull back," the Ghost said, then hesitated. "It should, at least. All of this is only theory, for obvious reasons."

"That's not particularly reassuring."

"It's the only chance we have," the Ghost said. "We have to take it."

"What happens to the Beast's bodies? Do their minds return?" Winter frowned. "When I tried to catch the Beast with Infernivore in one of its other bodies, the body just . . . died."

"As I said, we only have theories, and I can't even speculate what might happen afterward. But . . ." The Ghost shook his head. "It does not seem likely that the taken will recover."

If that's true, that means Jane is truly gone. And Janus . . . Winter decided she wasn't ready to think about that. *We don't know anything for certain.*

"And . . ." She paused again, not sure she wanted to say it aloud. "What about me? If I invite the Beast into my body and destroy it?"

"Again, we don't know. It may be that Infernivore will devour the Beast entirely."

"But you don't think so."

The Ghost fixed her with his empty gaze. "They may destroy each other, and you in the process."

So this could be a suicide mission, even if everything works. Winter set her jaw. She'd set out after the poisonous Penitent with twenty-five soldiers and no guarantee of return, and that had been just to save Janus. *If it helps everyone in the Second—and maybe the world—then it has to be worthwhile, doesn't it?*

"I understand the burden we're placing on you," the Ghost said. "What we're asking. But you know—"

"I know. There's no other choice." *I'm getting a little tired of hearing that.* "Let's find the Eldest. I need to look at a map."

They reconvened in the high chamber after Winter had a chance to wash off the sweat of the day and wolf down a hasty meal. From the kitchen, she'd watched the Mountain people come and go, along with the handful of soldiers from the Girls' Own who'd survived the journey here. They'd long ago swapped their uniforms for Mountain homespun, and aside from their darker hair and halting Murnskai it was hard to tell the two groups apart.

A surprisingly good map was waiting when she rejoined the Ghost and the Eldest. Though they were self-reliant, the Mountain people weren't ignorant of the outside world—the Eldest had implied they had spies as far away as Mohkba, the Murnskai capital. So the map was a modern one, military precise on crisp waxed paper. It showed Murnsk west of the Votindri Mountains, a rough rectangle bounded by the mountains and the coast on its long sides, the river Bataria in the north, and the river Ytolin and the Vordanai border in the south. Two more large rivers, the Syzria and the Kovria, snaked across the center of the rectangle; Winter had crossed both with the Grand Army. Elysium and the Mountain were on the far eastern side of the map, nestled against the mountains.

"We cannot know where the Beast's core is precisely," the Ghost said. "But its limited range makes it possible to guess." He drew a circle with one gloved finger in the center of the map. "We know it has bodies near us in the north, watching for you, and we know Janus is at Yatterny in the south"—he tapped the city, at the mouth of the Ytolin—"so it follows the creature itself must be somewhere in between."

"I don't think I can just head directly for the core," Winter said. "I'd never make it."

"Agreed," the Eldest said. "Even aside from the Beast, the journey will be extremely difficult. The false winter unleashed by the Black Priests has wreaked havoc."

"And the tribes from north of the Bataria who came to fight the Vordanai are scattered across the whole region, preying on the peasants and one another." The Ghost looked up at Winter. "You're the strategist among us. I will defer to your judgment."

"I think I need to get back to Vordan," Winter said. "If I'm going to get to the core of the Beast"—saying that was easier than saying *Jane*—"then I'm going to need help. Marcus and Raesinia will understand what's at stake here. If the Beast is going to use Janus to raise an army, it'll be a hell of a lot easier if we have one, too."

"Taking too long is a risk," the Ghost said. "The Beast's power grows the longer we wait."

"A necessary risk, I think," the Eldest said. "I agree with Winter. But I do not think you can return to Vordan the way you came."

Winter glared at the map. Janus' army had followed the most direct route north, along the Pilgrim's Road to Elysium. Trying to go back that way would lead through the center of the region devastated by the fighting and the weather, as well as being the most obvious possibility for the Beast to guard against. *And even if I make it, Janus and his army will be on the Vordanai border, between me and home.*

She nodded. "That leaves two options. East"—she pointed off the edge of the map, beyond the mountains—"or northwest. East means taking the road to Mohkba and then south from there across the Sallonaik."

"It would take months," the Ghost said. "All the way to Mohkba, south to the lake, and then down the valley of the Velt. And Mohkba is hardly safer than going directly south."

"That is where the Church fled," the Eldest said. "And now that Janus has claimed the emperor's throne, there may be fighting."

Winter had been thinking along the same lines. "That leaves northwest. Down the valley of this river"—she squinted to make out the tiny text—"the Gereia, until it joins the Bataria. Then down the Bataria to Dimiotsk on the coast, and hopefully to Vordan by ship."

"The chaos may have spread in that direction as well," the Ghost said. "And there's no guarantee there will be a ship at Dimiotsk going in the right direction."

"If not, I'll try to convince one." Winter shrugged. "I don't like it much, but I think it's my best chance of getting there alive." She looked up at the Ghost. "Would you be able to make it over the border and head directly to Vordan?"

The steel mask tilted quizzically. "Probably. I can travel as sand on the wind. Not fast, but nearly invisible."

"I want you to go south and find Raesinia and Marcus, then. They need to be warned what they're up against. You helped them once before, so they should be willing to listen."

"I should accompany you. You're our best chance—"

"I'm not going to have a chance if Vordan falls before I get there," Winter said. She gritted her teeth. "You called me the strategist here. One thing I know is that you always need a fallback plan. If I . . . don't make it, then the Thousand Names are the only chance left. Someone else will need to read Infernivore and try to stop the Beast."

"That would take time. And lives. Most who try to read a powerful *naath* will die in the attempt."

"It's better than *nothing*, which is what we'll have if the Beast gets its hands on the Names," Winter said. "Please."

Slowly, the Ghost nodded, slit eyes dark and fathomless. "But you cannot plan to travel alone."

"I suggest you speak to Alex," the Eldest said. "I have no doubt she would wish to accompany you."

"No," Winter said. "I can't ask her to do that. She barely made it out of Elysium alive." And she'd had to kill her lover Maxwell after he'd been taken by the Beast. "She deserves to rest."

"I think," the Eldest said with the hint of a smile, "that you may find it difficult to stop her."

"Obviously," Alex said. "You need me."

Winter hadn't spoken to her since they'd parted at Elysium. She'd seen her a few times, standing at the edge of the field where Winter was working, just watching. It was a reunion Winter had known would come eventually, but she'd been hoping for a little more time to settle her mind.

"I don't—I'm not going to pretend that I wouldn't be glad to have you along," Winter said. "But the chance of anyone coming back from this is small. You've already done so much, I can't ask you—"

"You don't have to ask," Alex said. She got up from her chair and started rooting around under her bed. "I'm volunteering."

Winter hadn't been to Alex's room before. It was inside the Mountain itself, not in the cluster of huts in the valley. A pair of arrow slits let in some light, but a lamp was burning even in daylight. There wasn't much to mark the room as lived-in, other than dirty laundry scattered across the floor and a few books stacked here and there.

Alex herself was seventeen, slim and pretty, with close-cut dark hair and an expression that always seemed on the verge of mockery. Much of her past was still unknown to Winter—she'd called herself the greatest thief in the world, and had apparently trained for that profession under a mentor before she'd been captured by the Priests of the Black. She and Abraham had broken out of their custody and fled to the Mountain, where they'd stayed until Alex had heard about Janus' war against Elysium and come south to offer her services.

Without her, Winter would be dead several times over—at the fight against the ice-wielding Penitent in the forest, and again when the blizzard had caught them in the mountains. After all that, she had to trust Alex, but she still didn't feel like she understood her. The girl didn't seem to be able to take anything *seriously*, but there was something beneath the surface that her laughter never touched.

"Anyway," Alex said, emerging from under the bed with a leather sack, "you know as well as I do that if the Beast isn't stopped, that's the end for all of us. Hiding here in the Mountain is just buying time. So if I have a choice between helping you and maybe dying, or putting my head under the covers until a tide of red-eyes starts climbing the walls, you can count me in." She shoved some wadded-up clothes into the sack, then looked up with a bright smile. "Does that make sense?"

"What about Maxwell?" Winter said.

"What *about* him?" There was a hint of real pain under Alex's facade, quickly erased. "He's dead, and I'm sorry about it. But it's not going to stop me from doing what needs to be done."

Winter shook her head. It was pointless to argue—the fact was, she needed Alex's help, and in any case, the girl was impossible to talk out of something once she'd put her mind to it. *I just wish, for once, that helping me could lead someone to a happy ending.*

Alex was still packing. There were a surprising number of hiding places in such a small room. Every little table and chair seemed to have something stuck to its bottom, and every pillow had a secret pocket. So far Alex had produced quite a few coins, several small tools whose purposes Winter didn't know, and an assortment of knives.

"Are you afraid the Eldest is going to come by and search the place?" Winter said, as Alex extracted a roll of silver Vordanai bits from a hollow candlestick.

"What? Oh." She looked down at the coins. "No. It's just habit. I don't like to leave too much stuff lying around." She shook her head and put the coins in her pocket. "So, where are we going?"

"Vordan, eventually," Winter said. "But we're going to have to take a roundabout route."

"And we think Janus has been taken by the Beast?"

"It's our best guess," Winter said. That was starting to sink in, like a shard of glass wedged in her chest slowly wiggling itself deeper every time she spoke the words aloud.

"Hell," Alex said, pulling the drawstring on her bag tight. "I was hoping to get the chance to thank him."

"I think," said a man's voice from behind Winter, "that the best way to thank him is to finish what he started."

Winter turned to find Abraham standing in the corridor, hands clasped at the small of his back. He wore the same loose robe that the Eldest and his priests did. Winter didn't know him as well as she knew Alex, but his healing demon had saved her hand from rot and spared the lives of several of her wounded soldiers. He had soft brown eyes and an easy smile that never seemed quite free of a deep sadness.

"What do you mean?" Alex said.

"From what Winter has told me, Janus wanted to free the world from the Priests of the Black. He might not have known it, but that meant dealing with the Beast one way or another. So it might be argued that this is the continuation of his mission."

Alex snorted. "There's a priest's argument if I've ever heard one. I was going to come and see you before we left—don't worry. I'm not sneaking out this time, remember?"

"No need," Abraham said. "If Winter will have me, I'm coming with you."

"You are?" Winter said. "Why?"

"For the same reasons as Alex, I suspect. This is the time to do what I can, if there ever was one. I owe my life to the Eldest and the people of the Mountain, and the best way I can defend them is by stopping the Beast." He looked down. "And there are some things in the outside world I left . . . unfinished. While the Priests of the Black hunted me, I didn't dare hope I might find some resolution, but if we are successful in defeating the Beast . . ."

"You realize the odds are high that we're going to die trying," Winter said.

"Of course." Abraham looked her in the eye. "I am fully prepared for that possibility."

"I'm not," Alex said. She crossed the room in a few strides and wrapped her arms around Abraham. "I can't tell you not to come. But you're not allowed to die, you understand?"

Abraham ruffled her hair playfully. "The same goes for you."

In a surprisingly short time—the Mountain people were nothing if not efficient—their little expedition was provisioned and ready. They had six horses, shaggy, short-legged mountain breeds that would be sure-footed on bare rock. The Eldest had insisted on loading them with as much food as they could carry, despite Winter's protests that they could resupply once they reached civilization.

"We have sufficient," he told Winter. "And I could not bear it if the world was consumed by the Beast because I was stingy with a loaf of bread."

Only the Eldest and the Ghost had accompanied them to the exit from the valley, a narrow crack in a sheer vertical cliff that was practically invisible from any distance. From here, Winter could see the whole thing laid out in front of her, neatly terraced fields and wide stretches of pasture dotted with grazing sheep. *Such a calm place, so close to Elysium.* She still couldn't believe it, sometimes.

"I will convey your warning to Queen Raesinia," the Ghost said. "I pray that we will meet again in Vordan, Winter Ihernglass. The hopes of the world go with you."

Winter had thought about adding a message for Cyte, as well, and decided against it. *She probably thinks I'm dead by now. Either I'll get to see her when I make it to Vordan, or I won't, and at least she won't have to live with false hope.* She extended her hand, and the Ghost shook it carefully. At the back of her mind, Infernivore raised its hackles at the close contact with another demon, ready to spring forth at Winter's command.

"Good luck to you, too," she said, stepping back.

The Ghost nodded and raised his arms. Wind swirled around him, carrying the hot, dry taste of the desert, incongruous in this mountain hideaway. Sand rose into a whirlwind, obscuring him from view, and then streamed off into the air, leaving behind nothing but a bare patch of earth.

"That would be very convenient," Alex said, looking down at her hands. "If my demon could do that, it would have saved me a lot of trouble."

Winter turned to the Eldest. "My soldiers," she said. "They can stay?"

The old man nodded. "Of course. The Beast has no reason to hunt them. And if you succeed, they can even return to Vordan. We don't need to hide if the Black Priests have been destroyed."

And if we fail, it won't matter. Winter suppressed a grimace. "Thank you."

"You are doing God's work, Winter Ihernglass," the Eldest said. "I pray that He will protect you."

"I thought it was God who sent us the Beast of Judgment?" Winter said.

"He did," Abraham said. "But He also sent us the means to keep ourselves safe."

"God can be sort of a jerk that way," Alex said.

CHAPTER FOUR

RAESINIA

Mistress Lagovil sniffed haughtily and drew herself up. With her hair piled on top of her head in elegant disarray, she was intimidatingly tall, a head and a half higher than her queen. Raesinia had to fight not to hunch her shoulders like a child being scolded.

"I see no reason why war, if there even *is* to be a war, should interrupt the social calendar," she said. "Your father, may God rest his soul, held the view that Ohnlei was a precious jewel, to be preserved from the storms and furors of the outside world. He would have insisted that the Autumn Fete proceed as scheduled."

"I'm sure," Raesinia said, biting back the rest of her response. In the privacy of her own head, she added, *Perhaps if he'd spent less time attending to the social calendar and more time paying attention to his wars, he might have won a few of them.* Raesinia had loved her father, who'd been as kind and loving a parent as she could have hoped for given the demands of kingship, but she had to acknowledge that military matters had not been among his talents. She cleared her throat and said, "But it's a matter of resources and popular opinion. A great deal of work still needs to be done here, and expenditures must be kept to a reasonable level while war is still a threat. The people will not tolerate a court that pampers itself while soldiers starve."

"In your father's day," Mistress Lagovil said, "we were more concerned with what people of *quality* thought."

"Times have changed," Raesinia said grimly. *We had a little bother with a revolution, you might have noticed. They nearly burned your precious palace down. Maybe it would have been better if they had. Then I could start from scratch and not put up with this—*

Mistress Lagovil had the look of someone willing to continue the argument indefinitely, but thankfully at that point there was a rap on the door.

"Eric Vandalle to see you, Your Highness," said Barely from outside.

"Finally," Raesinia said, cutting off Mistress Lagovil before she had a chance to protest. "Excuse me. I've been expecting him."

"Very well." The frosty look on the head of staff's impeccably made-up face said that the discussion wasn't over, but she stood and walked stiffly to the door, making the palace livery look as martial as a soldier's uniform. Raesinia waited until she was gone and Eric had stepped in to take her place before she relaxed.

"I should ask Marcus if the Girls' Own needs any officers," she said, to no one in particular. "I can just see Mistress Lagovil screaming her troops into line to repel a cavalry charge."

Eric started to snigger, remembered himself, and turned it into a cough, then struggled to regain his impassivity. Raesinia gave him a few moments, then said, "I don't suppose you actually have anything important to report?"

"I do, in fact," Eric said, trying for dignity. "A message from Deputy—that is, from *Minister* d'Andorre. He has, as of this morning, been confirmed in the post of Minister of War, and would greatly like to meet with you in his offices."

"That's why he's been putting me off," Raesinia muttered. She'd been trying to meet with d'Andorre for a week. Once again, she found herself deeply missing Sothe. Alek Giforte was competent, but she was certain Sothe could have done better. And Sothe would have had d'Andorre kneeling on the palace carpet instead of inviting *her* over to his ministry like some kind of supplicant.

Careful, careful. She couldn't afford an open rift with the Deputies now, however obstreperous they might be. *At least they've finally picked someone, and he's a known quantity.*

More news had trickled into the capital in the weeks since Janus' announcement, and none of it was good. Janus had ridden south, to where part of the Grand Army had been left to guard the frontier. The divisions there had all declared for him immediately, without more than token resistance on the part of loyal officers. Reports had also confirmed that an unknown number of Murnskai troops marched with Janus, apparently under his command. All in all, it meant that the would-be emperor had collected an army at the northern frontier that was at least equal to the loyal Grand Army in size, if not larger.

Marcus had not been idle, of course. Garrisons, frontier posts, and training camps had been stripped to bring the divisions camped north of Vordan City up to strength, though the process was far from complete and many of the new recruits were raw. Other units were on their way, summoned from as far afield as the eastern border, but they would take weeks to arrive. The city was restive, with pro-Janus demonstrations almost every day, and the Armsmen had been worn ragged preventing riots. *This can't go on.* There would have to be a clash, sooner rather than later. *And God help us if we don't come out on top.*

The Ministry of War was one of the big stone buildings that stood along the grand drive leading up to the front gates of the palace. Standing in front of it, Raesinia could look over her shoulder and see the ruined shell of the Cobweb, former headquarters of Duke Orlanko's Ministry of Information. *Hopefully, the sight will remind d'Andorre what can happen to ministers who get too big for their boots.*

Smartly uniformed guards escorted Raesinia, her two attending soldiers, and Eric into the building and up to the top floor. The minister's vast office faced a huge picture window, looking out across the palace grounds. D'Andorre had already settled himself behind the leather-topped desk, but he had the decency to rise at his queen's approach. Raesinia waved for him to sit, though she herself remained standing; if she'd sunk into one of the heavy armchairs, her head would barely have shown over the edge of the desk, and she didn't want him literally looking down on her.

"Minister d'Andorre," she said. "That is correct, yes? I only just received the news of your appointment."

"It is," d'Andorre said. "My colleagues in the Deputies voted yesterday evening."

"Do you know if they've come to a decision on my request to appoint a supreme commander?"

"They have." D'Andorre steepled his fingers. "I'm afraid they have rejected it, Your Highness."

"They must see that we have to do *something.*"

"That is clear to everyone," d'Andorre said. "The Deputies-General is only concerned that, in our haste, we will repeat the mistakes of the past. The creation of the post of First Consul was, after all, one of the primary reasons for our current difficulties."

Raesinia gritted her teeth, but she couldn't really deny that. "Then who will command?"

"The Deputies have appointed a military committee, chaired by myself, to oversee the army."

"So instead of repeating the mistakes of the Consulate, you want to repeat the mistakes of the Directory?"

"There's no danger of that, Your Highness. Strict safeguards have been put in place, I assure you." He spread his hands. "I am merely a representative of my colleagues, not a power unto myself."

"In that case, you, or the committee, or the entire Deputies, need to *get moving*. Janus is accumulating supporters by the day, and every hour we sit here doing nothing makes us look weak. We have to act."

"I understand that, Your Highness."

"Then give Marcus the order to march!"

"Ah." D'Andorre gave a tired smile. "I wondered when we'd come to that."

"They're making a mistake," Marcus said.

Raesinia sat in his tent, in the uncomfortable camp-chair, staring across the big table at him. Between them was a large-scale map of Vordan, with stacks of paperwork pushed to the side.

"Look," he said. "Janus is coming south. He needs to take Vordan City, obviously. He could push southeast, here"—he stabbed a finger at the map as though it had offended him—"through the passes at the head of the Vor. That's the most direct route, but it's rough country, with a lot of fortified towns and little rivers to hide behind. It'd be very hard to bring an unwilling opponent to battle.

"Instead, he's pushing southwest, down the valley of the Pale." This time he tapped the map more thoughtfully. "Open country, fewer rivers. Good terrain for a field battle, where Janus excels. He wants us to go after him. He needs a quick decision."

"*We* need a quick decision," Raesinia said. "If we let him do as he likes, anyone on the fence is going to want to join the winning side. We need to confront him."

"Not if it means playing directly into his hands."

"Janus isn't divine, Marcus," Raesinia said gently. "Not *everything* we do is part of his plans."

"I don't know if I'd bet on God Almighty against Janus bet Vhalnich," Marcus said grimly. "I'm telling you that if I take the army to the Pale, I can't guarantee—"

"They don't want you in command," Raesinia said. "That's what I came here to tell you."

There was a long pause. Marcus looked down at the map for a moment, then over at the papers, as though seeking inspiration.

"I'm sorry," Raesinia said. "I tried to get d'Andorre to reconsider. But as far as the Deputies is concerned, handing the army that's going to fight Janus over to his closest subordinate is too dangerous, no matter how loyal you claim to be. Even with the queen vouching for you, apparently."

"So who are they putting in charge?" Marcus said. "One of the other division commanders?"

Raesinia shook her head. "They've summoned General Thomas Kurot from the southern coast. Apparently, he served well against some holdouts during the revolution and basically sat out the war against the Directory. He's supposed to be some kind of prodigy, and he's never even met Janus."

"That's . . ." Marcus suddenly looked very tired. "That's going to be a disaster. Sending some back-ranker who's hardly tasted gunsmoke up against Janus bet Vhalnich? We might as well pack it in."

"That's why I need you to go with him," Raesinia said.

"I thought you said the Deputies didn't want me along."

"They don't want you in command. I was able to persuade d'Andorre that it would be foolish not to use you in some capacity, though even that wasn't easy." Raesinia grinned. "I may have implied that the troops might mutiny if they tried to march without you."

Marcus snorted. "I think you overestimate my popularity." The brief moment of humor faded and died as he considered the situation for a moment longer. "So where do they want me?"

"Commanding the Second. It seemed like a neat solution. They need a general who understands their . . . unique circumstances."

"And that's supposed to be me?" Marcus shook his head. "I should refuse."

"I don't think you can refuse an order from the Minister of War."

"I can resign," Marcus said, jaw set. "God knows that would be a relief."

"D'Andorre might call that treason."

"Then he's welcome to court-martial me," Marcus said, voice rising. "After everything I've done—"

"I know." Raesinia cut him off. "I may not be a military man, but I understand pride. I know it must be hard for you."

"It's not about *pride*." Marcus laughed bitterly. "Spend enough time with Janus and you soon get used to swallowing your pride. You're asking me to take responsibility for a division, under a commander I don't have any faith in. That means ordering my men—men and women—into fire when I don't have confidence their sacrifice is going to be worthwhile. I can't do it."

Raesinia swallowed past a lump in her throat. "Marcus . . ."

"I'll resign," he said, suddenly animated. "I'll stay here with you. I'm sure Alek can find some use for me with the Armsmen, and you're going to need all the help you can get keeping the city under control."

"None of that will matter if Janus takes Ohnlei," Raesinia said. "What I need is for you to be on the scene when things start to happen. Please, Marcus."

Marcus stared at her, jaw working.

"Why me?" he said eventually. "You know I'm no match for Janus."

"The Deputies don't trust you," Raesinia said. "But I do."

And it'll be safer for you with the army. The soldiers loved Marcus almost as much as they loved Janus. If he stayed, once they departed he'd be at the mercy of the politicians. *And if things go wrong and they start looking for scapegoats, you'll be much too convenient.* At the height of the revolution, anyone of Borelgai or Murnskai extraction risked being strung from a lamppost by an angry mob. It wasn't much of a stretch to think that Janus' former subordinates might face the same fate when it was his army approaching.

"If Kurot won't listen to me, I'm not going to be able to help," Marcus said after a long silence.

"You know the other division commanders. If you work together . . ."

"That sounds dangerously close to suggesting mutiny."

"I wouldn't go that far. Just . . . guide him."

"Saints and *fucking* martyrs." Marcus slumped in his chair. "This is insane."

"There's another thing," Raesinia said. "Maybe you're right about Janus. If someone *is* using him, you'll be in the best place to do something about it. That could put an end to the whole thing at a stroke."

"That's a long shot," Marcus said.

"It may be the best we've got."

Another pause. After a moment Marcus pushed himself to his feet.

"All right. Tell them I'll take the Second. Let's hope this Kurot is willing to listen to reason."

"Thank you, Marcus." Raesinia stood up as well. "I wish I could come with you."

"*I* don't. It's been a few hundred years since the queen's place was on the battlefield."

Raesinia circled the table, feeling Marcus' eyes on her. "I know. But it was . . . simpler when we were away from Ohnlei."

"I suppose." He looked uncomfortable. "Those were unsettled times. I think we were . . . confused."

Raesinia fixed his gaze with her own. "What do you mean?"

"Just that . . . I don't know." He shook his head. "Forget it."

"No. Be straight with me, Marcus. Have you changed your mind about what you said to me?"

"No! Of course not." He looked away, cheeks burning under his beard. "I just meant that I wouldn't hold you to any promises that you made in the heat of the moment. I understand that political realities can be difficult."

"Marcus."

When he wouldn't look at her, she stepped closer and grabbed the front of his uniform. Surprised, he bent toward her, and she kissed him as thoroughly as she knew how. After a moment his arms came up, wrapping around her shoulders and pulling her close. Raesinia felt her heart beat faster as she was pressed against him, and she locked her hands together at the small of his back. His beard tickled her cheek.

"Believe me," she whispered when he finally broke away for breath, "I intend to hold you to every word. I love you, Marcus. And as soon as this *nuisance* is dealt with, we're going to figure out how to do something about it." *And to hell with what Mistress Lagovil and the rest think.*

The Grand Army of Vordan—henceforth to be called the Army of the Republic, according to a hastily promulgated proclamation from the Deputies—unfolded itself from the camp north of Ohnlei with a ponderous slowness, like a bear ready for hibernation but prodded into action. It was still midautumn, the leaves gloriously red and gold on the trees, and the weather remained warm and clear. But there was a fragility to it that hadn't been there at midsummer, a sense that the storms and frosts of winter might blow in at any moment.

Ironic, Raesinia thought, *given what happened to us over the summer.* This time, she hoped, there would be no Penitent Damned putting their fingers on the scale.

The columns were supposed to have started moving at dawn, but it was past noon before the vanguard was finally on the road, Give-Em-Hell's light cavalry riding in neat squadrons in front of the long, thin column of plodding musketeers. At intervals came the battalion flags, the silver eagle of Vordan on a blue field snapping in the breeze. Cannon rumbled by, teams of horses harnessed to the covered ammunition carts called caissons with the guns themselves, pointing backward and down, attached to the rear by their trails. More carts, carrying the tents, baggage, and other supplies, came down the road in a dense mass, protected by long lines of heavy cavalry riding beside them.

Raesinia had witnessed quite a few such departures. This was far from the worst showing a Vordanai army had made, although she had to admit Janus' Grand Army had been prettier as it had left for the north. Many of these battalions had been filled out with fresh recruits, some of whom still lacked proper uniforms, and sergeants screamed at them where their lack of marching practice was obvious. Here and there, the line contracted to a tight knot until an officer hurried along to sort out the disturbance.

It's always like this, Raesinia thought, trying to suppress a flutter of nerves. Traffic jams and mix-ups were par for the course when armies were on the march—after bearing witness to what Marcus had to do to keep roughly on schedule in Murnsk, she was amazed they ever got anywhere at all. Still, she couldn't help but think in terms of omens.

Enough. She turned away from the scene and back toward the little cluster of people behind her. They were on a grassy hilltop, overlooking the line of march. Besides Eric and the two guards, there was a small crowd of Deputies, city notables, a few curious nobles, and foreign dignitaries assembled. Raesinia spotted Duke Dorsay and headed in his direction.

"Your Highness," he said with a modest bow.

"We need to talk."

He looked over his shoulder as the crowd began to break up into smaller knots of conversation; then he shrugged and started walking away from the others. Raesinia fell in beside him.

"I suspect I know what you want to talk about," Dorsay said. "But I'm very much afraid I'm going to have to disappoint you."

"I'm not going to beat around the bush," Raesinia said. "You and I managed to keep Vordan and Borel from each other's throats. Surely it's in your interests to help us now. If Janus takes over, it will mean war with you sooner or later."

"No one doubts that," Dorsay said. "And you know you have my personal sympathies. But it's more complicated than that." He sighed. "We received a packet from our government this morning."

"That's quick work." The speed of the Borelgai packet ships was proverbial, but even so. "Are you certain they had all the information?"

"Enough for preliminary instructions. All work on the treaty is to be suspended, for now."

Damn. She'd expected that, but she'd been hoping the Borels wouldn't act quite so soon. "So we're just going to be left hanging?"

"I imagine they expect you to communicate your needs to the ambassador, so that whatever assistance is required can be a part of the negotiations when they resume."

"You think you have us over a barrel, so you're going to wring out more concessions, in other words."

"Not me, Your Highness." Dorsay looked genuinely unhappy. "My position here has been brought to an end. I will be returning to Viadre on the first available ship."

"What happened to Georg and his desire for peace?"

"We may not have a Deputies-General, but neither is Georg an absolute despot." Dorsay sighed. "I can only assume there has been a realignment at home. I'll know more once I arrive." The duke kicked at a tuft of browning grass. "Assuming I'm permitted to remain at court. They may pack me off to the country again, which I have to say would suit me well enough. I'm too old for this nonsense."

"It's going to take too long," Raesinia muttered, half to herself. Time to talk to the Borelgai ambassador, time for the message to go to Viadre by ship and back again, however many times it took to come to an agreement. "By the time any help even sets out from Borel, it could be too late."

"I know. I have tried to impress upon Georg that military affairs rarely wait on a politician's timetable."

"There must be something we can do to speed things up."

Dorsay shrugged. "Not unless you can convince Georg he needs a Vordanai vacation, and I sincerely doubt that you can. He hasn't left the palace grounds in years, the lazy wretch."

She thought, briefly, of the flik-flik lines, the signaling technique that Janus had brought back from Khandar. Their operation required extensive training, however, and all the operators Vordan possessed were going along with the army, to lay out a line keeping General Kurot in contact with the capital. *We should have more of them. And permanent stations, and—* And they would, someday. But here and now there wasn't time, even if she was willing to reveal military secrets to the Borels.

Or maybe there's something in the Thousand Names. Feor, the Khandarai priestess, had students studying the ancient archives. But from what Raesinia knew of magic, coming up with something so eminently practical so quickly was unlikely.

"That's it," Raesinia said.

"What, getting Georg to go on vacation?"

"The other way around," Raesinia said. "Duke Dorsay, I think it is about time I saw Viadre."

"I'm telling you, Your Highness," Dorsay said, as they neared the Borelgai ambassadorial suite, "this is a bad idea."

"I agree," said Eric, on the other side. "The Deputies will have a fit."

"You have no idea what the court in Viadre is like," Dorsay went on. "I'd take any battlefield you care to name over that nest of vipers, and I've seen my share of both."

"They'll say you don't have the *authority*," Eric said. "What's the good of going there yourself if the Deputies won't approve the deal you work out?"

Raesinia stopped in her tracks, forcing the two of them to come to a hurried halt. She'd changed out of her riding leathers and into a full formal dress, whose layers of velvet and silk added considerably to her bulk. They rustled as she turned on the two men.

"First of all," she said, "the court doesn't scare me. Politics around here haven't been exactly *safe*, you may have noticed." *And I was at the center of the revolution,* she added mentally. *"Nest of vipers" doesn't begin to describe it.* "Second of all, the Deputies have already given their approval to the treaty in outline. All that's under discussion is the details."

"They won't see it that way," Eric said. "Military assistance was *not* what they had in mind!"

"Then they're welcome to explain that to Janus," Raesinia said, "or argue with me after we've won."

"But who's even going to *conduct* the negotiations?" Eric said. "You?" At Raesinia's arched eyebrow, he stuttered, "N–n–not that you're not a fine negotiator, but do you know enough about the subjects? I know *I* can't follow half of what goes on when they get into trade agreements and shipping rights."

Raesinia glanced at her two bodyguards. Barely was trying hard to keep a straight face at Eric's discomfiture, but Joanna was definitely grinning. She felt like grinning back.

"As it happens," she said haughtily, "the Minister of the Treasury has agreed to lend me one of his experts." *Or he will, once we ask him.* "Between us we should be able to handle the major issues."

"Your Highness, please." Dorsay lowered his voice. "You may be putting yourself in danger."

"I'm sure His Majesty would never lower himself to harming a guest," Raesinia said. *And danger or not, this is what I can do to help.* Marcus was out there because *she'd* asked him to go, begged him over his best instincts. *If there's anything I can do to protect him, I have to try.* She grinned. *Besides, what's the worst they can do, cut my head off? They'd be very surprised at the results.*

She started walking again, reaching the door to the ambassadorial suite before her escorts had a chance to say another word. The Borelgai Life Guards opened the door and stepped out of the way, coming to attention. Ihannes Pulwer-Monsangton waited by the big table, wearing his diplomat's grin.

"Your Highness," he said. "It's an honor."

"Thank you for receiving me on such short notice," Raesinia said, sweeping in. That was one thing to be said for formal dresses, she had to admit—they made for dramatic sweeps. "You got my note?"

"I did indeed." Ihannes' smile widened.

"And?"

"While my instructions from His Majesty do not *specifically* address this eventuality, I am sure that I'm not going outside the bounds of my authority to say that he would welcome your visit as a sign of the increased cordiality between our two nations." Ihannes cocked his head. "And, of course, it would be more convenient for any negotiations that might arise."

"Then His Majesty will receive me?"

"In due time."

Raesinia felt her heart sink, expecting some excuse for indefinite delay. But Ihannes only waved a hand theatrically.

"His Majesty is, of course, extremely busy, and arranging the appropriate celebrations will take time. But I'm certain that the relevant members of the government would be at your disposal immediately."

"Perfect," Raesinia said. She'd expected more of an argument from the ambassador, truth be told. *Perhaps even he realizes this is a crisis.* "I want to leave as soon as possible."

"In part that depends on how much of an escort Your Highness plans to bring," Ihannes said. "The packet sails tomorrow evening, but space is limited."

"It won't be much," she said. "Fewer than a dozen, including myself. Is that acceptable?"

"Ideal," Ihannes said, so quickly Raesinia wondered if she'd made a mistake. But bringing a regiment of soldiers along wouldn't put her any less at the Borels' mercy if they decided to turn on her. "In that case, I must begin preparations at once. If you'll excuse me?"

"Of course. Thank you, Ambassador."

Ihannes bowed again, and Raesinia retreated. Dorsay hurried in beside her.

"That man," he whispered, "is not your friend, however much he smiles. Don't forget that."

And you are? Raesinia looked down at the flustered duke. He'd always been honest with her—always *seemed* honest—but he had to have his own agenda, the same as anyone else. *I'll have to watch him, too.*

"Believe me," she said, as her bodyguards resumed their places at her shoulder. "I'm used to it."

CHAPTER FIVE

MARCUS

Getting an army on the road after a long time in camp was always difficult. It seemed to take even veterans only a few weeks to forget everything they'd ever known about how to march, which meant that order had to be carefully established all over again—road space allocated to prevent traffic jams, carts and other transport accounted for, patrols and sentries assigned, and distances plotted. Having lots of fresh recruits made things worse. The cavalry patrols would be kept busy rounding up those who'd gotten lost or dropped out of line. Fortunately, they had at least ten days' march before they reached the Illifen passes, which meant there'd be time to get the fresh troops into some kind of shape before they had to worry about the enemy.

All of this, Marcus had been expecting, and much of the staff work had already been done. What he hadn't planned for was the attitude of the other senior officers, who were suddenly ill at ease whenever he was around. It was as though he'd been diagnosed with some horrible disease and nobody quite knew how to talk to a dead man walking. *Or they're worried it might be contagious.* Even Val showed the signs, though he made a dutiful effort to pretend nothing was wrong.

Only Fitz was immune, which was not surprising. He shook his head when Marcus asked him about it.

"It's not that they don't trust you," Fitz said. "Most of the officers don't care much what the Deputies think. It's more that they expect you to be upset about it, and so they're walking on tiptoe."

That made sense, Marcus thought. *They do look a little bit like children who know Daddy's ready to explode about something.* It didn't make it any less irritating, though. General Kurot was on his way from the south, but Raesinia had insisted the march begin immediately, so it had been Marcus' responsibility to set things in motion. Once that was done, though, he happily passed over command to Fitz and reported to the division that was from now his only responsibility.

Every unit, Marcus knew, had its own character, its own customs and rituals, a culture that grew as men died or retired and fresh ones were brought in. That spirit could be a powerful motivator—troops would fight harder for a group they felt like a part of than for a gang of strangers—so it was, in most cases, to be encouraged. But it put a new commander in a ticklish position, expected to exercise authority but ignorant of the social ramifications.

How much worse is it going to be when half the division is women? Marcus didn't feel like he understood women at the *best* of times. The usual solution was for the new commander to lean heavily on his immediate subordinates. *Let's hope they're willing.*

Each divisional camp was separated from the others, so the army spread out over a considerable stretch of country. They were marching alongside the river Marak, which ran calm and black to the east, flowing in lazy curls to ultimately join the Vor. Around it stretched the heart of Vordan, land that had been farmed and cultivated for centuries. Fieldstone walls surrounded orchards and pastures, plots of vegetables and chicken coops. As the sun went down, lights twinkled behind the windows of cheerful little farmhouses like fireflies coming to life in the gloom. An occasional copse of gnarled old trees still stood, black against the purpling sky. After the harsh wilderness of Murnsk, this flat green land felt like paradise.

Marcus rode alone to the Second's camp, pleased to see the lights of a well-spaced sentry ring surrounding it. He waggled his lantern at the nearest as he approached, and the sentry's lantern bobbed in return. As he got closer, he made out the shape of a young woman leaning on her musket in the weary pose of sentries everywhere. She straightened a little as he rode up, then came fully alert at the sight of the general's stars on his shoulders.

"Sir!" She snapped a sharp salute. "Welcome to the Second Division, sir."

"Thank you, ranker." Marcus swung out of his saddle, trying not to show his aches. He'd improved a bit, but he'd still never quite gotten the hang of horses.

"Is your escort coming up?" the sentry said.

"It's just me, for the moment," Marcus said. "My baggage is still on the carts. I imagine it'll be along eventually. If you could take me to your commander?"

"Of course, sir. Follow me."

Marcus led his horse after the ranker, up a slight rise. Rows of tents followed the familiar pattern, nicely regular and without a lot of extraneous clutter, which was a sign of good discipline among the junior officers. As Marcus expected, he was taken to the center of the camp, where the command tent was pitched alongside the company baggage and the artillery park. More sentries saluted as they approached.

"Colonel Cytomandiclea should be inside, General d'Ivoire," the ranker said, a little louder than was necessary. Marcus grinned, remembering Fitz pulling a similar trick to give him a few moments' warning when Janus dropped in unexpectedly. He handed her the reins and scratched at the tent flap.

"Come in."

Marcus ducked inside. It wasn't as large as his army command tent, but it was laid out in a similar fashion, with a map table and a bedroll stowed in one corner. Leaning over the table was a slender young woman, her long dark hair falling forward from her shoulders as she frowned in concentration.

The ranker's warning had apparently been lost on her. Marcus cleared his throat, and she looked up.

"What—oh!" She came to attention, crisp and professional, and saluted. "Column-General d'Ivoire. Welcome to Second Division. I'm Colonel Cytomandiclea. Please call me Cyte, if you like."

Marcus acknowledged her salute and smiled. "We've met. Before that mess at Gilphaite."

"Of course, sir." She smiled back cautiously. "I wasn't sure if you remembered me."

Marcus was tempted to say that he hadn't met *that* many female officers, but on second thought reckoned it might be impolitic. He coughed to cover the pause, and scratched his beard. "I've, ah, received good reports of your work here."

"Thank you, sir. Colonel Giforte has seniority, but I was the head of General Ihernglass' staff, so I've been doing the planning and paperwork." She shook her head. "I'm glad you're here. Before we go into action, I mean. I'm . . . not a line officer."

"I take it you have no objection to continuing as head of staff?"

"No, sir."

There was an awkward pause. Marcus felt trapped. One set of instincts saw a young woman and prompted him to make polite conversation; another, military set told him there was work to do. *Pretend you're talking to Fitz, damn it.* He gritted his teeth. *How did Ihernglass* manage *this?*

"I'll read the strength reports when I get the chance," Marcus said. "Anything I should be aware of, in general terms?"

"Nothing major, sir." Cyte seemed as eager as he was to move on. "We took on a lot of new recruits in the last few weeks, including a big draft of men for the Third Regiment. Colonel Giforte's ordered extra camp guards to make sure everyone stays in good order."

"Good idea."

"She also said she wanted to see you, sir," Cyte said. "When you arrived." She paused. "At your convenience, of course."

"I'll pay her a visit. Can you arrange for the colonels to join me for dinner? And yourself, of course."

"Yes, sir."

"My things should be arriving at some point. You can just move them in here." A thought struck him. "You do . . . ah . . . have your own tent, don't you?" It wouldn't be at all unusual for a staff lieutenant to sleep in a tent with his commander, but in this case the thought had Marcus' face going red.

"I have my own, sir." If Cyte noticed his discomfiture, she didn't say anything. *Of course she does. This used to be Ihernglass' command. He'd have had the same problem. Unless . . .* He stamped firmly on that line of thought.

"Good. That's good." Marcus patted his uniform vaguely. "I'll go and see Colonel Giforte, then."

"Of course, sir. With your permission, I'll stay here and sort some of this paperwork."

"Thank you, Colonel." Marcus turned away, shaking his head.

The First Regiment—otherwise known as the Girls' Own—had a sort of camp within a camp, complete with its own inner ring of sentries. They waved Marcus through, and he headed for the command tent. Women, in uniform and out, straightened up and saluted as he passed. He did his best not to stare. One contingent must have freshly returned from bathing in the nearby stream—some of them were wrapped in blankets and others . . . less so. Marcus could have sworn they saluted with particular vigor and barely hidden grins. But apart from the bathers—and the shapes of the underthings drying on the laundry lines—there wasn't much to distinguish the camp from any other regiment's, with muskets stacked neatly, cook fires burning, and dice and card games in progress.

Outside the command tent, Colonel Abby Giforte was easy to spot, striding up and down spitting fire in the face of a pair of cowed-looking lieutenants.

"—I don't care what Captain fucking Jathwhite told you," she was saying. "I've got the maps from the general and they're quite fucking clear. Tell him his idiots will have to move their goddamned horses."

One of the lieutenants, a tall, willowy girl who couldn't have been older than twenty, said pleadingly, "I know, sir, but he might be more willing to listen if you would just come and talk to him—"

"I have better things to do with my time," Abby said. "And so do you. Balls of the Beast, you need to learn not to let some second-rate moron push you around because he's got stripes on his shoulder and a cock between his legs. Get back there and tell him to move, and don't let him alone until he fucking gives the orders. Got it?"

The other lieutenant, a shorter, slightly older woman, was grinning broadly. They saluted together and hurried off. Marcus waited while Abby let out a long breath and looked around.

"What's everyone staring at?" she said. Then, catching sight of Marcus, she raised an eyebrow and offered a sloppy salute. "Made it at last, General?"

"My apologies for the delay," Marcus said. "I'm told you wanted to see me." He nodded after the retreating lieutenants. "Are you having trouble?"

"Trouble?" Abby looked confused for a moment, then barked a laugh. "That's just training. Lieutenant Koryar has spent most of her life getting what she wants by smiling at people. She needs to learn there are other ways."

"I see," Marcus said. "Then you had something else you wanted to talk about?"

Abby's eyes narrowed, and she sighed. "You'd better come inside."

Her tent was a mess, which was an impressive achievement considering it could have been up for only a few hours. There were no tables, and a few leather maps were spread on the floor. A small pile of clothing sat in the middle of the bedroll, including a large uniform shirt with a distinctly masculine look. Marcus tried not to show any reaction, but Abby clearly caught him looking and raised an eyebrow, as though daring him to comment. When he said nothing, she nodded slowly, as though he'd passed a test.

"Column-General d'Ivoire." She heaved another sigh. "I apologize if I was rude."

"Don't worry yourself, Colonel." He tried a tentative smile. "I've had worse."

Abby smiled herself, very slightly. She was at least a decade younger than Marcus, in her early twenties, with a short shag of brown hair and a heavy dusting of freckles.

"It's all for the girls' sake," she said. "They expect a bit of a hard-ass at the top. Since Jane's dead and General Ihernglass is . . . away, that has to be me. Cyte isn't really the type."

Marcus had to agree that it was hard to imagine the slight, soft-spoken captain as a martinet. "I understand. And I'm sorry about General Ihernglass."

"Don't be," Abby snapped. She started to speak, paused, and then said deliberately, "*He* is alive. And he'll catch up to us eventually. For the moment I imagine he has something more important to do."

Marcus nodded, not wanting to argue. "So, what did you need to see me about?"

"I just wanted to be clear where we stand." Abby frowned, looking up at Marcus. "You know that most of the women in this regiment joined up to follow Jane and Winter."

"I know." Jane Verity, the street tough turned officer who'd been widely rumored to be Winter's lover, had ultimately betrayed Janus and been imprisoned for it. She'd later died, under somewhat mysterious circumstances. "I'll do my best to follow their example."

"Good. Winter was always very clear about the Girls' Own being an equal part of the division."

"You're afraid of the other regiments taking advantage?" Marcus looked sympathetic. "I'll speak to the colonels and make it clear it won't be tolerated—"

Abby snorted. "We can take care of ourselves on that front, General. Not that we need to—we've got them pretty well trained by now. It's *you* I'm worried about."

Woman or not, being an officer demanded a certain code of behavior. Marcus fixed Abby with a frosty stare. "You're concerned about my ability?"

"I have no doubts as to your ability," Abby said. "We all know what you did in Murnsk after the river flooded. I'm more worried about your character."

Marcus, who'd unfrozen slightly, resolidified. "My *character*?"

"That you might have some crazy ideas, like maybe keeping my regiment off the front line, or sending us where you think it's going to be *safe*." Abby grinned. "Winter always said you had an excess of chivalry. I'm telling you that if you try to apply that to us, you're going to have a lot of angry soldiers on your hands."

Ah. Marcus paused uncomfortably. Winter wasn't wrong, he supposed. Marcus had opposed the creation of a female unit, back in the beginning, out of a visceral feeling that letting women put themselves in harm's way went against everything he was supposed to stand for. Janus hadn't shown any such scruples, however, and it had been hard to maintain his opposition in the face of the enthusiasm of the Girls' Own and other volunteers. Then there'd been Andy, who'd served as his aide all through the coup and the Murnskai campaign, until she'd been killed during the retreat. Her name still brought him a pang of guilt, though she'd chosen her own path every step of the way.

"General Ihernglass . . . has known me a long time," Marcus said. "But I like to think I'm capable of learning, at least a little bit. I can't pretend I'm completely comfortable, but I promise I won't hold this regiment back." He shrugged. "I'd be a fool if I tried to. You're widely agreed to be the best skirmishers in the Grand Army, and any commander who was handed a weapon like that and didn't use it would deserve to lose his battles."

"Good. That's what I wanted to hear." Abby's grin widened. "I'll hold you to it, General."

"Please do," Marcus said. "Now, may I ask *you* a question?"

Abby raised her eyebrows again. "Of course, sir."

"My guess is a lot of your . . . soldiers joined up because of Janus, too. Are we going to have any difficulty now that he's on the other side?"

Abby gave that some thought, then shook her head. "I don't think so. We might have, once, but the old hands have been through two campaigns together now. We owe one another more than any commander, even Janus. And the latest batch of new recruits is from after Janus resigned as First Consul."

"What if Winter Ihernglass turns up at Janus' side?"

Abby's smile faded. "That . . . might be difficult. But I don't believe Winter would ever fight against Vordan."

I might have said the same about Janus. Marcus decided not to press the point. Despite Abby's optimism, the odds were that Winter was dead, his frozen body lying somewhere in the Murnskai mountains along with so many others.

"All right." Marcus looked around. "I suppose I'd better see if my baggage has arrived. Was there anything else?"

"No, sir. Not for the moment."

"Good." He hesitated. "Your father sends his regards, by the way." He hadn't, in so many words, but Marcus felt certain he *would* have, if asked.

Abby laughed. "My father and I have agreed to a truce. I pretend we're not related, and he pretends I don't exist."

"He's a good man. We wouldn't have gotten through the coup without him."

"I'm sure he is. Maybe one day he'll be okay with the fact that his daughter is a good soldier." She shrugged. "You can tell him I said hello, if it'll make you happy."

"I doubt I'll see him soon, but I'll keep that in mind—"

There was a scratch at the tent flap, and Marcus paused. A woman's voice from outside said, "Messenger for the general, sir!"

"Come in," Abby snapped.

A moment later a boy ducked through the tent flap. He was a corporal, but no older than sixteen. His wide eyes suggested he'd absorbed the same scene Marcus had outside, but been a bit less polite about staring.

"Sir. Sirs." He came to attention. "Message for Column-General d'Ivoire."

"That's me," Marcus said. "What is it?"

"Compliments of Column-General Kurot," the boy said. "He's arrived, and he wants to talk to you as soon as possible. I'm to take you to him, if you're ready."

Marcus had hoped for another day or so to get settled in to his new command. *No such luck, apparently.* Though it was probably a good thing from the point of view of the army as a whole. *At least Kurot keeps a quick pace.*

"Then let's not keep the general waiting," Marcus said. "Lead on."

The new commander of the Army of the Republic had clearly only just arrived, but his staff were unpacking with impressive efficiency. A large command tent was already up, and others were rising around it. Several carts full of neatly labeled and organized supplies stood nearby. Marcus' guide brought him to the central tent and scratched for entrance, and was greeted by a barked "Come!"

Marcus nodded to the boy and stepped inside. Column-General Thomas Kurot sat at a folding table behind a portable writing desk. Very little else had been unpacked yet, but the table was already prepared with maps and a set of tiny wooden soldiers, complete with long rakes for moving them about. Beside the map stood a chessboard, pieces carved from black and white marble, apparently abandoned midgame.

Kurot himself was in early middle age, his brown hair fading to gray and receding toward a bald spot atop the dome of his skull. He wore thin, squarelensed spectacles, which combined with a peaked nose to give him an owlish look. Deep blue eyes gave a strong impression of intelligence. Marcus saluted, finding the reflex a little rusty.

"Sir," he said. "Column-General Marcus d'Ivoire, reporting as ordered."

"General d'Ivoire." Kurot looked up, and his smile held genuine warmth. "Please. Come and sit."

Marcus crossed the room, a little uncertainly, and pulled out a folding chair near Kurot. The general looked him over a bit longer and gave an approving nod, as though he liked what he saw.

"Let me first say," Kurot began, "that it's an honor to serve with you. I have read your accounts of the Khandarai campaign with great interest, and I've heard many stories from the more recent Murnskai expedition."

"Thank you," Marcus said.

"And let me also say that I appreciate the difficult position you've been placed in."

"I'm not sure what you mean."

"I am, of course, technically junior in rank to you, having received my promotion to Column-General only recently. By rights it ought to be you in command of the Army of the Republic."

"The Deputies-General believe you are the best choice," Marcus said non-committally.

"We both know that has more to do with your perceived affinity for the former First Consul than with anything else." Kurot spread his hands. "An army can have only one commander, General d'Ivoire, and I don't pretend that I'm unhappy to have been granted charge of this one. But I want you to know that I appreciate the depth of your experience, and I plan to rely on you a great deal. The Deputies may not trust you, but I know better."

"Thank you, sir."

"How long did you spend with Vhalnich?"

"Practically from the beginning," Marcus said. "Although I was here in Vordan during the Velt campaign."

"Ah, yes. When he conquered mighty Antova in only a few days." Kurot frowned. "A pity. I would have liked to hear more of that. But no matter. You must have formed an impression of him."

"I . . ." Marcus hesitated. Whether Kurot trusted him or not, it wouldn't do to seem *too* friendly with the man who was now an enemy of Vordan. "I had his trust, I think. And I understood him, at least a little. I'm not sure anyone has the full picture. Janus is a very secretive man."

"So I understand. Secretive, prone to drama, with a tendency to conspiratorial thinking." Kurot flashed a smile. "I've been studying him, of course. One should always know as much as possible about one's opponents. Would you call him a genius?"

"It doesn't quite fit, sir, but it's as close as I can get. It seemed like things that would elude an ordinary person were just *obvious* to him."

"So it often is, with geniuses and great commanders. Janus is as interesting a case as I've ever studied. *Nearly* great, we might say. Like a cracked gemstone. Flawed, but still intensely brilliant."

Marcus frowned, but said nothing.

"The Velt campaign was a masterpiece," Kurot went on. "And the Khandarai campaign will be taught in military schools for centuries. But under extreme pressure, he clearly starts to fray a bit. Murnsk was not such a great success, after all."

It was very tempting to speak up—Janus had, after all, destroyed every enemy army that had come against him except for Dorsay's slippery Borels, and only the magically turned weather had halted the march. But that seemed impolitic, so Marcus merely concurred with a "Yes, sir."

"Did he talk to you about his art of war?" Kurot said.

"A little, sir. But only in broad terms."

This apparently excited the general so much that he had to stand up and pace. "We'll have to go over what he said. Every word." He waved a hand at the maps. "It will be a pleasure to finally face an opponent who understands the rules of the game. Hunting rebels in the south is necessary, but I take little pleasure in it. They're simple creatures, by and large. You set the trap and wait until they step into it. No, I imagine Vhalnich will be a different sort of player altogether."

"I'd expect so, sir," Marcus said, swiveling in his seat.

Kurot's gaze went to the game board. "Do you play chess, General d'Ivoire?"

"Not since the War College, sir."

"Pity. I think every important truth about war can be found in chess. All this"—he gestured again at the map and the little soldiers—"is contained in this simple board, if you have the eyes to see it. Move and countermove is the very essence of war." He looked up. "I'm sure Vhalnich told you the same."

"I can't say he did, sir. But Janus never attended the College."

"Of course. An amateur. All the more astonishing, really." Kurot went quiet, lost in thought.

"Did you want to discuss plans, sir?" Marcus prompted.

"Time for that later," Kurot said dismissively. "We won't even reach the passes for days. No, I just wanted to meet you face-to-face. Clear the air, as it were."

That's what everyone seems to want today. Marcus suppressed a sigh. "Thank you, sir. But if there's nothing else, I had better get back to my division. I'm still introducing myself to the colonels."

"Of course, of course. For the moment, the marching schedule remains as you've so kindly laid out. I'll send you any changes of plans." Kurot smiled again. "And let me know if you want to brush up on your chess. I'd be happy to show you a few tricks."

"I'll keep that in mind, sir."

By the time Marcus returned to the Second Division camp, dinner was well under way. Light streamed from the command tent, and loud voices were audible from inside. Marcus swept in and found a half dozen people sitting around the big table, with a steaming platter of meat and a plate of bread sitting between them.

"Finally," said a handsome young man. "I thought my stomach was going to tear itself in half."

"Oh, come off it," Abby said. She sat at one corner of the table, leaning back in her chair. "You've been eating like a king all week."

That was certainly true, Marcus reflected. Being in rich, friendly territory was an unaccustomed luxury for an army on the march, and the locals were happy to sell the quartermasters all the food they wanted. For the moment, hardtack and army soup had been replaced by beef, pork, and fresh bread.

"Let me make it my first official order," Marcus said, "that no one should ever wait for me to eat dinner. Please, get started."

A laugh went around the table, and the assembled officers relaxed and began loading their plates. Marcus tossed his jacket on the bedroll and sat at the head of the table, with Cyte at one side and Abby on the other.

"Would you mind doing the introductions?" he asked Cyte. "I still need to put names to faces."

"Of course." She set down her knife and fork and pointed at the young man next to Abby. "Colonel Parker Erdine, of the cavalry."

Erdine doffed an imaginary cap and bowed, silky brown hair falling around his face. "An honor, sir." He had the air of a dandy, but from what Marcus had read he'd proved himself a hard fighter.

"You know Abby," Cyte went on. "Colonel David Sevran commands the Second Regiment."

Sevran was a solid, serious man with pockmarked cheeks and an unflappable look. Marcus nodded to him and said, "You commanded a battalion under Ihernglass in the Velt campaign, didn't you?"

"I did," he said. "Most of those men are still with the regiment. They're solid soldiers."

"Good to hear." Marcus turned to the oldest man in the room. "I presume you're Colonel Blackstream, then?"

"You presume correctly," Blackstream drawled. He wore his age well, with long white mustaches and gray hair pulled back into a complicated braid. Marcus knew he was a War College man, who'd been a captain at Vansfeldt when Marcus had been a nineteen-year-old lieutenant. "Fourth Infantry Regiment, sir. We won't disappoint."

Winter had written that Blackstream seemed to get along well with the other officers, even if he was a bit dour. Marcus watched his expression for any hint of jealousy—Marcus was, after all, a considerably younger man who'd advanced much farther in the same career, and that kind of professional rivalry was stock-in-trade for prerevolutionary officers—but the man's face was hard to read. Marcus made a mental note to keep an eye on him, and turned to the other side of the table.

"This is Colonel Martin de Koste," Cyte said. "Commander of the Third Regiment."

"Honored," de Koste said, inclining his head. He was tall and neatly dressed, with the attention to detail and etiquette that came from a noble upbringing. Of all the colonels of the Second Division, he was the one Marcus was most inclined to mistrust. Winter had written that de Koste practically worshipped Janus. *I'll have to see if there's a way to have a quiet word with him.*

Aloud, Marcus said, "And of course Colonel Archer and I go all the way back to Khandar. The good old days, eh?"

"The old days, at any rate," Archer said, grinning. He was a boyish-looking fellow, with smooth cheeks and golden hair. Despite the impression of youth, he was an experienced artillerist, and a student of the Preacher's methods. Marcus wasn't certain if Archer shared the old cannoneer's religious tendencies as well.

"All right," Marcus said to the table at large. "I'll keep this brief. It's never easy joining a new command, and I know it's never easy getting a new commander. Winter Ihernglass was one of the best soldiers I ever had the privilege to lead, and this will always be his division. I consider myself to be just looking after it for the time being."

There were smiles around the table, and Abby leaned back in her chair, looking satisfied.

"I know the thought of fighting Vordanai doesn't sit right with a lot of you, and I can't say that I like it, either," Marcus went on. "Janus bet Vhalnich was . . . a friend. But anyone who takes up arms against the queen and the people of Vordan needs to be stopped, no matter how great their previous services. I still hope this will somehow be resolved peacefully, though I admit that seems unlikely. If it does come to fighting, I want every courtesy extended, every surrender honored, in accordance with the civilized laws of war. Most of the men we'll face are just obeying their officers' orders, the same as ours."

Colonel Erdine was nodding vigorously, but de Koste was scowling. *Interesting.*

"In that vein," Marcus said. "I want to make one point very clear. This is Vordan, and we are Vordanai. That means *no* looting or pillaging will be tolerated, under any circumstances. Is that understood?" There was a round of nods. "Please communicate that to your men. We're here to protect the people, not abuse them." Marcus looked around the table again. "That's all I've got, for the moment. Any questions?"

"You went to meet with Kurot," Abby said. "Did he tell you anything about the plan?"

"General Kurot assured me he'd fill me in when the time came," Marcus said.

Blackstream looked sour. "Do you really think he'll be a match for Janus?"

"I'm sure he'll do fine," Marcus said. "He's . . . very clever."

Abby and Cyte exchanged looks. "Clever" was usually not a good trait in an officer. Clever officers got people killed. *But that's what I said about Janus, back in the beginning. Kurot deserves a chance.* He ignored the traitorous voice in the back of his mind that said against Janus bet Vhalnich, one chance was all you usually got.

CHAPTER SIX

WINTER

That morning, they skirted another little ridge, veering north to avoid a rocky knuckle of ground that reared up between two valleys, covered with stunted, skeletal trees. The land to the west of the Votindri Range, against which Elysium nestled, was folded like a carpet shoved against a wall. Every quarter mile brought them into a new valley, heavily forested where the trees could get purchase on the rock.

It would have been bad enough if they could just *follow* one of the little streams, but they were still on the wrong side of the watershed. All the tiny trickles ran south, eventually merging into the river Kovria, which veered into territory known to be under Janus' control. Up ahead was a line of hills, dark and forbidding. On the other side, they'd be in the basin of the Bataria, and things would get easier, or so Winter told herself. *At least we won't have so much up and down.*

Her legs burned already. After the Murnskai campaign, she'd thought she was inured to hard marching, but this cross-country trekking through forests and over hills was more difficult than traversing even the worst roads. The uncertain footing wasn't helping—the trees had shed their leaves with unaccustomed haste in the sorcerous freeze, and now that it had warmed they were decomposing into slime.

The forest, in general, didn't seem to have weathered the brief spate of unnatural blizzards well. Some trees had tentative buds, but others seemed dead in truth, or determined to wait out the true winter. The valley floors were choked with debris, rocks, and broken bits of wood. Abraham said these came from the breakup of ice dams and the resulting floods. He'd proven to be quite the authority on the natural world, in fact, while Alex was almost cheerfully ignorant.

"I still say it would have been easier to go south," Alex said now, breathing hard. "We're walking *away* from where we want to be."

"This way we're more likely to get there in one piece," Winter said. "If we go south we've got half the Vordanai army and God knows how many Murnskai between us and Vordan."

"We could get past them," Alex said. She raised one hand, and her power gathered a globe of darkness at her fingertips.

"And if the Beast finds us?" Abraham said. He carried a long stick in one hand and used it to probe the muck as he walked. "You told me what it was like at Elysium. It will not give up easily."

Alex went quiet. Winter stifled a sigh. They'd had the same conversation a number of times since they'd left the Mountain days before. She was glad for the company, and she couldn't exactly *blame* the girl, but . . .

Abraham, on the other hand, rarely spoke but was always worth listening to. He'd already pointed out several places where edible mushrooms grew and the tracks that might lead them to beaver dens. At the moment their packs were still laden with dried meat and berries, but the mushrooms had been welcome, and eventually hunting might be necessary. *We have a long way to go.*

He paused beside Winter, stick outstretched, and wrinkled his nose. Alex, up ahead, half turned.

"What's wrong?"

"I can smell something," Abraham said. "Something dead."

After a moment, Winter could, too, the sick-sweet stench of rotting meat infiltrating the cleaner smell of decaying leaves.

"Another deer?" she said. They'd passed several corpses, all in an advanced state of decomposition, not even torn much by scavengers.

"Probably," Abraham said. He sniffed again. "I think it's up ahead."

"I see it," Alex said. "It's not a deer."

Either Abraham's sense of smell wasn't as good as Winter's, or—more likely—his time working with the sick had bred a certain tolerance. Either way, he was the only one who could approach the body. Alex and Winter stood together, upwind and a little way off, and watched.

Winter had had—unfortunately—quite a bit of experience with *fresh* corpses, but this one represented new territory for her. The body sat at the foot of a tree as though it had simply taken a rest one day and never gotten back up. The skin was sloughing off, and the flesh beneath was black with rot, to the point where Winter couldn't tell where the remnants of the clothes ended and the body began. Bits of pale bone peeked through around the face, and the eyes were gone, leaving only empty holes.

"Still some scavengers around," Abraham said, kneeling in front of the vile thing. "Probably crows. It'd take more than a freeze or two to get rid of them."

"Why are you messing with that thing?" Alex said. "Please don't tell me you think we ought to bury it."

"I'd like to, but the ground's too rocky," Abraham said. "No doubt the forest will take care of it soon enough. But I'd like to see if I can figure out who this was."

"Why?" Alex said, then saw that Abraham had picked up a smaller stick to poke the body. "Oh, saints and martyrs." She turned away, making a retching sound.

"Because if there's one person out in the middle of nowhere, there might be more," Winter said.

"Exactly." Abraham bent a bit closer. "This was a woman. Middle-aged. Wearing some kind of robe, nothing fancy. Probably Murnskai, by the hair." He straightened up, tossed the stick aside, and shrugged. "Any idea why she'd be out in the woods?"

"Refugee from the war?" Winter said.

"We're pretty far north," Abraham said. "And you'd think a refugee would run to a town, especially if she was alone."

"Maybe she was with a larger group, and she died on the way," Alex said, still not looking around.

"And they just left her like this?" Abraham shrugged. "It's possible, I suppose."

"Maybe bandits cut her throat and left her as a warning," Alex said. "Can we please move on?"

There weren't any bandits in these woods, Winter reflected. Bandits needed prey, and here there was no one, just endless miles of forests and hills. She'd always known Murnsk was a vast country, but she hadn't appreciated how much of it was no-man's-land, undisturbed except for the occasional trapper. She'd read that in the north, the Murnskai territory didn't end at a border so much as peter out amid the tundra, where the nomadic tribes acknowledged no king or emperor.

The smell of the corpse faded after a few minutes' walk. It was Alex who spotted the next one, propped against a tree like the first. This one seemed like it had been outside longer, and there wasn't much left but bones and scraps of dark fabric. They gave it a wide berth by common agreement, and kept moving.

The third corpse was a bloated thing that looked like it had been drowned, lying among a pile of broken wood where a flood had washed it. Winter and the others looked down on it from the hillside above.

"This is getting weird," Alex said.

"One body might be coincidence," Abraham agreed, "but this many means there was a group of people here."

"If it was a big group, we ought to have seen tracks. Campsites, maybe," Winter said.

"I think this one is a soldier," Alex said. "Look at his collar."

Winter was unwilling to get closer, but even from this distance she could see that the jacket the body wore had a military look. "I think you're right."

"The last one looked more like a peasant," Abraham said.

"Weird," Alex repeated.

After that they found bodies at least once every few hours. Some of them had been dead for a long time, leaving little clue as to their identities, while others seemed more recent, still clothed and waxy-skinned. They seemed to come from every walk of life—young men and old women, peasant girls and Murnskai soldiers, servants in drab linen and even a white-robed Sworn Priest. Except for the ones that had been obviously moved by animals or floods, every body looked at rest, as though they'd all taken a seat and waited there to die.

"Sacrifices, maybe," Alex said. "The Trans-Batariai do human sacrifice."

"None of them seem to be *wounded*," Abraham said. "Poisoned, maybe?"

"There's another." Winter pointed. A man in a long gray coat sat slumped against a leafless trunk, head lolling. "It looks pretty intact. Abraham, do you think you could figure out how he died?"

Alex made a face, but Abraham nodded. "If something's killing people out here, I think we ought to know what it is."

They trudged through the muck of dead leaves to the body. It had been an older man, with a huge, wild white beard and a fur cap. A hunter, Winter guessed, by his clothing. There was no blood on him, and his posture gave no indication that he'd been in pain. He must have died relatively recently, since there was still a hint of color in his flesh.

Abraham poked the corpse with his stick, and it wobbled. He grunted. "Still fresh."

Winter knelt next to it. The eyes were open, staring off to the east. *Have they all been looking east?* She felt like every body they'd found had been *facing* them, more or less. *Something about the rising sun—*

The dead face twitched, eyes blinking once. Winter startled, falling backward. She scrambled on her backside away from the thing, her mind filling with visions of a temple under the Khandarai sands. *Corpses rising, their eyes filled with green light, smoke leaking from their mouths . . .*

These eyes weren't green. They were red, glowing from within. The man's head wobbled, struggling to face Winter. His lips moved, flesh splitting as they formed silent words.

Winter, the nearly dead man mouthed, and the eyes glowed brighter. *Found. You.*

Then the lights faded.

"Winter!" Abraham had rushed to her side, stick raised, looking at the corpse. "What happened?"

"Not dead," Winter said, breathing fast. The sight of those crimson eyes had sent her back to that horrible night in Elysium. "Not . . ."

"Looks dead now," Alex said, darkness shrouding her hands as she approached. "Want me to spear him to make sure?"

"He was one of *them*," Winter said. "A red-eye. The Beast."

"Oh." Abraham's voice was very quiet.

There was a *crunch* as a spear of pure shadow flashed from Alex's hand, impaling the man's skull and the tree behind it.

"Just to be sure," she said.

But Winter knew the damage was already done. She could picture it all too clearly—in her mind's eye, hundreds of heads snapped around, hundreds of pairs of glowing red eyes narrowed. *Found you.*

"It's the Beast," she said. "All the bodies. It's been sending them into the woods to watch for me. Just letting them wait until they freeze." She forced herself to take a long, slow breath. "It knows we're here."

"Balls of the Beast," Alex swore, then frowned. "I mean, *fuck*. What now?"

"Now we run," Abraham said softly.

Winter nodded, heart thudding in her chest. Across the dead forest, she imagined the baying of hounds.

This far north, the nights were coming early. Up until now, they'd camped at dusk, keeping a relatively leisurely pace. There was a lot of ground to cover, and rushing it early on would only risk injury.

No more time for that, though. Her lungs were on fire and her legs were lead weights, but she pushed on, switchbacking up the rocky slopes as they climbed toward the range of hills that separated the two rivers. Alex kept up, but Abraham was starting to flag, leaning on his stick. Winter pressed on until the sun dropped below the horizon, painting the clouds a fiery orange, and then called a halt.

"Give me a moment," Abraham said, leaning against a tree. "I'll be fine."

"We can't keep running forever." Winter wasn't sure if *she* could press on much longer. "Even if the Beast knows where we *were*, it doesn't know where we're going. Depending on how close its other bodies are, it may not be able to follow."

"We'll have to keep a watch," Alex said, looking around in the gathering darkness. "And no fire."

Winter nodded glumly. Despite the lifting of the magical cold, the autumn chill was rapidly setting in, with nightly freezes. *At least it's still dry.* Pushing through wind and snow had nearly gotten her whole company killed once, and she wasn't eager to try it again.

They had a tent, a clever, lightweight thing from the stores at the Mountain, but they'd been keeping it stowed. The Eldest had provided thick wool blankets, and while Winter begrudged their size in her pack, they'd turned out to be worth their weight in gold. Alex unfolded one, while Abraham shucked his pack and slid to a seat with a sigh.

He's exhausted. Alex was evidently more used to this kind of travel than the young healer. *She walked half the length of Murnsk with a hole in her side to get to me, after all.* Still, fatigue was evident in her movements. Winter found a rock to sit on and shrugged out of her own pack, shoulders aching.

"I'll take first watch," she said. "Get some sleep."

"I'm not going to object," Alex said. "Wake me in a few hours."

Winter nodded. Abraham already had his eyes closed, head tipped back against the tree. With practiced ease, Alex slid in close beside him and pulled the blanket tight around them both. Within minutes, she was asleep.

There was a closeness between them that made Winter a little envious. It wasn't romantic—more like long familiarity and a history of shared hardships. She couldn't help but wonder what they'd gone through before reaching the Mountain. *Someday I may get the chance to ask.* She pulled out her own blanket, wrapped it around her shoulders, and settled in.

Not falling asleep was a challenge. The wool made a warm, tight bubble in the chilly darkness, and Winter wanted nothing more than to hunch in on herself and let consciousness drift away. She forced herself to shift position occasionally, letting drafts of cold infiltrate her cocoon. The pain in her legs and shoulders subsided to a dull, throbbing ache, and the sweat that had sheathed her skin turned cold as the sunlight faded away.

There wasn't much to see after the light leeched out of the world, but she didn't dare close her eyes. Overhead, the sky was a solid mass of stars, cut by the bone-like bare branches of the trees all around. To the east, the mountains made a jagged line on the horizon.

What the hell am I doing? She'd forced herself into motion when the Steel Ghost had returned, but everything still felt *wrong*. Unreal, somehow. Even when she'd been freezing to death, before Alex had guided them to the Mountain, she'd felt like she'd known what she was doing it for. Janus had explained everything—the war, the Priests of the Black, the desperate need to reach Elysium and put an end to it once and for all. Standing in his tent, it had all seemed so clear.

Now Janus was gone, and her certainty had gone with him. The plans she'd made with the Eldest and the Steel Ghost seemed like a thin reed in comparison, sandcastles built by children in ignorance of the tide. The Beast of Judgment was out there, getting stronger. The idea that she could stand against it—stand up to the terrible wall of human flesh that had come for her in Elysium—

God. Tears dried on her cheeks, cold in the night breeze. *What I wouldn't give for a nice set of orders.* No need to worry about purpose or direction, just a point on a map to aim for. *And good soldiers to march with, good officers to command . . .*

And Cyte. The thought of what they'd had, so briefly, made Winter's chest hurt like she'd been run through with a bayonet. She'd never had those feelings for anyone but Jane, never thought she *could*. After Jane's betrayal had torn her apart, she'd thrown herself into her responsibility to her soldiers, certain that it was all she had left. *Cyte showed me there's more than that.* The way she'd shaken when they'd first kissed, desperate and terrified at the same time. The way she'd grabbed at Winter, pulling her close like a drowning man clutching driftwood.

Now Cyte was a thousand miles away, if she was still alive. *And Jane's body is being used by a thing that wants to destroy the entire human race.*

Maybe I should have stayed at Mrs. Wilmore's. If Janus had died in the desert, maybe none of this would have happened. She felt Infernivore shift deep inside her.

How bad could it be, being a farmer's wife? Half the world seems to manage it. She tried to imagine herself kissing a fat, bearded man, cooking his meals, raising his children. *My children.* The images felt impossibly alien, like something happening on the far side of the moon.

Infernivore shifted again. It was uneasy in the presence of Alex and Abraham, who both had powerful demons of their own. *Though it seems to have gotten used to them—*

Her eyes snapped fully open. *Something's out there.*

Wood went *crunch*, very faintly.

Slowly, Winter extracted one arm from the blanket and fumbled her pack open. There was a pistol there, buried under the wad of her extra shirts, and beside it a tin box of cartridges. She pulled out first one, then the other. Then, freeing her other arm, she went through the familiar ritual—pull out the paper cartridge, bite off the end with the ball, sprinkle powder into the pan and make sure it closed, pour the rest down the barrel, spit the ball after it, and jam the whole mess home with the small ramrod. She'd done it so often her hands worked automatically, the salty tang of powder on her lips as familiar as the taste of blood. When it was done she got to her feet, the gun leveled, her thumb on the hammer.

For a long moment there was silence. Winter might have thought she'd imagined the sound, but the growing restlessness of the demon in her soul was unmistakable. Infernivore couldn't quite detect the Beast the way it could find other demons—probably because the Beast was spread among so many bodies— but it still sensed *something* when the creature got close. She held her pose, turning slowly, eyes searching among the faint shadows cast by starlight.

Two points of red blossomed in the darkness, as bright as twin fires.

"Found you." An old man's voice, speaking in Vordanai, his tone singsong. "Knew you'd have to come out. Couldn't hide forever. Not Winter Ihernglass."

Winter pulled the hammer back and slid her finger around the trigger. *There could be more than one.* She kept the gun aimed at the glowing eyes as she backed toward Alex and Abraham.

"Did they tell you it was your duty to come for me? Your destiny?" The Beast's laugh was more of a strangled cough from a desiccated throat. "Maxwell knew a great deal about the Eldest and his people. They love to talk about duty, don't they?" The creature coughed again. "Fools."

"Alex?" Winter murmured. When she got no response, she kicked the girl with her heel. Alex yelped. "Get up. It's found us."

Fuck was Alex's first coherent word. She struggled to free herself from the blanket. "How many?"

"Don't know," Winter said. "Get ready to run."

"What's the point?" the Beast said. The red-eyes were getting closer. "You know how this has to end. You can kill and kill until you stand atop a hill of corpses. Run to the ends of the earth. What's it going to gain you?" Another *snap*, a twig somewhere breaking. "Better to let me take you. That's what Jane wanted, you know. The chance to be with you forever. Would it be so terrible?"

"I'd rather die," Alex said, pushing to her feet.

"So would I," Winter said.

Would you? said a tiny, traitor voice. *Giving up control would be so* easy. *No more decisions. No more weight on your shoulders.*

"You'll get the chance," the Beast said. "We're a little too far out for me to eat you. So unless you come along quietly, you'll have to make do with being torn to pieces." Another coughing laugh. "Poor Jane will be so disappointed."

Winter gripped the pistol tighter. She heard the blanket rustle behind her and guessed that Alex and Abraham were on their feet. She sighted carefully on the red eyes—

Another twig *snapped*, off to the right. Winter spun on her heel, straightened her arm, and fired. The shot was shatteringly loud in the still forest, echoing over and over, and the flash partially obscured Winter's vision. She could see that she'd been on target, though—a woman who'd broken from cover a dozen yards away had taken the ball high in the chest and gone down. She was stick thin, dressed in rags, with long, wild gray hair and open sores on her arms. *Another one of the Beast's bodies. She must have been out here for some time already. It doesn't even bother to give them proper clothes . . .*

Winter's body was moving faster than her stunned brain. Her saber was tied to the side of her pack; she reached down, scooped up the bag, and tore the weapon free. More people, at least half a dozen, emerged from the trees all around them, closing from every direction. Winter tossed the useless pistol away and raised her blade.

"Alex! Watch my back!"

"On it!" Alex said, followed by the *hiss-crunch* of her power spearing through flesh and bone.

One man was coming straight at her, while two more figures closed in from the sides. Winter, slashing in a diagonal arc, stepped forward to meet the attack rather than be trapped between them. The heavy blade connected with the man's face, raking across one glowing red eye and through his nose in a spray of gore. His hands came up, grabbing for the weapon, and Winter hastily yanked it back, slashing off two fingers.

Saints and fucking martyrs. The pain from wounds like that would put an ordinary person on the ground, but the red-eye didn't flinch, just came forward again with blood still spraying from the cuts. Aware she had only a moment before she was surrounded, Winter feinted high, then kicked him in the chest when he reached up for the sword again. He staggered backward, losing his footing on the slippery ground, and she spun away just in time for two pairs of groping arms to miss her. Another man, in the leathers of a hunter, collided with a teenage girl in the tattered remains of a parti-color dress. They both turned on her, and Winter gave ground. *Oh, Karis Almighty . . .*

They're already dead. No minds inside those bodies. The girl's pale, dirty face was something out of Winter's days at Mrs. Wilmore's, grubbing with the other inmates in the gardens or scrubbing the floors. *Except it's not a girl. It's the Beast, the Beast, the Beast.*

It took her a moment to realize she was shouting. The girl came at her, and Winter grabbed her bony wrist with her off hand, pulling her forward and off-balance. A smooth blow of the saber ripped across the girl's neck, and her head lolled back with a spray of arterial blood. She tottered, fell to her knees, and then collapsed, arms groping toward Winter's feet.

Dead is still dead. These weren't the monsters of the temple, whose broken bodies had been animated by magic. They were human, more or less, with their souls hollowed out and replaced by the Beast's controlling intelligence. They might not feel pain, but they bled and their bodies failed.

The hunter shifted to the left, trying to force Winter to move in the other direction. A quick glance told her that the first man, one remaining eye still aglow, was crawling toward her, leaving a sticky trail of blood. Winter went the other way instead, ducking under the hunter's outstretched arms and letting her trailing hand slash him across the belly. She kicked him from behind as he stumbled forward, and he fell among his own viscera, twitching like a landed fish.

"Winter." Abraham's voice. "I think we need to leave."

Winter looked up. Three more people lay dead off to her left, speared neatly through the head. Alex was gathering up her pack, and Abraham already had his on. He was pointing down the hill, into the valley, and Winter turned in that direction.

Red lights, like distant torches, but always in pairs. Dozens of them, spread through the forest, flickering as they moved among the trees. Glowing eyes, every gaze locked in one direction.

We're dead. There were too many, far too many. The sea of lights went on and on.

"Winter!" Alex said nervously.

"Higher," Winter said. "If we can get over the hill, maybe we can lose them on the downslope. Find somewhere to hide." She looked from Alex to Abraham, and both of them looked back at her with trust in their eyes. *They think I know what to do.* Winter wanted to laugh and cry at the same time.

The night seemed to last forever.

At some point, Winter realized the Beast was driving them, chivying them as it had back in Elysium. The red lights were always visible, a cordon of flickering eyes, behind them but drawing ever closer. It didn't *have* to show its position that way; it could hide the glow. But it served the Beast's purpose that they exhaust themselves running.

Unfortunately, it's damned good tactics. Winter, Abraham, and Alex could tire and fall. The Beast's bodies would push themselves to the physical limits of exhaustion, and if they collapsed, there were always more.

They climbed until they reached the spine of the hills, breath puffing in the chill night air as they scrambled across patches of bare rock to reach the line of the forest on the other side. During the day, at a leisurely pace, the change from ascent to descent might have represented some relief, but now it only made things more difficult. Starlight barely picked out the ground ahead, and revealed nothing but slippery mud or shifting rocks that could easily swallow an ankle.

For a time they lost sight of their pursuers, and Winter allowed herself a splinter of hope. Then, pausing for a desperate swig from her canteen, she saw the flicker of red on the hilltop.

Abraham had long ago gone silent, his face pale and limbs trembling. Even Alex was panting for breath, her short hair spiky with sweat.

"We should . . . find somewhere . . . to make a stand," Alex said. "Make sure they can only come . . . one way. We could hold them off."

"Forever?" Winter shook her head. "If we stop moving, it'll just bring up more bodies."

"We can't keep this up, either." Alex watched the red lights disappear momentarily, then emerge again. "Maybe we can double back? Punch through them?"

"Maybe." But Winter didn't think there was much chance. The problem was that the Beast was a *single* opponent, not a collection of individuals. Individuals would get confused, in the cold and dark. She could try to bluff them, disorient them. But the Beast . . . "We can't *punch* through. If even one of them sees us, it'll know what we're trying. We need somewhere to hide. Look for a . . . a cave, or something."

Alex nodded. It was a slim hope to cling to, but better than nothing at all.

No caves were immediately in evidence, not that Winter was confident she'd be able to see one in the dark. They picked their way down the slope, then alongside a streambed, staying out from under the trees to make the best use of the light. *Can the Beast see in the dark? Or is it leaving a trail of broken bodies behind it?*

"There's something up there!" Alex's finger stabbed out, pointing at the ridge ahead of them. "I saw someone moving."

"Then we're dead," Winter said. "It's got us surrounded."

"No red," Alex said. "Could it be someone else?"

Winter was about to ask who else would be out in the woods in the middle of the night, but at that moment a pair of shapes burst from the underbrush, eyes blazing with crimson light. *Clever bastard,* Winter had time to think. She'd counted on more of a lead, but the Beast had obviously let its fittest bodies range ahead of the pack. These two were both big brutes—stocky, heavily built men with the look of laborers. One of them came directly at Winter, and the other went for Alex.

Winter clawed for her saber, while Alex raised her hands. A spear of darkness stabbed out, but exhaustion had slowed Alex's reflexes, and the red-eye lurched sideways, taking the bolt in the shoulder instead of the head. An instant later it was on top of her, slamming into her with a body blow that carried her off her feet. They hit the ground together with a clatter of stones.

The second red-eye got within arm's length of Winter before she got her sword free, and she backed away, slashing wildly. The weapon hacked a gash in the thing's arm, which he completely ignored. Winter sidestepped and lunged, sliding the saber in under the red-eye's armpit. It slipped between his ribs, burying itself almost to the hilt, and as he collapsed it was torn from her grasp.

Hell. She didn't bother to try to retrieve it from the thrashing body, just turned and ran for Alex. The girl was on her back, with the big man kneeling on her, both hands pressed against the back of her head. As Winter closed, Abraham slammed his stick against the red-eye's skull with all his strength, but the thing didn't do more than sway. *All right, then. How about this?*

Winter grabbed the creature by the back of the neck and unleashed Infernivore. The demon flowed eagerly through the contact, trying to grab hold of the thread of otherworldly energy that animated the red-eye. As it had before, though, the Beast withdrew from its vessel. The big man slumped forward, suddenly limp, and Infernivore wrapped itself back around Winter irritably, deprived of its prey. Winter felt a sudden gut punch of fatigue, as though she'd just finished a sprint. She shook it off, grabbing the corpse by the shoulders and rolling it off Alex.

"Abraham!" Winter went to one knee beside the girl. There was blood on her scalp where she'd hit the ground, but more worrying was her ankle, which had bent entirely the wrong way under the red-eye's weight. She was breathing, but she didn't seem conscious. "She's hurt!"

Abraham scrambled in beside her and laid his hands on Alex's back. He closed his eyes, concentrating hard.

"Her skull's not fractured. Nothing more than bruises, except the ankle." He looked up at Winter. "I can put it back together, but . . ."

"We don't have time." Winter turned. No glowing red eyes were visible behind them, but she saw moving shadows in the underbrush. More of the Beast's bodies, closing in. "Can you carry her?"

"Not for long." Abraham's lips were pale. "I'm not strong enough. I'm sorry."

"Wouldn't work anyway. Too slow." Winter walked over to the now-still red-eye and yanked her saber free, wiping the blood on the dead man's shirt. "Heal her. As fast as you can."

"You should go on," he said abruptly. "Leave us. I'll help her and then . . . find somewhere to hide, like you said."

I knew he would try that. She hadn't known Abraham long, but he seemed the self-sacrificial type. *Why else would he even be here?* "No."

"Winter, please." His face was a mask of anguish. "If you don't get there—"

"I *know*, damn it." She slashed the saber through the air. "What are my chances of making it by myself? This isn't sentiment; it's tactics. If you get Alex up, she *might* be able to kill enough of them with her power that we'll have a chance."

"I don't think it'll be quick enough—"

"Try!" Winter snarled.

If we're all going to die, the hell if the last thing I do will be to abandon my friends. She turned to face the woods.

A gaunt woman in peasant's skirts stepped out of the shadow. Then a boy, another priest, several farmers, a pair of girls who looked like sisters. A dozen, more. Eyes glowing from within with the lights of hell.

"What did I tell you?" the woman in the lead said. "There's only one way this can end. Though I enjoy a good chase."

Winter wanted to say something, some cutting last words, but nothing came to mind. *What does it matter? No one's going to remember.* She raised her saber for a moment, then let the tip fall. *The Beast doesn't care how many of these poor bastards I kill.* Her throat was tight. *What's the point of* anything—

Something long and heavy flashed out of the darkness and hit the red-eye in the chest. It was a spear, thrown hard enough that the tip emerged from the small of the woman's back. She tried to speak, but when she opened her mouth, only blood emerged. She toppled a moment later, and the rest of the red-eyes charged.

They were met by more spears, a ragged volley, arching over Winter's head to plunge down among the minions of the Beast with devastating effect. Most of the red-eyes went down at once. Those that kept coming ran into a tide of black-and-white figures, more spears in their hands. A farmer fell, clutching at the ruin of his throat. One of the girls ran right at Winter, but someone intercepted her with a kick, hurling her to the ground. Before she could rise, another figure stabbed down with a spearpoint, once, twice, three times. The girl went still.

Who . . . ? Winter felt her fuzzy, sleep-deprived mind struggling to keep up. *Someone* helped *us?*

She backed up, until she was standing beside Alex and Abraham. Abraham had his head down and his eyes closed, deep in his healing trance. Alex had yet to move.

The newcomers fanned out. There were a lot of them, at least a score. It was hard to see much in the starlight, but they seemed to be short and bulky, though they moved with a lithe grace. Winter saw pale skin and dark hair, and flashes of white fur. Every hand held a spear, and most of them had several more strapped to their backs.

Those spears were leveled at her. The points didn't gleam as metal would have, but she had ample evidence they were sharp enough.

O-kay. Now what? Whoever these people were, they hadn't hesitated to cut down the red-eyes. *Since they haven't spitted us yet, they must be waiting for something.* Winter cleared her throat, then hesitated. *I doubt they speak Vordanai or Hamveltai.* She'd worked on her Murnskai during the campaign, but it was weak compared to Alex's or Abraham's. *Still better than nothing.*

"*Kaja . . . sevet . . .*" Winter concentrated on the tricky consonants of the northern language. "*Kdja svet Murnskedj?*" Do you speak Murnskai? "*Vordanedj?*" she added hopefully.

One of the figures took a step closer. "*Sveta Murnskedj.*" It was a young woman's voice, with a different accent than Winter had heard from the Murnskai she'd met on the road north. "*Dost'av ohk va? Tul fuhr'nos?*"

Damn. The first part was "Who are you?"; simple enough, but the second, *Tul is . . . sun? Sun look? Sunray?* She glanced at the bodies littering the edge of the forest, and realization dawned. *Sun eyes. Red-eyes.*

"*Hja, hja, hja. Tyv tul fuhr'nos.*" We kill the red-eyes. Winter drew a line across her throat, hoping they might understand if she'd gotten the word wrong. "*Tyv!*"

The points of the spears lowered a fraction.

Abraham opened his eyes and sagged.

"Hey!" Winter said. "Is she all right?"

"She'll be fine," Abraham said, sitting down heavily. "The break was more complicated than I anticipated. I had to guide several splinters of bone back into place." He looked down at Alex with a faint smile. "I don't know how many times that makes it that I've put her back together."

He let out a breath and looked up, smile fading.

"Who . . . ?"

"I'm not entirely sure," Winter said. "But they haven't killed us yet."

The newcomers were in the process of setting up a camp, several hundred yards away from where they'd slaughtered the red-eyes. Winter had done her best to explain that Alex couldn't be moved yet, and wasn't sure if she'd gotten the point across or not. Regardless, five of the spear-wielding warriors had stayed to watch them, weapons not pointed but not stowed, either.

"I tried to tell them that you'd be able to speak to them once you were finished," Winter said, after she'd explained. "I'm pretty sure I messed that up, though. But they were willing to wait once they saw Alex was hurt."

"Are they all women?" Abraham said, looking at the guards.

"Possibly," Winter said. She'd been having a difficult time making much out in the darkness, but some of the faces definitely had a feminine cast. "Is it safe to carry Alex a little way?"

Abraham nodded. "She may not wake up for a while, but she's not in danger."

"Can you ask them if we can move over to their camp, then? I think they're getting a fire going."

Abraham got to his feet and waved at the guards, who approached warily. He spoke, a rapid-fire stream of Murnskai, which they answered excitedly. One of them broke away and hurried off toward the camp.

"She says it's all right," Abraham said, "but that we're not to try to run away."

"I don't think I'm up to running anywhere," Winter said. "Help me with Alex."

Between them, they managed to get Alex upright and her arms slung around Winter's neck. Winter hefted the girl—surprisingly heavy, despite her slim frame—and trudged toward the camp, with Abraham hovering behind her and the four guards maintaining a watchful distance.

The women—they *were* all women, as far as Winter could see—setting up the camp went about it with the efficiency of long routine. By the time Winter arrived and set Alex down, they had a fire burning merrily, and small, steep-sided skin tents were going up in concentric rings around it. The ground was higher and flatter than where the fight had taken place, and some distance from the edge of the forest, so a sentry would have plenty of warning in case of attack.

In the light of the flames, she got a clearer view of their—*captors? Rescuers? Maybe both.* The appearance of bulk came from the thick furs they wrapped themselves in, including long cloaks that could be wound about their middles to stay out of the way in combat. Sewn into the dark leather of these garments were many smaller, paler objects. *Bones,* Winter realized, after watching for a few moments. They were arranged in neat patterns, expanding spirals or flower-like blossoms, the way a fine lady of Vordan might have her dresses sewn with pearls. The women wore their hair long, but tied up tight, with more bones worked into the weave.

The language they spoke among themselves wasn't Murnskai, though it was similar enough that Winter could hear the occasional familiar word. Abraham's eyebrows went up at the sound of it, and he leaned close to Winter and spoke under his breath.

"I'm not certain, but I think these are Trans-Batariai."

Winter frowned. Tribesmen from beyond the river Bataria had dogged the army's steps after the unnatural snows had begun—the Vordanai had called them the "white riders" for the color of their furs. She explained this to Abraham. "I only saw a few up close, but they didn't look like these people. And we never saw any women."

"A different group, perhaps?" Abraham shrugged. "Their language is supposed to be closer to what the original inhabitants of this land spoke before the Children of the Sun invaded. Murnskai comes from mixing it with Mithradacii."

"So what are they doing here? We're still well south of the river."

"No idea. I suggest we ask them."

Once Alex was arranged on a blanket by the fire—she mumbled something and curled up tighter in her sleep, which was encouraging—Winter and Abraham sat next to her, soaking up the welcome warmth. Spearwomen watched them with unabashed curiosity, but no one spoke until another woman emerged from one of the little tents on her hands and knees.

She looked young, in her late teens—all the Trans-Batariai did, now that Winter thought about it—but she obviously carried some authority. She had a small, round face, with the dark hair that seemed universal among these people. A ragged scar, healed into a shiny ribbon, went from her eyebrow up to her hairline. She looked Winter up and down, then strode over, putting on a fierce scowl.

"*Hja tifet Murnskyr,*" she said. "*Hja tifet tul fuhr'nos.*" *You are not Murnskai. You are not red-eyes.*

Winter nodded eagerly and looked at Abraham. "Tell her we're . . . travelers."

Abraham spoke, and the woman replied. Winter realized her Murnskai wasn't as bad as she'd thought—Abraham was mostly comprehensible. It was clearly a second language for the spearwomen, or possibly a different dialect.

"She asks if it's only the three of us," Abraham said. "Or if there were more who were lost to the red-eyes."

"Just the three of us," Winter said. "Please thank her for saving us. We would certainly have died without her help."

Abraham translated. "She says that killing demons is the shared duty of all humans," he said when she'd finished. "She would help her worst enemy against the red-eyes."

"Ask her what she's doing here," Winter said. "If this land is where her people normally live."

The spearwoman shook her head before Abraham had finished speaking. She talked at length, and Winter felt like she got the gist, though she waited for Abraham to translate before replying.

"She says they came south because the Blessed Ones told them there was a threat to the Holy City. A vast army gathered, like she'd never seen before, and fought with heathen invaders." Abraham coughed. "From the context, I think that's the Vordanai."

"There must have been more fighting after I left," Winter said. "I wish we knew what the hell *happened*."

"According to her, the enemy were driven back in fear. But the weather was terribly cold—maybe *demonically* cold is a better translation—and the Trans-Batariai suffered badly. They split into smaller bands to return home, but then the cold weather vanished and all the rivers flooded. While they were trying to find their way, the red-eyes appeared and started attacking."

Winter winced. She could imagine it all too well—the army of bodies the Beast had gathered at Elysium fanning out across Murnsk in search of more raw material, spreading like flame across a dry field.

"Are there more of them?" Winter said. There were thirty or forty spear-women in the camp, she guessed. "A larger group nearby?"

"No," the spearwoman said, which Winter understood without translation. "We were separated. The others were killed or taken." She looked anxious, staring at Abraham, and after a moment she blurted out something that Winter couldn't quite follow.

"Oh dear," Abraham said.

"What?"

"The others told her I was helping Alex. She's asking if I'm a healer. One of their people is badly hurt."

"Do you think you could help her?"

"I'd have to examine her, but . . ." Abraham looked down at his hands, and his voice softened. "I won't leave someone to die if I can help it. But if they consider my gift to be demonic, there's no telling what they might do. We know they serve Elysium."

"On the other hand, they seem to serve the Priests of the Black," Winter said. "Which might mean they know all about the Penitent Damned." She shook her head. "I don't know. I can't order you, but—"

"I'll do it," Abraham said. "I'd do it regardless. I just wanted to warn you."

He said this to the spearwoman, who nodded and gestured toward the tent. Winter went along with them, after one last check on Alex, and no one seemed to object. The flap at the front of the tent was low enough that she had to enter on her knees, and it was a tight fit for the three of them plus the patient, who was buried under a heavy pile of furs.

"I'll need to look at her," Abraham said.

The spearwoman nodded and gestured for him to get on with it. Abraham pushed the furs aside, revealing a girl a year or two younger than the leader. She was naked, and Winter felt herself flush slightly, but Abraham looked her over with a clinical detachment. A bandage, crusty with blood, was wound around her stomach, and seeing the placement of the wound made Winter's heart sink. When Abraham untied the bandage and raised it gently from the skin, the sudden stench was all the confirmation she needed.

Gut wound. And a bad one, by the look of it. Any cutter from the Second Division gathering wounded would have left this girl where she lay in favor of those who might have a chance to survive. A wound to the muscle might heal clean, and if a limb was injured it could be amputated, but a puncture to the viscera meant festering and a long, nasty death as sure as sunrise.

Winter suddenly was back in another tent, on another continent. Bobby had taken a similar wound, after making Winter swear never to take her to a cutter. At the time, Winter had been foolish enough to imagine she might be able to do something about it on her own. Graff, a veteran sergeant, had disabused her of that notion, and only Feor's sorcerous intervention had saved Bobby's life. *For a while.*

She shook her head and wiped at the tears pricking her eyelids. *The question is, is this woman as naive as I was? Or has she guessed that Abraham has something more than ordinary healing to offer?*

The spearwoman was looking down at the girl, and her fierce expression was gone, replaced with an overwhelming grief. *She's desperate.*

"Please help her," she said in Murnskai even Winter could understand. "My sister."

There was a long moment of silence.

"I'll do what I can," Abraham said. "But we need to be alone."

The woman nodded and crawled out of the tent without another word. Winter hesitated for a moment.

"You're sure about this?" she said. "She knows that's not a wound anyone can live through. Which means she's going to know—"

"It doesn't matter now," Abraham said, looking down at the dying girl. "She's here. I'm here. I can't just ignore her."

Winter nodded slowly.

"We'll deal with the consequences when they happen," Abraham said. He let out a long breath. "Wait outside, please. It's easier with no one watching."

Winter pushed her way out of the tent on her hands and knees, clambering awkwardly to her feet beside the spearwoman leader. Someone had draped a fur blanket over Alex's shoulders, and she looked comfortable enough. The rest of the spearwomen were still going about the business of setting up the camp, but throwing frequent glances in their direction.

"He'll help your sister," Winter said, in her halting Murnskai. "He is . . . a very good healer."

The spearwoman nodded vaguely. She was staring into the forest, in the direction the red-eyes had come from. Winter followed her gaze, searching for movement, but there was nothing but the dead trees.

"What's your name?" Winter said. "I'm Winter."

"Winter." The woman frowned, and touched her chest. "Letingerae."

"Letin . . . gah . . . ray?" Winter struggled with the unfamiliar syllables. The woman grinned, for the first time since Winter had met her.

"Leti," she said. "I'm Leti."

"My friends are Alex and Abraham," Winter said, pointing. "What's your sister's name?"

Leti looked away. "Vess."

"Winter?" Abraham's voice came from within the tent. "You can come inside now."

Leti pushed through the tent flap so quickly the whole structure shook, Winter worming her way in after. Abraham was undoing the bandage from Vess' middle, using it to scrape at some of the dried blood and pus. Even through the grime, it was clear that there was unbroken skin underneath, and the girl's breathing was visibly eased. Leti's eyes widened.

"She will sleep for a long time," Abraham said. "A day or two, maybe. And we will need water, to clean her. But she will be fine."

"You . . ." Leti paused, swallowing hard. "You are—" And then a word Winter didn't recognize.

"What'd she say?" Winter said.

"It means . . . Blessed One, maybe?" Abraham frowned. "I'm not sure I understand the theology."

"It doesn't sound like the sort of thing you kill someone for being," Winter said.

Abraham nodded and said in Murnskai, "I think so. I may not understand you properly."

"She will live." Leti looked down at her sister. "She will really live?"

Abraham nodded. "She will live."

"I will clean her." The spearwoman didn't look up. "We will find you a tent. You are welcome to share our fire."

Winter closed her eyes and breathed a prayer of thanks to anyone who might be listening.

CHAPTER SEVEN

RAESINIA

Raesinia had never been out on the ocean before. The river Vor was deep and wide enough that oceangoing vessels could come as far north as Vordan City, and she'd been aboard a few of those—most notably the *Rosnik*, where she'd been captured by Ionkovo during Maurisk's coup. Once, as a girl, she'd gone with her father to Vayenne, at the mouth of the river, and seen the harbor there.

That trip had taken several weeks, with frequent stopovers for official functions along the way. The *Prudence* made the same voyage in a little less than two days, even accounting for several halts at military checkpoints. Raesinia was no judge of ships, but the courier *looked* fast, sleek and streamlined as a dolphin with two masts whose spars seemed absurdly overlarge. She'd taken them downriver with only a few sails deployed, giving Raesinia the impression of a spirited horse eager to get out of the stalls and into a field where it could work up a gallop.

Certainly, she moved well compared to the fat-bellied merchantmen they passed along the way. *Prudence* had no room to spare. Aside from her small crew, she carried only passengers and a sack of diplomatic correspondence from the Borelgai embassy. Even the Queen of Vordan was asked to share a cabin, though the captain had offered up his own accommodation for her use. Raesinia didn't mind sharing with Cora, though, especially since the girl was in on her secret and Raesinia didn't have to pretend she could sleep.

Cora didn't sleep much, either, as far as Raesinia could tell. She'd hardly been able to sit still since she'd first heard about the voyage. Their destination, Viadre, was the capital of Borel, and as far as trade and finance were concerned practically capital of the world. To someone like Cora, for whom the stock books of the Exchange were light reading, visiting the great markets of Viadre was the next best thing to visiting the kingdom of God.

Besides Cora, Raesinia had brought the minimum entourage she thought she could get away with: Barely and Jo as her personal guards, a pair of maids chosen by Mistress Lagovil, and Eric. Duke Dorsay was on board, and the Borelgai ambassador, Ihannes Pulwer-Monsangton; and with their staff and guards along as well it was no wonder the *Prudence* felt decidedly cramped. Raesinia spent as much time as she could on deck, staying out of the way of the crew and marveling at the speed with which the coastline slid by.

Once they'd cleared Vayenne's breakwater, the courier had started her run in earnest, hoisting so much canvas that Raesinia expected them to be lifted out of the water entirely. Winds were apparently favorable, and they ran northwest, within easy view of the rumpled Vordanai coast. Ihannes had told her they'd keep on like that all around the bulge of western Vordan, past Enzport and Ecco Island, until they passed the jutting peninsula of the Jaw and struck out northeast across the Borel Sea.

Raesinia couldn't have said exactly where they were, at the present. The coast all looked the same, little port towns and river mouths, cliffs and rolling hills. She leaned against the rail near the bow of the ship, watching the waves and the clouds. Off to her left, the ocean went on and on into the infinite distance, until blue-gray sky and gray-blue water met at the horizon. Somewhere in that general direction was Khandar, and the mysterious southern kingdoms on the other side of the Great Desol. *Maybe I'll get to visit, after my official death.*

Raesinia shook her head. Something about the sight sent her thoughts in melancholy directions. She looked over her shoulder at Barely and Jo, her everpresent shadows. Barely looked cross, as usual, but Joanna was staring out over the water with a dreamy expression.

"It's beautiful, isn't it?" Raesinia said.

Barely gave a little start, then shrugged. "It's all right, I guess." She looked up at Jo. "No ocean in Desland. We'd never seen it before we got to Vayenne."

Jo's hands moved, her eyes staying fixed on the horizon.

"She says she never thought it would be so big," Barely translated. "Like there's nothing but water in the whole world."

"Not far from the truth, I suppose," Raesinia said. She pushed herself back from the rail, then shook her head when the two of them made to follow. "Stay here. Get some rest."

"We ought to stay by your side," Barely said. "I don't trust the Borels." Jo nodded emphatic agreement.

"I trust Duke Dorsay, for whatever that's worth," Raesinia said. "I don't think we're in danger until we land in Viadre."

After that, though, is another story . . .

"I understand your reasoning, of course," Dorsay said, steadying himself with a hand on the wall. "I just wish you'd been a bit more . . . circumspect."

They were in Raesinia's—formerly the captain's—cabin, the largest space on the ship with any semblance of privacy. The wind had picked up, so the air was a mass of creaking, groaning wood and straining ropes, mixed with the shouted commands of the sailors struggling to keep the sails in the right places. It was all gibberish to Raesinia, but the racket provided enough cover that she felt like they could be reasonably sure they weren't overheard.

Unfortunately, the constant sway of the ship left them both rolling back and forth like wobbling jellies. Dorsay seemed unaffected, but there was a distinct queasiness at the pit of Raesinia's stomach. *The binding heals me from everything else. Can't it do something about seasickness?* She did her best to put it out of her mind.

"You know we didn't have time to be diplomatic," Raesinia said. "The army is on its way to confront Janus as we speak. Aid that arrives weeks after the decisive battle is no better than no aid at all."

"Yes, yes," Dorsay said. "I *have* fought a campaign or two of my own, young lady."

"What I don't understand is why Georg"—she'd adopted his habit of familiar reference to the King of Borel—"isn't being more helpful. He sent you and your army to Murnsk to stop Janus, with the authority to make a deal with me if that's what it took. Why hesitate now?"

"If it were entirely up to Georg, I believe he would send help at once. But the situation is more complicated."

"You've said that before." Raesinia sat on the bed, which was bolted to the floor, in the hopes that it might help with her stomach. It didn't. "Maybe you'd better explain. Borel doesn't have anything like the Deputies-General."

"Not officially, no." Dorsay sighed and stroked his famous nose. "There's a group of nobles who serve as advisers to the king. They call themselves the 'Honest Fellows,' possibly in jest. Some of them are from old families, others are merely vastly rich, but together they represent the most powerful forces in the realm. The ordinary business of the government is handled by one of them, or their subordinates, with the permission of the king."

Raesinia frowned. The way they talked about him in Vordan, she'd always imagined the King of Borel as a tyrant, with no checks on his authority. *I should have known that politics is politics, wherever you go.* "And these Honest Fellows don't want to help?"

"Some of them might. Some might complain about the cost. Others might prefer that Vordan weaken itself with a long civil war." Dorsay scowled. "I am convinced that there is a faction that *wants* us to continue the war with Vordan, presumably because they have interests in the armaments industry. A few might prefer to deal with Janus than risk your notions about 'votes' and 'Deputies' spreading across the Borel Sea. The point is that a majority among the advisers would like Borel to stay well clear for the present, especially now that Janus is no longer threatening to march on Elysium."

"Was that true when you brought your army to Murnsk?"

"More or less. Georg can, of course, overrule the Honest Fellows when he wishes. In that case, he knew that if he did nothing and Elysium was destroyed, the peasantry would be incensed." Dorsay coughed. "I may have had something to do with it as well. I spoke in favor of intervention at some length."

"But now you don't think he'll be willing to act again."

"As I said, the case is no longer as clear. It . . . may be possible to persuade him." Dorsay's gaze went distant for a moment. "But he will demand concessions, and you may not be able to agree."

Raesinia nodded slowly. "And I take it our friend Ihannes works for the nonintervention faction?"

"Decidedly so. His patron is Fredrick Goodman, one of the Honest Fellows and possibly the wealthiest single individual in Borel. If not the world. He leads the voices who argue against any action that might impinge on state coffers."

"Lovely," Raesinia muttered. "Well, I'm sure he and Cora will have a great deal to discuss."

Cora was standing at Raesinia's shoulder, bouncing on the balls of her feet, as the *Prudence* arrived at the mouth of the river Brack. It was a cold, blustery day, with a spitting rain falling from low-hanging clouds to moisten the deck and everyone on it. Despite the weather, there was no question of remaining below. The port of Harborside was one of the wonders of the world.

Viadre proper straddled the Brack somewhere upstream, protected from the swells driven by cold northern winds blowing across the Borel Sea. In ages past, Harborside had been a separate town, where ships too big to ascend the shallow river could shift their cargo to flat-bottomed barges. Over the years, Viadre had sprawled into the countryside, tendrils of streets and buildings reaching out to engulf the nearby communities, until places like Harborside were part of the city in all but name. The old docks, with their wood piers and crumbling stone breakwater, had been cleared away more than a hundred years ago.

Their replacement was built on a massive scale. The Brack let out into a wide bay, with three channels to the sea separated by a pair of small islands. The old breakwater had protected only a portion of this space, and ships had been forced to ride at anchor around the islands, with frequent wrecks when the winds grew too high. The *new* breakwater closed off the bay completely, two of the channels blocked by massive wood-and-tar palisades anchored to stone pilings. More walls flanked the main channel, including a mobile barrier that could be swung closed at need in high seas.

With the bay protected from ocean swells, docks had sprung up like fungus, spreading out from the river mouth in both directions. Stone quays served His Majesty's Navy and other official ships, while wooden piers of every possible description belonged to trading companies and other concerns.

All of this Cora explained to Raesinia as the captain slowed the *Prudence* and carefully navigated the harbor entrance. She was unable to help herself, so Raesinia bore it stoically. To her, the breakwater looked like the outer wall of an old-fashioned hill fort, rising out of the water instead of clinging to a mountaintop. But there were no defenses here—no hoardings, no embrasures for guns. It was a deliberate statement, she decided. His Majesty's Navy was protection enough for Borel, and always would be.

The harbor inside the breakwater made its own kind of statement. Raesinia had often seen the docks in Vordan City and marveled at the complexity of commerce, the sheer number of people hurrying about in what looked like absolute chaos but was actually a strange kind of order. It had always reminded her of an anthill, that same busy sense of motion. But if the Vordan City docks were an anthill, then Harborside was the city rising around that anthill, utterly dwarfing it.

The ranks of docked vessels went on *forever*, stretching out as far as she could see through the curtains of falling rain. They came in every possible variety and combination of colors, shapes, and sizes, an endless forest of masts with sails tied tight around their spars. Raesinia recognized a few men-of-war, flying the muddy red Borelgai flag, but the ensign of every nation she'd ever heard of was represented, along with quite a few she hadn't. Small boats scurried around them, propelled by sweating, swearing oarsmen wrapped in brightly colored oilcloth.

"That's a Hannamen junk," Cora said, bouncing higher and higher as they came closer. "They're from the southern kingdoms! And that one's a League warship. It has to be at least a hundred years old. And—"

"Your young companion knows her ships," Duke Dorsay said, coming to stand with them at the rail.

"She's here in her capacity as an official of the treasury," Raesinia said. "But I find she knows just about everything."

"Not everything. I—" Cora flushed and stopped bouncing, then looked awkwardly at Dorsay. "Thank you, Your Highness. I'm sorry if I was overexcited."

"Don't worry on *my* account," Raesinia said, flashing her a smile. "Just remember what we came here for."

Cora nodded, her eyes going beyond the line of ships. "Viadre." She looked at Dorsay again. "Will the Great Market be open in the rain?"

Dorsay snorted. "If it closed whenever it rained, we'd only have a market four days a year. You know the saying about Borelgai seasons? We have three."

"Cold rain, colder rain, and snow," Raesinia finished. "No wonder your people have such an affinity for the sea. You practically have to swim even on land."

"Exactly. I'm the odd one because I prefer a good horse to a deck under my feet." Dorsay laughed uproariously.

Raesinia wondered if they'd have to fight for a berth, but the courier ships had their own pier, patrolled by red-uniformed guards. The *Prudence* docked with no delays, and the captain made a ceremony of handing over the official courier bag to a waiting mail coach, which took off at a gallop. Another pair of carriages, considerably more ornate, had been provided for the queen and her escort. Raesinia, her guards, and Eric took one, while Cora and the servants accompanied the baggage. The driver set a sedate pace, and Raesinia looked out through rain-glazed windows as they wound through Harborside. Viadre had a very different look from Vordan City, quite apart from the constant rain—the houses were almost all brick, instead of timber and plaster, and they had many stories and steeply canted roofs.

"I've met with the ambassador," Eric said, opening a folded sheaf of paper.

"While a formal reception will take some time to arrange, he assures me that His Majesty will want to welcome you immediately. We'll go directly to the palace."

"Cora will want to go into the city and see the market," Raesinia said, most of her attention still on the window. It seemed like such a gloomy place. *How do they live without ever seeing the sun?* "I assume we won't talk about anything important today?"

"Ah . . . probably not, Your Highness." Eric looked down at his papers. "Word of our coming has only just arrived, so I imagine they'll want to discuss among themselves before setting up a meeting of consequence."

"What about these Honest Fellows? The king's advisers. Do you know anything about them?"

Her tone must have been harsher than she intended. Eric's eyes widened. "O-only a little, Your Highness. I can, of course, have more information prepared."

Once again Raesinia found herself wishing for Sothe. If her old friend had been at her side, Raesinia would never have gone into a meeting without knowing who was present and what their allegiances were. *Not to mention a standing offer to have them quietly killed.* It wasn't that she approved of assassination as a political tactic, but the knowledge made her a little more comfortable. It wasn't Eric's fault, of course. *He's a fine political adviser. He's just not the Gray Rose.*

It took close to an hour to make the trip to the palace, which the Borelgai referred to simply as the Keep. Unlike in Ohnlei, the estate of the Borelgai kings was in the very center of their capital, not far from the site of the Great Market. Where Ohnlei was a creation of the modern age, laid out by Farus V in an effort to compete with his father's glory, the Keep was an actual fortress, built for defense in a time before cannonballs. The curtain wall stood thirty feet high, studded with square towers and lined with a crenellated battlement. Raesinia saw dark figures walking back and forth atop it, keeping watch as the king's men might have done five hundred years before. The carriage passed underneath a mammoth gatehouse, through a tunnel that felt more like something bored out of native rock.

Ohnlei had always seemed to Raesinia to be a place of air and light, with enormous, expensive windows and mirrored halls, vast grounds set with perfectly manicured plants and elaborate fountains. The Keep felt claustrophobic by comparison, crammed in behind its ancient stone walls like a dense city block instead of a country estate. Beyond the gatehouse was a large square, lined with tall brick buildings. Streets led off to the left and right, and Raesinia could see more structures packed cheek-by-jowl, right up against the walls. Ahead, a wider road led to the Keep proper, what had been the inner sanctum of the old fortress.

This, at least, had been modernized, though the facade still looked appropriately medieval. Broad windows and dozens of chimneys hinted at more up-to-date comforts, and the steady glow of gaslights illuminated the entryway, protected by stained-glass covers from the endless rain. Borelgai Life Guards, distinguished by the white furs on their shakos, stood to attention as the carriages passed by, ignoring the splashes from the iron-rimmed wheels. Another gate loomed.

They finally halted in a covered yard, the rain drumming on the roof overhead. A black-liveried servant, flanked by a pair of Life Guards, bowed deeply as the carriage door opened and Raesinia descended.

"Your Highness," he said, his voice a deep rumble. "Welcome to the Keep. I regret that we have only lately been informed of your visit and so cannot receive you in the fashion you deserve."

"I understand," Raesinia said. "News can scarcely outrun one of your courier ships, after all."

"His Majesty has been informed of your arrival and has indicated he would be pleased to receive you in private. However, he asked me to convey that if you wish to retire for a time beforehand, he will not take offense. He understands the rigors of travel are taxing."

Raesinia looked down at herself. Her dress wasn't exactly informal, but it certainly wasn't the sort of thing in which one would ordinarily choose to meet foreign royalty. Moreover, it was still slightly damp from the rain and a bit rumpled from the ride. Mistress Lagovil would have insisted that she change into something more suitable, and probably bathe.

The hell with it. The whole point of this visit was that she wasn't here to observe diplomatic niceties. *Maybe being a little unkempt will impress the king with the urgency of the situation.*

"I would be happy to attend on His Majesty at once. Can someone show my servants to our chambers?"

"Of course."

"Eric," Raesinia said over her shoulder. "Get everything set up, would you? And see that Cora has an escort to the market."

"But—" Eric decided that this wasn't the place to argue. "Yes, Your Highness."

"Do you two need a rest?" Raesinia said to Barely.

She shook her head. "Not unless you need us to put on dress blues."

"Later." She turned back to the servant. "Lead the way, then."

"I am Sebastian Carter, majordomo." He bowed again. "It's my pleasure to be of service."

Sebastian led them rapidly down a series of corridors. It seemed to Raesinia that this was not the part of the Keep normally shown to foreign dignitaries, since some of the halls they traversed were quite plain, with no carpets and only whitewash on the walls. Eventually they emerged through a discreet servants' door into something more recognizable as royal splendor, with the arms of Borel alternating with the Pulwer crest every few yards along the walls. A double door at the end of the hall, attended by another pair of Life Guards, was carved with an elaborate bas-relief of a ship in heavy seas.

The guards opened the doors at a gesture from Sebastian, and the major-domo stepped aside, letting Raesinia precede him into the room beyond. It was large and somewhat gloomy, with thick red carpets and dark wooden paneling, and the air was a haze of sweet-smelling smoke. A crowd of men, perhaps two dozen, stood in knots against the walls. They were dressed in suits and waistcoats, all dark, sober browns and grays, with only the flash of jeweled collar studs to provide a touch of color. Long-stemmed pipes were ubiquitous, each drooling a thin thread of smoke to add to the general fog.

"Her Royal Highness, Queen Raesinia Orboan of Vordan," Sebastian boomed, from behind her.

A bow, barely more than a nod, rippled through those assembled. Raesinia looked around, feeling a bit lost in a sea of gray beards and drooping sideburns.

At the other end of the room, a man stood up. His suit was black and his waistcoat threaded with silver. He looked like all the rest, with one exception—an elaborate gold double circle pinned to his chest, set with a spray of pearls and bearing a dark red gemstone the size of an eye. He had a pipe in one hand and something like a walking stick in the other.

This, Raesinia realized, was the King of Borel. She had pictured him as some version of her father, swathed in colorful silk and velvet; certainly there had never been any question, in the court of Farus VIII, of a visitor mistaking who was supposed to be the center of attention. Georg Pulwer clearly had different standards for the majesty of a monarch than Mistress Lagovil. *He looks more like a banker than a king.*

"Queen Raesinia," Georg said. "Please forgive this poor greeting. We only received word of your coming quite recently."

"My apologies for not sending word ahead," Raesinia said. "Events have caught us off guard."

"Don't they always?" Georg said. This was apparently supposed to be a joke, because it produced a round of dutiful laughter among the others. "In any event, welcome to Borel, and my sympathies on what must be a trying time." He raised a hand and beckoned, without looking. "Let me introduce my sons. This is Crown Prince Rupert."

"Honored, Your Highness." The crown prince shuffled forward. He was a large man, well into middle age and not carrying it well; Raesinia might have guessed him to be of the same generation as his father. He carried a similar black-and-silver walking stick, but where Georg's seemed decorative, Rupert leaned heavily on his.

"And this is Second Prince Matthew," Georg went on.

"Your Highness." Matthew sketched a deep bow. He was much younger than his brother—probably not yet thirty—slim as a sword, and had a well-trimmed beard and no sideburns. Instead of his father's and brother's somewhat fleshy features, he had a thin face with sharp cheekbones and icy blue eyes. Rather handsome, Raesinia thought, but something in his expression seemed hostile.

"I look forward to getting to know both of you," she said. That seemed safe. "I regret to say, however, that this is not merely a social visit. You're aware of the most recent developments?"

Georg nodded. "The return of Vhalnich, you mean?"

"Yes. It was with the assistance of your servant the Duke of Brookspring that we were able to thwart him the last time he reached for power. It must surely be in the interests of both our nations that he be stopped again."

"Of course." Georg's mustaches twitched in what might have been a smile. "It's the duty of all civilized peoples to stand together against a tyrant, especially one as dangerous as Vhalnich has proven to be. We will not be found wanting in that duty. Borel will be at your side in this hour of need, never fear."

Some unspoken cue prompted a short round of applause from the onlookers. Raesinia frowned. She'd hoped for an audience with less of, well, an *audience*, where Georg might be persuaded to speak a bit more candidly. *Still, he seems willing.* She bowed slightly in appreciation.

"Thank you. If your fleet can be assembled within the week, then—"

Georg cut her off with an upraised hand. "I must refer you to my advisers for the details. Fredrick?"

One of the men standing by stepped forward and bowed as low as his ample stomach would allow. "At your service, Your Majesty."

"Please discuss the necessary arrangements with Queen Raesinia."

"Of course." Fredrick turned to Raesinia. He was heavily bewhiskered, eyes almost lost above a substantial nose. "If you'll follow me?"

They had this planned. Raesinia smelled an ambush, but she had no choice except to smile graciously and go along. She checked reflexively to make sure Barely and Jo were still behind her, though she didn't really expect to be physically assaulted. *Fredrick hardly looks the type.*

Sebastian, walking ahead of them, opened a door nearby. It led to a small sitting room, where two armchairs were positioned in front of a fire, already burning. A table between them held a silver tray of pastries.

"Have a seat, Your Highness," Fredrick said. "I'm sure you're tired from your journey."

Cautiously, Raesinia settled into one of the chairs, and Fredrick lowered himself heavily into the other. He rubbed his knees with his palms, shaking his head.

"The knees are always the first to go, when you get to my age," he said. "If you want my advice, Your Highness, you'll enjoy them while they last."

"I'll keep that in mind." Raesinia almost started when Sebastian appeared at her elbow, offering a glass of wine. She took it and sipped politely.

"Did you have good weather for your journey?"

"Tolerable," Raesinia said. "Your captain made excellent time."

"The courier captains pride themselves on it. And what do you think of Viadre?"

"I haven't really gotten a good look," Raesinia said. She sat up a little straighter. "Can we skip the small talk, please? It *has* been a long journey, and as I said to His Majesty, time is of the essence."

"I see." Fredrick gave a heavy sigh. "Fair enough."

"You're Fredrick Goodman, I take it?"

"Humble merchant and one of the Honest Fellows. At your service."

And possibly the richest man in the world. "His Majesty seemed eager for us to work out the details of your assistance."

"As to that," Fredrick said. "My colleagues and I have been in conference with His Majesty since we received word of your arrival. While we of course sympathize with your situation, we agree that there are certain . . . injustices that must be redressed. Until that happens, Borelgai assistance to Vordan will be more in the character of moral support than anything . . . tangible."

Raesinia narrowed her eyes. "What sort of injustices?"

"Financial ones." Fredrick steepled his fingers. "To put it bluntly, Your Highness, you owe us a great deal of money. The Vordanai crown borrowed heavily from many upstanding citizens of Borel in the period before your father's death." His whiskers twitched. "You have my condolences, by the by. Afterward, your new . . . Deputies declared the debts of the previous government null and void. This was a source of great hardship in Viadre and no doubt contributed to our recent unpleasantness before you and the Duke of Brookspring resolved matters."

"I'm sure something can be arranged as part of the treaty," Raesinia said. "But aid must come first. Troops are in the field as we speak."

"From my position, surely you must see why that seems unwise. Once Janus is defeated, what is to prevent your government from repeating its act of fiscal dereliction?" He shook his head. "No. The Honest Fellows are agreed. A firm pledge on the debt issue must come prior to any assistance." Fredrick leaned forward, his smile showing yellowed teeth. "You must agree, that's only reasonable?"

". . . and you should see the system they have in the commodity pits," Cora said. "There's so many people packed in so tight, all shouting at once, that nobody can hear a damn thing. So the pit bosses take orders entirely by *gesture*. They have a whole language and hand signals, and it's considered as binding as a paper contract! Can you imagine making an agreement to deliver a million bushels of wheat just by going like this?" She bent her fingers into an L shape and waggled her thumb.

"It'd certainly make me more likely to keep my hands in my pockets," Raesinia said.

She was only half listening. Cora had been telling her about the wonders of the Viadre markets since she'd returned, and she required little more than the occasional nod to continue her gushing commentary. Raesinia's mind kept returning to her brief meeting with the king.

I have to see him again. In private this time. Dorsay had been right about Fredrick Goodman. *If he really represents the majority of the Honest Fellows, then our only chance is for the king to override them. But*—

She became aware that Cora had stopped talking, and blinked. "Sorry. What?"

"I asked if you'd made any progress," Cora said. "I know you said nothing important would happen today."

"Honestly, I'm not sure," Raesinia said. "The king was . . . polite, but that's about it. But I met with Fredrick Goodman afterward."

"What'd he say?"

Cora settled into the heavy leather armchair across from Raesinia while she recounted their conversation. The suite the Borelgai had provided for her use was comfortably furnished, though in the same gloomy fashion as the rest of the Keep, paneled in dark wood and equipped with solid, heavy furniture. Oil paintings of old men in antique costumes stared down from the walls. Eric was already asleep in his room, and Raesinia had insisted that Barely and Jo take some time to rest as well. Cora's energy, however, was apparently inexhaustible.

"That's . . . not going to work," Cora said, when Raesinia told her about Fredrick's insistence on the restoration of prerevolution debt.

"I guessed that we wouldn't be able to afford it," Raesinia said.

"It's not that," Cora said. "I mean, it *is* that—we already have more debt than we can really afford—but it's not *just* that. Toward the end of your father's rule . . ." She trailed off, blushing slightly.

"You don't have to dance around it," Raesinia said with a sigh. "I know he made some bad decisions."

"It wasn't really his fault," Cora said. "Orlanko put Rackhil Grieg in the Ministry of Finance, and everyone knows he was a Borelgai puppet. A lot of the loans the Crown took on his watch were on very unfavorable terms, deliberately, to improve profits for the Borels. The Deputies could never accept them, treaty or no treaty."

"Wonderful." Raesinia shook her head. "Let's hope this is just Goodman's opening offer. He has to be willing to negotiate—we may need his help, but he certainly won't get his money if Janus takes over."

"I'll talk to him," Cora said. "We need to narrow down exactly which loans he's talking about, and—"

There was a knock at the door. A heavily accented voice, one of the Life Guards outside, called, "A visitor, Your Highness. The second prince."

Raesinia and Cora raised their eyebrows simultaneously.

"Did he say anything about coming to meet you?" Cora said.

"Not that I recall." She pushed herself out of the chair. "I suppose it would be rude to leave him waiting in the hall."

She opened the door, half expecting to find the prince at the head of a whole procession. Instead he was alone except for the ever-present Life Guards, hands thrust in his pockets, ruining the line of his dark gray suit. His expression made it look as if he'd just eaten something foul.

Have I offended him already? Raesinia put on a blank expression. "Prince Matthew. What a pleasant surprise."

"Your Highness," Matthew said. "I wanted—that is, I would be honored . . ." He trailed off with a scowl, took a deep breath, and started over. "If you're not too tired, I would be pleased to invite you to dinner."

"Dinner?" The sky visible from the suite's windows was a uniform gray, and Raesinia realized she had no idea what time it was. "Tonight?"

"Or another time. I am . . . eager to get to know you."

He doesn't look it. The second prince had all the excitement of a man walking to his own execution. *So what's going on?* The little she'd learned from Dorsay hadn't included anything about where the princes fell in relation to the king and the Honest Fellows. *Better to play it safe until we know more.*

"It will have to be another time," she said with an ostentatious yawn. "It really has been a trying day. I hope you won't be offended."

"Of course not," Matthew said. He seemed pleasantly surprised. "I'll call again, Your Highness. Enjoy your evening."

"Thank you," Raesinia said. She watched, mystified, as he turned away, trailing his personal guard.

"What was that about?" Cora said, peeking over the back of her armchair.

"I have no idea," Raesinia said as she pulled the door shut. *But I think I'd better find out.*

CHAPTER EIGHT

MARCUS

There was a scratch at the tent flap. Marcus set down his pen with some relief and looked up. "Yes?"

"You wanted to see me, sir?" Cyte said.

"Please. Come in."

After nearly a week on the march, Marcus was settling in to his new routine. In truth, it was a relief to have a smaller force to worry about than the entire Grand Army, and General Kurot and his staff had been doing a competent job thus far. The Army of the Republic had proceeded by easy stages away from the river and up toward the Illifen passes without more than the usual number of entanglements, traffic jams, and stuck wagons.

Marcus had been trying hard to get to know his colonels and learn some of the peculiarities of their units. Every command had its eccentricities—the intercompany handball games that were a regular feature of the Second's camp life were a new wrinkle, for example—and, for the most part, they were harmless. *But not always.* He frowned as Cyte slipped inside.

"Something wrong, sir?"

"Maybe." He cleared his throat and steeled himself. "I have become aware of an . . . improper relationship between Colonel Giforte and Colonel Erdine."

"Improper, sir?"

"A sexual relationship."

"Ah."

"I realize it's a serious charge, but I'm quite certain." Marcus felt himself flushing a little. *Hell of a thing to have to talk to a girl about.* "When I was at Colonel Erdine's tent, I encountered Colonel Giforte in a state of undress." He'd damn near walked in on the two of them in the act, by the look of things.

"I see, sir." A faint smile played at the corner of Cyte's lips.

"Were you aware of this?" Marcus said.

"More or less, sir. I think it's . . . common knowledge."

"I thought that might be the case," Marcus said. "I have the highest respect for both of them as officers. Ordinarily a stern reprimand would be appropriate, but I wondered if General Ihernglass had a special procedure for this kind of . . . affair. Given the First Regiment's unique situation, I mean."

"Of a sort, sir. He was generally willing to turn a blind eye. Provided, of course, the liaison did not involve soldiers in the same chain of command." She was definitely smiling now. "I think it's safe to say that Abby and Erdine are . . . not unique, sir."

"I should have expected as much." Marcus sighed. "It's not going to be good for discipline in the long run."

"From what General Ihernglass told me about the Colonials, it wasn't uncommon for the officers to keep women," Cyte pointed out.

Marcus had to admit there were several establishments in Ashe-Katarion that he'd frequented. He grimaced. "That wasn't . . . regulation. And, of course, with only men in the regiment, we didn't have to deal with any relationships between soldiers."

"That's . . ." Cyte paused, and apparently decided not to comment. "In any event, sir, so far it hasn't caused problems in the Second. Do you plan to change General Ihernglass' policy?"

"I suppose not." He shifted uncomfortably. "I assume Colonel Giforte and her soldiers have . . . that is, they won't . . ."

"They have appropriate protection, sir," Cyte said. "And Colonel Giforte is very firm if there's even a hint of coercion or commerce involved."

"That's good. We can't have the regiment turning into a brothel."

"The Girls' Own takes care of its soldiers, sir."

"Good, good." Marcus let out a long breath, feeling like he'd surmounted a difficult obstacle.

"Was that all?" Cyte said with a broad grin.

"I've had this note from General Kurot," Marcus said, tapping his pile of papers. "There have been several attempts at defection intercepted by the sentries, and it's possible others were more successful. Marching against Janus . . ." He shrugged. "What's your sense of the Second? Are we likely to have problems in that respect?"

"I doubt it, sir. Speaking frankly, it was always more Winter's division than

Janus'." She looked a little uncomfortable. "I have to admit, sir, that there's been a little talk about you. Not that the soldiers doubt your loyalty, but . . ."

"I understand." Marcus was getting used to those suspicions, unfortunately. "Is this talk anything I should worry about?"

"No, sir." Cyte straightened up. "Of course not."

"You haven't offended me, Colonel. Don't worry."

Marcus got out of his chair and walked around the table, brushing papers out of the way until he could see the map. The present position of the Army of the Republic was marked in grease pencil, along with most plausible guesses about where Janus' army might be, moving slowly down the Pale toward Alves. He found his finger drawn, once again, to a spot not far from their line of march, just this side of the mountains.

"I understand you were fairly close to Ihernglass," Marcus said.

"Y-yes."

"He trusted you."

"I like to think so." Cyte leaned over the table to follow Marcus' gaze. "Is there a problem, sir?"

"Ihernglass told me that there were a few soldiers in his command that understood the . . . full extent of what happened to him in Khandar. He implied that you were one of them."

"You mean his, ah, more unusual service?"

The hell with it. "I mean magic, Colonel. General Ihernglass told you about magic. The Thousand Names and the Penitent Damned and the whole rest of that Karis-damned lot."

Cyte didn't even flinch. "Yes, sir. We were attacked by Penitents several times during the Velt campaign."

"Good. I need someone who isn't going to think I'm crazy. Is there anything important on the schedule for tomorrow?"

"Not particularly, sir. We're third in line of march, so it should be an easy day."

"Anything Colonel Giforte can't handle without you?"

"No, sir." Cyte looked curious. "Why?"

"I want you to come with me on a little side trip."

His finger tapped the map again. The tiny castle was labeled in the smallest type the mapmaker had been able to find. Marcus had to squint to read it. *Mieranhal.*

It felt like an invitation to disaster, riding away from the column, even though Marcus had gone through proper channels and informed everyone who needed informing of his brief absence. *It'll be days yet before we're in any real danger.* Even Janus, with his reputation for doing the unexpected, wouldn't force a march over an inhospitable mountain pass in hostile territory just for the sake of a little bit of surprise. *Probably.*

He'd fought off all efforts to provide an escort, ostensibly for the sake of morale. This was, after all, still Vordan, and senior officers shouldn't need guards to ride around the countryside. He was just as happy not to have to explain himself to anyone but Cyte, though. They started early and rode southwest at an easy pace. Marcus was glumly unsurprised to note that Cyte was a far better rider than he was, but an amiable trot down a sleepy lane was a trip even he could handle.

"Have you spent much time in the country, Captain?" he said, as they turned to follow the road around the curve of a hill. The mountains were startlingly close, looming blue and vaguely unreal in middle distance. Between here and there, the land rose into increasingly steep hills, the farms of the flat bottomland giving way to orchards and pasture.

"No, sir," Cyte said. "City girl for the most part."

"I'm the same. Closest I got was my time at the War College." He looked up at the mountains. *It feels like I could reach out and touch them.* "Pretty, I suppose."

"Yes, sir." Cyte hesitated. "Where exactly are we going?"

"Mieranhal." Marcus waved a hand. "This is all Mieran County. Mieranhal is the county seat."

"Oh!" Cyte looked around with new interest.

"You've been here before?"

"Never, sir. But Mieran has a fascinating history. Linguistically, it's an isolated dialect, unrelated to the Mithradacii that—" She stopped. "Sorry, sir. I studied ancient history at the University, before the revolution."

"No need to apologize," Marcus said. "In fact, I'd be obliged if you'd give me the short version."

"The *short* short version is they're a bunch of mountain people who fought like hell and managed to hang on to their land when everyone down in the valleys was overrun. The Mierantai rulers swore fealty to the Tyrants, and later to the kings of Vordan, but they kept their own customs and language. They've been basically keeping to themselves for thousands of years."

"Interesting." From a military perspective, Marcus could see it. This kind of hilly country would be a nightmare to fight in, especially against a canny enemy who knew the ground well.

"Yes, sir. They're supposed to have the oldest surviving examples of pre-conquest script and architecture." She cocked her head. "I assume you're not here for the historical significance?"

"In a way. But I'm interested in more recent history." Marcus shifted in his saddle, already feeling the aches. "This is where Janus bet Vhalnich grew up."

"Of course," Cyte said, sounding irritated she hadn't made the connection. Her eyes went wide. "You think he might be in communication with someone here?"

"I doubt it, actually. But I'm hoping we can find someone who knew him when he lived here."

"Why?"

"I don't want to prejudice your opinion," Marcus said. "But keep your ears open, and I'll explain later."

They didn't reach Mieranhal until well after midday. The roads had an irritating tendency to curve, following the shoulders of the hills to maintain a shallow grade but making it very easy to get lost. Fortunately, Cyte was excellent with maps, and they only had to backtrack twice. Both sides of the road were planted with trees, mostly craggy little apple trees standing in neat rows, their leaves just starting to change from green to yellow. A cheerful young man sitting on a fence post offered them each an apple as they passed, and another for each of the horses. Marcus bit into his as he rode and found it just the right balance of sour and sweet.

Orchards gave way to rocky pastures as they climbed higher, dotted here and there with sheep. Marcus was starting to think they'd taken another wrong turn when they came around a switchback and found their destination looming directly in their path, as though it had snuck up on them. Mieranhal was an ancient stone building, more manor house than true fortress. It had been added to extensively over the years, modern wings sprouting off the original structure, including wooden outbuildings and several plaster-walled cottages. More orchards and vegetable gardens stretched out behind it, and Marcus saw two girls leading a flock of sheep around the back. As they got closer, several dogs began barking.

The front doors were mammoth things that looked like they'd require a team of dozens to open. Marcus reined up in front of them, not sure exactly what to do, but a smaller door around the side creaked open. A young man stepped out, holding the leash of a large, jowly dog that was sniffing the air entirely. To Marcus' surprise, the man smiled and transferred the leash to his left hand to make a proper salute.

"Saints and martyrs!" The voice, with its harsh accent, brought a spark of recognition, but it wasn't until the man came closer that Marcus placed the face. "Marcus d'Ivoire. And risen so high I don't even recognize the stars on your shoulder."

"You're Lieutenant . . . Uhlan, wasn't it?" It had been only a year since they'd worked together in Vordan City, thwarting Maurisk's attempted coup, but it felt more like a century. Uhlan had been one of the Mierantai volunteers who'd served as Janus' bodyguards and trusted aides.

"Yes, sir. Though not a lieutenant anymore, glad to say. Resigned my commission. Just Medio bet Uhlan, at your service."

"It's good to see you," Marcus said. "This is Colonel Cytomandiclea, of the Second Division. She's serving as my aide at present."

"He's got a knack for finding pretty girls to be his aides," Uhlan said to Cyte. To Marcus, he said, "What happened to Andy? She finally get tired of you?"

"She died," Marcus said, feeling a twist in his guts. "In Murnsk. She saved all our lives."

"Ah, shit." Uhlan shook his head. "Sorry. And here I am keeping you in the yard. Hyllia!" When a girl's head popped out of a window, he shouted, "Get someone out here to take care of the officers' horses, and fetch drinks." He looked back at Marcus. "You'll stay for dinner, I hope?"

"I'd love to," Marcus said.

It turned out that Mieran County was one of those places that took their hospitality seriously. No sooner had Marcus and Cyte knocked the dust from their boots and come inside than they were whisked to a comfortable sitting room and provided with mugs of hot apple cider, plates of cheese and bread, and some kind of dried meat so doused in hot pepper it made Marcus' eyes water.

Uhlan sat with them, chatting amiably as servant girls brought the food and drink. Marcus remembered the Mierantai volunteers as being a taciturn lot, but Uhlan was much friendlier here, on his home ground.

"My family has been in service to the counts for generations," he said, when Cyte quizzed him about his history. "Since the lance-and-shield days, if you believe the stories my grandfather told me. *His* father formed the first Mierantai Volunteers to fight with Farus IV. Since then it's been sort of a tradition."

"You went home after the coup," Marcus said. "When Janus became First Consul."

"He said he didn't need us anymore." Uhlan sipped at his cider. "He always felt guilty about calling us out, I think. He takes his responsibility toward the county seriously, and he knows we've all got families waiting for us. We're not professional soldiers."

The Mierantai had seemed professional enough when Marcus had fought beside them, deadly accurate with their long rifles and admirably disciplined. Marcus reached for more bread and surreptitiously checked to see if the servants had left the room. When he was satisfied they were alone, he said, "I assume the news has reached you here."

Uhlan smiled dryly. "We're not *that* isolated, General d'Ivoire."

Marcus glanced at Cyte. "You haven't had any contact with him, have you?"

"No." Uhlan shook his head. "Some of the boys wanted to go and find him, but we talked them out of it."

"Would you go, if he called?" Cyte said.

"Don't imagine I haven't thought hard about it," Uhlan said. "He's been a good master to everyone in Mieran, but we swear an oath to keep the county safe. This emperor business . . ." He shrugged. "He ought to know better." After a pause, he cocked his head. "Did you come out here just to ask me that? You're not the first officer to come around, you know."

"Someone else was here?"

"A pair of them," Uhlan said. "One came in uniform and asked around. The other tried to do a bit of spying, but that gets hard in a place like Mieran, where everyone knows everyone. We told 'em both the same I'm telling you."

Probably Alek Giforte's men. The former Armsman was trying to put Vordan's intelligence service back together, and it made sense he'd send someone here.

"That's not really why I came," Marcus said. "I was hoping to find out a little more about Janus."

"Why?" Uhlan's face was still friendly, but there was a sharp edge to his tone. "He's your enemy now, isn't he?"

"I'm . . . not sure." Marcus looked at Cyte again. "You're right. He *ought* to know better. And some of the things he's said to me make me wonder . . ."

He shook his head. "I can't explain it well. But I'm trying to understand why he would turn on all of us the way he has. I wouldn't have said it was possible."

"What're you hoping to find?" Uhlan said.

Marcus shook his head helplessly. "A reason, maybe. Just . . . something."

The Mierantai looked at him for a long time, hard eyes unreadable. Then his face split in a grin again, and he shrugged.

"Can't see the harm," he said. "And I know you, General d'Ivoire. *You* would never betray a friend."

I already have. Marcus felt a stab of guilt, remembering Janus imprisoned in the barn outside Polkhaiz. It had been the right decision, backing Raesinia and peace instead of helping Janus continue the war, but Janus' face at that moment would always be etched in his memory. *Is that why he's doing this? Is it my fault?*

But his instinct said no. *It doesn't make sense.*

"Thank you," Marcus said.

"Hyllia?" Uhlan raised his voice. After a few moments, a servant girl opened the door and poked her head in. "Take General d'Ivoire and his friend up to see Gravya, would you? Tell her I said she can trust them."

Hyllia bobbed politely. Marcus finished his cider and set it aside, then followed her back into the hall and on a winding path through the house. They passed under a stone arch and into one of the older sections, where warped, cloudy glass in the windows cast strange patterns of light on the walls and the floorboards were polished smooth and almost black. A faint dusty smell hung in the air.

The girl rapped at a wooden door with flaking blue paint, knocking a few chips to the floor. "Mistress Gravya?"

"Yes?" The response was an old woman's. "Hyllia, dear, is that you?"

"There's visitors, Mistress Gravya," Hyllia said. "Master Uhlan asked if you'd speak with them. He says you can trust them."

"Visitors?" The door opened, revealing a tall, iron-haired woman in her sixties. She wore a practical brown dress and thick spectacles, and a white cap was pinned to her neat bun. She took in Marcus' and Cyte's uniforms, and her eyes narrowed behind her glasses. "Soldiers? What would soldiers want with me?"

"My name is Marcus d'Ivoire," Marcus said. "This is Colonel Cytomandiclea."

"That's a mouthful," Gravya said, looking critically at Cyte. "You're a woman."

"Yes, mistress," Cyte said. "And you can call me Cyte, if you like."

"We'd like to ask you some questions about Janus," Marcus said. "What he was like when he was younger."

"Oh, for heaven's sake," Gravya said. "He was a boy like any other boy. There were no comets at his birth or anything like that."

"I realize that. He . . . is a friend of mine." Marcus lowered his voice and fought off another pang of guilt. "I was hoping you could tell me about Mya."

The old woman went very still for a moment, staring intently at Marcus. Her hand came up and patted her bun, as though reassuring herself her cap was still in place.

"Hyllia, you can go," she said. "I'll bring the officers back when we've finished."

"Yes, mistress." Hyllia bobbed again and hurried off, apparently glad to be away from these strange visitors.

"He never talks about Mya," Gravya said. "Not to anyone he doesn't trust completely."

Another stab of conscience. Janus hadn't *known* he'd been talking about Mya; he'd been delirious, dying of a supernatural poison. Marcus forced himself to nod solemnly.

"All right," Gravya said, suddenly decisive. "Come along."

She swept out of her room and led them off down the corridor again. It went deeper into the oldest part of the house. Eventually they climbed a narrow stairway, accompanied by a chorus of creaks and groans.

"I keep telling Medio someone ought to clean up here," Gravya said. "But there's always something else to do, and not enough hands to do it. That's the thing about an old pile like this; some part of it's always falling down. I'm not so different, I suppose." She gave a bark of a laugh.

"You knew Janus well, then?"

"Of course. I practically raised him. His parents both died when he was a baby, you know. We all raised him, the servants here at Mieranhal, but I was his tutor." She snorted. "To the extent he needed such a thing."

"And who's Mya?"

"Nearly there."

They reached a door, which Gravya opened. It led to a dimly lit room at the top of the house, attic rafters fading into darkness overhead. A long, moth-eaten carpet spread out underfoot. Gravya took an oil lamp from a hook on the wall, lit it expertly with a match, and turned up the flame to reveal a gallery hung with paintings in heavy, ornate frames.

"The other thing about an old pile like Mieranhal," she said, "is that nobody ever throws anything away. You stash it somewhere, just in case you need it. Or someone else needs it, three generations down the line. It's not as though we're short of space!" She raised the lantern and started to walk, then stopped in front of a painting. "Here. Look at this."

Marcus looked. The painting was a big portrait, well captured and thick with detail. The background was a large kitchen, with dozens of figures preparing food. In the foreground were two children, standing side by side, looking up as though they'd been captured in the act of doing something naughty.

The boy on the right seemed about six years old, with a round face and a lick of dark hair. In the crook of one arm, a small gray kitten was nestled, looking up at him inquisitively. On the left, an older girl, perhaps twelve, held a saucer of milk. The resemblance between them was uncanny—her hair was long and brown, and her face sharper angled, but the eyes were the same. Huge gray eyes, with a strange depth the painter had expertly captured.

"That's Janus," Gravya said. "And Mya. The night of the winter feast, they snuck into the kitchen to find treats for the cat. Janus had been hiding it in his room, because old Woodsmark had said he couldn't have one. I forget why. Cook caught them, but the poor cat looked so sad she kept it secret anyway." Gravya smiled. "Mya asked for the picture to be painted, later. She had a mischievous streak a mile wide, that girl."

"She's his sister?"

"His older sister." Gravya touched the painting with one gnarled hand. "This was painted not six months before she died."

PART TWO

INTERLUDE

JANUS

The hardest thing to fathom about the mind of the Beast was the way that space inside was, or more precisely was *not*, connected to the physical world. Janus had at first assumed that the silver lines far "below" were something like a map of the Beast's bodies in physical reality. When he'd investigated, however, it had proven considerably more complex. The threads were a network, reflecting in their topology the timing and manner in which new bodies had been added. But they also changed over time, as the bodies moved. It was a fascinating puzzle.

It was not that Janus was immune to the confusion and introspection that might normally be expected from someone who had discovered he was now, at best, a disembodied mind. He was only human, after all, or at least had been. But he went through the introspection and despair with the quick efficiency he expected of himself in everything and got them over with so he could move on with making what he could out of the situation.

Step one had been convincing the Beast that he could be of some use as an independent personality, both for obvious reasons of self-preservation and because it might provide useful avenues in the future. Janus had done this almost automatically, once he'd fully appreciated the circumstances that had been thrust on him. It even made sense, from the Beast's point of view. Its mind was vast, but still in an important sense singular—it could pay attention to only one thing at a time.

At the moment, its focus was in the north, dedicated to the pursuit of Winter Ihernglass. Her use of Infernivore to destroy one of its bodies had reminded the demon of its vulnerability, and if it had been human Janus would have described it as enraged. All across northern Murnsk, red-eyes were on the move, converging slowly on Winter and her small band of fugitives. It would take time to gather enough bodies for an assault, especially considering the capabilities of Winter's companions.

This left the Beast caught between two fires. The range at which it could control its bodies was increasing, but it still had limits. Its core, the body that had once belonged to Jane Verity, had to shift farther and farther south to retain control of the red-eyes with Janus' army, including Janus' own body. A battalion of bodies guarded the core, bringing it a constant stream of fresh subjects to convert, but sooner or later the Beast was going to have to decide between the war in the south and its pursuit in the north.

If Winter was killed, or the Beast gave up the chase, it would be able to devote its full attention to the south. Once the core came close enough, the red-eyes would be unleashed on the densely populated Vordanai countryside, enslaving everyone they could reach. That was to be avoided, if possible. For the moment, Janus was satisfied with his progress—by convincing the Beast to use his own body as a figurehead, he had advanced its timetable for the southern war and brought about this split. *I need to take advantage of it while it lasts.*

He was looking for something—if *looking* was a word that applied to a disembodied mind wandering an entirely metaphorical space—the echo of a voice. He'd "heard" it before, briefly, but the Beast's attention had been on him and he hadn't been in a position to investigate. Now he crossed and recrossed the area in which he'd been hovering, hunting for the elusive sound. Just finding the "same" place had been an extremely nontrivial exercise, but now he was sure he had it right. *Consider how fast the threads readjusted, expand the search radius, keep moving—*

Got it. Down at the very edge of hearing, a woman's voice. Different, somehow, from the non-sound by which the minds in here communicated— real sound, coming in from the *outside*. He moved in circles, following it when it got louder, homing in on the source.

". . . don't think that's possible." He recognized the speaker. "You know that . . ."

It faded into unintelligibility, still barely audible. Janus cast about for the source of the sound. He found another mind, visible in the mindscape of the Beast as a tiny whirl of cloud and movement, like a miniature storm. It was smaller than himself, and felt incomplete, as though it were only a part of a whole person. But—unlike every other mind he'd encountered here—it had some kind of *connection*, visible as a hair-thin thread of brilliant crimson, snaking away into the depths of non-space.

He'd made a good guess about what that connection might be. Now, examining the mind, he could see that guess had been right. *But can I use it?*

Manipulating other minds, here in the mindscape, was a matter of exerting pure will. This was a quality that Janus had never lacked, which probably explained his continued survival. He pushed his attention into the smaller mind and found it composed of a chaotic whirl of thoughts and impressions. At the center, that familiar voice. Janus grabbed hold of the connection, *twisted* it into reverse. He could feel something happen at the other end.

"If you're there," he said, pushing his words down the link like a memory of human speech, "please answer quickly. I don't think I have long."

". . . who is speaking?" Very faint, but understandable.

"This is Janus bet Vhalnich, and there isn't time to explain everything—"

Later, Janus approached the enormous, black-walled hurricane that was the primary personality of the Beast. It was still directing its bodies in their pursuit of Winter, though Janus could see at a glance that it would be some time before an assault was practicable. *She'll get through.* He had every confidence in Winter.

"Vhalnich." The mental voice was similar to the Beast's, but not quite the same. More feminine, more singular, where the Beast was a choral roar of many blended into one. "Still fighting the inevitable."

"Jane Verity," Janus said. "I thought you had long ago been subsumed."

"I think I have." There was no visible structure to her mind separate from the Beast itself. Just one whirling cloud among a hurricane. "But I kept a little of myself apart. Just to enjoy this."

"Hunting Winter?"

"*No.* Seeing you trapped at last." Jane's voice was bitter. "It won't be long. Winter will join me, and we can finally be free. Free of the world. Free of *you.* How does it feel, monster?"

"One of us is a monster," Janus said. "I invite you to consider which."

Jane fell silent as the Beast's primary attention shifted, noticing Janus' presence. The hurricane bulged and spun, producing a pull on Janus' mind-stuff he could feel like a strong wind.

"You venture close, for one who wants to remain whole," the Beast said.

"I had a thought," Janus said. "I have been observing the progress of the army accompanying my former body, and I can't help but notice it is decidedly unsatisfactory. From your point of view, of course."

"Winter is more important. I have time to deal with Vordan and the Names."

"Of course. But Vordan will have dispatched an army to intercept, and Marcus d'Ivoire will be with it. He is a fine soldier, and without strong leadership he might well be successful. That would delay our project considerably."

"*Our* project, is it?"

Janus would have shrugged, if he'd had shoulders. "My existence is contingent on your continued pleasure. All of your projects are by definition mine as well."

"I cannot leave Winter to escape."

"I know. Hence my suggestion—allow me to control my former body, and the others with the army. Those yet to be converted will be expecting 'Janus' to issue commands."

"None of the other minds have attempted to control a body." The Beast sounded fascinated. "You can do it?"

"I believe so. I have studied the mechanism. I would not proceed without your permission, of course."

"That could be useful." The Beast had every bit of knowledge and skill of all of its continuants, and it could see the advantages immediately. For all that it was in some ways limited, it was still terrifyingly capable. "But I cannot help but think you find some advantage for yourself."

"What advantage could I gain, in here?"

"Misplaced loyalty to former friends, perhaps?" The Beast's voice was a roar. "I should tear you apart and find out."

"You can do so, of course. But then I will be unable to assist."

There was a long pause.

"Go," the Beast said. "If you can. But I will be watching."

CHAPTER NINE

MARCUS

"They were six years apart," Gravya said. "Janus' mother never recovered from his birth, and the old count followed her a year later. She was always his strength, I think. He was a kind man, but not a hardy one."

The old woman stood at an iron stove in the dusty sitting room, expertly building the fire. Marcus, sitting in a tattered but comfortable chair, felt a bit awkward letting her wait on them, and Cyte apparently had the same thought, because she said, "Can I help at all, Mistress Gravya?"

"Oh, no, dear. It's just something to do with my hands. Helps me think. Habit, you know?"

Cyte, frowning, settled down into the chair opposite Marcus. Marcus said, "So Janus never knew his parents?"

Gravya shook her head. "He had us—the house servants—and he had Mya. That was all. They were inseparable from the time he could walk. I called myself his tutor, but it was Mya who taught him to read and write. I just filled in what she couldn't be bothered with. Not talking with your mouth full and the like." She laughed and poked the fire, sending up a shower of sparks. "Most days it was just the two of them, going wherever they wanted, all over the estate."

"What was Mya like?" Marcus said. "Was she as smart as Janus?"

"Hard to say," Gravya said. "She was smarter than anyone in the house by the time she was ten, that's for certain. And she was . . . good at understanding people, better than he was." She transferred a cast-iron pot to the stove top and set to stirring. "You're his friend, so you must have seen how he can be a bit . . . distant?"

"From time to time," Marcus muttered, which made Gravya laugh again.

"He hasn't changed, I take it. Once when he called for me in the middle of the night, I told him off for waking me, and he said he'd forgotten that I needed to sleep. Other people just don't always *register*, you know? He's lost in his own head."

"Mya wasn't like that?"

"Oh, no." Gravya stopped stirring for a moment, lost in memory. "If anything, she understood too well. She couldn't bear seeing anyone suffering, and she *knew* when they were hurting, even if they didn't know it themselves. You couldn't lie to her, not ever. She would always know." The old woman sniffed, and started stirring again. "Once when she was nine, one of the stableboys played a prank on her, dirt down her dress or some such. She spent all afternoon devising a way to get back at him, a sort of hunter's trap in the yard that dumped him into a pile of pig shit. But then, when everyone was laughing at him, she broke down and started to cry. She understood how it made him feel, she told me later, and she couldn't stand it."

"She sounds like a kind soul," Cyte said.

"She was, I think," Gravya said slowly. "Difficult, sometimes, and with strange ideas. But ultimately kind."

"Strange ideas?" Marcus prompted.

Gravya was quiet for a moment, taking dried leaves from a small box and grinding them between her fingers to sprinkle in the pot. She sniffed again, and, apparently satisfied, resumed stirring.

"She read a lot," the old woman said finally. "They both did, of course, but by the time she was twelve Mya had read every book in her father's library and sent away for more. She loved history, but she was never satisfied with it. She always said that she could have done better." Gravya shook her head. "For a while she and Janus would play with toy soldiers, over and over. She would get angry and shout at him if he wasn't good enough, even though he was only six. They would draw, not like ordinary children draw, but . . . diagrams, charts, that sort of thing. I asked what they were doing once, and Janus told me they were inventing a new kind of king. Then Mya shushed him. She was getting to that self-conscious age, poor thing. Poor girl."

"Was it the Red Hand?" Cyte said. Marcus blinked, surprised, but when he added up the dates it worked out. The plague had swept through Vordan City, brought by ships from the east, and worked its way out into the country, the worst epidemic since the age of tyrants.

Gravya nodded. "It was worst on children, you know. That was always the

cruelest part. They both caught it, and for a time we thought they would recover, but Mya took a sudden turn for the worse. Janus . . . didn't react well.
At first he kept demanding to see her, no matter how we tried to explain it to
him. Later he burned all their papers, all the work they'd done together, and
nearly set fire to the house. Sometimes he'd stop eating for days at a time. He
went into the library and started reading. He knew Mya had read all the books,
and I think it helped him feel closer to her. But he just . . . stayed there.

"We were worried sick about him. He'd never really recovered from the
Red Hand, and he was so thin you could see his ribs. He'd get sores, sometimes,
from not washing properly, and he'd ignore food until he fainted. I finally
figured out that he'd run out of books—he'd read everything in the library ten
times—so I would have peddlers bring in a cartload and refuse to hand them
over until he'd taken care of himself. That got him washing and eating, at least,
but he still wouldn't go outside."

"I remember going through a similar phase," Cyte said. "Though it wasn't
quite that bad." She chuckled, to show it was joke, but Gravya merely continued stirring. Awkwardly, she continued. "How long did this go on?"

"About eight years." Gravya dipped a small cup into the pot and held it in
one hand, waiting for it to cool. "Sometimes we could convince him to leave for
a few days, a week. But something would always set him off again, and he'd be
back in the library before we knew it. I practically beggared us buying new books
for him. Eventually we ran out of room, and I could at least sell off the old ones.
He still looked like a scarecrow, those big gray eyes in such a hollow face. It broke
my heart." She blew across the cup, tasted the contents, and downed the rest.

"That doesn't sound like the Janus I know," Marcus said.

"It's not." Gravya poured from the pot into three waiting mugs and handed
one to Marcus and one to Cyte. "Try this."

Marcus sipped. Almost too hot to drink, it was clearly based on the apple
cider he'd had downstairs but with something else added, a dark, subtle flavor
with a hint of spices. When he inhaled the steam, he could smell cinnamon and
other things he couldn't identify.

"It's wonderful," he said.

"I make it for him whenever he comes back," Gravya said. "My special
recipe. He says he can never quite get it right himself."

"What happened to him?" Marcus said.

"I don't know." Gravya sipped from her own mug. "Something changed
when he was twelve. Maybe it was because that was how old Mya had been

when she died, but I don't think so. I've always figured it was something in the books. Something he *found*." She shook her head. "We were bringing them in by the cartload by then, just buying whatever the vendors in the city had handy. He read everything anyway, so we weren't picky. I think he read something that . . . affected him."

Gravya laughed. "Not that I believe in magic or anything like that, you understand. But it was like he'd found a *purpose*. He came out of the library the next day and started taking exercise. At first he could scarcely run around the yard without falling over, but he kept at it, every day. He learned to ride, to fight with a sword, anything else anyone could teach him. And he sent off for more books from the University, whole courses' worth. Mathematics, philosophy, war. Always war. He liked history as much as Mya did."

"And he never told you why? What he was doing?" Marcus said.

"No." Gravya stared into her mug. "He would talk to us, and he was always polite. But there was this feeling that he wasn't paying attention, not really. He was always . . . somewhere else." She sighed. "Eventually he left. Traveled for a while and then went to court. He must have impressed the king, because he stayed in the palace. He'd come back here from time to time and help us manage things. He designed a new way to lay out the orchards, you know? Said it would work better because it would make the bees happier. I don't know why he thinks he knows what makes *bees* happy, or how you could tell if they were."

"Did it work?" Cyte said.

Gravya laughed sharply. "Of course it did. You've met him. Everything he does works."

"You said he doesn't talk about Mya," Marcus said. "Has he said why?"

"At first I thought it was because he wanted to forget," Gravya said. "He had us put all the pictures of her away, and he never mentioned her. But I don't think he *can* forget. I think it was for everyone else to forget, if that makes any sense. Almost nobody outside Mieranhal knows she even existed." She cocked her head. "That's why I was so surprised he told you."

"So was I," Marcus said honestly. "He's normally very . . . private."

There was a long pause.

"Well," Gravya said, with false brightness. "Drink up. I'm sure Medio will want you for dinner."

Uhlan did indeed insist on Marcus and Cyte staying for dinner, which was simple, delicious, and offered in vast quantities. Afterward, there was still enough daylight left to make it to the next town, and Marcus gave his military duties as an excuse to avoid any further hospitality. He and Cyte rode through the gathering twilight, winding down the hilly paths. The shepherds were all gathering in their sheep, and the apple orchards cast long shadows.

"We'll spend the night at Gyff," Marcus said. They'd passed it on the way up, and he recalled a small inn. "If we start at dawn tomorrow, we should be back with the army by the time they make camp."

Cyte nodded. She was silent for a moment, then said, "You wanted me to draw my own conclusions."

"I did." Marcus looked around, but there was no one within earshot. "Have you?"

"There's not *that* much to draw a conclusion from. Janus found something in his books that gave him a purpose in life. Since you asked me about magic, I'm guessing you think it's something to do with that."

"It makes sense," Marcus said. "When Janus came to Khandar, he *knew* the Thousand Names were there. There was a moment when he thought he'd lost them—" He shook his head. It had been one of Janus' rare, spectacular rages; only Marcus' intervention had prevented him from torturing an old woman to death.

"Why did he want them?"

"I know the story he told me," Marcus said slowly. "Princess Raesinia had—has—a problem of a magical nature." He looked up. "I don't need to tell you this is all strictly secret, do I?"

"Of course not," Cyte said.

"Winter knows most of it. Raesinia, obviously. A few others have bits and pieces." He frowned. "In any case, the king asked Janus to help his daughter. A few years later Janus is assigned to command in Khandar, by the king's personal intervention. He told me—well after the fact, of course—that he'd been looking for the Thousand Names to help Raesinia. He thought that she would never be safe as long as the Priests of the Black were hunting for stray magic, and with the Thousand Names he'd have the power to take them on."

"Given Winter's history with the Priests of the Black and the Penitents, I can't say that I disagree with him," Cyte said. "But you said that's the story he told you. You don't believe it?"

"I think it's true, as far as it goes," Marcus said. "But there's a piece missing. Why would the king pick Janus to help his daughter unless he already had some familiarity with magic and demons?"

"Janus is a genius," Cyte said. "Maybe the king saw that."

"It's possible. But I think Janus was already searching for that kind of information. He said to me once that it was out there, if you knew where to look, and I think he was looking. I think he's been looking ever since his revelation at age twelve."

"What do you think he found then?"

"I'm not sure. Maybe just something that convinced him magic was real, that demons really existed." Marcus looked sidelong at Cyte. "Did you believe any of that, before you saw the truth for yourself?"

She watched him carefully for a moment. "The Church has always said demons are real."

"In a vague sort of way. But did *you* believe it?"

"No." Cyte shrugged. "I haven't believed since I was a little girl. It always seemed too . . . comforting to me. Too much like a fairy tale."

"It must have been a shock finding out you were wrong."

"It took some getting used to." Cyte smiled slightly. "But just because magic and demons are real doesn't mean the rest of it is. What about you?"

"I suppose I believe in God. And in Khandar there were always odd rumors going around. I got used to the idea that there might be something strange in the world. When it finally hit me, it was a shock, but I got over it pretty quickly." He grimaced. "Although it took some time to heal. But now imagine you're someone like Janus."

"That's not easy to imagine."

"Granted. But try. You believe in a world that you can understand. It has rules, laws. You study history, engineering, mathematics, and so on. And then one day you find something that convinces you that there's *more*, things that don't fit in with any of the laws you know about."

"It does seem like it would be a shock," Cyte said. "You think that everything he did after that was a reaction to finding out about magic?"

"Maybe. There's one more piece."

"When he told you about Mya." Cyte had the air of someone who'd been waiting to ask the important question. "What did he say?"

"I wasn't entirely straight with Gravya," Marcus said. "Janus had been poisoned by a Penitent, and he was feverish. Not in his right mind."

"That was when Winter left," Cyte said. "To track down the assassin."

"Exactly. I was taking care of Janus myself, especially after we got cut off by the river. He would . . . talk."

"About Mya?"

"I didn't always understand him, but he mentioned her name. He called out to her, telling her not to leave him."

"That makes sense, since he was so upset by her death."

"That wasn't it, though." Marcus frowned, trying to recall the exact words. "He told me the world was as thin as the scum on the surface of a bowl of soup, and that far underneath there were . . . continents of shadow. And that she—Mya, I think—is down there somewhere." He paused. "He said he had a fishing line."

Cyte sucked in her breath.

"He said," Marcus went on, "that she outshone him like the sun against a candle. And that we had to *help* her, and to do that he had to get to Elysium. He said something was waiting for him there. He called it 'my demon.'"

Disclosing a friend's most private thoughts, Marcus felt simultaneously burdened by guilt and lightened for having someone else to share the secret. He watched Cyte's face as she worked through it.

"How can he want to help Mya?" Cyte said. "Is it possible that she's still alive, somehow? That something happened to her, some demon, and Janus wants to undo it?"

"I thought that at first. It's one reason I wanted to come here. But the story doesn't match up." Marcus shook his head. "I don't think he could have kept something like that from Gravya and the others, not when he was only six years old. And he didn't have his revelation for another six years."

"So . . ."

"I think that Mya died," Marcus said. "And that Janus still thinks he can help her."

There was a long, uncomfortable silence.

"That's insane," Cyte said.

"Is it?" Marcus said. "Do you know that for certain? I mean, I would have agreed with you two years ago. Since then I've seen dead bodies rise as monsters and watched a woman tear stone apart with her bare hands. Who am I to say that there's no way to bring a girl back to life?" *Look at Raesinia.*

"But . . ." Cyte shook her head.

"He leaves Mieranhal. Reads everything he can find about magic, and figures out that if there *is* a demon that can do what he wants, it's going to be at Elysium, with the Black Priests and their Penitents. He also finds out that the Thousand Names exist, so when he has the chance he gets the king to assign him to the Khandarai expedition."

"Because he knows it's a threat to the Black Priests," Cyte said slowly. "So that there'll be a war with Murnsk . . ."

"And he can march on Elysium with the army behind him."

The sun was nearly gone from the sky. Up ahead, Marcus could see the lights of Gyff, warm and welcoming. The shadows of their horses stretched out, flickering along the road.

"You really think it's possible?" Cyte said. "That he *planned* all of this?"

"I know that if anyone could have done it, it's Janus bet Vhalnich." Marcus shrugged uncomfortably. "But I think something's gone wrong."

"When he didn't make it to Elysium, you mean."

"More than that. If all this is true—and that's a big *if*—then what's the sense in what he's doing now? Declaring himself emperor and marching *south*, toward Vordan, instead of back to Elysium?"

"Maybe he wants to secure Vordan before going back for another try. Or maybe there's another step we don't understand." Cyte sighed. "Or maybe we're spinning our wheels, and he's just in love with power for its own sake."

"It's possible." But Marcus remembered Janus on the march north, even before he'd been poisoned. The single-minded focus. *He was willing to sacrifice the whole army if it got him to Elysium.* "Or maybe someone else is pulling the strings."

"I don't think Janus would ever serve as a puppet," Cyte said.

"The Penitents got to him once," Marcus said. "Maybe they did it again."

Cyte gave Marcus a long look. "You want to believe that, don't you?"

He did. He couldn't deny it. *Because if it's true, then my betrayal isn't a betrayal. We're marching to save Janus, not to destroy him.* "That doesn't make it wrong."

"It doesn't." She gave him a wan smile. "Just be careful. One of the lessons of history is that you should always be the most skeptical when the evidence lines up just the way you want it to."

"We have that one at the War College, too," Marcus said. "When things look too good to be true, it's probably a trap."

And if there's one person who could set a trap like this, it's Janus bet Vhalnich.

CHAPTER TEN

WINTER

"Upstream," Leti said decisively. "There'll be a place to cross."

"How do you know?" The Murnskai words still came slowly to Winter, but her vocabulary was improving, and she'd adapted to the peculiar dialect Leti and the others used. She needed Abraham to translate only when the conversation got particularly abstract.

"Deer tracks. They'll have a way over."

Leti pointed. They were standing by the side of a small river, running deep and fast in a narrow gorge. Trees overhung it on both sides, and bright green shoots were poking up through the sludge of plants killed by the sudden frost. There was nothing that looked like tracks to Winter's eye, but she'd learned to trust Leti's experience. The Trans-Batariai—they called themselves Haeta—took for granted a level of wilderness expertise Winter couldn't have matched in a lifetime.

"Come on." Leti led the way upstream, bounding easily over the rocky ground. Winter followed, more cautiously, careful of her footing on the slime-slicked stones. They scrambled up a short slope, while the river roared beside them. Sure enough, beyond a pair of massive boulders the water grew calmer, spreading out into a wide, shallow section that would be easy to ford.

Winter's nose wrinkled at the smell of rotting meat, and she was immediately on guard. They hadn't found any of the Beast's bodies for days, but that certainly didn't mean it had given up. Leti smelled it, too, and pointed to the piled debris that had jammed together between the two rocks. A deer's head was visible, eyes gone and skull showing through gaps in the fur.

"Floods." Leti shook her head. "This land went mad. We should never have come here."

"You can say that again," Winter said. The unnatural freeze and subsequent thaw had wreaked terrible havoc in the wild, and she could only guess how bad it had been for the people who lived here.

"I can?" Leti said, puzzled.

"Never mind." Idioms were tricky when neither of them was speaking their native language. "We should find the others and tell them to come this way."

"Yes." Leti looked at the sun, which was well past the meridian. "We will camp on the other side."

The Haeta traveled in one main group, where they traded off carrying the tents and other supplies, with pairs of scouts thrown out ahead and behind. Their pace was deceptive—they didn't seem to be rushing, but Winter often found herself hard-pressed to keep up. Despite the speed of the column, Leti never had any trouble finding her way back to it, apparently possessing an intuitive map of the local terrain that Winter entirely lacked. As usual, Winter followed her lead, and soon they crested a ridge and found the bulk of their group. A pair of girls at the front, carrying their spears and without packs, waved to Leti and shouted something in their own language.

"Winter!" Alex jogged over. The girl was apparently none the worse for wear after her misadventure with the red-eyes, and once again Winter sent up a silent prayer of thanks that Abraham had insisted on coming along.

"Hi, Alex. You keeping up?"

"More or less." Alex shook her head and tugged at the straps on her pack. "I can see why they use those little tents. They seem a lot easier to carry."

"Any sign of red-eyes?"

"None of the rear guard have seen anything," Alex said. "If they're there, they're staying well hidden."

"They're there. The Beast isn't going to just give up, and we can't hide our trail with this many people."

"We're moving pretty fast," Alex said. "They may have trouble matching our pace."

"We need to sleep," Winter said grimly. "I'm not sure they do."

The rear of the party came into view, the last few warriors also unburdened by packs and carrying spears. Abraham was among them, limping slightly. He'd replaced his broken walking stick, and after some discussion the contents of his pack had been distributed among the others, but he still trailed the rest of the group.

"He's getting better," Alex observed. "Another week and he'll be as fit as the rest."

"Or he'll trip and break a leg," Winter said. "And then we'll have to carry him. It's a shame he can't use his power on himself."

"I've had that thought before," Alex said darkly. The pair of them had fled across Murnsk together, Winter knew, and hadn't had an easy time of it. Neither of them liked to talk about it, and Winter hadn't pried.

"Leti said we're camping on the other side of the stream, just ahead. Nearly there." Winter nodded at Abraham. "I'll go cheer him up."

Alex grinned. "Cheering Abraham up is like trying to fill a pond with pebbles."

"I'll try anyway. You go on ahead."

"Yes, sir!" Alex managed a reasonable salute, and jogged toward the head of the column, where Leti was talking with Vess in the Haeta language. Winter dropped back until she was walking beside Abraham, who took a few moments to notice she was there.

"You've done a lot of these marches," he said, wheezing a bit. "Haven't you?"

"I suppose I have," Winter said. It still felt odd, sometimes, to think of herself as a veteran. *We've crammed a lot of fighting into the last two years.*

"How often does it happen," Abraham said, "that somebody's legs actually fall off?"

Winter grinned. "Never, to my knowledge."

"Then I think I might be a unique case." He paused, leaning on his stick. "I spent too much time reading and not enough running back and forth in the snow, apparently. Or whatever it is the rest of you did."

"You're doing better than half my recruits," Winter said. "The first serious march of the Velt campaign, we had to send the cavalry back every night to round up the stragglers, and it sometimes took until morning."

Winter wondered, abruptly, where those recruits were now. The Steel Ghost had told her the majority of the Vordanai army had returned home, but Raesinia would have to respond to the threat Janus posed. *Are they marching again? Is Abby with them? Is Cyte?* Between the two of them, at least the Girls' Own would be in good hands. *And Marcus will find a way through. He always has.*

Abraham had said something, and she'd missed it. Winter blinked and shook her head. "Sorry?"

"I said, tell me we're nearly there."

"We're nearly there," Winter said obediently. "There's a stream up ahead. We'll camp just on the other side."

"Thank God." Abraham paused again, breathing hard, then looked over his shoulder. The Haeta rear guard were catching up with them, but the young women were still some distance away. "I didn't get a chance to ask about the plan."

"What plan?"

"Our plan. How long are we going to stay with the Haeta?"

"As long as we can," Winter said. "We'll be safer from the Beast."

"We will," Abraham said, starting his trudge forward again. "What about *them*?"

Winter grimaced. For all that the Haeta had been enemies of the Vordanai, Leti and her people hadn't been anything but helpful. It was hard, knowing she might be putting them in danger. "I hope it'll be safer for them, too," she said. "I don't think the red-eyes will leave them alone if they catch up, do you?"

"I doubt it," Abraham said. "But they're still following *us*."

They're following me, Winter thought, but didn't say it. *At least Alex and Abraham got into this with their eyes open.* "We can stick together until we make it to the river, at least. Then we can try to find transport downstream, and they'll want to head north anyway. That might get us clear of the Beast, at least for a while."

Abraham nodded. Winter couldn't tell if she'd convinced him, or if he was just too tired to argue. Either way, they walked in silence until they came to the stream, where several Haeta waited to show them the shallowest place to splash across. The water had the bitter cold of snowmelt, and Winter was glad for the thick, waterproof boots they'd given her at the Mountain. On the other side, tents were already going up on a small rise.

Leti has good instincts. The wilderness aptitude of the Haeta extended to building a camp—they could have their small, steep-sided tents up in a matter of minutes, and a fire going in a few minutes more. Everyone seemed to know their assigned roles without being told, and performed them with only minimal supervision.

It was all the more impressive because of how *young* they were. It had taken Winter several nights to realize that Leti, who couldn't be older than twenty, was easily the oldest of the Haeta warriors. The youngest, gangly, wide-eyed girls with spots, looked like they were about fourteen, and the majority were somewhere in between. *Not that we didn't have plenty of young ones in the Girl's Own, I suppose. But we didn't send them off by themselves.*

Alex was already working on setting up their own tent, larger than the Haeta's and considerably more cumbersome. Winter joined in, letting Abraham sit on a stone and guzzle ice-cold water. By the time it was up, some of the Haeta had started cooking. They carried rations, dried meat and roasted vegetable cakes, but the advance guard doubled as hunters, and they had considerably more success than Winter and Alex had. A variety of rabbits, squirrels, and other small creatures had been brought down, and the young women now rapidly skinned them and set the meat to cooking. The smell made Winter's stomach rumble.

Leti and her sister, Vess, sat near the fire, their part in the night's chores apparently done. Vess was speaking urgently in low tones, and Leti nodded periodically, as though distracted. At Winter's approach, Vess looked up and said something sharp. Leti turned and beckoned; Vess, disgusted, spat what sounded like a curse and stalked off through the camp.

"Did I do something wrong?" Winter said.

"She doesn't trust you," Leti said. "She thinks I am a fool for allowing you to travel with us."

"That doesn't seem very gracious, after Abraham saved her life," Winter said, settling down on a damp stone. The warmth of the fire beat against her clothes, gradually seeping in.

"Do not think ill of her. She worries that you helped her only to gain our trust. She would happily have died if it meant saving the rest of us." Leti looked into the flames. "In truth, the priests might agree with her. I was the one who acted . . . against tradition. I could not stand to watch her die."

"The priests are in charge? When you're back home, I mean."

"In peacetime, yes. When we are called to war, the tribe elects a warleader, and each cohort follows suit."

"Is that how you got to be in charge?" Winter hesitated. "Sorry, I don't mean to pry. I'm just curious."

"I understand. I hope you will not mind answering some questions as well." Leti's smile was shy. "You are the first southerner I have met, except for the representatives of Elysium. I must say you are not what I expected."

"Of course. I'd be happy to." Though, Winter reflected, she might have to be careful with some of her answers. Leti had accepted that Abraham was a Blessed One, so apparently the theology of the Haeta was not as black-and-white on the subject of magic as that of the Black Priests they served. But she still had no idea what that entailed, or what might cast doubt on that status.

Leti said, "To answer your question, yes. I had the honor of being elected
to lead this century."

"Are all the warriors of the Haeta so young?"

Leti laughed. "No, of course not. We are warriors of the second line." She
seemed to be struggling to find good words in Murnskai. "It means . . . those
who have only just passed their blooding, and lack experience. We accompany
the warhost, but serve as scouts and camp guards, unless the warleader deems
it a true emergency."

Winter nodded, understanding. *A bunch of recruits after all. Girls on their first
adventure, out for seasoning. And it turned into a nightmare.* "So how did you end
up out here by yourselves?"

"Some of it I still do not understand," Leti said. "We came south in the
summer. It should have been four moons, at least, to the first snow. But the
blizzards came suddenly, as hard as they are in the farthest north of our land.
We suffered badly." She looked around at the circle of tents. "There were a
hundred in our century when we left home."

Winter had counted thirty-four Haeta, including Leti and Vess. She lowered her eyes respectfully.

"There was a battle against the heretics," Leti said. "At the river Kovria.
Many fell on both sides. Afterward, the heretics moved south, back toward their
own lands, and the warleader said our task was done. But as we came north,
the weather worsened. Our century was forced to take cover in a blizzard or
freeze. When we emerged, there was no sign of the others, and the snow had
obliterated their tracks." She shook her head. "The weather improved soon
after, but that was when the demons came. What you call the red-eyes. Some
of them wore the forms of our own people, some Murnskai soldiers, some
common peasants. But they are driven by unnatural spirits."

Winter nodded. *That's as good a description as any.* "And you've been working your way home since?"

"Yes. It has been slow. We are too few to fight, and bands of red-eyes and
Murnskai soldiers wander the forests. But we are close now. A few more days
and we will cross the river and be in friendly lands." Leti sighed. "I only pray
to God others made it home as well."

"I hope so, too," Winter said. She was surprised to find that she meant it.
The Haeta and other Trans-Batariai tribes might have fought the Grand Army,
but they'd been as much victims of the Black Priests as the peasants who'd

slaughtered their own children to keep the Vordanai from stealing their souls. *Elysium has a great deal to answer for.*

"And you?" Leti said. "The business of a Blessed One is his own, of course, but it is unusual to meet anyone this deep in the forest."

"We were fleeing the red-eyes," Winter said. "Actually, our story isn't so different from yours. I was seeking the . . . Blessed One with a small band of companions when the weather turned." That wasn't *precisely* true—they'd been chasing the Penitent who'd poisoned Janus, but they'd certainly ended up finding Abraham. "Many of us were killed. Our goal now is to reach the river Bataria and find a ship, and we thought keeping to the woods would be safer. We didn't know the red-eyes were waiting." She hesitated, then added, "It's possible they are seeking us." *Let her think it's Abraham they're after. At least she's been warned.*

"Demons have a great hatred for Blessed Ones," Leti agreed. Winter breathed a silent prayer of thanks that this was apparently plausible. "Have you always been his attendant?"

"No," Winter said. "I was—I am, I suppose—a soldier. An officer, actually."

"A soldier?" Leti's brow creased. "The priests told us that in the south women were not permitted to fight."

Winter thought about going into the story of her disguise, and how some people knew and other people didn't. Ultimately, she decided it was too complicated to explain—*frankly, I have trouble keeping track*—and didn't make much difference.

"That was true for a long time," she said. "But things have changed recently."

Leti smiled. "Perhaps there is hope for southerners yet, then."

Winter grinned back. "Perhaps there is."

After dinner, Winter retired to her tent. Most of the Haeta did the same, though a few would trade off sentry duty throughout the night. *I should offer to take my turn.* It was only fair, though she was sure the woods-trained warriors would be better lookouts. So far no one had asked her, and she'd been so tired in the evenings that she hadn't pressed the issue.

Abraham was already sound asleep, rolled up in his blanket. Alex lay under hers, but she sat up as Winter came in.

"Listen," she said, before Winter could speak.

Winter paused, head cocked. The distant chuckling of the stream was audible, and the whistling of the wind in the leafless trees.

"What—" Winter began, and Alex waved a hand for quiet.

Another sound reached them, a low moan, followed by a quick yelp, faint but distinct. Winter raised an eyebrow.

"Not *that*," Alex said. "That's just the Haeta having sex. They do that a lot."

"They do?"

"Sure. You haven't noticed?"

"I haven't been paying close attention," Winter said archly.

"They don't always sleep in the same tents," Alex said. "I don't know if they have some kind of rotation or draw lots or what. If you ask Leti, they might be willing to include you—"

Winter fixed Alex with a glare, and the girl went quiet. After a moment, she said, "Sorry. That was . . . sorry. I know you and Cyte . . . I mean, I'm sure when you get back . . ." Alex ran down again, took a deep breath, and added, "Sorry."

"So if we're not playing voyeur," Winter said, after a moment's silence, "what am I listening for?"

"It's—there!" Alex went quiet, and Winter listened as well. The sound was on the edge of hearing, a long, mournful howl, fading rapidly into echoes. It was followed by another, and another, until it was difficult to tell where the howling ended and the echoes began.

"Wolves," Winter said. "Is that a problem?"

"I'm not sure," Alex said. "It sounds like there's a hell of a lot of them."

"It's a big forest," Winter said uneasily. She didn't know much about wolves. Almost all her time in the wilderness had been spent in the company of marching armies, where wildlife usually wasn't much of a concern.

"The thing is," Alex said, "I haven't heard any up until now."

Winter frowned. "Maybe they've just been keeping quiet."

"Maybe." Alex shook her head. "Mention it to Leti? Just to ease my mind."

"I will."

"Thanks."

Alex lay back down. Winter undressed in the dark and slipped under her own blanket. The thick wool the Mountain people had provided warmed up quickly, and she pulled it tighter with a contented sigh. Her legs burned, but her stomach was full, and for a moment she felt almost calm. *Maybe it's being in a proper camp again. There's something about knowing there are people all around you.*

"I really am sorry," Alex said quietly.

"I forgive you," Winter said. "Honestly. Just go to sleep."

Outside, the howls went on.

They saw the first of the wolves the next day, just a glimpse of a long gray body through a break in the decaying undergrowth. Winter, walking near the front of the column, pointed in time for the Haeta nearby to catch a glimpse of it.

"I heard them howling last night," Winter said to Leti. "I didn't realize they were so close."

"Howls at night are very hard to place," Leti said. "But don't let them worry you. Wolves will not attack humans. Most likely they follow us hoping to make a meal of our leavings."

Winter nodded. The flash of gray was gone, and she couldn't see any others. *I think we have more to fear from the Beast than from anything that lives in these woods.* She shook her head, looking back over the marching column, and trudged on.

Sometime later, her curiosity finally got the better of her. "Leti, can I ask you something about your people?"

"Of course."

Leti had taken to spending most of her time beside Winter on the march. Winter had noticed Leti didn't talk much to her fellow Haeta, who were otherwise constantly chattering in their own tongue. She wondered if it was a social dynamic she didn't understand, or simply the difficulty of being the one in charge. *I certainly know how that feels.*

"When your girls go to their tents for the night, they . . . hmm." Winter's Murnskai vocabulary wasn't really up to this particular challenge, at least while remaining polite. *I suppose I could always ask Abraham.* "They, ah, touch one another?"

"Of course, if they are lovers." Leti cocked her head, frowning. "It is different in the south?"

"Sort of. I mean. Most women don't take . . . other women as lovers."

"It is expected for members of a warhost to take lovers among their century," Leti said. "It is the same among the men. It increases their tenacity in battle."

"What happens to them when they get home?"

Leti shrugged. "Most leave such things in the wilds where they belong. Warriors of the second line can expect to have their husbands presented to them soon after their blooding, when they become full adults."

"I . . . see."

Winter had never been able to guess what lay in store for herself beyond the end of the war. At times—many times—she'd despaired seeing the end of the war at all, told herself that it wasn't even worth thinking about. She and Cyte had pointedly never talked about it, about what might happen once peace finally returned and the rules of civilized society rolled over the Girls' Own like a tide.

It felt like an indulgence to even consider it now. *After all, even the Steel Ghost said I probably won't survive using Infernivore on the Beast, assuming by some miracle I make it that far.* But, Winter thought, she was owed a little self-indulgence.

I'm sure Raesinia would help us. It wasn't like Winter had any profession, outside the army. *Surely the queen could find me a sinecure, though. And then . . .*

She couldn't even picture the "and then." Her mind rebelled. She'd been taking her life one day—one *hour*—at a time for so long that she couldn't imagine what it would be like without danger. When she could assume today would be more or less the same as yesterday and tomorrow. *Settle down? Raise children?* That was what people *did*, as far as she knew, but . . .

"There's another one," Leti said.

"Hmm?" Winter looked up and saw the wolf, standing on a rocky outcrop, staring down at the passing column with steady interest.

"They usually aren't so eager to show themselves," Leti said, looking back. "I wonder if there's something wrong with it."

"It looks . . . thin," Winter said. Her skin prickled. The wolf's ribs were clearly visible, and its coat was patchy. Its tongue lolled, breath steaming in the chilly air.

Three Haeta, led by Vess, came running up the length of the column. Seeing Winter standing beside her sister, Vess hesitated for a moment, then strode forward.

"Wolves," she said. "A dozen or more at the rear of the column, following close."

"Wolves will not attack humans," Leti repeated, though now she didn't sound quite as certain.

"Wolves don't gather in packs larger than a half dozen, either," Vess said.

"I think," Winter said, "that the rules may have changed." She had an image of packs stalking through the empty forests, with most of their usual game fled or dead and rotting. *Getting hungrier and hungrier, until . . .*

She looked around. They were on relatively open ground, a rocky hillside leading down to a winding stream. A few miles farther on, the stream curved across their path, and beyond it was another ridge, huge chunks of tumbled stone rising above the trees.

"I think we need to move a little faster," she said carefully. She wasn't sure how well Leti would take advice from a strange foreigner. "If we can get to the forest, we can put our backs to those rocks."

"She's right," Vess said, though her expression was pinched. "In the open they will surround us."

Leti nodded. She was trying hard to look decisive, Winter thought, but it made it easier to see how young she was, her big eyes just a fraction too wide. Vess, half a head shorter and several years younger, seemed more calm. Leti shouted something in Haeta and sent her sister to the back of the column to spread the word.

Winter herself fell back, looking for Abraham. She found him and Alex together, watching apprehensively over their shoulders. Two wolves were visible, walking at an easy pace well behind the rear guards, their gray fur flecked with white patches.

"Did you ask Leti about—" Alex said.

"Yes," Winter said.

"And are we worried?"

"*Yes.* We need to move fast. Abraham, can you run?"

"Run?" He groaned. "I can try. Not for long."

"I can carry him, if we need to," Alex said. "I've done it before."

"Good," Winter said. "Make sure he keeps up. If anyone gets left behind . . ." She looked back at the wolves again and shuddered.

The Haeta had adopted a faster pace, each girl alternating between a jog and a walk. The rear guards pulled in, staying within a quick sprint of the rest of the column, and the scouts in front pushed farther ahead. The precision of it all made Winter think of the Grand Army, and she wondered how many drills these young women had had to go through. Abraham stumbled along, puffing, with Alex staying protectively by his side. Winter went back to the front of the group, where Leti was calling to the others.

"It may not be enough." Vess spoke, unexpectedly, from beside Winter. "If they attack, it will be at twilight, when they are hardest to see."

Winter glanced at the sky. The sun was already well down toward the horizon. Under ordinary circumstances, they'd probably have camped on the near side of the stream.

"We'll make it." She tried to sound reassuring. Vess only glanced at her sourly and slunk away.

The clouds were changing to a delicate pink when the scouts reached the stream, the rest of the column descending the hillside close behind. From above, Winter could see the two girls on scouting duty look at the water and then at each other. One of them stayed put, while the other sprinted back up the slope and called at the top of her lungs in Haeta.

"What?" Winter's heart was in her throat. "What did she say?"

"It's too deep," Leti translated, staring down at the stream. "We'd have to swim, or find another place to cross."

"We don't have time to find another place to cross." If Vess was right, they didn't have time for anything.

"Swimming water that cold and fast is too dangerous," Leti said. She bit her nail nervously. "They may not even come today, or at all. We should—"

Someone shouted. Winter looked up and saw it was the scout who'd remained behind. A dozen low, gray shapes had sprouted on the slope, as if by magic, half of them facing the column while the rest closed in a circle around her. She stood with her spear out and her back to the river.

There was more gray, on all sides, dappled shapes running through the long shadows. *Oh, damn. Saints and fucking martyrs. How many of them are there?* More shouts came from the back of the column.

"Don't just stand there," Leti said to the warriors closest at hand. "Help her!"

No. Winter could see it unrolling before her, as though someone had drawn the pictures. A disorganized rush, and the charge of the wolves from behind. Melee and red ruin. *No, no, no.* The animals were faster, loping easily to match the humans at a dead run. *They'll circle us, just like cavalry around an infantry battalion, looking for a weak spot—*

The first group of warriors ran at the wolves in front of them, spears raised. The animals broke and scattered, easily keeping ahead of the humans, but others circled in behind. The lone scout, meanwhile, swung her spear back and forth, keeping the wolves in front of her at bay. From Winter's vantage, though, she could see it was only a game. *They can rush her whenever they want. They're keeping her apart to break up the herd.*

"Call them back," she said to Leti. "Call them back now."

"Jaesja will die!" Leti said.

"We're *all* going to die if we don't get into formation!" Winter said. "Call them back *now*."

"But—"

"Leti!" Vess shouted, from somewhere behind. "They're coming!"

The rear of the column had turned into a confused mass, brandishing spears to fend off a dozen wolves advancing slowly with hackles raised. Winter could already see others working their way around the sides.

A square. Not a square, even—no need for it without muskets. *A circle.*

"You're supposed to be warleader," Winter said. "That means—"

"I know!" Leti said. It was almost a scream. She continued in her own language, and the band of hunters paused, hesitating.

The wolves shadowing them chose that moment to pounce. A dozen of them rushed in, coming from all sides, teeth flashing as they bit at shins and ankles. One of the girls went down with a scream as an animal bit into the back of her leg, dragging her off her feet. A moment later a spear stuck it in the side, and it let go with a whimper. Another wolf writhed, pinned to the dirt, but more were closing.

"Back!" Leti shouted. "All of you, get back!"

The scout, Jaesja, was screaming something, and the girl who'd fallen shrieked in pain. But the rest of the warriors obeyed, sprinting back toward the main group. The wolves faded away, parting to let them through, then closing in behind.

"A circle," Winter said urgently. "Your people must know the formation. When you fight horsemen, you make a circle, with spears facing out."

Leti stared at her blankly, and Winter cursed the language barrier. She gestured, miming a spearpoint, until the girl's eyes lit with understanding. Leti called out commands, and the effect on the Haeta was almost instantaneous. They'd been in danger of becoming a mob, but the sound of clear orders brought them to their senses, and within a minute they'd formed into a circular formation, each with spear leveled.

The wolves who were toying with Jaesja tired of their game. One of them darted for her, a feint to draw her spearpoint, and when it retreated another tore out her hamstring. As she fell, jaws closed on her throat, spraying red. The warrior who'd gone down in the first rush had rolled onto her back, groping for her spear, but three animals were on her before she could use it. Her screams rose in pitch as they tore at her, ripping her furs and then her skin. A muzzle came away drenched in red, and her shrieks turned to a low mewling before they mercifully ceased. More wolves closed in, ripping and tearing as they fed, and Winter gagged and looked away.

Around the circle, wolves paced back and forth. Periodically one of them would close in, sensing weakness, and spears would jab in its direction.

"We can't keep them away forever." Vess again, appearing at Winter's elbow. "If we had archers, we could pick them off, but now they only need to wait for us to tire."

"They . . ." Leti couldn't tear her eyes away from the dying scout. "I . . ."

Winter grabbed her shoulders and turned her forcibly. They stood in the small clear area inside the circle, with Alex and Abraham. Everyone else was turned outward, spears raised. *No reserve,* said the part of Winter's mind that always thought tactically. *Nothing to repair a breach.*

"She's right," Winter said.

"What do we do?" Leti said. "If we break and run, they'll kill us all."

Why is she looking at me? *Why do they* always *look at me?* It felt like the most natural thing in the world, but Winter could already feel the weight on her shoulders. *Why is it always my responsibility?*

Complain later. Survive now.

"Alex!" she said. "Are you two all right?"

"So far," Alex said, watching the wolves.

Winter went to her side and spoke quietly. "I think you need to start picking them off."

"Are you sure?" Alex said. "The Haeta might not see my power as kindly as they see Abraham's."

"If you don't, we're all dead. I've got another five rounds for my pistol. That's not going to be enough."

"Okay." Alex shook out her hands. "Give the word."

"Leti!" Winter called. "Alex will try to hurt them. Tell everyone not to panic, no matter what happens."

"How?" Leti said. But Vess was already shouting in Haeta, and after a moment Leti joined her.

"Do it," Winter said to Alex.

Alex raised her arms, globes of darkness enveloping her hands. She sighted carefully, between two of the Haeta warriors, and a lance of pure shadow licked out. The pair flinched back in alarm, but the beam had already passed them and gone on to spear one of the circling wolves through the head. The animal crashed to the ground, blood spurting. The other wolves around it paused, uncertain. That made them easier targets, and two more black lances snapped across the field, leaving two furry bodies in their wake.

"She . . ." Leti said, staring. "She is . . ."

"A Blessed One," Winter said. "Like Abraham. They are companions."

"This is not the power of a Blessed One," Vess growled.

As the dead piled up, the wolves were growing agitated, fleeing from where Alex's attention was directed. She followed them, turning in a slow circle, her beams scything out whenever she had a clear shot. Some of the Haeta gave alarmed shouts, but others were cheering every dead wolf.

Driven by desperate starvation, the wolves charged, two dozen of them in a tight group. They hit the side of the circle across from Alex, dodging the protective spears and leaping at the girls. Three of the animals went down, but their corpses dragged the spearpoints away, and the rest poured through. One Haeta girl was bowled over as a wolf slammed into her, her scream dissolving into a gurgle as it ripped out her throat with one efficient motion. Others struggled as the animals grabbed their arms or legs, dragging them to the ground.

No reserve, Winter thought. *Except one.* She drew her saber and charged. The first wolf, tearing at the fallen girl, didn't see her coming, and her blow to its neck nearly took its head off. It collapsed, twitching, and she spun to face the next one. The animal backed away from the blade, while two more circled her, staying low. Winter gave ground and caught one of them with the tip of her blade, drawing a bloody line on its flank. It yelped and retreated, but the other came in from behind, slamming into the back of her legs. She lost her balance and fell, scrabbling away on her elbows as another wolf loomed in front of her.

No sooner did she manage to focus on the yellowed fangs than the animal was gone, picked off its feet by a thrown spear. With a yell, Leti closed, driving off another wolf with rapid thrusts of her weapon. Vess came in behind her, spearing a wolf that tried to circle around. The pair of them pushed forward and closed the gap in the circle, while behind them Alex's lances of shadow skewered the wolves that had gotten inside.

A few seconds later, and the wolves were breaking, peeling off in ones and twos and slinking into the deepening shadows. Alex blasted another one off its feet, and its pained cry spurred the rest into full flight. Between breaths, they were gone, leaving only corpses behind.

"Winter!" Leti said. "Are you hurt?"

"Fine, I think," Winter said. *Somehow.*

She took Leti's outstretched hand and hauled herself to her feet. The Haeta still maintained their circle, spearpoints raised. Abraham and Vess were working where the wolves had broken into the formation. The girl whose throat had been torn out was beyond saving, but several others were down with nasty bites to arms or legs. Winter silently thanked God once again for Abraham. *Otherwise we'd be carrying them the rest of the way.*

"I think," she said slowly, "that we made it."

"They won't be back soon," Leti agreed. She barked a command in Haeta, and the warriors put up their spears. Someone gave a cheer, and a few others picked it up, but the celebration seemed half-hearted. Most of the girls were either looking at the dead or staring at Alex.

Leti, though, was looking at Winter. She wiped her sword on a dead wolf and sheathed it, feeling suddenly self-conscious.

"What now?" Leti said.

Vess was looking at her, too, Winter realized. And quite a few of the others. She gave a heavy sigh.

"Make camp closer to the stream," she said. "With a nice wide berth between us and the nearest cover, and torches for the sentries. Do what you need to do for the dead."

Leti nodded eagerly and started giving orders in Haeta. Vess stared for a moment longer, her expression unreadable, then turned away. Alex, the black glow gone from her hands, came over to stand by Winter's side.

"Am I cursed?" Winter said in Vordanai.

Alex seemed to understand immediately. "The curse of competence," she said, and clapped Winter sympathetically on the shoulder.

CHAPTER ELEVEN

RAESINIA

"What about you, Prince Matthew?" Raesinia said.

"Hmm?" The prince looked up from his plate.

Raesinia gritted her teeth and tried to remind herself that throwing a bread roll at the Second Prince of Borel probably wouldn't be diplomatically appropriate. Instead she repeated herself, a little louder.

"I asked about your interests outside court. We were discussing my readings in philosophy . . ."

I was, anyway. It was a bit exhausting making conversation for two.

They sat in the second prince's private dining room, which had the same opulent-but-oppressive feel as the rest of the Keep, with a huge, dark wooden table and claw-footed leather chairs. In this case, the decor was reinforced by the attitude of the second prince himself, who was doing a very good impression of a little boy who'd been dragged to church by an overbearing parent. He picked at his food and responded mostly in monosyllables, leaving Raesinia to keep up a running monologue.

At least he was telling the truth about his chef. The food was impressive, even by the standards of the Queen of Vordan. Borelgai cuisine tended to be bland by Vordanai standards, with lots of boiled meat, vegetables, and heavy brown sauces, but whoever the second prince had hired took these pedestrian staples and made them exquisite. The main course was a steak as thick as Raesinia's wrist, with some sort of green sprouts she didn't recognize crisped in honey and butter, and a sauce that was—well, she didn't know what it was, other than delicious. She'd briefly paused her one-sided conversation to devour it all. Raesinia was hardly a gourmand, but she knew when she was in the presence of a master.

Unfortunately, compliments on the cooking only got her so far in terms of filling the awkward silence, hence the attempt at soliciting something—anything—that might be of interest to the sullen prince. He looked up, frowned, and then returned his attention to dissecting his meat.

"Nothing that would interest you, I'm afraid," he said.

"I have a very wide range of interests," Raesinia said immediately. "I'd love to hear how you spend your time."

"It's . . . a bit embarrassing, to be honest," the prince said. "My father reprimands me for my disreputable friends."

"That sounds delightfully wicked," Raesinia said.

"Nothing so entertaining," he said. "We pass most of our time drinking and smoking. Oh, and gambling on billiards."

"That must be fascinating," Raesinia said, seizing on the opening. "Billiards always struck me as a game of skill. There must be a great deal of strategy to it."

"I wouldn't know," the prince said. "I'm terrible at it. Really, I only play to please my friends."

Raesinia sat back in her chair, leather creaking beneath her, and admitted defeat. A few more moments passed in silence while the prince chewed, and then the door at the far end of the hall opened, admitting a pair of servants carrying delicate iced sugar confections. *Dessert. Which means this ordeal is almost over.*

You'd think I was the one who'd badgered him *to have dinner.* Despite his ambivalence on their first encounter, Second Prince Matthew had been persistent, repeating his appeal for Raesinia to dine with him until she'd run out of excuses. She'd come into the meeting ready for anything—treachery, underhanded offers, even an attempt at seduction. Instead, the prince had been morose and listless. *So what's the point?* If there was a game being played here, it was a very subtle one.

The confections were as incredible as the rest of the food, literally melting on the tongue, sticky-sweet. Raesinia wondered aloud where they got the ice, but the prince only shrugged. *Can he really be such a dullard?* Rumor could be deceiving, of course, but what she'd heard about the prince suggested a lively if somewhat irregular mind.

Finally, Matthew announced that he was tired, and Raesinia practically bolted from the chamber. Barely and Jo were waiting in the foyer, with a couple of Life Guards. All four soldiers stood as Raesinia came in.

"Back to my chambers, please." She turned to the servant hovering behind her. "My thanks for a lovely evening."

The man bowed, his expression a little pained. Raesinia swept out, bodyguards at her heels, into the Keep's endless miles of gloomy corridor.

"Did they feed you?" Raesinia said.

Jo waggled her eyebrows, and Barely patted her stomach. "Oh, yes," she said. "Damn well. Makes up for having to make small talk with the Life Guards all evening."

"They can't have been worse than the prince," Raesinia said.

Jo made a sign, and Barely laughed. "I don't know. How many different ways can you answer the question, 'You're girls, so you can't really be soldiers, can you?'"

"Reminds me of Cesha Dzurk." Raesinia rolled her eyes. She'd been around the pair from the Girls' Own for so long that she sometimes forgot women in uniform were an unspeakable oddity in a place like Borel. "You know, if you ever get tired of explaining yourself, just tell me. You can go back to the Girls' Own and Abby can send someone else to take a turn."

"Thank you, Your Highness, but I'd only fret about you." Barely laughed at something Jo signed to her. "Besides, the food here's a lot better."

Eric was waiting in her suite's outer room, absorbed in his ever-present notebook. He jumped to his feet when Raesinia entered, but she could tell by the set of his features—not to mention the dark circles under his eyes—that he didn't have good news to share.

"All right," she said, waving away the maid who scuttled up to offer her tea. "Let's hear it. You visited them all?"

"All the members of the Honest Fellows who are currently in the Keep," Eric said, looking down at his notebook. "Which is all of them except for Count Summerfeld, who is yachting for the next month, and Count Issenstrad, who is dead. Um." He licked his finger nervously and flipped back a page. "I thought there was some confusion on that point, but I was assured by everyone I spoke to that the count remains a member in good standing of the Honest Fellows despite his . . . indisposition."

"So what did the *living* ones tell you?"

"Mostly they told me to talk to Goodman. A few expressed sympathy but said they couldn't act without him. The others didn't seem very friendly to Vordan." He sighed. "Apparently Master Goodman's hold over the Honest Fellows is as complete as Duke Dorsay led us to believe."

"And Goodman? Did you see him?"

"I did." Eric flipped forward a page. "He . . . doesn't seem to like me. As he put it, 'Why should I bother talking to a clerk?'"

Raesinia gritted her teeth. Fredrick Goodman had some very definite ideas about who he should be meeting with. She was starting to wish she'd brought Count Strav, just so she'd have an elderly, bearded figurehead to make Goodman comfortable. He'd see Raesinia, but clearly he didn't take her authority seriously, and he'd flatly refused to talk to Cora. *Which, being fair, is a little more reasonable. I wouldn't believe Cora was running the treasury of a major nation if I hadn't put her there myself.*

"Did he get over himself long enough to talk about our proposal?"

"He said it was 'absolutely unacceptable.'" Eric traced a finger over his notebook. "He said that there was going to be no negotiation except on the basis of Vordan acknowledging the validity of prerevolution contracts, and terms could be worked out with the debt holders. Anything less would amount to 'accepting outright theft.'"

"Balls of the Beast," Raesinia swore, flopping into an armchair. She hadn't really expected more, but she'd hoped Goodman would at least provide some avenues for negotiation. Cora had worked overtime coming up with a debt settlement she thought Vordan could afford—and the Deputies-General might approve—which had revolved around treating the overall amount owed from before the revolution as a block but ignoring the terms of individual loans.

That was the version Raesinia could follow, anyway. She hadn't been looking forward to a laborious back-and-forth between Cora and Goodman, but now she apparently wasn't even going to get *that*.

"The Duke of Brookspring sent a message," Eric said, after a moment's silence. "He asked to see you when you have a free moment."

"That's something," Raesinia said. "Maybe *he* has good news."

Duke Dorsay did not, in fact, have good news.

His quarters looked much like hers, gloomy and elegant, with nothing of his personality in them. He only lived at the Keep in times of crisis, he explained.

"Until this business came up, I hadn't left Brookspring in years," he said. "It's on the western coast, across the mountains. You must come visit someday. In spring, preferably. We get snowed in through the winter, but spring is beautiful. It's only a small manor, but it hums along neatly."

"Honestly, I feel like we might as well go there now," Raesinia said. "We'd make just as much progress."

"I wouldn't bother, unless you like sitting inside watching the rain." Dorsay sat at his table, breaking nuts with an iron-handled nutcracker and picking the meat from the debris. The *cracks* made Raesinia think of musket-fire. "Chin up. I know you're frustrated, but some things take time."

"I would like it if you didn't treat me like a child," Raesinia snapped. "I'm not throwing a tantrum because I didn't get a pat on the head. People are going to *die*, Dorsay."

"I appreciate that." Another shell broke with a *crunch*. "But I'm trying to get you to understand that not everyone else does."

"How can they not understand what Janus' return means?"

"Borelgai, I'm sorry to say, have traditionally taken a somewhat *distant* view of matters on the continent. There's a school of thought that says you people are always killing each other, so why should we trouble ourselves? Not that I agree with it," he added hastily. "But it's the psychology of the matter. It lacks *urgency* for someone like Goodman."

"What about the king?" Raesinia said. She started to pace back and forth in front of the table. "He sent you to Murnsk. You said yourself he doesn't want war."

"He doesn't want to return to the old wars of religion," Dorsay interjected. "Georg isn't foolish enough to think that we'll have peace forever. World affairs simply don't work that way, I'm sorry to say."

"But he at least knows the danger Janus poses. Why won't he speak with me?"

"That I don't know." Dorsay leaned back in his chair, resting his hands on his stomach. "Georg hasn't been confiding in me of late, I have to admit."

"If I could just talk to him alone, we might get somewhere." Raesinia shook her head. "God knows I understand how hard it is to have a reasonable conversation with half the court looking on."

"In Borel, private audiences with the king are considered a high honor," Dorsay said. "Giving one to you would amount to a tacit endorsement of Vordan. Georg may not be ready to go that far."

"Tell him I don't care if he makes it public or not. I'll sneak through the back garden if he wants me to." *Or jump off the top of a tower,* some part of her mind prompted, with a hysterical giggle. "But as it stands we're getting nowhere. Goodman isn't going to budge unless we give him some reason to think we won't eventually be forced to meet his terms."

"Unfortunately, events seem to be playing into his hands," Dorsay said.

"You've had news?" Raesinia said eagerly.

"A courier ship came in," the duke admitted. "Though some of the reports are vague. It appears the Army of the Republic has crossed the Illifen passes at last and begun debouching into the valley of the Pale."

"About time," Raesinia muttered. By the standards of Janus' campaigns, Kurot's march was cautious at best. "What about Janus?"

"The so-called Imperial Army has reached the outskirts of Alves. To date, they have avoided any fortified places too large to storm, but they seem to be pushing hard for the city. It was not yet under siege when our messengers left, but may well be by now. Our man there reported the defenders are determined to hold out." He shrugged. "Of course, from this far away, we have only a narrow view. And out of date, even via courier ship."

"Saints and fucking martyrs," Raesinia growled. *It could be* over *by now.* If Kurot moved quickly, he might have already fought a battle against Janus. The threat could be past. Or, conversely, disaster might have overtaken the Army of the Republic. *Marcus could be dead.* Her throat tightened.

Marcus knows what he's doing. But he wasn't in command. She'd sent him out, *begged* him to go, under the authority of a man she knew almost nothing about. *Damn, damn, damn.*

I should be there. She was tempted to drop everything, forget about Borel, and just *go.* Surely there was a ship in the harbor that would take her across the Borel Sea, and from there she could make her own way. *Then at least I'd know what was happening. Marcus and I could be together.* All that stopped her was the knowledge that it wouldn't *help*; on a battlefield, she'd only be an encumbrance he'd feel obliged to protect. Here, at least, there was *some* chance of doing good.

"I will petition Georg again on your behalf," Dorsay said. She wasn't sure how much of her conflict he'd read on her face, but his tone had softened. "Perhaps he's simply busy with affairs of estate."

"Thank you," Raesinia said. "And thank you for the news." Without Sothe, she felt blind.

"It's nothing." Dorsay shook his head. "You know, some generals like to say they'd relish a confrontation with a brilliant opponent, the opportunity to match their mind against one of the best."

"You want a chance to fight Janus?"

"Good God, no. Those men are idiots. Give me stolid morons for enemies, every time. The only certain thing when two 'great' generals do battle is that a lot of poor soldiers are going to end up dead." He sighed. "If Janus takes power, sooner or later Georg will send me over to fight him, unless I spoil things by dying first. Maybe that'll be my plan, if it comes to it. War is a young man's game anyway."

"If you did have to fight him, how would you do it?"

"Ideally by having a hell of a lot more men than he does." He grinned wolfishly. "Which is why I'm working so hard on your behalf, you see. Much better to have half the Vordanai on my side than all of them fighting against me."

Raesinia wasn't certain if Dorsay's pleas had an effect, or if the news that matters in Vordan were reaching a head had knocked something loose, but the message she'd been waiting for arrived the next day, delivered by an impeccably uniformed footman.

"His Majesty cannot grant you an audience, of course," the young man said, with an air of insufferable authority that made Raesinia want to punch him. "But if you were to take a walk in the rose garden this afternoon, you might get a chance to share a few words with him. Coincidentally, you understand."

"I understand," Raesinia said.

The footman sniffed, bowed shallowly, and departed. Raesinia spent the rest of the morning with her maids, sorting through the clothes she'd brought from Vordan. Another place she missed Sothe—she'd always been able to ignore the issue of how to dress, because Sothe had instructed her on what was best for any given occasion. *I really did rely on her too much,* Raesinia thought. *Not that she didn't deserve my trust, but having the same person responsible for assassinations and my wardrobe is putting too many eggs in one basket.*

In the end, given the fashions in Borel, she decided on something sober and understated, practically mourning wear by Vordanai standards. Dressed and equipped with the appropriate jewelry, she had the Keep servants direct her to the rose garden. This turned out to be at the top of a building that had once been a gatehouse, so getting there meant climbing a narrow spiral stair up several flights. Jo and Barely tromped along behind her, their heavy boots slapping on the ancient stone.

A pair of the ever-present Life Guards waited in the upper chamber, in front of a sealed door. They bowed to Raesinia.

"You may view the gardens," one of them said, in heavily accented Vor-danai, "but your companions must remain."

Barely started to object, but Raesinia cut her off with a shake of the head. "I understand. Wait here, please."

The other guard opened the door, and a blast of warm air hit Raesinia in the face. She stepped through into a glass-windowed greenhouse that perched atop one of the old walls and was barely wide enough for two people to walk abreast. It was considerably warmer than the rest of the Keep, and much more humid. Condensation dripped down the glass panels overhead, sliding drops of water leaving clear trails in the fog. Planters lined both sides, with vines climb-ing wooden trellises. Some of the flowers were in bloom, despite the late season, and colors from blood red to blue-white were everywhere. Enormous blossoms drooped on their stalks, and the air was heavy with their sick-sweet scent.

About halfway along the walk stood the King of Borel, alone. He wore a dark suit, as before, and the ruby pin that seemed to be a badge of office. He was examining the flowers, one by one, lifting them up gently and running his fingers over the petals. From time to time he would write something in a small notebook, licking his fingertips to turn the pages.

"Your Majesty," Raesinia said.

"Your Highness," the king said. His notebook snapped closed. "Shall we dispense with the honors while in private? Georg will suffice."

"Raesinia, then," she said. "Thank you for seeing me."

"I'm sorry it took so long," Georg said. "I assume Dorsay explained the difficulties."

"He did, and I appreciate the problems. Believe me when I say I wouldn't have pressed if the situation weren't urgent."

"I understand." Georg waved a hand. "But indulge my pride for a moment. What do you think of my roses?"

"They're beautiful," Raesinia said. Truthfully, she wasn't terribly fond of flowers, and these seemed a little overpowering. "They're so . . . large."

"A gardener once told my grandfather that roses would never grow in Borel. Grandfather didn't know anything about plants, but he didn't like to be told no. Stubbornness runs in the family, you see." Georg's mouth quirked, not quite a smile. "Grandfather gathered the cleverest men in Borel and offered a prize to anyone who could help him grow roses. This greenhouse is the result, and seventy years later we have the biggest roses in the world."

"I can believe it," Raesinia said.

"An ordinary greenhouse wouldn't do, apparently. We don't get enough sun here. The air is warmed by water pumped up from a boiler, which also keeps it from drying out. And we've bred, over the years, for varieties that will tolerate our gloomy days." He shrugged. "It's the Borelgai way. We make do, muddle through, carry on. Eventually we get where we're going." He ran his fingers through his side-whiskers. "I imagine it seems slow-paced to a hot-blooded continental."

"Your Majesty—" Raesinia hesitated. "Georg. Troops are in the field as we speak. I don't think my desire for haste is unreasonable."

"Of course it isn't," Georg said. "I was merely trying to provide a bit of . . . context."

There was a long pause. Raesinia took a deep breath, wet air dragging at her throat. Before she could speak, the king cut her off.

"You're aware that the relationship between our nations has always been difficult."

"The War of the Princes," Raesinia said.

"And the War of the Twilight Strand before that. And the Three Year War, and on and on. Sometimes it seems we are destined to be in conflict."

"I don't believe in destiny," Raesinia said. "What matters is what we do, here and now. When Dorsay brought his army against Janus, it would have been easy to think they were destined to fight it out. But Dorsay told me he didn't want war, and he told me *you* didn't want it, either."

"There's war, and then there's war," Georg agreed. "Our genteel little scuffles are nothing next to the sanguinary contests of yesteryear. Your First Consul seemed determined to bring back the bad old days."

"I agreed with Dorsay then. It wasn't easy. Janus had been a friend to me, and his popularity in the army and among the people is immense. But I wanted peace, too, and so I took a chance." Raesinia hesitated. "Now I need you to take a chance. Help us finish what we started."

"You're so certain our help is required?"

"If Janus truly has Murnsk on his side, yes. Even if not, his record in the field is enough to ensure that I won't underestimate him."

"Some might say you already have."

"How so?"

"You could have executed him when you had the chance." Georg raised an eyebrow. "Harsh, but such are the exigencies of the sovereign."

"I can't say it didn't occur to me," Raesinia said. "But his support among the people was too strong. He agreed to return to his estate, and we sent guards to make sure he stayed there. We thought that would be enough." She shrugged. "Obviously we were wrong."

"So it appears." Georg looked down at one of his flowers, a huge specimen the color of red wine. "You understand, then, the danger of going against the will of your people."

"That's why we have the Deputies-General," Raesinia said. "To express the will of the people."

"Here in Borel, things are a little different. I have the Honest Fellows."

"Forgive me," Raesinia said, "but I didn't think they represented anyone but themselves."

"It's . . . complicated. Sometimes it seems like everything in Borel is complicated." Georg looked back up at her. "The Honest Fellows represent the opinions of people *like* themselves. If they did not, if they were out of step, they would not retain their positions."

"So they represent lords, bankers, and traders."

Georg nodded. "In other words, everyone who matters."

"In Vordan, the Deputies give a voice to *all* the people."

"Do they?" Georg smiled faintly. "I should like to see that. But in Vordan, when the people are upset, they take to the streets and storm the prisons. Here in Borel we have not had such . . . disruptions. But if the lords, bankers, and traders are upset with me, they have ways of making their displeasure known that are just as efficacious, if considerably quieter. I cross them at my peril, for all that armies march at my command. After all, armies need to be fed, and the money for gunpowder must come from somewhere."

"You *can* overrule the Honest Fellows, though. You've done it before."

"When I thought the reward merited the risk. Or if I was convinced they would come around to my point of view in the end."

"So what's the reward?" Raesinia felt like the garden was tightening around her, the heavy air almost numbing. She shook her head to clear it. "I don't think you brought me here just to say you couldn't contradict Goodman. What are you looking for?"

"You've met my son Matthew, I understand."

Raesinia blinked. "I have. We had dinner last night."

"You got along, I hope?"

"He was . . . polite." Raesinia's eyes widened. *He can't be taking this where I think he's taking it.*

But he was. The king looked down at her gravely and clasped his hands behind his back.

"He has expressed great admiration for you," he said. "And he remains, somewhat to my distress, unmarried. As do you, I believe."

Raesinia stared at him, searching for words.

"You will need a consort, of course, if the house of Orboan is to continue," Georg went on. "And aside from my personal considerations, a union between you and Matthew would guarantee ongoing peace between Borel and Vordan."

"Your Majesty . . ." Raesinia said, then shook her head. "I'm not sure what to say."

"Surely you must be aware that a continuation of the family line is an expectation of those in our position?"

"Of course," Raesinia said. "But given the crises since my father's death, I haven't given the matter much thought."

"Perhaps it's age that gives one perspective," Georg said, with another small smile.

I'm getting really sick of people telling me how being older helps them understand. Raesinia's trained reflexes kept her features neutral, but she felt her teeth clenching. "I take it Matthew knows about this offer?"

"He does. And he approves."

No wonder he's been so persistent. "I hope you're not expecting an answer right away. I will need to consult my advisers."

"Oh, without a doubt. But now you have my offer. If you want me to go against the best recommendations of the Honest Fellows, then I need to know that what I'm getting will be worth the price. A guarantee of peace is the only thing that will serve." He inclined his head. "Have a pleasant evening, Your Highness. I hope to hear from you soon."

Bastard, Raesinia thought as she paced the floor of her foyer. *Conniving bastard.*

Eric had taken one look at her expression and scuttled back to his own room, and her maids were similarly employing themselves elsewhere. Even Barely and Jo were standing guard in the corridor, out of sight. *When did everyone become so worried about my temper, anyway?* She kicked a small footstool and gave a smile of satisfaction as it caromed off the wall, leaving a gouge in the paneling.

The king must have told Goodman about his "offer." If not the specifics, then at least enough for the merchant to know that he could take a hard line and not risk having his monarch overrule him. *In fact, better for Georg if Goodman pushes hard. If we can't afford to meet the Honest Fellows' conditions, then I have no choice but to take Georg's deal or go home empty-handed.*

The door to the suite opened, and Cora blew in. She was wearing new clothes, a dark blue dress with clever little accents in lighter-colored silk, and silver jewelry. With her hair tied up neatly, it was a reminder that Cora was really quite pretty, or would be once she lost the gawky angularity of adolescence.

"Raes!" she said. "You won't believe what's happening in the market."

"I don't know," Raesinia said. "Right now I can believe almost anything."

Unlike the others, Cora was sufficiently oblivious not to notice the tension in Raesinia's tone. "Vordanai debt contracts are *everywhere*. It's madness. Apparently someone worked out a legal form that allows for the creation of negotiable paper based on the resolution of an existing debt, even if the debt itself is nontransferable. They got it approved by whoever manages that here, and a week later every merchant in the market is buying and selling the things."

"In Vordanai, please," Raesinia said, closing her eyes. "*Simple* Vordanai."

"They're betting on our debt," Cora said. "Making a contract that says one person owes another a hundred eagles when such and such a debt is paid. Which means the value of the *contract* is somewhere between a hundred eagles and nothing, depending on whether you think the debt is likely to be paid and when. I think information is getting out of the Keep to the market, and someone found out that you and Goodman were talking about what will happen to all that old debt, so they figured out a way to speculate on it."

"Really?" Raesinia sighed. "Bad enough that I have to argue with that idiot, but now people are *betting* on how well I'll do, like I'm some kind of racehorse?"

"More or less," Cora said.

"So what are the odds?"

"Six and a half," Cora said promptly. "Varying a bit for the specifics, of course." At Raesinia's look of incomprehension, she explained. "That means a contract with a face value of a hundred eagles is selling for six and a half eagles. If you want racetrack odds"—she screwed up her face for a minute—"it's about fifteen to one that we'll get to an agreement."

"And have you been putting any money down?"

"Not yet," Cora said. "But I was thinking. I still have credit at the markets here, from back when we broke the Second Pennysworth Bank in the revolution. I could—"

Raesinia held up a hand, her patience reaching an end. "Is this something that's going to help us with Goodman?"

"Probably not." Cora deflated slightly. "I take it he didn't like my proposal?"

"You don't know the half of it," Raesinia said. As briefly as she could, she summarized the meeting she'd had with the king. Cora's eyes went wide.

"The way I see it, they're playing us between them," Raesinia said. "Goodman pushes hard, which makes it more likely that the king gets what he wants. Or else we give in, and bankrupt the country trying to pay them back."

"Or we agree and then renege, and the rest of our creditors pull out," Cora said. "Half of Vordan would collapse, and that's if the Borels *don't* declare war."

"The hell of it is, I see Georg's point." Raesinia's anger was fading now that she'd put things out in the open. It left her cold and numb, like her blood was draining away. "This *is* the best way to assure Borel's interests in Vordan, once Janus is beaten."

"It's ridiculous," Cora said, toying nervously with her new silver bracelets. "He can't *actually* expect you to marry a man you've barely met, right? It's like something out of ancient history."

Raesinia frowned. It was hard to explain that she'd always expected *some* kind of arranged marriage. *It may be ancient history for ordinary people, but queens don't usually get the luxury of choice.* On the other hand, over the past few months she'd allowed herself to believe it could be otherwise.

"I don't know." Raesinia stopped her pacing and flopped into an armchair. "Maybe he's right."

"Who? The king?" Cora shook her head. "You can't be serious!"

"He's offering us an out." Raesinia tipped her head back and looked at the ceiling. "You've said yourself we'll never be able to come to terms with Goodman."

"He seems unlikely to budge," Cora admitted. "But aren't you forgetting something?"

"What?"

"Marcus!"

Marcus. With his rough beard and kind eyes, a tough skin wrapped around a soft vulnerability that made him deliciously easy to tease. *Marching into battle, where I sent him.*

"You love him, don't you?" Cora said.

"I think I do," Raesinia said. "I don't have a lot of points of comparison."

"Then you have to marry *him*," Cora said, as though that concluded the argument. "Not some prince who can't even hold a decent conversation."

Raesinia had an image of last night's dinner repeated for eternity. It was like a vision of a particularly vicious hell.

"I always knew we'd have problems with the court and the Deputies," Raesinia said. "The people may love Marcus, but he's still a commoner. Commoners don't marry queens."

"I think queens marry whomever they want," Cora said. "Otherwise what's the point of being queen?"

Raesinia closed her eyes and let her head sink against the overstuffed cushion. "Sometimes," she said, "I really wonder."

CHAPTER TWELVE

MARCUS

Crossing the Illifen passes was considerably easier than Marcus had expected. These were old, tired mountains, worn gentle by the passage of years, a far cry from the craggy peaks of Murnsk. They used the High Gap, steepest of the three available routes, but even this was a gentle enough slope that the teams pulling the wagons and guns didn't struggle. A good road ran from the banks of the river Marak, which dwindled into something more like a stream, and wound its way through the foothills of the mountains before passing through the gap.

Marcus was glad to see that Kurot had ordered Give-Em-Hell's light cavalry ahead of the rest of the army. Janus was still supposed to be a hundred miles off, but even a small advance force at the far end of the gap could have caused serious difficulties. Fortunately, the riders reported no contact with the enemy, and the great blue stream of the Army of the Republic flowed over the saddle between the rounded heights and into the valley of the Pale.

Abby had reported no serious difficulties while he'd been away. According to Cyte, she'd never been filled in on the supernatural side of General Ihernglass' activities, so he didn't share his suspicions or what he'd learned at Mieranhal. He badly wanted to talk it over with Fitz, but he hadn't been let in on the secret, either, and Marcus was wary of involving anyone who hadn't seen proof firsthand. *If someone had come to me with this story, I'd have probably thought they were crazy.*

The second night out of the pass, an unseasonable thunderstorm blew in, drenching the ground and frightening the animals. It had died to a steady drizzle when a scratch came at Marcus' tent flap, which turned out to be a lieutenant on Kurot's staff, bearing an invitation. The Column-General wanted a council of war.

"General d'Ivoire." Kurot's voice was warm as he came around the map table. Marcus saluted, but Kurot waved it away and shook his hand. "I hope your errand went satisfactorily."

"Perfectly, sir. Personal business. Sorry to be away from the column."

"Nothing to worry about." Kurot smiled genially. "I knew you'd be here when it mattered."

He gestured for Marcus to take a seat. Fitz and Val were already there, and shortly after de Manzet ducked in, shaking the rain from his jacket and murmuring apologies.

Kurot waved him off. "Welcome, General de Manzet. I believe this completes our little ensemble, since General Stokes is still in the field."

He stood across the table from them, looking down at the map. His little wooden soldiers were deployed across it, a tight bunch in blue with a handful of horsemen and cannon. Across from them were figures dyed a deep burgundy. On one corner of the table stood the general's ever-present chessboard, where a game was in progress.

"The latest reports from our scouts are in," Kurot said, sliding cavalry figures of both colors across the table. "Our patrols have crossed swords with Vhalnich's outer cordon, and we still don't have his precise dispositions. But his general intentions are obvious." He began laying out red infantry on the map, behind its protective screen of cavalry. "His main body seems to be concentrated in the angle between the Daater and the Pale, with the intention of laying siege to Alves."

Marcus looked at the map. The winding river Daater flowed roughly east to west, up to the point where the Pale slashed down diagonally from northeast to southwest. Between them they made an angle like a wedge of cheese. Alves, the largest city in the Pale valley, was pressed into the point of that wedge, where the two rivers met.

"Alves has strong, modern fortifications," Kurot went on. "It will not fall quickly. On the surface, this appears to present a golden opportunity for us to advance and attack Vhalnich's forces while they are pinned against the city."

Marcus opened his mouth to speak, but Fitz got there first. "Where Janus is involved, sir, nothing is as it appears on the surface."

Kurot smiled. "As you say, General Warus. All things considered, I believe this is a trap." He paced, as though to survey the situation from every angle, then went to the chessboard. Pursing his lips, he pushed a pawn forward one space.

Theatrics, Marcus decided. *Is he hoping we're going to be impressed?*

"The Daater is passable at several points," Kurot said. "The Pale is deeper, but Vhalnich has control of several bridges upstream. Once we commit to attacking his army, which will no doubt be dug in, I would expect flanking forces to fall on us from both directions in a classic double envelopment."

De Manzet scratched his nose. "The timing on that would be tricky. It's a risky plan."

"Exactly the sort of bold maneuver Vhalnich is known for." Kurot adjusted his spectacles, smiling slightly. "It's always worth knowing the character of your enemy. Having anticipated his moves, you can remain one step ahead."

"We're not going to attack, then?" Val said.

"Not directly. Amateurs think of war in terms of battles, General Solwen. Professionals think about lines of supply." He picked up another figure, a stylized wooden wagon, and placed it astride the Pale upstream of Alves. "Janus is drawing his supplies from depots in the north, captured when the divisions at the frontier went over to him. His lines of communication run down the west bank of the Pale for the most part, protecting them from interference as long as the bridges are blocked. But at some point"—he tapped the wagon—"they needs must switch to the east bank to support his siege.

"This is his point of vulnerability, gentlemen. He hopes that we will charge ahead, taking the bait, and attack him head-on. Instead we will strike here. Part of our force will proceed to Alves, appearing to fall into the trap. When he springs it, our main force will fall on one of his flanking columns and destroy it, while our detached force makes a fighting retreat. We will seize this bridge and block his line of supply, and then he will be forced to engage us on our terms or starve."

It looked very neat, the blue soldiers slipping in behind the oblivious reds. Marcus was reminded of diagrams from his textbooks at the War College, which was undoubtedly what Kurot had in mind. He glanced surreptitiously at his fellow officers. Fitz' face was guarded, as always, but Val looked skeptical, and de Manzet was deep in thought.

"Comments?" Kurot set his wooden soldiers down and smiled, though the expression seemed a little forced. "I do not expect you to obey like slaves. You are all"—he glanced at Marcus—"experienced officers."

Marcus cleared his throat. "It seems a little . . . complicated."

Kurot's smile became even more strained. "Military operations often are."

"You assume that Janus will react as you expect," Fitz said. "And this force serving to spring the trap"—he indicated the most forward of the blue soldiers—"could be in serious danger if Janus ignores the threat to his line of communication and presses his attack."

"He won't," Kurot said. "The cardinal sin of any general is underestimating his adversary, and I do not intend to commit it. Vhalnich is too good a commander to simply allow his flank to be turned. If he committed to attacking the bait force, he might destroy it, but we would be in a position to capture his entire army. No. He'll come north to fight once it becomes clear he's in danger."

"What about Alves?" Val said. "There must be a bridge there, and supplies."

"Messengers have gotten out of the city in small boats," Kurot said. "Colonel Vinkers is in command there, and he is certain of his ability to hold out for at least another four weeks. In the very worst case, I have ordered him to demolish the bridges and fire the magazines before surrendering. Vhalnich will not escape that way, have no fear."

That seemed to be the last of the objections. After a moment of silence, Kurot straightened.

"Very good. Detailed orders will be on the way before nightfall, gentlemen. The diversionary force will be yours, General Solwen, including much of the cavalry reserve. General d'Ivoire, you'll have the lead for the attack against Vhalnich's flanking force, when it shows itself. The rest of the army will follow and be ready to deal with Vhalnich's primary attack. We complete our approach march tomorrow, and barring any unexpected developments, the plan goes into effect at first light the day after."

All four generals rose and saluted. "Yes, sir."

"God be with you all," Kurot said. "Vordan is relying on your valor."

"It's hard to know what to think," Val said, hunkering a little deep into his coat. He and Marcus rode together back up the road from where Kurot and his staff had camped. The rain was only a drizzle now. "If something goes wrong, I'm the one who's going to be up the creek."

"If it works, you're the one who's going to get all the credit," Marcus pointed out. "Tip of the spear and all that."

"Kurot will get the credit, you mean." Val shook his head, a dribble of water running out of his cap. "Let him, honestly. As long as my men come back alive."

"He seems to be taking Janus seriously, at least."

"I suppose." Val hunched his shoulders. "I can't help but wish you were in command, Marcus. What would you do if you were in Kurot's place?"

"I'm trying not to think about it," Marcus said. "Panic, most likely."

Val laughed. "I don't think you've ever panicked in your life."

You didn't see me when dead men rose up with glowing green eyes, Marcus thought. But he said, "You just need to be careful. Remember you're not intended to fight a major engagement, just give the impression that you're ready to. And Give-Em-Hell will be there."

"There's that. After what happened in Murnsk, half the army thinks he's practically superhuman." He brushed his horse's mane with one hand, sodden hair squelching. "I have a bad feeling, is all."

"You always have a bad feeling, Val. It's just nerves. Remember that tactics exam where you took class first?"

"I threw up just beforehand. In my boot." Val smiled faintly. "Had to chuck it out the window and take the test in one sock."

"Exactly."

"There's a little bit more riding on this than drinks at the Hafhouse, though."

"I know." Val had changed, too, Marcus realized. You couldn't hold the lives of thousands of men in your hands and *not* change. *Not unless you're Janus bet Vhalnich, I suppose.* "I think when we're done you won't have to buy your own drinks for a long time."

"There's a happy thought. Adrecht would have volunteered for the assignment just for that."

Marcus laughed and clapped Val on the shoulder. Ahead, he could see the lights of the Second Division camp, and he waved to his old friend and turned off the road. His horse squelched across the sodden fields. He acknowledged the sentry's challenge and then her salute as he came closer, and threaded his way through the outer ring of tents to his own.

Cyte was waiting for him, and mercifully she'd thought to save him a plate from dinner. Pork, apples, and some kind of bitter greens reminded him of the food from Mieran County, though the preparation was less artful. *Enjoy it while it lasts.* When they went on the attack, they'd probably be moving too fast to gather supplies, and the army would go back on good old dried meat and hardtack.

"Anything I should know about?" Marcus said, chewing vigorously. He swallowed and reached for his canteen.

"Not really, sir. A few out sick, but fewer than last week. The new recruits are toughening up. Colonel Erdine is complaining that the weather is hard on his horses."

"Tell him that when I figure out how to give orders to the weather, I'll take care of it."

"Noted, sir. Any new orders from the general?"

"Mmm," Marcus said, mouth full. After a moment, he went on. "I'm expecting written orders soon, so I don't know how much I can tell you. But you can pass the word that we should expect action before long."

Cyte nodded grimly. Everyone had known that was coming, of course. But to the recruits, the immediate prospect of combat was always something they had to work themselves up to, and it was better to warn them than to let it take them by surprise. *Even the veterans could be forgiven for worrying a little, going up against Janus. I sure as hell do.*

When the written set of orders arrived, Marcus was amused, though unsurprised, to find that they were both thorough and verbose. His line of march was spelled out in detail, complete with approximate times he was expected to reach certain landmarks and where his nearest supports would be positioned at each stage. If Marcus had sent it across an instructors' desk at the War College, he would have received extra marks. After years in the field, though, all he could do was wonder what would go wrong first.

Rain, it turned out. Rain mixed with dirt made mud, and mud was a soldier's worst enemy.

He'd hoped the thunderstorm would pass on, giving them clear weather, but more gray clouds rolled in behind it. It rained all the next day, not the torrential downpour of the night before but a steady, solid curtain of water. Marcus ordered an early start, but it wasn't long before the familiar problems started to trickle in. Thousands of marching feet churned even the stoutest road into mush. Wagons got stuck, guns foundered, and horses injured themselves. Traffic jams grew from these seeds and stretched on for miles.

Val's Third Division had the lead, and the schedule called for them to reach Grenvol on the Daater by noon. In fact, Val's outlying pickets made contact with Give-Em-Hell's cavalry, holding the town, closer to two thirty, and he wasn't actually crossing the bridge until after three. That took longer than expected, too—whoever had written up the timetable hadn't accounted for the bottleneck the narrow bridge presented. Marcus' troops, who were next in line, had plenty of time to close up ranks before it was their turn to file over the churning water. A few civilians came out to cheer them on, but the rain seemed to have dampened everyone's spirits.

The march went on until long after dark, but even with the lengthened hours they ended up well short of their planned campsite, still between the Daater and the small river Ixa. General Kurot was waiting when Marcus finally arrived at the camp himself, soaked through and spattered with mud after a day spent herding soldiers and finding crews to rescue bogged-down equipment.

"General d'Ivoire," Kurot said. He had a rain cape with a raised hood, keeping the damp from his uniform, though spray still fogged his spectacles.

"General Kurot," Marcus said. "The last of my division is coming in now, sir."

"We are still short of the Ixa," Kurot said. That was the scheduled jumping-off point for the move against Janus.

"I realize that, sir," Marcus said, and gestured at the heavens. "We've been lucky to get this far in this mess."

Kurot's lips were pressed into a thin line. "Then it is your opinion that it is impossible to regain the original timetable?"

Is he joking? "Yes, sir," Marcus said cautiously. *It's not my opinion; it's a fucking fact.*

"Very well." Kurot let out a breath and closed his eyes, with the air of someone taking the high road. "We will allow one more day to get across the Ixa, and plan the attack for the morning of the day after tomorrow."

"Understood, sir!" Marcus said.

"I will inform General Solwen." Kurot inclined his head. "I expect better results tomorrow, General."

The rain stopped around midnight. That was cheering, but it would be some time before the mud dried out, and the next day's march suffered from most of the same problems. Despite Kurot's admonition, Marcus was pleased with the way the Second Division handled the adversity. The veterans in the Girls' Own and the other regiments didn't complain when he rounded up teams to haul lines or lift guns. They just rolled up their sleeves and did it, and that attitude spread to the recruits. Several times Marcus responded to a call for help to find that a passing company had pitched in unprompted, unsnarling the line before he even needed to intervene.

"A little mud is nothing," he heard one older woman telling a wide-eyed young man, "when you've been to Murnsk and seen blizzards in July."

Cavalry patrols returned regularly, reporting running skirmishes with their opposite numbers. They were unable to penetrate the enemy cordon, so Janus' exact position was unknown, but the orientation of his cavalry screen told them that he was still somewhere around Alves. Meanwhile, Give-Em-Hell's men worked hard to prevent anyone who got within sight of the Army of the Republic from getting away. That would be especially crucial in the morning, when Val's division would split off for its diversionary march west.

That night, after shedding his mud-spattered clothes, Marcus reread his orders for the next day and sent for Cyte. She turned up promptly, her boots flaking dried mud whenever she moved.

"Sorry, sir," she said. "Haven't had the chance to brush them."

"Don't worry about it." He tapped the orders. "We're leading the charge tomorrow. There's a town called Satinvol with a bridge over the Pale. Kurot wants us to take it by nightfall."

"Understood, sir."

Marcus frowned. He didn't like this next part, but however he twisted himself there didn't seem to be a way out of it.

"If the enemy has dug into the town itself," he said slowly, "in your opinion, which regiment would be best suited to handle the attack?"

"The Girls' Own, sir," Cyte said, without hesitation. "They have the most experience in loose-order tactics. General Ihernglass generally deployed the entire regiment as skirmishers, with Sevran's Second Regiment leading the close-order assault."

"That's what I thought," Marcus said. *So tomorrow I'm going to order a bunch of young women to charge into musket-fire.* He clenched his jaw. *I promised Abby I'd do what's best without being . . . old-fashioned about it.* It still felt *wrong*. "All right. We'll see where they make their stand, assuming they decide to put up a fight at all."

He found himself desperately hoping they wouldn't, that the clash between blue and blue could be delayed just a little bit longer. But he could read a map as well as Kurot could, and Satinvol was the closest upstream crossing to Alves. *He's not wrong. If we take it, we'll be well and truly on Janus' supply line. I just hope that's not exactly where Janus wants us.*

The next morning, the drummers woke the camp as soon as the first hints of light infiltrated the eastern sky. As the gray faded slowly to pale blue, the Second

Division shook itself out, like a dog emerging from a pond. Tents were struck and left in piles for the baggage train to collect. The regiments formed up on the road to Satinvol. In the lead was Erdine's cavalry, charged with scouting ahead and keeping the column from being surprised. Then came the Girls' Own, two thousand young women in columns of companies for quick marching. They called cheerfully to one another in the predawn light, taunts and half-eager, half-anxious banter. Some soldiers responded that way to the prospect of combat, Marcus knew. He could see others staring at their shoes, as though intent on memorizing every detail, or murmuring prayers, or checking and rechecking their kit.

Behind them came Archer's divisional artillery, one battery of twelve-pounders and one of six-pounders, still limbered to their caissons, facing backward. Marcus wanted the guns in position as soon as possible, though it risked slowing the overall march if they got snarled. Archer knew his business, though, and the alternative, to arrive with no supporting artillery, would be much worse.

On the other side of the guns was Sevran's Second Regiment, a unit of "royals" who'd been in service since before the revolution. In theory, anyway—in practice, Marcus guessed that casualties and replacements meant only a fraction actually had been around that long. It was part of their mystique, though, the image of themselves that the veterans passed down to the new recruits, and it showed in their neat uniforms and well-dressed ranks, in the way they held themselves superior to the sloppier volunteers. The line of blue continued down the road, out of Marcus' view, but he knew that de Koste's Third Regiment and Blackstream's Fourth were waiting for the men in front of them to step out. Nine thousand soldiers, give or take, holding themselves ready for Marcus' order.

He'd commanded a larger force in Murnsk. But somehow it didn't change the feeling of power, the sense of potentiality, of enormous energy coiled and ready to be hurled like the thunderbolt of a pagan god.

The sun finally crested the mountains to the east, a sliver of gold breaking clear of the peaks. Marcus, sitting uncomfortably astride his horse, beckoned to Cyte and watched enviously as she brought her mount over with barely a touch on the reins.

"Signal the advance," he said. "Then go to Erdine and remind him that I want him to be careful. It's four hours to Satinvol, but if Kurot's right and Janus' troops are advancing, we could end up in a meeting engagement anytime before then. Make sure we've got riders ready to send back for support."

"Sir!" Cyte saluted, turned her mount, and hurried off.

A few moments later, the drums trilled for attention, then settled into the steady rhythm of the marching pace. The Girls' Own started forward, each battalion's drummers picking up the rhythm, and then the guns rumbled into motion. Within minutes, smooth as a parade, the whole division was advancing down the road. *General Ihernglass certainly kept them in good shape.* Marcus got his horse moving, staying by the side of the road ahead of the artillery.

The country they were moving through was farmland, with the crops mostly already harvested, so he had a good view as the sun rose higher. Hedges divided the fields on either side of the road, with a few small farmhouses and the occasional village visible in the distance. Up ahead, he could see the cloud of dust and occasional flashes of blue from Val's Third Division, moving roughly perpendicular to his own course. In accordance with Kurot's plan, Val was taking the road southwest to Alves, to convince Janus that the enemy was obligingly strolling into his trap. Behind Marcus, invisible through the dust of his own trailing battalions, the rest of the army was scheduled to fall in, with Fitz serving as a rear guard ready to blunt the other half of Janus' theoretical double pincer.

Stop, Marcus told himself firmly. It was easy to fret about the overall situation, but that wasn't his role at the moment. *There's nothing I can do for Val or Fitz.* What was important today was what was in front of him, the mission of the Second Division and what the enemy might do to stop him. He tried to recapture the proper state of mind for a subordinate commander—the firm resolution that if things *did* go badly wrong it wouldn't be because his own part had been fucked up.

The sun crawled higher. They passed through the crossroads where Val had turned off, a village of a couple dozen homes whose inhabitants had either fled or hidden. Beyond it was a slight ridge topped by a few trees, and after confirming with Erdine that his men had already been over the ground, Marcus trotted to the top of it to take advantage of the slight elevation. The Pale valley was very flat here, sloping gently down to the river with only a few hills like this one, and even from its modest height Marcus could see quite a long way. Ahead of him, the fields unrolled for miles, until they reached the broad, sparkling band of the river. He could see Satinvol, a dense cluster of houses, with several high-steepled churches. Between his leading battalion and the town, there was nothing but more fields—no marching soldiers, no sign of defenses.

So the envelopment Kurot anticipated either isn't coming or hasn't arrived yet. There could be soldiers out there, lying in wait behind hedges, but Erdine's cavalry screen would flush them out. He pulled out his spyglass and focused it on Satinvol, but at this distance he couldn't make out much more than a mass of buildings. *If they're on this side of the river, that's where they are.* His assignment, if no enemy presented themselves for a field battle, was to take the Satinvol bridge. It was possible Janus would yield it without a fight, but Marcus doubted it.

As the column wound past, he came down from the hill to rejoin it, looking for Cyte. When he found her, he waved her over and said, "Tell Erdine to push a squadron forward all the way to Satinvol, but not to get too close. If he gets shot at, he should come back. If not, ask him to look and see if the houses have been prepared for defense—loopholes, barricades, that sort of thing."

Cyte nodded and rode off. Marcus glanced at the sun. It was barely nine in the morning, and already the day felt old. Ahead of him, the Girls' Own were singing a marching tune he didn't recognize. Whether they'd heard it somewhere or invented it themselves, it was in the grand tradition of soldiers' road songs in being spectacularly filthy, and Marcus found himself grinning despite the tension.

Erdine's answer came back almost an hour later. The colonel himself rode up, falling in beside Marcus, and saluted flamboyantly. The huge feather in his cap quivered with each step of his horse, and the polished silver and brass on his uniform glittered.

"Sir!" Erdine said. "Report that we got within a hundred yards of the outskirts of Satinvol, sir, and then we were fired on by sharpshooters. One man wounded, not seriously. I observed soldiers in Vordanai uniforms among the houses, and definite signs that the position had been prepared for defense."

Balls of the Beast. Marcus had been afraid of that. Storming a defended town was always a nasty business, and there was no way of knowing how many enemy there were or what reinforcements they might have available. "No sign of troops outside the town?"

"No, sir. We haven't seen anything larger than a rabbit since we left this morning."

"I want you to send a rider back there under flag of truce. Tell him to ask for whoever's in charge, and deliver a message from Column-General d'Ivoire. The town of Satinvol is likely to become the site of fighting today, and in respect of the fact that we are all Vordanai fighting in Vordanai territory, I request that he deliver this warning to the civilians and urge them to evacuate as quickly as possible."

"Understood, sir." Erdine hesitated. "You don't think that's going to warn them of our intention to attack?"

"I think they already know about that, Colonel. We can't cross the river any other way, so we have to come straight at them. Besides, it's the only decent thing to do." *I have enough on my conscience as it is.*

"Yes, sir!" Erdine nodded, feather bobbing, and rode off. Marcus called for a runner, and found himself facing a girl no more than fourteen years old. *She still rides better than I do.*

"Find General Kurot," he said. "Tell him we've encountered nothing short of Satinvol, but the enemy has dug in there and intends to defend the town. I'll begin the assault as soon as my troops are in position. Anything he can spare from the artillery reserve would help, but we absolutely must have at least a battery of howitzers."

"Got it, sir!" The young soldier turned her horse about and kicked it to a gallop, back down the road the way they'd come.

A mile short of the town, Marcus took the column off the road and got ready for combat. He told Abby to throw the first battalion of the Girls' Own forward as skirmishers, pairs of soldiers spreading out over a wide front. The second battalion stayed formed up as a reserve, with the other regiments taking up formation beside it. Archer unlimbered his guns from their caissons and hooked the teams to the cannon themselves, dragging them forward across the furrowed, muddy earth. The Girls' Own front line advanced in time, staying ahead of the artillery.

The first shot came from the enemy's lines, a flower of gray smoke blooming from the gap between two houses. Marcus could see the cannonball in flight, seeming to hang motionless in midair at the apex of its trajectory for a moment before descending with shocking speed to hit the ground in a spray of earth. It bounced, landing again in another miniature explosion, and then again, the interval steadily decreasing like that of a rock skipping across a pond. The range was much too long, though, and the ball came to a halt well short of the approaching lines. Marcus imagined some lieutenant being scolded for opening fire too early, giving away the concealed gun's position.

If they have a lot of artillery in there, this is going to be a tough nut to crack. He'd managed to put it out of his head that it was his own people across the field, commanded by his old commander and, maybe, friend. They were just "the enemy," as usual, once the cannon started to roar. *We're going to need those how-*

itzers. He was still ahorse, near where the Girls' Own reserve was waiting, watching the guns bump across the uneven ground.

Archer deployed the first half battery at eight hundred yards, long range for twelve-pounders. On the other hand, he didn't have any target smaller than a house, so accuracy wasn't really necessary. The teams were well trained, and before long the six guns were shrouded in smoke. Hollow *booms* echoed across the field, weirdly out of sync with the muzzle flashes. It took only a few tries before the cannoneers had their solid shot plowing into the buildings on the outskirts. Plaster billowed from every hit, and roofs caved in or sprayed fragments of slate tiles. Marcus devoutly hoped the civilians had heeded his warning.

The second half battery went into action at five hundred yards, close enough to bowl shots into the buildings end-on rather than arcing them down at a high angle. In the town, someone's patience cracked, and all at once the defending artillery opened fire. Marcus counted a dozen or more muzzle flashes, earth flying up all around Archer's batteries to mix with the smoke. Archer's men adjusted their aim in turn, shots probing the smoky rubble for the flashes of their opponents. An isolated cannon was a hard target to hit, though, and at this range the duel could go on all day.

Marcus didn't intend to wait that long. The Girls' Own kept advancing, a thin, uneven line of blue. A few of Erdine's horsemen, keeping an eye on the town, retired past the advancing skirmishers with waving caps, trotting back toward the rest of the cavalry. Marcus' hands tightened on the reins as the women closed the range.

At two hundred yards, the defending cannon gave up trying to hit Archer's long-range guns and switched to canister, spraying musket balls like giant shotguns. The skirmishers made for poor targets, but a few blue-coated figures began to fall, punched backward off their feet or collapsing in place like broken puppets. Archer's second battery, the six-pounders, went into action, slamming canisters of their own back at the enemy positions. Marcus' mind filled in the sounds of breaking glass and the *pock, pock, pock* of balls tearing into plaster.

A hundred and fifty yards, and the defending musketeers opened fire. That was very long range, which meant the commander in the town either was incompetent or had no concerns about running out of ammunition. Marcus guessed the latter—certainly if Janus had anticipated a defense of this position, he would have made certain it was well stocked. The Girls' Own held their fire until half that distance, one of each pair of skirmishers bringing her weapon up to sight and fire, then ducking away to reload while her partner took her turn. From this vantage point, the enemy were invisible except for the smoke puffing out of the damaged buildings, but they had to be getting the best of the exchange. The fields offered only scattered rocks and hedges for cover, not loopholed buildings and stone walls.

Archer's first half battery, farthest out, had fallen silent, and Marcus could see the teams reattaching themselves to the guns, getting ready to close the range. *Good man.* After another few moments, Marcus turned his horse and rode over to the second battalion of the Girls' Own, waiting in close order while their companions fought and died. Sevran's Second Regiment was just behind them, and Sevran himself was on foot with Abby, watching the distant flashes of the fighting.

"Sir," Abby said, as Marcus approached. "My girls need support."

"So they do," Marcus said. "Colonel Sevran?"

The colonel came to attention. "Sir?"

"Storm those houses, please. Close columns."

"Yes, sir." Sevran gave a crisp salute. "We'll have them for you in thirty minutes, sir."

He jogged off, and moments later the drummers of the Second Regiment started up. Abby looked up at Marcus.

"I hope you haven't forgotten your promise," she said.

"There'll be plenty of action for everyone," Marcus said grimly. "Once we get past the outskirts, it'll be house to house. I want half of the Girls' Own left fresh for that."

He knew the soldiers closest in the ranks could hear that, and it was rapidly passed by whispers down the line. Abby nodded, also hearing the whispers, and raised her voice. "We'll sharpen our bayonets, then."

There was, as Marcus had expected, a second defensive line ready behind the first.

Sevran's attack, delivered with considerable skill and courage, had driven a wedge into the enemy line. Despite the gaps blown in their ranks by the canister and musketry, the Second Regiment had kept its formation until the last moment, then charged in a mass with lowered bayonets up the streets and into the ruined houses that marked the border of Satinvol. Archer's gunners, closer now, switched their fire to the edges of the spreading conflict, and more houses began to show the scars of cannonballs.

When it became clear to the defenders that Sevran's men could not be dislodged, they pulled back through the streets of Satinvol to a second set of positions. The Girls' Own skirmishers followed them carefully, the rattle of musketry almost continuous as the contest of ambush and counterambush began. Marcus could see almost nothing now, just a few ruined buildings and the rising smoke, but he could imagine it—small assaults, rushes of a dozen or two dozen men and women at a time, a building captured or lost, fierce battles for possession of a shed or a back garden.

Girls who ought to still be under their mothers' skirts lying bloody and broken in back alleys, or clutching shattered limbs, or screaming as their guts are ripped open by bayonets . . .

He swallowed hard. *They want to be there. They* demanded *it. It's war.* But it still felt like a monstrosity.

True to his word, though, he'd ordered the second battalion of the Girls' Own in when the attack bogged down. Abby went with them, walking ahead of her troops, waving them into position with her sword. Marcus moved closer himself, now that the enemy guns had pulled back, and brought the Third and Fourth Regiments with him. Fighting in towns was always devilish business. A formed unit, under its commander's tight control, could deliver a charge with considerable impetus, but it wasn't very long before it would get tied up in a hundred tiny battles. And getting a unit *out* again once the battle had started was nearly impossible. So skirmishes had a tendency to take on a life of their own, becoming a maelstrom that sucked in well-ordered troops and spat out dazed fragments.

A colonel from the artillery reserve arrived, leading a battery of a dozen howitzers. The squat, wide-barreled guns looked more like cook pots than cannon. They were designed to lob powder-filled bombs in a high trajectory, and were direct descendants of the catapults that had hurled stones over the walls of medieval castles. Howitzers were notoriously inaccurate, but in a situation like this, with the enemy pinned to his defenses, they were just the thing. Marcus quickly set them to firing at the inner perimeter of Satinvol, just in front of the bridge, where the enemy reserves and supplies had to be massed. Soon fires were burning in several places, columns of black smoke rising to mix with gray drifts rising off the battlefield.

Noon came and went. Marcus had only the most tenuous grasp of the shape of the battle, relying on hurried reports from commanders who knew only what they could see on one particular street. Janus' troops were falling back, but they hadn't cracked yet. Whenever things seemed stuck, Marcus fed in a fresh battalion from his rapidly dwindling reserve to get the attack moving again. By four in the afternoon, he was feeling, if not sanguine, then at least reasonably confident. *If Janus had a big reserve to throw into a counterattack, he'd have used it by now.* The narrowing enemy front was rapidly contracting to the footing of the bridge itself, and a counterattack over the bridge would be suicidal.

Not that Marcus expected to actually cross. Destroying bridges once you had no further use for them was standard practice, and he fully anticipated Janus would have left orders to demolish the span once his defenders had bought all the time they could. Only a quick rush could hope to take a bridge intact, and the drawn-out struggle had left no chance of that here. *That was inevitable, though. At least we'll have cut his supply line as intended.* The rest of the battle didn't seem to be going according to plan, or indeed happening at all. There was no sound of artillery from behind him, no clouds of smoke rising from the southwest. If Janus was still in front of Alves, he hadn't marched to keep Kurot out of his rear.

As if thinking the man's name had summoned him, a mounted party came into view from the east, picking their way across the shot-torn fields. Marcus had moved his command post to just outside the town, not far from where the cutters had set up their aid stations. Casualty parties were still fetching the wounded from the parts of Satinvol that had fallen under his control, and the usual horror of triage and treatment had begun. Marcus could see Hannah Courvier, the Girls' Own's regimental cutter, prowling the lines of blue-coated bodies, bloody to the elbows like a monster from a children's story.

"General d'Ivoire," Kurot said as he rode up. Fitz was with him, and several staff officers Marcus didn't recognize. Kurot's face was an icy mask, and his voice dripped impatience. "Report your progress."

"Sir." Marcus saluted. "We've taken most of the town on this bank of the river, sir, and we're approaching the bridge. The enemy was expecting us and was heavily dug in. We've captured four guns and prisoners from at least five regiments."

"You're behind schedule," Kurot snapped. "My calculations show that you should have had the bridge by noon if no enemy force came forward to confront you in the field."

"With respect, Column-General, the enemy have been buying time, and doing it as well as I'd expect of Grand Army soldiers. But it won't be long now."

"It had better not be," Kurot said. "I suggest you move forward, General d'Ivoire, and discover what's causing the delay. Apply the whips if necessary."

"Sir—" Marcus gritted his teeth. "Yes, sir. As you say."

Kurot rode off without a word, his staff trailing him like the tail of a kite. Only Fitz remained, dismounting and beckoning to Marcus. They walked a few steps away from the nearby soldiers, and Fitz spoke in a low voice.

"He's in a foul mood," he said. "Janus hasn't been playing along."

"I gathered that," Marcus said. "What's happened? Any word from Val?"

"He's engaged Janus' pickets, but there's been no serious fighting, so he's still pushing forward. But scouting reports are confused. Some of them say that Alves has already fallen, betrayed from within or overtaken by demons." Fitz waggled his eyebrows. "Others tell us the city is still holding out. Kurot doesn't know what to think."

"If Alves *has* fallen and Janus has the bridge there, this sideshow isn't worth any more lives," Marcus said.

"He doesn't believe the city could fall so quickly," Fitz said. "And if it did, he's certain the defenders would at least have demolished the bridge."

"He may be right," Marcus said. "They're certainly fighting hard here."

Fitz nodded. "He's got us moving south, to link up with Val tomorrow morning. I imagine you'll bring up the rear once you're finished here."

"Thanks for the warning," Marcus said. He looked around for Kurot and saw the general inspecting the one battalion of Blackstream's troops that remained in reserve. "I'd better go forward and see what's happening before he decides to take command himself."

"Good luck," Fitz said. "And be careful."

Satinvol was like something out of a nightmare. Cannonballs had wreaked havoc on the outskirts, punching through walls and cracking beams, leaving the houses leaning drunkenly against one another or lying in shattered piles of rubble. Broken roof tiles were everywhere, littering the streets like gray hail. Smaller craters from musket balls pocked the plaster.

Bodies lay all over, clustered behind temporary barricades or sprawled in the street. Almost all of them were dressed in blue, which to Marcus' eyes made the field look like the site of a particularly one-sided massacre. It was impossible to tell who had been on which side, except when the broken rag doll shapes were women. There was, as far as Marcus knew, no Girls' Own on the other side. The sickening smell of torn guts and blood mixed nauseatingly with the gritty tang of powder smoke.

Casualty teams hurried back and forth, searching the bodies for those with a spark of life. In the Girls' Own, this duty was carried out by women too young or too small to hold a musket in the line, and Marcus kept running into children in blue uniforms carrying stretchers. They ignored him, rolling bodies off a pile to get to the source of the groans coming from underneath, heedless of the sticky, thickening blood coating their hands. Marcus' throat was tight.

As he approached the bridge, the sound of musketry got louder. Not eager to wander into the line of fire, he got directions from a passing soldier, and followed a back alley to reach Abby's command post. She was crouched behind a barricade made from a wagon pulled sideways across the alley entrance, a couple of Girls' Own soldiers with her. Beyond was a street liberally scattered with bodies, facing a tall, square building standing on its own. Past that was the footing of the bridge, a gently sloped stone span that crossed the wide river in three low arches.

"General," Abby said. "Keep your head down, please."

"What's going on?"

"I gather that's the rivermaster's office," Abby said. "Three stories tall and mostly stone. They've turned it into a blockhouse, and it's a real bastard. Got to be a couple hundred men left in there."

"You've got men—soldiers—around the sides?" Marcus said. He could see puffs of smoke rising from the buildings there.

"Working on it," Abby said. "We're in range of the bridge now. Nobody is getting out of there alive unless we let them."

"You've asked them to surrender?"

"Twice. Dog-fuckers won't even acknowledge a truce flag. They just keep firing."

Marcus frowned. That didn't sound like Janus.

"What are you doing here?" Abby said, while he looked the situation over.

"Kurot sent me to hurry things along," Marcus said with a grimace. "His words, not mine."

"I've lost at least a hundred soldiers trying to charge that thing. If he thinks I'm throwing any more lives away, he can get fucked." Abby shook her head. "Archer's bringing up a couple of twelve-pounders. Once he's ready, we can blast the bastards right out of there."

"Don't change the plan on my account. How long until he gets here?"

"Shouldn't be long. I'll go find him. Stay here, and by all the saints, keep your head down. The bastards have been taking potshots, and they're pretty damn good at it."

Abby turned and ran back down the alley in a crouch, with a lieutenant in tow. A sergeant and two rankers remained with Marcus, pressed against the barricade. Musketry cracked and rattled all around.

The sergeant was a big woman, around Marcus' age, broad-shouldered and heavily muscled. She looked at him with undisguised curiosity, while the two young rankers kept their eyes averted. Marcus shifted awkwardly under her attention, not sure if he should speak.

"Hell of a day," she said eventually.

"It is," Marcus answered lamely.

"Hope this bridge is worth it."

Marcus could only nod. *General Kurot thinks it is.* That was the only answer he had, and what kind of an answer was that?

He was saved the trouble of further conversation by the *boom* of a cannon, close by. An explosion of masonry and stone splinters cascaded from the side of the rivermaster's office, quickly obscured by a cloud of dust. A second shot clipped a corner off the roof, spraying broken tiles.

Abby must have found her guns. Now she would offer surrender again—no matter *how* dedicated they were, no soldiers would want to die in a collapsing building, unable to fight back. *They'll have to give in—*

Three sets of big doors along the base of the building opened at once, and a crowd burst out at a dead run. For a moment Marcus thought the place was already falling in on itself and they were scrambling to get clear. But every one of them had a musket in hand, with bayonet fixed, and they weren't shouting for quarter.

The half second of shock let them get out into the street. Then Abby's voice, shrill with alarm, rose over the field. "Fire! *Fire!*"

Muskets roared, an impromptu volley that fringed the street with fire and smoke, Second Division soldiers shooting from every window and alley facing the blockhouse. The oncoming men, caught in the open, were scythed down by the dozens. The shock would have broken any charge Marcus had ever seen, but this one seemed impervious, the attackers stepping over the broken bodies of their comrades as though they weren't there. They were coming in a furious mass straight across the street, right toward—

Right toward me. Marcus backed away from the wagon. His three companions had all fired and were frantically reloading their muskets. Marcus tore his
pistol from its holster, checked his sword, and waited.

"Get to the rear, sir," the sergeant said, slamming her ramrod home. "We'll
hold—"

Marcus shook his head. Before he could reply, the first of the attackers
scrambled up and over the barricade, musket held in one hand. Marcus sighted
carefully and shot him in the chest as he stood up. He toppled backward without a cry, and two more men replaced him, clawing their way up the wagon
and edging forward. They raised their weapons like spears, and for a moment
Marcus thought there was something wrong with their eyes. They glowed red
from the inside, like they'd been replaced with hot coals.

The sergeant finished loading, shouldered her weapon, and shot one of the
men. The second one, dressed in Murnskai white instead of Vordanai blue,
dropped off the wagon in front of her, and she slammed him in the face with
the butt of her musket. Bone crunched, and he went down. But another three
were already climbing, while musket-fire went on and on from the buildings
all around them. *How many can be* left? *How can they keep coming?*

One of the rankers, a small, mousy girl with long brown hair, shot wildly
and missed. The other, a brawny teen built more like the sergeant, managed to
catch one of the next wave of climbers, his head disintegrating in a shower of
bone. The three on the wagon jumped down, coordinating with the ease of
men who'd fought together before, though one was Vordanai and two Murnskai.
The sergeant gave ground, parrying the stroke of a bayonet, and the two rankers
stepped up beside her. Marcus drew his sword and joined them as two more
attackers came over.

For a few moments, he lost his awareness of the larger situation in the heat
of thrust and parry. The attackers were good, quick and well trained, working
together smoothly and apparently completely without fear. Marcus got the better
of one of them, getting around his bayonet and breaking his arm with the pom-
mel of his saber. His wounded opponent closed in, taking a deep cut to the side
but fouling Marcus' stance, and he was forced to jump sideways to avoid being
skewered by another. In the clear for a moment, he saw the sergeant bury her
bayonet in one man's chest only to be struck from behind—the man whose jaw
she'd broken had levered himself up and thrust his own weapon into the small of
her back, heedless of his injury. She stiffened and stumbled forward, and two
more attackers cut her down. The mousy girl was bleeding, her left arm hanging

useless, and the other ranker was cornered. Her attacker tossed his weapon aside, grabbing her by both shoulders and pulling her close as if for a kiss.

Marcus charged, saber swinging. He chopped through one assailant, spun, and put his weight behind a swing that took the ranker's attacker in the neck and nearly removed his head. He crumpled in a welter of blood, and Marcus spun back to the other ranker just in time to see the remaining enemy bat her weak parry aside and spear her in the gut with his bayonet. Shouting with rage, Marcus opened the man's back with a downward slash, his dirty white Murnskai uniform turning crimson as it soaked up the gore. The mousy girl, hand pressed to her wound, slowly slid down the wall of the alley, leaving a smear of blood when she tried to prop herself up. He looked at him, and then behind him, and her mouth moved in a warning.

Marcus lurched sideways. Not far enough. A bayonet jabbed into his left shoulder, a hot spike of pain that left him breathless. He spun away, the weapon tearing free from the wound. His saber was already coming around, and he was expecting to see another man in dirty blue or white—

It was the ranker, the brawny teen, musket in hand. She'd just bayoneted him, and she was winding up for another try. Her eyes glowed bright enough to cast flickering shadows.

Marcus' arm moved automatically. He sidestepped her thrust and rammed his saber home, blade going in just under her breastbone. She let her weapon drop and stumbled forward, hands grabbing at his arms. As her breath bubbled in her throat, she tried to pull herself *up*, raising her crimson eyes to stare into Marcus'. He felt paralyzed, one hand still on the saber embedded in her chest. The red light grew brighter, nearly filling the world.

Then the girl's legs gave out, and the moment was broken. She collapsed, sliding off of Marcus' sword, and flopped motionless in the dirt.

Saints and martyrs. For a moment all Marcus could see was red. *What in the name of all the* fucking *saints was that? Why would she . . . ?*

The other ranker moaned. Marcus shook himself and went to her side. She was sitting up against the wall of the alley, breathing in quick, ragged gasps, one hand pressed over the hole in her gut, fingers already slick with blood. A glance told Marcus that she was finished, if not immediately from loss of blood then later, when the gut wound festered. But he crouched beside her anyway, shrugging out of his coat and laying it over her, gripping her free hand with his own. Her head turned toward him, eyes very wide, and he waited as her breath came slower and slower until she finally went still.

Behind him, from the direction of the river, there was a dull *boom*, much louder than a cannon-shot. Marcus didn't need to hear the sounds of stone tumbling into water to know what that meant. Janus' men had blown the bridge.

The battle of Satinvol was over.

CHAPTER THIRTEEN

WINTER

In the three days since the lupine assault, Winter had heard a few more howls in the night, but they hadn't seen any sign that the animals were still close. Three Haeta had died in the attack, but those who'd been wounded had all recovered, thanks to Abraham's talents. The revelation that Alex, too, was a "blessed one" had most of the Haeta behaving uncertainly around their three southern allies, but no one seemed ready to suggest that they turn against the power that had saved them all.

Leti increasingly deferred to Winter, asking her advice whenever they came to a fork in the path or needed to choose where to camp. It made Winter uncomfortable—she had no *right* to be giving orders to the Haeta—but it made things easier, especially since the rest of the young women obeyed Leti without question. They held their course northwest as best the terrain would allow, crossing another ridgeline and beginning a long, slow descent. The forest here hadn't suffered as badly from the abnormal weather, and some of the trees were still green. Hunting got better, with the occasional deer added to their diet of rabbits and squirrels, and the scouts occasionally brought back wild vegetables.

On the third day, they broke through a patch of tangled underbrush and found the river Bataria spreading out in front of them, wide and frothy brown. Meltwater from upstream had clearly swelled it beyond its usual banks, and they made an early camp in a clear meadow well above the river's edge. Winter helped Alex and Abraham set up their tent, impressed as usual with the speed and efficiency of the Haeta's camp skills.

She'd gotten to know a few of them, despite the language barrier. Most of the Haeta understood quite a bit of Murnskai, but didn't speak it as well as Leti and Vess, and seemed embarrassed to try. When she found herself standing watch or walking beside them, though, she tried to coax them to speak a little, and she tried to at least learn their names. There was Gina, beanpole thin and sharp-eyed; Yath, with her red hair and clever fingers, always working on complicated knots and braids; placid Ulli, with her lazy eye. They couldn't tell her much about themselves, but she got a vague sense just by watching them at night. She found herself envying the easy camaraderie, the feeling of shared skill and shared danger.

She wondered, sometimes, if she'd have felt less apart if she'd been born among them. *No need to put on a disguise to go into the army here.* And either the "Tyrant's Disease"—the technical term, Cyte had taught her, for when women slept with other women—was very common among them, or their standards were just . . . different. It was a pleasant fantasy, which Winter acknowledged was certainly no more than that. *No doubt they have their own set of problems. Every one of these girls is going to go home and marry some man her priest has picked out.* She was uncomfortably reminded of Jane, sold to Ganhide like a sack of meat. *I hope it's not that bad.*

There was guilt there, too. *We didn't call them here.* But the Haeta had come because of the Vordanai invasion, along with many others. *We didn't bring the blizzards. We didn't unleash the Beast.* But it was possible none of it would have happened if Janus had stayed south of the Ytolin.

Since they'd set up camp earlier than usual, the scouts had had a chance to range farther afield for food. They'd come back with a deer, assorted smaller game, and clusters of wild onion and mushrooms. The Haeta set to work with a will, skinning and gutting, and Winter left them to it. *The best I can manage is army soup.* Instead, she stood by the river, staring pensively at the distant far bank and trying to think.

"Winter." Leti sounded hesitant, as though she didn't want to intrude.

"It's all right," Winter said, beckoning her over. "I'm just trying to figure out what we do next." She shook her head at the brown, rushing water. "The river isn't normally this wide, is it?"

"No. In fall it can sometimes be only a trickle. But even in spring I have never seen it so deep."

"I don't suppose you know of a convenient ford nearby."

Leti shook her head. "We crossed at one on the way south, but that was many miles to the east of here." East was the way they'd come, where the Beast might be following. "In any case, I doubt it is passable with the water so deep."

"We certainly can't swim it," Winter said. "And I wouldn't trust any boat we could build in *that*."

Leti nodded silently. Winter watched her for a moment, then looked back to the water. *They always look to me for answers.*

"We'll follow the bank and head west," she said, trying to sound authoritative. "What we really need is a small ship and someone to sail it. That way we can drop you off on the north bank and get ourselves downriver. There must be towns and villages along here, and we can bargain with them."

"They are spread thin this far east, but yes," Leti said.

I hope we find something sooner rather than later. Every day the Beast grew stronger. More immediately, Winter would feel a lot better when she was able to put distance between her and the red-eyes behind them. *Still, we've been lucky. We'd never have gotten this far without the Haeta.*

"Winter," Leti said again.

"Something wrong?"

"No." The girl's face scrunched up, and she took a deep breath.

Winter cocked her head. "What?"

"I thought . . ." Leti looked down. "Would you care to share my tent tonight?"

"Your . . ." That took a moment to sink in. "Oh."

"I know you don't share our ways," Leti said quickly. "But I thought you might . . . like to try."

Winter ran a hand through her hair—it was getting longer than she liked, out here in the wilderness—and stared at Leti. She was pretty, though Winter hadn't thought about it much until now. Compact and athletic, with small breasts and lean muscles, dark hair pulled back in a short braid. Her eyes were wide and blue.

There's no reason I shouldn't. She and Cyte had never spelled out the parameters of their relationship, after all. And in all probability Winter would never see Cyte again—even if she made it back to Vordan, she still had to confront the Beast, and one way or another she doubted she was coming back from that. *So what's the harm?*

Logical, she supposed. And yet she didn't find herself tempted. It wasn't that Leti was too young—there was only half a decade between them, after all—or that she didn't find her attractive, in the abstract, but—

"I'm sorry," Winter said. "I appreciate the offer, but I can't."

"To be with another woman is so terrible for you?" Leti's eyes shone with tears.

"It's not that. I'm . . ." *Taken? Married?* "Promised. To someone else."

Leti frowned. "But . . ." She stopped, shook her head. "Southerners are strange people."

"I agree," Winter said. "I hope I haven't offended you."

"No." Leti shrugged, though her expression betrayed her casual tone. "You have every right to refuse. And perhaps it is for the best."

"Maybe." Winter looked back up the slope, sniffing the air. She patted Leti on the shoulder. "Come on. I smell dinner."

The evening was a pleasant one, with plenty of food for once and a merry fire. Some of the Haeta danced while others sang and clapped along. Some, Winter couldn't help but notice, slipped off in pairs to their tents. Leti retired early, alone, and as the sun sank down into the water of the Bataria, the girls who were left at the fire began to drift away to their own pursuits. Abraham had long since gone to sleep, and Alex, sitting in the dirt beside Winter, was yawning.

"I wish we had a better map," Winter said. The one they'd brought from the Mountain showed only the rivers and a few major cities. "We could be walking for weeks before we find civilization."

"Probably not weeks," Alex said. "The Murnskai army has regular garrison posts along these rivers for courier traffic, though I have no idea if they're still manned."

"If not, let's hope they've left their boats behind," Winter said. "Even a sturdy rowboat would be something. We could take the Haeta over the river in shifts."

"Better than staying on this side," Alex agreed. She yawned again. "Coming to bed?"

"Not quite yet," Winter said. "I want to think for a while."

"Suit yourself." Alex dug her elbow into Winter's ribs. "Abraham told me one of the Haeta propositioned him in very unambiguous terms. He asked for my help telling her that she's, ah, barking up the wrong tree."

"He's not interested?"

"Abraham?" Alex raised her eyebrows. "I suppose there's no reason you'd know. He has—had—a lover, who was taken away by the Church. A boy named Peter. Abraham talks about going to find him someday."

"Ah," Winter said. *Is that the Tyrant's Disease, too?* She wondered if they ought to compare notes, but was certain she'd never be able to bring it up. "Well, the Haeta seem to respect that we have different ideas about that sort of thing. I don't think you'll have difficulty."

"We'll find out." Alex clambered to her feet. "Good night, then."

"I'll be in soon."

Alex wandered off, leaving Winter alone, staring into the slowly fading fire. It popped and crackled, and in the darkness beyond the camp the forest was alive with rustles and soft animal noises. Somewhere, an owl hooted. There were sentries out there, too, but the Haeta had a way of disappearing into the woods when they kept watch, quiet as any nighttime hunter.

"Southerner."

Winter nearly jumped at the sound of the voice. She looked up to find Vess crouching beside her, hands held flat to the fire, warming herself on the last embers.

"Yes?" Winter said, feeling uncertain. Vess had been the only one who'd voiced a worry about the nature of Alex's powers. On the other hand, since the ambush, she'd been a little warmer, if not actually friendly. Her face was set in a perpetual scowl, but it was less often aimed in Winter's direction.

"Leti spoke with you this evening," Vess said. "She invited you to spend the night with her."

"She did," Winter said carefully.

"I do not know you, Winter Ihernglass." This time the scowl was very definitely directed at Winter. "My sister may be wet for you, but do not think you have earned my trust."

"Your sister's virtue is safe, if that's what you're worried about."

Vess snorted. "If she ever had such a thing, she discarded it ages ago, and happily. It is her heart that concerns me."

"Her heart?"

"Leti is . . . a good person. Better than I am. She strives to see the best in others, and reflecting her, they become better in her presence. It is why she was chosen to lead us, and why she will lead the tribe one day." Vess pressed her lips together. "But it makes her vulnerable, you understand? To betrayal. She looks up to you, and if you disappoint her it will hurt her badly."

Winter stared into the fire, suddenly uncomfortable. "I never asked her to." *I never asked any of them to.*

"In the crisis, when she froze, you acted. That night, after she cried in my arms, she talked about you. She sees you as . . . who she would like to be." Vess cocked her head. "You are not just a soldier, I think. You are a leader."

"I am," Winter admitted. "Or I was."

"Then you understand."

All too well. It was easy to put herself in Leti's place, in command of an expedition that had turned into a disaster, with all the people who once might have joked with her instead looking at her with that terrible *need*. The hunger for someone who *knew what to do*, who would make things better. Bobby's face—from back in Khandar, before war and pain had aged her—floated through Winter's mind, bringing a stab of guilt. *The way she looked at me . . .*

There was a long silence. The fire popped, settling.

"I'm not sure what you want me to do," Winter said. "If you want to try to convince her she's wrong, you're welcome to."

"It's too late for that now," Vess said with a sigh. "You must live up to her expectations instead. Be the woman she wants you to be, Winter, or you will answer to me."

"I'll try." *I always try so hard.* It felt like a hundred ghosts mocked her as she said the words. And behind them all, Jane. *Not a ghost but something worse. The heart of a monster.*

Vess' eyes narrowed. "I believe you will."

Winter wanted to ask what she meant, but Vess suddenly looked up. A moment later Winter heard it, too, the sound of running feet. One of the Haeta, an older girl named Qwor, burst into the light, spear in hand.

"Red-eyes," she gasped out, and then more in her own language that Winter couldn't follow. Vess shot up.

"What's happening?" Winter said.

"Gina is missing," Vess snapped. "Qwor saw red lights on the hillside. They have found us."

More sentries reached the camp, shouting, and the Haeta began to emerge from their tents. Many of them were half-clothed or wearing nothing at all, but they picked up their spears regardless, strapping the quivers of spares across bare skin. Alex crawled out of her tent, with Abraham following.

Leti was nowhere in sight, and everyone was looking at Winter.

Saints and fucking *martyrs.* She could feel Vess' stare on her back.

"Torches!" she shouted. "Get some light on the perimeter. Set them and then *back off.* They may have muskets—"

Leti emerged from her tent a few minutes later, still fighting her way into her furs, but it changed little. Instead of coming to Winter for orders, the Haeta looked to Leti, and Leti looked to Winter. Their little band hunkered down and braced for the onslaught of red-eyed slaves of the Beast.

It never came. Once, Winter caught sight of a pair of crimson lights, shining in the darkness, but that was all. Minutes passed and then hours. She organized shifts, kept half the Haeta ready while the others got dressed and packed their tents. By dawn they were shivering and exhausted, but there was no option except to push on.

There was no sign of Gina, the girl who'd vanished. A band of Haeta found where at least two men had caught her, but they'd carried her deeper into the forest, with no sign of whether she was alive or dead. Leti wanted to go after her, and Winter had to take her aside.

"Gina's gone," she said, swallowing hard. *Live up to her standards. But what does that mean?* "Worse than gone. She's one of them now."

"One of *them?*" Leti's eyes widened. "The red-eyes?"

Winter nodded. "They are . . . a kind of demon. You know that. If they catch you and stare into your eyes, they can transform you into a demon, too. The same body, but the mind is gone."

"That's . . ." Leti looked like she wanted to be sick.

"I know." Winter hesitated, then added, "They are a plague. I can't say too much, but my companions and I are trying to stop them. We must reach the mouth of the Bataria."

It would have been a ridiculous story, of course, if Leti hadn't already seen Alex's and Abraham's supernatural powers. As it was, guilt flooded through Winter as she saw the girl's expression change, her horror hardening into a sense of renewed purpose. *It's true,* she told herself. *We are trying to stop them, even if I haven't filled in all the details.* But she still felt like she was abusing Leti's trust.

They slogged through the next day, following the bank of the river, where the forest was a little thinner. This land had clearly never been cultivated, which made Winter wonder just how far from civilization they were. She'd been in Murnsk long enough, though, to know the line between humanity and the wild could be abrupt, and she hoped and prayed they'd run into it sooner rather than later.

That night Winter directed the group to a rocky outcropping, where they could put their backs against something solid. Instead of lone sentries, they kept watch in shifts, staring at a perimeter of makeshift torches for signs of movement. They saw points of glowing red, now and then, well off in the dark beyond pistol range. The Beast was there, watching.

"It's not strong enough to rush us," Alex said quietly. "So it's trying to wear us out, slow us down. It must have more bodies closing in."

Winter nodded. Inwardly, she wanted to scream, to rush out and tear the things to shreds. Only it wouldn't help. *How can you* fight *something like this?* It was too *big* a task, like trying to dig up a country with her bare hands. No matter how many bodies they killed, the Beast would only send more, a never-ending flood spreading out across the world.

They struggled on through the next day, and the next, setting the pace as fast as Winter dared. Every moment they were stopped, she felt the jaws closing around her, the hidden tide of red-eyed monsters getting closer. Leti had circulated her description of what the Beast could do, and as a result none of the Haeta complained when she asked them to walk longer or push harder. A few of the younger girls collapsed, and the others carried them. Abraham was practically a ghost at the end of every day, white-faced and trembling, and Alex stuck close to his side, looking worried.

But no matter how far or how fast they went, the red lights were waiting for them in the darkness.

This can't go on. It was a killing pace. *One more day,* she told herself. *One more day. If we don't reach some kind of civilization, we'll have to risk a longer halt, recover some strength.* Even the Beast's bodies couldn't run *forever.* They still tired, still wore out, even if they could ignore pain. *One more day.*

Then, on the fourth day, one of the scouts came back to report a curl of dark woodsmoke rising against the cloudy sky.

"They have ships," Alex said.

"Boats," Winter said, although she had to admit she wasn't entirely sure of the difference.

Whatever they were, there were two of them tied up to a stone pier, bobbing in the fast current of the Bataria. They had one mast each, and locks for several sets of oars. Winter thought they looked like something between a ship's longboat and a proper sailing vessel.

They were looking at a small fortress, presumably one of the Murnskai army garrisons Alex had mentioned. It had an outer palisade of logs strapped together, with a wooden wall walk and a pair of gates. Inside was one large stone building, grim and official-looking, surrounded by a scatter of makeshift wooden shacks and lean-tos. In addition to the smoke rising from the chimney of the central structure, several smaller fires contributed thin strings of gray.

The hillside they stood on was some distance away, and overgrown enough that Winter was reasonably certain they wouldn't be spotted. Around the fortress, though, the forest had been cut back, leaving a clear field of fire.

Leti squinted, shading her eyes. "I see men on the walls."

"Are they in uniform?" Winter said.

"I think so. White uniforms."

"Murnskai army, then." Winter had half expected the fortress to be held by bandits, but apparently the garrison was still in residence. "When you were fighting the heretics, did you work with them?"

Leti shook her head. Vess, crouching beside her, looked sour and said, "The priests told us we were serving in the same cause but that the southerners were too blind to see it. We stayed apart from them where we could and killed them when we had to."

"They don't seem to be expecting trouble," said Alex. "There's only a few men on the wall."

Winter made a quick count of the buildings she could see and the number of fires, and frowned. "There could be at least a hundred of them in there, though."

"Wait for nightfall," Vess declared. "We can go over that wall easily in the dark, kill the guards before they can cry out."

"Then what?" Winter said. "Slaughter them all in their beds?"

Vess nodded. "Now that the heretics are gone, there is no reason for us to consider them allies. We have often fought the white-coats."

"We don't necessarily need to kill all of them," Alex said. "Just steal their ships. If we can get over the wall, we can just go to the pier and help ourselves."

"Getting our supplies over the wall would be difficult," Vess said.

"Capture a gate, then," Alex said.

"Too dangerous." Vess set her jaw. "If they are alerted, we will be too few to fight them."

Leti was looking at Winter. *Live up to her standards,* Winter thought.

"We should try to talk to them," she said. "I don't want to massacre anyone, if we can help it. And they need to be warned about the red-eyes."

"They won't listen," Vess said. "And once they know we're here, they'll be on guard. We'll lose our chance."

But Leti was nodding. "Even if we take them by surprise, attacking is risky. If one guard shouts, we could all be killed. I think it's worth trying to talk."

Vess looked from her sister to Winter. Her expression said, *Of course you do.*

Winter cleared her throat. "Besides, do you know how to sail a ship like that?" The two Haeta shook their heads. "I certainly don't. If we can convince them to evacuate before the red-eyes get here, they might be willing to help."

"We can manage the ships," Vess said stubbornly. "Logs float downstream. I'm sure we'll be able to."

"With the river running so fast, I wouldn't bet on it," Alex said. "Logs don't mind being flipped over."

"We'll talk," Leti said decisively. "I will go." She looked at Winter almost shyly. "Will you accompany me?"

"Of course," Winter said. "Bring a few more warriors. Not too many. We don't want to scare anyone. But just in case."

"I'll come," Alex said, but Winter shook her head.

"Stay with the camp," she said. "If the red-eyes see we've split up and decide now is the time for another try, you're the best chance of stopping them."

"I will—" Vess said, but Leti interrupted her in her own language. An argument ensued, but after a few moments Vess sighed, got to her feet, and stomped back in the direction of the camp.

"What did you tell her?" Winter asked.

"That she should stay behind," Leti said. "If something goes wrong, she will have to lead the others."

"Let's hope it doesn't come to that."

In the end there were five of them: Winter, Leti, red-haired Yath, and a pair of sisters named Elka and Seka. They circled around the cleared area so as not to approach from the direction of their camp and then walked slowly and deliberately toward the fortress.

Whether or not they were expecting trouble, the guards on the wall weren't blind. It wasn't long before they spotted the small group, and a half dozen of them gathered to watch as the five women came closer. Winter stopped the others a bit outside musket range and waved to the watching soldiers. When one of them cautiously waved back, she cupped her hands to her mouth and shouted in Murnskai.

"Greetings! We'd like to speak to someone in authority, please!"

The answer drifted back, almost inaudible. "Who are you?"

"Travelers!" Winter paused, then added, "We don't want any trouble!"

There was an animated discussion among the soldiers, and several of them disappeared. The others stared, but didn't speak, and for a long while nothing happened. Leti shifted impatiently, but Winter, more familiar with the ways of soldiers, gestured for her to wait. *They'll have to find the command, explain the situation, convince him it requires his attention . . .*

Five minutes was actually faster than she'd expected. The front gate swung open, and four white-uniformed soldiers emerged, followed by a man in a dark cloak. He wore a uniform underneath it, Winter saw as he approached, of a considerably more impressive cut, adorned with silver and gold braid. His cloak was black leather, lined on the inside with soft, dark fur. He had blond hair that fell loose to his shoulders and a narrow, suspicious face with a neat blond beard. A pistol and a short sword hung at his belt, while the men with him carried muskets with bayonets fixed. *Not taking any chances, is he?*

When he was perhaps twenty yards off, he stopped, eyeing the group of women with open curiosity. His eyes lingered on Winter, and he raised an eyebrow.

"You're not one of them," he said, his Murnskai strangely accented to Winter's ears. "But by your voice you're not Murnskai, either."

Winter shook her head. "I'm from the south." *No need to specify Vordanai, what with the war . . .*

"A foreigner." His mouth twisted. "So, what is a foreign woman dressed in rags doing in the company of four girl savages?"

Winter glanced down at herself. "Rags" might be pushing it, but she had to admit she didn't look imposing. She'd patched the gear she'd gotten at the Mountain with pieces provided by the Haeta, and the result was warm but didn't look pretty. She shrugged.

"It's quite a story," she said. "I'll be happy to tell it to you, if you like."

"We shall see." The man strolled forward, and his escort followed, though they looked unhappy. "Do your companions speak Murnskai?"

"I do," Leti said. "I am Letingerae, of the Haeta."

"Remarkable," the man murmured. "I am Captain Evar Kollowrath, commander of Fort Penance."

"And I'm Winter Ihernglass." She didn't think her fame was enough that she had to worry about being recognized.

"And what do Winter Ihernglass and her savage friends require of His Imperial Majesty's army?"

Winter took a deep breath. "We need passage downriver, as soon as possible. We saw your ships. We'd like to use them."

One of the soldiers standing beside Kollowrath sniggered. The captain merely smiled broadly.

"Really? Is that all?" He waggled his eyebrows. "You don't want a hot meal and a bath while you're at it?"

"There are . . . people behind us. A small army. They're killing everything in their way." Winter had explained to Leti that the Murnskai wouldn't believe in demons. She had to admit, though, that this story wasn't as convincing. "I suggest you come with us."

"Abandon our posts, in other words," Kollowrath said. "Give up this fortress, with which His Imperial Majesty has entrusted me. Take over His Imperial Majesty's river couriers for my own use, on the word of an indigent young woman and a pack of northern barbarians." He raised his hands. "Why not?"

The man at his shoulder, a big, heavily bearded fellow, whispered something in the captain's ear. Kollowrath turned scarlet.

"Rumors and exaggerations," he spat. "And if you contradict me in public again, Sergeant, you'll be on ice duty for a month. Is that clear?"

The sergeant stepped back. Winter met his eyes and saw his frustration. But he muttered, "Yes, sir."

"We will not be abandoning the fortress," Kollowrath said, turning his attention back to Winter and the others. He came closer, until he was just a few strides from her. "If some 'army' of brigands wants to take it, I invite them to try. They will find His Imperial Majesty's soldiers ready for them."

"Fine," Winter said. She turned to Leti. "This was a mistake. Let's go."

"Now, wait." Kollowrath was smiling. "I don't want it to be said that I'm uncharitable. If you and your companions wish to shelter within the walls, I'm sure something could be arranged."

"Sir," the sergeant said.

"What kind of arrangement?" Winter said. Though, looking at Kollowrath's face, she had a sinking feeling she already knew.

"The kind I imagine a group of young women alone on the road makes on a regular basis," Kollowrath said. He stepped closer to Seka, who stiffened. The girl didn't understand much Murnskai, but she could read Kollowrath's tone.

"Sir!" the sergeant said. "We should go back—"

"Stop," Leti said.

Kollowrath ignored both of them. He moved beside Seka and stroked her cheek with one hand. "I've never bedded a northern girl, you know," he mused, fingers sliding down her arm. "They say they're wild—"

Elka, Seka's sister, raised her spear. Winter saw her moving as though in slow motion, and her own hand came up as she shouted in Murnskai, knowing the girl wouldn't understand. Leti barked something in Haeta, and Elka hesitated, her weapon pointing at Kollowrath. Then the world went white, and Winter's ears were ringing with the blast of a musket going off at close range.

For a moment everyone was still. The spear clattered from Elka's fingers, and she brought her hand up to the hole in her furs, just below her collar. When she pressed it against the wound, red spurted around it. She blinked, and collapsed.

As if that had been a signal, everyone moved at once. Seka screamed, snatching up her own spear. Kollowrath scrambled backward, his face a mask of terror, and the sergeant was shouting something. The soldier holding a smoking musket backed away, while his companions raised their weapons.

"*Run!*" Winter screamed.

The closest soldier blocked Seka's spear thrust with his musket, slashing his bayonet diagonally across her stomach. Leti was going for her weapon, but Winter grabbed her arm, her legs feeling slow and clumsy. Dirt slid under her feet as she turned, her boots tearing through the tall grass. She shouted again at Yath, who'd drawn her own spear, but the girl was already pivoting on one foot for a throw. The weapon whipped out and caught the soldier who'd shot Elka, several inches of bloody spearhead emerging from the back of his neck. He fell to his knees, clawing at the spear as he choked and gurgled.

"Back to the fortress!" Kollowrath said, voice high with panic. "Back!"

Yath turned to run. Another musket went off, and she toppled with a grunt. Leti saw, and half turned herself, pulling Winter with her.

"Leti—"

"We can't—" Leti began.

Seka's guts were sliding out of her, but she had a long knife in her hand, jamming it over and over into the soldier's ribs. The sergeant and his two remaining men were following their commander back toward the gate. One of them had snatched up an unfired musket from his companion and turned to sight on them. Winter flung herself down, pulling Leti alongside her, just as the weapon went off with an earsplitting *crack*.

She buried her face in the dirt, tasting it on her lips, listening. There was a short shriek, a soft gurgling noise, and then only the sound of retreating boots fading into the distance. Winter raised her head, brushing soil from her face.

"We have to get out of here," she said. "Kollowrath will send more men. He'll—"

She stopped. Leti didn't move.

No. Not again. Winter was back in Bobby's arms, huddling against the motionless statue. At the regimental aid station, watching as Hannah Courvier removed arms and legs. Signing the strength reports, counting the dead. *No, no, no . . .*

Leti lay facedown, arms splayed, with a hole the size of a gold eagle in the back of her head. Winter dropped to her knees, eyes filling with tears.

Again.

They always trust me. And then they die.

She wasn't sure how long she lay there. Eventually, something drove her to her feet, the part of her mind that kept her alive while the rest was broken. Kollowrath would be back, with more men, and she couldn't be around when he arrived.

Leti was dead. Elka was dead, eyes still open in blank, blank surprise. Seka was dead, along with the Murnskai soldier who'd killed her, tangled together in a gory mess. The soldier with the spear through his throat had long ago stopped twitching.

Yath was alive, the musket ball having punched clean through the meat of her thigh but missed the bone. She sat up when Winter staggered over, and gritted her teeth while Winter tied a makeshift bandage around the wound. It still leaked blood, but Yath managed to stand up with one arm around Winter's shoulder, and they made reasonably good speed to the edge of the wood. Looking back, Winter could see soldiers running along the wall walk, but the gates were still closed. *Lucky for us Kollowrath's a coward.* She wanted to sob, but it stuck in her throat.

Once they made the tree line, Winter found a hidden spot in the crook of a dead log, and laid Yath down. The girl was white as a sheet, and Winter didn't think she'd make it all the way to camp.

"Back," Winter told her, gesturing. She didn't know how much Murnskai Yath could understand. "We'll come to bring you back. The others."

Yath's eyes closed. Winter turned and ran in the direction of the camp, cursing her decision to come so far from it, to come here at all, to involve anyone else in her *fucking* life and its ongoing disasters. She ran until there were spots of gray at the corners of her vision, and she almost didn't notice that she'd arrived. One of the sentries shouted at her to stop, and she pulled up short, breathing great gulps of air.

"Alex! Abraham!" Winter ignored the sentry, who couldn't understand her, and raised her voice. Before long, her two companions came running, followed by Vess and a dozen nervous Haeta. Alex pulled up short, eyes widening.

"Winter, are you—"

There was blood spattered all over her, Leti's and Yath's and who knew who else's. "I'm fine," Winter said. "Yath's hurt badly. Take Abraham to her as fast as you can." She described the dead tree.

"I can run," Abraham said. "My legs are doing better—"

"I can go faster," Alex said flatly.

"I know." Abraham looked a little green, but he nodded. "Go ahead."

Alex put one arm around his waist. She raised her other hand, and a beam of darkness shot out into the forest, anchoring to a distant tree with a *crunch*. She took a running start, jumped, and let the beam contract, carrying her and Abraham high above the forest floor in a long arc. Another beam snapped out, pulling them farther along, and then they were out of sight, moving much faster than a sprint.

They'll save her, if she can be saved. Winter's legs wobbled, and then she was sitting. She was still breathing hard, and her lungs still burned.

Vess pushed forward, past the sentry and the other Haeta.

"What happened?" she demanded. "Where're Leti and the others?"

Winter hesitated. *She might kill me.* At that moment, she couldn't have said she would have begrudged Vess that. *I made the decision. I took Leti along. My fault.* It rang in her ears. Not just Leti but all the others, Bobby and Jane and names she'd shamefully forgotten. *My fault.*

"Dead," Winter said. "The Murnskai . . . attacked us. Yath and I escaped, but the others . . ."

She shook her head and closed her eyes, waiting for the scream, the bright pain of a knife at her throat. *My fault.*

"Winter?" Alex's voice.

Winter opened her eyes. Overhead was the battered canvas of her tent. She lay on her bedroll, curled up on her side. When she tried to stretch out, her abused muscles protested, cramping hard. Alex leaned over, looking worried, as Winter slowly forced her legs to straighten.

"Should I get Abraham?" Alex said. "He's worn out, but—"

"I'm okay," Winter panted. "Just . . . never run quite that far." She closed her eyes. "What about Yath?"

"She'll be fine. We got there in time." Alex hesitated. "There were soldiers out by the gate, dragging . . . people inside. You're certain none of the others might have . . . ?"

"Yes," Winter said. "I made sure, or I wouldn't have left them there."

"Of course," Alex said quickly. "I'm sorry. Leti was . . . She seemed kind."

"She was." *Kind, and young, and stupid enough to put her trust in me. Just like you.* "What is Vess doing?"

Alex looked away. "You should rest."

"Alex. Tell me."

"She's planning to attack the fortress," Alex said.

Winter sat up abruptly, then doubled over, clutching her stomach as more cramps seized her.

"That's crazy," she coughed out. "There's got to be a hundred men in there, and they'll be on guard. She and the Haeta will be killed."

"I know!" Alex said. "That's what I told her. But she's not listening to me anymore."

"I have to talk to her." Winter groped around the bedroll for her coat, breathing hard. "I—"

Alex put a hand on her shoulder. "Wait. At least a little while." She got to her feet. "It's at least two hours before sunset. I'm going to get Abraham, and we'll see if he can help with your pain."

Winter nodded wearily. *I'm not going to be able to talk sense into Vess if I can't stand up.* She lay back down, slowly and carefully, while Alex slipped out of the tent. Distantly, she could hear raised voices, arguments in the Haeta language. She recognized Vess' voice, cold and hard.

Blame me if you need to, Winter wanted to tell her. *You don't have to get yourself killed.*

Abraham came in, thin-faced and worn in his battered traveling clothes. He knelt beside Winter and smiled.

"Are you sure you're up to this?" Winter said. "I'll live."

"I'm fine," Abraham said. "Alex worries too much." He shook his head. "Having her carry me like that is just . . . a little hard on my stomach."

"I can imagine." Winter remembered the terrifying descent from the tower at Elysium, being supported only by Alex's power and a few scraps of rope. "Thank you for helping Yath."

"Thank you for pushing so hard to get to us quickly," Abraham said. "She had lost a lot of blood. I'm not sure she would have survived much longer." He put his hands on Winter's shoulder and hip and closed his eyes. "Now, be quiet for a moment."

Winter closed her eyes, too. Infernivore perked up, as it always did when someone who carried a demon touched her. She'd grown so used to Alex's and Abraham's presence that she barely sensed them anymore unless they were very close by, but physical contact came with the awareness that only an effort of will would be required to send her demon surging into their bodies.

Abraham's power slowly flowed into her, like cool water running just under her skin. The cramps in her muscles eased, and the burning faded away. She took a deep breath, relishing the lack of pain along her ribs, and blew it out.

"There." Abraham took his hands away, and she opened her eyes. "I can't fix everything, but you should be in a lot less pain."

"Thank you," Winter said. She sat up, this time much more comfortably, and stretched. "You really do have an incredible gift."

He bowed his head. "I think I agree with you, though I haven't always thought so. There are times when it's brought me . . . hardship." He looked up again. "It's been much the same with you, I imagine."

"My demon?" Winter looked at her hands. "I suppose so."

"Your demon is not your only gift. You would never have come this far if it were."

She snorted. "In that case, my 'gift' is a lot of luck and a knack for getting other people killed."

"Leti," Abraham said.

"She's only the latest. Ever since they made me a sergeant in Khandar, I've just been trying to keep my head above water." Winter felt her eyes filling with tears again. "Bobby trusted me. She's dead now, along with most of the rest of my company. I found Jane again, dragged her and the girls from the Leather-backs into this. Now most of them are lying in graves somewhere between here and Desland. I pulled Jane into a life she couldn't face, and it broke her. I led twenty-five brave women to Elysium when Janus was hurt and left a trail of frozen corpses behind me. And then I led the ones who were left to the fucking *Beast of Judgment*." Winter's jaw trembled, and tears were running hot down her cheeks. "And now Leti. Saints and fucking martyrs. She . . ." She shook her head. "Why? Why do they trust me? Why do *you* trust me? I don't know what the *fuck* I'm doing. You and Alex ought to go back to the Mountain, before . . . before . . ."

Her throat went tight, and she couldn't say any more. It was like Abraham's words had been a lance, pressed into an angry boil of guilt until it burst. She'd never said it out loud before, the ugly truth, only kept it in the privacy of her skull.

Abraham was silent, and Winter was suddenly certain he was horrified. He'd trusted her, too, after all, put his faith in her. *Now he knows better. I'm just a gibbering mess.* She wondered if he'd just *leave*, take Alex and go. *Better for both of them.*

She wanted, very badly, for Cyte to be by her side. To feel her arms around her and pull her close. At the same time, she was glad her lover was a thousand miles away. *Because she put her faith in me, too.*

"There were times," Abraham said slowly, "when I thought the world would be better off without me. I hurt people—sometimes on purpose, sometimes without meaning to, sometimes just by being who I am. If I hadn't met Alex, I don't know . . ." He stopped, took a deep breath. "Once we made it to the Mountain, I talked to the Eldest about it."

"Did he give you some pious platitude?" Winter said.

She'd meant it to hurt, but he sounded unruffled. "He told me I'd have to work it out for myself."

Winter snorted. "Priests and Mages."

"I did a lot of thinking," Abraham went on. "When we weigh up the balance sheet of our lives, it's always easy to see the costs. People we've hurt, mistakes we've made. But the other side of the balance can be harder to make out. How do you measure what *didn't* happen? Friends who *didn't* die because of something you did, wars that didn't start, cities that never burned. That has to count for something, doesn't it?"

"You can't know what would have happened," Winter said. "Maybe everyone would have been better off."

"It's possible," Abraham said placidly. "But you can't know that for certain, either. Out of all the possible worlds, we can't know if this is the best, the worst, or somewhere in between. But it's the one we've got." He shrugged. "The Eldest didn't have an answer for me, and I don't have one for you. But I can say why *I* chose to put my faith in you. You have your gifts—intelligence, leadership, your demon—but more important is that I trust you to try to do the right thing."

"More fool you," Winter said, wiping angrily at her eyes.

"Perhaps. But I suspect Bobby and all the others would agree with me. Not that you always succeed, but that you always try." He got to his feet. "You're here, after all. Trying to save the world."

Winter was silent. Abraham bowed his head and left the tent.

The sun was nearing the horizon when she emerged, hair washed and face wiped clean. Alex and Abraham were sitting on the ground outside the tent, talking quietly. They both jumped up at the sight of her.

"Winter!" Alex said. "Are you feeling better?"

"A little," Winter said. She still felt like there was a storm inside her, but she was floating atop it, not drowning in the waves. She caught Abraham's eye. "Thank you."

"Like I said"—he smiled—"I don't have any answers."

Neither do I. But it didn't matter, not now. *There are people who need saving. One step at a time.* "Where's Vess?"

"She and the others are scouting the wall," Alex said. "I tried to talk sense into them, but Vess won't listen. She said that tomorrow night she's going to attack."

Tomorrow night. That gave them twenty-four hours. "You said you could get us into the fortress if you had to," Winter said.

"Meaning the three of us? Sure. Probably not *everyone*, not without someone noticing." Alex paused. "If Vess is intent on doing this, we might be able to sneak in and steal a boat in the confusion."

"I'm not going to abandon them," Winter said. "I'm not even going to abandon the damned Murnskai, if I can help it. Not when it's hell on earth coming up behind us." *Although a certain captain may find all his limbs broken.*

"So what, then?" Alex said.

"We find a way to get everyone out of here," Winter said. "And then we convince Vess to take it."

Chapter Fourteen

RAESINIA

"You knew," Raesinia said as soon as the door to Dorsay's suite closed behind her.

"I suspected," Dorsay said mildly. He wore a brown silk robe and his hair was ruffled, but he seemed unperturbed at finding the Queen of Vordan in his chambers first thing in the morning.

"Why didn't you tell me?"

"It's not my place to reveal Georg's plans, especially when he hasn't consulted me about them." Dorsay shrugged. "I did warn you not to come here."

"You didn't warn me he had a marriage alliance in mind."

Dorsay waved her to one of the armchairs. After a moment of stubborn irritation, Raesinia sighed and sat down, and he settled in opposite her.

"Georg is the kind of man who takes opportunities when they present themselves. If Janus had remained quiet, no doubt he would have concluded the treaty with Vordan in good faith. When the situation changed, however, it gave him the chance to ask for more."

"Goodman has been insistent about that," Raesinia said.

"I'm sure he has. That's the stick. I wasn't sure what the carrot would be, but it makes sense."

Marrying some prince I barely know is supposed to be the reward? "Why does it make sense?"

"The crown prince has only one son, and he is known to be sickly, while the prince himself grows weaker by the year. It seems increasingly likely that the Pulwer dynasty will not continue down *that* branch of the tree. The second prince is healthy and presumably fertile, but so far has refused every potential match. You are young, unmarried, and in need of heirs yourself." Dorsay shrugged. "Given the course of recent events, Georg is also eager to move Borel away from Elysium's orbit. An alliance with Vordan, cemented by something as strong as a marriage between the monarch and the prospective heir, would be a good way to accomplish that."

"You think this offer is genuine, then?"

"Oh, certainly. Georg is an honorable man."

"No king is an honorable man," Raesinia snapped. "Not if he wants to keep his throne for long."

"Fair," Dorsay conceded. "But he does *try* to keep his promises. The alliance would be popular with the merchants, which would make Goodman and his friends less ruffled about being overruled. From Georg's position, I can certainly see the advantages." Dorsay steepled his hands. "And from yours, I have to say."

"*Advantages?*" Raesinia glowered. "You're not serious."

"From a purely political point of view, of course. You are young, and your power is insecure. If you married Prince Matthew, then Borel would have a powerful incentive to make sure you kept your throne, which can only assist in dealing with domestic opponents. You would receive the aid against Janus you came for. And you clearly must marry *someone* soon, in any event."

"I know," Raesinia said. "I'm just . . ." *What? Not happy about having my body bargained with like a broodmare?* "Unprepared. I hadn't thought to address the problem of marriage until things were more settled."

Dorsay raised an eyebrow. "Well, we are where we are, and we needs must make the best of it."

"You think I should accept, then."

"I wouldn't dream of telling the Queen of Vordan what she should do. All I can say is that it seems to be one way of achieving what you came for, at a cost your nation is willing to bear." He got to his feet. "It's time for breakfast. Would you like to join me?"

Raesinia declined, as graciously as she could, and headed back to her own chambers. Barely and Jo fell into step behind her, as usual, but she was so lost in her own thoughts she hardly noticed them.

He's right, damn him. Taking the king's offer *was* the logical thing to do. It would accomplish everything Dorsay said, securing Borel's aid now and in the future. *All at the price of, what? Sleeping with a boring dimwit? Women have done far worse for far less.*

The problem, of course, was that it wasn't that simple. Prince Matthew didn't know about her supernatural problem, and there was no telling how he'd react if he found out. Raesinia planned to "live" only a few more years in any case, before her agelessness became too obvious to deny. Any heir would be too young to rule at that point, so she needed a husband she could trust with the throne. *I would trust Marcus with Vordan. But Matthew?*

Then there was the matter of the child. Raesinia had no idea if she *could* conceive, in her current state, but she strongly suspected not. She hadn't had her monthly flows since Orlanko and the Black Priests had made her read the name of her demon. If she couldn't age, or even get drunk, she doubted pregnancy was an option. With a husband who was in on the plot, that was a problem that could be circumvented, but if she had to deceive him about the parentage of his child on top of her other secrets . . .

It can't work. Something would go wrong, and then everything *would fall apart.* She paused outside the door to her own suite and caught her breath. *I can't take Georg's offer, whatever Dorsay thinks.* She felt a little better having arrived at the decision without invoking purely personal reasons. *My need to be with Marcus can't trump the good of the whole country. But it won't work* anyway. She nodded decisively. *We just have to find something that will.*

Eric and Cora returned just after noon from yet another round of meetings with Goodman and his clerks. The servants, at Raesinia's orders, had laid out a cold lunch, so there was food waiting when the two of them came in. Cora, as expected, went straight for the buffet and started loading up a plate with little sandwiches and the tiny egg-and-vegetable pies the Borelgai were so fond of. Eric, moving a little slower, tossed his ever-present notebook into one chair and then slumped into another.

"Do you need something to eat?" Raesinia said.

"Something to drink, for preference," Eric muttered. He sat up a little straighter. "I'm sorry, Your Highness. Thank you, but no. Not at the moment."

"I take it you didn't make much progress."

"*Much* would imply any movement at all," Eric said. "Talking to Master Goodman is like arguing with a wall. He listens politely, then repeats his position verbatim."

"It's actually impressive how consistent he is," Cora said, from the table. "You can tell he's an expert."

"I don't know how you can be so cheerful," Eric said. "He's been unbearably rude to *you* from the beginning."

"'M used to it." Cora had popped a whole hard-boiled egg into her mouth and was chewing furiously. "People usually are. I think Raes was the first person who took me seriously."

"People are stupid," Raesinia said. She turned from Eric to Cora. "So, you don't see any chance of getting to an agreement we can actually afford?"

She shook her head. "He doesn't have any reason to give us one unless something changes. If Janus has a setback, maybe we could threaten to walk away."

"That's the problem," Eric said gloomily. "It's hard to negotiate when you haven't got any leverage."

Cora laughed. "Well, if we need leverage, at least we're in the right city."

Raesinia blinked. "I'm sorry?"

"Oh. It's a joke." Cora swallowed and set her plate down to gesture. "In finance, *leverage* can also mean *debt*. Because it helps you lift more than you otherwise could, you know? And Viadre has the largest debt markets in the world." She caught the look on Raesinia's face and sighed. "Not a great joke, I guess."

"No," Raesinia said. Something was whirling at the back of her mind, the core of an idea. *It's not all there yet, but . . .* "You said you still had credit to your name here, right?"

"Some," she said. "Quite a bit, actually, but not on the scale we need. Not if we're talking about the national debt."

"But you could grow it. With leverage."

"Y-yes." Cora turned away from the buffet to face Raesinia. "Probably. It might not be easy."

"I know you can do it," Raesinia said. "From now on, that's your main assignment."

She met Cora's gaze and saw the flicker of worry in the girl's eyes. Raesinia forced herself to look confident and watched as Cora drew herself up. It was manipulation, pure and simple. Cora couldn't let her friend down, and so if Raesinia had confidence in her she'd try her damnedest regardless of how she felt. It was the sort of trick Raesinia had employed all her life—she thought about Ben, with his puppy-dog crush on her, and how she'd used him to further the revolution—and she felt only a faint twinge of guilt. *That's what being a queen does to you.*

"It'll take some time," Cora said. "I don't know if I can get anywhere fast enough to be useful."

"I understand. Just try." Raesinia grinned. "You're obviously not getting anywhere with Goodman, so you might as well do something productive."

"Even if she can make some money," Eric said, "where does that get us?"

"I'm not certain yet," Raesinia said. "But the markets are Goodman's game board, and it can't hurt to have a few more pieces." She looked back at Cora. "Is there a way to make sure what you're doing can't be traced back to us?"

"I can set up a trading company," Cora said. "It won't be bulletproof, but at least it won't be *obvious*. We'll need the structure if we're taking on debt anyway."

"Good. Get started building it, and I'll figure out what we're going to do with it when you've finished."

"Got it." Cora already looked energized. She snatched a last sandwich and beckoned to Eric. "Come on. I'm going to need you for some of the paperwork."

When another invitation to dinner with the second prince arrived, Raesinia wasn't sure whether she ought to accept. What decided her, in the end, was the thought of the food—a second chance at Prince Matthew's chef was too good to pass up. *And now that I know what the game is, maybe I can get a better handle on what he thinks of it.*

The prince opened the door to his suite himself, stepping out the way and bowing low as she came in. His suit was dark blue this time, subdued enough that it emphasized the startling light blue of his eyes. For her part, Raesinia had dressed carefully to avoid anything that could be considered flirtatious; the last thing she wanted was to give the impression that she was falling for the second prince's charms. Her dress was high-necked and sober, with a minimum of jewelry.

"Your Highness," Matthew said. "Thank you for coming."

"Prince Matthew." Raesinia tried a tentative smile. "Given the quality of the food, I'm afraid I couldn't resist."

"Arnat is a wonder, isn't he?"

The prince shut the door and gestured her toward the hearth, where there were two of the heavy claw-footed chairs that infested the Keep. The big table was set for two, Raesinia saw, but there were no servants in evidence, or even any Life Guards. The suite felt deserted. Her eyes narrowed. *He wouldn't think of trying anything, would he? Even a prince can't be* that *stupid.*

A table between the two chairs held a bottle of wine and a pair of glasses. Prince Matthew poured while Raesinia sat, welcoming the warmth of the crackling fire. She took the wineglass when he offered and sipped politely. Matthew took a long drink and sank into his chair.

"Is something wrong?" Raesinia said.

"No, not really. I just wanted a chance to talk in private before we eat." He looked over his shoulder at the silent dining room. "Your Highness, I owe you an apology."

"For what?"

"For the way I treated you last time."

"You were—"

"I was deliberately rude, dull, and boorish." He sighed. "You didn't deserve any of it, and I want you to know that I'm sorry."

"Well." Raesinia looked down into her glass for a moment, thinking hard. "Apology accepted, provided you tell me *why*."

"I was . . . irritated at my father's scheming, and I took it out on you." He ran one hand through his hair. "I should have understood that you didn't ask for this, either."

"You know about the offer he made me, then."

He nodded. "From what I heard, you had no idea what he intended."

"You thought I did?"

"I've known of Father's intentions for some time," Matthew said. "When I heard you were coming to the Keep, I thought it had all been arranged in advance."

"I assure you I had no thoughts along those lines," Raesinia said, a little stiffly. "My goal is to secure your father's help against Janus."

"I know." He sighed again. "I suspect I've made rather a mess of things."

"I take it," Raesinia said, "that you're not enthusiastic about this marriage plan."

Matthew shook his head. "No offense intended, Your Highness. But I had hoped to marry someone I've known for more than a few hours."

"Likewise. But surely you can tell your father no?" In the old days fathers might have had a right to decide on marriages without a son's permission, but surely Borel wasn't *that* backward.

"It's . . . more complicated than that."

I suppose he is the king. "So you were hoping . . ."

"That you'd be so disgusted you'd laugh in his face." He chuckled. "I suppose the fact that you didn't is a compliment, of a sort."

"You were very convincing as a boor," Raesinia said. "But I need your father's help."

"That's how he likes to operate," Matthew said bitterly. "Getting himself into a position where he has what everybody needs and then exacting his price."

Raesinia set her wineglass down and looked across at him. The second prince cut a lean, handsome figure in the light from the fire, shadows playing across his brooding features.

"Are you going to take his offer?" Matthew said, after a moment.

"That gets right to the heart of things, doesn't it?" Raesinia said. "I'm not any more eager to marry you than vice versa. No offense."

"None taken," Matthew said, waving vaguely.

"But at the moment we are precariously balanced. If the war goes well, I may be able to push back. If it goes badly . . ." She shook her head. "You know him better than I do. Is there any chance of convincing him to accept an alternate solution?"

"The man has a mind like a limpet. He grabs on to an idea and doesn't let go, not for anything." Matthew stared morosely into the fire. "He hates fighting with his advisers. If you can get Goodman on your side—"

"That seems unlikely. Master Goodman is convinced we owe him quite a lot of money."

Matthew winced. "That's always a bad position to be in."

There was an awkward silence, broken by the *pop* of wood collapsing in the fire.

"Still," Raesinia said. "It's nice to know we have a common cause."

"Even if we don't have any way to actually do anything about it?" He looked up. "Sorry. I suppose you're right. Come, let's have dinner, properly this time. I promise not to be boring."

A pull on a bell cord brought the servants running, and Raesinia thought she detected some aggrieved looks as they hurried to get dinner started. True to his word, Matthew was transformed, utterly unlike the clod he'd convincingly impersonated the other night. He told hunting stories while uniformed waiters brought in a delicate soup garnished with rings of shellfish, and managed to make Raesinia laugh hard enough that she knocked a half dozen empty shells across the room. The second course was greens with a lemon sauce, and Matthew segued into a lengthy anecdote about a friend's amorous misadventures.

"... so he says, 'I'd love to, my lady, but the dogs are still down there!'" Raesinia barked a laugh, and Matthew beamed. He really was a born storyteller, able to perfectly imitate the tone of an aggrieved housewife or anxious innkeeper. His narrow face seemed to come alive as he talked, and Raesinia was reminded for a moment of Danton Aurenne, the spellbinding orator who'd been the focal point of the revolution. She was fairly sure there was no magic at work here, though. Her binding hadn't given her any twinges of warning.

"It was all right in the end, of course," he went on. "He ended up marrying poor old Rosalind, and Ella eventually found her merchant's son." Matthew went quiet for a moment, perhaps reflecting that his choice of subject might not be ideal under their current circumstances. He cleared his throat. "I understand times have been quite interesting in Vordan of late as well."

"*Interesting* is not the word I'd use," Raesinia said. "*Terrifying*, maybe."

"Was it as bad as they say?"

Raesinia paused. There were some stories she couldn't tell, of course. How she'd escaped from Ohnlei by jumping off a tower and breaking her head open every night. The time she'd been shot in the head by a Concordat traitor and spent hours pinned on a rock like a butterfly, upside down and underwater. How she'd been kidnapped by the Penitent Damned called Ionkovo, and how she'd turned the tables on him later in a spectacularly gory fashion.

I can't tell him anything, can I? It wasn't just the magic and the secrets she had to keep. Looking at Matthew, with his pretty blue eyes and stories about climbing over rooftops to help friends meet their lovers, felt like staring into a different world. It was a world she'd been born into, a world she'd been *meant* for, but it had been taken away from her by disease and dark magic. *I was supposed to be like him.* Not frivolous, exactly. It wasn't his *fault.* He'd just never been down to the sharp end, where things balance on the edge of a knife and pretenses are stripped away.

"It was . . . pretty bad, yes." Raesinia blinked and shook her head.

"I'm sorry," Matthew said. "Obviously it's something you'd rather not think about."

It's not that, Raesinia thought. *It's just something I can't inflict on* you.

Instead, she took a deep breath and told him a story from the old days, before her brother had died. It was a good story, which ended with an arrogant wine steward getting his comeuppance in a stable full of horseshit. Telling it made Raesinia miss Dominic more than she had for years. It had been ages since she'd even thought about her brother. It seemed strange now that there had been a time when he'd been the most important person in her world, after her father. *I would have done anything to get their approval.* They'd gotten in trouble for shoving the wine steward, but a little scolding from her tutor was worth it if she made Dominic smile.

It felt, for one evening, like she'd been allowed to visit the world she'd lost.

Clever, handsome princes who made her laugh, spectacular food, the quiet bustle of servants moving all around. It was life as it might have been.

"Thank you," she said, when the dessert plates had been cleared away. "This was a wonderful evening."

"It was," he said. There was a touch of sadness in his eyes. "Let me apologize again."

"You've apologized enough for last time—"

"Not for that. For my father." Matthew shook his head. "I wish we'd been able to meet under better circumstances."

"We'll figure something out," Raesinia said, aware that there were still servants all around them.

Matthew nodded distantly, but his expression was resigned. *He thinks there's nothing we can do. That I'm going to have to take Georg's offer, and we'll have to go through with it.*

It made her even more determined to escape from the trap the Borelgai had laid. *On top of everything else, Matthew doesn't deserve to be used like this.*

CHAPTER FIFTEEN

MARCUS

The orders had come in just after dark, as the Second Division was settling back into camp. Marcus scanned through them, suppressing a groan. *Another dawn march. Another battle tomorrow.* He turned the page. *At least we won't be right in the middle of it.*

"Thank you," he told the young lieutenant who'd brought the pages. "Tell General Kurot I understand, and we'll be ready."

"Yes, sir." The young man looked around curiously. Cyte and Abby were in the tent with them, looking over the big map, along with several Girls' Own sentries. This courier clearly found the idea of women in uniform fascinating.

Marcus cleared his throat. "That'll be all."

"Ah. Yes, sir." He straightened, saluted, and left the tent. Marcus glared after him.

He should go visit the cutters. Casualties from the fighting at Satinvol were still being brought in by the stretcher teams combing the town. Those who could be saved had been evacuated already, so now the work mostly came down to giving the badly wounded a somewhat more comfortable place to die. Meanwhile, Hannah Courvier and the other cutters worked nonstop, the floor of their tent slick with blood, the pile of amputated limbs outside growing ever larger as the bone saws sang.

All of the Second's regiments had lost soldiers, but it was the casualties among the Girls' Own that hit Marcus the hardest. *I can't help it, damn it. I'm supposed to* protect *them, not march them into danger.* Thinking about it made him angry with himself, angry with Janus, angry with everyone. It was almost enough to make him forget what had happened on the enemy's last charge.

Magic. It had to be magic. That Girls' Own ranker had turned on him, and he was certain the glow in her eyes had been real. *Janus must have . . . something. Some power. Maybe he found what he was looking for.* The voice at the back of his mind—the one he tried to ignore, because he knew he *wanted* what it said to be true—said, *Maybe something got to* him. *Maybe he's not to blame for all this after all.*

"More good news, sir?" Abby said.

Marcus blinked and shook his head. He handed her the orders, and while she read he said, "We're going to be moving out at first light again. You'd better spread the word."

"Understood, sir." Cyte saluted. "I'll make sure the colonels get the message."

"You believe this, sir?" Abby said, when Cyte had slipped out of the tent.

"Which part?"

"That we're going to be able to trap Janus against Alves."

The orders called for a fast march southwest, pushing through whatever got in their way. With the Satinvol bridge destroyed and the Alves bridge presumably still in friendly hands or at least demolished, Janus would be left with no way out, and his supplies would be diminished by days of siege and fighting. The Army of the Republic, by contrast, was still receiving supplies and reinforcements over the passes. Kurot had carefully assigned forces to guard those lines, but Janus had made no attempt to interfere. *As though he doesn't mind walking into the trap.*

"It seems . . . possible." Marcus shifted uncomfortably. He didn't want to speak against a superior directly, but . . . "Janus is tricky. You know that. I wouldn't be surprised if he's got something up his sleeve."

"Me either." Abby sighed. "We gave about as good as we got yesterday. It's not easy, fighting our own people."

"No, it isn't," Marcus said. "Is morale holding up in your regiment?"

"I think so. The girls feel . . . not good, never good after something like this, but happy to have done their part." She cocked her head. "Thank you, by the way. For keeping your promise."

"It's . . . only fair." *Even if it does give me nightmares.* "Your performance was excellent. General Ihernglass would have been proud."

"I'm only sorry you were in danger," Abby said. "I never expected those mad bastards to try to break out."

"No one did, myself least of all." Marcus hesitated. "Any idea who they were? They seemed to have a mix of uniforms—I saw Vordanai, Murnskai, and some in civilian clothes."

"Nobody seems to know," Abby said. "We didn't capture any of them alive, not one. And the Vordanai soldiers from other regiments just know they're some kind of personal guard for Janus, but not the name of their unit or how many there are."

It feels wrong. Janus' old Mierantai Volunteers had been almost fanatical in their master's defense, but he didn't think even they would have thrown away their lives like that. *It has to be magic.* He wished Raesinia were here. *Cyte knows. Maybe I can talk to her about what she's seen.*

That would have to wait for tomorrow, though. The light was draining from the sky, and fatigue from the day's fighting dragged at Marcus' limbs like lead weights. He made his apologies to Abby, and she saluted and left the tent. Once she was gone, the full force of exhaustion fell on Marcus, and he barely made it to his bedroll before he was asleep.

The drums woke him what felt like minutes later. He sat up with a groan, blood pounding in his head. Before he managed to push himself to his feet, there was a scratch at the tent flap.

"Sir?" Cyte's voice, sounding inhumanly good-natured for this early in the morning. "Are you awake?"

"Getting there," Marcus said. *Maybe I'm getting old.*

Blessedly, Cyte had brought coffee. His favorite was still Khandarai style, dark and thick with a kick like a mule, but when he was feeling fragile he had to admit the milder Vordanai variety had its appeal. Breathing in the rich scent and taking the first few scalding sips had an almost magical effect, and by the time he reached the bottom of the cup he felt almost human again. Cyte stood to one side, quietly watching his transformation.

"Thank you," he said. "I needed that."

She smiled only slightly. "Of course, sir." *Has she been taking lessons from Fitz?*

"Everything on schedule?"

"We should be ready to break camp in the next half an hour, sir."

"I'd like to have a word with the colonels before we take the command tent down."

"I'll let them know, sir."

Within a few minutes, they had all gathered: Abby, Sevran, de Koste, and Blackstream, Erdine for the cavalry and Archer for the artillery. Cyte joined them, too, and stood quietly by the tent flap. Even the large command tent felt crowded with so many gathered around the table.

"In another half an hour, we'll start our advance," Marcus said. "We're the far right of the line, so our flank should line up on the Pale. Colonel Black-stream, that's you. Colonel Giforte, the First Regiment will be skirmishing in front. Colonel Sevran, you'll be on our left. General Warus' division is next in line, so make sure to maintain contact."

He drew their attention to the map. The field on which the battle would be fought—always assuming there *was* a battle, of course—was roughly trian-gular, a wedge formed by the convergence of two rivers. The top was the wide, deep Pale, uncrossable except at a bridge. The bottom was the smaller Daater, narrower but still a significant barrier. The city of Alves with its fortifications occupied the tip of the wedge, pointing west. The open end of the triangle was held by Kurot's army, stretching in a line from Satinvol on the Pale to the Daater. Somewhere in that narrowing triangle, Janus' army was waiting for them.

On the map, a position somewhat ahead of the line was marked in pen-cil. That was where Val's Third Division had made camp the night before. They'd marched farther than expected, surprised by the lack of resistance. Now they were dangerously overextended, and Marcus was glad Kurot was moving quickly to bring the rest of the army up in support. He tapped the map with his finger.

"We're to advance into line with the Third Division, then hold position and wait for orders." He looked around the room at the colonels. "General Kurot knows we fought hard yesterday, and he's planning to make the main effort with his left." The two divisions there, under de Manzet, hadn't fired a shot the day before. "Our job is just going to be to hold the line and keep Janus' left in play. No heroics, understand?"

"We seem to be stretched a little thin," Blackstream said, frowning at the map. "Kurot hasn't left much of a reserve."

"He hasn't got a choice," Sevran said. "It's a wide front, and he has to cover it or else risk Janus slipping past."

"It'll narrow as we advance," Erdine said. "We'll be fine."

"None of that is our concern," Marcus said. "Let General Kurot worry about it. We need to make sure everything goes well *here*. You should all have the written copies of your orders. Any questions?"

There was a brief silence.

"Well, then," Marcus said. "Let's get moving."

Dawn broke to find the division on the move, long columns winding south-west, with the baggage train still packing up the camp behind them. Erdine's horsemen were out front, probing for the enemy, and behind them was the Girls' Own, sweeping through the fields in skirmish order.

Marcus, riding beside Cyte, was glad to see that yesterday's fighting hadn't cracked the division's discipline. Despite the casualties, and the fatigue the soldiers had to feel, their formations were clean and they made good time. It helped that the sun was out and the mud had finally started to dry. While the Girls' Own were spread out, picking their way through harvested fields and over the drystone walls that separated them, the other three regiments stuck to the Alves-Satinvol road, which ran more or less parallel to the river.

For the moment there was no sign of the enemy. Marcus kept looking across the river, expecting to see troops on the move there, but either the Pale was too wide or there was nothing to see. There was no sign of Alves yet, either. The only other force he could see was Fitz Warus' First Division, advancing roughly in the same direction a mile or two to Marcus' left. That was heartening, too. Not that he'd had any doubt about Fitz' punctuality, of course, but it was always good to know the allies who were supposed to be covering your flanks were actually in place.

"Do you really think there'll be a fight today, sir?" Cyte said.

"You doubt it?" Marcus said, looking back at her. "The enemy certainly showed willing at Satinvol."

"If Kurot is right, then we've got Janus cornered." She shrugged. "I suppose that just seems a little too easy."

"Even Janus makes mistakes, Captain," Marcus said. Though, truth be told, he'd been thinking the same thing. "But let's be careful anyway."

By nine in the morning, it was clear the day would be hot, a last breath of summer as fall wore on. The advance was leisurely, with regular halts for water. Kurot hadn't expressed any urgency, and after their exertions yesterday Marcus didn't want to overstrain his soldiers. Still, he found himself fretting. When the smoke from the Third Division's camp became visible beyond Fitz, he breathed a sigh of relief. His biggest worry had been that Janus would take the chance to snap at Val while he was stuck out on a limb.

"Come on," he told Cyte. "We're going to see General Solwen. If the enemy have been up to anything, he'll know the latest."

Barking a brief order putting Abby in command until he returned, Marcus turned his horse up a convenient farm track, threading between stone walls and making his way parallel to the front. Cyte followed him, as usual much more comfortable in the saddle. They got stuck briefly at a junction clogged by First Division baggage wagons, but after a bit of swearing on the part of the sergeant directing traffic, a passage was cleared. Another backcountry trail led up to where the Third Division had spent the night.

"Odd," Cyte said, as they rode closer.

"What's odd?"

"Scouts." She nodded at a pair of cavalrymen, carbines in hand, sitting on their horses in the middle of a field. "Seems a waste of manpower to have scouts facing east."

"Val can be a little paranoid," Marcus said. "Besides, he doesn't know for sure when the rest of us will turn up. You're not the only one who worries about Janus trying something tricky." He waved at the pair of troopers, who didn't seem to notice.

The Third Division's four regiments were still forming up around their camp, soldiers filing into formation, the regimental flags snapping in the slight breeze. Sentries had spotted Marcus and Cyte, and a small delegation of officers accompanied by a couple of troopers mounted up and came out to meet them. Marcus didn't see Val among them.

He's busy. Got a late start, as usual. Marcus looked back at Cyte again. She was watching the approaching riders with an odd expression. *Something seems . . .*

Marcus looked closer, and felt the blood drain from his face.

The banners are wrong. Not the flags themselves, which were just the usual Vordanai eagles, but the banner staffs. Val, peacock that he sometimes was, had paid out of his own pocket for bronze-banded staffs with silver caps before the Murnskai campaign had begun. All four regiments here were holding ordinary wooden staffs.

He looked back at the approaching party. There was a captain and two lieutenants, none of whom he recognized. He didn't know every officer in the Third Division by sight, but he was familiar with most of the members of Val's staff. *So where are they?*

This isn't the Third Division.

The simplicity of the ruse took his breath away. *But why not?* Both sides of the war used the same uniforms, the same flags. From a distance it was impossible to tell one body of men from another. *And anyone who gets up close . . .*

"Cyte," Marcus hissed under his breath. When she didn't look around, he repeated it a little louder. "Cyte, keep looking ahead."

Sir? Cyte mouthed, eyes locked.

"When I say go, I want you to turn your horse around and head back the way we came, as fast as you can. If we get separated, head for General Kurot's command post."

She nodded, very slightly, and didn't ask why. *Perfect.*

They were about fifty yards from the oncoming group of riders. Marcus loosened his pistol in its holster.

"*Go!*" he shouted, sawing back on the reins.

His horse objected, bucking, before he got it under control. Cyte, slightly behind him, turned in a smooth circle, accelerating rapidly up to a canter. Marcus pulled his pistol, aimed in the general direction of the approaching officers, and fired. At fifty yards, on the back of a bucking horse, they might as well have been on the moon, but the flash and bang threw them into confusion for a few moments. Once he had his mount headed in the right direction, he applied his spurs.

Despite his instructions, Cyte had slowed long enough to let him catch up, and she came up to gallop only when he drew alongside. Behind him, he could hear shouts of alarm, and then a bellow.

"Stop them! Fire!"

A half dozen carbines went off at once, and Marcus ducked instinctively. He could hear the *zip* of balls, but nothing came close. A man on a galloping horse was a hard target. *They're going to have to try to ride us down.* He looked over his shoulder, trying to assess whether pursuit was forming up—

"General!" Cyte shouted.

Marcus looked forward again to see the two cavalry troopers they'd passed earlier pounding out of the field and onto the road. Now he understood why they were there, and he swore as he fumbled for his saber. The weapon was designed to be used on horseback, but *Marcus* hadn't been, and he barely got the sword drawn without dropping the reins. A trooper had swung in behind him, raising his carbine. Marcus jerked his horse's head to one side in an inelegant dodge as the weapon went off, a cloud of smoke briefly enveloping the galloping trooper. The man dropped back, controlling his horse with his knees in a way Marcus could only envy, and drew his own sword.

Cyte, up ahead, rode alongside the second trooper, weaving as he leveled his carbine. The soldier fired, and Cyte dropped sideways. For a heart-stopping moment Marcus thought she'd been hit, but she'd only leaned over, hanging off the side of her mount like a trick rider. She swung back up, veering away from her attacker as he drew his sword.

Oh, damn. Cyte's weapon of choice was a slim rapier—appropriate for her physique, but practically useless on horseback. Marcus dug his spurs in harder, trying to catch up to her, but his suffering mount was already giving him all the speed she had. Then the trooper behind him closed in, and Marcus didn't have time to worry. It required all his attention to ride and parry at the same time, steel ringing off steel once, twice, three times before the soldier pulled to one side.

The other trooper came at Cyte, weapon raised. As he swung, she cut in front of him, forcing his mount to stumble in the moment his attack left him off-balance. One of his legs came free of his stirrup, and the trooper dropped his sword and clung desperately to his saddle as he tried to right himself. His horse slowed, falling behind.

Cyte dropped back herself, toward Marcus, drawing her slim weapon. Marcus moved toward the remaining trooper before he noticed her, and sabers clashed again. With his clumsy sword work Marcus couldn't maintain the offensive for long, and the cavalryman was getting the better of him when Cyte came alongside and slid her rapier in between his ribs. He went stiff as she whipped the sword free, then slumped forward over his mount's neck, the horse slowing in confusion. *I guess you can use a rapier from horseback if you know what you're doing.*

"How'd you know?" Cyte said, sheathing her weapon. Marcus didn't even *try* that trick at a full gallop.

"Know what?" he said, feeling a little dazed.

"That General Solwen had turned traitor!"

Marcus shook his head. "He hasn't!" It felt obscurely important to defend Val's honor. In that moment, it first occurred to Marcus that his friend was probably dead, or at the very least a captive. His throat went tight. "I'll explain later! General Kurot needs to know before it's too late."

By the time they reached Kurot, perched on the crest of the tallest hill in the area, it very much looked like it might be too late.

From the slope, they could see the whole battlefield stretching out before them. Marcus could understand why Kurot had chosen this spot, although it was a little far from the line. It offered an unparalleled view, from Marcus' own troops on the far right to de Manzet's on the left. And, directly ahead of them, the camp of the "Third Division."

Marcus' escape must have told whoever was in command there that the game was up. His four regiments were forming up and turning to their right, ready to descend on de Manzet's line. At the same time, more blue columns were advancing from the front, silver eagle flags fluttering. De Manzet was about to be under attack from two directions, every commander's worst nightmare.

"General!" Marcus reined to a halt on the hilltop, his horse blowing. Kurot was surrounded by his staff, staring through a spyglass at the surprise attack below, looking from the map to the terrain and back again in consternation. A corporal came over to take Marcus' reins, and he got down, legs aching. He gave his mare an apologetic look. "Take care of her, will you?"

The corporal nodded and led the exhausted horse away. Marcus hurried in Kurot's direction. "General Kurot!"

"General d'Ivoire." Kurot was staring through a spyglass. "I'm surprised to find you away from your men."

"I went to the Third Division, sir, to confirm that General Solwen understood today's plan." Out of the corner of his eye, Marcus saw Cyte come up to his side.

"Ah." Kurot lowered the spyglass. "That explains the timing of his treachery. I daresay he's sprung his trap a little early."

"It's not him, sir. That's not the Third Division. They must have been ambushed, and Janus snuck his own men into place."

"That's impossible," Kurot snapped, then frowned slightly. "He'd have to know our plans in detail. If someone is feeding him information—" The general's brow furrowed for a moment, and then his expression cleared. "No matter. Whether it is the Third Division or a set of impostors, the damage is done, and it is for us to handle it."

"Tell de Manzet to retreat," Marcus said. "Give-Em-Hell can cover him with an attack on the flanking division, and Fitz and I will fall back to match. We'll form a solid line to meet whatever Janus has coming."

Kurot's face darkened. "I appreciate the *advice*, General, but I believe I know my business here." He raised the glass again. "If we retreat, without the Third Division we cannot hope to seal the gap between the rivers. Janus can maneuver around us and escape."

"But—"

"Furthermore," Kurot said, "his forces must necessarily be low on supplies, as we are now in possession of their lines of communication. This has the feel of a last, desperate gambit."

It doesn't. This is how Janus fights his battles—with every means at his disposal. Marcus shook his head. *Kurot isn't listening.* He straightened up.

"What do you want me to do, sir?"

"Push forward. I will detach General Stokes to your assistance. You and General Warus are to break through whatever's in front of you and advance to the Daater and the gates of Alves."

"What about de Manzet?"

Kurot clearly didn't like being questioned, but he grated, "He will be ordered to hold his ground, and the artillery reserve will support him. Once you get in the rear of the forces opposing him, they will be compelled to surrender."

"I don't think Janus *will* surrender—"

"He will *have to*," Kurot snapped. "He has made his move. It is a clever one; I admit it. But I have the countermove, and once he sees that he is outmatched, he will be compelled to give in. Even Janus bet Vhalnich is not immune to the rules of war!"

"Yes, sir," Marcus said. *God save us from clever officers.* All he wanted now was to get back to his men before things got worse. "Understood, sir. I will convey your instructions to General Warus."

"Please do." Kurot stared down at the developing battle. "You are dismissed, General."

The walk to the base of the hill was hard on Marcus' aching thighs, burning with the unexpected strain of the chase. They got new mounts for the ride back to the Second Division, and Marcus could swear his was glaring at him suspiciously. *Maybe bad news gets around, even among horses.* He patted the animal, and it chuffed.

The distant rattle of musketry, broken by the deeper boom of cannon, rolled in from below. The battle was getting started.

"Sir?" Cyte said. "Do you think Kurot's plan will work?"

"It's our job to make it work, Captain." Marcus sighed. "If we can."

"Understood, sir."

"Thanks, by the way. For saving my neck back there."

Cyte grinned. "You're welcome, sir."

Shortly after he returned to his own troops, Marcus gathered the colonels and sent a messenger to summon Fitz. He explained the problem, and Kurot's plan. Fitz raised one eyebrow, speaking volumes, but nobody objected. As he'd told Cyte, that wasn't the way things were done.

"Start pushing ahead," Marcus told Abby as the meeting broke up. "If you run into anything solid, fall back on the other regiments and wait for orders. When Give-Em-Hell gets here, we'll see if we can press a little harder. And stay in contact with Fitz' people on your left."

"We'll handle it," Abby said. "Don't worry."

And they did. The Girls' Own fanned out, pressing ahead of the columns of the other regiments. Before long, scattered musketry rose out of the gently rolling fields and stone walls, enemy skirmishers putting up a racket. It wasn't a serious effort to stop the advance, only slow it, and as the Girls' Own came on, the opposition fell back. Marcus told Colonel Erdine to assist, and his squadrons rode out to back up the line, charging at knots of the enemy whenever they were flushed from cover. Behind this running battle, the three columns of the formed regiments kept moving, and by watching the smoke on his left Marcus could tell Fitz was keeping pace.

They were making ground, not quickly but steadily, and only a trickle of casualties was coming back to the aid stations. Marcus watched from whatever vantage he could find, accompanied by Cyte and a swarm of young soldiers ready to carry messages. For the most part, though, he didn't have to interfere. *Which is perfect. The less I have to do, the better.*

They all heard Give-Em-Hell coming before they saw him, the ground drumming with the sound of thousands of hooves. As dust rose from the road behind them, a small group of horsemen approached. Feeling a little anxious, Marcus turned his spyglass on them and was relieved to see the familiar, diminutive figure of the cavalry commander in the lead. A few minutes later, Give-Em-Hell reined up and slipped out of his saddle, accompanied by several officers Marcus didn't recognize. The cavalry had been reinforced and reorganized since the Murnskai campaign, though Marcus knew they hadn't completely made good their heavy losses.

"Good to see you, General," Give-Em-Hell said. His bowlegs gave him a bit of a swagger. "Nice day for it, eh?"

"Better than rain, anyway," Marcus said. "Did General Kurot explain things?"

"Only that I was to come to your assistance," Give-Em-Hell said. "And that something's happened to Val and the Third."

Marcus had been doing his best to put that out of his mind. "That about sums it up. We're driving on to Alves."

"Excellent!" the cavalryman roared. "Give me a few minutes to get my lads together, and we'll give 'em hell!"

For once, the horseman's straightforward approach was entirely appropriate. Marcus nodded, pointing. Up ahead, the line of smoke that marked the front was climbing a low ridge.

"According to the map, that's the last real obstacle between here and the city outworks," he said. "Once Abby clears it, take your heavies up there and charge down the other side. If there's nothing in the way, don't stop until you get to Alves. If you run into squares, hold back, and I'll send some artillery to support you."

Give-Em-Hell nodded. "These rebels haven't got any horsemen worth a damn. We'll give them a good kicking."

"I want your light cavalry over on Fitz' left," Marcus said. "Make sure nothing comes at us from that direction."

That open flank had been gnawing at Marcus' mind. His right was hard against the river Pale, but his left—the left-hand side of Fitz' line—was in the air, facing the gap where Val's Third Division had been. The enemy who'd replaced those troops were supposed to be fully engaged with de Manzet, but he didn't want them turning about and suddenly hitting Fitz' line end-on. *We're getting dangerously strung out.* It was an inevitable consequence of Kurot's orders, and the same would have to apply to Janus' forces, but to an experienced commander it felt like an itch he couldn't quite reach, a faint premonition of danger. Sending a division of light cavalry to cover the gap was applying a flimsy patch at best, but it would at least serve to warn him if things were about to go sour.

"Easy enough," Give-Em-Hell said. "Though they'll be unhappy to miss out on the fun."

"There'll be fun enough for everyone by the time we're done," Marcus said.

"Right!" Give-Em-Hell roared, grinning hugely. He spun around and scrambled back on his horse. With his officers in tow, he headed back down the road, toward where the first squadrons were just coming into view. They were cuirassiers, intimidatingly big men on big horses, with steel helmets and polished breastplates like medieval knights. They sent up a cheer at the sight of their commander approaching, and Give-Em-Hell acknowledged them with a wave.

Marcus caught Cyte smiling after them. "You've worked with the general before, I take it?"

"Yes, sir. At Jirdos."

It was easy to underestimate Give-Em-Hell, with his short stature and manic attitude; Marcus had, for years. But in his element, with a proper cavalry force behind him instead of the crippled remnant the Colonials had had, he was formidable. *Yet another talent Janus picked off the garbage heap.*

Marcus relocated his command post to the ridge, in the yard of an abandoned farmhouse, as the heavy cavalry began their attack. It was an impressive array, nearly four thousand horsemen in flashing armor, swords drawn, riding downhill in three successive lines. They passed through the Girls' Own, who sent up a wild cheer, and bore down on the line of enemy skirmishers. There was no question of trying to hold *this* back. The blue-uniformed soldiers broke and ran, or hunkered down into cover. The Girls' Own followed on the heels of the cavalry as fast as they could, taking prisoners as enemy soldiers who'd sheltered under hedges poked their heads up.

So far, so good. From here Marcus had an excellent view. He could see the hill on which Kurot had waited, well behind them now, and the smoke rising from where de Manzet's battle was continuing. Ahead was the Pale, and—not too distant now—the city of Alves. He could see into its streets: tall, narrow buildings, with church spires rising above them, silver double circles shining in the sun. Closer to them were the fortifications, including a modern star-shaped earthen rampart with outlying ravelins, walls sloped to deflect cannon-fire and studded with embrasures where its own guns could fire out.

Further to the left was the twisty, narrow line of the Daater. This held his attention because he could see troops moving along the river road, not skirmishers but heavy, formed columns of infantry with accompanying artillery. He guessed there were two regiments, maybe more—most of a division, at least, apparently marching away from Alves and toward the ongoing battle with de Manzet. They seemed to be in some confusion, and Marcus could readily imagine why, scouts frantically reporting the charging cavalrymen.

"There's no camp," Cyte said, coming up beside him.

Marcus frowned. There was nothing to indicate where Janus' troops had spent the night. "Maybe they packed everything."

"We should still be able to see where they were. You know what a campsite looks like after we leave."

Marcus nodded slowly. "You're right." Wherever they'd sheltered last night, it hadn't been on the field. *And that means . . .* "Alves has fallen."

"Oh, damn," Cyte said. She shaded her eyes and looked down at the advancing horsemen. "Should I send a messenger to Give-Em-Hell?"

"Do it," Marcus said. "Hurry."

Cyte swung astride her horse and rode down the ridge. Marcus raised his spyglass again, tracking the Pale as it passed behind the city and beneath its fortifications. It was difficult to see through the clutter, but—

There. He didn't have a view of the bridge footing itself, but a section of the span was visible, and a steady stream of wagons was passing across it. *Brass balls of the fucking Beast.*

That meant the worst-case scenario, the one Kurot had dismissed yesterday, had happened: Alves had not only fallen to the enemy, but had fallen so quickly that the defenders hadn't had time to demolish the crucial bridge. *Which means all the fighting we did yesterday was for nothing.* Janus already had another crossing for his supplies, closer and more convenient. *He only defended Satinvol because he knew he could bleed us.*

That, in turn, meant that de Manzet would be facing not opponents short on ammunition after a long siege, but fresh, well-armed troops coming at him from two sides.

"Rider!" Marcus shouted. "Two of you!"

A young man and a woman hurried over, both wearing lieutenant's stripes. Marcus turned to them and spoke fast and quiet.

"Ride to General Kurot. You'll have to backtrack and swing wide. Tell him Alves is in enemy hands and they've got the bridge. We are *not* going to be able to attack Janus from behind." Any attempt to do so would be inviting a strike at his own rear from whatever troops remained in the city.

The pair looked on with wide eyes.

"Tell him I advise—" Marcus stopped, shook his head, then said, "Tell him I *request permission* to withdraw and extend my left to link up with de Manzet. I should be able to take some of the pressure off him. If we can hang on until nightfall, we can pull back a little farther and stabilize the line. You've got all that?"

They both nodded, the girl swallowing hard.

"As soon as you get there, send two riders back with a report on what's happening, and then wait for Kurot's response. Go!"

They went, scrambling down the back side of the ridge. Ahead, plumes of smoke rose from the city walls, followed moments later by the dull boom of guns. Give-Em-Hell's advancing cavalry halted, milling in confusion, as what was supposed to be a friendly fortress opened fire on them. *At least they didn't try to bait them close.* At that distance, the damage to the cavalry would be slight. *Unless Give-Em-Hell does something really, really stupid . . .*

Marcus held his breath. But even the redoubtable General Stokes apparently drew the line at asking his troopers to ride against a fortress in the face of canister fire. Instead, the cuirassiers turned about smartly and fell back the way they'd come, until they were out of range of the heavy guns on the walls. *Thank God.*

To the south, the troops he'd glimpsed along the Daater were forming up in line but so far showed no signs of advancing. Marcus' and Fitz' divisions were out on a limb, with the Pale on one side, hostile Alves and that line ahead of them, and enemy on the other side with just a light cavalry screen to stop them. The only option was to fall back, but Marcus didn't dare, not yet. He was, very roughly, where Kurot had wanted him, and if the general proceeded on that assumption, moving out of position would be a disaster.

What I wouldn't give for a flik-flik line right now. Marcus looked back down the hill, in the direction his messengers had departed, and waited.

When riders arrived, it wasn't from General Kurot, but from the left. Fitz Warus in person led a small group of light cavalry troopers, surrounding a bedraggled-looking lieutenant with the insignia of Kurot's staff. Marcus hurried down to meet them, grabbing Cyte along the way.

"General," Fitz said, swinging off his horse. He waved the troopers away, and only the lieutenant dismounted.

"Fitz." Marcus nodded at the lieutenant. "Have we got new orders?"

"Not exactly." Fitz was generally the definition of imperturbable, and Marcus didn't know if he'd ever seen the younger man truly rattled. The grim tone in his voice spoke volumes. "You'd better hear this."

Marcus exchanged a look with Cyte. The lieutenant came forward, face pale.

"Th-the last I saw General Kurot, he and the rest of his staff were falling back northward. Enemy infantry broke de Manzet's line along the Daater and pushed in his flank. A cavalry charge came within a few minutes of getting us all." He shook his head. "I got separated. I thought I'd had it when your cavalry found me."

"How bad is it?" Cyte said. "Is de Manzet still in action?"

"Bad," the lieutenant said. "At least one whole division is gone. The Eighth was still fighting, last I saw, but they were close to surrounded." He looked on the verge of tears. "You have to attack, General d'Ivoire. Turn and break through to de Manzet."

Too late. Much too late. That was what Marcus had suggested to Kurot hours ago, catching the false Third Division between hammer and anvil. Kurot had sent him in search of a larger victory, though, and now the chance was gone, the anvil broken. *And we are well and truly fucked.*

"Someone get this man some water," he said aloud, and a corporal jumped to obey. Once the lieutenant had been led away, Marcus called for a map and unrolled the small, leather-backed version he used in the field. It didn't tell him anything he didn't already know, but he stared at it anyway, in hopes of some kind of revelation.

"This is bad," Cyte said.

"That," Marcus said, "is a considerable understatement."

"Indeed," Fitz murmured.

Kurot had expected to put them across Janus' supply line. Instead, with the entire left flank of the army swept away, Janus was now squarely astride theirs, between Marcus' troops and the road back to the Illifen passes and Vordan City. It hadn't even been a complicated trap, just a simple application of force at the enemy's weakest point. *Damn Kurot. I knew he was too clever for his own good.*

"Under other circumstances," Fitz said, "I'd say this was the time to start asking the enemy commander for terms of surrender."

"No," Marcus said. *Raesinia is counting on me. I'm not giving up yet.* "Not unless there's no other choice. Are you facing any pressure yet?"

"Nothing substantial," Fitz said. "But my flank is open. There's nothing stopping them from circling around and attacking from three sides."

"So we have to move before they can get themselves organized," Marcus said.

"Move *where*?" Cyte said. "You can't be thinking of attacking the city."

"And they'll be waiting for us to attack toward de Manzet," Fitz added. "Those troops along the river will pounce as soon as we turn our backs."

"So we hit them first," Marcus said. "Push right through them and cross the Daater. Then turn about and hold the line of the river against anyone who tries to follow."

Cyte frowned at the map. "Is there even a crossing?"

"Not a bridge," Marcus admitted. "But there's a couple of fords marked here."

"We'll never get wagons across," Fitz said. "And even the guns will be difficult."

"Forget the wagons. Once we're past the river, we can get fresh supplies from the towns to the south. Janus hasn't reached them yet. Their depots should still be full."

"Even if we manage it," Cyte said, "we won't hold the river line. Not for long. If nothing else, Janus can march down the Pale and outflank us."

"We'd have to fall back south," Fitz said.

"Exactly," Marcus said. "We'll retreat, as slowly as we can manage. As long as we keep him in play, Janus can't turn away and head for Vordan City without splitting his forces. That gives Queen Raesinia time to put together a defense."

Cyte shook her head. "You really think she can come up with something?"

"There are still troops coming in from the frontiers, recruits in training." Marcus gritted his teeth. "I'm not giving up unless she says so. This is the best we can do to help her."

"I agree," Fitz said. "But there's still at least a division in our way."

"Then let's get started."

Some hasty reorganization followed. The Girls' Own, driven by Abby and the shouts of dozens of frantic sergeants, double-timed back past the rest of the division, shifting the skirmish screen to the rear. A detachment went to the baggage troops, stripping the wagons of everything that could be carried and freeing the horses for use as pack animals. The light cavalry of the reserve remained on the left, sending regular reports on the steadily diminishing sounds of battle from the direction of de Manzet's divisions.

One of Fitz' regiments was assigned to the left as well, forming up to watch for any attempt by enemy infantry to push inward from that direction. Blackstream's regiment performed a similar duty on the right, facing the walls of Alves. That left five regiments—Sevran's, de Koste's, and three of Fitz'—to push forward. Opposing them were three regiments, which Marcus' scouts reported as being from the old Tenth Division. Marcus knew the commander, General Beaumartin, only distantly, but he wondered if the man was still in charge or if he'd been replaced with someone more pliable. *Or is he doing the job with glowing red eyes?*

Ten battalions against six. Not ideal odds, for an attack against a prepared enemy. Marcus' best asset was Give-Em-Hell and his horsemen. *If he can be persuaded to stick to the plan.* He'd given his orders, with particular emphasis on when to charge and when *not* to charge, and now all he could do was hope they'd be carried out.

There was no convenient hill close enough to get a good view, so Marcus' escort had commandeered a farmhouse, breaking down the door to find it empty. Marcus couldn't help but wince at the tromp of muddy boots over the neat rugs and well-swept floorboards. Upstairs, one of the two small bedrooms held a crib piled with stuffed animals, while the other was overrun with toy wooden soldiers. He wondered, briefly, where the family had gone. *Alves, probably.* But with Alves fallen to the enemy, who knew what was safe anymore?

Cyte found the trapdoor that led to the roof, and climbed the ladder ahead of him. The slate tiles were steeply sloped, forcing them to crawl on hands and knees to get to the edge. Then they sat, legs dangling, and Marcus produced his spyglass. In the yard below, a half dozen riders waited, ready to relay his messages.

At this point, though, that was mostly a formality. Trying to exert moment-to-moment control over an attack this size, with more than ten thousand men involved, was an exercise in futility. That was the job of the regimental and battalion commanders, and all he could do was trust that they did it properly. Marcus spent half his time looking north and east, waiting for the trouble he knew would come when Janus' victorious troops sorted themselves out and turned in his direction.

Artillery on both sides had already opened fire. The enemy had at least two batteries, smoke billowing from where the cannon were set in front of the infantry. Marcus' five regiments were arranged in a line, each with one battalion behind the other. For the moment they were still in column, the companies of each battalion stacked up one after the other for easy marching.

Archer's guns responded, blasting away at the enemy from in between the advancing columns. As at Satinvol, he kept half of them on the move while the other half fired, gradually closing the distance. That meant his fire was less effective, though, compounding the effect of the enemy's thinner formation. Columns might move faster, but when a plunging cannonball skipped through one, it could sweep away a dozen men at once, while the strung-out line the enemy had adopted meant a hit was far less devastating. Guns were more vulnerable on the move, too—Marcus saw one of Archer's six-pounder teams take a hit, the solid shot slamming through the horses and leaving gory wreckage in its wake.

A cloud of dust announced the arrival of Give-Em-Hell and his cuirassiers, their wedge-shaped formations pounding onto the battlefield on the extreme right. He was advancing slowly, keeping pace with the infantry. One by one, the enemy gunners shifted their fire—massed cavalry was a tempting target, even easier to hit than infantry in column. Balls crashed and bounced among the horsemen, and broken men and mounts began to litter the ground behind their advance, like a slow drip of blood from a wound. Injured men staggered away, looking for help, while broken animals ran wild or screamed their agony, their cries drowned under the ongoing cannonade.

Marcus felt his admiration for Give-Em-Hell ratchet up another notch. It couldn't have been easy to restrain himself under that fire, but the cavalry attack would be useless if it was pressed too early, before the toiling infantry had the chance to get into range. The horsemen continued their slow, measured advance, matching their pace to that of their comrades in the ranks.

Smoke obscured much of the enemy line, but there was enough of a breeze that Marcus could get an intermittent view. The dull *boom* and the flash of the guns changed timbre as the infantry reached four or five hundred yards and the artillery changed to canister, switching targets back from the cavalry pressing on the flanks. Sprays of musket balls cut swathes from the oncoming battalions, leaving corpses piled in mounds of blue. The ranks tightened up, Marcus' mind filling in the monotonous cries of the sergeants to close the gaps. *Nearly there.*

With Fitz' customary timing, his battalions halted to deploy into line, and Sevran and de Koste followed suit. Companies fanned out, marching sideways and then forward to convert the squat column into a long, thin formation that could bring maximum firepower to bear on the enemy. As they went through their evolution, canister and solid shot continued to rain down. Archer's guns moved forward while the infantry was halted, and they switched to canister themselves, spraying shot across the enemy line. *They're taking hits, too,* Marcus had to remind himself. It was always easier to see the effect on your own side than on the enemy.

He glanced at Cyte. She was looking to the east, where the Girls' Own was watching the rear.

"Anything?" he said.

"A little fighting, by the smoke," Cyte said. "Nothing serious yet."

Marcus nodded grimly and turned away. *All right, Give-Em-Hell. This is it.*

At the moment the infantry started to move forward again, Give-Em-Hell's men spurred their mounts, plunging ahead. They swept forward from the right of the infantry in a diagonal line, spreading out into separate wedges by squadron. Blasts of canister emptied saddles and sent horses crashing down in crimson ruin, but the momentum of the charge was too much to stop. As the cuirassiers closed, the cannoneers abandoned their pieces, scrambling back to take shelter among the infantry.

Well trained as they were, the enemy infantry formed themselves into squares, each battalion closing up into a rectangular diamond shape bristling on all sides with muskets and fixed bayonets. The cavalry flowed around these tight formations, unable to press their charge home into a wall of steel, and the rattle of muskets joined the sound of cannon as the squares opened fire. More cuirassiers fell, washing over the squares like a wave around standing rocks, then falling back in much the same fashion. The cavalry retreated in good order, though losses had clearly been heavy, and they'd failed to make any impression on the squares. Give-Em-Hell's men rallied outside of musket range, squadrons forming up again under the shouts of their officers.

The time they'd bought had been enough for the infantry to cover three hundred yards. As the enemy cannoneers hurried to return to their pieces, the lead friendly battalions halted and delivered a volley, scything through the artillerymen and sending many of them running back the way they'd come. Once they'd reloaded, the infantry continued to advance, until they were within easy musket shot of the enemy squares. Then, as the two formations faced off, the true killing began.

Marcus had been in this kind of fight before. It was like living in a nightmare, the world obscured by smoke, the enemy visible only by the flashes of their muskets. Men fell, shrieking or crying or with hardly a sound. There was no avoiding death, no dodging or parrying, just the mechanical drill of load, shoulder, and fire, hoping like hell that the enemy broke and ran.

Thanks to the cavalry charge, however, Marcus' troops had a distinct advantage in firepower. They already had more battalions engaged, and the enemy were formed in squares, with half their weapons pointing uselessly to the rear. The opposing battalion commanders could try to re-form their units under fire, a difficult task at the best of times, but they risked opening themselves up to another sudden charge from Give-Em-Hell, whose men hovered off to one side waiting for the opportunity. To make matters worse, Archer's guns were close now, slamming double canister into the tightly packed squares.

They didn't have things entirely their own way—one of Fitz' battalions broke, formation disintegrating as its men fled for the rear—but in the end the pressure told. One by one the squares began to waver and then to give way, walls of bayonets faltering as soldiers ran from the unrelenting storm of shot. Marcus watched them go, and found himself smiling as he mouthed words along with the distant cavalry commander.

"All right, boys, give 'em hell!"

The cuirassiers swept forward, crashing among the disorganized, routing enemy to complete their destruction, slashing left and right with their sabers. There wasn't much room for the panicking soldiers to run, with the river Daater so close behind them. Where they bunched up, the cavalry surrounded them, and Marcus saw large groups throwing down their weapons in surrender.

"Sir," Cyte said. "I think it's starting."

He turned around. Powder smoke was rising all along the line in the rear, and the sound of artillery, so lately fallen silent ahead of them, was now taken up behind.

"Saints and martyrs," Marcus muttered. "It would have been nice to have a little rest."

This late in the season, the Daater was wide but slow. Even still, what was marked on the map as a ford was barely shallower than the rest of the river, and the scouts Marcus sent across were wet to their armpits when they reached the other side.

"Not going to be easy," Fitz said.

They were standing on the riverbank, with Give-Em-Hell, Cyte, and a small escort of troopers. The crossing was a little upriver from where the fighting had been, but there were still blue-uniformed bodies scattered here and there, cut down by the cavalry in the pursuit. Musketry cracked and rattled behind them, as the Girls' Own gave ground.

"We need to make sure nobody gets ahead of us." Marcus shook out the map. "There's a bridge upriver at Mezk, and another crossing of the Pale down at Josper. Our only safety is going to come from staying far enough ahead of Janus' army that they can't surround us." He looked at Give-Em-Hell. "Pull your light cavalry back and put them across the river as fast as you can. Split them into two divisions and have them block those two bridges. Destroy them if you can, but if they're defended, just block the crossing." He shook his head. "I know I'm asking a lot of you and your men. Again."

"My boys are up to it," Give-Em-Hell said, eyes twinkling. "What about the heavy divisions?"

"They cross next and form up on the far bank. If any enemy make it to the crossing—" Marcus grinned. "You know what to do."

"Right! Understood, sir."

Marcus turned to Cyte. "Send to Archer. I want his guns across as soon as the cavalry is clear. If they get stuck, use men from the infantry to help haul them, whatever it takes. Set up on the far side to support the crossing."

That wouldn't hold for long. Two batteries of cannon could make the crossing hot, but Janus could bring up enough guns of his own to smother them with fire. The majority of the Army of the Republic's cannon had been with the army reserve, and that had been supporting de Manzet. *If Janus captured the whole thing, he won't be short of artillery.*

"After the guns," he went on, "the infantry start crossing, carrying our supplies." Some gear—tents and uniforms, sealed barrels of salted meat—could stand a ducking. Those would be easiest. Others, especially powder, the men would have to carry above their heads to keep dry. "We'll contract the perimeters as we get men across. The Girls' Own will bring up the rear."

Cyte nodded and hurried off. Give-Em-Hell was already dictating orders to his own officers. Marcus caught Fitz' eye.

"Damned fine work, that last attack," he said. "That could have been a lot worse."

"Thank you, sir," Fitz said. "I'll pass that along to my men." He paused. "How long do you plan to stay ahead of Janus?"

"As long as we can," Marcus said. "We've got plenty of room to maneuver. How far is it to Enzport?"

"Three hundred fifty miles, give or take," Fitz said.

"If he follows us that far, *then* we can surrender," Marcus said. "But he won't. Destroying this army won't win him the war. He won't let himself be distracted from the prize."

Fitz nodded. Marcus looked down at the map again.

"God damn," he muttered. "I feel like I'm back in Murnsk." *Retreating over another river, watching a wall of water bear down on me—*

"You got your men out of that," Fitz said. "You'll get them out of this, too."

"I didn't get them all out," Marcus said quietly. *Not Andy, and not a lot of the others.*

"At least this time," Fitz said, "a flash flood seems unlikely."

Marcus refrained from saying that it had seemed unlikely *then*, too. In any event, the weather showed no signs of supernatural meddling as the retreat went on. The light cavalry streamed past, a river of men on horseback, each squadron with a string of remounts bringing up the rear. They saluted or waved their carbines to Marcus as they went past. The heavy cavalry followed, splashing water dampening the battle-stained cuirassiers' brightly colored uniforms.

As he'd predicted, getting the guns across was the biggest headache. The river bottom was soft and muddy, and the small six-pounders were submerged to the axle. Again and again, they got stuck and had to be hauled out by teams of heaving infantrymen with ropes. In the end, though, they lost only one, a twelve-pounder whose axle snapped when it became inextricably mired in the mud. Marcus ordered it abandoned, and the retreat went on.

All this time, from the north, the sound of musketry got closer. Fitz ordered one of his regiments to disperse as skirmishers, to thicken the line of the Girls' Own, while the rest of the troops made the slow crossing. It wasn't long before the smoke of the running firefight came into view, then the soldiers themselves, men and women stopping to load, fire, and then run back to the next piece of cover as answering flashes came from the hedges and fencerows.

If Janus had possessed a good cavalry division, he might have been able to punch through the skirmish screen and strike at the vulnerable, disorganized troops making the crossing. But the cavalry reserve had remained loyal to Give-Em-Hell. Marcus kept a few squadrons of cuirassiers on the near bank, to counterattack if Janus decided to try something, but the assault never came. For the most part, the enemy seemed satisfied with their day's work. *As well they might be.* At least two-thirds of the Army of the Republic was scattered or captured, with the remaining third in full flight away from the capital.

The sun was sinking toward the horizon when the last of the infantry started the crossing. The wounded who could be moved had already been evacuated with the cutters. Those who couldn't, or who weren't expected to survive, had been left behind in the company of a few volunteers to surrender. Abby finally arrived, with the last few companies of her soldiers, as the sky flamed red. She had a bloody bandage on one arm and was coated from head to toe in powder grime.

"Sir!" She saluted despite her injury. "This is the last of us."

Marcus looked over the few dozen women who accompanied her. There were a few men in cavalry uniforms, too, though their horses were nowhere to be seen.

"Time to put a river between us and them, I think," Marcus said. "Are you all right to cross, or do you need to ride?"

Abby looked at the bandage on her arm and snorted. "I'm fine, sir. Cutter just a got a little overenthusiastic." She hesitated. "You should know, sir. Colonel Erdine brought some of his men up to reinforce the line. He was hit while we were falling back. He's . . . dead, sir."

Erdine, the cocksure cavalryman with the plumed hat. *Her lover.* Marcus shook his head. "I'm sorry."

"Goddamned gallant idiot," Abby said, quiet enough that Marcus wasn't certain he'd been supposed to hear. She took a deep breath and raised her voice. "All right! Everyone, over the river!"

Marcus waded across himself with the rest of them, the water warmer than he'd expected. On the other bank, they were lighting torches as the sun faded. Cannon were parked atop the riverbank, silent sentinels watching for anyone who might try to follow.

Marcus didn't think they would, not here and not tonight. *But they'll come. And we'll buy time.*

I just hope Raesinia can do something with it.

CHAPTER SIXTEEN

WINTER

Just after midnight, Winter, Alex, and Abraham left the abandoned Haeta camp and struck out through the forest, swinging wide to avoid running into Vess and her band. After a lengthy detour, they turned toward the fortress again, breaking out of the tree line and crossing the clear ground close to the river. There was a jumble of rocks here to use as cover, and the sentries on the wall were easily visible by the light of their torches. By timing their moves as the men made their rounds they were able to reach the base of the log palisade without being spotted.

"Take Abraham up," Winter told Alex. "I can climb the rope."

Alex nodded, and Abraham, looking resigned, suffered himself to be once again tucked under her arm. A beam of darkness anchored them to the wall with a soft *crunch* of wood, and Alex let it take her weight as she walked up one of the logs. Winter pressed herself tight against the wall, listening. She heard a gasp, then a *thump*, but no screams. A moment later, a knotted rope hit her on the shoulder, and she began to climb. Her legs still screamed at the effort. *Maybe I should have had Alex carry me, instead.*

At the top, Alex and Abraham stood on the wall walk over the sprawled body of a uniformed Murnskai guard. Alex shrugged apologetically.

"He was waiting on the steps," she said. "I don't think he managed to warn anybody."

"Is he dead?" Winter said, stretching her legs as cramps threatened her aching muscles.

"Just asleep," Abraham said. He looked uncomfortable. "My power can be . . . applied to things other than healing, in an emergency."

"This whole damned trip is an emergency," Alex said.

"If it means we don't have to kill the people we're trying to help, I'm all for it," Winter said. "Come on—let's get off this wall and under cover."

Inside, the fortress was less organized than it appeared. The central building was three stories tall, made of stone and clearly a military structure. But the space inside the walls was crowded with smaller buildings, wooden shacks, lean-tos, and tents. Some had the uniform look of army-issue shelters, but most did not. A few fires were still burning, and Winter could see people sitting around them, despite the late hour. *Keeping watch?*

"Camp followers?" Alex guessed.

"More likely refugees," Abraham said. "Between the weather and the Beast, people are scared. Some of them probably fled to the nearest army post."

Winter guessed their number at a few hundred, along with perhaps a hundred soldiers. A rickety wooden stair led down from the wall walk and into the camp, and she threaded her way among the tight-packed shelters. The presence of the refugees was helpful—it meant, if they were careful, no one would automatically assume they were intruders. *Now if we can only find what we're looking for.*

She wasn't sure, exactly, what they *were* looking for. Something about the way the sergeant had reacted to Kollowrath, as well as her own experience with aristocratic senior officers, told her that the bulk of the garrison probably wasn't particularly dedicated to the captain. *If I can convince them that the Beast is coming and that we all need to flee together . . .*

"There's the ships," Alex said. "Plenty of guards, though."

The stone pier on which the two sailing vessels were docked was indeed heavily guarded, with a couple of bright lanterns and at least eight men on watch. *They're worried about the refugees trying to steal the ships.* Unless they decided to simply attack the garrison, there would be no sneaking out that way.

"We need information," Winter muttered. "Follow my lead, and try to look pathetic."

Alex looked down at her battered clothes, then over at Abraham. "That shouldn't be hard."

Winter picked a fire with only one person beside it, an old man in creased leathers, with a long rifle leaning against his shoulder. He wore a fur hat and had long, greasy gray hair. She saw him tense as they approached, then relax slightly, his hand falling away from the rifle.

"Hello, friends," he said in Murnskai. Winter silently gave thanks that she'd been practicing with the Haeta. "I don't know you."

"We just arrived," Winter said. "May we share your fire for a few minutes?"

He gestured laconically. Winter sat, the heat feeling good on her aching legs, and Alex and Abraham settled down beside her. The old man looked at them curiously.

"You're a long way from home," he said.

"That's the truth," Winter said, nodding. "I've been traveling a long time."

"Going somewhere?"

"Just . . . away."

"I know that feeling," the old man said. He grinned, showing a total of perhaps five remaining teeth. "I'm Fyotyr."

"Winter," Winter said. "I wanted to ask you a few questions, if I could. About what's going on here. I didn't expect there to be so many people."

"No one did. Everyone thought they were the only one with the idea of running to the army when the summer froze or when the demons came stalking." Fyotyr spat into the fire with a sizzle. "I've been to the garrison many times. It's on my route east, when I go that way. But I've never seen it like this."

"What are the soldiers going to do with everyone?"

"They don't know, God help them." Fyotyr shook his head. "That bastard Kollowrath would put everyone out of the gate and let the demons take them, but Lieutenant Dobraev and Sergeant Gorchov have more sense. If it were up to Dobraev, we'd have been gone from here days ago, but Kollowrath insists on waiting for orders from high command. Orders!" He snorted. "The world has gone to hell—anyone should be able to see that. Blizzards and demons and now Vhalnich says he's the new emperor. What's the sense of holding down a little fort in the middle of nowhere?"

Dobraev. As she'd expected, that was the man she needed to talk to. *It sounds like he already wants to evacuate. We just need to convince him to take us along.*

"Why is there such a heavy guard on the boats?" Alex said. "Are they afraid someone is going to steal them?"

"Some of the refugees already tried," Fyotyr said. "Kollowrath was furious. He ordered the sails and oars stripped and stored in the keep so it wouldn't happen again. I think he's terrified but can't bring himself to admit it."

"What about this morning?" Winter said. "Somebody told me there was an incident."

"Some savages wanted to take shelter." Fyotyr shrugged. "I heard it was a trick. Two soldiers were killed. Now we have them to worry about, on top of the demons."

"You don't seem very concerned," Abraham said mildly.

"Eh," the old man said, "I've seen worse days. This is Murnsk. If we got excited over every little catastrophe, we'd never be stopping." He leaned forward. "Now, what brought you all the way out here?"

Winter spun him a tale about sick parents, a trek for medicine, and a journey that went awry in foul weather, with Alex adding a few creative details where necessary. It seemed to satisfy Fyotyr, who nodded solemnly.

"You're a good child," he said. "If only my own sons had such respect for their father."

"I don't even know if Mother is still alive," Winter said. "If I can get back to Dimiotsk, then I can find my way home."

"Well. You're safer in here than out there, but I wouldn't count on leaving anytime soon. The worse things get, the more that stubborn bastard Kollowrath will dig in his heels." He waved a hand. "If you've got tents, spread them anywhere there's room."

"We will." Winter hesitated, then decided to push her luck. "Can you tell me where Lieutenant Dobraev is? I wanted to ask him for news of the army. I have a brother, you see."

Fyotyr frowned and pointed. "That's his shack over there. But don't wake him; he's worse than a bear. Try to catch him after breakfast."

"Thank you." Winter yawned. "We'd better find a little space for ourselves."

"Check the west wall. It's close to the privies, so the smell isn't great, but there should be room."

Fyotyr grinned, and Winter smiled back. She and the others slipped into the darkness, passing between tents and lean-tos until they were well out of sight of the old man.

"We're not actually going to sleep next to the toilets, are we?" Alex said.

"I think we may not be getting a lot of sleep tonight." Winter looked up at the keep, its solid stone bulk looming over the rest of the encampment. *That's where Kollowrath will be.* "First we need to have a chat with this Lieutenant Dobraev."

Dobraev had one of the nicer shacks, as befit an officer. It was built against the east wall, leaning on the palisade for support, tucked in neatly underneath the wall walk. Unlike most of the others, it had been there for some time, and someone had tried to make it proof against the elements. It was built out of awkwardly split logs, with the gaps stuffed with rags and a doorway covered by half a rug nailed to the top of the frame. It was big enough that Winter guessed it might even have two rooms.

A corporal stood by the door, hands cupped around a twist of something he was smoking. He wore Murnskai white, with a nonregulation fur cap on his head and a musket slung over his back. Winter didn't think he was much of a threat, but they couldn't afford for him to raise the alarm.

"How long will someone stay out when you do that sleep trick?" Winter said.

"As long as I want," Abraham whispered. "Up to maybe six hours."

"And how long does it take?"

"Once I'm touching them, just a couple of seconds."

"Good. Give our friend here a nap while I distract him."

Abraham nodded, face twisted as though he'd eaten something sour. *He doesn't like doing this.* Winter could understand that, but she was glad he was willing to work through his moral scruples when it counted. She took a deep breath and walked up to the guard, giving him an openly appraising look.

"Hello, Corporal."

The man—boy, really—frowned and pinched his smoke between two fingers. "Do I know you?"

"My masters and I came in last night," Winter improvised, "and we've got wares to sell. I see you're . . ." She waggled her eyebrows at the twisted paper, not really knowing if it was stuffed with tobacco or something more exotic.

The corporal grinned. "Oh, you're a saint. This is my last pinch." Then his eyes narrowed. "How much will it cost?"

"Not much," Winter said, as Abraham came up behind the boy and put one hand on his shoulder. The corporal started, then sagged, his eyes rolling up in his head. Before he hit the ground Winter caught him and dragged him into the shadows beside the shack.

"You two should do this sort of work more often," Alex said, strolling up behind them. "I could have used you back in my thieving days."

Winter rolled her eyes. She pushed the rug aside a fraction and found that a faint light emerged from within. There was a quiet clatter and the slosh of water.

"Someone's awake," she said. "Stay here until I call."

"What if he gives the alarm?" Alex said.

"Then we're in big trouble." Winter pushed the rug up and slipped underneath, as quietly as she could.

The interior of the shack was only dimly lit. As Winter blinked, she made out a very small iron stove with a tiny flame flickering in its box and a pot of water on top of it. A big man with a full, bushy beard crouched in front of it, dressed only in a nightshirt. He puffed gently into the firebox, encouraging the flame to catch.

Winter drew her pistol, aimed, and said quietly, "I'd really prefer not to kill you, but I will if I have to. Please stay quiet."

The man froze, hands on either side of the firebox. He turned his head, far enough to see the weapon in her hand.

"Stand up and raise your hands slowly," Winter said. "I promise you I just want to talk. If you don't do anything stupid, you won't get hurt."

He hesitated for a moment, and she could see that he was calculating the odds. Grab the firebox, fling it at her, dive out of the way—what would happen? *Nothing good,* she thought. *You have to know that.*

The man stood up. To Winter's surprise, she recognized him—he'd been the sergeant accompanying Kollowrath that morning. *The one who at least tried to stop this mess.*

"Where's Lieutenant Dobraev?" Winter said.

The sergeant stiffened. "If you want him, you'll have to go through me. Shoot and you'll have the whole camp down on you."

Now that her eyes had adjusted, Winter could see she'd been right about there being two rooms in the shack. The one they were in had the little stove, a larger fire pit beside it, and a few boxes and supply crates arranged to form a table. Another curtained doorway led to the other room, up against the palisade wall.

"You're the woman from this morning," the sergeant said. "The one who was with the savages."

"And you were with Kollowrath," Winter said. "Before the shooting started."

He frowned. "You killed two of my men."

"And your men killed three of my friends." Winter swallowed. "It was a mistake. Your captain is to blame, if anyone is."

"How did you get inside?"

"We'll get to that. You're Sergeant Gorchov?"

He nodded slowly.

"I'm Winter Ihernglass. Please believe me when I say I don't want to hurt anybody here."

"That's a little difficult to stomach when you have a pistol in my face."

"Would you have spoken to me if I didn't, or just called for the guard?"

"Fair, I suppose." His face darkened. "What did you do to Vlissy? If you've hurt him—"

"He'll be fine. He's just asleep, for now. My friends are keeping watch outside."

"More savages?"

"No." Winter fought down a twinge of guilt. "These are . . . other friends. Now, I really need to speak to Lieutenant Dobraev. Is he here?"

"Kila?" Another man's voice came from behind the curtain. "What's going on?"

"Nothing, Byr," Gorchov said. "Just making a cup of tea."

There were a couple of footsteps, and then the curtain was pulled aside. A younger man, blond, pale, and completely naked, blinked in the light and froze when he saw Winter.

"Tell him to stay quiet," Winter hissed.

"Don't scream, Byr," Gorchov said. "Not yet, anyway."

"Who exactly are you?" The young man, presumably the lieutenant, mustered as much dignity as he could given his state. "What are you doing here?"

"I'm trying to save everyone in this garrison," Winter said, letting a little bit of her frustration into her voice. "If I put the pistol down, do you think we could have a talk about that without anyone doing anything stupid?"

The two soldiers looked at each other, and Gorchov shrugged. "Your call, Byr."

"I think I would like that tea," Dobraev said. "And some pants, if the young lady wouldn't mind."

Winter felt obligated to watch Dobraev dress, in case he took the opportunity to try to send for help. The second room was just a messy sleeping area, with a single huge bearskin apparently standing in for a bedroll. Dobraev pulled on his trousers and a white uniform shirt, then came back into the other room amiably enough. Gorchov was at work on the firebox again, and Alex and Abraham sat at the makeshift table.

"Winter Ihernglass," Dobraev said. "Kila told me what you said this morning, about someone coming to attack the fortress."

"It's true," Winter said. "And you're not going to be able to stop them when they get here."

"No bandits have ever been bold enough to raid a garrison," Dobraev said.

"These aren't bandits. They're kind of . . . fanatics." Winter struggled for something the two men would believe. "After the weather and the war, lots of people have been displaced. Some of them have fallen in with a cult. They've been grabbing everyone they can and killing everyone who won't convert."

The two soldiers exchanged glances, and Gorchov nodded slowly.

"I've heard of things like that," he said. "In Novhora, when they had that terrible winter, they found whole villages turned to worshipping idols. Doing sacrifices in front of them."

"Why?" Dobraev said. By his accent, Winter guessed he was city-born. His speech was different from Gorchov's and the other locals'.

"People do stupid things when they get desperate." Gorchov turned back to Winter. "You really think they could take the fortress?"

"They're crazy, and there are a hell of a lot of them," Winter said. "We've been running for weeks, and they're not far behind us."

"Who are 'we'?" Dobraev said. "This morning I heard you had a bunch of Trans-Batariai. Now you have these two."

"The people who were with us this morning are called the Haeta," Winter said. "My friends and I have been traveling with them until now."

"Abandoned you, have they?" Gorchov said. "The savages can't really be counted on."

"They want to kill you all," Winter said bluntly. "As revenge for what you did this morning. One of the girls who died was their leader, and her sister is in charge now."

"We didn't intend to hurt anyone," Gorchov said. "And we lost men, too."

"I *know*," Winter said. She gritted her teeth hard enough that it brought tears to her eyes. "I'm just trying to get everyone through this, and killing one another isn't going to help." She gestured at Alex and Abraham. "That's why we're here. We came over the wall to see if we could work things out before the shooting starts."

"You came over the wall?" Dobraev said. "Just like that?"

"Alex is a thief," Winter said.

"The greatest thief in the world, actually," Alex said, cracking her knuckles. "This wasn't exactly a challenge."

"And you?" Gorchov said to Abraham. "I suppose you're the world's greatest lover?"

"I'm a healer," Abraham said. "And . . . a priest, of a sort."

"A thief, a priest, and . . . whatever you are," Gorchov said, looking back to Winter. "You come out of the wilderness with a mad warning, and you want us to—what?"

"Get everyone on the ships," Winter said. "Invite my Haeta friends inside as well. Get us all downriver and away from the crazy bastards behind us."

"Madness," Gorchov said. "We'd have to load the ships to the rails, and there'd be no room for supplies. We'd have to leave our guns, ammunition, everything."

"You'd be alive," Winter said. "Which is more than I can say for you if you stay here."

"You have to understand," Dobraev said contemplatively, "that this is no small thing you're asking."

"I understand," Winter said. "But you must know no orders are coming. Murnsk is in chaos. I doubt anyone remembers you're still here."

"It's a moot point in any case," Gorchov said. He turned to the firebox, where the pot had finally begun to boil, and began scooping the hot water into tin cups. "Kollowrath will never listen. Even if he believed there was an army of madmen coming, he'd say it was our duty to defend our posts."

"You don't agree, though," Winter said. "What purpose would it serve for you to die here?"

"It has been suggested," Dobraev said carefully, "among the common soldiers, that we would be better off moving to Dimiotsk. But the captain has made it clear that he views any such suggestion as mutinous."

"What if you were in command?" Winter said. "What would you do?"

Time seemed to stretch thin. Gorchov froze, a cup in each hand. Winter watched Dobraev's face. The young man gave very little away, but she could see the struggle.

"That seems unlikely," he said eventually.

"If something happened to Kollowrath—" Alex said.

Dobraev turned to her. "I'm not stupid, young lady. Nor am I entirely without honor. I will not sit and listen to you speak of murdering my superior officer, no matter how . . . misguided he may be."

"Besides," Gorchov said, "people here are on edge as it is. If the captain were found dead, this place would go mad."

Winter closed her eyes and thought hard. She'd read the Vordanai army regulations cover to cover, back when she'd thought they would be important for impersonating a soldier. Since then she'd learned that it was a rare ranker who even glanced at that dusty tome, but some of it had stuck with her.

"There must be circumstances under which Kollowrath would have to hand over command," she said. "If he were to be incapacitated with illness, say, authority would automatically descend to you as next ranking officer."

Gorchov finished with the tea and handed Winter a tin cup, almost too hot to touch. She rested it on one knee, still watching the lieutenant.

"If . . . that were to happen," Dobraev said, as though the words cost him a great deal, "then I would obviously have to evaluate the strategic situation. Including any intelligence about approaching enemy forces."

"And, speaking purely hypothetically, would you be willing to grant your protection to a group of Trans-Batariai?"

"In light of the . . . tragic incident this morning," Dobraev said, "I would feel honor bound to offer my assistance."

"Interesting," Winter said.

"Hypothetically," Dobraev said wretchedly. He glanced at Gorchov, who gave a shrug and handed him a tin cup.

Winter took a sip. The tea was really quite good.

"I'm sorry," Winter told Abraham, outside the shack. "I know you don't like doing this."

He sighed. "My goal is to save lives. Sometimes, in pursuit of that, I am required to do . . . a little harm." He flexed his fingers.

"You're sure you can do it?"

"Oh, yes. The only delicate thing is making sure the illness isn't a fatal one. Kollowrath seemed relatively young and fit?"

"From the little I saw of him."

"I, for one, wouldn't mind if you messed up," Alex said. "If the fight this morning really was his fault."

Winter had to admit she'd had that same thought. *Maybe we shouldn't have told Dobraev anything, and just made it look like Kollowrath died naturally.* But there would have been no guarantee then that anyone would listen to them. *And now we've tipped our hand. Dobraev is bright and honest. A dangerous combination, if he's not on board.*

"I'll wait here," Winter said. "Get it done as fast as you can. We're running out of darkness."

Alex nodded and loped off into the shadows, Abraham following at a more dignified pace. Winter settled her back against the palisade, staring up at the stone keep and fighting off exhaustion. She hadn't slept since the previous evening, not counting a few hours of exhausted unconsciousness. Every part of her ached, and her eyelids kept slipping downward.

She caught a glimpse of a dark shape clinging to the outside of the keep, but only for a moment. Winter tried to calm her racing heart. *Greatest thief in the world, remember? This is a walk in the park for her.*

At some point she must have dozed, because the next thing she knew her eyes snapped open at the sounds of footsteps. Alex was returning, grinning like a cat, with Abraham in tow.

"*No* problem," she said. "The shutters weren't even *locked*. I swear, people put a guard at the door and think they're safe; it's ridiculous."

"You did it?" Winter said.

Abraham nodded. "He'll be unconscious for at least a few days, and feverish for a while after that. But he'll live, if someone takes care of him."

"I'm sure Lieutenant Dobraev will make sure that happens."

"Now what?" Alex said.

Winter shook her head grimly. "Now for the hard part."

Alex once again lifted them over the wall, this time without Abraham having to incapacitate a guard. They crossed the cleared ground around the fortress as dawn was breaking and regained the cover of the trees. Alex led the way to where the Haeta were waiting, gathered at the edge of the woods to gauge the Murnskai defenses.

"I don't know what Vess has told them," Winter said. "So be careful—"

Wham. A spear sprouted, as if by magic, from the trunk of a tree just beside Winter's head, the shaft vibrating from the force of the throw. Two Haeta girls rose out of the underbrush, weapons ready. Alex raised her hands, but Winter threw up an arm to stop her.

"That was a warning," one of the girls said. "In deference to what you did for us. Vess has said you are no longer welcome."

"I need to speak with her," Winter said. "Please."

"She will not talk to you," the girl said.

"*Please,*" Winter said. "You're . . . Ceft, aren't you? And Huld, I remember the story you told the night after the wolves. The sad one, about the girl and the wolf-boy."

Ceft lowered her spear a fraction. "She has made herself clear."

"She's not thinking straight, and she's going to get you all killed," Winter said. "You see that. There's a hundred soldiers in that fortress, and hundreds more civilians. You can't fight them *all*."

"We can try," Huld said.

"Just take me to Vess. That's all I ask. If she doesn't want to talk to me, that's her decision."

The pair looked at each other. Ceft nodded slowly.

"These two will remain," she said. "Huld, watch them."

"Winter?" Alex said. "I don't like it. If Vess decides she wants to hold you responsible for Leti—"

"I know."

"You have more than your own life to worry about," Abraham said quietly. "Don't forget that."

"I *know*." Rationally, this was a poor decision. *We should have killed the guards, stolen a boat, and been away from here already.* But Leti and the Haeta had helped her, and Leti had paid the price that people who helped her always seemed to pay. *I'm not going to let her sister and her friends die, too.* "I'll be back soon."

Ceft stowed her spear and led Winter on through the forest. More Haeta were waiting, resting against rocks and trees, eating what was left of their dried food, and maintaining their weapons. They all looked at Winter as she approached, though she couldn't say what emotion she saw in their features. A few called to Ceft in their own language, but she waved them away.

"I told you she wasn't welcome here."

Vess was crouched in the dirt with two of the older warriors, sketching crude maps with a stick. She stood when she saw Winter, face frozen hard.

"I told her I wanted a chance to talk to you," Winter said, before Vess could take out her anger on Ceft.

"Then you've wasted your time," Vess said. "Leti listened to you and ended up dead. We're done taking your *advice*."

"So you're going to get yourself killed instead?" Winter spoke loudly enough that the whole group could hear. "You know that attacking the fortress is suicide. You're that eager to take a few Murnskai soldiers with you?"

"What choice do we have?" Vess snarled. "The red-eyes are close behind us, and ahead is only the river. I would prefer to fight my sister's killers and drag a few of them to hell than be devoured by demons."

"The man who killed your sister is *dead*, Vess. Yath put a spear through his throat." In truth, Winter didn't know that for sure—in the confusion of the fight, she had no idea whose shot had cut Leti down. "Yesterday morning was . . . awful. But it doesn't mean every Murnskai soldier deserves to die, any more than you do for killing some of them."

Vess snorted. "Words. We see where that got Leti."

"I can get you on the ships," Winter said, again loudly enough for everyone to hear. "All of you. You don't have to die here."

"Winter carried me from the field." Yath dropped down from a tree branch. One leg of her trousers was still ripped and stained with blood. "She ran here to fetch Abraham, and only by his power am I alive."

Vess turned on her. "And so you would follow her? Was being shot so exciting you're eager to repeat the experience?"

"The enemy commander," Yath said to Winter, ignoring Vess. "Kollow-rath. The one who said we would have to sell our bodies for safety. He was at the root of the killing."

"I know," Winter said. "Last night Abraham paid him a visit. He's no longer in command."

A murmur ran through the Haeta. Vess looked back and forth, furious.

"I've spoken to the new commander, Lieutenant Dobraev," Winter went on. "He's promised shelter and passage across the river for all of you."

"Lies," Vess said weakly.

Winter leaned close to her and spoke quietly. "Why would I lie, Vess? What would I have to gain? If we wanted to leave you behind, we could have done that already. I want to *help* you, damn it."

Vess' fists were clenched, but her eyes were bright with tears. "You should have helped my sister."

"I should have done a better job," Winter said. "But it's for her sake I'm here. She wouldn't want the rest of you to die."

"You don't get to talk about what she would have wanted."

"Then tell me I'm wrong."

Tears started to leak from the corners of Vess' eyes. She crouched, clutching her knees, head bowed, as sobs racked her small body. Winter looked to Yath, who sat down next to the girl and put an arm around her.

"Go and tell the white-coats we are coming," Yath said, to murmurs of assent from the others. "We don't want any more surprises."

Once again the two sides faced off in the tall grass outside the gates of the fortress.

This time all the Haeta were there. Twenty-nine young women, spears in their hands, standing in a single tight knot except for Vess and Yath, who came forward to speak to the Murnskai. Across from them stood Lieutenant Dobraev, unarmed. Winter knew that Sergeant Gorchov was waiting back at the gate with another detachment. She'd left Alex and Abraham there, too. *Hopefully, they can keep anyone from doing anything rash.*

"You command here?" Vess said. In the few hours since their last meeting, she'd regained her composure, though her eyes were still red. She avoided Winter's gaze, staring instead at Dobraev.

"I do," the lieutenant said. "Captain Kollowrath has been . . . taken ill."

"We wish only your help to pass to the other side of the river in safety."

"I believe I'm prepared to grant that," Dobraev said with a slight smile. He glanced briefly at Winter. "You're welcome to take shelter inside the walls until we've got the ships ready."

"We will not be attacked?" Vess said. "Not pressed into . . . service?"

"I give you my word as an officer," Dobraev said.

Vess nodded and took a long breath.

"I am sorry," she said, after a moment. "For your men who died yesterday."

"And I am sorry for your friends," the lieutenant said.

"Winter!" Alex shouted.

Oh, hell. Now what? Winter looked back to the gate and saw the girl sprinting toward her. She was gesturing wildly toward the forest. With a frown, Winter turned.

Points of light appeared among the trees, two by two, the malevolent crimson of a banked flame. First a dozen, then a hundred, on and on, spreading out along the tree line.

Oh, saints and goddamned martyrs. It knows we're getting away, and it's not going to wait.

"What the hell is that?" Dobraev said, following her gaze. The Haeta were already shouting to one another.

"Everyone inside!" Winter shouted. *"Now!"*

PART THREE

INTERLUDE

JANUS

Through one set of eyes, Janus watched long lines of blue-coated infantry marching wearily down the road. Through another, he saw colonels and generals debating at a map table, and he offered a few choice suggestions. Another, and he could ascertain personally how much progress a flanking column had made, and then back to the map table to update the estimate of their arrival.

It was the dream of every general since the beginning of time. To be everywhere, to see everything, to be able to speak across the miles without delay or fear of interception. To learn things as they happened, not hours later and filtered through the eyes and understanding of others.

He felt like a god.

This is all I would need. All the other powers the Beast possessed—its ability to take control of new bodies, the depth of knowledge it had gained from its thousand-year existence, everything—were unnecessary. *Communication, information, is* everything. *This is all I would need to conquer the world.*

He felt a moment's pity for poor Marcus d'Ivoire. The man was perfectly competent, and under ordinary circumstances Janus would have enjoyed the chance to match wits against him, though of course the outcome would be a forgone conclusion. But with the near omniscience of the Beast behind him, there was simply no contest. It was like fighting a blindfolded opponent.

The only thing that could catch him off guard was the Beast itself. He knew it was watching him, making sure he conducted the campaign in its interest. But he hadn't expected its sudden rage, pushing all the red-eyes in Satinvol in a desperate attempt to get to Marcus. Nor had he thought the Beast could capture new bodies at such long range, though he suspected the effort had cost it a great deal of energy. *It is not to be underestimated.*

Now its primary focus had withdrawn again, back to the north, where the pursuit of Winter Ihernglass was coming to a head. There was nothing Janus could do there beyond what he'd done already, not with the Beast paying such close attention; he could only put his trust in others, and hope. *Winter hasn't let me down so far.*

Instead, he took the opportunity to work on his letter. It was tricky work, since the Beast always watched him most carefully when he made use of his original body. A few words here and a few words there were all he could manage, written in haste when the demon's focus was otherwise engaged. He hoped the result would be legible.

"What are you doing?"

It was Jane's *voice*, inasmuch as there were such things in the strange mindscape of the Beast. Janus saw her hovering nearby, another miniature whirlwind like himself, held together by sheer force of will. *And, perhaps, madness.* What Jane had managed was even more impressive than his own survival—she'd apparently extricated herself from the Beast's core. *I suppose it no longer cares about her.*

"The Beast has found me useful," Janus said. "It cannot split its attention, so it has delegated some relatively unimportant tasks to me. I am prosecuting the campaign against the Vordanai army."

"You're killing them. Your old companions."

"It is my area of expertise," Janus said. "If I am not useful, I will be torn to pieces, as you well know."

"You'll be torn apart in the end anyway," Jane said tauntingly. "We all will. Our only peace will be inside the Beast."

"Perhaps. I choose to delay my fate a little longer, if I can."

"Why?"

"Why does anyone live another day when they'll have to die eventually?" If he'd had a body, Janus would have shrugged. "What are *you* doing, Jane Verity? I thought you had achieved your peace already."

"Winter will be here soon. The Beast will take her."

It will try. "I understand that's what's consuming its attention." He paused. "Is that it? You don't want to watch?"

"It will be . . . hard for her. At first."

Janus laughed. "As I thought. You truly are a coward, aren't you?"

"What?"

"You told me this was for her sake. That you and Winter could be together here, and happy. But you know, if you're honest with yourself, that it isn't true. Winter would never submit to the Beast, as you and I have. She will fight until there is nothing left of her but scraps."

"I will find the scraps," Jane said. "I will find her. I have until the end of time."

"Of course. Better that than risk her rejecting you again."

"She only rejected me because of *you*," Jane said. "Because you twisted her mind."

"Deceive yourself if you like," Janus said. "I know Winter better than that. Better, it seems, than you do, if you think she'll ever be happy here, as part of a monster."

"I will have her," Jane said. "Forever. And that's the end of it."

"Whether she wants you or not?"

"She wants me!" The last word rose to a screech, and Jane vanished, her whirlwind self zipping across the non-space. Janus watched her for a moment, then returned to his task.

In the real world, Janus bet Vhalnich picked up a pen and, without looking, quickly scrawled a few words on a sheet of paper, as though he were afraid someone was watching.

CHAPTER SEVENTEEN

RAESINIA

Raesinia had been present for quite a few of Cora's excited rambles, but this one was definitely worse than usual. This one had *diagrams*. They had started on one sheet of foolscap and spread off it in all directions, necessitating a raid on the writing desk in the other room for more paper and ink. Raesinia wasn't actually sure what the network of boxes and lines depicted—it could have been corporate structure, the interdependence of contracts, or the web of a drunken spider. She did her best to nod at appropriate junctures and chime in with enough questions to get the gist.

"—and once you've come to terms, you dictate them to one of the market scribes, and that's the end of it. Millions of eagles can move around that way in a few minutes. The Exchange in Vordan looks like a medieval fair by comparison." She shook her head. "Everything's public, too, by law. You can look at the record books, which can be very valuable if you know how to read them. For example, I'm certain Goodman and his cronies are leaking to the market; you can see the prices move every time we have a meeting. Which is probably illegal, but I'm sure we'd never pin it on him—"

"Is it working?" Raesinia interrupted. She'd gotten used to doing that, with Cora. The girl didn't mind, and it was the only way to get a word in edgewise.

"Is what working?"

"Your plan, to make more money." Raesinia had understood it only vaguely, something about speculating in derivatives related to Vordanai debt.

"Oh. Yes, so far. I'm still a long way from where I need to be to play on Goodman's scale, though. Even down in the trading pits, you can practically feel everyone pause when he walks by." Cora cocked her head. "Have you figured out what we're going to do yet? If we had a more specific objective I might be able to tilt things in that direction."

Raesinia shook her head. She didn't have a plan, precisely. More a sense that money was the water through which Goodman and people like him swam, the substance of their power; being able to manipulate it had to give her *some* kind of advantage. *Cora can think rings around Goodman. We just need to use it somehow.*

"Well, I'll keep things as they are, then," Cora said. "I've mostly been taking the buying end of the derivatives, because as a new concern traders are reluctant to take on the counterparty risk, even at a good rate. That limits us a little bit, but if our capital keeps expanding we ought to—"

The door opened. Raesinia stood up, a little relieved, until she saw the expression on Eric's face. He looked like someone who'd been told he had only weeks to live.

"What's wrong?" Raesinia said. Even Cora stopped chattering.

"You'd better read this," Eric said.

He handed her a folded page, written in a neat hand she didn't recognize. Raesinia scanned it, and her breath caught in her throat. She read it again, more carefully, hoping that somehow she'd gotten it wrong the first time.

After what felt like a hundred years, she looked up.

"You've seen this?" she said. But of course he had; it was written on his features.

He nodded. "It's all over the Keep, Your Highness."

"What is?" Cora said. The bubbly excitement of moments before was gone. "What happened?"

"There was a battle near Alves," Raesinia said, keeping her voice level. "General Kurot's army was beaten badly. Much of the army was shattered, and the general was captured. Marcus is leading what's left of the Army of the Republic south, with Janus' army in pursuit."

At least he's alive. Though the terse notice seemed to shatter all her hopes, she clung to that. *Marcus is alive. Or he was, when this was written.*

"I don't understand why he would retreat *south*," Eric said. "Why not east toward Vordan City? Surely—"

"*Surely* he had his reasons," Raesinia said. One thing her strategy sessions with Marcus had taught her, back in Murnsk, was that there were always realities on the ground that couldn't be appreciated by looking at a map. "I'm not going to critique Marcus' moves from five hundred miles away. Kurot's, either, for that matter. There'll be time for recriminations later." *Assuming Janus doesn't send us all to the Spike.* "You said this is all over the Keep? You're sure?"

"Yes, Your Highness," Eric said. "I overheard some of the staff discussing it in the hall."

Damn. It was too much to hope they'd be the *first* to find out, but it would have been nice not to be *last.* "Go and tell the king's secretary I need to speak to him at once. Tell him it's very urgent."

"Of course," Eric said. He hurried away, nearly dropping his notebook in his haste.

"What are you going to tell him?" Cora said. Raesinia turned to her, trying to keep the turmoil off her face. The confidence Cora had when dealing with the markets was gone, and she was just a scared teen, looking for reassurance. "This isn't going to make our position any stronger."

"I know," Raesinia said grimly. "I'm going to ask him if his offer is still open."

"Why?"

"Because if it is," she said, "I'm going to take it."

"Ordinarily, the king reserves this part of the day for private business," said the officious young footman who'd been assigned to escort Raesinia. "He very much dislikes being disturbed. So please keep your interruption as short as you can."

"I'll do my best," Raesinia ground out. Some of it had to be down to cultural differences, but she was certain now that the staff in the Keep were being deliberately disrespectful. "Thank you for bringing him my message."

"He *has* expressed an interest in you," the footman said, in a tone that implied he couldn't understand why. "This way."

They were in a part of the Keep that Raesinia hadn't visited before, which she assumed to be the king's private apartments. They passed through a large reception room, complete with an ornate throne, and went through a door at the back of the dais. A short corridor led to a smaller, plainer room, half occupied by an enormous wooden writing desk in the shape of an L. Two smaller desks were wedged into the corners. The king sat behind the big desk, flipping rapidly through the pages of a document and scrawling the occasional note in the margins, while the smaller places were occupied by clerks who copied out the monarch's hasty notes more legibly.

"Queen Raesinia," Georg said, not looking up. "Give me a moment."

Raesinia gritted her teeth. *Let him play his power games if he has to.* "Of course, Your Majesty."

The footman bowed and took his leave. Georg reached the end of his document in a few more moments, signed the bottom with a flourish, and slid the stack of pages across the desk. One of the clerks jumped up to take it.

"Clear out, please," the king told his secretaries. "I'll call when I need you."

They both bowed and slipped away. Raesinia stood facing the king across the vast expanse of hardwood. There was nowhere to sit, and Raesinia wasn't sure she wanted to. *I won't be here long.*

"I assume you'd prefer to skip the preliminaries," Georg said. "You've heard the word from Vordan, and so have I."

"Yes."

"You never gave me an answer to my proposal."

"Is it still on the table?"

Georg grinned slyly. "Master Goodman would chastise me. When your opponent's position becomes more desperate, he would say, take the chance to put the screws to them. Should I demand some territory, perhaps? Trading concessions? I'm sure he could think of something."

"Your Majesty—" Raesinia tried to keep her voice calm, but something must have shown on her face, because Georg barked a laugh and held up a hand.

"My apologies," he said. "Yes. The offer stands. I take it you've . . . considered?"

"I have." Raesinia stood up a little straighter. "I will marry Matthew, if you are willing to help."

"Excellent." Georg's smile widened. "I'm sure you will be very happy together."

"I'm sure," Raesinia said. "Let's talk about the terms of your assistance."

The king leaned back in his chair. "It will take some time to assemble troops—"

"Your Majesty, we don't *have* time. This news is days old at best."

"I'm well aware," the king said. "As I was about to say, a land force will take some assembly, but it should be practical to dispatch a navy squadron and transports immediately. They will sail to Enzport and up the Pale, rendezvous with General d'Ivoire's army, and make arrangements to evacuate it by sea. I assume that would resolve the immediate difficulty?"

"It would." Something unclenched in Raesinia's chest. *We're not there yet,* she told herself. "Thank you."

"For what it's worth," Georg said, "I appreciate your position. And I truly think this is the best possible outcome. Vhalnich is dangerous, and he needs to be crushed. Now stability is assured."

"Let's save the victory celebrations for later," Raesinia said. "I would appreciate it if you would send those ships at once."

"Of course. I'll need you to write out orders for your garrison at Ecco Island to allow our ships past. It wouldn't do to begin our partnership by shooting at one another, would it?"

Raesinia fought down her gorge as the scribes came back in. One of them wrote at her dictation, then presented her with the finished product to sign and seal. Her hand was shaking, blurring the shape pressed into the wax.

Then she was being escorted out of the king's presence by the same officious footman. She didn't even look at him, didn't want to see his superior expression. When he returned her to Jo and Barely, it was obvious they both knew something was wrong, but Raesinia ignored them, too. She stalked back to her suite, went into the drab bedroom, slammed the door, and threw herself on the too-hard bed.

It's not so bad. It'll be a few years at most, anyway. Then I have to disappear. She and Marcus might still manage to be together, if he was willing to disappear with her. She wasn't certain if she was willing to inflict that on him, though, nor if she really wanted to watch him get old and die while she lived on. *But this marriage is . . . nothing. Just a brief interlude. Prince Matthew isn't even such a terrible person.*

It didn't feel that way, no matter how she rationalized it. It wasn't Matthew that was the problem, or even marrying him, in the abstract. It was the knowledge that, in the end, she'd failed.

Duke Orlanko had intended to set her up as a puppet, a convenient body to occupy the throne while he ruled, complete with a terrible secret he could hold over her to maintain control. Everything she'd done since the start of the revolution had been in order to escape that fate, to regain control of her own destiny and break the hold that Orlanko and his backers had on Vordan. People had died—a great many people—along the way. Some of them had been her friends. Some of them had died in her arms. Raesinia herself had had her brains blown out, been shot, stabbed, drowned, smashed, and otherwise abused; if her particular situation meant that none of that was fatal, it still wasn't *pleasant*.

All of that, to get to a place where she could make decisions about her own life. *And now I'm back where I started.* Not Raesinia, just the queen, a convenient body to wed and breed, a pawn on the game board of nations. *And I doubt I'll even be able to do that satisfactorily.*

She imagined telling Marcus what she'd done and why she'd done it. He'd understand, from a logical perspective. Perhaps even agree that it was the right course, to save Vordanai lives, including his. *But will he forgive me?* She thought not. Marcus could recognize when a coldly rational decision was the correct one, but he could never truly bring himself to accept it. If she married Matthew, whatever the reasons, he would feel betrayed. *And I can't say he'd be wrong, because I feel like a traitor.*

Raesinia curled up on the bed, on top of the sheets, and cried in a way she hadn't for a very long time. Eventually she stopped, not because she felt better, but simply because she felt empty.

I wish Sothe were here. Not for her organizational talent, her spying, or her fighting skill. Just because no one else had been with her from the beginning, and understood.

Eric knocked at the door, calling for her. Then Cora, her voice full of concern. Then Duke Dorsay. Raesinia just pulled the sheets around her and lay still. *Go away. I gave him what he wanted. Can't I have some peace?*

Eventually—the curtains were drawn, and she had no idea what time it was—the lock clicked, and the door swung open a fraction. Raesinia frowned, blinking against the brighter light from the outer room, and looked up.

"Cora?" she said.

It wasn't Cora. It was Sebastian Carter, the tall, black-clad majordomo, with a pair of footmen hovering behind him.

"Your Highness," he said, pushing the door open wider and bowing. "I apologize for the intrusion. We weren't sure if you were well."

"I'm fine," Raesinia said. "I would like to be left alone."

"I understand that," the majordomo said. "However, as you are being moved to new accommodations, I will need you to come with me."

"New accommodations?" Raesinia's eyes narrowed. "These are fine."

"A new suite," the majordomo said, as if she hadn't spoken. "Where you can be with the second prince."

"What?"

"His Majesty was most insistent," Sebastian said. "Your staff will be moved to their own quarters nearby, of course, so you may have privacy."

"This is ridiculous. We aren't married *yet*."

"Those are His Majesty's orders," Sebastian said, as if that answered everything.

"I'm not doing it," Raesinia said. She felt like there were ants crawling across her skin. "In fact, I'd like my things packed." She'd gotten what she wanted from Borel, if not in the way she'd hoped. *There's no reason for me to stay here.* "I need to return to Vordan."

"I'm afraid that won't be possible," Sebastian said. "The king gave very specific instructions. You are welcome to go anywhere in the Keep, but I will have to ask you not to leave until your union to Prince Matthew has been formalized."

"He's holding me *prisoner*?" Raesinia slid off the bed and stalked over. "That's ridiculous. I am the Queen of Vordan. I demand to see the king at once."

"I'm afraid he's very busy," Sebastian said, as imperturbable as a mountain lake. "But I will inquire as to when he might have the time."

She glared. "Are you really going to move me by force?" She wondered where Barely and Jo were. Probably in the corridor, not knowing anything was wrong. They'd take on this butler, she was certain, but what would that accomplish in the long run besides possibly getting them killed?

"You are free to go to your new quarters, or not, as you choose, Your Highness. But I'm afraid the cleaning staff need to access this suite now that your things have been moved, so we can prepare it for other guests."

She almost laughed. It was such a prosaic way to present a demand. *Presumably if I stand here, they'll just clean around me.*

The despair that had afflicted her was rapidly transmuting into rage. *Georg obviously has been taking his lessons from Goodman.* Twist the knife while you had your opponent down. *Fine.*

"As you wish, of course," she said. "Please show me to my new accommodations."

And let's see what Prince Matthew has to say for himself.

To her annoyance, Prince Matthew was nowhere in evidence when she arrived at her new apartments. They were somewhat larger than the old suite, with a single master bedroom, a dining room, a study, and servants' quarters. No servants were in evidence, either. Raesinia tracked down Cora, who had rooms in the next corridor, and did her best to reassure her. Then she went back and settled in to wait for her newly acquired fiancé.

Second Prince Matthew came in sometime after dinner, still smartly dressed but ever so slightly disheveled, his hair delicately mussed and his steps weaving a bit across the tiled floor. He opened the door and grinned, as though Raesinia were a surprise gift.

"Well, then," he said. "I *thought* I knew the way back to my room, but the footmen assured me that I was mistaken. This isn't the apartment I remember, but I can't say it isn't an improvement."

"Hello, Your Highness," Raesinia said.

"Please." He came inside and leaned against the door until it closed. "No need for formality. I understand there's been a change in our relationship since this morning."

"I have agreed to your father's proposal that we should be married, yes," Raesinia said. "I wasn't expecting him to move us in together. Is that *normal* in Borel?"

"Not really, no. But Father approaches the breeding of heirs in the same way he approaches the breeding of hounds. Just put the dog and the bitch in the same cage for a while and wait for them to fuck." He rolled his eyes. "He's a born romantic."

Raesinia stared fixedly at the prince. "I have no intention of obliging him. Just so we're clear. And if you have any other ideas—"

"You wound me," Matthew said, hand trying for his heart and missing. "I would never take advantage of a helpless woman, much less one like yourself, who I assume is capable of ripping my balls off."

Raesinia fought a smile. "Let's hope we don't have to test that."

"I shall sleep," Matthew announced, "on the sofa. I'm sure it is comfortable."

He walked across the room to the ornate sofa against one wall and flopped onto it facedown, though it wasn't long enough to accommodate his lanky frame.

After a moment he said, voice muffled, "It is not comfortable."

Raesinia finally had to smile, just a little. "I'm sure we can figure something out."

"You are the soul of courtesy." Matthew rolled over. "Are you angry with me?"

"No," Raesinia said, surprised to find that she was not. She had been, before he came in, angry with him and his father and every Borelgai. But something about his exaggerated self-pity reminded her that he was as much a victim in this as she was. *More so. I had a choice, and I got something out of it, even if the terms weren't to my liking.* "I'm angry at your father."

"Being angry at my father is my stock-in-trade. I recommend it. It's kept me looking youthful all these years."

Raesinia smiled a little wider at the joke, which was more relevant than Matthew knew. She said, "Are you angry at me? I feel like you'd have every right to be. I did say I wasn't going to take your father's bargain."

"I suppose I could be, but it seems like a lot of effort." His expression softened. "And I understand your situation. I heard the word from Vordan."

"Apparently everyone did," Raesinia muttered.

"Keeping secrets is not among Borelgai virtues," Matthew said. "In the Keep least of all." He sighed. "If I blame anyone, I suppose it's my father, but at this point it's hard for me to hate even him. He's just . . . a fact. Like the rain and the fog."

"Can I ask you something?"

He shuffled himself up on the sofa, so he was at least partially upright. "Of course."

"Why can't you say no to him on this? From what he told me, you've refused marriages before."

The second prince's lips thinned. "It's . . . personal."

The Queen of Vordan and the Second Prince of Borel, caged together. Something in Raesinia's mind rebelled at the thought that, between them, there was *nothing* they could do.

She got up from her seat at the table, picked up one of the heavy chairs, and dragged it across the room, to face the couch. The prince watched her curiously as she set it down and then sat facing him.

"There has to be a way out of this," she said carefully. "I'm not sure how, but I'm pretty certain I'm going to need your help."

"That seems unlikely," Matthew said. "I'm not good for very much. Unless you need to throw a party."

"It's not just that I'm unhappy with the idea of this marriage," Raesinia said, ignoring him. "There's a man I'm in love with. His name is Marcus d'Ivoire."

Matthew blinked. "The general?"

Raesinia nodded. "He wasn't so high-ranking when we met. And . . . it's hard to explain. We went through a lot together."

"Raesinia." Matthew sat up a little straighter, and the cynical humor left his face. "Why are you telling me this? I take it no one else knows."

"A few people do. My friend Cora." She shook her head. "I'm telling you because I want you to trust me. If we're going to work together and beat your father, we're going to need that."

"We won't," Matthew said. "We can't. Believe me, no one has fought him longer or harder than I have."

"Why?"

"Look," Matthew said, the ironic twist of his lip sliding back into place. "Keep d'Ivoire around. I certainly won't raise a fuss. Be discreet and we can all get what we want."

"*He* wouldn't accept that," Raesinia said. "Marcus is . . . old-fashioned sometimes."

"Then I guess you'll have to poison me," Matthew said. "It shouldn't be difficult. I drink quite a lot."

"Matthew, please. I might be able to help you, but—"

He sat up all the way, glaring at her. "Why would you think that? Do you know my father?"

"I don't," Raesinia said. "But I *am* the Queen of Vordan. I have . . . resources you might not. What can it hurt just to talk about it?"

"You'd be surprised," Matthew said darkly. Then he sighed and put his face in his hands. "Why not? Half the Keep knows by now, I'm sure. Like I said, Borelgai and secrets."

"I'm from Vordan," Raesinia said. "And we can keep secrets."

Matthew snorted, then took a deep breath.

"There's a man I'm in love with," he said.

Ah. Raesinia tried to keep any surprise off her face. "I see."

"His name is . . . not important. You wouldn't know him. He's in the Life Guards."

"And your father found out?"

Matthew nodded miserably. "We kept it secret for years. I have a reputation as a wastrel, so nobody pays close attention to the company I keep. While my brother was healthy, my father didn't care. He thought he'd have all the heirs he needed. But when he got sick . . ."

"The king started pressuring you to marry."

"And when I kept turning him down, he got angry, and started investigating."

"He told you he'd send your lover away if you didn't go along with this," Raesinia guessed.

"Worse than that. There's all sorts of duty he can send a Life Guard to where he's likely to get killed. I . . . can't risk that. Even if we can't be together." Matthew swallowed hard and forced a smile. "I should have told you from the beginning. If we go along with Father's plan, maybe he'll let me choose my escort. Then you can have your lover and I'll have mine, and we'll be a perfectly happy couple."

"Your father won't allow that," Raesinia said. "He'd be worried people would find out."

"I know." Matthew's smile faded. "But what else am I supposed to do?"

Leverage, Raesinia thought. "Your father has a hostage to hold over both of us," she said. "We need something we can hold over him."

"Unless you've got a spare heir to the throne lying around, I doubt you'll come up with anything." Matthew cocked his head. "You could always just leave once he's dispatched the ships you wanted."

"That only helps in the short term. I still need him to keep Janus from taking the kingdom." She sighed. "Besides, he's decided I'm a prisoner in the Keep. I can't even visit the city, much less take a ship."

"That, at least, I guarantee is a bluff," Matthew said.

"How can you be sure?"

"Father's desperate to avoid another war with Vordan," he said. "He's still paying for the War of the Princes. That's the point of all of this, in the end, in addition to getting him an heir who seems likely to live out the decade. He wants to tie Borel to Vordan." The prince looked pensive. "If you walked out the front gate, I doubt he'd really be able to stop you. Not without causing an incident that might lead to war."

"Fair enough. He knows he's got the promise of aid to keep me chained here anyway." Raesinia frowned. "The king has debts? I thought Borel was a rich country."

"*Borel* is extremely rich. The *Crown* is very poor. It's traditional." Matthew waved a hand. "How do you think Goodman got so powerful? He paid for practically half the fleet. That's why Father won't cross him unless he knows he's got something to gain."

"Goodman," Raesinia said, half to herself. "Goodman is the key to this. He has to be."

"He's the richest man in the world," Matthew said. "He's central to quite a lot of things."

"I mean that if we can get leverage on Goodman, then we can put pressure on your father."

"Good luck. The other merchants have been trying to tear Goodman down for years. If it could be done, one of them would have found a way. It's a dog-eat-dog world, as they're so fond of telling one another."

Raesinia was thinking about the Second Pennysworth Bank, the proud marble facade that had seemed so impenetrable until the mob arrived. *And the way the panic spread.* Cora had talked about it, something she hadn't quite understood at the time, but—

"You have friends," Raesinia said abruptly. "The best people in Borel, I expect."

"I like to think," Matthew drawled, "that I am not unloved."

"They're rich?"

"In Borel, *best* and *richest* are basically synonymous," Matthew said. "Why? Do you need money?"

"Not exactly," Raesinia said. "But I might know someone who does."

"Raes, are you sure you're okay?" Cora said. "I can't believe they stuck you in the same *room* with him."

"I told you, I'm fine," Raesinia said.

She looked around, feeling a little paranoid. The second prince had warned her that the Keep servants in their new rooms were probably spying for his father, and she assumed the same was true of those in Cora's new quarters. To avoid them, she'd come with Cora to one of the castle's inner courtyards, where dour statuary brooded on well-trimmed lawns. Given the near-constant drizzle, they were not frequented, and by taking shelter away from any doors, they had as much privacy as they were likely to get.

"I'm fine," Raesinia repeated. "Prince Matthew is . . . well, a gentleman. More important, he's on our side. He doesn't want this marriage any more than I do. He's going to help us."

"Help us how?" Cora said. "If we break off the marriage, the king will refuse to send aid, won't he?"

"Not if we can get Goodman behind us."

"That doesn't seem very likely," Cora said. "He's the one who's been pushing to wring us dry."

"You said that as a new company, without any backers, you had trouble getting access to investors," Raesinia said. "If someone important—Prince Matthew, say—were to offer his support, that would help, wouldn't it?"

Cora nodded slowly. "It would certainly *help*. But, Raes . . ." She hesitated. "Even with a lot more capital, it would take a long time to put us on a sound enough footing to have real influence in Borel. I'm not a magician. I'm sorry."

Cora looked pained, and Raes impulsively put an arm around her shoulders.

"I know," she said. "I rely on you too much as it is, and *I'm* sorry. I promise I'm not going to demand the impossible." Raesinia put on a mischievous grin. "Forget about a sound footing and success. How long will it take you to *fail*?"

CHAPTER EIGHTEEN

MARCUS

"They're persistent," Cyte said, watching the white-uniformed soldiers gathering themselves for a third try. "I'll give them that."

"That's one word for it," Fitz said.

Marcus grunted. "Some might say *stupid*."

"That's another," Fitz said.

They stood on a hillside, the high point of a ridge that rose out of the rolling farm country south of Alves like a pillow stuffed under a bedsheet. Behind them, to the south, was the river Reter, a slim waterway too easily crossed to provide much of a barrier. In front of them, low plains stretched north to the Pale.

The three Murnskai regiments had arrived just after noon and had been battering themselves against the hillside position ever since. Marcus had light cavalry patrolling to either side, watching for outflanking maneuvers, but so far there'd been nothing, just this headlong assault. It was almost painful to watch.

The approach to the hill, fifteen hundred yards or so of low grass, bare earth, and the occasional stone wall, was already strewn with Murnskai dead. They were scattered everywhere, but piled up in drifts where the enemy battalions had made their farthest advances. In the lull between attacks, Marcus ordered his own casualties picked up and taken south, where the advance guard and the baggage train were still pushing forward.

"Here they come," Cyte said. She offered the spyglass to Marcus, but he waved it away. He didn't need to watch this close up.

Six enemy battalions, depleted from their earlier attacks but restored to some semblance of formation, marched forward. Their commander had apparently decided to deploy in depth, in three lines of two units abreast. To either side of them came a couple of small guns, four-pounders, which Marcus' men had dubbed yappers for how they sounded a bit like excited terriers. The Vordanai army had dismissed such small cannon as nearly useless decades ago, but the Murnskai still clung to them.

Archer's twelve-pounders opened up at a thousand yards, solid shot plunging down from their elevated position at the crest of the hill to wreak its usual havoc on the packed ranks of men. The Murnskai had already deployed into line, coming on like they were on a parade ground, but a good shot would bounce through two or even three of the battalions, carrying away victims as it went. More white-uniformed bodies dribbled from the rear of the formation, adding to those already carpeting the grass, the battalions shrinking toward their centers as they came on.

As the enemy closed, the six-pounders joined the chorus, doubling the volume of fire. The yappers fired back, but the range and the slope defeated them, and Marcus couldn't see that they were having any effect. He wondered if the Murnskai commander just wanted to hearten his men with the noise and the smoke. If so, it wasn't working—the rear battalions were already looking shaky, formation loosening as they were hit again and again. As he watched, one of them dissolved, soldiers breaking and running for the rear while officers on horseback rode in to try to rally them.

And still they came on. The guns switched to canister, throwing clouds of musket balls, cutting chunks out of the Murnskai ranks. Another battalion broke, and another. One of the yapper batteries had come close enough that its shots began whistling overhead, but the two regiments of Vordanai—Sevran's and one from Fitz' division—waited stolidly behind their guns, unperturbed.

"About now, I think," Marcus said.

Cyte yelled to the drummers, and they beat out a new rhythm, transmitting the command. Archer's guns fell silent, and the line of Vordanai infantry moved forward, positioning themselves in front of the cannon. The remaining Murnskai were less a distinct formation at this point than a tightly packed mob, three remaining battalions dissolving into a dense mass of men with their standards at the center. As they came within musket range, two battalions of Vordanai stood in neat lines to oppose them. On either side of the line, another battalion moved forward, angling inward like a swinging door, forming a C shape with the Murnskai at the center.

"*Fire!*" The command went up from a hundred throats, on both sides at once. Six thousand muskets went off with a roaring, tearing rattle, and the whole front line was instantly blanketed with a dense bank of off-white smoke. It didn't take an expert's eye to see that the Murnskai were getting the worst of it, pressed together in an awkward blob instead of a well-dressed line, raked by fire from both sides. Men fell in the Vordanai ranks, but enough white-uniformed soldiers dropped that their corpses began to form a rampart. By the third volley, the Murnskai were wavering, and the fourth put them to flight; they streamed down the hill like a flock of frightened sheep, leaving only the ghastly piles behind.

"They won't be trying that again," Fitz said. "Not today, at any rate."

Marcus nodded. The Murnskai officers didn't seem to be having much success rallying their men, who were spreading out into the fields or streaming up the road the way they'd come. Cyte snapped her spyglass closed and stowed it.

"Sir," she said, pointing over his shoulder. Marcus turned and saw a horseman in the uniform of a light cavalry sergeant approaching. The man saluted without dismounting.

"Something to report?" Marcus said.

"Yessir. Got a column pushing south from Mezk. At least a division, possibly two."

Marcus closed his eyes, visualizing the map that was at this point burned into his brain. Traveling due south from Mezk would take them around the end of the Reter, neatly outflanking his current position. *Just as expected.*

"That's long enough, then," Marcus said. He turned back to Cyte. "We're pulling out. I want everyone over the river by sundown. Get the baggage train on the road for the Vlind first thing in the morning."

"Yes, sir," she said. Her salute was still crisp, though her drawn face and the bags under her eyes spoke volumes.

Marcus had to imagine he showed the same signs of weariness, as did almost everyone in what was left of the Army of the Republic. They'd been marching hard since the disaster at Alves, from first light until well after the early-autumn twilight, sometimes stumbling into camp by torchlight. Even for troops accustomed to the harsh pace Janus had demanded of his men, it was difficult, and for the new recruits it was pure torture. They were losing men every day, soldiers abandoning their units or simply dropping by the side of the road, and Marcus didn't know whether to call it desertion or illness born of exhaustion.

What they'd bought, with all this pain, was a little distance from their pursuers. Janus was whipping his pursuing columns hard, but bringing an enemy to battle when he was determined to evade was one of the trickiest coups in grand tactics. So far Marcus had been able to avoid it, moving steadily south and west to keep Janus' pincers from closing around him. When he found a good position for defense, as he had today, he turned part of the army about and faced down Janus' vanguard, giving the slower elements time to increase their lead. Sometimes their pursuers paused, waiting for support to come up; more often, as they had today, they threw themselves into the teeth of the defense and came away bloodied.

But it couldn't last. The moment the Army of the Republic stopped moving, it would be surrounded and overwhelmed by Janus' more numerous forces. Marcus could turn and swipe at his pursuers, but not make a real stand, not without committing to an all-out battle he was sure to lose. So every day they went back, and every day a few more men were left by the side of the road or melted into the darkness.

"We're hurting them," he said to Cyte, as they rode through the twilight toward the Reter. "We have to be hurting them. But they keep coming." He shook his head. "It doesn't seem like Janus."

"He never struck me as particularly sentimental about losses," Cyte said. "Given his advantage in numbers, maybe he's just willing to accept the casualties to wear us down?"

"It's not that I think he'd balk at the casualties," Marcus said, frowning as he struggled to articulate his feelings. "It's not that this way of fighting is too *ugly* for him. It's worse than that. It's *inefficient*."

"A capital sin," Cyte deadpanned.

"It is, for Janus. This is the man who spent the last hours before his execution writing out letters to be delivered in the event of his rescue. He never *stops*. It's not like him to waste time and lives bashing us head-on when he could get us some other way."

"Maybe there is no other way," Cyte said. "Maybe you've thought of everything and this is all he's got left."

"Somehow," Marcus said grimly, "I doubt it."

It occurred to Marcus, as they rode into the camp, what it was that bothered him about Janus' strategy. *He doesn't need to attack to wear us down. We're doing that to ourselves.*

The campfires were burning, and the air was thick with the scent of grill-

ing meat. Most of it, Marcus knew, was horsemeat. The killing pace was consuming horses faster than it did men, and Marcus had given orders that none
of those that fell were to be wasted. Supplies were desperately low as it was.
The towns along the Pale had depots of powder, fodder, food, and other military necessities, but their commanders—*cowardly, fence-sitting traitors*—had been
reluctant to hand over their stocks to the fleeing Army of the Republic. Marcus
had seriously considered taking them by force, but in the end he couldn't bring
himself to storm a friendly outpost. *They're afraid of Janus. If he wins, he might
come looking for the names of the officers who helped us.*

Instead, his men had been forced to forage, as though they were in enemy
territory. There was no shortage of food in this rich country, but the farmers
and merchants of the villages were understandably reluctant to surrender their
surpluses to the army's bottomless need. They were even less happy about giving up their horses, but Marcus' foraging parties gave them no choice in the
matter. The artillery and baggage needed to move, and the cavalry needed
remounts. He'd told the men to keep records of where they'd gone, so Queen
Raesinia could make the losses good after the war, but he couldn't blame the
farmers for not trusting his promises.

The command tent was set up in its usual place, though the camp layout
had become increasingly sloppy as the march went on. Marcus and Cyte rode
in as a slow drizzle began to fall, handing the reins of their mounts to a waiting
corporal and slipping inside before the real rain began. Fitz was already there,
along with Give-Em-Hell for the cavalry. Since Marcus was now in overall
command, he'd nominated Abby to represent the Second Division. She arrived
a few minutes later, shaking rain off her coat. Cyte unrolled the big paper map
on the camp table and sat in front of it, marking their new position and the last
reported location of Janus' forces in grease pencil.

"All right," Marcus said. "Give me the bad news."

"Had a skirmish with a local militia today," Give-Em-Hell said. "A gang
of farmers and their sons with shotguns and hunting rifles. We told them we
were foraging in the name of the queen, and they said we were just a bunch of
thieves." He snorted. "Not a patriotic bone in the whole yellow bunch. They
scattered quick enough when I called up the cuirassiers."

"It's still not a promising sign," Marcus said. "If the whole country starts
to rise against us, we'll starve."

"They won't," Give-Em-Hell assured him. "I'll come down like a thunderbolt on any hint of trouble, and word will get around."

Marcus hesitated. The harsher they were, the worse it would be in the long term. *But we won't get to the long term if we starve in the short term.* The only saving grace was that their breakneck pace might keep them ahead of the wave of indignation.

"Do your best to keep things peaceful," Marcus said. "Try not to use force if you don't have to."

He turned to Fitz, who raised one eyebrow. "Nothing to report that I didn't say yesterday," he said. "Sick lists are way up, and desertions are getting worse. If this keeps going, it will get a lot easier to feed my division."

"It's the same in the Second," Abby said, settling down at the table with a weary sigh. "The Girls' Own is holding up, but Sevran says there's ugly talk among his men."

"Mutiny?" Give-Em-Hell said. "You can't stand for that, sir. Pick an example and give—"

"They don't want to fight for Janus," Abby said. "They just want to stop marching, and I have a hard time blaming them. They say we should have surrendered after Alves." She looked up at Marcus. Her eyes were dull and flat. "It would help if we could tell them where we're going."

"You can read the map as well as I can," Marcus said. "We haven't got the strength to hold the line of the Vlind. If we can make it as far as the Rhyf, then maybe—"

"That's another hundred and fifty miles," Abby said. "We're not going to last that long."

"She's right," Fitz said quietly.

Cyte finished marking up the map and sat back. They all stared at it, lost in thought.

What can I tell them? That, in the end, they were just buying time? *If we surrender, Janus will be free to march on Vordan City.* This way they were luring his forces farther and farther south, far from where they would need to be. Every step they took following the Army of the Republic was a step they'd have to retrace. *Raesinia can assemble new armies. Get help from the Borels. Something.* But he doubted that sentiment would go far to fill empty bellies or soothe aching legs.

"We'll go as far as we can," he said. "That's the long and the short of it. I don't intend to waste the lives of our men—if Janus surrounds us, we'll surrender. But while we can march, we'll march."

"Well said, goddammit," Give-Em-Hell roared. "Never give in while you've got an ounce of strength left!"

"I'll tell Sevran," Abby said, then muttered, "though I'm not sure if he'll pass that along."

"Once we cross the Vlind," Fitz said, "I suggest we shift to a more westerly course. We'll have to screen the Pale crossings, but I think that will be substantially easier than pressing south into hill country. We may even be able to ease the pace somewhat if General Stokes can delay the enemy flanking columns."

"It's an idea," Marcus said. "But . . ."

An hour of discussion followed, the gritty details of marches and foraging assignments, spoiling attacks by the cavalry and what could be risked. A sergeant came in with steaming bowls of army soup, prepared by the old reliable method of boiling whatever you had in a pot until it was soft. Marcus wolfed his down mechanically, not paying enough attention to notice the flavor.

There was no resolving many of the questions, not unless the situation changed radically, and eventually they simply ran out of energy for further argument. Even Give-Em-Hell's indefatigable impetus was flagging. And while Fitz seemed, on the surface, as impervious as ever, he withdrew into himself, answering only in clipped, precise monosyllables.

"Enough," Marcus said. "Get some sleep. We'll pick this up later."

No one argued. In a few moments, only he and Cyte remained in the tent.

Two days to the Vlind. Marcus looked down at the map. There were a few rivers between the Vlind and the Rhyf, but none of them large enough to present a strategic barrier. *If we make it to the Rhyf, it's only another hundred miles to Enzport.* He didn't dare say that out loud to the other commanders. Even Marcus had to admit that making the trek, at their current pace, seemed impossible. *But it's our only choice, apart from surrender or a glorious last stand somewhere.* Enzport had a deepwater harbor and modern fortifications. Once inside, the army could be supplied by sea, and keep Janus tied down in front of its walls indefinitely.

"I'm worried about Abby," Cyte said, after an interval.

"Oh?" Marcus said.

"Erdine's death hit her harder than she's letting on. She's . . . not coping well."

Marcus had almost forgotten about the loss of the colorful cavalryman. It was the all-pervading effect of exhaustion—anything that wasn't crucial to immediate survival fell out of his mind almost at once. The cavalry detachments of the divisions had been merged into Give-Em-Hell's depleted command, so he hadn't had to worry about finding a replacement.

"She seems to be attending to her duties," Marcus said.

"She's working herself to death," Cyte said. "She doesn't sleep more than four hours a night, and she's barely eating. At this rate, she won't last."

Marcus shook his head. "What do you want me to do? I can't afford to tell her to take a few days off."

"I know. She wouldn't do it anyway. It's just . . . Jane's gone, Winter's gone, and now Erdine. The Girls' Own is all she has left."

"Can you talk to her?"

"Me?" Cyte hesitated. "I can try. It would be better if it were Winter."

"Winter's not here," Marcus said gently. "And I doubt it would help, coming from me. Try."

Cyte nodded jerkily. "I'll do my best."

"What about you?"

"Sir?"

"How are you holding up?"

She gave him a level gaze. "I'm tired, sir. We're all tired."

"Take care of yourself as best you can." Marcus sighed and rubbed his temples. "God knows I couldn't keep all this running without you."

They crossed the Vlind at a town called Zeckvol, a dot on the map no one had ever heard of. It turned out to be a few streets' worth of plaster-and-timber buildings, a brick church, and a bridge. Only the last mattered to Marcus. No inhabitants were in evidence, the townspeople all having either fled or taken shelter.

The bridge was a short wooden span, beams anchored to a rock in the middle of the river. Fitz looked at it thoughtfully as he and Marcus reined up on the east bank, while the infantry filed across in a long, bedraggled procession of weather-beaten blue.

"Shouldn't take much, sir," Fitz said. "A little powder and it'll burn nicely."

"Good." It wouldn't make the locals happy, but there was little choice. Give-Em-Hell's light cavalry were ranging up and down the river, burning or blowing up every bridge they could find. If Janus' army wanted to cross, they'd need to use a ford or take a long detour.

Cannon rumbled across, hitched to the back of their caissons, their metal-shod wheels making the planks rattle.

"If this slows Janus down," Fitz ventured, "maybe we can afford a short march tomorrow. Give the men some rest and the foragers more time to work."

"Maybe," Marcus said. He wasn't optimistic the river would hold their pursuers for long. "The cavalry will keep watch to see where they cross."

They sat in silence for a while, as another infantry regiment began crossing.

"I hope Val had the sense to surrender," Marcus said.

"I'm sure he did," Fitz said.

What that would mean for him, Marcus didn't know. He hadn't ever known Janus to mistreat a prisoner, apart from one near catastrophe in Ashe-Katarion. But there was the strange red-eyed *thing* to consider. *Hell. He was always the one who dealt with all this mystical nonsense.*

"Sir!" A light-cavalry trooper rode up, his mount spattered with mud. Behind him was a lieutenant Marcus didn't recognize. "There's a messenger," the trooper said, indicating the other man. "From the . . . ah, enemy, sir."

"Lieutenant Virson, Ninth Division." Virson saluted.

Marcus straightened up in his saddle and glanced at Fitz. "Where'd he come from?"

"Rode into the cavalry screen about ten miles back carrying a white flag, sir," the trooper said. "General Stokes said I should bring him here."

"Well done." Marcus turned to Virson. "You've got a message?"

"Yes, sir. The emperor presents his compliments and requests a meeting with General d'Ivoire at a time and place of the general's choosing. I can return with the general's answer, or any messenger with a white flag will be conducted safely through our lines."

"Did he say what he wanted to meet about?"

"No, sir," Virson said. "That's all the information I have."

"Thank you." Marcus jerked his head, and he and Fitz turned their mounts away from the lieutenant and put their heads together. "What do you think?"

"It could be a trap, of course," Fitz said. "But I think it's unlikely."

"I agree," Marcus said. "Not that I would put it past Janus, but what good would it do him to take me out? You'd just take over."

"I think it's more likely that he hopes to offer us terms of surrender," Fitz said. "The chase must wear on his army as much as on ours, even if his supply situation is better. Perhaps he thinks he can persuade you to give in."

"Which I have no intention of doing," Marcus said. "In which case, why bother meeting?"

"If I might make a suggestion, sir," Fitz said. "He's given you the chance to specify the circumstances of the meeting. We may be able to get a slight advantage from that. If you say that the meeting will take place here at sunset,

on the Zeckvol bridge, and stipulate that our scouts will watch for the approach
of any substantial force . . ."

"Then he won't be able to move into town today," Marcus said. "And we
can still demolish the bridge afterward. So it will slow him down."

"Not very much, I'm afraid," Fitz said. "His army is large enough that he
can search for another crossing at the same time. But it keeps him off the direct
route."

"Good idea, regardless." Marcus looked back at Virson. "Let's see if they
go for it."

Virson readily agreed to the terms, adding only that Janus wanted the right
to have a squadron of his own troopers inspect the meeting place beforehand.
That seemed reasonable, and likely to produce even more delay, so Marcus
assented and sent Virson hurrying back toward his own lines. By the time the
sun was approaching the horizon, the bulk of the Army of the Republic was
well to the west, pushing hard to put distance between themselves and the river.
Marcus remained behind, with Cyte and a squadron of cuirassiers as escort,
along with a pair of Archer's artillerists to handle the demolition of the bridge.

The sound of hooves on packed earth alerted them to the approach of the
enemy. A dozen mounted men came into view, not proper cavalry troopers but
infantrymen, their muskets long and awkward on horseback. They dismounted,
stared at their opposite numbers on the other side of the bridge for a while, then
cautiously came forward to check for traps.

Marcus sent one of his escorting cuirassiers to meet them, to confirm that
everything was ready. The man came trotting back, waving the okay, and
Marcus slid off his horse and stretched his aching legs.

"You're sure you don't want me to come along, sir?" Cyte said.

"At this point it would take more renegotiation than I'm comfortable
with," Marcus said. "Besides, if it comes down to it, you're probably more
important to the army than I am, and I don't want to risk you."

"Sir—"

He held up a placating hand. "I don't think there's actually much risk. Janus
may be a traitor, but he wouldn't do all this just to get to me." Marcus snorted.
"It's not *efficient*, after all."

Cyte lowered her voice. "What about what we discussed after Mieran
County? If he's not really in command?"

"Then things might get interesting," Marcus said. "If there's any fighting,
you know what to do."

"Come and rescue you?" She gave a half smile.

"If you can. But you have to make sure to burn the bridge. We can't give them an easy crossing."

"Understood, sir." Cyte looked up. "Here he comes."

A lone figure in a long blue coat had ridden up to the line of escorts on the other side of the river. He dismounted, handing the reins to one of the soldiers, and started across the bridge. Marcus did the same, trying to project confidence and adjust his pace so they met in the center.

The last time he'd seen Janus, the general had still been recovering from the effect of a supernatural poison inflicted on him by one of the Penitent Damned. At the moment, Marcus thought, he looked even worse than he had in the depths of his feverish delirium. His enormous gray eyes seemed bigger than ever, standing out in an already-lean face that had thinned until it was nearly a skull. There was stubble on his cheeks, something Marcus had never known Janus to tolerate, not even when they were in prison. His hair had grown, hanging to the nape of his neck in an unkempt bundle.

"Hello, Marcus," he said.

"Janus." The reflexive *sir* was hard to avoid, but Marcus was determined not to let his automatic deference get the better of him.

"You're looking well."

"That's a lie," Marcus said, smiling a little. "And you look as bad as I feel."

"We may both be getting too old for war." The smile that crossed Janus' face, there for an instant and then gone, was like a punch in the gut, utterly familiar on this strange, shrunken version of his old friend. *This may have been a bad idea.* Marcus straightened a little and tried to keep his tone businesslike.

"This meeting was your suggestion. Did you have something to propose?"

Janus sighed. "Very well. Shall we go through the script?" He cleared his throat, like a stage actor preparing a monologue. "General d'Ivoire, it should be clear to you that further resistance will only result in the useless destruction of life without any change to the eventual outcome. As your countryman and, I hope, your friend, I call on you to surrender to prevent a further effusion of blood, and I assure you that you and the men under your command will be treated with the greatest respect." He cocked his head. "And now you say—"

"Go to hell," Marcus ground out. He was remembering that Janus could, at times, be incredibly irritating.

"Or words to that effect."

"Queen Raesinia trusted me with this command. I don't intend to disappoint her."

"From what I hear, she didn't trust you, but rather that fool Kurot."

"She had her reasons," Marcus said.

"I'm sure."

This time Janus' smile was venomous, and Marcus felt anger rising. He clenched his fists. "Don't. How can you do this to her?"

"For what it's worth, I'm sorry she's involved. But it had to be done."

"Why?" Marcus said. "You told me that your goal was the destruction of the Priests of the Black."

"They were a threat," Janus said. "And they had to be eliminated."

"That's it? In the end all that matters is gathering power for yourself?"

"Of course," Janus said, with that summer-lightning smile. "Read your history, Marcus. Nothing else has ever—"

"Liar," Marcus snapped. "You're not in it for power, and you never were."

"Oh?" Janus cocked his head. "You know me so well?"

"I went to Mieranhal," Marcus said. "Gravya told me your story."

There was a long pause. Beneath them, the river splashed and gurgled. A cavalry horse snorted and stamped a foot. Behind Janus' eyes, Marcus could almost see the gears turning, the clockwork mechanism swinging into a new configuration.

Then Janus blinked, and there was something else. Deep in the center of his huge gray eyes, inside the pupils, Marcus swore he could see a faint red spark. Another blink and it was gone.

"She told you . . ." Janus said, after a while.

"About Mya."

"Ah."

"You mentioned her," Marcus said, flushing a little in ridiculous embarrassment, "when you were feverish. You told me . . . bits and pieces."

"I'm surprised you got her to talk. The Mierantai are a notoriously close-mouthed lot."

"Lieutenant Uhlan vouched for me."

"Of course." Janus' lip quirked. "And now you think you understand me?"

"I'll never understand everything. But it's all for her, isn't it? The Thousand Names, and then the march on Elysium. All of it."

"If it had worked," Janus said, with a hint of his old fire, "it would have been worth it. You can't understand, Marcus."

"Why not?"

"Because you think *I'm* a genius," Janus snapped. "It's like a cat trying to understand the works of Voulenne."

"I appreciate the comparison," Marcus drawled.

"I . . . apologize." Janus let out a breath. Something passed over his features, some emotion Marcus couldn't guess. It was gone in an instant, and he was himself again.

"What I can't figure out is the point of all *this*," Marcus said. "If it's all for Mya, what does *this* get you?"

"The next best thing, perhaps." Janus looked away, down at the river.

"You are . . ." Marcus shook his head. "Enough. We've established that I'm not going to surrender. Is there anything else?"

"I suppose it won't help to remind you what you owe me," Janus said.

"What about what you owe *us*? All of Vordan?"

They glared at each other, a few yards apart, and there was another awkward silence. Then Janus stepped forward, one hand extended.

"As you wish, Marcus. If this is how it has to be."

For a moment Marcus considered ignoring him, just turning away. It would be a nice, dramatic gesture. But he still couldn't bring himself to hate this man, who'd brought him so far. *It doesn't make* sense. He stepped forward and clasped his old commander's hand.

"I wish things were different."

"So do I," Janus said. Oddly, he refused to meet Marcus' eye, fixing his gaze instead on the buttons of his coat. "So do I."

Then he was walking away, hands tucked into his pockets. Marcus stared after him, then down at the palm of his hand, where a single much-folded sheet of paper had been pressed.

CHAPTER NINETEEN

WINTER

"Inside!" Winter shouted. "Everyone inside *now*!"

Lieutenant Dobraev looked at her, startled. "What—"

Fortunately, Sergeant Gorchov had more sense. "Back to the gate!" he thundered, in a voice that would have done credit to a parade-ground instructor. "At the double!"

Dobraev took the hint and started to run, and his escort followed. Vess and the Haeta needed no further urging. They sprinted for the gate, overtaking the more heavily laden Murnskai soldiers. Winter, following behind, sent up a silent prayer that the guards on the walls wouldn't interpret this as an attack. But there was no repeat of yesterday's disaster—either Dobraev had been careful with his instructions, or Gorchov's shout had carried clear back to the wall.

Alex and Abraham stayed with Winter, who slowed a little as she turned to look behind them. From the trees an army had emerged, a strange, ragged force whose only common trait was their battered condition. There were Murnskai soldiers in muddy whites and Vordanai men in stained blue. Peasants—men, women, and children—in leather and homespun, their outfits ragged and torn. Hunters with fur caps, scruffy-looking bandits, priests in red and white robes whose distinctions had been erased by the mud.

Quite a few of them carried muskets, Winter was surprised to see. *It must have decided it needed a stronger force to get to me.* The Beast had nearly waited too long, and now its prey was on the verge of escaping.

They passed through the big timbered gate, and Dobraev waved frantically to the guards, who shoved the log barrier forward on its rope hinges. When it was in place, they slotted two iron bars across it, each the size of Winter's arm. Deeper in the fortress, a bell was ringing, a tinny clamor of alarm.

"To the wall!" Dobraev was shouting. "Every man to the wall! We are under attack!"

There's too many. She'd gotten only a glimpse of the Beast's force, but there had to be hundreds of red-eyes. "You won't be able to hold the wall," Winter said urgently. "We have to get the ships ready and fall back—"

"With all respect, *Miss* Iher_nglass," the lieutenant said, his expression rigid, "I am most appreciative of your warning, and your removal of my oaf of a commanding officer. But this is an hour for *soldiers*, so I would appreciate it if you would stay out of my way."

"I—" Winter shook her head, frustrated. *Weren't you just complaining about being in charge?* She shook her head. *Not the time. People are going to die.*

She left Dobraev and went to the Haeta, who were huddled together in a clear space among the shacks and lean-tos. The soldiers who ran past gave them curious glances on their way to man the wall walk, where the *cracks* of musketry were already sounding. Alex and Abraham stood at the edge of the group, waiting anxiously for Winter.

"Just in time, huh?" Alex said.

"It was waiting for us," Winter said. "It must not have been certain it had enough bodies, so it held off."

"It certainly looked like enough," Abraham said. "Do you think they can hold the wall?"

"No," Winter said shortly. "We need those ships ready to sail, with everyone on board. Fyotyr said the sails and oars were taken to the keep. Abraham, do you think you can talk to the refugees? There must be a few sailors here. Get as many as you can to help you get those ships ready."

"I . . . can try," Abraham said, taken aback. "There'll be a rush to get aboard once they know what we're doing."

"Let them. But no cargo, only the people. We're getting everyone out of here." Winter glanced over her shoulder at the wall, now wreathed in smoke. A white-coated Murnskai soldier pitched backward off the wall walk with a scream and landed hard in the mud, and others scrambled to take his place. "Alex, go with him in case anyone tries to get in the way. Do *not* let those ships leave until everyone's aboard."

"Got it." Alex pointed to the keep. "Come on. Let's find some oars."

"Won't they have everything locked up?" Abraham said.

Alex rolled her eyes. "Greatest thief in the world, remember?"

The two of them ran off. Winter turned back to the wall, watching the flashes of musketry, waiting for the inevitable.

"They're coming over!" one of the Haeta shouted. Hands appeared above the edge of the log palisade, spindly, underfed figures lifting themselves over the barrier. The Murnskai troops converged with bayoneted muskets, driving them back, but soon more red-eyes were reaching the top at another spot, and then another.

Come on, Dobraev, Winter thought. *You have to see this isn't going to work.* Under normal circumstances, a soldier at the top of a wall had a considerable advantage over one at the bottom. But this wasn't a stone fortress wall, or even a ditch and scarp as one might find on a modern fortress, just a set of lashed-up logs. It was an easy climb for anyone with a knife or a hatchet. The defenders were harder to hit than the Beast's musketeers lined up below, but the attackers were indifferent to wounds or casualties, and outnumbered their opponents several times over.

Making matters worse, the circuit of the wall was too long for the relatively small numbers Dobraev could call on. He had no reserve, nothing to plug a breakthrough. The first penetration of the Murnskai lines would be the end of the battle.

Unless we do something about it. One of the attacks was being pushed back, but at another spot, to the left of the gate, the Beast had made a lodgment on the top of the wall. The musketeers outside were concentrating their fire there, bringing down the white-coated soldiers who ran to drive the attackers back, and the few who made it found themselves struggling hand-to-hand with vicious red-eyes. More of the Beast's bodies dropped from the wall walk into the courtyard, their path into the fortress blocked by only a handful of soldiers.

"Vess!" Winter shouted.

She expected another argument, but Vess was smarter than that. The girl raised her spear and pointed, and the Haeta charged with a roar. Winter drew her saber and went with them, reaching the knot of red-eyes just as the last of the Murnskai were cut down.

The enemy were armed as variously as they were uniformed, carrying everything from sharpened sticks and cudgels to muskets and swords. They turned, fluid as the singular creature they were, to face this new threat, but it did them little good. The front rank of Haeta girls hurled their spears in mid-sprint, a volley that hit hard enough to punch men off their feet. The warriors had time just to grab another spear from their quivers before they met the red-eyes, a solid line of spearpoints against which the Beast's creatures hurled themselves as uselessly as the wolves had days before. Unlike the Murnskai, the Haeta had fought the red-eyes and knew their strengths. Winter, trotting up behind the line, watched as the girls carefully finished each downed opponent, knowing that the Beast's creatures could ignore wounds that would cripple a human.

There was the sharp *crack* of a musket. A girl stumbled, clapping a hand to her throat, then collapsed in a heap. The shooter was on the wall, where a dozen red-eye musketeers were loading with inhuman speed. Another group was pushing down the stairs beside the gate, shoving the Murnskai soldiers back. The red-eyes were willing to accept a bayonet thrust to the gut to get their hands on an opponent, disarming the enemy with their own bodies. The Murnskai wavered, and Winter saw Lieutenant Dobraev running to steady them.

"Byr!" The scream came from Sergeant Gorchov, engaged in his own desperate fight above the gate itself. He struggled to cut himself free, but red-eyes swarmed over the wall on both sides.

Winter gestured with her sword, then charged, hoping Vess and the others would follow. She reached the stairs alongside Dobraev. The Murnskai soldier in front of her slumped to the ground, groaning, and a heavyset peasant woman with a long stick bulled right over him. Winter deflected her downward stroke with one arm and ran her through, then kicked her back into her fellows. A young man with sunken cheeks and carrying a boat hook came forward to take her place, and Winter hacked at him wildly, driving him off-balance. Dobraev, fighting beside her, managed a strike to his throat, and the young man sank to his knees with a gurgle.

A half dozen Haeta arrived, and Winter grabbed Dobraev and spun out of the way as the spearwomen pressed the red-eyes back up the stairs. The rest of them were attacking the musketeers on the wall walk with thrown spears, or climbing up the rickety shacks that backed against the wall to get a handhold and pull themselves up to the palisade. The first girl to make it got a bayonet in the eye and dropped back to the ground, where she lay twitching, but two of her companions grabbed the bearded red-eye who'd stabbed her and pulled him forward, too. He hit the ground headfirst, but the Haeta below took no chances, descending on him with knives flashing.

Winter turned Dobraev to face her. The lieutenant looked dazed, blood spattered across his face, pupils tiny pinpricks in a sea of white. She took him by the collar and shook him roughly, and he gasped, a little color returning to his cheeks.

"Get your men off the *fucking* wall!" Winter shouted.

"You don't know what you're talking about—" the lieutenant began.

Winter snarled. "I am a *goddamned division-general*, and I have been in more battles than you have ever *fucking heard of*. Now give the order before I bash you on the head and give it myself!"

Dobraev took a deep breath, pulled away from her, and shouted.

"*Down from the wall!* Kila, get the men down into the courtyard!"

Sergeant Gorchov answered with a roar, swinging his sword with such violence that he decapitated a red-eye entirely in a spray of gore. Winter spoke urgently into Dobraev's ear, and the lieutenant shouted more instructions. The Beast had concentrated its attacks around the gate, where the defenders were heavily engaged, but the men farther along the wall were free to move. They came down the stairs at a run and lined up in the courtyard, muskets ready. At the lieutenant's signal, the Haeta and Gorchov's few remaining soldiers pulled back, ceding the wall to the red-eyes. As soon as they were clear, the Murnskai opened fire, pinning the red-eyes to their newly won position with a withering volley of musketry.

Answering shots came from the top of the wall, the few survivors using piles of the dead and dying for cover. That was more than the defenders had down in the yard, and Winter waved them back, in among the shacks and lean-tos. In the shadow of one of these insubstantial buildings, she caught her breath. The Murnskai found cover and returned fire, and musket balls *thock*ed into earth and wood all around her.

A bloodied Gorchov staggered over to her and Dobraev and grabbed the lieutenant by the arm. Dobraev stared at him.

"Kila. Kila! Are you all right?" he said.

"I'm fine," Gorchov snarled. "Most of the blood is Vasil's, brave little fool. Who *are* these monsters? I saw a girl of twelve throw herself onto a soldier's bayonet so an old man could dash his brains out with a footstool!"

"They're mad," Winter said. "I told you. They don't value their lives, and they don't feel pain."

"Demons," Gorchov muttered.

"There's no such thing as demons, Kila," Dobraev said. "They die the same as men." He straightened up. "We can pull back to the keep."

"*No,*" Winter said. "You're not listening. We can't hold them off. They're not going to give up. They'll keep coming until we run out of ammunition, if nothing else works. We have to *get out of here.*"

"The ships," Gorchov said. "Kollowrath stripped the sails and oars."

"I sent Abraham and Alex to get help from the refugees," Winter said.

"It'll take too long," Dobraev said. "Once they get the gate open, they'll swamp us."

"We fall back," Winter said. "A fighting withdrawal." She gestured at the cluttered yard. "One shack at a time."

"There's still too many," Gorchov said. "We're down to fifty men, plus your . . . warriors." He eyed the Haeta.

"I may be able to help with that," Abraham said. Winter turned, surprised, and saw him trotting over with at least two dozen men behind him, old Fyotyr in the lead. The newcomers were all refugees, dressed raggedly, and most had only clubs and knives for weapons, but they shouted their enthusiasm.

"What about the ships?" Winter said.

"We found some sailors. Alex is keeping watch," Abraham said. "When they saw what was happening—"

"We want to fight," Fyotyr said. "If I am to die today, better to die like a man than huddling like a sheep."

"Some of the women wanted to fight, too," Abraham said quietly. "The men wouldn't let them."

"There are spare muskets and ammunition in the keep's armory," Dobraev said. "They can help run it forward."

"Tell them," Winter said, and added in Vordanai, "And if any of them decide they want to use those muskets themselves, I'm certainly not going to stop them."

It took thirty minutes before the ships were pronounced ready for the swollen, fast-flowing river, thirty minutes purchased in blood, step-by-step. As Dobraev had predicted, the red-eyes soon got the gate open, despite concentrated fire from the Murnskai musketeers that left dozens dead in the gateway. Once they did, a tide of them flowed in from outside the fortress, and the musketry got considerably less one-sided. The Murnskai were forced back through the camp, giving ground as the red-eyes assembled and charged, a line of powder smoke marking the front.

Without the refugees, the fight would have been hopeless. The civilians picked up the muskets that fell from dead soldiers, providing fresh bodies for Dobraev to throw into the line. Now that he had the right idea, he was skilled enough that Winter left him on his own, sticking close to the Haeta. She and Vess led them wherever the red-eyes threatened to break through, blunting their attacks long enough for the line to pull back. The price they paid was terrible, the girls whom Winter had come to know falling one after another, cut down by musket-fire or gutted with bayonets.

They were fighting around the base of the Keep when word finally came. The stone walls provided cover for musketeers who fired weapons reloaded by refugee women huddled in its lee. A refugee girl grabbed Winter's arm to get her attention.

"Alex says the boats are ready!" she shouted, almost inaudible above the battle racket. "She says to come *now*; the sailors don't want to wait!"

Winter locked eyes with Vess, who waited nearby with a dozen surviving, blood-stained Haeta. "Go board," she said. "Don't let them leave without the rest of us."

Vess grinned savagely and pointed with her spear, and they took off at a run. Winter found Dobraev and shouted the news in his ear. The defenders disengaged, gradually at first, a few men turning to fire to keep the red-eyes at bay while the rest hurried ahead of them. When the Beast realized what was happening, its creatures surged forward, ignoring musketry and opposition, ignoring wounds, ignoring *everything*.

"*Run!*" Winter screamed. "*Now!*"

They ran, dodging through the camp, all organized resistance gone. A soldier tripped over a tent line and vanished, trampled by the horde of red-eyes. There was scarcely any firing now, just a mad scramble to escape. Winter thought her heart would burst, her lungs sawing at the air, Dobraev leaping nimbly over a broken crate just ahead of her.

Then there were no more shacks, and the stone pier was in view. The two ships, packed from bow to stern with a dense mass of humanity, rode dangerously low in the water. They'd pulled away from the pier, held in place by only a few straining lines, with cargo nets dangling from their sides into the rushing water. The soldiers were throwing away their muskets and jumping, swimming out to get a hold on the nets and haul themselves up.

At the ship's rails, a handful of muskets fired, bringing down a few red-eyes out of the horde. Winter didn't stop to look. She pounded down the pier and flung herself into the water. It was shockingly cold, momentarily driving the breath from her lungs, but she felt her boot touch the sandy bottom and push off again. A few floating steps, and she got hold of a net and pulled herself up with arms that suddenly felt as strong as wet paper. Someone grabbed her. She looked up to find Sergeant Gorchov grinning broadly, his beard crusted with blood.

On the deck, someone took an ax to the lines, and the ships sprang into the current. They ran out the oars, sweeping hard to keep themselves steady in the swift-flowing river. Behind them, the red-eyes hit the shore and started to swim, and for a horrible moment Winter thought it had all been useless. But even the Beast couldn't drive flesh and blood beyond its ultimate limits, and the Bataria was in full flood. Most of the red-eyes that went in the water were swept under and away, and the few that closed with the ships were summarily dispatched with musket shots.

We made it. Winter stared at the crowd of monsters remaining on the shore. *Saints and fucking martyrs. We actually made it.* She looked across the rope net and found Vess, soaked and huddled against the hull. *Some of us.*

They put in at a rocky beach on the north bank, fifty miles downstream from the fortress. Many of the soldiers made it only as far as the shallows before collapsing from exhaustion, unable to do more than lie in the water and struggle for breath. It fell to the refugees who'd stayed out of the fighting to drag them ashore and get fires built. The north bank of the Bataria seemed to have no trace of civilization, and thick woods came down almost to the river, so firewood, at least, was plentiful.

"We're going to be pretty hungry by the time we get to Dimiotsk," Alex said.

She and Abraham had helped Winter, whose arms had been cramping so badly she hadn't been able to get herself loose from the net. Now, seated beside the blaze of the fire with a cup of warm soup cradled in her hands, she was starting to feel alive again.

"Most of the refugees brought something in their packs or their pockets, but we made them leave all the heavy baggage behind," Alex went on. "It'll be two or three days to the city, at least."

"We'll survive," Abraham said firmly. "And some of the sailors said they might be able to fish."

Winter nodded slowly. Alex, crouching beside her, peered at her a little closer.

"Are you sure you're all right?" she said. "Abraham, do you want to take a look at her?"

"She's exhausted," Abraham said. "Leave her alone, Alex."

"I'm fine," Winter said. She unfolded her fingers from the tin cup of soup with some effort and took a sip. It was thin, but wonderfully warm. "Just . . . cold."

Alex nodded. Abraham clapped her on the shoulder, and they moved off, talking quietly. Winter stared into the depths of the fire, watching the logs slowly crumble, until she heard a soft grunt and looked up to find Lieutenant Dobraev sitting nearby.

"Your friend is quite the healer," he said. "He tended several men I had despaired of, and they all seem much improved."

Winter nodded. "He's . . . very experienced."

"Such wisdom in a man so young." Dobraev shook his head. "I do not pretend to understand you, Winter Ihernglass, or what happened here. I am not sure I ever will. Are you truly a general?"

She nodded.

"In what army?"

Winter didn't think she could lie to him at this point. "Vordanai."

"I guessed as much. The famous Girls' Only division."

Correcting him seemed pedantic, so Winter only nodded again.

Dobraev shifted, holding his hands up to the fire. "No need to tell anyone else, I think. I am not even sure if we are still at war with you. I have heard rumors . . . of many things. When we reach Dimiotsk, I will report to the colonel there for orders. I imagine you'll have time to slip away before then."

"Thank you," Winter said.

"It would be poor form to turn you in after you saved my life, and the lives of my entire command."

"*Some* of your command," Winter said.

"True. But without your warning, we all would have been slaughtered by those . . . fanatics."

Maybe. Winter couldn't be sure. *If I'd never come here, would the Beast have destroyed the fortress? Or would it simply never have bothered? Am I helping people, or just mitigating the catastrophe I drag in my wake?* She took a long breath, thick with the scent of woodsmoke.

"For what it's worth," she said, "I'm glad I could help."

"What will your Trans-Batariai friends do?"

"Continue north, I imagine." *I should talk to Vess.* Somehow the thought of standing up, right at the moment, was unbearable.

"Tell them they are welcome to continue down the river with us, if they would like to put more distance between themselves and the enemy." Dobraev looked over his shoulder toward the river. "Will they build boats, do you think?"

"I don't know. I don't think so. But when we get to Dimiotsk, I would advise your superiors to be ready. They'll be coming sooner or later." *They'll be coming for everyone, sooner or later.*

"Oh, believe me, I plan to. Mohkba needs to be told."

"Will Kollowrath cause trouble, when he recovers?"

"I doubt it." Dobraev looked pained. "Apparently the men I sent to retrieve him from his sickroom in the keep disobeyed orders and fled directly to the ships."

Oh. Winter swallowed. For all that the captain had nearly gotten her killed, she wasn't sure he deserved to be left for the Beast. *No one deserves that.*

"We will spend the night here, I think," Dobraev said. "The ships are too heavy to risk the river in the dark."

"Keep a watch," Winter said. "Just in case."

"Believe me," Dobraev said, looking over his shoulder again, "I plan to."

There were no tents, besides those the Haeta carried, and few blankets. Winter ended up stretched out on the hard ground beside Alex and Abraham, pressed tight together against the chill with a couple of ragged cloaks thrown across them. The watch fed the fires all night, keeping off the worst of the cold, and Winter woke feeling stiff and achy but otherwise much improved.

The trappers among the refugees had erected a few snares, and they had rabbits for breakfast, though not nearly enough to assuage Winter's hunger. She chewed the last of the jerky from her own pack and told herself it was only two days to the city. *We'll manage.*

As soon as it was light enough to see clearly, Dobraev busied himself getting the party back aboard the boats. Somehow this was much more difficult without the threat of the red-eyes pushing everyone forward, and arguments broke out about who would get what space. Sergeant Gorchov had his hands full breaking up shoving matches. A few of the trappers and other folk used to the wilds quietly melted away, preferring to chance it in the forest rather than stay with the noisy crowd.

Winter watched, waiting for her turn. There had been no sign of the Beast attempting to cross the river, but most of the Murnskai soldiers were still standing guard, muskets at the ready. In the midst of the dead fires from last night's camp, the small group of Haeta were checking their packs and preparing to depart. Glancing at them, Winter saw Vess looking back at her, and she suppressed a sigh. *I can't put it off forever.*

As Winter came over, Vess stood apart from the others, her pack already on her back, a spear in hand. Including her, there were seventeen Haeta girls left, half of the group that had rescued Winter from the Beast's pursuit. Yath was dead. Clever Yuil, Nish with her quick hands, soft-spoken, wide-eyed Boli—

Enough. Listing them won't bring anyone back. Winter forced a smile.

"You're going north?" she said.

Vess nodded. "I know this territory. It is not ours, but it is not far to Haeta land. And the tribes close to here will not be unfriendly."

"Good." Winter hesitated. "Dobraev offered to take you to the city. It might be safer. I don't know if the red-eyes will come over the river."

"If they do, we will kill them," Vess said matter-of-factly. "I will warn my tribe when we return."

Winter nodded. There was an awkward silence. "I'm sorry," she said, after a moment.

"For what?"

"For putting myself in charge. I . . . tried. But . . ."

"Winter." Vess shook her head, struggling with herself. "Leti . . . would have wanted this. For everyone to escape together, however much it cost us. I told you that you had to live up to her expectations. I think you have done so."

"Thank you."

Vess turned to look over her warriors. "We should go. The farther I am from this place by nightfall, the more comfortable I will feel. Good luck to you."

"And to you."

"I hope your blessed friends find what they're looking for."

So do I, thought Winter. She gave a slight bow, which Vess returned awkwardly. At command in their own language, the Haeta formed up. A few of the girls waved to Winter as they headed north at an easy trot. Winter waved back, then turned to the river.

Alex and Abraham were waiting for her, some distance away from where the crowd around the ships was finally thinning.

"The Haeta are gone," Winter said.

"I'd almost rather walk with them to the city," Alex said. "At least then we'd have something to eat."

"I don't think you could convince them to go to the city," Abraham said.

"I know." Alex sighed, and gestured at the overcrowded ships. "I'm just not looking forward to *that*."

"They're safer this way," Winter said. "I'm the one the Beast is following. The farther they are from me, the better."

"It's not your fault the thing hates you," Alex said.

"It's just a fact," Winter said.

"You did the best you could," Abraham said.

I always do, Winter thought. *And then people die.* Abraham caught her eye with a knowing look, and she half smiled. "I know. The paths not taken."

"One step at a time," Abraham said.

"What?" Alex looked at them. "Nobody's going to fill me in?"

"It's just . . . something we talked about," Winter said. "Come on. Let's get aboard."

CHAPTER TWENTY

RAESINIA

The room at Grindel's was considerably cheerier than the dour chambers of the Keep. Raesinia had wondered if Borelgai were just allergic to color, but apparently the merchant elite allowed itself more license than the royal family, at least in private. Grindel's was a private club on the top floor of a building near the Great Market, with enormous windows that looked out over the bustling activity on the surrounding streets. The market building itself was something like an enormous cobbled square, covered by multiple peaked roofs but open on all sides. A steady stream of carriages pulled into a circular drive at one end, while people milled in crowds on every side, struggling to make their way under the roof and out of the rain. Out of sight were the pits, where speculators lined the rails calling or gesturing to catch the attention of the dealers working at the bottom.

Raesinia was curious to see it all, actually, but according to Cora, visiting the market itself was considered something of a faux pas for a serious merchant; it implied that one didn't have people one could trust to take care of one's interests. It was for hirelings to scuttle and shout in the pits. *Real* business was transacted high above, in the private chambers of the clubs like Grindel's, which topped the buildings that ringed the Great Market.

From the outside, there was nothing to distinguish the club from the offices below it, save for the wide windows. Visitors arrived by the elevator, a device Raesinia had never encountered before—a wood-paneled box that rose smoothly through ten stories, powered, Matthew told her, by a team of oxen in the basement. If one's name were on the list, the dark, severe doors of the club were opened by a footman, revealing a considerably more lively interior. It wasn't Ohnlei—where it often felt like someone had gone berserk with gold leaf and mirrored glass—but there were oddities everywhere. Tall wooden figures, elaborately carved, alternated with statues of animal-headed gods from Khandar. Shelves held brilliantly colored glass and jewelry from Hamvelt, silk banners from the Old Coast, and strange bronze weapons that Raesinia guessed had come all the way from the Southern Kingdoms. Paintings in every possible style adorned the walls, in a variety of gaudy frames.

It was a monument, in other words, to the power of commerce. The wealth and beauty of the world, brought to Borel and mounted for display, like lions and tigers in a menagerie. Vordan was poorly represented, all things considered, and Raesinia felt vaguely offended.

"Vordanai art is out of favor at the moment, I'm afraid," Prince Matthew said when she asked him about it. "Fashion has dictated that the Hamveltai schools are in this year, though that may be growing stale." He chuckled. "If you really want to see the influence of your country, visit the kitchen and the cellar. Vordanai cheese and wine never go out of style."

They'd come from the Keep in a covered carriage, and Raesinia had worn a hood and veil, which Matthew had assured her was common for noble ladies who didn't wish to be recognized. The king had agreed to permit her to leave the palace provided she was in the company of the second prince, though she didn't doubt there were discreet watchers following in case she decided to make a dash for the harbor.

Not that Raesinia was inclined to do so. It wouldn't be enough to get away from Georg. She needed his cooperation, especially with Duke Dorsay and a Borelgai naval squadron already on the way to rendezvous with Marcus' beleaguered forces. *We need our leverage.* Cora and Eric were at work elsewhere, helping to acquire it. But this was a task that Raesinia could only attend to herself.

The room to which the footman led them was one of several lined up at the edge of the club, where the windows looked into the Great Market. It was small but comfortably furnished, with a polished rectangular table, a sofa, a liquor cabinet, and a glassed-in shelf displaying a set of jeweled human skulls no doubt obtained by some Borelgai trader in a far-off land. At Matthew's direction, Raesinia took the seat closest to the corner, leaving her hood up and her veil down.

"Just like last time," he said quietly, sitting next to her. "Let me do the talking unless they ask you a question."

Raesinia suppressed a sigh. Once again, she was *on display. At least this time it's by choice.* "Are you and the duke close?"

"We've had our differences, but we used to be inseparable," Matthew said. "He's gone *respectable*, I'm afraid."

"And he's rich?"

"Oh, yes. Half the nobles in Borel are in debt up to their eyeballs, but the Farings own a successful shipping company and several banks in addition to their ancestral estates. If he signs on, I think we'll be most of the way there."

Raesinia nodded and went quiet as there was a polite cough outside the door. A moment later the latch clicked, and a man in a dark suit came in. She'd seen so many Borelgai aristocrats over the past few weeks that there was a certain interchangeability about them, the same well-cut grays and blacks, the same sober ties, the same vaguely ridiculous hats. This one was younger than average and clean-shaven, with blue eyes and a mouth that already seemed on the verge of an ironic smile.

"Finny," Matthew said, getting up and extending a hand.

"Matty," the man said. They shook enthusiastically, and the visitor swept off his hat. "It's been too long."

"Not my fault," Matthew said. "I keep sending you invitations."

"Yes, well, the wife doesn't approve of your invitations anymore," the visitor said. "She says you're decadent."

"I have always striven to be," Matthew said. "It's good to know that my efforts have borne fruit."

The visitor barked a laugh, then turned to Raesinia. "And who is the young lady?"

"We'll, ah, get to that," Matthew said. "Have a seat, would you?"

"A mystery, eh? How exciting." He bowed in Raesinia's direction. "I am Phineas Faring, Duke of Highwatch. At your service, my lady."

"Thank you, Your Grace," Raesinia said. "I apologize for being unable to introduce myself."

"Believe me, I'm familiar with Matty's taste for theatrics." Phineas slid into a chair. "So, what's all this about? Your letter was most insistent that you had an opportunity that was not to be missed."

"If anything, I understated the case," Matthew said. "But first I need your word that, yes or no, nothing I'm about to say will leave this room. You know how sensitive these things can be."

"Perfectly. My word as a gentleman." Phineas leaned forward slightly. "So?"

"Vordanai debt," Matthew said, pronouncing the words as though they ought to be a revelation.

Phineas sighed and sat back. "Oh, Matty. You too?"

"I'm not the first to approach you?"

"My boy, you're not even the tenth. Everyone and their uncle seems to be betting on whether our friends to the south will pay their bills. I've had a half dozen asking me to buy bonds, and a half dozen more insisting I should be selling them short."

"But you haven't taken a position."

"No." Phineas shook his head. "The whole thing is a touch *volatile* for my tastes. Armies in the field, and all that. Who knows which way it will go? I might hazard ten marks just to be sporting, but—"

"What if I told you that I know which way it will go?"

"Matty." Phineas looked like someone had given him a lemon to suck. "Please. If you need money, just be honest and ask me as an old friend. I know you and your father haven't been on good terms."

"He's not the only connection I have in the Keep."

Matthew half turned, which was Raesinia's cue. She raised her veil and pulled back her hood, nodding respectfully at Phineas.

"Raesinia Orboan," she said.

"Raesinia—Raesinia *Orboan*?" Phineas practically leapt out of his seat. "The Queen of Vordan?"

"And," Matthew said smoothly, "my fiancée."

"Oh," Phineas said, settling rapidly. "Oh, I *see*. That's . . . *very* interesting."

Raesinia could practically see the gears turning behind his eyes. As Matthew went into the actual sales pitch, Phineas kept looking back to her, tilting his head as though trying to see her from a different angle.

We've got him.

". . . and I'm confident," Matthew said, "that, given our unique advantages, the company will be able to keep ahead of the pack."

"Confidentiality?" Phineas said.

"Assured. Our shares are already trading in the market. If I sign these over to you"—Matthew raised a satchel, which contained a thick stack of gilt-edged documents—"you can deposit them with your favorite deniable broker, and there will be no connection visible between us. The staff here is known for perfect discretion."

"They are indeed." Phineas eyed the share certificates like a hungry man watching a steak browning in a pan. "And how much were you thinking, Matty, my old friend?"

"Two hundred thousand marks at minimum. Below that and we'll need to cut too many people in—"

"Make it five hundred," Phineas said. "I'll run it through my box at Three Crowns Bank. You know the one?"

"Oh, yes." Matthew smiled. "You won't regret this, Finny."

"I'd better not." Phineas grinned. "You have no idea what the wife would say."

"Does it bother you?" Raesinia said, when they were back in the carriage and rattling their way toward the Keep.

"Does what?"

"Doing this to your old friends."

"They're not my friends," Matthew said. "They're the boys that I got drunk with, or cousins I saw at my father's parties. None of them care about me. The less popular I am with my father, the less I hear from them. Strange how that works." He rolled his eyes. "I don't have many real friends, and none of them are rich enough for this sort of thing."

"I'm glad you won't be troubled by pangs of conscience, then." Raesinia found that she was, a little. Phineas had seemed like a nice enough person. *If things go badly, we're going to make a lot of lives very miserable.*

She gritted her teeth. *Let them complain to Georg. I'll do what I have to.*

The carriage rattled under the looming gatehouse and around to a rear drive, one of several that led into the labyrinthine bulk of the Keep itself. Jo and Barely were waiting to escort Raesinia to the courtyard, where she met Cora.

"I wish you'd let us come with you," Barely said, as they walked through the wood-paneled corridors, past the stiff-necked Life Guards. "Anything could happen out in the city."

"I appreciate that," Raesinia said. "But anything could happen in here. If Georg wants to hurt me, we can't stop him, and I can't imagine anyone else daring to cross him now."

Joanna signed something, and Barely gave a bitter laugh.

"What did she say?" *I'm really going to have to learn to understand her.*

"Old proverb," Barely said. "The quickest way to die is to underestimate your enemies. The second quickest is to overestimate them."

Raesinia snorted.

Cora was waiting beside a decorative stream, near where it ran into a grated archway and under the wall. Barely and Joanna kept watch for interlopers, though the yard was empty except for the occasional hurrying servant. Cora was bouncing on her heels.

"Is he in?" she whispered.

Raesinia nodded and held up five fingers. Cora's face lit up.

"Five hundred thousand marks." Her eyes went glassy as she calculated. "Banks require ten percent in equity. We've been getting our derivatives at four or five percent, less handling fees, a little for . . ." She went quiet. "Call it a hundred million, give or take a million."

"Give or take a *million*?"

Cora shrugged. "The exact rate is hard to predict."

Raesinia shook her head. When they'd paid five thousand eagles for Danton Aurenne, that had seemed like a fortune to her. It probably *was* a fortune to almost anyone. The amounts Cora talked about now felt dreamlike and unreal.

"*Are* there even a hundred million marks?"

"You mean physical coins?" Cora laughed. "Almost certainly not. If you count bank deposits, outstanding credit, metal value of—"

"Never mind." Raesinia pressed her hands to her temples. "Is it enough?"

"I think so. I'll need a couple of days to put the appropriate transactions through."

"Then what?" The broad outline of the plan had been Raesinia's, an idea that would never have entered Cora's tidy, rule-abiding mind. Once it had come to actually implementing it, though, she'd been dependent on Cora's acumen. *As usual.*

"Then we move to the next step," Cora said. "The warning shot."

Raesinia's negotiations with Goodman had taken on a slightly dreamlike quality as well.

Officially, her engagement to the second prince, and the deal that had brokered it, was still a secret. But there seemed to be no secrets in the Keep, and it had become clear almost immediately that Goodman knew everything. Raesinia knew that he knew, and vice versa, which meant that they were both well aware that their meetings had become a farce. Goodman continued to stick to his guns on the matter of Vordanai debt, even while he knew that his monarch was preparing to overrule him.

Maybe it's just for public consumption. There had to be *some* people in the Keep who didn't know the secret, and probably a lot more outside. It would look strange if the negotiations stopped, especially after the king had ordered the navy dispatched to Vordan's aid. *Or else he's maneuvering against Georg and the other Honest Fellows.* By maintaining his resistance, Goodman might be intending to show that he wasn't willing to be bullied, or possibly he was setting himself up to win future concessions from the throne.

It was impossible to know, and for Raesinia's purposes it didn't particularly matter. All it meant was that she had to sit through sessions that had long since become utterly rote. She would be on one side of a table, with Eric beside her, and Goodman would be on the other with a gaggle of aides. Raesinia would read her statement, which contained an offer to negotiate a settlement on Vordan's prerevolution debts. It was the most generous offer Cora thought they could afford, but it was clearly unacceptable to Goodman, who in turn would read his own statement about the sanctity of contracts and his unwillingness to impose burdens on private bondholders.

Then they would bow to each other and leave through opposite doors. Inevitably, there was a small crowd waiting outside, kept at bay by Jo and Barely. Nobles and other palace hangers-on congregated in hopes of a quick word from Raesinia, who ordinarily didn't oblige them. Today, however, she paused as a young man in a smart suit stepped in front of her and begged her pardon.

"Your Highness," he said, when he saw she was looking at him. "I'm Count Edward Holish. I was hoping to invite you to a small gathering—"

There was a general clearing of throats, and other gentlemen stepped forward, some of them waving introductory cards.

"—a dinner—"

"—perhaps you'd enjoy—"

"—a tour of the harbor—"

How popular we are. Now that the king's offer was widely known, it was clear that her favor suddenly had considerable value. Hence the self-serving courtiers pushing and shoving to present their invitations and the steady stream of perfumed envelopes making their way to her door.

"I'm sorry, gentlemen," she said, a bit more loudly than was really polite. "I'm afraid my business here requires all my time at the present." She allowed a little exasperation into her voice, and shook her head. "Not that we seem to be making much progress!"

"Your Highness!" Eric said, not having to work hard to feign shock.

Raesinia put on a guilty expression, like she'd been caught talking out of turn. The whispers had already started by the time Eric and her guards hustled her around the corner and out of sight.

They went straight to Cora's suite to wait for results. It didn't take long—after an hour, Cora came bounding in, grinning gleefully.

"It's working," she said. "I think a dozen messengers must have gone straight to the market. Vor River Trading—that's us—has dropped almost thirty percent in the last forty-five minutes. And the securities market as a whole is down nearly twenty percent. It's a bloodbath."

"When does the next message go out?" Raesinia said.

"Soon," Cora said breathlessly. "There's still two hours until the market closes. I'm going to go see what happens."

Raesinia would have liked to go herself, but that would have tipped her hand. Instead, she returned to the room she shared with Matthew and kept waiting. The second prince was at the market, reassuring his friends and distributing Raesinia's message.

This was the part that had most worried her. She'd seen, back in the revolution, that once fear and panic were unleashed, they could prove almost impossible to stop. Her statement this afternoon, the seemingly banal admission that negotiations were going poorly, had been taken as the symbol it had been meant to be. If negotiations collapsed, Vordanai debt would be worthless, and companies that speculated in Vordanai debt—like their own VRT—would be in serious trouble.

The new message said that Raesinia remained committed to finding a mutually acceptable solution to the debt problem, and hinted in the most oblique possible terms that she was aware of the conditions in the markets in general and concerned about VRT in particular. This would probably go over most heads, but the friends of Second Prince Matthew, who had bought into the venture on the strength of his promise that he had Raesinia's support, would hear it loud and clear. It *should* turn things around, making today's scare brief. *If greed is stronger than fear.* That seemed likely—this was Borel—but . . .

Raesinia didn't relax until Cora returned, sending Barely over with a note. "VRT stable at -9, broader market -3. Hornets buzzing." The last referred to Goodman and his friends among the Honest Fellows, whose market activities Cora had been observing. The wild fluctuations had no doubt alarmed them, and Raesinia felt that she could count on them to take the appropriate steps.

So far, so good.

"It's Master Goodman," Barely said through the door. "He wants to see you immediately."

"We have a conference scheduled for Thursday," Raesinia said, feigning confusion. They were in Cora's room, sitting behind the heavy dining table.

"This is not an *official* meeting." Goodman's voice was muffled. "This is urgent. And I suspect you would prefer to be discreet."

I *would prefer to be discreet, would I?* She kept her voice neutral and hid her smile. "Very well, I suppose. Let him in." She got up, exchanging glances with Cora.

The door opened. Goodman was in his usual suit, but there was something very slightly off, his cuffs uneven and his tie askew. For him, Raesinia suspected, this was the equivalent of turning up to work stark naked. He pushed into the room, and she had to give ground rapidly to avoid a collision. He glared at her, ignoring Cora completely.

"I expected better," he said. "I don't know why. In retrospect, this is exactly the sort of pathetic grubbing so typical of Vordanai. But I thought that being royalty meant you'd have at least the pretense of honor. More fool me, I suppose."

"My dear Master Goodman," Raesinia said, pretending shock. "What exactly are you implying?"

"We can drop the act, as long as we're alone."

"We're not alone," Raesinia said. "I think you know my companion Cora?"

Goodman waved a hand impatiently and sighed. "If I must spell it out, I'm referring to your involvement in the Vor River Trading concern. Do you deny it?"

"I suppose it would be silly to try, seeing as you seem so certain."

"Believe me, I didn't want to do this." Goodman took a deep breath, steadying himself on the back of a chair. "The thought that a member of one of the great royal families of the continent—albeit one fallen on hard times—would stoop to entangling herself in *trade* out of pecuniary interest was the farthest thing from my mind. However, after the events of the last few days and my own investigations, it has become clear to me that you have done exactly that, and furthermore have used your privileged position to profit from our private discussions. I am, frankly, ashamed, and I suspect His Majesty feels likewise."

Goodman took a deep breath as he finished this speech, and Raesinia gave him a moment to recover. She walked to the sideboard, where there were several dusty bottles of amber liquor.

"Would you like a drink, Master Goodman?"

"I would not," Goodman said stiffly. "I ask again. Do you deny any of this?"

"Let me see if I understand what you're accusing me of. You think that I fed information from our negotiations to this trading company, in order to unfairly make money for myself in the market?"

"That is exactly what you did," Goodman said. "And it is highly illegal under Borelgai law, I might add."

"Would this be a good time to point out that Vor River Trading has not, in fact, made any money?" Raesinia poured a tumbler half full of sticky spirit, and carried it back to the table.

"I don't see that it matters," Goodman said. "I never accused you of *competence* in your crimes."

"I see. So, what do you intend to do?"

"In light of your agreement with His Majesty, I am prepared to be lenient," Goodman said, swelling visibly. "The concern will be wound up immediately. You will be confined to the Keep until your marriage, with or without an escort from the second prince. Your companions"—he glanced derisively at Cora—"will be returned to Vordan by the first available vessel."

"And the creditors?"

"What? What creditors?"

"The creditors," Raesinia said patiently, "of Vor River Trading. As I said, the concern has done poorly. If it's wound up, I doubt there will be enough to pay its debts."

"Don't expect me to believe you honestly care," Goodman said. "But His Majesty will, I'm sure, make your creditors whole." He smiled nastily. "I imagine we'll recoup our losses from Vordan eventually."

"Oh, good." Raesinia turned to Cora. "How much would that be, do you think? In round figures."

"In round figures?" Cora's lips moved soundlessly. "Six hundred, maybe seven. Certainly not more than eight . . ."

Goodman rolled his eyes. Cora counted, ostentatiously, on her fingers, and then grinned.

"Yes, that's about right. Call it seven hundred million marks."

The merchant's face clouded. "What sort of nonsense is this?"

"We've had quite an influx of investors of late," Raesinia said. "And with Second Prince Matthew vouching for us, your banks have been more than happy to extend credit, which has allowed us to leverage those investments—that's the term, isn't it? Leverage?"

"You've *lost* seven hundred *million marks*?"

"We haven't lost it yet," Cora said. "It's invested in the market for Vordanai debt derivatives."

"We bet on Vordan's not having to pay, in other words. For some reason there was no shortage of investors willing to take the other end of that bet. So if Vordan *does* pay out in the end, we'll be in quite the hole."

"I see," Goodman said grimly. "Clearly I underestimated your capacity for dishonor. And this is supposed to force my hand, is it? Make me grant you a favorable deal?"

"Something like that," Raesinia said.

Goodman grinned like a snake. "Passing clever, I'll admit. But contracts are just paper. If the king declares them invalid, your little attempt at blackmail goes up in smoke."

"That would be very interesting," Raesinia said. "Cora, do you want to explain this part?"

"Well," she said cheerfully, "first of all, those contracts are pledged as collateral to the banks, in exchange for the loans that paid for them. So if they go up in smoke, then a lot of angry creditors are going to come looking for VRT."

"That is hardly my problem."

"What they're going to find," Cora went on, "is that our accounting has been . . . well, a bit irregular. Specifically, we've sold more shares in the company than actually exist."

"A lot more," Raesinia said.

"Each mark of income is about thirteen thousand percent overpledged," Cora agreed. "There are a lot of investors holding a lot of paper that will suddenly be worth essentially nothing. When they find out, there'll be a panic."

"You—" Goodman looked from Cora to Raesinia and back again. "You didn't. That's absurd."

"I suppose I'm just not very good with numbers," Cora said.

"Given the size of the company, if VRT goes down hard, the whole market in Vordanai derivatives is going down with it," Raesinia said. "Once it gets out where our loans came from, there'll be runs on the banks. And then the banks that lent to those banks, and so on."

"Including the Yellow Shield Bank," Cora said. "They're one of our largest creditors. And I believe you're the majority owner, aren't you, Master Goodman?"

"Do you have any idea what you've done?" Goodman said. "If a *breath* of this hits the market—"

"Then everything collapses like a house of cards. That was more or less the point." Raesinia picked up the tumbler again. "Are you sure I can't offer you that drink?"

This time Goodman took it. He dragged one of the chairs away from the table, sank into it, and downed half the liquor in a single swallow. He coughed, then slammed the glass down, amber slopping over the rim. A muscle jumped in his cheek.

"You stupid little *girls*," he snarled. "Playing with things you can't possibly understand."

"I would say we understand them considerably better than you."

"You'll face justice for this. Queen or not. The people will demand it." His lips tightened. "You'll never see Vordan again."

"It's possible," Raesinia admitted. "That will mean war, of course. Which, as I understand it, is the one thing Georg is desperate to avoid. Are you ready to explain to him what's happened?"

"On the other hand," Cora said, as though she were just thinking of it, "Georg might welcome the prospect of a general collapse. He could repudiate the Crown's debt fairly easily under the circumstances, couldn't he? Bad news for anyone who'd lent him money, of course."

Goodman had gone very pale, and he flinched visibly at this last shot. When he reached for the sticky tumbler again, Raesinia knew they'd won.

"What do you want?" he whispered.

"Tell the king that my marriage to the second prince is off. In addition to the squadron already dispatched, he's to follow through on his promise to send an army to help defeat Janus, which we agree is in everyone's best interest."

"I think," Goodman said, "that I might—"

"I'm not finished," Raesinia snapped. "You'll also agree to Cora's plan for repayment of Vordan's debts, which she assures me is the most generous we can afford."

"Ah." Goodman swallowed. "Anything else?"

"Ihannes Pulwer-Monsangton is to be replaced as ambassador to Vordan by Second Prince Matthew. He gets to name his own escort from among the Life Guards."

Goodman looked briefly puzzled, then shook his head. "And what do I get in exchange for all of this?"

"Once we're back in Vordan, Cora will wind down VRT. Slowly, so as not to cause a panic. I suggest you take steps to suppress the market in Vordanai debt speculation, so when the details are announced it doesn't rock the boat too much."

"Of course," Cora added, "if you change your mind, then we can simply go public with VRT and flip the table."

"His Majesty won't like it," Goodman said.

"My understanding is that you have considerable influence with the king," Raesinia said. "I suggest you use it."

Goodman glared at her for a moment, then gulped the rest of the liquor from the tumbler and bowed his head.

"Another messenger," Barely called.

"Tell him we're not interested," Raesinia said. She was watching as Matthew's servants packed up her things, which had gotten a bit disorganized when they'd been hurriedly moved from her old quarters. *I don't remember bringing so many dresses. I suppose I wasn't paying much attention when we packed.*

"He's got fancy gold braid all over him," Barely said. "Says he's the chief herald, or something like that."

"Chief herald?" Raesinia said. "What does he want?"

"Says you've got to come and see the king."

"Tell him I don't think I do."

Raesinia's heart beat a little faster as the voices outside the door grew louder. She was aware she was playing a dangerous game here—push Georg too far and he might lash out, consequences be damned. But she wanted him to be clear on how much their positions had changed, and she couldn't help but take a little personal satisfaction. *I don't like being dictated to.*

Eventually the chief herald left, and the packing continued. Matthew was already down at the docks, arranging their passage. Raesinia didn't intend to waste another hour, now that she'd gotten what she needed. *The sooner we can be back in Vordan City, the better.* God only knew what the Deputies-General had been up to in her absence.

"Your Highness?" Barely said.

Raesinia rolled her eyes. "If it's another messenger, tell him—"

"It's the king," Barely said. "Do you want me to tell him to go away?"

Well. There was such a thing as pushing too far. *Though I'd love to see the look on his face if Barely told him to get lost.* "Let him in, I suppose."

The door opened. The two maidservants bowed low as Georg came into the room, muddy red jewel gleaming on the breast of his suit.

"Your Highness," he said.

"Your Majesty." Raesinia turned to the servants. "Would you give us a few minutes, please?"

They bowed even lower and hurried out, relief written all over their faces. Raesinia turned back to Georg, who stood staring at her for a moment, hands clasped behind his back.

"It's not done, you know, for the king to visit a guest," he said. "I don't know what you did to the chief herald, but the man is practically apoplectic. He's always had a somewhat fragile disposition."

"I didn't think we had anything left to discuss," Raesinia said. "At our last meeting, you made it clear I could deal with you, or deal with the Honest Fellows. As Master Goodman has proven accommodating . . ." She spread her hands.

"Oh, yes. He told me all about it."

"*All* about it?" Raesinia couldn't suppress a slight grin.

"He required some prompting, I must admit." The king started to pace the length of the foyer. "I could, of course, simply have you all arrested."

"I went over that with Goodman," Raesinia said, keeping her voice nonchalant. "It's possible. But it would mean war."

"Only if you are the Queen of Vordan. If I were to come to an accommodation with Vhalnich . . ."

"I'm sure he'd be happy to entertain the offer. Much as the wolf is happy to listen to the sheep profess their loyalty." She shrugged. "Also, it's possible that the secrets of VRT might find their way to the market if anything were to happen to me. Just a . . . hunch."

Georg snorted. Reaching the wall, he turned back to Raesinia, eyes narrow. "You've thought of everything, haven't you?"

"I do my best."

The king sighed, rolling his shoulders, first one and then the other. Raesinia watched him warily.

"Was it such a burden," he said eventually, "to have to marry my son?"

"Your son is a wonderful person," Raesinia said, a little surprised. "But he made it clear he had no interest in marrying *me*. And I have my own feelings to consider."

"Those who sit on a throne can rarely afford the luxury of feelings," Georg said. "If you don't understand that now, you will someday. Assuming you live that long."

"I wonder if it's not the other way around," Raesinia said.

"I'm not sure I understand."

"There was a time when I told myself my feelings didn't matter. I did what I had to for the throne, for the people, for my family." She waved a hand. "Look where it's gotten us. I can't say for certain I would have gone a different path, but . . . at some point cold reason takes you only so far." *I realized that in Murnsk, standing on the bridge, watching Marcus run the other way. When I held my hand out . . .*

"It's a nice sentiment," Georg said. "I hope you don't wind up paying dearly for it."

"I've paid a great deal as it is, Your Majesty."

He shook his head and turned to the door. "Good luck, then."

"Your son has promised me he'll write to you," Raesinia said.

Georg paused, his back turned.

"You might want to try listening to him," she said. "Just a bit of advice, from one monarch to another."

"I'll keep it in mind," Georg said.

Part Four

INTERLUDE

JANUS

He felt the Beast's primary focus sweeping toward him, a hurricane moving over the mindscape, scattering the floating wisps of thought like dandelion puffs. Janus had to work harder to hold himself together, exerting his will to keep his thoughts from being torn apart and drawn into the ravenous maw.

Winter has escaped. If Janus had still had anything like breath to hold, he would have let it out. *If she's made it to Dimiotsk, then she'll be in good hands. That's one piece in place.*

"Vhalnich," the Beast said, its voice a shriek of immaterial wind. "I am disappointed."

"How so?" Janus said, holding himself at a steady distance from the dark wall that marked the Beast's core.

"You had the opportunity to kill or capture the leader of the Vordanai army, this Marcus d'Ivoire. You didn't make the attempt. Should I suspect you of . . . sentiment?"

"I judged the risk too great," Janus said. "No sentiment was involved."

"Risk? We are beyond such things."

Janus' nonexistent lips twisted into a brief smile. *As you proved so handily in the north?* He'd only been able to watch that chase from afar, but it was clear the Beast had botched the pursuit, at first by being overeager and then by waiting too long. *It's used to thinking of "risk" in terms of its own existence. But even the Beast can have setbacks.*

"Marcus would have come to the meeting only if my body was there. If I tried to take him, it's quite possible my body would have been killed in the attempt."

"What of it?"

"It's irrelevant to me, of course, except inasmuch as it affects your plans. Our supply of bodies in the south has been depleted by the battle, and it is only through my body that we retain the loyalty of the soldiers you have yet to incorporate. If that body were lost, things would become . . . chaotic."

"Hmm." Janus felt the increased stress of the Beast's attention.

"You told me you wanted Vordan City taken as quickly as possible, and the Thousand Names seized. I am working only to achieve that end. Now that Marcus' army has fled out of range of the Illifen passes, we can leave a small force to watch him as we take the bulk of our troops directly toward Vordan City. I don't think what's left of the Army of the Republic will put up much resistance."

"Good," the Beast growled.

"If I may be so bold, I suggest bringing your core body south, now that the north is no longer of such . . . interest. Having it close by will enable us to secure more bodies quickly once Vordan falls."

"I have already begun the journey," the Beast said. "When the city falls, I will feast. And with the strength that grants me, I will make the world tremble."

Janus said nothing. *Once the shot is fired, all you can do is wait and see if it will hit the target.*

CHAPTER TWENTY-ONE

WINTER

"Take the knife," Jane said, as though instructing a friend in how to carve a roast. "Put the point of it about here, and press it in, upward, as hard as you can."

She stood, naked and beautiful, in front of Winter. Jane as she had once been, well muscled and full breasted, long hair hanging to the small of her back like a curtain of dark red silk. Jane as she ought to be, not the shaven-headed, scrawny thing Winter had seen in the pontifex's office in Elysium, with eyes that glowed red from the inside.

There was a dagger in Winter's hand, long and gleaming. She raised it to Jane's throat, her arm trembling. The point shook until it came to rest in Jane's skin, just above her collarbone, its prick drawing a single bead of blood.

"Oh, no," Jane said, with a playful smile that cut like a knife. "Not me. You had your chance at that."

Her hands came up, surrounding Winter's own, and with gentle but unstoppable strength they pushed the dagger across the space between them, until Winter felt the tip touching the skin of her throat.

"That's it," Jane said. "Press it in, upward, as hard as you can."

"I can't," Winter said. "There's something I have to do first."

"Defeat the Beast?" It was Bobby's voice, from behind her. "You think that matters to me?"

"To me?" Leti, just behind Winter's left shoulder.

"It matters to *me*," Winter said. "If I can save everyone . . . if I can save Cyte . . ."

"Even if you end up dead?" Cyte strode out from nowhere and crossed her arms. She was naked, too, her body slim beside Jane's, her hair black instead of red. "You know that's what it's going to take. You felt it the first time you confronted the Beast."

"If you'd been willing to make the sacrifice then, none of this would be necessary," Jane said.

"I might still be alive," Bobby mused.

"So would I," Leti said.

"I *know*," Winter hissed. "I know. This time . . ." She looked down at the dagger, then raised her chin, tensing her shoulders. "This time I'll do what needs to be done."

The blade sank into her flesh as though it belonged there.

Winter opened her eyes slowly, the lids gummy with sleep.

Her throat still stung from the dagger's thrust. She brought one hand up, groggy, and felt for the wound, but there was nothing. *Of course.* The nightmares had followed her for years, all the way to Khandar and back again. *Why should they stop now?*

She shifted, shoulders aching where she was propped at an awkward angle. She lay against the rail of the ship, wedged beside a coil of rope. That she'd managed to sleep regardless was a testament to her exhaustion.

Even the slight movement brought a rumble from her stomach, and the shaky, hollow feeling that came with it. She'd had nothing but half a handful of dried meat in the last day. Everyone aboard the ships was hungry, but Winter and Dobraev had agreed to make straight for Dimiotsk, and not risk another stop looking for supplies that likely weren't available in any case.

This close to the coast, the river had opened out into a broader, slower flow, and the sailors had agreed it was safe to continue by lantern light after dark. They'd seen no other ships, and few lights on the shore. *We should reach the city early tomorrow.* Winter glanced up at the sky, which was starting to lighten. *Today, rather.*

She stood up, thighs and calves aching, and did her best to stretch. With the departure of the Haeta and those refugees who'd decided to take their chances on land, the ships weren't quite jammed to capacity, but it was still close. The deck was littered with sleepers, and she knew they were packed tight in the hold as well. She could see the lantern of Dobraev's ship a few dozen yards away, sails drooping. The wind had been weak, and they'd relied mostly on the current and the oars. *At least the rain has held off.*

Turning to the bow, she could see more lights, twinkling in the darkness like a swarm of fireflies. Winter walked in that direction, following the rail, stepping carefully over sleeping bodies. The sun rose over the horizon, and the sky went from gray to purple and began shading into blue. Ahead, the lights started to wink out, disappearing like the constellations with the sunrise, and the prosaic reality of the city of Dimiotsk was revealed.

The river Bataria broadened at the mouth into a wide bay, letting into the Borel Sea. The northern curve of the bay was lined with tall, rocky cliffs, but south of the river the land was flatter, and there a hard-bitten city had grown up. *City* was, in fact, perhaps too grand a term—it was more like a country town writ large. The buildings were made of logs, with leather covering the window openings. With no shortage of space, they sprawled back from the riverfront with only the loosest suggestion of a street plan. Only the Sworn Church was built of brick, sporting a tall spire topped with a silver double circle.

Docks, most of them decidedly decrepit-looking, stretched out into the river like the grasping, skeletal fingers of a corpse. Farther along, where the water was deeper, a more substantial set of moorings provided space for ocean-going ships. The harbor was somewhat protected from the sea by a string of barrier islands, barely visible as lumps in the ocean.

One whole section of the bay was devoted to lumber, a vast field of tree trunks lashed side by side and floating like a carpet stretching from the dock to the breakwater. A ship was taking some aboard with a crane, pulling them dripping out of the water and lowering them into its hold. The forests of northern Murnsk were famous, Winter knew. She wondered if the trade was hurting—they certainly hadn't passed any lumbermen.

A light flashed from the other ship. Sergeant Gorchov, who was in the bow, watched it for a moment and then looked over his shoulder.

"The lieutenant says we'll dock here," he said. "He has to proceed on to the fort afterward, to report, but there's no need to drag this lot with us." He gestured at the refugees.

"We don't need to get permission from someone?" Winter said.

Gorchov snorted. "In Dimiotsk? Not likely."

This turned out to be correct. They simply found a dock that looked like it wouldn't collapse and they tied up, ignoring the furious protests of the crew of a small fishing boat who had been aiming for the same space. Gorchov exchanged scatological retorts with the fishermen over the rail, apparently in a fine mood, while the sailors dropped the cargo net over the side. The refugees swarmed off, despite the soldiers attempts to keep things orderly. *I can't blame them,* Winter thought. *I'd want to get the hell away from here, too.*

The second ship docked nearby, unleashing a similar tide of desperate humanity. Winter saw Lieutenant Dobraev climbing down the net, hand over hand, and walking along the shore toward their vessel. Alex and Abraham had emerged on deck, looking as bedraggled and hungry as Winter felt. She turned to Gorchov.

"Thank you for all your help, Sergeant."

He shrugged and scratched his beard in a way that reminded Winter so much of Marcus that she almost laughed. "It's nothing. I should thank you. That bastard Kollowrath would have kept us there until we died at our posts." He glanced down at the lieutenant. "I'm glad you could talk some sense into Byr."

Winter smiled. "Glad I could help."

Climbing down the cargo net was one more insult to aching muscles, but she managed it well enough. Abraham had more trouble, though Alex swarmed down with the agility of a spider and hopped lightly to the dock. Winter turned to Dobraev as Abraham gingerly dismounted.

"It . . . might be possible for you to come to the fort," the lieutenant said. "The colonel may be understanding. And . . ." He gestured at the three of them, who had nothing more than the clothes on their backs and the saber at Winter's belt.

"We'll be all right," Winter said. She wasn't at all certain of that, of course, but it was clear that Dobraev didn't think highly of his chances of explaining them to some Murnskai colonel. *No need to make his life any harder.*

"If you say so," he said, relieved. "Thank you, once again. None of us would have survived if not for you."

Winter nodded silently. *You wouldn't have been in* danger *if not for me.* But she didn't say it. *It might not even be true. The Beast would have come here eventually.*

"If you are unable to find a ship," Dobraev said, "get a message to me at the fort. I will see if there's anything I can do."

"Thank you," Winter said. "I will."

There was an awkward pause. Dobraev looked up at Gorchov, who was leaning on the rail of the ship, then back to Winter. He grinned, straightened, and gave her a crisp salute.

"Division-General," he said.

Winter nodded, as she had to so many salutes. Dobraev turned and hurried aboard the ship. Gorchov said something in his ear, putting one big arm around his shoulders, and they both started laughing.

"We made it," Winter said. She looked at her companions. Abraham was grave, while Alex grinned, eyebrows raised.

"We made it," the girl agreed. "So, now what?"

It turned out that they hadn't been the only group with the idea of making for Dimiotsk when things went sour. The city was almost as full of refugees as the fortress had been, but there was no garrison to keep things orderly. The smell of the place was overpowering, whatever sanitary systems normally served the city having long since been overwhelmed.

They worked their way inland from the river docks, angling in the general direction of the deepwater harbor. The streets were crowded, a dense mass of people pushed to the center of the crooked alleys by the crude shelters against the walls of every building. More people were sleeping in the open, huddled under blankets or cloaks. At the intersections, hawkers called out, drawing queues for roast potatoes or fresh bread, but the prices seemed shockingly high, all the more so when Winter remembered that the Murnskai imperial was roughly two and a half Vordanai eagles.

"There must be inns, right?" Alex said, glancing around at the press of desperate humanity. "Any harbor has to have somewhere for people to stay and eat."

"I don't think we can afford an inn," Winter said. "Actually, I'm not sure we can afford *anything*. If I sell my saber, maybe—"

Alex tossed a small purse in Winter's direction, and Winter reflexively snatched it out of the air. It was heavier than it looked, and a brief glance inside showed her the dull gleam of gold. She quickly stuffed it deep in her pocket and drew close to Alex.

"How long have you been hiding *that*? Since the Mountain?"

"About five minutes. And there's more where that came from." Alex looked back at Winter over her shoulder and raised her eyebrows. "Greatest thief in the world, remember? Cutting a purse isn't exactly a challenge."

"But . . ." Winter looked around at the desperate refugees and lowered her voice. "You can't steal from these people."

Abraham, pulling up next to them, nodded vigorously.

"Of course not," Alex said. "They haven't got any money! I got that off the angry-looking merchant with the bodyguards two streets back."

"I'm not . . ." Winter took a breath, catching the whiff of roast potato, and found her hunger rapidly overcoming her moral qualms. "Just don't steal from anyone who doesn't look like they can afford it, all right?"

Alex grinned. "Think of it as their contribution to saving the world from the Beast."

Abraham let out a long-suffering sigh and muttered something that might have been a prayer.

By the time they reached the harbor front, Alex had harvested three more purses, from what she assured her companions had been very deserving-looking targets. They found an inn, nameless and unmarked except for a painted sign of a man climbing into bed. It was guarded by a broad-shouldered mountain of a man with a stout cudgel at his belt. Winter slipped the bouncer a silver coin to demonstrate that the three of them weren't as indigent as they appeared, and he grunted and stepped aside.

The inn was a large, two-story building, a rarity in Dimiotsk, with a common room on the main floor and ship-style bunks cramming a single big space upstairs. The prices were absurd, as Winter had predicted, but there was enough gold in the purses Alex had cut for at least a few days' room and board. They sat at a table made from planks nailed over a barrel and told the proprietor to bring them lots of everything.

She wasn't expecting much, but apparently there was plenty to eat in Dimiotsk, if you could afford it. Most of it was fish, bowls of thick chowder followed by something pink-fleshed and fried crispy. Thick, crusty bread topped with pork fat accompanied the seafood, along with a dark, bitter beer. The first round only managed to take the edge off Winter's hunger, and she called for more, which the smiling, potbellied man who ran the place was only too happy to bring.

As the proprietor was laying out another set of iron skillets, Winter said, "A question, if you don't mind?"

"Of course, honored guest." The man was beaming. *He ought to be, for what we're paying him.*

"We're looking for passage on a ship south, to Vordan. Do you know any captains who might be taking on passengers?"

The innkeeper's face fell. "You have not heard?"

"Heard what?" Alex said, sucking the meat from the bones of her last course.

"There is war on the sea. The Borelgai king has sent ships to aid the Vordanai child-queen against our new emperor. Wise captains are staying close to shore and the guns of His Imperial Majesty's forts."

"The Borels have attacked Murnskai ships?" Winter said.

"Not yet, that I have heard, but it cannot be long."

Winter swore silently. "I'd pay generously. Do you know anyone who might be willing to risk the danger?"

"Captain Fyrnor of the *Black Cat* has always been a little bit mad," the innkeeper mused. "But even he would have to be *very* well paid to risk the Borelgai navy."

"I see." Winter waved the man away, ignoring his apologies. She looked around—the common room was mostly full, and the sailors and merchants were making quite a bit of noise. Quietly she said, "That doesn't sound promising."

"If you need me to steal enough to bribe a pirate, it might take a few days," Alex said. "Just finding someone with that much cash is going to be the hard part."

"At that point," Abraham said, "why not just steal the ship?"

"And a crew to sail it?" Alex said. "I'm no seaman, but I know that an ocean voyage is a long way from a quick jaunt down the river."

"We'll figure it out," Winter said, lifting something out of the skillet. "Anyone have any idea what this is?"

"Looks like a bit of gristle," Alex said.

"Fish guts?" Abraham hazarded.

"Barnacle," a woman's voice said. "A bit like a snail. Not bad with butter."

All three of them looked up. A slim figure in a hooded cloak stood beside the table, though moments earlier Winter could have sworn they'd been alone. She let one hand drop to the hilt of her saber, while she popped the barnacle into her mouth with the other.

"You're right," she said, after a moment of thoughtful chewing. "It's not bad. Now, would you mind telling us who you are?"

"You don't recognize me, Winter Ihernglass?" The voice *did* sound familiar. "I've been waiting for you."

Winter's eyes narrowed. "I'm not in the mood for games."

"Fair enough." The woman drew back her hood, revealing olive skin and short, dark hair. "Better?"

"Rose," Winter said. She'd been part of the group that had gone into the Vendre, the night of the revolution. Afterward, the queen had introduced her by another name. "Or is it Sothe?"

"Whichever you prefer," Sothe said.

"You know her?" Abraham said.

"I saw her, too," Alex said. "Back with the army. She was some kind of attendant to the queen."

"Something like that," Sothe said, with the hint of a smile.

"How can you have been *waiting* for us?" Winter said. "No one outside the Mountain knew we were coming here."

"That is . . . a very complicated story," Sothe said. "We have quite a lot to talk about. But you won't need to find a ship."

"Why not?"

"Because I have one ready," Sothe said. "And, from what I understand, it's important that we leave immediately."

Winter wasn't sure what to expect when Sothe led them to the harbor. Experience told her that things rarely worked out quite so conveniently, but if they were walking into a trap, she couldn't figure out *why*. Sothe was an expert assassin, as Winter could personally attest. *If she wanted to kill me, walking up and announcing herself doesn't seem like the right way to do it.* And, as best as Winter had been able to tell, Sothe was utterly devoted to Raesinia.

Unless she's been taken by the Beast. But this close, she ought to be able to sense if Sothe was a red-eye. Infernivore was uneasy, but no more than usual in the company of Alex and Abraham. Just to be certain, she caught Alex's eye, indicating Sothe. Alex raised an eyebrow and then, understanding, shook her head.

The harbor was mobbed, a press of humanity that set Winter's teeth on edge. Fishermen had set up shop along the waterfront, dumping loads of still-flopping fish in the mud and accepting shouted bids. Armed guards stood alongside them, bearing swords and cudgels. More guards maintained a strip of clear space in front of the stone piers where the smaller ships were docked. Sailors worked, loading or unloading cargo, deaf to the shouted pleas from the refugees who crammed as close as they dared. *We're not the only ones who want a way out of here.*

Out in the bay, larger ships were anchored, and small boats were rowed back and forth. From here, Winter could see the tip of the chain of barrier islands, where the largest of the desolate rocks had been converted into a stone-walled fortress. Murnskai flags flew above its walls, and from the mast of the warship lying at anchor just below it. She wondered what sort of reception Dobraev had gotten when he reported to the commander.

Sothe slipped easily through the press, never shoving but hardly slowed at all, and Winter had to work hard to keep up. They seemed to be headed to the end of the row of smaller vessels, where a sleek, two-masted ship was being watched by a particularly unfriendly set of thugs. Looking at it, Winter felt something shift at the back of her mind, a slight change in Infernivore's attention. She grabbed Alex and pointed. Alex paused for a moment, eyes narrowing. Then she nodded grimly.

After a few more minutes of difficult progress, Winter pushed free of the last rank of refugees, emerging onto the muddy strip of ground the thugs guarded so jealously. Sothe stood between two of the men, speaking quietly and pointing to Winter and the others, and the guards raised no objection as Winter came forward. Alex was a step behind her, and had one hand on Abraham's shoulder.

"This is your ship?" Winter said.

"This is the *Swallow*," Sothe said. "Captain Kerrak . . . owes me a favor."

"You trust him?"

Sothe cocked her head, considering. "Let's say that I trust him to know where his interests lie."

"And they lie in taking us to Vordan?"

"If I tell him they do, yes." Her smile was disturbingly predatory.

Winter stepped forward, away from the line of guards, and lowered her voice. "And are you aware that you have a demon aboard?" This close, it was unmistakable.

"Of course," Sothe said blandly. "How do you think I knew where to find you?"

Winter gave her a blank look, then glanced back at her companions.

"I think," she said carefully, "that you had better explain."

The *Swallow* was long and narrow, with smooth, clean lines. Winter, who knew nothing about ships, got the impression of speed and power, and the crew worked with practiced efficiency. Sothe led them across the deck, which was littered with boxes, ropes, and nautical paraphernalia, and through a narrow doorway into a cabin at the rear of the ship. It held a large table, bolted to the floor, a couple of locked cabinets, and a few chairs. A round window gave a view of the bay.

"We're taking on fresh supplies," Sothe said. "But the captain assures me we'll be ready to sail by the evening tide."

"Is it true that the Borelgai navy is stopping Murnskai shipping?" Alex said. "Will we be able to get through?"

"I'm not sure," Sothe said. "But it shouldn't be a problem. *Swallow* has a Borelgai flag and papers if we need them. And, if it comes to it, I don't think any warship could catch us."

"The demon," Winter said. "And what you're doing here."

"Of course," Sothe said. "Wait here for a moment. I'll get her."

She slipped out through the narrow door. Winter looked at her companions.

"I don't need to say that this feels suspicious, do I?" Abraham said.

"She's not a red-eye," Alex said. "And neither is the demon here, I think. It doesn't feel the same as the Beast."

"If this is a trap," Winter said, "it's a very strange one. The Beast wants to kill me, so why lure us all the way here?" She hesitated, then added, "Sothe is an assassin, and a damned good one. If she wanted us dead, she's chosen a very roundabout method."

"Just because she's not working for the Beast doesn't mean she's on our side," Abraham said. "Be careful."

Alex flexed her fingers ostentatiously, and Winter nodded.

"If it comes to that," she whispered, "I'll take the demon. Don't take your eyes off Sothe."

She straightened at the sound of footsteps in the hall. Sothe reappeared, followed by a slender young woman in a long gray robe. She was thin to the point of illness, sallow and hollow-cheeked, with dark hair cut boyishly short. A fading bruise colored one side of her face an ugly yellow-green. Old knife scars surrounded her eyes, and her eyelids hung slack over empty sockets. Sothe held her wrist and guided her forward until her outstretched hand found the back of a chair.

"This is Ennika," Sothe said, shutting the door behind them. "She's a Penitent Damned."

Winter tensed. Deep in her mind, Infernivore thrashed and strained. But this sick-looking blind girl was a far cry from the masked killers of the Church she'd faced before, and she forced the demon down. "I assume she's not dangerous?"

"I'm not dangerous," Ennika said in fluent Murnskai. "I'm broken. Useless." She felt her way around the chair and sat down. Winter did likewise, and the others followed suit. Sothe patted Ennika's shoulder gently as she went by.

"I'm going to assume," Sothe said, "that you don't have much information about what happened to the army after you left."

Winter shook her head. "I know there was some kind of peace, and then Janus declared himself emperor, but that's about it."

"The full story will have to wait for another time," Sothe said. "Suffice to say, we came to an accommodation with the Borelgai after the weather forced us to retreat. Certain elements in the Borelgai camp were unhappy about this, most especially Duke Orlanko."

Alex's hands clenched into fists. "Orlanko was there?"

"He was a guest of the King of Borel," Sothe said. "The faction in their court that wanted war saw him as a potential candidate for a puppet ruler of Vordan. When the other faction won out, Orlanko attempted to stop them with his usual subtlety."

"He tried to murder everyone," Winter guessed.

"Precisely. Fortunately, Marcus d'Ivoire and I were able to thwart him. Duke Dorsay's faction won out, and Orlanko fled."

"Damn," Alex muttered. "Damn, damn, *damn*."

Abraham touched her shoulder. "There'll be another chance," he said.

"Orlanko hurt you?" Winter said.

"His thug Andreas killed the closest thing I had to a father," Alex grated. "Then he handed me over to the Penitent Damned, and they kept me drugged and chained to a fucking cart for a thousand miles."

Ennika bowed her head, her shoulders hunched.

Sothe cleared her throat. "If it helps," she said, "Andreas is dead. I trapped and killed him during the revolution. And I was just as determined to make sure Orlanko did not escape justice for his crimes. I followed him when he fled from his Borelgai protectors and I cornered him and the last of his minions in Vorsk." Her face was perfectly calm. "I killed them all."

"He's dead?" Winter said. "Orlanko's dead?"

Sothe nodded. "For certain."

Alex let out her breath with a hiss, her hands still clenched tight.

"I found Ennika among Orlanko's entourage," Sothe said. "She was his link to the Black Priests."

"What do you mean, link?" Winter said.

"Paired demons," Ennika said in a low voice. "My sister and I both intoned their names, and our minds were linked. What one of us thought, felt, or heard could be known instantly by the other. There are many such demons, and we who bear them serve the pontifex and the Church by passing on their words in secret." Her lip twisted. "Orlanko was never worthy of such trust."

"I thought she might be useful," Sothe said. "So I kept her alive and brought her with me."

"Even though I *told* you," Ennika said. "I *told* you that I was broken."

"Explain it to them," Sothe ordered.

Ennika took a deep breath. "My sister. She's . . . gone."

"Dead?" Abraham said sympathetically.

"*No,*" Ennika said, voice thick with frustration. "I would feel it if she died. She was . . . taken. Vanished. I don't know how to explain it. The link wasn't severed; it's just . . . empty."

"Where was your sister?" Winter said, certainty rising in her mind.

"Elysium. One half of every link was kept in Elysium, while the other was sent out into the world."

Winter looked at Abraham, and his eyes went wide.

"The Beast," he said. "She was taken by the Beast."

Sothe nodded. "We had no idea at first. I had . . . other tasks to perform, but I kept Ennika with me."

"I told you to kill me," Ennika said, sounding like a sulky child.

Sothe ignored her. "Until one day she felt something over her link again."

There was a long silence.

"The Beast *talked* to you?" Winter said.

"No," Ennika said. "It's more complicated than that. The Beast has more than a single mind."

"I don't pretend to understand what's happened," Sothe said. "But apparently it is possible for a mind taken over by the Beast to retain its . . . integrity, so to speak, and some sort of independent existence. One of these independent minds discovered a way to use Ennika's link, through some remnant of her sister."

"She's not dead," Ennika said. "Worse than dead. Broken into pieces, but still *knowing* . . ." She trailed off, head bowed.

"How do you know it's not the Beast itself, trying to trick you?" Abraham said.

"Precisely what I thought at first," Sothe said. "The explanation he offered seemed . . . far-fetched. But after several conversations, I was persuaded that it was, at least, a lead worth following, especially in light of events. The entity claims to be working against the Beast, and he told me that the most important thing was that I come to help *you*. He kept me apprised of your progress, which he could apparently observe through the Beast's bodies. I came here, with the *Swallow*, to wait until you arrived."

"That's . . ." Winter shook her head. "I don't know. It seems mad."

"Who was he?" Alex said. "This entity. You said he was a mind inside the Beast?"

"I can't know for certain, obviously," Sothe said. "But he *claims* to be Janus bet Vhalnich."

CHAPTER TWENTY-TWO

MARCUS

The Army of the Republic came to rest, at last, behind the line of the river Rhyf.

In the end, they didn't have much choice. The sick lists had burgeoned with each dawn-to-dusk march, and more horses broke down with every passing mile. Wagons were consolidated, and then consolidated again for lack of teams to pull them, inessential supplies left behind and wounded who could barely walk turned out to fend for themselves. By the time the Rhyf came into sight, a broad ribbon of silver in the midafternoon sun, there were barely enough animals to pull the guns.

If they'd tried to keep on at that pace, Marcus was certain there'd have been a mutiny. Instead, they'd crossed the river at a midsized town called Gond and made camp in the fields outside it on the south bank, much to the dismay of the local farmers. The townspeople had been even less happy when Colonel Archer began laying powder against the bridge supports, ready for a quick demolition.

Give-Em-Hell's light cavalry remained on the north bank, keeping the enemy scouts back. The next morning, while the exhausted infantry rested in its camp, cavalry detachments and engineers rode east and west along the river, looking for crossings. By nightfall they'd identified three more bridges and one possible ford. Marcus ordered the former prepared for destruction, and artillery dug in around the latter.

If we have to make a stand, he reflected, looking at the map that night, *it's not a bad position.* The Rhyf was narrow but deep, without many easy crossings. *As long as we get enough warning, we can shadow any force on the north bank and be waiting if they try to get over the river.* Pushing through a river crossing in the face of determined resistance was one of the bloodiest prospects in warfare, even with a big advantage in numbers. *Which Janus has, of course. But at least we can make it difficult for him.*

As the reports trickled in from the scouts across the river, though, he began to think the situation had changed. The batch that was waiting for him in the morning only confirmed it. Give-Em-Hell wrote that they'd clashed with a few enemy patrols, but that Janus' force was making no serious effort to push through their screen and reach the Rhyf. Marcus sent new orders, then went in search of Cyte.

The camp was a mess, by any standard. Instead of neat rows, the battalions had set up their tents in loose clusters, grouped only vaguely by regiment and division. A faint, nasty scent on the morning breeze made Marcus wrinkle his nose; they'd clearly gotten sloppy about latrine placement, too. *We're going to have to do something about that.* Staying in a camp with bad sanitation was asking to be decimated by disease.

It could wait a day or two, though. They'd had only a day and a night so far to recover from the grueling march. Everywhere he looked, Marcus saw soldiers sitting in groups, cooking or playing cards, but generally simply enjoying *not* being on the move. The men were still noticeably thinner than they'd been at the start of the march, but the halt was already doing wonders for morale. Two days ago, on the other side of the river, his passage through the camp had been greeted with apathetic silence or ominous grumbling. Now soldiers cheerfully saluted as he went past, though usually without actually getting to their feet first.

Soldiers in the Girls' Own camp directed him to the cutter's station. This was a large tent whose sides could be rolled up for easy access, with a few long, low tents alongside where the wounded could be sheltered. After a battle, it would be a nightmarish scene—every soldier, Marcus included, shuddered at the singing of the bone saw, and he'd seen arms and legs piled up like firewood and enough blood to turn the dirt to mud.

Fortunately, at the moment there wasn't anything so dire going on. Hannah Courvier, a middle-aged woman with the long-suffering expression of a schoolteacher, sat on a crate behind a makeshift desk while a line of Girls' Own rankers waited to see her. Those who saw Marcus saluted, a wave that progressed down the line. The woman at the head, a solidly built sergeant, was bent over the desk whispering urgently to the cutter.

"—every time I take a shit," Marcus heard as he got closer. "I—"

He cleared his throat, and they both looked up. The sergeant saluted, her cheeks coloring, but Hannah just sighed and leaned back.

"Problems, Captain Courvier?" Marcus said.

"About what you'd expect after a march like that," Hannah said. "But we've got to do something about the latrines—"

"I know," Marcus said. "When you're done here, find General Warus and tell him I asked you to take care of it. He'll get you some men to dig new ones."

"Thank you, sir."

"Have you seen Colonel Cyte?"

Hannah nodded at the first of the tents housing the wounded. "In there."

The tent flap was low enough that Marcus had to bend nearly double to enter. It felt like a tunnel, dimly lit, both sides lined with bedrolls. The women who occupied them were in various states of disassembly—a few seemed intact, except for bandages, but most were missing pieces, hands and feet, arms and legs. Some were unconscious, the telltale angry red of infection creeping up from their stumps. Others sat up, talking, playing cards, or reading by candlelight. Once again a wave of salutes went through them at the sight of Marcus.

Marcus took a deep breath to steady himself, then regretted it. The whole place smelled of vomit and the sick-sweet stench of rotten flesh. He nodded acknowledgment to each soldier as he passed, working his way along the line until he found Cyte. She was kneeling beside a young ranker whose right arm ended just below the shoulder. The girl was examining a sheet of paper while Cyte took notes.

"Cynthia's dead," the girl said. "For sure. At Satinvol."

Cyte nodded, pen moving.

"And someone told me Elly—Elsbeth—dropped out with a bad ankle and stayed in a village we passed." The girl's face clouded. "You're not going to punish her, are you?"

"No," Cyte said. "Don't worry."

"Those are the only ones I know." The girl handed the list back. "Sorry."

"You've been very helpful," Cyte said. She looked up at Marcus, then back to the girl. "Thank you. I'll be back."

"Captain—" Marcus began.

"Let's get out of here first," Cyte said quietly. "If you don't mind."

That was fine with Marcus. They walked back to the flap, both hunched over, and slipped back out into the morning sun. Cyte led him a few steps away from the line of people waiting to see Hannah. She stretched, arching her back with a distinct *pop*.

"What are you doing?" Marcus said. "Looking for someone?"

"Just updating army records," Cyte said. She showed him the notebook, which was covered in a list of names with little notes about their current status—dead, wounded, missing—and how certain it was. "On the march the bookkeeping fell by the wayside."

"You can let it fall a little farther, if you like," Marcus said. "I promise I'm not about to order a surprise inspection."

"I'd . . . rather not, sir." Cyte shook her head. "We had a similar problem in the retreat from Murnsk. By the time we got around to tallying things up, there were a lot of soldiers we just couldn't account for. This way people have an easier time remembering. It . . . makes it easier when it's time to tell the families, sir."

"Ah," Marcus said awkwardly. He wondered if Fitz had done something similar back when they'd worked together. *Almost certainly. He just made sure I never noticed.* "Well. Thank you."

"Of course, sir. It's my job. And . . . it helps, a little." She held the notebook close, like she was worried it might escape.

War. It put people through unimaginable stresses, and they each had their own way of dealing with it. *Better this than crawling into a bottle, that's for sure.*

"I'm sorry you had to come and find me, sir," Cyte said, straightening up. "Is something wrong?"

"Nothing urgent. But we need to figure out what we're doing next." He put his hand in his coat pocket, where there was a single much-folded slip of paper. "And that means I need to show you something."

Back in his own command tent, Marcus spent a few moments flipping through the map case. He finally selected a large-scale one that covered the whole of Vordan, laying it on the table atop the smaller-scale maps of the Pale valley. Then, while Cyte watched with interest, he fished out the piece of paper and unfolded it. The edges had gone furry with wear.

"This is . . ." He looked down at the page and hesitated. "I don't know whether to believe it or not. But I think you need to see it. No one else knows."

"Sir? Why me?"

"Because you're the only one here who knows about . . . magic, and the

Priests of the Black, and all that damned nonsense." He handed her the page. "I got this, in secret, from Janus. When he came to talk to me on the bridge."

Cyte blinked, and read the note. He couldn't see it from where he was standing, but Marcus had read the thing so often he had it memorized. It was written in a slightly awkward hand, sometimes running letters together, sometimes stretching them out. Some of the sentences were at an angle, or above or below their neighbors, giving the impression of something that had been written in fragments by someone who couldn't see what he was doing. But the writing was Janus'. Marcus would have known that careful script anywhere. It read,

> Marcus—
>
> I must beg your forgiveness. I have very limited freedom of action, and my mind is not my own. This note is a risk, but I must reach you.
>
> Winter is the key. I am trying to bring him to Vordan City. Find him, help him, trust his judgment. He understands what needs to be done.
>
> Know that I am doing what I can. The Beast is watching.
>
> —J

"I don't understand," Cyte said. She let the note fall to the table, and Marcus saw her hand was trembling. "*Janus* gave you this?"

"In secret."

"Who could have been watching? You were alone!"

"I know," Marcus said. "When we stormed Satinvol, I . . . saw something." He described, as calmly as he could, what had happened in the final assault, the girl who had turned on him with her eyes glowing red. Cyte didn't immediately tell him he was insane, which he guessed was a good sign.

"At first I wondered if I'd just remembered it wrong," Marcus said. "Things happen, in battle. Or maybe she was a genuine traitor. But that light . . ." He shook his head. "Then I got this. So what if it's true? What if there is some kind of demon, something that can control people?"

"The Beast," Cyte said flatly. "As in the Beast of Judgment?"

"Maybe."

Cyte looked down at the note, expressions warring on her face. "It could be lies," she said carefully. "Maybe Janus has truly gone mad."

"It's possible. An aftereffect of the poison." Marcus sighed. "If not, though, it explains why he would do all of this. 'My mind is not my own.' Something is *using* him."

"If it's not madness, then Winter is still alive," Cyte said. Her hand tightened on the edge of the table. "He's *alive*."

"I know."

There was a long silence.

"I have to go to Vordan City," Cyte said. "I have to know. If he . . . If he needs help, then I should be there."

"The question is," Marcus said, "how do we get there?"

He gestured down at the map. From their current position on the Rhyf, it was a little more than four hundred miles to Vordan City in a straight line. Unfortunately, that line crossed the densest and most impenetrable part of the Illifen Range. The shortest route, through the passes they'd crossed by on the way west, meant going through Janus' army. That left the south, skirting the edge of the mountains before turning east to slog across the Vor valley. *Call it six hundred miles.*

"At any kind of reasonable pace, it would take months," Marcus said, as Cyte's brow furrowed in concentration. "Even forcing the marches with plenty of food, forty or forty-five days, and there's no way this army could sustain that."

Cyte said nothing. Marcus put a finger on their current position, then shifted it north slightly, toward where Janus' army was lurking.

"There's another problem," he said. "I think Janus isn't following us anymore."

She looked up. "The scouts reported enemy cavalry looking for us."

"They're not pushing hard enough. If he really meant to hit us here, he'd be searching for a place to cross the river, and he wouldn't let us brush him off. It's possible he's looping around our flank, or pulling some maneuver I haven't thought of, but I wouldn't bet on it." He traced a line north, toward the passes. "I think he's left a cavalry force and some blocking troops, and taken the bulk of his army toward Vordan City."

"Which means that it's not just a matter of getting there," Cyte said. "We have to make it before Janus if we're going to do any good."

"It's not possible," Marcus said flatly. "He's got the inside track, and we're not going to be able to outmarch him."

"Then what?"

"If we want to keep him out of Vordan City, there's only one thing I can think of." He tapped the map. "We attack. Whatever Janus has left in front of us, we smash it, and threaten to come down on his rear. He'll either have to turn around and fight, or let us cut off his supply line in the pass."

"Now you're sounding like Kurot," Cyte said. "I don't think Janus is worried about supply lines. He can live off the land, the same as us."

"It might be harder in the mountains." Marcus pursed his lips. "If he keeps marching, we can stay behind him. If the forces in Vordan City can hold him up at all, we might be able to catch him between us."

"Or," Cyte said, "he'll get irritated and annihilate us. Considering he has something like double our numbers."

"That's the downside," Marcus admitted. "It would slow him a bit, but . . ."

"I have another idea," Cyte said. "But I don't think you're going to like it."

"I'm listening," Marcus said.

"We head downriver until we find a boat. Take it to the Pale, and down to Enzport. Get a ship there, sail around the coast and up the Vor to Vordan City. It'd be a hell of a lot faster than marching overland."

"Faster for a few, maybe. There probably aren't enough boats on the Rhyf to get us to Enzport, and there *definitely* aren't enough ships at Enzport to get us to Vordan. Not after the war and the Borel blockade."

"I know." Cyte locked eyes with him. "You and I could go. A few soldiers you trust. Leave the army with Fitz."

"I can't abandon my men," Marcus said. The response was almost automatic. "Certainly not with the enemy still just over the river."

"You said yourself that you didn't think Janus was following us."

"I could be wrong!"

"If they do attack, would Fitz do a worse job than you would?"

He'd probably do better. Marcus shook his head. "That's not the point. It's my responsibility."

Cyte nodded, as though she'd expected that, and took a deep breath. "Then I'll go."

"Alone?"

"If necessary. Or with a small escort, if you'd like to assign one."

Marcus frowned and scratched his beard. "The army needs you, too."

"*Someone* has to act on this." Cyte pushed the note across the map. "That's why you brought me here, isn't it?"

"I needed another perspective—"

"And I need to find Winter," Cyte said. There was a quiet desperation under her controlled voice. "Please, Marcus."

Was this what I had in mind all along? Marcus sighed. "Have Abby give you an escort. However many you think you'll need. I'll write you orders authorizing you to requisition any form of transport you need, for however much that's worth, and as much gold as I've got on hand."

"Thank you," Cyte said. She straightened up, blinking away tears. "I'll find him, I swear."

"I have a feeling," Marcus said, "that is going to be the easy part."

Cyte had been insistent on leaving before nightfall, taking a half dozen Girls' Own troopers on horses reluctantly donated by the cavalry. Marcus told Fitz and the others that she was on important business, but no more than that. *Better to keep them focused on our own situation.*

That situation was, at best, tenuous. The locals were getting increasingly angry about the army's requisitions of food, horses, and fodder. There hadn't been any outright violence yet, but the farmers were more likely to hide their reserves than offer them up freely. Marcus ordered the foragers to range farther afield, where they hadn't covered the ground so thoroughly, but that would be a temporary measure. Sooner or later, the army would have to move, or starve.

When it did move, he faced a similar choice to the one he'd outlined for Cyte. They could march to Enzport, and hope that enough supplies could be brought in by ship to feed the army indefinitely. That would be the safest course, but it meant abandoning any hope of putting pressure on Janus, which would put them out of the war for all practical purposes. Or they could march south and east, taking the long way to Vordan City, meaning months on the road and no guarantee there would be a capital left by the time they got there.

Or we could attack. Marcus found himself drawn, more and more, to that option. He almost laughed aloud when he realized why. *It seems like something Janus would do.* But it would mean, of course, the risk—even the probability— of disaster. *And our last chance to help Raesinia.*

That night he slept poorly, dreaming of the dead. Adrecht and Jen Alhundt, Andy and Hayver, Parker Erdine and the girl he'd killed at Satinvol. Gaunt and desiccated, they all staggered toward him, their eyes alight from within with a horrible crimson glow.

That's wrong, Marcus told them.

Why? said Jen, her rasp of a voice a parody of the one that had whispered in his ear at night.

I've seen the dead walk, Marcus said. *Their eyes were green.*

They all started to laugh.

He awoke to a scratch at his tent flap, with the light of dawn just barely brightening the canvas. Marcus groaned and sat up, his shoulders stiff and aching.

"What?" he shouted.

"It's me, sir." Cyte's voice.

"Colonel?" Marcus shook his head, trying to clear it of sleep. "What are you doing here?"

"Didn't get very far before we ran into someone looking to talk to you, sir."

Marcus blinked and sighed. "Maybe this will make sense after I've had some coffee."

"I've got some ready," Cyte said. "I think you need to come with me right away, sir."

True to her word, Cyte handed him a steaming tin cup as he emerged from his tent. Marcus drank, ignoring the heat, and let the bitter stuff settle into his stomach. Cyte waited patiently. The six women who'd been escorting her were nowhere to be seen.

"All right." Marcus breathed deeply, inhaling the smell of the coffee. "You want to explain this?"

"Just follow me, sir. We left everyone out past the sentry line."

Bemused, Marcus walked after Cyte through the slipshod camp. There were details digging new latrines already, he noticed. *Hannah doesn't waste any time.*

The sentries saluted as they passed. Cyte led the way down the river front, up a small rise with a copse of trees at the top. A number of horses were tethered there, and Marcus saw women in blue uniforms, as well as a knot of men in familiar muddy red. *Borelgai.* No sooner had he recognized the white-furred shakos of the Life Guards than a short, hawk-nosed figure was striding across the damp grass, hand extended.

"General d'Ivoire! No one I'd rather see in these circumstances, believe me."

"Duke *Dorsay?*" Marcus said. He looked down at his coffee cup, then took another long drink. "I'm not still asleep, am I? Don't answer that. What are you doing here?"

"Like I told the colonel, I've come looking for you," the duke said. "We've had a hell of a time getting any accurate information."

"That means my cavalry are doing their job," Marcus said, still feeling bewildered. "*Why* are you looking for me?"

"It's a long and complicated story," Dorsay said. "But the short version is that your queen asked me to. When news of the battle at Alves reached us in Viadre—"

"Raesinia's in *Viadre*? Why—" Marcus stopped. "I think you're going to have to give me the long version."

"Later. Right now, the important thing is that I've come to help."

"I'll take any help I can get," Marcus said. "How many troops have you brought?"

"We're a little light on troops at the moment, I'm afraid," Dorsay said.

"But he's got something better," Cyte said, her eyes shining.

"Well. Yes." Dorsay cleared his throat. "The First Squadron of His Majesty's Royal Navy is anchored about ten miles downriver. Six frigates, a flotilla of heavy transports, and a few support craft. We'd originally planned to ascend the Pale, which our charts say should be clear all the way to Alves, but when we heard you were on the Rhyf, we thought we'd get as close as we could. The river's not deep enough to come farther." He shrugged. "We have six men-of-war as well, but we had to leave them at Enzport. Not really designed for river work, I'm afraid."

It took Marcus' mind a few moments to catch up to this. He drained the rest of the coffee.

"How many men will fit in your transports?" he said.

"Twenty thousand, with a fair bit of baggage," Dorsay said mildly. "More if we heave everything over the side."

That's the whole damned army. "And what were you planning on doing once you found us?"

"Extracting you from your current predicament," Dorsay said. "We'll sail north, around the Jaw, and make for Nordart. From there we can supply easily from Borel by sea. When I left, your queen was working out the terms of the alliance with Georg, but when they've finished dickering, I imagine we'll bring over some of our troops to even up the numbers. From there we can liberate Alves, cut Janus off from the north, and find a way to corner him."

"Nordart," Marcus said. That was a thousand miles in the wrong direction. He shook his head. "No. We have to get back to Vordan City before Janus does."

Cyte, at Marcus' side, nodded emphatically. The duke scratched his hawk-like nose.

"I'm not sure that would be wise," he said, speaking carefully. "As I said, I haven't brought any fresh manpower. Even if we make it to Vordan City before Janus, do you think you can hold it? My impression was that you were rather roughly handled at Alves."

Marcus winced. "That might be an understatement. We're down to two divisions, more or less."

"And Janus has, according to our intelligence, received a fresh infusion of men from Murnsk, including a large contingent of cavalry. So the odds against us would be something like three to one."

"Not *that* bad, surely," Cyte said. "They won't have been idle in Vordan City. I'm sure there'll be fresh troops waiting for us. And we can call out a citizens' militia. That's what carried the day in the revolution."

Marcus, who'd been at that battle, remembered it a little differently, but he didn't want to undermine Cyte's argument. Instead he added, "There were troops on the way to Vordan City from the south and east that didn't arrive in time to join the army, too."

"Still not enough to match Janus' numbers, though," Dorsay said.

"No," Marcus admitted. "But we'll have the advantage of the defensive."

"*If* we arrive in time."

Marcus exchanged a look with Cyte. *I can't exactly tell him we need to be there to help Winter stop some mystical Beast that can take over people's minds.* Marcus gritted his teeth in frustration. *There has to be something.* Having the help they needed materialize so miraculously only to take them the wrong way was intolerable. *Dorsay, clever, cautious Duke Dorsay. Of course he wants to wait, plan, reinforce.*

"I think," Marcus said, "if we don't get to Vordan City before Janus does, it's not going to matter how many men we have."

"If the city falls, it can be retaken," Dorsay said with a dismissive wave.

"With respect, Your Grace, you're not Vordanai. When was the last time Borel was invaded?"

"Mmm. Seven hundred years ago? Seven hundred fifty? I've forgotten my histories."

"Vordan City isn't just another city," Cyte said, joining in eagerly. "It represents the legitimate government of Vordan to our people, and that's exactly what Janus is claiming to be. If he takes it and starts issuing orders from Ohnlei Palace, most of the country is going to go along with him."

"I'm not sure I could even vouch for my own men, in that case," Marcus said. "Raesinia would be just another exile, and with only the Borelgai backing her it would be easy for Janus to turn sentiment against us. Foreign puppets are never popular."

"You see how well it worked for Orlanko," Cyte added.

Dorsay looked from one of them to the other, clearly distressed. At last he said, "You really believe this? That this is the only way?"

"I do," Marcus said. Somewhat to his surprise, he meant it. "Right now our greatest enemy is the idea that Janus is invincible. If we let him take the capital, by the time we get around to fighting him, nobody is going to believe he can be beaten."

Dorsay snorted. "Are you entirely certain he *isn't* invincible? He certainly gives a good impression of it."

"I would know better than anyone, Your Grace."

The duke let out a long sigh. "Well. My orders are to assist you, and I suppose we can interpret the specifics as . . . suggestions. If you want to defend Vordan City, I don't think I can stop you. But if you lose, you may waste all Raesinia's hard work in securing a Borelgai army. Georg won't commit soldiers to a lost cause."

"Let's hope it doesn't come to that." Marcus grinned. "We've got no time to waste. I'll get my men on the march today."

"Splendid. I'll return to the fleet and prepare the transports." Dorsay returned the smile. "It *is* good to be working with you, General. Glad to have the chance to repay the favor you did for me."

Dorsay bowed slightly and went off toward his guards. Marcus turned to Cyte.

"Well done," she said. "I didn't think we were going to convince him."

"Me either. But I think he genuinely wants to help. He's tangled with Janus before."

"Do you think it's true that some of ours would switch sides if Janus took Vordan City?"

"Maybe. I suspect we'd see a lot of quiet desertion, at the very least."

"What's this favor you did him?"

Marcus shrugged. "I saved his life from Orlanko's assassins, back in Murnsk."

Cyte's eyes widened. "And you didn't think cashing in *that* chip would help?"

"Not with Dorsay," Marcus said. "Not if he thought it was the wrong thing to do."

Cyte looked after the duke, who was being helped onto his horse by his guards, then back to Marcus. "If you say so. What now?"

"Now," Marcus said, "we need to break it to everyone that they're going to be getting on board a bunch of Borelgai transports."

As Marcus had expected, this did not go over well.

"You can't trust the Borels," Colonel Blackstream said, bristling. "Once we're on the transports, we'll be completely dependent on them. They could ship us to Khandar for all we could do about it."

Blackstream was old enough to have served in the War of the Princes, Marcus reflected, which made his distrust natural enough. He and the other colonels of the Second Division had gathered in the command tent, along with Cyte, Fitz, and Give-Em-Hell.

"Not *completely* dependent," Fitz said mildly. "I imagine we'll still have access to our weapons, and we'd considerably outnumber the crews. We could take the ships, if necessary."

"And if we did," Blackstream shot back, "what about the men-of-war? They could blow us out of the water, no trouble."

"Why would they *bother*?" said de Koste. "If the Borels wanted us out of the way, they could just leave us here in the middle of nowhere."

"I'm more worried about what will be waiting for us at the other end," said Sevran. "Forgive me, sir, but are you certain it's wise to go straight to Vordan City? Perhaps we could send messages ahead and ask any forces there to meet us at Vayenne while we wait for Borelgai reinforcements."

"Bah," Give-Em-Hell said. "What's the use in waiting? They'll come for Vordan City, and we'll be ready. You boys hold the line against the first charge, and then we'll ride out and give 'em hell!"

"Against three-to-one odds?" Sevran said.

"We've faced worse," Give-Em-Hell shot back.

Cyte leaned close to Marcus' ear as the argument went on. "Aren't you going to remind them who's in command here?" she murmured.

"Let them have it out first," Marcus said quietly. It was something he'd learned in Khandar, when his status had been more like first among equals as senior captain. People were far more likely to give in to authority *after* they'd worn themselves out in argument than when they were full of fight. "Besides, I can't say they don't have a point. We can't tell them about Winter."

"*Enough.*" To Marcus' surprise, it was Abby's voice that cut through the rising chatter. To this point, she'd been quiet, but now she stood with her hands flat on the table. "*Of course* we're going back to Vordan City. Your queen heard that you were in difficulty, and she managed to pry a fleet out of the *Borels*, for God's sake, and sent it to come get you. Now she needs you to get back into the fight." She looked around the circle. "Are you going to say no?"

"You trust the Borels?" Blackstream said.

"I trust Raesinia," Abby said. "And I trust the general. That's enough."

"Damned right!" Give-Em-Hell said. "As long as we get to Vordan City in time to find a few remounts, the cavalry will be ready for anything."

Sevran looked at Blackstream, then at Marcus, and shrugged. "If those are your orders, General."

"They are," Marcus said. "As Colonel Giforte said, the queen has asked us for help, and I don't intend to let her down." *Not again.* "We march in the morning. Duke Dorsay said it's ten miles to the ships, and I want our men embarking by tomorrow evening."

There was a chorus of "Yes, sir!" and a round of salutes. The colonels stood and filed out, but Fitz lingered for a moment.

"You know that Sevran is right, of course," he said. "The numbers are against us. And Vordan City is not defensible. Not that I'm questioning your decision."

"I'm aware of the numbers. They were against us in Khandar, if you recall."

"In Khandar, Janus was on *our* side." Fitz smiled thinly. "I'll start working on a plan, shall I?"

"I'm hoping we'll have more to work with," Marcus said. "But we won't know until we get there. So yes, it can't hurt to start thinking about it."

"Understood, sir." Fitz saluted, and slipped out through the flap, leaving only Cyte at the big table. Marcus sat down next to her with a sigh.

"Do you have any idea how to organize an army to board transports, Captain?" he said.

"No, sir. I imagine you'd have to think about provisions, fresh water—"

"And a hundred other things, I'd wager. Hopefully, Dorsay's people have a little more experience."

"We'll get there, sir. Don't worry."

"I'm not worried. Not about that, anyway. Too many other things to worry about."

"Understood, sir," Cyte said with a smile. "Was there anything else? I should draw up marching orders for tomorrow."

"Go ahead," Marcus told her. "And thank you, Colonel. For all your help."

"Of course, sir." She smiled, a surprisingly cheerful expression on her serious face. "I'm glad I don't have to leave the army behind."

"So am I, believe me. I'd never get all the paperwork done myself."

Cyte laughed, saluted, and left. Marcus sat for a while, staring at the maps and stray papers on the table. His thoughts went north, to Borel, and Raesinia.

She went to Borel. *To meet with the king and ask for his help.* If he knew Raesinia, she'd asked quite forcefully, and it apparently had worked. *Typical. I'm scraping to keep the army alive, and she casually produces a fleet out of nowhere to rescue us.* For a moment the need to see her, to hold her as he had after she'd come to his rescue in Murnsk, was nearly overpowering.

I should ask Dorsay when she's coming back. It would be safer for her to stay in Viadre if Vordan City was going to become a battlefield, but for a moment Marcus allowed himself to think selfishly. *Maybe she'll lead the reinforcements herself, like one of the warrior queens of old.* The image of Raesinia in medieval plate armor with a winged helmet was simultaneously so incongruous and so fitting that he laughed out loud.

The next morning it was raining again, a light mist that was just enough to add a layer of slime to the surface of the roads and make everyone clammy and miserable. Cavalry patrols trooped across the Gond bridge at regular intervals, pulling back across the river, and the artillerists retrieved their fuses and powder barrels from the bridge to the relief of all concerned. The infantry packed up their tents and began the long trudge to the west, following the curve of the river.

This time, Marcus rode ahead instead of keeping his normal position in the middle of the column. He and Cyte stayed with the cavalry vanguard, to meet with Dorsay and organize the loading. As the day wore on, though, Marcus found himself afflicted with superstitious worry, as though yesterday had been some kind of dream. The haze of the rain didn't help, rendering everything farther than a few dozen yards away misty and ghostlike. *Marching forever toward help that never comes would be a pretty good hell for an entire army,* he thought. There were stories in the *Wisdoms* . . .

Silliness, of course. But it was still with a sense of relief that Marcus heard the call from the forward scouts that they'd sighted the first masts. A few minutes later he could see for himself, a row of them looming out of the mist like huge, naked trees. The transports, big boxy things that seemed as seaworthy as bathtubs, were anchored just off the bank. Farther out, a sleek frigate prowled, looking like a predator beside its ungainly prey. The muddy red of the Borelgai flag flew from the stern of every vessel.

Marcus sent messengers back to the column, giving more precise directions, then rode ahead with Cyte. They found Dorsay standing with a small group of men in unfamiliar, ornate uniforms, which Marcus guessed were Borelgai navy. At the sight of him, they took off their overlarge hats and inclined their heads.

"General d'Ivoire!" Dorsay said as Marcus dismounted. "Everything went smoothly, I trust?"

"So far," Marcus said. A Life Guard came forward to take the reins of his horse. "Colonel Cyte has information on how much space we'll need for the various units. Who should she be talking to?"

"Sub-Captain Gale is handling the logistics." Dorsay beckoned, and a younger man, less impressively uniformed and hatted, stepped out from behind the others. His superiors were eyeing Cyte with mixed expressions of mirth and horror, and one of them whispered something that set the others to chuckling. Cyte studiously ignored them, but Marcus felt himself going red.

"These gentlemen," Dorsay went on, "are the captains of our frigates. Captain Neilson, of the *Swiftmark*, Captain—"

Another chuckle was too much for Marcus.

"Yes," he said. "My chief of staff is a woman. If you find this difficult to accept, I suggest you get over it quickly."

"Sir—" Cyte said.

"My apologies, madam," one of the captains said.

"It's just a bit . . . unusual for us," said another. "Borel has never been quite so *desperate* that the frailer sex has needed to take up arms."

Cyte straightened up. "I suggest you not repeat that comment when the rest of the army gets here. We have a couple thousand women with muskets, and they're quite used to making fools of men who think of them as frail."

"Quite right," Dorsay said blandly. "We fought them at Gilphaite, and you'd better believe that was a bloody mess."

The smiles on the captains' faces were gone, but they made no further comments. Cyte went off with Sub-Captain Gale to compare lists, and Marcus endured the rest of the introductions, though none of them stuck in his mind. More Vordanai cavalry was starting to arrive, and he set them to marking out an area where the army could stop and erect its tents. *We'll be at least a day getting on board. No sense getting wet until then.*

"You're very thorough, General d'Ivoire," Dorsay said approvingly. "We'll have some time on our hands once we set sail. I hope we get the chance to compare notes." He winked. "And it's possible a bottle or two of Hamveltai *flaghaelan* may have come into my possession."

Marcus grinned. "I think I would like that very much, Your Grace."

"We can raise a glass to your queen," Dorsay went on. "She's due congratulations."

"Congratulations?"

"On her marriage to Second Prince Matthew." Dorsay slapped Marcus cheerfully on the shoulder. "The price of the alliance, I imagine. Georg drives a hard bargain, but if she got a fleet and an army out of him in exchange for a marriage, I think he may have got the short end of the stick for once!"

CHAPTER TWENTY-THREE

RAESINIA

"Well," Raesinia said.

"Well." The second prince gave a crooked smile. "It was a nice engagement while it lasted."

"Surprisingly pleasant," Raesinia agreed, grinning back at him.

They were standing in the same foyer where Raesinia had confronted Georg. Trunks full of Raesinia's things sat by the door, waiting to be hauled to the docks.

"You're sure you wouldn't rather come with us?" Raesinia said. "I can't imagine you want to spend any longer here than you have to."

"Unfortunately, I can't simply vanish from the capital on a moment's notice," Matthew said. "I have affairs to wind up and friends who need tearful good-byes. It won't be long before I grace your Ohnlei Palace with my presence, I assure you."

"If your father tries anything—"

"I've got the letters," Matthew said. Cora had written out instructions for a few different contingencies. "And the duplicates are somewhere safe. My friends know what to do."

The threat that they could still bring the Borelgai economy down, even once Raesinia and Cora had left the city, *should* be enough to keep Matthew and his lover safe from the king's reprisal. Still, Raesinia felt uneasy. "Make sure *he* knows what will happen. Just in case."

"I will." Matthew looked down, uncharacteristically at a loss for words. "Your Highness—"

"Raes," Raesinia said. "My friends call me Raes."

"Raes, then." The prince swallowed. "I don't know how I can possibly thank you for this."

"You don't have to," Raesinia said. "We couldn't have done it without your connections."

"You didn't have to do it at all. You could have married me, gone back to Vordan, and let me drink myself to death. You didn't have to . . . care."

"Well." Raesinia's smile broadened. "I'm sure, as ambassador, you'll find some way to make it up to me. You can't be worse than Ihannes. He has a smile like a carnival mask."

"It does have a mechanical look to it, doesn't it? Like there was some kind of clockwork inside his head keeping it wound up." Matthew let out a breath. "For what it's worth, then. Thank you."

"Thank you, Prince Matthew." Raesinia bowed slightly. "I look forward to seeing you at court."

"Of course you do. I make a stunning addition to *any* court." He struck a pose, and Raesinia laughed out loud.

After a carriage ride through the city, shrouded as usual in mist and rain, they were back at the docks. The *Prudence*, the same courier that had brought Raesinia to Borel, was assigned to bring her home. Eric, Cora, and the other servants followed in her retinue, along with a small packet for the Borelgai embassy in Vordan City. With so few passengers and no cargo, the captain assured her that they would make excellent time.

That turned out to be the case, thanks to a southerly wind that heralded the onset of winter. *Prudence* sped through choppy seas, rounding the Jaw and down the western coast of Vordan. They were headed, not directly back to Vordan City, but for Enzport at the mouth of the Pale. If nothing had gone terribly wrong, that was where Duke Dorsay's squadron would be, and the prospect of an early reunion with Marcus was impossible to resist. *It's not far out of the way, in any event,* Raesinia told herself. *And we need to get the latest news on the war.*

Cora kept herself occupied reading—she'd gotten a small crate full of new texts in Borel, which at the rate she was going looked like they'd last until roughly the end of the week—while Eric seemed to enjoy the break from the pressure. But the waiting wore on Raesinia. There was only so long she could spend on deck, watching the foam-flecked waves rise and fall, or down in the chart room staring at the maps. She tried to read, but couldn't concentrate. *There ought to be something I can do to be useful.* But the crew certainly didn't need her help, and without more information there wasn't much planning that could be done.

It was with some relief, therefore, that she watched Ecco Island slide into sight. It was a mountainous hump, rising out of the ocean like the domed back of a turtle, with only scattered greenery on its rocky slopes. A few people lived there, she knew, mostly raising sheep, but the only permanent settlement was on the landward side, at the naval base. As they hugged the north coast of the island, she could see the bumpy shapes of brick embrasures at the tops of the cliffs, where the shore guns that had closed this route to enemy vessels were emplaced. Those guns were gone now, dragged away and spiked by the Borelgai when they'd invaded the island during the war and not yet replaced by a revolutionary government that needed every cannon it could manufacture for the army.

Past the island, the southern peninsula swung up like a lower jaw, creating a bay the shape of a long, narrowing funnel. It made for a magnificent harbor, the best in Vordan: shielded from ocean storms by the bulk of the island, deep enough for the largest ships, and big enough to float the navies of the world. Before the War of the Princes, the largest squadron of the Vordanai navy had been based here, as well as their primary shipyard. The Borelgai had smashed the former and burned the latter, and kept the place under very effective siege, though neither city nor island had actually fallen. After Vansfeldt and the peace that followed, Vordan's navy had been officially disbanded. Enzport was still a center of commercial shipping, but the naval shipyard had never been rebuilt.

For the people who'd lived through that time, looking out their windows must have made for an awful reminder. Once again, Borelgai men-of-war lay at anchor in the Enzport harbor, red flags snapping from their sterncastles in the brisk breeze. They were huge ships, towering over the slender *Prudence*, their high, slab-sided hulls broken by three horizontal lines of gunports. Men bustled about in their rigging, climbing the ropes and spars.

Behind those behemoths was the rest of the fleet, a flock of wider, lower transports with lean frigates at the edges like sheepdogs. The civilian ships of the harbor gave the whole group a wide berth. Enzport was mostly on the north bank of the Pale, and the docks there were crowded with merchantmen and fishing vessels. If she hadn't just come from Viadre, Raesinia might have been impressed at the sight.

Colored flags ran up the mast of the closest warship in response to a similar string flying from the *Prudence*. Sothe, Raesinia reflected, would have been able to decode them.

"Your Highness." A young crewman, obviously overawed by the rank of his guest, edged up to where she stood against the rail. "With your permission, we'll tie up to the *Dominant*, and you can go aboard. Duke Dorsay and General d'Ivoire are waiting for you."

Marcus. She was so close now. She stared up at the mountainous ship, trying to pick him out along the rail. "Of course. Proceed."

He saluted and ran off. *Prudence* tacked expertly to come alongside the larger vessel, then ropes were flying down from *Dominant*'s deck, and the courier's crew worked hurriedly to bring the two together. A few minutes later, a long ladder unrolled from the man-of-war. Raesinia waved off any offers of help and grabbed the rungs, pulling herself up the side of the larger ship.

The men at the top of the ladder were clearly not prepared for this, and stepped back in some confusion at the sight of the queen herself awkwardly straddling the rail before she managed to get herself over. They stood stiffly at attention as she brushed herself off, immaculate in their red-and-white navy uniforms. After a polite interval, a tall man in a more elaborate uniform stepped over and bowed, doffing his bicorn.

"Your Highness," he said. "My name is Captain Charles Brixton. Welcome to the *Dominant*, flagship of the First Squadron."

"Thank you, Captain."

"We have your cabin prepared, if you'd like."

"I was told Duke Dorsay and General d'Ivoire are aboard," Raesinia said, her heart thumping a little faster. "I'd like to see them."

"Of course. I believe they're in the chart room." He snapped his fingers at a waiting sailor.

"My staff and bags will be coming over as well," Raesinia said, as she followed the man. "Make sure they get settled."

Brixton bowed again. Raesinia followed the sailor across the crowded deck, dodging barrels, coils of rope, and assorted tools. Carronades, small, short-barreled cannon, were mounted at intervals along the rail, intended to fire grapeshot onto an enemy deck during a close encounter. A tight spiral stair led belowdecks, into a narrow corridor toward the ship's stern.

The chart room was larger than any space aboard the *Prudence*, with a big table and dressers full of maps, notes, and cartographers' tools. At the moment, the *Dominant*'s own paper charts had been pushed aside, replaced with the unrolled leather maps that the army used in the field. Standing around the table were Duke Dorsay, General Fitz Warus, and the young woman captain Raesinia recognized as Winter's second in command.

And Marcus. He looked much as he had when Raesinia had last seen him, beard well trimmed, uniform neat and clean. She realized she'd expected to be charging to the rescue again, as in Murnsk, and to find him battle-worn and exhausted. *He must have been here at least a week, if Dorsay kept to the timetable,* she told herself. *Don't be silly.* He looked up at her, and his eyes widened, but just for a moment. Then he was staring at the map again, and something had gone tight in his face.

"Your Highness," Dorsay said, stepping around the table with a warm smile. "Welcome. Your journey was clearly swift. I hope it was uneventful as well?"

"Entirely," Raesinia said. "And I'm glad to see everything has gone according to plan on your side."

"Not *entirely* according to plan, but well enough," Dorsay said. "We had to send the transports a considerable distance up the Pale, which put us a bit behind schedule. But we're here now, and that's what matters."

"And the army?" Raesinia said, looking directly at Marcus. "What's their condition?"

He looked her in the eye, his face rigid with military discipline. Raesinia's throat went thick. *It's not just that we're in front of the others. Something's wrong.*

"We have the First and Second Divisions," Marcus said. "Along with some stragglers and detached units from the rest of the army, and the cavalry reserve, though we're very short on horses."

"The other divisions were destroyed?" The shock of that overcame Raesinia's worry about Marcus. *That's tens of thousands of soldiers.*

"We don't know," Marcus said. "When our left flank collapsed at Alves, there was a rout. Some units were probably dispersed, others mostly taken captive. Some may have changed sides." He shook his head. "Unfortunately, we don't have a great deal of information."

"And Janus?" she said.

"There the picture has cleared up in the last few days," Fitz said. "Though I'm afraid it still isn't good. Reports have reached us that his main force is, indeed, pushing through the Illifen passes. There are some garrisons there, and the positions are strong, so it may take a little time. But there's no question of stopping him completely. Once he's on the other side, it's an easy march down the Marak to the Vor and Vordan City."

Dorsay cleared his throat. "General d'Ivoire has been very insistent that we make all haste for Vordan City. We were, in fact, planning to weigh anchor tomorrow. But I must repeat to Your Highness what I told the general—I don't believe that we'll have the strength to fight a battle when we get there, not without waiting for reinforcements from Borel. My own suggestion was Nordart, but perhaps a rendezvous at Vayenne—"

"Your Highness," Marcus said. "Before we discuss strategy, I need a moment with you in private."

"There are decisions that must be made immediately," Dorsay complained. "If we plan to switch the rendezvous to Vayenne, we should dispatch the *Prudence* with orders—"

"Please, Your Highness," Marcus said. "It's important."

"Is there somewhere General d'Ivoire and I could speak alone?" Raesinia said. Her heart started beating faster again, and she felt her cheeks flush. She gritted her teeth. *I'm the Queen of Vordan, for God's sake, not a lovesick schoolgirl.*

"Of course," Dorsay said with a sigh. He gestured to the door. "Follow me."

Down the hallway from the chart room was a well-appointed cabin—not, in fact, very different from the room Raesinia had occupied at the Keep in Viadre, except with all the furniture bolted to the floor.

"This is the commodore's quarters," Dorsay said. "While I'm technically filling that role on this expedition, we thought it best to reserve them for you."

"Thank you, Your Grace." Raesinia glared at Dorsay, her expression fixedly polite, while he bowed and backed out of the room.

"Raesinia—" Marcus said, when the duke was gone.

That was all he got out before she was on him, standing on tiptoes to reach his mouth with hers, her arms wrapped around his shoulders. For a moment he went stiff, and then he relaxed slightly, kissing her, his hands sliding up her flanks.

All right, she conceded. *Maybe I am a lovesick schoolgirl.*

He pulled away, pushing her to arm's length, and stared as though she'd grown an extra head. Raesinia felt her cheeks flush further, but she stubbornly met his gaze.

"You didn't tell me you were going to Viadre," Marcus said.

"The opportunity came up after you left," Raesinia said, with a twinge of guilt. It was only half-true, since she could have sent him a messenger. She hadn't wanted to distract him, or deal with his inevitable objections. "I thought it was where I could do the most good."

"And you were right, clearly." He waved at the ship around them. "A navy squadron and an army to follow. That's impressive negotiation."

Something clouded his expression for a moment, and he took a step back, looking away. Raesinia frowned. "Marcus?"

"I'm sorry." He took a deep breath. "I wanted to tell you I understand."

"Understand what?" Raesinia's hand went to her mouth. "Oh God. Dorsay told you."

Of course he did. He had no reason not to. When he'd left Viadre, Raesinia's engagement to Prince Matthew had been settled fact, not publicly announced but certainly not much of a secret. And the duke didn't know about her relationship with Marcus, of course. *Why wouldn't he tell him?*

Raesinia hadn't been exactly planning to *keep* the whole episode from Marcus. She'd just hoped that she'd be able to explain it a little later. *Maybe that was foolish. Damn, damn, damn.*

"I understand," Marcus repeated, all wounded dignity. "You're the Queen of Vordan. I told you back at Ohnlei that I knew it might come to this, that you'd have to put the interests of the state before your personal feelings—"

"It's the opposite, damn it," Raesinia burst out. "It wasn't until after I heard about Alves that I . . . No one knew what had happened to you, or whether you were even still alive. And—" She shook her head frantically. "It's not important. Marcus, it doesn't matter—"

"You did what you had to—"

"*It doesn't matter,*" Raesinia said, a bit louder than she'd intended. "Because it's off. The engagement, the marriage—it's all off."

Marcus stopped, looking like she'd shone a lantern full in his face. "Off?"

"Canceled. Crossed out. Not happening."

"But . . ." Marcus swallowed. "Dorsay said . . ."

"Dorsay doesn't know. We left Borel almost as soon as I worked it out, and the courier ships are faster than anything else afloat. He hasn't gotten the news yet, though I'd wager there's something in the mailbag for him."

"Isn't that going to be . . . bad?" Marcus said. "If the marriage was the price of this alliance, then can we still trust the Borels?"

"We found another way to convince the king." Raesinia couldn't help grinning.

"How?"

"Financial fraud and complex derivatives, mostly. It's a long story." She took a deep breath. "The point is, Marcus, that I am *not* going to marry the

Second Prince of Borel. Not now, and not ever." She stepped forward. "I thought that I had to choose between loving you and saving your life. Between political expedience and personal feeling. You know what I decided?"

"What?" Marcus said, looking a little overwhelmed.

"The *hell* with that. I'm not giving up *any* of it. Not without a fight."

"Um. Good?"

He'd been retreating in front of her, she realized, and now he was backed against the bulkhead, hands raised as though she had a sword at his throat. Raesinia grinned and pressed herself against him, kissing him furiously. His arms went around her waist, pulling her close, and this time he didn't push back.

"I hate to be the one to say this," he murmured, his lips brushing her ear. "But Duke Dorsay is waiting for us."

"I know." Something in Raesinia's body ached in unfamiliar ways, deep and sweet. It was more effort than she was prepared to admit to pull herself away. She was breathing hard. "Sorry."

"No, um, need to apologize," Marcus said.

"There was . . . something." Raesinia tried to force her mind back outside this room and away from the body standing so temptingly close. "You wanted to talk to me. About why we need to go to Vordan City."

"Right." Marcus took a deep breath. "I told Duke Dorsay it was because Vordan City and the palace are the symbols of the legitimate government and if Janus takes them he may win the support of the people. And that's . . . true, probably. But there's more than that."

Raesinia cocked her head, waiting.

"It's not just Janus we're up against. There's some kind of demon involved. The Beast. Winter Ihernglass is on his way back to Vordan City, and he has some kind of a plan for stopping it." He shook his head. "It might be the only chance we get."

"The Beast? Like the Beast of Judgment, from the *Wisdoms*?"

Marcus shrugged. "Your guess is as good as mine."

"Who told you all this?"

"Talk about a long story," he muttered.

"The short version," Raesinia said.

"Janus did."

"Janus," Raesinia deadpanned. "Who has declared himself emperor and gone to war against us."

"We think the Beast is controlling him somehow. It explains a lot."

"And you trust him?"

"I . . . don't know."

"But you're willing to bet your life on this anyway," Raesinia said. "All our lives, maybe. The kingdom."

Marcus was silent.

"Tell me one thing," Raesinia said. "Janus is your friend. I know it's hard for you to think he would turn on us. Tell me this isn't just what you *want* to believe."

"It's not that," Marcus said firmly. "It's not *only* that, at least. I believe there's more going on than we understand." He paused. "And when it comes down to it, I suppose I *do* trust Janus. Even when he's on the other side."

"I'm going to need you to explain exactly where that conviction comes from at some point," Raesinia said. "But if you're certain, then I'll back you. I can come up with plenty of other reasons we need to fight at Vordan City."

"Thank you," Marcus said. He hesitated for a moment. "And . . . thank you for what you did in Borel. For coming to rescue me. And for not giving up."

Raesinia kissed him again. *Duke Dorsay can wait.*

By the time evening fell, the *Prudence* had been dispatched for Vordan City with messages for the Deputies and the garrison, and Duke Dorsay and his captains were making preparations for the fleet to leave in the morning. The duke hadn't been happy about Raesinia's choice to side with Marcus, but he'd seemed to expect it. *Maybe he knows more than he's letting on.*

Once the strategy session had broken up, Raesinia gathered what she thought of as the conspiracy, everyone who knew that magic was real. With Winter gone and Sothe missing, this amounted to herself, Marcus, Cora, and Cyte, whom Marcus introduced as his second in command. Raesinia watched the captain with interest. She remembered Cyte, vaguely, as one of the student radicals who'd been there the night they stormed the Vendre. But that memory was of an anxious, insecure girl, inclined toward melodrama and heavy eyeshadow, and nothing at all like the calm, professional soldier before her now.

Marcus and Cyte went through what they'd discovered, their visit to Mieranhal and the nature of Janus' obsession. When Marcus told the story of the battle of Satinvol, where he'd been forced to kill a girl who'd fought by his side, she could hear the emotion in his voice, and she reached out to take his hand.

He started slightly at her touch and gave her a questioning look, but she only smiled. *I've had enough of hiding.*

Raesinia read the note Janus had written, in his familiar, precise script. *"My mind is not my own."* It *did* fit, in a way. *Or is he only playing us all, again?*

"I thought Karis got rid of the Beast of Judgment," Cora said. She was sitting on the bed, hugging her knees, and Raesinia felt another twinge of guilt for getting her involved. Genius or not, this was a lot to lay on someone her age. "Isn't that in the *Wisdoms*?"

"We don't know what this thing is," Cyte said. "Only that it can control people."

"But not completely," Raesinia said. "Janus seems to be able to fight it."

"Only a little bit," Marcus said. "And it's not just controlling his body, either. It was definitely Janus leading the battle against Kurot. He took us to pieces."

"So it takes over someone almost completely," Cyte said.

"And it can spread from one person to another?" Cora said. "Like at Satinvol."

"Feor might know more," Raesinia said. "We can talk to her as soon as we get to Vordan City."

"What happens if Winter doesn't come back?" Cora said. "Or if he's too late?"

"He'll be there," Cyte said. Her tone brooked no argument.

"Even assuming he does," Marcus said, "we need to think about what happens if he hasn't got a magic bullet. Suppose Winter takes care of this Beast, and leaves the army for us to deal with?"

"I left orders for soldiers to be gathered at Vordan City," Raesinia said. "If the Deputies-General haven't screwed things up, there should be *some* reinforcements waiting. Beyond that . . ." She shrugged.

"There's no point in speculating," Cyte said. "We don't have enough information. Once we know what resources we have to work with and how much time we have, then we'll see."

"It might not hurt to start looking for a place to mount a defense," Marcus said. "We know the basics. It has to be a strong position somewhere north of the city."

Cyte sighed. "I'll look over the maps. It'll give me something to do until we get there, at least." She got to her feet. "Your Highness, General. If you'll excuse me, I'm going to get some sleep."

"Me too." Cora yawned.

They left the cabin. Just for a moment, Raesinia thought she detected a conspiratorial glance between them.

"She's impressive," Raesinia said.

"Cyte?" Marcus said. "I agree. I don't think we'd have gotten this far without her."

"She and Winter . . ."

Marcus nodded. "From what I hear."

"Then for her sake I hope you're right, and this isn't all some trick of Janus'."

"Me too." Marcus shook his head. "Cora really helped you beat the King of Borel?"

Raesinia snorted. "More like *I* helped *her*. And mostly just because I've got a nastier mind than she does." She grinned. "She helped us track down Maurisk's people, remember?"

"I knew she had a head for figures," Marcus said. "But . . . you'd better make sure she never falls into the wrong hands."

"Don't worry. Cora's a good person. If not for my bad influence, I think she'd be entirely virtuous."

Marcus chuckled. "That's reassuring."

They sat quietly for a moment. There was something in the air, a hum of tension Raesinia could practically feel in her bones.

"Well," Marcus said. "I should go get some sleep myself."

"You could," Raesinia said, swallowing. "Or you could stay."

"Stay?" Marcus said. "In your cabin?"

"Stay," Raesinia repeated, watching him carefully. *He can't be that* dense. "In, as you say, my cabin."

"Ah." Marcus glanced at the door. "People will notice."

"I don't care anymore." Raesinia took a deep breath. "With everything you and I have been through trying to save this country, I think we're entitled to . . . some latitude, don't you?"

"That's one way of putting it."

Raesinia got out of her chair and went over to him. Sitting, he was only a little taller than she was, which made it easy to lean in and kiss him. This time, Marcus didn't pull away.

When they broke apart at last, Raesinia reached for the hem of her shirt. Thankfully, her shipboard wear was considerably less formal than the dresses she'd worn in the Keep, and she was able to pull it and her undershirt over her head in one smooth motion, without spending an hour undoing tiny buttons.

Marcus stared, his expression suddenly unreadable. Raesinia felt her skin pebble into goose bumps, and she fought a sudden urge to cover herself. Spending her whole life being dressed by servants had left her without a lot of body modesty, but here, now, she suddenly wished she was a little more . . . mature. *Why couldn't I have died a year or two later?*

"Marcus?" Raesinia said.

"Sorry." He shook his head gently. "It's just . . ."

"Am I not . . . ?" Raesinia swallowed hard. "Is it too strange? The way I look?"

"What?" He bounded out of the chair and wrapped his arms around her, pulling her close with a surprised squeak. "No. Raes, *no*. You're beautiful."

"Then what's wrong?"

Flushing under his beard, he looked down at her. "I just thought . . . You really want this? With me?" He gestured at himself with one hand. "I'm not . . ."

"Oh, for God's sake." Raesinia rolled her eyes, then went in for another kiss, standing on her toes. Marcus' hands gripped her shoulders and slid down her arms, his thumbs brushing inward across the slim curve of her breasts. Raesinia shivered.

"I should warn you," she said, her mouth near his ear. "I have no idea what I'm doing."

"Really?" He stood up a little straighter. "I thought you spent a year slumming it at the University. You must have learned *something*."

"I mean, I understand the . . . mechanics. But I never thought it really applied to me."

"Well," Marcus said, leaning toward her again, "I'm not an *expert*. But I can offer a little instruction."

"That's good," Raesinia murmured. "A queen should really be properly educated."

CHAPTER TWENTY-FOUR

WINTER

The *Swallow* was every bit as fast as Sothe had claimed. Captain Kerrak—a tall, thin, nervous-looking man who Winter was increasingly certain was a smuggler—pointed out the landmarks of the Split Coast as they went past. The great expanse of western Murnsk, which had seemed so vast and intractable when the Grand Army had been marching through it, slipped by them like a dream. Salavask and Vorsk, both port cities like Dimiotsk, and then Yatterny on the Vordanai border. From there their course swung west, through the narrow Borel Sea that separated Borel from Vordan. The massive cliffs of the Jaw loomed on their left, glimpsed through a haze of rain on a choppy sea.

The days were getting colder, and the wind stronger, though the captain assured them it would be weeks yet before winter storms might imperil the *Swallow*. They sighted few other ships, especially once they were close to the Vordanai coast. A couple of fishing vessels and some local traders. Once, a Borelgai frigate came into view on the horizon, but either its crew didn't notice them or the rumors of blockade were false after all; Captain Kerrak didn't even have to run up his false colors.

Poor Abraham had it worst. Something in the motion of the ship, the endless rise and fall on the waves, played havoc with his stomach, and he spent most of the first few days with his head over the rail. After that, matters improved somewhat, although whether that was because he had gotten used to it or because he simply had nothing left in his guts wasn't clear. He spent most of his time in silent contemplation, tucked away in a nook by the rail.

Alex, on the other hand, was having a wonderful time. She climbed the rigging as easily as any seaman. The *Swallow*'s sailors, who Winter found to be a pretty taciturn lot, were taken with Alex almost to a man, especially since she was willing to hurl colorful insults as quickly as any of them. A few of the young men seemed to have more than simple camaraderie on their minds, which worried Winter only for a moment. *Alex can take care of herself.*

As for their hosts, Ennika spent all her time closeted in the forward cabin, which she shared with Sothe. The assassin was more visible, talking with Captain Kerrak and spending time on deck, but after a few days Winter got the distinct sense that Sothe was avoiding her, inasmuch as it was possible to do so on a ship the size of the *Swallow.*

Winter had expected to be bored, but she found the journey oddly restful. Her mind had been whirling, full of plans and contingencies, ever since the Steel Ghost had returned to the Mountain. Sitting on the deck, with gray-green ocean extending to the horizon and her ears full of the creaks and groans of a ship under sail, she felt . . . peaceful.

As long as we're aboard, there's nothing I should be doing. The enforced waiting meant a break from the guilt, the knowledge that every minute she delayed might mean disaster. *We're going as fast as we can, for once.*

Eventually they turned south, rounding the tip of Vordan. Winter stood at the rail, watching the sun sink slowly into the western sea. Captain Kerrak's sailors shouted things to one another, incomprehensible nautical jargon for the most part, but it all sounded cheerful. Abraham had a book in his lap, but as best Winter could tell he was asleep, head propped against a water barrel. Winter looked up to see Alex padding over, wearing a broad grin.

"Enjoying the breeze?" she said.

"Something like that," Winter said. "Did you need something?"

"Do you think you could let me have the cabin for the next hour?"

"Let you have . . ." Winter frowned.

"The door doesn't lock," Alex said. "I didn't want you to, ah . . ."

Her eyes went to the narrow stair that led belowdecks. A young sailor was waiting there, olive-skinned and handsome, lounging against a post as he chatted to his colleagues. Winter raised her eyebrows.

"Ah," she said.

"Yeah," Alex said.

"I'll be here," Winter said. "Enjoying the breeze."

"Great." Alex's smile widened. "It, um, may be more like an hour and a half."

Once again Winter wondered if she should comment. Once again she decided Alex could take care of herself. "Go ahead."

"Thanks." Alex clapped Winter on the shoulder and hurried off. The young sailor said something to her, and then they were both laughing as they went down the stairs.

Winter wondered what it would be like, to spend an enjoyable hour or so in the intimate company of a near stranger for no better reason than that you found them attractive and willing. It was hard for her to imagine, like trying to picture living on the ocean floor. But Alex was a very different person, and she'd led a very different life.

A few moments after Alex vanished, Sothe appeared, wearing only tight leggings and a leather vest despite the chill wind. The assassin went through a complex exercise routine twice a day, a set of smooth, deceptively fast movements that were half dance, half combat. The sailors had cleared a space near the stern for her to use, but instead of heading that way, she came in Winter's direction.

"Ennika had another . . . message," Sothe said quietly. "She wanted to talk to you."

"To me? Why?"

"I don't know." Sothe sighed and crossed her arms. They were covered in old, whitening scars, from tiny cuts to a long, jagged wound that must have laid open her biceps. Winter tried not to stare.

"Well." Winter used the rail to pull herself up. "I've got nothing to do. I'll see what she wants."

"Thank you." Sothe hesitated. "After I've finished, I think we need to talk, too."

"Strategy? I'm not sure we have enough information."

"Not exactly. It's . . . complicated." Sothe shook her head. "Later."

A bit bemused, Winter went down the steps and to the forward cabin shared by Sothe and Ennika. That took her past her own door, and the noises from within made it abundantly clear what was happening *there*. There were no secrets on a ship as small as the *Swallow*. She did her best not to listen and knocked on the door to Ennika's cabin.

"Come in," the blind girl said.

The room was much like Winter's own, with two bunks, one above the other, and a small table in one corner. Everything was fixed in place, as a precaution against rough seas. Ennika sat on the lower bunk, her sightless eyes aimed at the ceiling, running her fingers against the pages of a book.

"It's me," Winter said, after a moment. "Sothe said you wanted to talk."

Ennika nodded. "Sit, if you like."

Winter did, wedging herself awkwardly sideways on one of the immobile chairs to face the bed. Ennika turned a page, tracing a few more lines, then set the book aside.

"Can you really read that way?" Winter said, fascinated.

"There are special books, with raised letters," Ennika said. She leaned forward, holding out the book to Winter. "This one is just an ordinary copy of the *Wisdoms*, though."

Winter took it and opened it to a random page. It was blank, or nearly so—the letters that had once been there had been worn away by the passage of Ennika's fingers, until only traces of ink remained.

She handed it back. "If you can't read it, then why . . . ?"

"I know the *Wisdoms* by heart," Ennika said. "I don't need to be reminded of the words. But tracing it out is . . . a comfort."

"How old were you when they took your eyes?" Winter realized a bit too late that the question might not be polite, but Ennika didn't seem to mind.

"Five or six, I think. I don't know my real birthday. It was just after my sister and I spoke the names of our demons and formed our bond. Once they knew we would live, our eyes were put out, so that we would not compromise the security of the Priests of the Black with what we saw."

"Saints and martyrs," Winter said. "That's horrible."

Ennika shrugged. "*Ahdon ivahnt vi, Ignahta Sempria.* What's done to me in this life is only a small taste of what I'll receive in hell, when my time is up."

"You really believe that? That you're damned for eternity because of what they made you do when you were a little girl?"

"I chose to do it," Ennika said. "I was young, but not unaware."

"You can't have understood," Winter said. "Not really."

"I understood enough. I wanted to help people." She shrugged again. "I probably would have ended in hell in any case, you understand. My sister and I were living on the streets before the priests took us. We would have been whores, or worse. This way, I can at least save the souls of others. Or I thought I could."

The Priests of the Black have a lot to answer for. It was bad enough that they captured, tortured, and killed those who were born with demons through no fault of their own. *But to take innocent children and feed them* this *line of nonsense . . .*

"I have been trying," Ennika said, "to make sense of what's happened. The Beast's return. At first I was in despair. I would have taken my own life, if Sothe hadn't stopped me."

"At first? You've changed your mind?"

Ennika nodded. "I talked with Janus. If it is Janus who touches my mind, where my sister once was. He asked me if all this was not also part of God's plan. The Lord tested mankind once before, when the Beast of Judgment first came, and Karis proved equal to the challenge. Now He tests us again, and we have you."

Winter sat up straighter. "Wait, wait. I'm not a prophet."

"I know. It may be that you fail and the Beast will bring about the end of man. That, too, would be part of the plan. But my role in it, my purpose, will be fulfilled. It's not an accident that I'm here, with you."

"It's sometimes hard to tell the difference between God's plans and Janus'," Winter said dryly. "Is that why you wanted to see me? To talk theology?"

"No. Janus gave me a message for you. He said that the core of the Beast is coming south, toward Vordan City, and that this is where you will have your chance." She frowned. "He also said that if you fail, you will not get another. If the Beast takes Vordan City, it will grow so fast that it will be unstoppable."

"If I fail, I'll probably be dead."

"And in hell," Ennika agreed. "So it won't matter much to you. But that was the message."

Winter bit back a sarcastic response. "Fine. It's good to know we'll have one chance at this, at least. Was there anything else?"

"Not from Janus." Ennika's hands went tight in her lap. "I . . . wanted to ask you something."

"You—" Winter frowned. "Go ahead, I suppose."

"Your demon, the Infernivore. It tears the demons from others and devours them, correct?"

"More or less," Winter said uncomfortably.

"When we reach Vordan City, will you use it on me?"

"Use—you *want* me to take your demon?"

Ennika nodded solemnly.

"Why? I thought it was all part of God's plan."

"My part will be finished soon. And when Janus is not speaking to me, there is . . . emptiness where my sister's mind once was. A gap. It pulls at me all the time. I can't . . ." She brought her hand to her head. "I can't explain it well. But I can't live with it."

"I'm not sure using Infernivore on you would be any better," Winter said. "Everyone whose demon I've taken has ended up dead, one way or the other. You might not survive. It could break your mind."

"As I said, I was going to kill myself in any event, to get away from the pain." Ennika smiled slightly. "Suicide is a sin, of course, but once one is bound to hell regardless, what's another sin? But I am not . . . eager to die. If there is a chance, I would like to take it." Her smile faded. "Though if it breaks my mind, I hope you will . . . take pity on me."

"I . . ." Winter shook her head, realized Ennika couldn't see it, and cleared her throat. "Let me think about it." The girl had helped them—that was undeniable—but . . . *I don't know.*

"Thank you," Ennika said. "I understand it may be difficult for you. I will inform you if Janus contacts me again."

Since her own cabin was still decidedly occupied, Winter spent some time in the chart room, staring gloomily at the maps. From the course the captain had plotted, the *Swallow* was small enough to make the ascent of the Vor all the way to Vordan City. That would be considerably faster than riding overland, assuming the wind cooperated. Nautical charts were very different from the campaign maps she was used to, and she was just trying to work out the meanings of some of the more obscure markings when she heard someone in the corridor. Sothe, a bucket in one hand and a towel in the other, paused in the open doorway.

"I talked to Ennika," Winter said. "Janus told her we need to get to Vordan City, and he'll try to give me an opening."

"Good to know." Sothe was damp with sweat after her exercise, her short dark hair plastered to her skull.

"You said you wanted to talk to me, after."

The assassin gave her a long, unreadable look. "I suppose this is as good a time as any. Come on."

Winter followed Sothe back to her cabin. Ennika was gone, above decks for a change. Winter had noticed the crew of the *Swallow* was very solicitous of the blind girl, and she wondered briefly what Sothe had told them about her. *Maybe nothing.* If Captain Kerrak was in fact a smuggler, then he'd have cultivated a crew who were comfortable not asking questions.

Sothe set the bucket down, shut the door, and reached for the buttons on her vest. She paused, glancing at Winter, who shrugged, a little uncomfortably.

"I must admit I've never liked being aboard ship this long," Sothe said, nimble fingers working down the row of buttons. "It's . . . confining. I'm only really comfortable when I have an escape route ready."

"Never go to Khandar, then," Winter said. The monthlong voyage to and from the distant colony had been pure misery.

"I don't intend to, if I can help it." Sothe shrugged out of her vest. Underneath, she wore only a linen wrap around her breasts. The skin of her stomach and back was just as heavily scarred as her arms, the records of decades of battles written in pale, crisscrossing lines.

Sothe undid her wrap, dipped her towel in the bucket, and started wiping herself clean. She sighed heavily.

"And, of course, you can't get a proper bath." She shook her head. "I suppose I'm getting soft in my old age."

"Someday," Winter said, "I'll be done with marching around and living in tents. And then there'll be baths."

"Every soldier's prayer," Sothe said, with a slight smile.

"Not *every* soldier," Winter said. "Most of the ones I've known would probably be more worried about food and wine than baths."

"Fair enough."

Winter looked away as Sothe stripped off her leggings. "So, what did you want to talk to me about?"

"I wanted to apologize."

"For what?"

"For . . . well, for avoiding you, to be honest. I've been trying to make a decision, and it's been . . . difficult."

"It's all right," Winter said. "I haven't exactly been a social butterfly."

"Do you mind if I ask you a question?" There was the creak of a chest, and a rustle of cloth.

"If you like."

"You seem to have given up your male disguise."

"I . . ." Winter hesitated. "Alex and Abraham already knew, and I didn't count on running into anyone from Vordan. It seemed easier."

"Then you plan to resume it? Once we get back to Vordan City?"

"I'll have to," Winter said.

"You don't want to?"

"It's not really a matter of wanting," Winter said. "I started pretending to be a man so I could get into the army. After that it just kind of . . . kept going."

"But the Vordanai army includes women now. You could, in theory, reveal yourself." The bed creaked as Sothe sat down. "I'm dressed, by the way."

Winter turned to face her, taking the same sideways seat in the chair she had earlier. Sothe had changed into a long, loose shirt and trousers. *All in black, of course. I wonder if she ever wears any other color?*

"I could," Winter admitted. "But I've fooled a lot of people for a long time. They might not be happy about it."

"Who? Raesinia knows. I assume your officers in the Second Division do."

"Some of them," Winter said. "Cyte and the Girls' Own."

"Then whose reaction worries you? The other generals'?"

"I suppose it's mostly Marcus," Winter said. "He's . . . a little old-fashioned at times."

"I suspected as much," Sothe said, crossing her arms.

"Why? Is it important?"

"In a way." Sothe sighed. "I find myself in a complicated position."

"That involves me?"

"Indeed. I have information that . . ." She broke off. "How much do you remember about your past?"

"My *past*?" Winter said, now thoroughly confused. "You mean Mrs. Wilmore's? The Prison? I assume you know I was there."

Sothe nodded. "What about before that?"

"Nothing," Winter said. *Fire.* But that was only a dream, or the memory of the dream of a frightened little girl.

"Would you want to know more about it, if you could?"

Winter shrugged. "I suppose so. I've never thought much about it. Most of the girls at the Prison had the same basic story—families who were dead, or in jail for debts, or petty criminals."

"There is . . . a little more to it." Sothe shifted on the bed. "Your parents are dead, but they were not criminals. They were labeled as traitors by the Concordat, but that was . . . a lie."

"Wait. You *know*? How? Where did you find out?"

"I was asked to investigate." Sothe took a deep breath. "You know I once worked for the Last Duke."

"I'd gathered that," Winter said carefully.

"When the Cobweb burned, the primary records of the Concordat were lost. But there were—are—backups, duplicates. Partial, but still extensive, scattered in various safehouses and secondary headquarters. I imagine there's almost no one left who has the proper ciphers, but I do. I went looking."

"Who asked you to look?"

"I'll come to that," Sothe said. "I found your records. I have your history— your real name, your family. If you want it."

Winter stared at her for a moment in silence. Sothe looked away.

"The trouble," the assassin said, "is that I . . . owe this person, the one who asked me to look. But when I found it, I realized I owed you, too. I can't just deliver up your secrets without asking you."

"That hardly seems like a Concordat attitude," Winter muttered.

"I have learned . . . quite a lot from Raesinia," Sothe said. She sounded earnest. "I believe this is part of it. So, if you want me to, I will destroy what I have learned. I cannot promise that it will not come to light in some other way, but it seems unlikely. Your past will remain unknown. Or else I can give it to you and leave the rest of the choices in your hands."

There was another long pause.

"Balls of the Beast," Winter said. "This is making my head hurt."

"It is a common issue in the intelligence business," Sothe said. "There is information you might wish not to know. But you cannot decide whether you wish not to know it until you know it. And so on."

"Well. You'd better tell me. Otherwise this is going to drive me insane."

Sothe let out a breath. "As you wish. Your parents were upper-class Vordan City merchants. They owned property and businesses that the Last Duke wanted for his own interests. He directed his agents to kill your family and make it look accidental."

"Fire," Winter said. "There was a fire, wasn't there?"

Sothe nodded. "There was. You were four years old. Your parents were killed, but a dedicated servant got you out of the building in time. She suspected the Concordat were involved, and hid from the authorities. By the time we found you again, she had placed you at Mrs. Wilmore's. She died not long afterward."

"Is that all?" Winter gave a nervous laugh. "I thought you were going to tell me I was the lost princess of Borel or something."

"You had an older brother," Sothe said. "He was away from the house that day, at the War College."

"A brother?" Something in Winter's stomach churned. "Is he still alive?"

"Yes," Sothe said. "Your name at birth was Ellie d'Ivoire. Marcus is your older brother."

It felt like an eternity passed, though Winter supposed it could only have been a couple of seconds. She blinked, and swallowed on a suddenly dry throat.

"Marcus?" she said. "*Our* Marcus?"

"Yes."

"But he's . . . older."

"By a decade."

"And . . . I can't . . ." Winter shook her head, squeezing her eyes shut. "You're *certain?*"

"Reasonably. I have the records from Mrs. Wilmore's, copied before it burned down. And surveillance reports from Concordat agents."

"Does Marcus know?"

"He knows that his sister is alive." Sothe tensed up. "For most of his life, he assumed that Ellie died with his parents. It was one reason he volunteered to be posted to Khandar, as far from Vordan City as he could get."

Exactly what I was looking for when I escaped, Winter thought numbly. *I suppose it runs in the family.*

"After the revolution and the fall of the Concordat," Sothe went on, "Marcus obtained some information from the archives." She frowned. "I am not entirely certain how he broke the ciphers, but my assumption is that Janus was involved. His knowledge of such techniques is . . . extensive. In any event, Marcus became aware both that Ellie was alive and that the Concordat agent called the Gray Rose was responsible for the deaths of his parents."

"And you volunteered to help him find out?" Winter said. "Out of the kindness of your heart?"

"No kindness was involved," Sothe said. "I was the Gray Rose."

"You?" Winter stared. "You mean . . . you . . ."

"I did not strike the match. But I was responsible. The operation was under my command." Sothe looked at the floor. "In those days I did not . . . question my orders."

Winter found her throat too thick to speak. *It's not every day someone tells you that your parents were murdered and in the next breath confesses to being the murderer.*

"When Marcus discovered the truth, I gave him the opportunity to kill me," Sothe said. "It seemed just."

"He wouldn't do it," Winter managed. "Not Marcus."

"No. Denied that route, I decided that I would find his missing sister, if she was still alive. When the army went south, I remained in Murnsk, visiting old Concordat safehouses."

"And killing Duke Orlanko."

"Indeed. It was not long after I found the records that Janus contacted me through Ennika. That was when I realized that, while I had been seeking the truth for Marcus, I could not in good conscience inform him without telling you first."

"Thank God for the conscience of assassins," Winter said.

Sothe flinched slightly. "I admit that mine is, perhaps . . . rusty. But I am doing my best to come to terms with it."

"So, now what?" Winter said. "*I'm* supposed to tell him? 'Surprise, I'm your sister. Oh, and by the way, I'm a woman.'" Just thinking about it made her stomach turn.

"It's a possibility."

"No, it isn't. It's insane."

"Why?"

"Because . . ." Winter wasn't quite able to articulate what she meant. "Can you imagine what he'd do?"

"I think I can. What, exactly, are you afraid of?"

"He's . . . the head of the army, for one thing. He could . . ."

"Expel you?" Sothe cocked her head. "Does that seem likely?"

It didn't. The truth was, Winter had no idea what Marcus would do. She couldn't picture how he'd take the news, because he seemed so determined to avoid it. He was practically the only one who hadn't figured out her secret, one way or another, because he didn't *want* to see it.

"Saints and fucking martyrs," Winter said. "I need to think about this."

"I know," Sothe said, still infuriatingly calm. "That's one reason I didn't allow myself to delay too long. There is some time yet before we reach Vordan City. If you wish, you can tell no one. Or I can tell Marcus the truth myself, although . . . that might entail some difficulties."

"Difficulties?"

"When he let me go, he said that if he ever saw me again, he would kill me."

Winter snorted. "I've seen you fight. Don't tell me you're afraid of Marcus."

"Not afraid of him, no. But it's a confrontation I would prefer to avoid."

"Of course." Winter laughed out loud. "Well. I don't even know if I should thank you."

"There's no need to," Sothe said. "In fact, you have every right to be angry with me."

"For killing my parents, or for telling me about it?"

"Perhaps both," Sothe said.

As the sun sank into the western sea and the clouds flamed pink and orange, Winter staggered back to her own cabin like a drunk. *Not drunk,* she thought. It was more like one of the times she'd gotten cracked on the head and felt the world spin around her and refuse to settle.

Brother. What does that even mean? Marcus was a comrade, maybe even a friend, though she'd never been as close to him as to Jane or Cyte. *Bad examples. But how am I supposed to think of him now? As family?* She had very little idea what that meant. The closest thing she'd had to family was Jane. *And we know how that ended.*

Alex was asleep in her bunk, naked under a knit blanket, her handsome sailor nowhere to be found. Winter climbed up to her own bunk and lay down fully clothed, trying to make sense of the mess churning behind her eyes.

Maybe it would be best not to tell him. It felt like taking the easy way out. *But if I'm going to face the Beast, and probably going to die, would it really be fair to him? To give him his sister back and then snatch her away again?* On the other hand, Marcus knew Ellie was alive, so if she *didn't* tell him the truth he'd keep thinking she was out there somewhere, maybe keep searching. *Sothe can tell him, after I'm gone. Then it won't matter anymore.* But that would be just as cruel as the other way around.

She must have fallen asleep, because she dreamed of fire. Marcus was there this time, not the child he must have been but as she knew him now. She ran from room to room in a burning house, feeling her skin blacken and char, calling his name. He called back, sounding close but somehow always out of reach.

When she woke, dawn was breaking, and her clothes were damp and chilly with sweat. Strangely, though, she felt better, empty but purified. She rolled out of bed and dropped lightly to the floor, finding Alex already up and sitting cross-legged in her bunk, eating a dried roll with a piece of cheese. She had another, which she offered to Winter. Winter accepted gratefully, her stomach reminding her that she'd missed dinner yesterday.

"Thanks."

"Mmm," Alex said, then swallowed. "You must have been exhausted. I tried to wake you at shift change."

"I was," Winter said. "Just . . . a lot on my mind, I think."

"Well, if you're looking for a little stress relief, I definitely recommend passing the time of day with seaman Goltov." Alex grinned and stretched like a cat, then paused. "Though I suppose you wouldn't see the appeal, would you?"

"He certainly seemed . . . attentive," Winter managed.

"He is that," Alex said. "Doesn't talk much, but definitely attentive."

"Can I ask your opinion on something?" Winter said.

"Of course."

"When we get to Vordan . . ." Winter hesitated. She wasn't ready to talk to anyone about Marcus, but . . . "You know that I spent my time in the army disguised as a man."

"Pretty effectively, too," Alex said, then paused again. "Um. That was supposed to be a compliment."

Winter waved it away. "I haven't bothered since we left to find Janus, since everyone already knew. When we get back . . . I'm not sure if I should keep pretending."

"Who else knows?"

"Raesinia. Sothe. Janus. Cyte. Abby and the others from the Girls' Own. Feor."

"So everyone, essentially."

"Except for Marcus, and the other generals."

"I'd tell them. What the hell, right?" Alex grinned again. "I mean, you're the only one who can save them from the Beast. If you aren't in a position to tell everyone to fuck off, then no one is."

"That's a point. You don't think . . ."

Winter stopped. She didn't know *what* she expected to happen. She'd spent nearly four years now wearing the disguise, and for three of those years not being discovered had been her overriding concern. It had burned itself into her mind, that discovery would mean disaster. And for a ranker in the Colonials, under the vile sergeant Davis, it would have: expulsion from the army if she was lucky, rape and murder if she wasn't.

But Davis was dead. Winter had carved his throat open herself, the day Janus had found out her secret, when he'd shocked her by taking it in stride. Since then she'd risen higher and higher, though some part of her mind stubbornly refused to take credit for any of it. *I'm lucky, and basically competent. And I have good friends.* Whatever it was that fueled her success, it had made her a division-general, second only to Marcus and Janus in the army. *So what, exactly, are they going to do to me?*

"Winter?" Alex said. "Sorry. I didn't mean to be . . . glib. I know this is serious."

"No," Winter said slowly. "I think you're right."

"Oh, good," Alex said. "In that case, I'll take all the credit."

A few days later, the *Swallow* reached Vayenne, at the mouth of the Vor. Winter had seen the city before, briefly, on her return from Khandar. It was a pretty, orderly place, all white-tiled houses in neat rows facing the sea. The river Vor, wide and slow here, emptied into the sea past Fort Cevant, whose guns dominated the harbor. The fortress was perched on a rocky promontory on the eastern side of the river, with massive brick-faced walls studded with embrasures on the seaward side and star-shaped earthworks facing the land, a monument to Vordan's perpetual paranoia about a seaborne ascent of the river.

Swallow dropped anchor in the mouth of the river, directly under the fort's guns. As the ship swung gently in the current, a longboat launched from the base of the cliff, pulled toward them by a dozen oars.

"Nothing to worry about," Captain Kerrak said, when Winter and her companions gathered at the stern to watch. "Everyone checks in with the fort before going up the river, unless you fancy eating a few rounds of hot shot. Our papers are in order."

Even so, Winter found herself looking up nervously at the fortress. On its cliff, it would be all but immune to cannon-fire from the river, while subjecting enemies to deadly plunging shots from its heavy guns. *No wonder the Borels never tried to invade this way.*

The longboat came alongside, and a short, balding man in livery climbed deftly aboard, followed by a pair of soldiers with carbines. Captain Kerrak greeted the man warmly, and handed over the leather packet with the ship's papers. Winter was fairly certain she saw the gleam of a coin when the harbor official opened it, which he made disappear as efficiently as a street magician.

"Well," he said after thumbing through the sheets, "this all seems to be in order. Have you called at any ports since Murnsk?"

"No, sir," Kerrak said. Hearing Vordanai spoken aloud was strange for Winter, after all this time in Murnsk. She'd even taken to using Murnskai with Alex and Abraham. Kerrak's accent in Vordanai was so atrocious that she suspected it was an affectation. "You can see, nowhere since Dimiotsk."

"You haven't heard the news, then," the harbor agent said, handing the packet back. "If you're planning to go all the way to Vordan City, you may want to reconsider."

"Why?" Winter blurted out. The harbor agent turned to stare. "What's happened?"

"A passenger," Captain Kerrak said hastily. "Bound for Vordan City. If there's news, we'd certainly appreciate hearing it."

"There's war that way," the agent said flatly. "Or will be soon. A Borelgai fleet sailed up the Vor, bold as brass. I never thought I'd see the day." He shrugged. "The queen herself was with them, they say. And General d'Ivoire. They've gone to Vordan City to have it out with Vhalnich. Emperor Vhalnich," he corrected hastily. "I wish they'd get it over with already."

There were a dozen questions Winter wanted to ask, but Sothe gave her a hard look, and she held her tongue. *We'll find out when we get there. No sense causing trouble now.* Kerrak thanked the agent, and he went back over the side with his guards. A few minutes later, *Swallow* was heading up the Vor, cutting smoothly through the dark water.

"How long until we get to Vordan City?"

Captain Kerrak shrugged uncomfortably. "Depends entirely on the wind. We don't have oars, and we're too heavy to tow. If it turns directly against us—"

"Then we'll make other plans," Sothe said.

"We have to get there before Janus does," Winter said, when they'd stepped away from Kerrak. "Ennika was clear on that. If the Beast gets its hands on Vordan City, then it'll be unstoppable."

"We will," Sothe said. "Worse comes to worst, we can use the post stations."

"I thought that needed a royal warrant," Winter said. She'd come up that way the last time, with Janus and Marcus.

"I can put one together in a few hours, if we need it," Sothe said. "But we'll stay with the *Swallow* as long as we can. Captain Kerrak knows his business." She paused. "Are you . . . feeling better? I—"

"I'm trying not to think about it," Winter said shortly. "We'll see what the situation is when we get there." *Marcus is still alive, at least. Does that mean Cyte is, too? Abby and the rest? How much fighting has there been?*

"A commendable attitude," Sothe said. "It never helps to develop plans with incomplete intelligence."

Almost there. Winter stared up the length of the river. *Then what?*

CHAPTER TWENTY-FIVE

MARCUS

The *Dominant* was such a large ship that, on water as calm as the river Vor, it was easy to forget that you were aboard a ship at all. Raesinia's cabin had a proper bed, a table, and a sideboard with bottles of liquor slotted into neat racks. It wouldn't have looked out of place in a high-class inn.

It was an odd feeling, traveling in such comfort despite the dire circumstances, but Marcus wasn't complaining. The bed, especially, he appreciated. Both for sleep—the aches and *pops* of his joints reminded him he was getting too old to spend so much time under canvas—and for . . . other reasons.

He propped himself up on one elbow, sinking deep into the feather mattress, and looked down at Raesinia. She lay beside him, half-covered by a sheet, eyes closed, breathing gently. He couldn't help but marvel at her. *She looks so . . . delicate.* The fine bones of her face, the soft hollows of her neck and the sweep of her collarbone, the rise of her small breasts, her tiny wrist and the thin fingers of her hand. She looked like the slightest pressure would snap her in two, like something unbearably fragile and precious, a statue made out of paper-thin porcelain.

She would laugh at that description, of course. And the truth was that she was anything but delicate—in her body but, more important, as a person. Marcus reached out to brush her cheek gently, and her eyes snapped open.

"I'm not asleep," she said. "Just so you know. I don't sleep."

"Not ever?"

She sat up and shrugged, sheet falling to her waist. "Not since the binding. The last time I was unconscious it was because someone had literally blown my brains out."

Marcus winced. "I wish you wouldn't be so casual about—"

"Getting killed?" Raesinia grinned impishly. "It's a defense mechanism. If I took it too seriously I'd never stop screaming."

"I suppose," Marcus said. "Still."

"Sorry." She leaned over and kissed him. "I'll try to keep your delicate sensibilities in mind."

She slid out of bed and walked naked to the sideboard, where there was a jug of water. Marcus turned over to watch her. She was clearly aware of the way his eyes lingered, but pretended not to be, in a way that Marcus found incredibly endearing.

"We'll make Vordan City today," she said. "This morning, if the wind holds. We made it."

"We made it," Marcus agreed. "But we still don't know how close Janus is."

Raesinia downed a glass of water, nodding. "We're going to be very busy for a while, that's for certain."

She raised an eyebrow. Marcus looked puzzled for a moment, then grinned.

"Do we have time?" he said.

"We can try," Raesinia said. "You seem . . . interested."

Marcus looked down to find the sheet pulled tight across his waist, making his rising interest obvious indeed. He laughed and kicked it aside, rolling out of bed and meeting Raesinia halfway across the room. He wrapped his arms around her, picked her up—she was so *light*, like she was barely there at all—and kissed her, as she happily put her arms around his neck. The Queen of Vordan was nowhere to be found, at moments like this. There was only the laughing, lively, beautiful Raes, whom he'd started to fall in love with the night they'd snuck into Exchange Central, who'd trusted him with her direst secrets, who'd come to his rescue a half dozen times. Who was lithe and warm against him, inexperienced but full of enthusiasm.

There was a knock at the door.

"*Fuck,*" Raesinia said quietly. Then, a bit louder, "Yes?"

"Your Highness," said a Borelgai-accented voice from outside. "We've reached the edge of the Vordan City harbor, and we've received a messenger from shore. He says that we do not have permission to approach and that the shore batteries will fire on us if we try to go past the pilings."

Raesinia gave an irritated sigh. "Aren't we flying my flag?" she said to Marcus.

"These *are* Borelgai ships," Marcus said. "Those defenses were built against this exact scenario. It's hard to blame them."

"I'll have to go ashore and convince them." Raesinia unwrapped herself from Marcus, and he lowered her gently to the ground.

"We don't know exactly what kind of reception we'll get," Marcus said. "Maybe it would be best if you stayed aboard."

"Marcus," Raesinia snapped, fixing him with a stare. "Please listen carefully for a moment, would you?"

"I—" He caught her expression. "I'm listening."

"I love you," she said matter-of-factly. "And this, what we've had, has been better than I could have ever imagined. I don't plan to give it up anytime soon. *But*"—her smile returned—"if you start using it as a reason to try to treat me like I'm made of eggshells, I am going to personally beat you black-and-blue. Understood?"

Marcus couldn't help but smile himself. "Understood. I can't promise I'll *never* do that, but feel free to swat me if I do."

"I don't need your permission to swat you. I'm the fucking queen." Raesinia rose to her toes and kissed him.

"May I at least come with you? A military presence may be useful."

"Of course." She looked at him and sighed. "I suppose you'll have to get dressed, though."

RAESINIA

Sitting in the longboat beside Marcus, with a crew of Borelgai sailors and a few Second Division soldiers as an honor guard, Raesinia had to work to keep her face straight, fighting the urge to break into a big, silly grin. It was inappropriate, obviously. Her throne was in peril, her capital days or weeks from being invaded by a man who was at best a potential tyrant and at worst the plaything of who knew what dark power. Quite a few of the men and women traveling with her on the Borelgai ships would be dead before this was over even if everything went well. *And God knows what will happen to me if we lose.*

And yet. The time aboard the *Dominant* had made her feel happy. Not just satisfied in the knowledge that her country, her people, or even her friends would survive, but happy in her own right. This had not been a common occurrence in Raesinia's life, at least after her illness and her brother's death. There hadn't been much time as she went from one crisis to the next—Orlanko, Maurisk, the Priests of the Black, and now Janus himself. Only a few times—talking with her friends at the Blue Mask, laughing with Marcus as they roamed the city, incognito and free—had come close.

There was also sex, of course. It was honestly something Raesinia hadn't known if she'd be capable of. Her education on the subject had been scanty before she'd started associating with students and revolutionaries, and even afterward she'd been left wondering if the binding would allow her to enjoy it. *I can't get drunk, after all. Or sleep.* A little furtive, solitary experimentation had been inconclusive. So it had been a relief to discover that whatever changes the magic had made to her body, they didn't interfere in *this* case.

In fact, the closer they'd come to Vordan City, the more she'd found herself wishing the voyage could last forever. No sooner had the thought occurred to her, though, than she banished it. *I'm still the queen. My people need me. And we're going to win, damn it, and then Marcus and I will marry and the* hell *with anyone who tells me it's inappropriate.* Then, at least for a few years, they could be together. *Until people start to wonder about me.*

The boat hit the water, and the rowers pushed it away from the *Dominant*, breaking Raesinia's reverie. The big ship was anchored just below the row of pilings that were Vordan City's first line of defense against a seaborne attack from the south. The huge stone pillars were anchored to the bottom of the river in a line from the north bank to the south, and mammoth iron chains could be threaded through metal loops atop them to close off the river.

All the contrast of Vordan City was on full display here. On the south bank, a small creek emptied out of a swampy stretch of land known as the Bottoms, a dumping ground for the very poorest of the city's rejects, those who couldn't find a place in even the cavernous, crime-ridden streets of Newtown. Shacks built out of scraps and driftwood stood on the few bits of solid ground.

On the north side, the riverbank below the pilings was home to what the public had dubbed the Fairy Castles, products of a trend among the Vordanai nobility to build their palatial homes in a style that suggested medieval fortresses. They had crenellated walls, big stone keeps, and tall, slender towers too thin for anyone to actually live in, combined with decidedly unmartial touches like huge colored glass windows and wide, well-tended gardens. Having recently been in the Keep, which had been an *actual* fortress, Raesinia found herself raising an amused eyebrow at these parodies. They were dark and shuttered, for the most part, the nobility having fled the city for country estates during the revolution and not yet returned.

Above the pilings, on both sides of the river, were the water batteries, brick-walled embrasures stocked with heavy cannon. The last time Raesinia had been there was when they'd boarded the *Rosnik*, sinking the Thousand Names in the river under the noses of Maurisk and his Black Priest allies. It hadn't been an *entirely* successful expedition, since Raesinia herself had been captured by Ionkovo. *Temporarily.* She permitted herself a small smile. *I got one up on him in the end.*

The longboat was rowed between two pilings where the chain had been lowered; it passed into the harbor proper and headed for the docks on the north side, beside the battery. Behind them were the South Docks, the riverbank lined with quays and piers that ought to have been bustling with traffic but were instead nearly empty. Obviously, the news of Janus' approach was not inspiring confidence. To the east, Raesinia could see the ugly spire of the Vendre, the prison where the revolutionaries had won their first victory. *Which I managed to fall off the top of, after Faro shot me in the head. In terms of memories, coming into the city like this is a seriously mixed bag.*

A short pier had been cleared for their arrival. At the foot of it were a score of blue-uniformed soldiers accompanying several civilians. When they got closer, Raesinia recognized Deputy d'Andorre, still in his blue suit with silver piping, though he was now wearing both his deputy's sash of office and a wide belt that glittered with gold thread.

A dockhand, looking overawed, rushed forward to tie the longboat up and then hurried out of the way. The Borelgai stayed put—Raesinia had talked to Duke Dorsay, and they'd agreed that she and Marcus should handle this on their own. Barely hopped nimbly out of the boat and lent her hand to Joanna, and then the pair of them assisted Marcus and Raesinia. The rest of the soldiers followed. D'Andorre and his men waited until they approached, and then the deputy offered a shallow bow, while the men behind him saluted.

"Welcome back, Your Highness," d'Andorre said. "The entire kingdom rejoices to see you safe."

"It's good to be on Vordanai soil again," Raesinia said. Her eyes went to the gold belt, which had the look of a badge of office. D'Andorre caught her gaze and smiled thinly.

"In your absence, the Deputies-General have done me the honor of naming me chief minister. They felt that the ministries required a . . . guiding hand, in the crisis."

"I see." Raesinia kept her face blank. *Is that a grab for power? Or just a reasonable precaution?* "Very well, Chief Minister. Our Borelgai allies require access to the harbor, so we can unload General d'Ivoire's army." She glanced at Marcus. "General d'Ivoire is hereby appointed to command of all Vordanai armed forces and particularly the immediate defense of Vordan City."

D'Andorre shifted his attention from Raesinia to Marcus. "Welcome, General. How many men are in your force?"

"Twenty thousand, give or take," Marcus said. "If you're worried about quartering them, rest assured we don't plan to remain in the city long—"

"It's not quartering that concerns me," d'Andorre said. "Are you aware that Emperor Vhalnich's approaching army is said to number nearly a hundred thousand men?"

"I seriously doubt that," Marcus said. "My information puts it closer to sixty thousand."

"Either way, it seems clear that we are not strong enough to engage him with a hope of success," d'Andorre said. "At least from my admittedly civilian viewpoint."

"There are more troops gathering in the city, are there not?" Marcus said.

"And the Borelgai are our allies," Raesinia added. "The fleet is here, and an army will join us as soon as it's able."

"Which will be too late," d'Andorre said. "The men in the city amount to perhaps ten thousand, and they are the sweepings of the depots and the greenest recruits. That brings the odds to a mere two to one. It's not enough, General."

"Unless you have a suggestion for securing more men," Raesinia said, "then I suggest you leave military matters to General d'Ivoire. He has already considered alternative plans—"

"The alternative is not a military one, Your Highness. It is political." D'Andorre had the grace to lower his head. "The Deputies-General has dispatched representatives to Emperor Vhalnich to request terms."

"Terms?" Raesinia blinked. "You're going to *surrender*?"

"It seemed to the representatives of the people to be the prudent course, for the good of the Vordanai nation," d'Andorre said.

"Obviously the situation has changed," Marcus said. "The Borelgai alliance—"

"Will not be enough," d'Andorre said. There was real emotion in his voice. "The emperor will be here before aid can arrive. Do you know what will happen if he takes Vordan City by storm?"

"Do *you*?" Raesinia said. "I don't know what he's promised you, but you can't be naive enough to imagine that Janus will let you keep your fancy new title. Or that *he'll* pay any mind to the Deputies-General once he's crowned himself by force."

"He hasn't promised me anything," d'Andorre said. He blinked, and Raesinia was shocked to see tears in his eyes. "Your Highness. Please believe I do not expect to benefit from this. Once we surrender, I would be a threat to the emperor. Exile is the best I could hope for, along with many of my colleagues." He paused to collect himself. "But I will not allow this city to be destroyed. The revolution and the coup were bad enough. If we surrender, the emperor will be merciful. If we force him to fight, God alone knows what he will do."

"Janus wouldn't destroy Vordan City," Marcus said. But there was a note of uncertainty in his voice that Raesinia well understood. *I would have said Janus would never turn against us. But maybe it's not Janus in control anymore.*

"The Deputies feel that the risk is unacceptable," d'Andorre said. "I will not demand that you surrender yourself, Your Highness. But we will not spend more Vordanai lives to save your crown. Take your fleet, return to Borel, and let the people of Vordan have peace."

"The hell of it is, I think he's sincere," Marcus said, when they were back on the *Dominant.* Raesinia paced the short length of the chart room, while he sat at the table.

"He is," she said. "At first I thought he was reaching for power, but it's worse than that. He thinks of this as a *self-sacrifice.* He's doing what has to be done for the good of everyone else." She ground her teeth.

"It *is* noble, from a certain point of view."

"Leave it to the Deputies to finally do something for the right reasons when it's totally the wrong thing to do." She looked up, heart pounding. "It *is* the wrong thing to do, isn't it?"

"Of course," Marcus said.

"I'm serious," Raesinia said, rounding on him. "Should we be considering d'Andorre's point? Am I such a better ruler than Janus that it's worth sending people to die for me?"

"Raes." Marcus stood up and came over to her. She leaned forward against his chest as he put his arms around her shoulders. "It's not just about you. You said it to d'Andorre—do you think Janus would put up with the Deputies-

General? If we give in, everything the people fought for in the revolution will be lost."

"The people were willing to make Janus First Consul," Raesinia said.

"Because he was good at winning battles," Marcus said. "That doesn't make him a good king. And we both know that's not the important point here. It's not just Janus we have to worry about."

The Beast. Whatever that is. She imagined a vast monster descending from the north to swallow Vordan whole.

After a few moments of silence, she pulled away from him and took a deep breath.

"Thank you," she said. "I didn't mean to . . . I don't know. I just thought . . ."

"I understand," Marcus said quietly.

And he does, Raesinia thought. On a battlefield, soldiers followed orders, and officers gave them, but they didn't decide *whether* to fight, whether it was worth it. That was reserved for queens and generals.

"All right," she said. "So d'Andorre and the Deputies are wrong. What are we going to do about it?"

"We could probably take the city, if we had to," Marcus said with a frown. "Unload the troops downriver, storm the water batteries from behind. Once we have men-of-war in the harbor, the Deputies would have to give in. But . . ."

"That would be worse than surrendering to Janus," Raesinia said. "If I have to take my own capital by storm, then *I'm* the usurper. Besides, between losses and desertion, we'd have no chance against Janus when he got here."

"Agreed," Marcus said. "So we have to get d'Andorre to change his mind."

"There are troops already in the city," Raesinia said. "What if you appealed to them, asked them to arrest the Deputies?"

Marcus sucked a breath through his teeth. "It's . . . possible. But I think they'd be just as likely to arrest *me*. These aren't veterans from the Murnskai campaign who know me. They're fresh recruits."

Raesinia nodded. "And if they split, then there'll be fighting in the city, and we're back to the first option."

"I doubt we can unseat d'Andorre in the Deputies," Marcus said. "Not in the time we have. And someone that self-righteous isn't going to take a bribe."

Raesinia thought about Cora and the mountains of gold she'd conjured in Borel. *A shame we used it already.* Even if they'd brought along a spare fortune, though, Marcus was probably right. *Honest men are the most frustrating.*

"We've done this before," Raesinia said slowly. "Forget about d'Andorre. We have to go over his head."

"Over his head?" Marcus raised an eyebrow. "Wouldn't that mean appealing to the queen?"

"We appeal to the *people*. He can't have made his plan for surrender public yet. The people of Vordan wouldn't give up so easily. If we turn them against him . . ."

"That might lead to fighting, too," Marcus warned.

"It won't," Raesinia said. "D'Andorre isn't Maurisk. He honestly believes he's doing what's right, and that means, as a Deputy, he can't stand against the people's will. He'll back down."

"That's . . . possible," Marcus said. "Are you certain you'll get enough support? The people of Vordan may not give up easily, but some of them were on Janus' side to begin with."

"No guarantees," Raesinia said. "But I think it's the best chance we've got." She looked down at the maps on the table, seeking inspiration. "How do we get the message out, though?"

"I think I may be able to help with that," Marcus said. "Let me see if I can talk to Alek Giforte. He was Vice Captain of Armsmen for years. He'll know how to whip up a crowd."

"You think he'll help?"

Marcus nodded. "He's a good man, and I guarantee he won't be happy about the surrender. We'll put the word around that you're going to speak tomorrow in Farus' Triumph."

Raesinia grinned. There was something appropriate about that; it had been in Farus' Triumph that Danton Aurenne had given the speeches that launched the revolution.

"Do it," she said.

"The only trouble is going to be getting you there," Marcus said. "D'Andorre's no fool. Once he figures out what we're up to, he'll keep a watch on the ships and be ready to stop you when you land."

"I have an idea there," Raesinia said. She sighed. "Now all I have to do is work out what I'm going to say."

Raesinia hit the water with a splash that set her skin to tingling. It was warmer than she'd expected, heated by the sun on the Vor's long progress south, murky with suspended dirt. She kicked downward, well below the surface, and let out all the air in her lungs in a stream of silver bubbles. Her chest started burning as she began to swim, her body screaming for air, but she had long since grown used to ignoring its importunate demands. She kicked steadily, feeling the slow tingle of the binding as it worked to repair the damage she was doing to herself. *At least I'm not* impaled *on anything this time.*

It was a long way to the south bank, and Raesinia wasn't the strongest swimmer. She tried to keep herself oriented, swimming diagonally against the current, but it was impossible to stay on a consistent heading in the muck. That was all right, though. D'Andorre couldn't watch the entire riverbank, and he'd expect to have plenty of warning to intercept any boats the *Dominant* put out.

For a while, suspended in featureless swirls of brown water, she felt like she wasn't making any progress at all. Then the riverbed came into sight, gradually getting closer as she approached the shore, until her feet started to stir up great clouds of river mud. Raesinia drew her legs in and stood up, her head breaking the surface of the water, and she finally let her body draw the breath it needed.

She stood there, chilly and dripping, while the binding worked its way through her and fixed whatever her suffocation had broken. When the tingling behind her eyes went away, she waded up the shore. It wasn't clear where the water ended and the land began, here. The Bottoms were a sucking, rotting bog, without much to distinguish between muddy ground and muddy river. By trial and error she found a patch sturdy enough to support her, then turned in a full circle. She oriented herself on the *Dominant*, easily visible at the head of the fleet. From there she traced the line she *should* have swum, and found the bone white dead tree Marcus had given her for a landmark. It was about a quarter mile up the shore. *The current must be stronger than I thought.*

She squelched in that direction, stumbling through mud that came up to her ankles and through occasional pools of stagnant water. As she got closer, she was relieved to see a one-horse coach waiting, with Marcus sitting on the driver's box, looking uncomfortable in civilian clothes and a high-collared coat. Raesinia waved to him, and he looked her over, then did a double take.

"Raes?" He jumped down from the box. "Good God. You look like . . ."

"Like I just swam the river and then walked through a swamp?" She wiped a glob of mud from her face and grinned. "I hope you found me a change of clothes. I don't think I want to address anyone looking like this."

"Of course." He opened the door to the carriage, and Raesinia was pleased to see a stack of towels sitting on the bench. "Alek should have everything ready."

Raesinia stepped up, and Marcus hurried to get the carriage turned around. He was an inexpert driver, but the horse was old and tired and they weren't in any hurry. They were on one of the many winding paths through the Bottoms, twisting and turning to stay on dry ground, and occasionally crossing an impromptu bridge of planks and logs. Before long they pulled out onto the River Road, a more official thoroughfare, which roughly paralleled the riverbank as it ran north toward the city.

The road passed just under the bastion of the southern water battery, which made Raesinia a little nervous, but there was no reason for anyone to suppose that a cheap one-horse cab held the Queen of Vordan and her highest-ranked general. Armsmen were out in force, with their green uniforms and tall staves of office, though traffic in the markets they passed through seemed to be sparse. The city felt like it was holding its breath, Raesinia decided. She couldn't guess if that boded well or poorly.

While they drove, she cleaned herself up a bit, utterly ruining several towels in the process. By the time they turned north to cross the Grand Span to the Island, she was merely grubby rather than dripping with mud, and she'd detached several leeches. The binding flared to life again, and the coin-sized holes they'd cut in her skin began to fade.

The road led directly from the foot of the Grand Span into the Triumph, but Marcus turned left, along a street of high-class hotels. He stopped in front of one called Montarn's and came around to open the door.

"Take this." He handed her his coat. "Just until we get upstairs."

She wrapped it around herself, concealing both her features and the filth that coated her. Marcus led the way into the hotel lobby and directly back to the stairs, with Raesinia hurrying after. She wondered how long it would be before the staff noticed the muddy footprints on their carpet. On the third floor, he brought her to a room and knocked, and the door was opened from within.

"Marcus?" Alek Giforte said. He wore his Armsmen uniform, and his face was pale and harried. "Did you bring— Oh! Your Highness. I didn't—"

"Don't worry about it," Raesinia said, waving a hand and flicking tiny bits of mud on the wall. "But I hope this place has a bath."

It did, it turned out, with hot and cold running water. *That* was certainly something she'd missed in her time at sea. She filled the tub once to wash off the mud, then let it empty and filled it again to soak for a few minutes in clean water so hot it made her skin flush pink. It took another few minutes to get her hair into some semblance of order.

Marcus had left her clothes just inside the bathroom door. As she'd requested, the outfit was nothing elaborate, a simple dress in dark blue and white, suggesting the colors of the Vordanai flag. A few pieces of silver jewelry completed the ensemble. *Alek has good taste,* Raesinia reflected, as she examined herself in the mirror.

She emerged to find the two men waiting nervously. Marcus had changed back into his uniform, complete with the column-general's stars on his shoulders. Alek got to his feet and bowed gracefully.

"Welcome home, Your Highness," he said. "I'm glad I could be of assistance."

"Marcus was certain you'd be reliable," Raesinia said. "I assume he's explained the situation?"

"Fully," Alek said. He shook his head. "There had been rumors that the Deputies were going to seek terms from Janus, but I had no idea they'd actually sent a messenger."

"How do the people feel about it?" At his slight hesitation, she added, "Be honest, please."

"People are . . . worried," Alek said. "Surrendering goes against the grain, obviously. But after the Battle of Alves, there's not a lot of confidence that Janus can be stopped. And of course there are some—a minority, but not an insignificant one—who support him. They're not open about it, but they're there." He grimaced. "We've had a hell of a time keeping a lid on things."

"And are we going to get a crowd today?"

"For a certainty," Alek said. "I only worry that we may get more than we bargained for. If enough Janus supporters turn up, we could have a riot on our hands."

"It wouldn't be the first time," Marcus said.

Raesinia nodded. "Let's get moving."

It had been a little more than a year since Raesinia had come to Farus' Triumph with Danton, though it felt more like half a lifetime. The huge square looked the same as it always had, with four small fountains framing a single enormous one and the pillar supporting the equestrian statue of Farus IV rising up behind it like a stone tree trunk. Halfway up that pillar was a disk-shaped stone platform, the traditional speaker's rostrum for anyone who wanted to address the crowds of Vordan City.

And the crowds were there in force. There was still time before Raesinia had planned to begin, but people thronged the square, pressing around the fountain into a tight mass that was slowly expanding toward the ring of shops and hotels that edged the open space. They came from all walks of life—neat, modest tradesmen; merchants from the north bank in suits that reminded her of her time in Borel; and swarms of laborers from the south bank in shabby linens and leathers. Armsmen were scattered throughout, creating small islands of calm, but the rest of the crowd surged and shoved, trying to get closer. A babble of voices made hearing all but impossible.

To get Raesinia to the platform, Alek had arranged a flying wedge of Armsmen, who pushed their way through the crowd with their staves. Inside the cordon, Raesinia walked slowly, feeling the stares of everyone they passed. Marcus was on one side, his posture stiff and correct, one hand on the butt of his saber. Alek Giforte was on the other, barking orders to his men as they advanced.

When they neared the base of the stairs leading up to the platform, Raesinia saw they were blocked off from the crowd by another cordon, this one of blue-uniformed soldiers. Behind them, sitting on the steps, was Chief Minister d'Andorre. He got to his feet and spoke to a nervous-looking lieutenant as the wedge of Armsmen got closer.

Raesinia grabbed Giforte's arm and dragged his ear close. "No violence!"

He nodded fervently and hurried forward to speak to his Armsmen. As the two groups came into contact, the soldiers closed ranks to keep the Armsmen out, and both sides began screaming at each other. Since the general racket made them impossible to understand, this produced very little result.

"Stay close," Marcus said, pushing forward himself. Raesinia followed just behind him. The soldiers stiffened as he came through the press, the insignia of his rank gleaming.

"What the hell is going on?" he said, his parade-ground voice loud enough to make himself understood.

"Sir!" The other soldiers quieted enough for the lieutenant to be heard. "I'm sorry, sir, but we have orders to keep the rostrum clear."

"Whose orders?" Marcus said. "Do they apply to the *queen*?"

"The chief minister's, sir." The lieutenant's face was very pale. "And they do."

"D'Andorre!" Raesinia shouted, into the tense pause that followed. "Can I have a word?"

The chief minister got to his feet, apparently heedless of the shouting, shoving tumult of humanity all around him. He came forward to stand beside the nervous lieutenant, and looked down at Raesinia.

"I wish you'd taken my advice," d'Andorre said.

"I'll bet you do," Raesinia growled. "Get your men out of the way before they get hurt."

"Are you willing to order Armsmen to attack Vordanai soldiers? Will they obey, do you think?"

"The Armsmen haven't got anything to do with it. What do you think will happen if I start shouting that the queen is here and the chief minister won't let her speak?"

D'Andorre's face paled. "You wouldn't."

"I was here during the revolution, Chief Minister. On the ground. I've seen the power of the mob. Have you?"

"I . . ." He shook his head. "Please. Don't do this."

"Do what? Give the people what they want?"

"They don't know what's good for them!" d'Andorre said. Despair was written all over his face. "Your Highness, I beg you. At least wait until we've received Janus' terms. They may be more lenient than we expect. Afterward—"

"Get out of my way."

Pushing past Marcus, Raesinia shoved between two Armsmen and pressed past the soldiers. One of them reached out to grab her, and she gave him her best glare. He faltered, looking back at d'Andorre, who only stared at her blankly. Raesinia shook the soldier off and went to d'Andorre's side.

"I'm only going to offer them a choice," she said. "If they choose you, I'll go quietly. You have my word."

"Your Highness . . ." D'Andorre shook his head. "If they choose you, then God help us all."

Raesinia turned away from him and climbed the rostrum. The steps seemed endless, winding around the pillar twice before they came to the speaker's platform. As she ascended, the noise of the crowd rose, shouts and exclamations merging into an enormous roar like that of a stormy sea crashing against the rocks. Raesinia reached the top step and walked out onto the small circle of stone. It felt a thousand miles high, high enough that the faces in the crowd were only dots in a pattern, a vast fabric of humanity that went on forever. Small flashes of blue and silver were everywhere, Vordanai flags in all sizes, waving wildly like a school of strange fish.

Her heart slammed in her chest, as though it were about to burst, and the air felt too thin. She'd spoken to her people like this once before, and it hadn't gone well. Only the arrival of the Colonials, the sudden restoration of hope, had turned the tide of opinion in her direction.

Last time she'd spent hours on her speech, reading classic texts, consulting books of rhetoric. This time she had a few lines she'd scrawled in haste the night before. There would be no last-minute arrival. She didn't have Danton's magic voice. *Just me.* She breathed in until her lungs creaked, let the air out in a rush, and held up her arms. Gradually, the crowd's shouts subsided, the noise level falling until it reached, not silence, but the closest equivalent a mob of ten thousand people could manage.

Raesinia stepped forward. She could feel the eyes on her, so many eyes, as though the concentration of attention was a physical force.

"People of Vordan," she said. In her own ears, her voice sounded wrong, thready and weak. *Do I always sound like that?* "I am Queen Raesinia Orboan, daughter of Farus VIII. This morning I returned to our city from Viadre, aboard the fleet that now waits outside the harbor.

"I went to Borel to look for help." A scattering of boos, quickly shushed. "I have as much reason for anger at the Borelgai as anyone. My beloved brother, Prince Dominic, was killed in the War of the Princes, and their pawn Duke Orlanko tried to remove me from the throne. But a queen must, above all, be practical, and trust others to do the same. I trusted that the Borelgai did not want to see Vhalnich on the throne, and my trust was rewarded." *After a fashion.*

A few cheers of "Vhalnich! Vhalnich!" broke out, mixed with "The queen! Long live the queen!" For the most part, the crowd was quiet. Raesinia felt sweat beading on her brow.

"The Borelgai have sent this fleet to return General d'Ivoire to Vordan City, and an army will soon follow. With their aid, I believe we can defeat the traitor who calls himself Emperor of Murnsk and Vordan. But on my arrival, I was informed by the chief minister that the war was over. The Deputies-General have asked Vhalnich for terms."

She paused to let that sink in. A wave of murmurs swept the crowd, punctuated by cheers for Vhalnich.

"What we've done here, since the revolution, isn't perfect," Raesinia said. "It's only just beginning. But I, for one, am interested to see where it goes. If we give in, it will all be swept away. The power of the people will be replaced by the power of the sword.

"The Deputies-General have offered to surrender their power. They say they are acting in the best interests of Vordan, and I believe them. Chief Minister d'Andorre is not an evil man." Raesinia took a deep breath and raised her voice. "But that power is *not theirs to surrender.* Nor is it mine. It's yours. It belongs to the people.

"If you are willing to give that up, to become part of Vhalnich's empire, then I will not stand in your way. I told Chief Minister d'Andorre as much. I do not want to ask anyone to fight, to die, for me." She stopped for a moment, turning in a slow circle. "But if you want to fight for Vordan, then I will fight beside you, to the bitter end. Believe me, it would be an honor."

She let her arms fall to her sides and then tipped her head in a bow. The quiet of the crowd took on a startled quality, as though they couldn't believe she was finished. People coughed. Clothes rustled.

"Vhalnich!" someone shouted. "Emperor Vhalnich!"

Raesinia swallowed.

"Fight!" A woman's voice. "Fight! Fight!"

"No surrender!" a man roared. When he said it again, there were a dozen voices alongside his. *"No surrender!"*

"Fight!" The shouting spread, deepened into a chant. "Fight! Fight! Fight!"

Feet began to stomp in rhythm. It began as a clatter, like a spray of rain pattering onto dry ground. As more and more people joined in, the sound grew louder, shaking the square, making Raesinia's teeth buzz in sympathy.

"Fight! Fight! Fight!"

Raesinia straightened up, sweat running freely down her face, mixing with tears. She raised her arms, and the crowd shouted its approval. Cries of her name mixed with shouts of "Vordan! Vordan!" and "No surrender!" The chant went on, like a heartbeat.

She turned around and walked to the stairs, concentrating on making a dignified exit. As soon as she'd left the platform, though, her legs went wobbly, and she stumbled forward, throwing out an arm to catch herself. Before she could fall, strong hands were on her shoulders, holding her up.

"You did it," Marcus said, barely audible over the chanting. "D'Andorre's run off with his tail between his legs."

Raesinia leaned into him, eyes closed. "I knew they would fight," she said. "Vordanai don't give up easily."

May God help us all.

"Now," she murmured, too quiet for anyone to hear, "all we have to do is win."

CHAPTER TWENTY-SIX

WINTER

The *Swallow* slipped into the Vordan City harbor as quietly as its namesake; it was one more small merchantman, unnoticed in the chaos. And chaos was certainly the order of the day. Six Borelgai men-of-war rode at anchor in the center of the harbor, under the cliff-like face of the Vendre, while smaller craft and transports were moored at every available north-bank dock.

The *Swallow* turned away from them and headed for the south bank. There, the docks were mostly empty. Commercial traffic, it seemed, was keeping its distance from Vordan City.

Alex, Abraham, and Winter watched the approach from the bow, while Sothe and Captain Kerrak conferred farther aft. Abraham looked eager and a little shocked, staring at the skyline in wonder.

"You've never been to Vordan City?" Winter said.

He shook his head. "I've never been to a *city*. Not since I can remember, anyway. I grew up in a village, and I stayed there until the Black Priests came for me." He glanced at Alex. "After we escaped, we went through a few towns, but nothing like this."

"It's certainly a far cry from the Mountain," Alex said, but there was a tension in her voice. Winter caught her eye questioningly, and Alex gave an irritated shrug. "Bad memories. I haven't been back here since they caught me and killed my mentor."

"Ah," Winter said. "Sorry to drag you through old pain."

Alex shook her head, then looked over her shoulder at Sothe. "Orlanko's dead. Andreas is dead. The Priests of the Black are smashed. And I'm still here." She forced a smile. "Why shouldn't I go where I like?"

"I'd say I'd give you a tour," Winter said. "But honestly, I feel like a stranger myself. If we could track Abby down, she'd be the one to show you the sights." She watched the empty docks slide past. "Though I suspect we won't have much time to spare."

"Afterward," Abraham said, laying a hand on her shoulder. Infernivore bridled at the contact, but Winter kept it in check, a practiced reflex by now. She smiled.

"Afterward," she agreed.

The *Swallow* was tied up at a sagging wooden dock in the shadow of the Grand Span, in front of a block of seedy warehouses. The crew secured the ship with quick efficiency, and ran out a gangplank. Sothe was talking quietly to Goltov, Alex's handsome sailor. He nodded, giving Alex a quick glance, then hurried down the dock and up the street.

"I'm arranging transport," Sothe said to Winter. "That will get you into the palace to see Raesinia. She'll be able to take care of things from there."

"You're not coming?" Alex said.

"Not . . . immediately." Sothe exchanged a look with Winter. "I have business to resolve first. But I'll see you soon enough."

"What about Ennika?" Abraham said.

"I'd be obliged if you'd take her with you," Sothe said. "When I first found her, I thought of her as a captive, but . . ."

"She doesn't seem to be much of a threat," Winter said. "And she's helped us."

"Exactly. I was hoping Feor might know a way to make her more comfortable, at least."

"Feor is the priestess you brought from Khandar?" Abraham said. "The one whose group held the Thousand Names?"

Winter nodded. "The Eldest thought they were the descendants of a group of Mages."

"Yes," Abraham said. "I suspect we will have a great deal to talk about. I wish the Eldest were here."

"He can come and visit," Alex said. "Afterward."

Afterward. Such an easy phrase. *If we win. If the Beast doesn't destroy humanity.* Even given all those ifs, it seemed unlikely that *she* would be around to see it. *That's why it's easy to make promises.*

After a few more minutes, a battered two-horse carriage came around to the base of the dock. Goltov got out, exchanged a few words with the driver, and jogged back toward the ship. Winter looked back at Sothe.

"Thank you," she said. "For helping me get here, and . . . everything else."

"I'm sorry I couldn't find you sooner," Sothe said. "You remember what to tell Raesinia?"

"I remember."

Abraham bowed respectfully to Sothe, and Alex waved. When Goltov arrived, Alex grabbed him and pulled him into a kiss, which attracted whistles and cheers from the watching crew. A crewman walked Ennika up from below, and Abraham took her arm, helping her down the gangplank and toward the waiting carriage. Alex and Winter followed.

The carriage driver, a burly, leather-coated man with a wide-brimmed hat, nodded respectfully to Winter as she opened the door.

"You know where we're going?"

"Oh, yes, miss," the man said with a chuckle. "Don't worry."

Inside the carriage, shades on the windows cut the glare from the afternoon sun. Ennika sat and ran her fingers over her nearly blank copy of the *Wisdoms*, while Alex and Abraham stared together out one window, Alex pointing out the landmarks as they passed by. They rattled over the Grand Span and through Farus' Triumph, the traffic in the great square not nearly what Winter remembered. From there they took the smaller Saint Vallax Bridge and followed the street through the wider, tree-lined thoroughfares of the north bank.

In Winter's pack, down under her spare clothes, was a small notebook into which Sothe had copied relevant details from the Concordat surveillance reports of Ellie d'Ivoire. Winter had read through them, weirdly guilty, like she was opening a window into someone else's life. Ellie's family had lived not far from here, in a solid, respectable house with a lawn and a front drive, like the ones they drove past. If Duke Orlanko hadn't issued the order for casual murder, this could have been Winter's life, growing up as a businessman's daughter in these safe, quiet streets. *Then what? Getting married to some merchant's son?* Or taking up the family business—after all, her brother had chosen a different career.

My brother. It was no use saying it to herself. It didn't seem *real. What do I do with a brother?*

Sothe wanted her to talk to Marcus. That was obvious, even if she wouldn't come out and say it. Her search for Ellie d'Ivoire was a self-imposed penance, but she wasn't willing to betray Winter's secrets in order to complete it. *Does it really matter, though? If I die fighting the Beast, then Sothe can do whatever she likes. And if, somehow, Winter survived . . . then I can think about what happens next.*

The northern boundary of Vordan City was difficult to place. The houses gradually grew larger, the estates more extensive, until they were riding along a country road rather than a city street. Small, well-manicured forests appeared among the elaborate gardens. Farther along, and the hedge-and-fence boundary of Ohnlei came into view, enclosing the vast royal estate that included the palace, Ministry buildings, and mansions of the favored elite.

Rather than going to the grand main gate, their driver took the carriage on a curving road that skirted the fence, coming to a much smaller and plainer entrance close to the palace proper. Two soldiers in the uniform of the Grenadier Guards stepped forward, and the driver presented his pass to them. Whatever it said, it must have been satisfactory, since they waved the carriage through.

"I wondered if we'd have trouble getting into the palace without causing an uproar," Abraham said. "Evidently not."

"Sothe was the head of Raesinia's security for years," Winter said. "I'm sure she knows every way in and out of here."

The carriage bumped along a gravel drive at the rear of the palace, past the bulk of the Prince's Tower. More guards were in evidence, but no one challenged them when they pulled up at what looked like a kitchen door. Winter and Alex got out, and Abraham helped Ennika down, while their driver opened the door without knocking and went inside. A few moments later he came back with a young woman in palace livery, who bowed.

"She'll take you up to the queen," the driver said. "Best of luck." He nodded again, hopped back on the box, and snapped the reins, the carriage's wheels spitting gravel as it got moving.

The young woman was even less talkative. She merely beckoned, and Winter and the others followed. They went through an empty kitchen and into a narrow corridor, which led to a servants' stair. From there they followed a twisting path Winter couldn't hope to replicate, never encountering another living soul. Their guide never faltered, and eventually they came to a door, which she opened to reveal a heavily decorated hallway, with cut-glass windows and thick blue-and-silver carpet. The door they'd come out of closed flush with the wall, so as to be nearly invisible.

Ahead was a much grander door, carved hardwood depicting an armored figure on a rearing horse. Two guards with muskets stood in front of it, staring curiously at the group of newcomers. Winter's guide held up a hand for her to wait, but Winter was already stepping forward.

"Barely!" she said. "Joanna!"

One of the guards, a tall woman, blinked and then made a rapid series of hand signs in the direction of her partner. The other, a short, skinny woman, stared at Winter, eyes going wide.

"Balls of the *fucking* Beast," she said. "Sir? *General Ihernglass?* You have got to be *joking!*"

"No need to stand on formality," Winter said, with a broad grin.

"Shit. Uh. Sorry, sir." Barely straightened to attention, joining Joanna, who was already saluting. "You're just the absolute last person I expected to step out of the woodwork."

"Believe me, I don't blame you." Winter looked over her shoulder. "Can you tell the queen I'm here? Quietly, please. I'm not eager to alert the whole palace."

"Of course. One moment."

Barely opened the big door enough to slip inside. A few moments later she pulled it wide and beckoned. Winter looked for the servant, but she'd slipped away, all in silence. With Alex by her side and Abraham and Ennika behind her, Winter went into the royal suite.

It looked more or less as she expected the queen's residence to look, with polished, gilded furniture and paintings of frowning nobility. Raesinia stood in front of her writing desk, grinning broadly. Winter resisted the urge to give her a nonchalant wave, and bowed instead. Alex and Abraham followed suit.

"Winter." Raesinia shook her head. "God Almighty. We hoped . . . but I didn't think . . ."

There were, Winter was astonished to see, tears in the queen's eyes. She coughed uncomfortably.

"I'm. Um. Sorry it took me so long." Stepping sideways, she waved a hand at her companions. "I think you've met Alex. This is Abraham, a healer from the Mountain, and Ennika, a . . . refugee. I wouldn't have made it without them."

"They all have demons? I knew I felt something in the palace."

Winter nodded.

"Welcome, all of you," Raesinia said. "Winter—"

"I know. We should talk, alone." Winter turned to the others. "If you don't mind waiting for a moment."

Alex was looking around with obviously avaricious eyes, as though she were totaling up the cost of the furnishings. Abraham nodded kindly and directed Ennika to a seat at a nearby table. Raesinia reached out and rang a small silver bell that hung from the wall.

"Eric will be here in a moment," the queen said. "If you need anything—drinks, food—just tell him."

"Thank you, Your Highness," Alex said.

Raesinia waved vaguely as she retreated to an inner room, with Winter following behind. This was her bedchamber, with a huge four-poster bed shrouded by translucent curtains dominating. Raesinia shut the door behind them and let out a deep breath.

"Not that I mind, obviously," she said, "but can I ask how you got into the palace without anyone telling me?"

"Sothe," Winter said. "She found us in Murnsk and brought us here."

"She's *here*?" Raesinia said.

"In the city, at least," Winter said. "There was business to take care of, apparently. But she told me to tell you that she's sorry and that she'll be there when you need her."

There was a long silence, punctuated by a soft *thump* as Raesinia slumped back against the closed door. The tears in her eyes threatened to overflow, and she wiped her sleeve across her face, sniffing.

"When I most need her," Raesinia said in a small voice. "I've needed her ever since she left. Idiot woman."

"I know the situation is . . . complicated," Winter said, shifting awkwardly. "Whatever she's doing, she has a good reason."

"Of course she does." Raesinia blinked rapidly and pushed herself away from the door. "God. I'm sorry. It's been a difficult few days."

"I understand," Winter said. "How much do you know about what's happening?"

"About the war, you mean?"

"About the Beast."

Raesinia stared at her. "How can you know about that?"

"I was there," Winter said. "When it escaped from Elysium."

"Escaped?" Raesinia shook her head. "You may need to start at the beginning."

There wasn't time to go over everything, of course. Even a summary took a while. Winter kept to the basics—the nature of the Beast, its ability to control minds, its unstoppable spread throughout Murnsk and its implacable pursuit of Infernivore. While she spoke, Raesinia walked slowly to the bed and sat down, as though she didn't trust her legs.

When Winter came to Ennika's role in the story, the queen brought her up short. "Janus? She said *Janus* spoke to her?"

"Yes," Winter said. "We weren't certain if we could believe that, but it's hard to think what the Beast has to gain by *pretending* to be Janus. I know it sounds crazy—"

"Not . . . entirely." Raesinia shook her head. "Marcus met with Janus, during the campaign in the Pale valley. Janus demanded he surrender, but while they were talking he passed him a note. As though he had to . . . slip it past someone. It said that Janus' mind was not his own and that you were our best chance against the Beast. That's the only reason I know the name."

"Saints and martyrs," Winter said. "So he really could be . . . alive in there? Aware? Whatever that means."

"And trying to help us," Raesinia said.

"Or trick us into helping *him*. I wouldn't put either past Janus," Winter said. But she had to admit the corroboration lifted some of her doubt. "And now he's coming here?"

Raesinia nodded. "With an army that's at least twice as strong as everything we've got."

"Ennika said the core, the Beast's original body, is coming with him."

"If we kill that, does it hurt the thing?"

"Not seriously," Winter said. "But if *I* can get to it with Infernivore, the Eldest at the mountain thought I might be able to destroy it for good. That has to be the chance Janus talked about." Winter took a deep breath. "If I push on north, I should be able to find it before he reaches the city. I don't know exactly what will happen if I succeed—"

"You'll never get close," Raesinia said. "Don't be stupid. The Beast *knows* this is a possibility, even if it doesn't know you're here. The core will be well guarded."

"What else can we do?" Winter said. "I have to try."

"We can figure out a way that gives you a chance at success," Raesinia said. "Which means not running off half-cocked. We may not be able to match Janus' numbers, but he'll have to at least deploy for battle when he comes against us, and that alone will give you an easier shot at the core." She got up from the bed, her face all decision. "We need to talk to Marcus. He's out there trying to bang the fresh recruits into some kind of army—"

"That may not be a good idea," Winter said, a little desperately. "Time could be important."

"Like I said, if we're only going to get one chance, we have to make it count. Besides, I'm sure there are other people you're going to want to see." Raesinia smiled again. "You're back from the *dead*. Do you have any idea—"

"*No,*" Winter said. "Please. You can't . . . tell people I'm here." *Cyte.* "I can't . . ."

The room shimmered. This time, Winter realized, she was the one on the verge of tears.

There was a pause. After a moment she felt Raesinia take her hand, pulling her to a seat on a velvet-cushioned chaise. The queen sat down across from her, cross-legged on an ottoman.

"Winter," Raesinia said. "What's going on?"

"I just . . ." Winter swallowed hard. "When I confronted the Beast the first time, at Elysium, it nearly devoured me at the same time I was using Infernivore to try to destroy it. Assuming I succeed this time, I'm not sure that it . . . won't succeed, too. I don't know if there'll be anything left of me afterward."

"Oh," Raesinia said. Her gaze was far away.

"It has to be done," Winter said. "I *know* that. If it's me or all of humanity, obviously it has to be me. I'm not . . . afraid." That was a lie. Sometimes she felt like she was nothing *but* afraid. "But the people in the Second Division, Marcus . . . they already think I'm dead. Wouldn't it be *more* cruel to them to come back for a little while and then to leave again?"

Raesinia sighed. "I don't know."

"Then I should stay quiet—"

"It might be more cruel, in the end," Raesinia interrupted. "But I do know that if you asked them, if you gave them the choice, they would want to see you again. However briefly you were going to stay."

Winter stared at her. Her throat was thick. Raesinia looked down, her hands interlocking in her lap.

"I'm hardly one to go around dispensing wisdom," she said. "Queen or not. I just thought . . ." She trailed off.

"You're right," Winter said. "They would want to see me." *I'm just scared.* Scared to see Marcus and of all that would mean. Scared to see Cyte again, and then face *not* seeing her. *And the others. Abby. Feor. Sevran. I can't just slink away.* Winter swallowed again and sat up straighter. "Your plan makes sense. If you're willing to help. "

"Good," Raesinia said. "I'll send a messenger to Marcus, and we can get started."

"Actually, I think I need to speak to Marcus alone. If you don't mind."

"Of course." Raesinia stood up, then looked back at Winter. "Do you need to try to find one of your old uniforms? The ones that, ah . . ."

Her disguise. Winter looked down at herself. She'd had the chance to wash all her clothes aboard ship, though they were still heavily patched and motley. Her traveling outfit wasn't particularly feminine, trousers and a loose shirt, but neither was it intended to conceal, like her tailored uniforms. Even her hair had grown out, almost to her shoulders.

"No," she said. Something inside her twisted. "I don't think so."

Winter sat in one of the palace's innumerable parlors, in a wingback chair beside a roaring fire that dispelled the late-autumn chill. Servants had brought a glass of wine—rather good wine—and a tray of fruit and cheese. She waited, tense as a cat, until she heard booted footsteps outside the door.

Marcus came in, brushing flecks of mud from the sleeves of his uniform coat. He'd aged visibly since Winter had last seen him, the dark circles under his eyes hardening into permanent fixtures, the hair at his temples and in his beard flecked with gray. He also seemed, in some indefinable way, *smaller*. In her memory, especially from back in Khandar, he loomed as enormous and solid as a mountain. This was just a man, a decade or so older than her and half a head taller, weary after a long day and short of sleep.

She wondered what he saw, looking at her. It took him a moment, and then his eyes widened. He closed the door behind him carefully.

"General Ihernglass," he said. "By God it's good to see you again."

"You as well, General d'Ivoire," Winter said. "You've talked to the queen?"

"She filled me in," Marcus said, crossing the room. "Though I have some questions for you about the Beast. I take it you've seen it in action."

"More than enough for one lifetime," Winter said. "But I need to talk to you about something else first."

"Something else?" Marcus frowned.

"It's . . ." She took a deep breath. "Go ahead and sit down. It may take a few minutes."

Marcus looked at her curiously, but took the other seat, stretching out to put his boots near the fire. Winter leaned across to pass him the second glass of wine, which he accepted gratefully.

"I see you're in your . . . female disguise again," he said, after a sip. "Good thinking. If Janus and the Beast are looking for General Ihernglass, they're hardly going to question a ragged girl."

Winter set her jaw. Marcus had seen her without her disguise once before, when she was working with Jane's Leatherbacks, and he'd had the same response then. *Sothe was right. He truly doesn't* want *to see.*

"First of all," she said carefully, "let's get that out of the way. This is not a disguise, Marcus."

"I mean . . ." He waved his hands vaguely. "It's not as obvious as last time, but—"

"I mean it is *not a disguise at all*," Winter said. "I am a *woman.*"

"You . . ." Marcus blinked. "You're . . ."

"Please don't make me pull up my shirt and demonstrate," Winter said.

"That, uh, won't be necessary," Marcus said hastily. He stared at her. "You're . . . I mean . . . since Khandar?"

"Since I was born, as far as I know," Winter said.

"How? How did you . . . ?"

"Do you really want to know?"

He thought about that for a moment. "No," he said. "Not really. But *why?*"

"Because you would have thrown me out of the army if I hadn't."

"I wouldn't have . . ." He shook his head. "I wouldn't have *thrown* you out. I would have made certain you were taken care of."

"I'm sure you would have, but that's not the point."

"Why join the army at all?" Marcus said. "Why would a girl . . . ? I mean, why would you *want* that?"

"You've been commanding the Girls' Own, I understand," Winter said. "Ask them."

"That's different," Marcus said. "I admit, at the beginning, I was . . . opposed to the idea. But the women in the Girls' Own joined up because they wanted to defend Vordan when it was under attack."

Or because it was the only way out of wherever they started, Winter thought. *Or out of a marriage they hated, or away from a father who beat them. Or because they wanted an adventure. Or a hundred other reasons.* But she remained silent.

"I understand that," Marcus went on. "When your country is in danger, sometimes you have to do things that . . . aren't usual. But you were in Khandar for three years before the Redemption, weren't you? God, you must have been what, eighteen when you arrived?"

"Twenty," Winter corrected.

"Why, then?"

"That's the second part. The more important part." Winter paused, gathering her courage. "I grew up in an institution. A school called Mrs. Wilmore's Royal Benevolent Home for Wayward Youth." From the way Marcus' face went still, she knew he recognized the name. "It . . . wasn't a good place, and I ran away. I wanted to get as far from there as I possibly could." She shrugged. "I don't know if I was in my right mind, to be honest. But the recruiting sergeants weren't hard to trick, and Khandar is a hell of a long way from anywhere." She let out a long breath. "Did Raesinia tell you how we got back to Vordan?"

"Only that it was difficult," Marcus said quietly.

"*Difficult* is one word," Winter said carefully. "We were stuck in a Murnskai port called Dimiotsk when Sothe found us. She had a ship all ready."

"Yes, she did tell me that. Janus talked to her, somehow, and told her to go and get you. But—"

Winter held up a hand. "While we were aboard ship, Sothe and I talked. She told me about your parents."

"Did she tell you," Marcus grated, "that she killed them?"

"She did. She also told me she'd been looking for your little sister, Ellie."

Another silence. Wood in the fireplace popped with a sound like a musket shot.

"Did you . . . ?" Marcus' voice was thick. "You were at Mrs. Wilmore's. Did you know her?"

"Not exactly," Winter said. "Marcus, she told me *I* am Ellie d'Ivoire."

She watched his face pale by several shades, blood running out of it like his throat had been slashed. His eyes never left hers.

"You?" he said. "E-Ellie?"

"I don't remember the name," Winter said. "I don't remember *anything*, really. Except fire." She took the small notebook out of her pocket, held it in front of her like a peace offering. "This is the information Sothe copied from the Concordat archives. It's . . . convincing."

"But . . ." Marcus blinked.

"Look." Winter shifted uncomfortably. "I don't know what to do with this any more than you do. I wasn't sure whether I could tell you I was a *woman*, for

God's sake. I don't know what this means, or how it affects us, but I just thought . . ." She paused for breath. "I thought you'd rather know than keep wondering."

Abruptly, Marcus got to his feet. Winter stood, cautiously, eyes still on his pale face.

"Marcus?" she said. "Please say something."

The last thing she was expecting was for him to lurch forward. At first she thought he was attacking her, mad as that sounded. By the time she realized he wanted an embrace, she was already twisting away, slipping under his outstretched arms, and backing rapidly against the wall. Her heart was pounding. Marcus looked at her, his arms falling to his sides.

"Sorry," Winter said. "I'm sorry. You . . . surprised me."

A log in the fireplace collapsed with a crackle. Marcus blinked, turned away, and left the room without a word.

A messenger found her not long afterward, and told her that General d'Ivoire was otherwise occupied for the evening, but would be available to see her tomorrow. In the meantime, the young ranker said, he would be happy to escort her to where the Second Division was being quartered.

"They're here?" Winter said, her heart still slowing down. "In the palace?"

"The officers have quarters here," the ranker said. "The rest are under canvas in the gardens."

"Is Cyte—is Captain Cytomandiclea here?"

"Of course. I can take you to her."

Once again Winter found herself walking through the complex maze that was the palace, though this time they stuck to the lavish main passages instead of taking the servants' corridors. Still as statues, the Grenadier Guards in the hall let them pass. Winter found herself subconsciously waiting for salutes.

She felt strange. Light, somehow, in the way she could be in dreams, as though each step might end with her floating away. Or like she'd walked off a cliff and was still in midfall, momentarily weightless until the ground arrived.

I told Marcus. My brother. It was strange to think that while the second half of her revelation had undoubtedly been what had shaken Marcus, it was the first half that had been the most difficult for Winter to nerve herself up to. *I learned who Ellie d'Ivoire was only a few days ago. I've been hiding who I am for more than four years.* Her mood shifted from a slightly hysterical calm to a certainty of imminent doom and back again every few steps.

Maybe this is a bad idea. Maybe I should find somewhere to sleep until I calm down. She wouldn't, though. Not now. She'd already taken the plunge by talking to Marcus. *Besides, it won't be long before rumors that I'm back start to spread.* The thought of Cyte finding out like that, before Winter had come to see her, made her quicken her steps.

The messenger left her in front of an imposing carved door, and bowed respectfully when Winter told him to go. His retreating footsteps matched the hammering of her heart as she raised her hand and knocked, almost inaudibly.

"Come in." Cyte's voice, harried and distracted. "If it's a note, leave it on the table."

Winter opened the door. Inside was a small suite, suitable for housing a minor noble and his servants. The main room had a large dining table, a sofa, and a couple of armchairs, all of which had been converted to serve as storage for stacks of paper and rolled leather maps. A big one, held flat by a pistol at one end and a sword belt at the other, showed the land north of Vordan City and was covered in grease-pencil markings. Cyte stood in front of it, looking down, comparing the map with pages from a loose pile and scribbling notes on foolscap.

She was just as Winter remembered her, slim as a dagger in her blue uniform, dark hair falling to her shoulders over too-pale skin. Her face bore the same signs of overwork and lack of sleep that it had in Murnsk, when Winter had left, though at least the weathering of the north had faded somewhat.

"Yes?" she said, without looking up. "Is there a message?"

Winter found that she couldn't speak, could only stare greedily. The soft, pale curve of Cyte's bent neck attracted her eyes like a magnet. A lock of dark hair slipped forward, and Cyte's hand came up automatically to tuck it behind her ear, a gesture so familiar that it made Winter's heart ache.

"If there's no message," Cyte said, turning, "then what's . . . going . . . on . . . ?"

She stopped, eyes wide, mouth open. Winter felt her cheeks flush under Cyte's gaze.

"Winter?" Cyte's voice was almost inaudible.

Winter nodded slowly. The air felt fragile, as though too forceful a movement might shatter the world.

Cyte crossed the room one step at a time, still staring. She stopped a few feet away, her throat working as she swallowed.

"I knew it," she whispered. "Even before we heard from Janus, I knew you were alive."

"I . . ."

Winter stopped. *What am I supposed to say?* That she'd felt no such certainty? That standing here, finally seeing for herself that Cyte had survived, released knots of tension she'd held for so long she'd almost forgotten it could be any other way? *That I'm not sure whether I want to laugh, or cry, or just kiss her until I run out of breath—*

Cyte solved that problem, stumbling forward the last few steps, wrapping her arms around Winter's neck like she was clinging to a life rope. Winter had the presence of mind to kick the door closed behind her, and leaned against it for support. Her arms went around Cyte's shoulders automatically, hands clasping at the small of her back.

They stayed that way for a long interval, the soundless shaking of Cyte's slim body the only evidence of her tears. Her face was buried in the crook of Winter's neck, and Winter gripped her tightly, as though sheer pressure could erase the time they'd spent apart.

"I'm sorry," Winter whispered into the mass of Cyte's hair. "I'm sorry I took so long."

Cyte's shoulders only shook harder. Winter held her close until the shudders subsided. Eventually Cyte took a long, slow breath and raised her head. Her eyes were red and puffy from crying, but her lips stretched in an awkward smile.

"God. I'm sorry." Cyte gave a laugh that sounded more like a hiccup. "You step through the door and I just—"

"It's all right." Winter squeezed Cyte a little tighter, blinking away tears of her own.

"You're okay?" Cyte said.

"I . . . think so." Winter sucked in a deep breath. "It's a long story. Are you . . . ?"

"I'm fine," Cyte said, when Winter trailed off. "It was touch and go a few times after Alves, but I'm still here."

Silence fell, tight and awkward. Where they were pressed together, Winter could feel Cyte's heart beating fast as a songbird's.

"You probably want to know what's happened to the Second," Cyte said, her eyes never leaving Winter's. "I have the . . . the strength reports, and . . ."

"What I want," Winter said carefully, "is to kiss you." *And never, ever stop.*

"Oh," Cyte said quietly. "I would, um, like that? More than . . . you know. Anything at all, really."

From the moment their lips met, it was as if Winter had been hit by a bolt of lightning, heat running through her body like a tide. Cyte's breath tickled her cheek as they staggered together across the room, unwilling to part even for an instant.

When they reached the sofa, Cyte swept several piles of reports onto the floor with a soft susurrus of sliding paper, punctuated by urgent gasps that Winter no longer knew who was making. Cyte sat down, breathing hard as Winter's lips slid down her cheek and along the delicate curve of her neck. One of Cyte's hands worked its way under her shirt, slipping up the curve of her back, sending waves of fire along her spine.

How could I have considered not telling her I was here? The fear that had driven her seemed incomprehensible now. *I might not come back from stopping the Beast. I might fail, and all of humanity might die with me.*

But for the moment, at least, I'm still alive.

They'd made it to the bedroom, eventually, after knocking over a few more of Cyte's carefully balanced piles of paperwork. After the initial rush had worn off, they'd had time for things like buttons. From the couch to the bed, the pieces of Cyte's uniform made a kind of trail interspersed with Winter's rough, dirty clothes. The bed was another big four-poster, with a down mattress that felt far too soft to be real. Cyte lay in the center of it, where they'd come to rest, her arms spread wide and Winter's head pillowed against her cheek.

Her breathing had soon taken on the soft rhythm of sleep, but Winter felt too keyed up for that. After a while she rolled out of bed as carefully as she could and padded naked across the thick carpet to the toilet. When she was finished, she ran hot water from the tap—hot, running water, that unimaginable luxury—and splashed it over her face and some of the more obvious grime. She went back into the bedroom, air cool against her damp skin.

Climbing back into bed, she paused for a moment, looking down at Cyte. With her eyes closed, some of the tension was gone from her face, making her look younger and more innocent. Her beauty brought a lump to Winter's throat. She let her gaze run across her, deliberately—milk-pale skin; small, perfect breasts; stomach hard and muscled from life in the field; the thatch of dark hair between her legs. Watching Cyte like this, acknowledging her desire for her, felt wrong, vaguely obscene. It added a thrill of the forbidden that pebbled Winter's skin into goose bumps.

She slid back into the bed, alongside her lover, feeling Cyte move sleepily as she draped an arm across her. Winter pressed her head against Cyte's and let her eyes close.

Is it really okay to feel like this? On its face she knew it was a silly question. But she couldn't help feeling like she needed permission, or else the universe was going to come down on her hard.

Well. If it does, then the hell with the universe.

When they awoke, it was well after sunset. Cyte got out of bed, stumbling and giggling in the dark, until she managed to find a candelabra in its nook and get it lit. From there, she bustled around the bedroom, lighting more lamps.

"Okay," Winter said, eyes on Cyte's naked backside as she bent over to retrieve her uniform shirt from the floor. "*Now* you can tell me about the Second."

Cyte laughed, and obligingly gave an abridged recitation of the events of the Pale campaign. Winter winced at her description of the fighting at Satinvol and Alves, the long march that followed, and the death of Colonel Erdine.

"Damn," she said. "He was a good officer, for all that he liked to puff himself up."

"I know." Cyte slid her trousers on. She still had her shirt hanging open, and Winter found the resulting half-dress incredibly appealing. "I'm worried about Abby."

"She's not taking it well?"

Cyte shook her head. "I don't know if they were . . . I mean, I don't think Abby had any illusions about their relationship. But it was something for her to hold on to, and now she doesn't even have that." She sighed. "You should see her as soon as you can."

"I will." Winter shook her head. "Though I don't know what I'm going to say."

"You don't have to say anything," Cyte said. "The Girls' Own is going to go mad just hearing you're back."

Winter hesitated. "I'm . . . not sure we should tell them."

"What?" Cyte turned. "Why?"

"There's something I have to do," Winter said. "It's—"

"The Beast?" Cyte said.

Winter blinked. "How do you know about that?"

"Marcus and I have been putting some pieces together," Cyte said. "Not everything, but enough."

"Then you know this is about more than whether Janus or Raesinia sits on the throne," Winter said. "I may be the only one who can stop it."

Cyte nodded. "And?"

"And . . . I might not be coming back."

"You're a soldier," Cyte said. "So am I. So are they. We understand what that means."

"That's not what I mean," Winter said. "Even if we win, even if I destroy the Beast, I don't know . . ." She fought a sudden hitch in her throat. "I don't want to hurt my friends more than I have already. I'm not sure I should have come *here*, but I . . . I couldn't . . ."

Cyte crossed the room in a few determined strides and crawled onto the bed, shirt still hanging open. Winter sat up, but Cyte put a hand on her chest and pushed her flat, propping herself on hands and knees.

"Winter," she said. "You are being an idiot."

"But—"

"Stop."

"You don't understand," Winter said, tears welling again. "My friends— the people I'm close to—they get hurt. They die. Sergeant Red, the women who followed me to look for Janus. The ones who came with me to Elysium. Leti and the Haeta." She knew those names would mean nothing to Cyte, but she couldn't stop them from pouring out. "Bobby. Bobby's dead, Cyte. She saved me, and then she died. I don't—I can't—"

"Please, Winter," Cyte said. Her voice had gone from hard to gentle. "Stop."

The words ran out. Winter lay still, breathing raggedly, staring up into Cyte's face.

"Do you know why the people around you get hurt?" Cyte said. "It's be- cause they're the same kind of person you are. People who put themselves in danger because they want to help others, or because they have a duty."

"But—"

"You think no one got hurt after you left? No one sacrificed themselves when we were fighting Janus at Alves?" Cyte's lip twisted, and she held up one hand, fingers an inch apart. "I came *this* close to getting my head shot off. You don't get to take responsibility for that."

"You wouldn't be here if it weren't for me," Winter said.

"You may have started me on this path," Cyte said, real anger in her voice now. "But I didn't have to keep going. Give us some *fucking* credit, Winter!"

"I'm sorry," Winter said. "You're right. I know—"

"You don't," Cyte said. "But I'm going to keep pounding it into your head until you do. You're a commander, but that doesn't make you a god. You can only do what you can." She took a deep breath. "You're going to stop the Beast, and you're going to come back. Just like you came back this time."

There was a pause. Cyte shifted and rolled onto her back, next to Winter. "Okay," Winter said.

"Good."

Another, longer silence.

"When I was riding away from the cavalry at Alves," Cyte said, quieter now, "I could almost feel them coming up behind me. I heard the shots going past. And . . ." She swallowed. "All I could think was that I couldn't die, because I had to be here when you got back."

"Oh, Cyte." Winter rolled onto her elbow, leaned over Cyte, and kissed her. "I'm sorry. Really sorry."

"Good." Cyte grinned. "Now. Did you say you went to *Elysium*?"

Winter flopped back. "It's a long story."

"I'm not going anywhere," Cyte said. "Get started."

CHAPTER TWENTY-SEVEN

MARCUS

There hadn't been any bottles of *flaghaelan* in the palace cellars, but Marcus had found a quite respectable brandy from the Transpale tucked in a cabinet underneath a stairway. He'd liberated the whole bottle, despite the scandalized look he got from the steward. Once the world had a pleasant rubberiness to it at the edges, he'd made his way to the Prince's Tower, where Raesinia had once had her chambers. It was dark and silent now, having been looted during the revolution and not yet refurnished, and he slunk through the too-empty rooms to the roof. There, on the chilly flagstones, was where Raesinia had regularly "escaped" from her own palace by throwing herself to the gravel below.

He leaned against the battlement, taking another swallow from the bottle and feeling it burn its way down his throat and into his churning stomach. After a few moments of silence, he coughed.

"Sothe," he said, and then repeated it in a shout. "Sothe! Where are you? I know you're watching me."

There was nothing but silence.

"Sothe!" He thumped the stonework with one hand, and winced. "You want me to sit here screaming your name all night?"

Something shifted in the shadow of a crenellation. Sothe's voice was soft. "You said you never wanted to see me again."

"Well, things have *fucking* changed, haven't they?" Marcus shook his head, sending the world spinning. "You found Winter."

"I did."

"And you found out he—she—was . . ." He couldn't finish.

"Your sister. Ellie d'Ivoire."

Saints and fucking martyrs. Just hearing the name out loud sent his heart racing, a mix of terror and anticipation and other emotions he didn't understand. *Ellie,* he told himself, trying for discipline. *My sister. Ellie. She's alive. Winter is my sister.*

It was no good. There were two people in his head. Ellie, four years old, smiling and clever. And *General Ihernglass*, enigmatic, competent, lethal in a crisis. A little girl and a grown man. A child and a soldier. Now the world was insisting they were *one and the same*.

Don't be stupid, he told himself. *What did you expect? That Ellie would still be four when you found her?*

But logic was a thin reed to cling to. He kept trying to push the two images together, like forcing a jigsaw puzzle piece into a place where it didn't fit, and they kept springing apart again.

What the hell am I supposed to do now?

"You might have told me," Marcus said. "That's why you found her, isn't it?"

The shadow shifted as Sothe nodded. "Once I became aware of her identity, I was . . . torn. I thought she deserved to make the choice herself."

Marcus had to admit he couldn't see the fault in that. *Balls of the fucking Beast. Could Winter really have chosen not to tell me? Let me live the rest of my life not knowing? It would have been easier for her, wouldn't it?*

"So, now what?" Marcus said. "Your conscience is assuaged? You've redeemed yourself?" He snorted.

"My conscience was never the issue here, Marcus." Sothe stepped out of the shadow, into the half-light of the torches on the walls. "I don't try to pretend I haven't done terrible things, or that I can make up for that. A person's life isn't like a ledger book, where this much good cancels out that much bad and all debts are paid. I will always be the person who killed at Duke Orlanko's command and never asked why." She bowed her head. "All I can hope for is to be someone else as well."

"And you think this helps?"

"I thought that I owed you the truth."

"Does Winter know?"

"Know what?"

"What you did to my—to *our* parents. That it was you who took her family away from her."

"She does. I think she is . . . still trying to understand how to feel about me."

Marcus leaned back against the wall, stone cool against his cheek. The bottle sloshed gently in his hand, but he suddenly wanted nothing more to do with it.

"What are you doing here?" he said. "Don't tell me you think this makes us even."

"I left after Janus resigned because I had unfinished business with Orlanko," Sothe said. "And . . . because I thought that perhaps Raesinia would no longer need my help. I have returned because I was wrong."

"What happened to Orlanko?"

"I killed him," Sothe said matter-of-factly.

"Good," Marcus muttered. He pushed himself back to his feet and turned to face her. "So, now what? I warned you—"

"That you would kill me if you saw me again." Something flashed between them. A knife, stuck point down in the crack between two flagstones, still quivering from the force of the throw. Sothe stepped slowly out of the shadow, light sliding off her black-clad form. "This is your chance. I will not abandon Raesinia, not now. If you wish to take your revenge, I offer you this opportunity."

Marcus looked down at the knife. In his inebriated state, he doubted he was much of a threat to Sothe. *No, let's not mince words. I'm no threat to her when I'm at my best, not unless I've got a company of sharpshooters backing me up.* He bent, with an effort, and pried the blade from the ground.

She watched him steadily, not even glancing at the weapon. Marcus shook his head.

"I can't," he said with a sigh. "You know I can't."

"I do." Sothe's lip quirked slightly.

"That hardly seems fair." He flipped the knife around and handed it to her, hilt first. She took it and slid it into some hidden recess of her costume.

"I'm not in the business of fair," Sothe said.

"I haven't forgiven you," Marcus said. "Just because I'm not willing to cut a woman down in cold blood doesn't mean I can accept what you did."

"I do not require your forgiveness," Sothe said. "You and I are both devoted to Raesinia in our own ways. I hope that we can at least agree on that."

Marcus nodded, letting out a breath that carried much of his tension with it. "Now what?"

"I am going to see Raesinia," Sothe said. "I had thought to stay away, but . . ." Uncharacteristic indecision showed on her face.

"Stay away? Why?"

"She relies on me more than she should," Sothe said. "I will not always be there to care for her."

"She trusts you."

"There should be more than one person in her life whom she trusts." Sothe cocked her head. "You will protect her."

It wasn't a question. *More like a command.* Marcus straightened automatically. "Of course. I love her."

"Good." Sothe's face relaxed, just slightly. "That's good."

"She wants a meeting tomorrow," Marcus said. "A strategy conference."

Sothe nodded. "The queen puts a great deal of faith in your ability."

"I keep thinking about Winter. She'll be there, of course." He shook his head. "How am I supposed to treat her? She's my little sister, but I hardly *know* her, not really."

"She's a soldier," Sothe suggested. "Like you. You may have more in common than you realize. Perhaps you can start from there."

RAESINIA

It was amazing how quickly things could become routine. Since she'd been old enough to walk, Raesinia had slept alone, in vast, cold beds as befit her status as Princess of Vordan. Her days with Marcus were brief by comparison, a bare instant, but now she felt his absence like a missing tooth. She'd grown used to lying beside him, warm and dreamy from their lovemaking, and listening to his breath gradually slow as he relaxed into sleep.

Before, she'd spent most nights working. Now she paced her bedchamber, nervous and irritable.

Winter really made it. Marcus seemed to believe the notes he'd received from "Janus," or whoever was truly pulling the strings, but Raesinia had been privately skeptical. But unless it was a trap of surpassing subtlety, the communications had been genuine. Winter was here, and with her a chance to defeat the Beast. *Or so we think.*

Raesinia's instincts told her they should be making plans at once, that there was no time to spare. She had to remind herself that ordinary humans needed sleep. *Winter's probably exhausted from her journey, and she said she had things to talk to Marcus about. And we're still waiting for Sothe.*

Sothe . . .

It was as though her thoughts were a summons. There was a quiet scrape at the window, which was Sothe's version of a butler's politely clearing his throat, a deliberate sound from someone who *could* have been perfectly silent. Raesinia turned and found her standing on the other side of the room, a slim, dark shape in the light of the brazier.

"Your Highness." Sothe bowed deeply.

"You're back." Raesinia walked around the untouched bed, snatching a candelabra from a table by the door. In its flickering light, Sothe's face was the same as Raesinia remembered, imperturbable and dispassionate, the faintest touch of sarcasm in her mobile eyebrows and severe features. She was dressed in the slightly scuffed black she always wore, capable of vanishing into the nearest shadow and no doubt full of hidden weapons.

"Where," Raesinia said through clenched teeth, "have you *been*?"

"I asked Marcus to give you a message," Sothe said. "Did he fail to do so?"

"He told me you were alive," Raesinia said. "That was *it*! Not where you were going or when you planned to return. Nothing!"

"Don't hold it against him," Sothe said. "I didn't tell him, either."

"And you couldn't have sent a *letter*? A message? A carrier pigeon?" Raesinia waved the candelabra in Sothe's face, scattering drops of wax on the floor. "I *needed* you."

"I am sorry, Your Highness. I thought . . ." She shook her head. "I had tasks to complete, and I hoped events would stay quiet for a time. Obviously, I was wrong."

"Damn right, you were wrong. I almost ended up married to the Second Prince of Borel."

Sothe raised one eyebrow. "A dire fate."

"He's not so terrible," Raesinia said, with an affectedly casual air. "It's his father who got on my bad side. The point is that it would have been nice to have a little help!"

"You seem to have escaped," Sothe said. "And, from what I hear, Cora and Marcus have been of some assistance."

"Cora has been amazing," Raesinia said. "And Marcus . . . yes. But they're not *you*. I . . ."

Raesinia's voice died. Wax pattered softly from the candelabra, and she sniffed and set it aside.

"Do you know how worried I was?" she whispered. "At first I would listen for you, after dark, when the castle got quiet."

"That was foolish," Sothe said, with a hint of a smile. "You know you'd never have heard me coming."

"And *then*," Raesinia said, ignoring her, "I thought you weren't coming back. That you'd been killed, doing—whatever it was you were doing. And I . . ." She rubbed her eyes with her knuckles. "I was so *angry*. And then guilty, for feeling angry, when you were lying dead somewhere, and here I was hating you for not being here, and—"

"I wasn't dead." There was something in Sothe's voice that might have been a touch of emotion, well suppressed. "I went looking for Orlanko."

Raesinia looked up. "Did you find him?"

Sothe nodded. "He won't trouble us again."

Orlanko. For all that he'd been the force behind the plot to usurp Raesinia's throne, it had been ages since she'd thought about him. *He seemed like such a nightmare a year ago.* And now he was gone, a roadblock smashed flat on Janus' rise to power, like so many others. *Like me, if we lose.*

And Sothe had hunted him down. *You could almost feel sorry for him. But not quite.*

"And then you found Winter and brought her here?" she said.

"It was considerably more complex than that. But yes, in essence."

Raesinia let out a long breath. "Well. You'll have to give me the full story sometime."

"Winter can tell you most of it. Marcus knows the rest."

"Why?" Raesinia felt the hairs on the back of her neck rising. "Where are you going? If you say you have more 'business' to take care of—"

"I have a part to play in stopping the Beast," Sothe said. "I am . . . not sure what will happen."

"Oh." Raesinia relaxed a bit. "If anyone will be fine, you will."

"Do not be so certain. I am . . . only human."

"Enough," Raesinia said, feeling something tighten in her chest. "No more of that sort of talk, understand?"

"As my queen commands," Sothe said, smiling. She bowed again. "What shall we discuss instead?"

"Send for something to drink," Raesinia said, forcing a grin. "We have a lot of catching up to do."

MARCUS

Marcus slept poorly, despite the brandy.

Ellie. He found himself going over his memories of his sister, and he was shocked at just how few he really had. In the long years of his exile, they had worn away, reduced to a few touchstones. A gap-toothed smile, an afternoon spent in the garden, a crying fit whose cause he'd forgotten.

Even if Ellie wasn't Winter—if it was some other girl—what kind of relationship would we really have? He tried to compose a picture of what he might have expected from a grown-up Ellie, but the features remained vague. *What would we talk about? What would she think of me?*

When he woke, tangled in the sheets of the too-soft bed, his mouth was dry and his head pounded. He'd spent most of his evenings in the queen's apartments, but last night he'd come back to his own, barely used quarters, a large suite that dwarfed his few possessions. Palace servants brought him water, filled his bath, and left a fresh, neatly folded uniform waiting for when he finished. He put it on, moving slowly to spare his head, and fixed the stars of a column-general carefully to his shoulders.

The conference was in a dining room that Raesinia had repurposed as a command center, with a huge map of Vordan City and the surrounding area laid out on the big, polished table. When he arrived, she was there, looking down at the finely painted details of Ohnlei, wearing a silver and dark blue dress that was somber enough to verge on mourning attire. At the sight of him, she smiled and cocked her head.

"Are you all right?" she said.

Marcus crossed the room and bent down to kiss her. "I'll be fine." *Eventually.* "Where is everyone?"

"On the way."

Sothe arrived first, all in rough black, moving silently to stand at Raesinia's side as if she'd never left. Then Cyte, neatly dressed and looking better rested than she had in weeks. And then, finally, Winter.

She was back in uniform, but something had changed. The fit was different—while her figure was modest, it nonetheless had unmistakably feminine curves. Her white-blond hair, grown down to the back of her neck in the time she'd spent away, hung around her ears and framed her face, making it look softer. Seeing her now, like this, Marcus wondered how he could have ever mistaken her for a man.

Winter herself seemed less than comfortable in her new attire, and was tugging awkwardly at her uniform jacket. She bowed to the queen and offered Marcus a crisp salute.

"Division-General Ihernglass, reporting," she said. "I apologize for the length of my absence."

"I believe I speak for all of us when I say that no apologies are necessary," Raesinia said. "Welcome back."

"Thank you, Your Highness. If you don't mind, I have several companions who I think should join us."

"Of course," Raesinia said. "I trust your judgment."

Winter went back into the corridor and returned with three others. Marcus recognized Alex, the young woman Winter had found on the Murnskai campaign, who'd accompanied her in her effort to find the Penitent who'd poisoned Janus. The other two were strangers to him. A tall, solemn young man in a priest's robe accompanied a frail girl with a strip of cloth wound around her eyes, and guided her to one of the chairs pushed up against the walls.

"I think you know Alex," Winter said. "This is her companion, Abraham, lately of the Mountain. He has his own demon as well." She paused. "And this is Ennika, once one of the Penitent Damned."

Raesinia caught her breath. "*Once* one of the Penitent Damned?"

"The Priests of the Black are destroyed," Ennika said. Her voice was surprisingly strong for such a thin frame. "The Penitent Damned are no more. There is only the Beast of Judgment."

"Ennika was a communicator, able to speak to her sister over great distances," Winter said. "Now her sister has been taken by the Beast. In a way we don't fully understand, Janus—"

"Some entity that claims to be Janus," Sothe put in.

"—indeed. The entity can speak to Ennika from 'inside' the Beast. So far, it has proven useful."

"I'm not sure I would believe it," Marcus said, eyeing the blind girl, "if not for the note Janus himself gave me."

"If anyone could plot his way out from inside a demon, it's Janus," Raesinia said. "Has he told you anything more?"

Ennika nodded. "But he said this would be his last chance to speak to me. He has . . . convinced the Beast to bring its core, the center of its power, along with its army as it marches on Vordan City. This will enable it to take over the bodies of everyone here without delay. But Janus says it provides Winter with an opportunity. The Beast believes she is still in the north, trying to find a way back to Vordan."

"Why won't Janus be able to speak to you again?" Marcus said. "Has something happened?"

Ennika shrugged. "His communication was never clear at the best of times. Perhaps my sister's soul has slipped from his grasp."

"Whatever the reason," Winter said, her tone still formal, "it's clear we can't count on his assistance. So the situation is this: somehow, I need to reach the core of the Beast and use Infernivore to destroy it."

"Can you identify the core?" Raesinia said. "What is it?"

"A person. The first one the Beast took over." There was a faint hitch in Winter's voice. "I can identify it."

"Even if it doesn't think you're nearby, I assume the Beast will keep the core well protected," Marcus said, looking at Winter for confirmation. She nodded, a momentary awkwardness as their eyes met quickly smothered under military professionalism.

"It will," she said. "It's possible that our best chance would come during a major battle, where the Beast's forces would have to deploy over a wider area."

"Which puts things back in the domain of the military," Sothe said.

"Do you want to go over the situation for everyone?" Raesinia asked Marcus.

"*Want* is putting it strongly," Marcus said with a grimace. He couldn't help darting a glance at Winter. She—*she*—was watching him intently. *Focus. Raesinia needs you more than ever.* He walked to the table and started to lay small wooden counters on the map.

"After Alves," he said, "Janus pursued my army south along the Pale for quite a distance. Our garrisons in the Illifen passes were enough to keep his detachments west of the mountains until he gave up the chase and marched his main force to push through. Unfortunately, we now believe he met with considerable reinforcements from Murnsk at this point, more than making good his losses in the campaign so far.

"He took his time reducing the forts on the east side of the pass, giving him a clean line of communications back to Alves that we can't interfere with. From there, as you can see, he had to deal with the Marak." On the map, Marcus traced the line of the river Marak, running almost due south from its source near the mountains to where it emptied into the Vor twenty miles downstream of Vordan.

"The terrain is better west of the river," Winter said. "Nice and flat, plenty of room to maneuver. Exactly what you'd want if you had an advantage in numbers. But . . ."

"He'd have to cross the river once he got here," Raesinia said. She grinned at Marcus. "I haven't entirely forgotten your strategy lessons."

"Exactly," Marcus said. "The Marak is wide enough to be a serious obstacle, and the Vor is even bigger. There are only a few bridges north of the city, and none to the south before Ohms. And he has to know by now that we have a Borelgai fleet backing us. Even if we can't get the men-of-war up the Marak, the frigates would make short work of a small-boat attack. Without his own fleet, he'd have to try to outmarch us in search of a crossing, and risk our striking at the pass to cut him off."

"Splitting his army would be inviting an attack," Winter said. "So he's coming down the east bank?"

"For the most part," Marcus said. "There's some cavalry on the west side, watching the crossings to make sure we don't slip around to his rear. But the bulk of his forces are coming due south, between the Marak and the Vor. From scouting reports, our best guess is that he has the equivalent of seven divisions, a bit more than sixty thousand men."

"And we have?" Sothe asked, in the ensuing silence.

This was what had been keeping Marcus up late at night, going over strength reports and recruiting estimates. *At least, it was what was keeping me up before Winter got back.* "We got out of Alves with two divisions, the First and the Second, plus fragments of other units that escaped the battle. Between depot battalions, garrisons from the south, and fresh recruits, we've got enough bodies to fill one more. With the cavalry reserve, that gives us about thirty thousand bayonets and sabers."

"Meaning we're outnumbered two to one," Raesinia said. "I'm not a military expert, but that sounds bad."

"What about civilian volunteers?" Sothe said. "That worked in the revolution."

"We'll use whatever we can," Marcus said. "But I'm skeptical they'll be much good against a seasoned army. In the revolution, our skirmishers caught the loyalists off guard, but Janus won't make the same mistake."

"We don't need to defeat Janus," Winter said. "If I can get to the Beast, that army should fall apart. And if I *can't,* then none of this will matter."

"You're going to need time to find the core," Marcus said. "It's no good if we're swept off the field at the first charge, which is what would happen if we just deployed in the open and waited for him."

"It sounds like you have an idea," Raesinia said, toying nervously with one of the red-painted counters.

"I see two possibilities, but I don't like either of them." Marcus took a deep breath. "The first is that we abandon Ohnlei and fall back to the city itself. Fortify as much as we can, fight house to house. Blow up the bridges to the island, when Janus gets that far."

There was a shocked silence. The ancient bridges of Vordan City were more than just a means of getting across the river—they were cultural artifacts, tying the kingdom to its ancient origins. Suggesting their demolition in the name of military expediency was close to sacrilege, especially since they were named for the holiest saints.

"We can't stop them," Marcus said after a moment. "Maybe if Vordan City had a proper wall, but it doesn't. But we can slow them down and make them pay in blood for every street. And it will certainly buy Winter the time she needs."

"No," Raesinia said. Her hand gripped the edge of the table, hard enough that her knuckles stood out in stark white.

"I know it seems cruel," Sothe said. "But if we win—"

"What's the good in winning if the city is rubble by the time we're finished?" Raesinia said. "We can't bring the war into the streets. Vordan City had enough of that during the revolution. I'd rather abdicate."

"The alternative isn't abdication," Sothe said. "It's losing all of humanity to the Beast."

"The queen is right," Winter said. "We can't have the battle in the city if we can possibly avoid it."

"What's the other alternative?" Raesinia said.

"It's riskier," Marcus said. "We deploy the army north of Ohnlei, close to the Marak, and dig in as much as we can. Janus won't be able to slip around our left, because of the river, and if he tries to go wide around our right we can pounce on his rear. He'll have no choice but to attack us. If we choose our position carefully, we might be able to hold out until nightfall, or until Winter succeeds."

"That seems logical enough," Winter said. "Why do you say it's risky?"

"Because Janus is *Janus*," Marcus said, with a bitter laugh. "General Kurot thought he had him locked in a trap, and look what happened to him. He could do a hundred things I haven't thought of and we'd be in no position to stop him. Once we pick our ground, we're committed—we can't maneuver without losing the advantage of our fortifications." He scratched his beard. "The only reason I even suggest it is because of the way he fought in the Pale valley."

"What way was that?" Sothe said.

"Carelessly," Marcus said. "As though the lives of his troops meant nothing to him. Whenever I served under Janus, he never spent blood recklessly, but now . . ." He shrugged. "If all he's concerned with is speed, he'll come at us head-on. Then we'll have our battle. If not, then we may end up like Kurot."

Raesinia took a deep breath, her face hardening.

"I think it's our best option," she said. "How long do we have?"

"Five days, at the minimum," Marcus said. "Longer, if Janus goes easy on his men, but when has he ever done that?"

"And have you picked out your site?"

"I think so," Marcus said. "I need to go and look it over personally."

Raesinia glanced at Winter, who nodded.

"All right," Raesinia said. "Then this is where we stop the Beast."

CHAPTER TWENTY-EIGHT

WINTER

Ennika held Winter's arm as they descended the steps into the palace basement, Alex and Abraham following behind. It was cool down there, a steady breeze blowing up from the dark, underground corridors. There were springs under Ohnlei, and their chilly waters were channeled through the walls to wine cellars and meat storage. The ubiquitous braziers were absent, and Winter carried a candelabra in her hand.

At the bottom of the stairs, a young man in a gray robe waited in front of a curtained doorway. He bowed at Winter's approach. She recognized him, distantly, as one of the students Feor had taken on when she'd been commissioned by the queen to study the Thousand Names. The lack of familiarity brought home just how long it had been since Winter had seen the Khandarai priestess. *She probably feels like I abandoned her here.*

"General Ihernglass," the young man said. "My name is Justin de Horat. The mistress is expecting you."

Winter nodded. "Is there somewhere Ennika could rest while we talk?"

"Of course." Justin extended his arm to the blind girl. "You'll find the mistress through the archive in the sanctuary. I'll find Miss Ennika somewhere comfortable."

He disappeared through the curtain, and Winter and the others followed. Beyond was a wide hallway with more curtained doorways off either side and a large arch at the back. Between the doorways, lining the walls, were the Thousand Names.

It had been more than a year since Winter had seen the ancient artifacts that had been the start of everything. They were eight-foot-tall slabs of steel, deeply incised with long strings of tiny, unfamiliar characters. Under the

Mountain, she'd seen a similar archive, and the Eldest had told her their un-wieldiness was intentional. Not only would the steel tablets be proof against the years, but their sheer size and weight made theft unlikely.

She knew now that they were the creation of the Mages, an ancient faction of the pre-Elysian church that held that the summoning of demons was not intrinsically evil. The Mages had worked to discover the names of demons, and inscribed their knowledge on tablets like these. But their enemies, led by the great Saint Elleusis Ligamenti, had won the power struggle, and the Mages were declared heretical. Some had survived by stealth, like the Eldest and his followers at the Mountain. Others had fled over the seas, taking their archive with them, and after a thousand years had become the secret cult that Winter and Janus had faced in the temple under the Great Desol.

Or so the Eldest claimed, at any rate. Winter was on shaky ground as far as theological matters went, and she wasn't sure how Feor would take being labeled as a devotee of a heretical Karisai sect. *She can talk it over with the Eldest, once all this is finished.* For the moment they had more practical concerns.

Abraham's eyes were wide and his hands twitched, as though he couldn't wait to examine the huge tablets. He leaned close to Winter and said, "It's true, then. What you said about the archive in Khandar."

"You thought I was making it up?"

"I just . . ." He shook his head. "The idea that it could be *found*, after so long, seemed incredible."

They pushed through the curtains at the end of the hall and into a large space, softly lit by ranks of candles. Like the chambers of the Eldest, it was simply furnished, with a circle of cushions on the stone floor the only conces-sion to comfort. They were all empty, save one where Feor sat, looking ex-pectant.

She'd grown, Winter thought, in the time since they'd last met. Not just physically, though a better diet had gone a long way toward filling out the half-starved girl Winter remembered. There was a confidence in her that hadn't been there before, a squareness to her shoulders and a steadiness to her gaze. Her dark hair was long and carefully plaited, and the gray cast to her skin marked her as Khandarai.

"Winter." She smiled tentatively and spoke in Khandarai. "Do you still remember my language?"

"Not . . . as well as I should," Winter answered haltingly. Both Alex and Abraham looked on, uncomprehending, and Feor laughed.

"Fortunately," she said, her Vordanai accented but smooth, "I have learned quite a bit of yours. Come, sit. I imagine we have a great deal to discuss."

"Quite a lot, yes," Winter said, relieved that Feor didn't seem to be angry with her. "This is Alex and Abraham, who accompanied me from the Mountain. That's a hidden enclave in the north—the Mages—" She took a deep breath. "I suppose I should start at the beginning."

Feor held up a hand. "Fortunately, we don't need to go back that far." She beckoned to another curtained doorway. "Come in, Jaffa."

The curtain twitched aside, and the Steel Ghost entered, candles gleaming softly on the brushed metal of his mask. Abraham let out a quick breath, as though he'd been waiting for this. Alex raised an eyebrow.

"Jaffa?" Winter said.

"Jaffa-dan-Iln was my name," the Ghost said. "Before I put on the mask."

"He came to me several weeks ago," Feor said. "Most unexpectedly, I might add."

"I have apologized for any difficulty I caused," the Ghost said. "But I dared not show myself to anyone else. Only Raesinia knew of my existence, and she had not yet returned."

"Once we'd established that he wasn't one of the Penitent Damned," Feor said, "he explained a great deal to me. I am not sure I completely accept his version of ancient history"—she looked sidelong at the Ghost and smiled again—"but our present circumstances seem clear."

"What have you been doing in Vordan?" Winter said.

At Feor's urgent beckoning, they took their seats, pulling the cushions into a tight circle. When he was settled, the Ghost said, "I came to warn Raesinia about the Beast, only to find that she was gone. It was urgent that the *naathem* in the city be alert for any of the Beast's bodies that might try to slip in, so I went to Feor. She and her students have been helping me keep watch."

"And you haven't told Raesinia you're here?"

"It seemed easier to deal with you," the Ghost said. "I am very pleased to see your journey was successful."

"It certainly wasn't easy," Alex said. "It must be nice being a sandstorm."

"It has its advantages," the Ghost said.

"The Beast pursued us," Winter said. "All the way to the Bataria. After that, it gave up and shifted its attention south. Or so Ennika tells us." At Feor's puzzled expression, Winter explained, briefly, what Sothe had told her about the Penitent Damned and her connection to the Beast.

"Remarkable," the Ghost said. "So it is possible for a mind to maintain its independence even after it is taken by the Beast."

"Or so it wants us to think," Abraham said. "I do not believe Ennika is lying to us, but the messages passed to her could be part of some manipulation."

"I just can't see the advantage for the Beast," Winter said. "If it is trying to lead me into a trap, it's taking a very long road to get there."

"And if it wanted to ambush you, it would have needed to suggest a particular time and place," Alex said. "Ennika hasn't given us anything like that."

"If we accept that this information is genuine," the Ghost said, "then Winter is right. The coming battle is our opportunity—maybe our only opportunity—to get her to the Beast's core, while it still believes she is in the north."

"That leaves us with two problems," Winter said. "First we have to find the core. Then we have to get me there, ideally with enough of a force that we can handle a few guards. The Beast may have to deploy its army to fight, but it will hardly be completely unprotected."

"You can leave the first task to me," the Ghost said. "I can travel fast and unseen. I should be able to locate our target."

"You can't take anyone with you, though?" When the Ghost shook his masked head, Winter sighed. "The core could be miles behind the lines. We could try to punch through with a cavalry force, but then it would know we were coming."

Winter looked at Feor. The young priestess went pale, and swallowed.

"You want to use my *naath*," Feor said quietly. "What your priests call the Caryatid."

"Bobby saved me when the Beast ambushed us at Elysium," Winter said. "She had wings, and she *flew*. It was . . ." Her throat went tight, and she forced herself to stay calm. "She was beautiful."

"Before that happened," Feor said, "she burned, didn't she?"

Winter nodded, not trusting her voice for a moment. Feor cast her eyes down.

"I have learned . . . a great deal since we left Khandar," she said. "There are more than just the *naath* in the archive. Mother never told me the true purpose of my power, only the barest outlines of what it could do."

"She hoarded knowledge like precious stones," the Ghost said. "A legacy of so many years in the shadows, perhaps."

"The *naath* I bear was once used to create temple guardians, in times of direst emergency," Feor went on. "A worthy woman would submit to the ritual, as you saw me do for Bobby. And then . . . before battle, she would step into the flames and emerge transformed. Endowed with great power, her mortal body purified."

"And then?" Winter said quietly.

"Such power cannot last. The life that flares so bright soon burns out." Feor's eyes were fixed on the floor. "I swear I did not know when you brought Bobby to me. I . . ."

"It's all right," Winter said gently. "She would have died if not for you. You gave her another year." She blinked away tears. "That has to be worth something."

"I've never heard of a demon that bestows power on others instead of the host," Abraham said. "But if they don't live long, it makes sense. The demon wouldn't want its own host to die." He shifted as Alex elbowed him in the ribs. "Apologies. I . . ."

Feor waved it away, looking up. "I felt it, when Bobby's power rose and died away. I wondered if it meant you had died with her."

"She saved me," Winter repeated. "And now that she's . . . gone, you can use the ritual again, can't you?"

"I . . . can." Feor bit her lip. "But as I said, if done properly, it means death."

"Can you make *me* into one of these guardians?" Winter's heart skipped a beat as she voiced the question, but she had to ask.

"No. *Naath* are jealous things. They will not coexist in the same body."

Winter let out a breath. "Okay. So we need someone who doesn't have her own demon."

"Is there not another way?" Feor said, looking around the circle. "I . . . do not wish to condemn another to death."

Winter closed her eyes for a moment. *Sometimes,* she thought, *it would be nice to be able to pray and mean it.*

"In a few days," she said, "thirty thousand men and women are going out to fight. Whatever happens, however clever Marcus' strategy is and however brave we are, people are going to die, by the thousand. Every time I give the order to take a hill or charge a battery, I know that some of those soldiers are not coming back. I'm not going to pretend it's an easy thing. But if we have a weapon that might save some of them and we have to sacrifice one life to use it, then I don't see how we can let it lie."

"You cannot order them," Feor said. "Not for this. I will not do it."

"Of course. It will be a volunteer," Winter agreed.

"Will you be able to find someone?" Alex said. "We're talking about a suicide mission."

Winter's mind went back to Murnsk, her desperate pursuit of the Penitent Damned and the way the Girls' Own soldiers had fought to be allowed to come along. She shook her head. "We'll manage."

The others left, Alex and Abraham back to the Second Division camp and the Ghost to his self-appointed patrol of the city. Winter remained, sitting across from Feor, while students brought them cups of hot coffee with lowered eyes. Winter told her story, for what felt like the tenth time, and Feor told her what had happened after the army had left for the Murnskai border.

"At first Janus asked for *naathem* to fight his enemies," she said. Her face was haunted. "My first student, Auriana, read her *naath*, but she was not ready. It . . . damaged her, her face and her limbs. She told me she was happy with the trade, but I knew I could not ask another to take that risk."

"At the Mountain, they test the children to see if they're strong enough to bear the demons they need." She remembered her visit to one such family, where a boy had taken on the burden his older brother had first attempted. "It doesn't always work."

Feor nodded. "I know the Priests of the Black simply sacrifice captives until they find one whose soul can bear the strain. Mother was . . . misled about many things, but she was not wrong about their cruelty."

"What happened to Auriana?" Winter said.

"She died," Feor said. "When the Penitent Damned took the Thousand Names, during Maurisk's coup. She held them long enough for the rest of us to escape."

"I'm sorry." Winter sipped her coffee, which was thick and strong, in the Khandarai style. Just the smell of it conjured up memories. "You're still teaching the others?"

"Yes. Some of them may be strong enough to bear a *naath*, with proper preparation. But it will take time. I fear we cannot offer you much assistance."

"What you're doing for us is enough," Winter said. "I know it can't be easy for you."

"It is not," Feor said. "But you are right, I think. The Beast is coming, and our lives are as dust. What I can do, I will."

"Mistress?" The voice from outside the curtained door was hesitant. "It's the woman who arrived with your guest. She demands to speak with you both."

"Of course," Feor said. "Bring her here."

A young man escorted Ennika through the curtain, guiding the blind girl until she reached one of the cushions beside Feor. She sat, and the student bowed and withdrew.

"Welcome," Feor said. "My name is Feor. I understand you've come a long way."

"I was hoping that you'd care for her here," Winter said. "I thought it might help her to be around people who understood her condition."

"Certainly. She's welcome to stay with us as long as she likes."

"We made a bargain," Ennika said, turning her covered eyes on Winter. "I hope you haven't forgotten."

"I haven't forgotten." *Though I might have wanted to.*

"A bargain?" Feor said.

Winter sighed. "Ennika wants to be free of her demon. She's asked me to use Infernivore to devour it. But when I took the demon from Jen Alhundt, she never recovered, and she died not long after. My other . . . experiences with it have been similar. I'd hoped that you might have learned something from the archive."

Feor frowned. "There is almost nothing on Infernivore in the archive. I searched, when I started to understand the tablets, but it has been used only a few times. Most who attempted it died at once."

"I am willing to take the risk," Ennika said. "I cannot live like this, with this hole in my mind where my sister should be. If I die, then at least we will be together in hell."

Feor looked a little alarmed at Ennika's casual reference to her own damnation. Her expression turned thoughtful.

"It is . . . possible that the experience would be less traumatic for a willing subject," she said. "The soul grips the demon as much as the demon grips the soul. If the soul were prepared to release the demon, perhaps the damage would not be so great."

"That's a slim chance to hang your life on," Winter said to Ennika. "You really want to go through with this?"

"Yes." The blind girl straightened. "I am ready."

"Wait," Winter said. "You mean *now?*"

Ennika nodded. "Janus has said he will no longer be able to communicate. I am not . . . of use, anymore." Her lip curved in a faint smile. "And if you intend to confront the Beast, then you will forgive me if I want to get our bargain fulfilled in advance."

That's fair enough. Winter looked down at her hands. "I suppose there's no reason to wait. Feor . . ."

"Come," Feor said, standing. "It's possible you will be unconscious for some time, Ennika. We should get you in a bed first."

The Khandarai priestess helped Ennika to her feet and led her out another doorway, through a basement passage. Winter followed, and found herself in a row of small cells, windowless and dry. Each was equipped with a bed, a chair, and little else, reminding Winter of a monastery. Feor guided Ennika to one of these cells and helped her to the bed, where she stretched herself out.

"You're sure there's no reason to wait?" Winter said quietly. "Nothing more you can discover in the archive?"

Feor shook her head. "We are in uncharted territory, I'm afraid. Try to be as . . . gentle as you can."

"I don't know how much control I have. But I'll do my best." Winter knelt, awkwardly, beside Ennika. "This will probably hurt. I'm sorry."

"I am accustomed to pain." Ennika held out her hand, and Winter grasped it. "Thank you for keeping your promise."

Winter squeezed the girl's fingers. She closed her eyes, letting herself feel the contact between them, the closeness of Ennika's demon. As ever, the proximity drove Infernivore to a frenzy, a lashing at the back of Winter's mind. She was so accustomed to holding Infernivore back, keeping it from leaping into Alex or Abraham at a moment's casual contact, that it took her a few seconds to lower her guard and set it free.

The demon didn't hesitate for an instant. As soon as Winter removed her mental leash, it surged across the boundary between Winter's soul and Ennika's, a torrent of energy passing through their linked hands. Winter could sense Ennika's demon, a small, frail thing in comparison to the bulk of Infernivore. Soon the predator was wrapped around it, like a python smothering its prey. Infernivore's energy spread through the other demon, changing it, incorporating it into its own substance.

In a bare instant, Ennika's demon was gone, and Infernivore retreated from her body and back into Winter's with the force of a tidal wave. Distantly, Winter heard Ennika scream, and her hand tightened on Winter's hard enough that her fingernails drew blood. She thrashed for a moment, back arching, and then collapsed on the bed.

Winter opened her eyes. Ennika was pale, her face beaded with sweat. When Winter let go of her hand, it flopped limply to her side. But she was still breathing, quick and shallow.

"That was . . . difficult to watch," Feor said. She was hugging herself. "For all that it may be our savior, Winter, your *naath* is . . . unpleasant."

"I believe it." Winter looked down at her bleeding hand. "Do you think she'll be all right?"

"I have no idea." Feor looked down at Ennika and shook her head. "My students and I will care for her body as best we can, but the damage is in her mind and soul."

Winter nodded grimly. *I doubt even Abraham can do much about that.* She got to her feet, feeling weary. "Let me know if she improves, or wakes up."

"I will." Feor paused. "And . . . the other matter?"

"I'll send you a volunteer," Winter said.

"I will be ready." Feor fixed her with a firm gaze. "Do not lie to them, Winter. They must know that there is no coming back from this."

Winter nodded.

The Grenadier Guard outside Cyte's quarters told Winter that Cyte was with Marcus, working on battle plans. Winter felt odd being there alone, like an uninvited guest in someone else's house, but as far as she knew no one had assigned her quarters of her own. *Not that we'll be here for long.* Talk was that Marcus wanted the army on the move in the next few days, to begin preparing the position he had selected to make a stand.

There wasn't much of Cyte's in the room, in truth, just the same few pieces of kit that she'd have with her in the field. The rest was palace furniture, solid and expensive, that looked badly out of place beside Cyte's battered writing desk and pack. Winter's own pack sat beside it, representing the sum total of her worldly possessions—a few scraps of clothing, her knives, cooking gear, and other odds and ends. She wondered what had happened to the rest of her things, everything that had been in her tent when she'd set out to the north. *Did they leave them behind in the retreat? Or are they packed away in some warehouse, lost in the army bureaucracy?* There hadn't been anything she particularly cared about, apart from a few souvenirs and her hand-tailored uniforms. *And I suppose I won't be needing those anymore, will I?*

It felt too early in the evening to go to sleep, but Winter didn't feel awake enough to do anything else. She sat at the big table and tried to read a few reports from Cyte's piles, but she could feel her mind wandering before she managed more than a couple of sentences. The second time her eyelids slipped closed, she leaned back in the chair with an exasperated sigh.

"Winter," said Sothe. "I need to speak with you."

Winter turned, startled but not really surprised to find Sothe in the room. The assassin stood by the window in her customary black.

"There's nothing to stop you from using the door, you know," Winter said.

"I prefer to remain unobserved," Sothe said. Then, with a slight smile, she added, "And it is important to hone one's skills whenever the opportunity presents itself."

"Your dedication is admirable." Winter gestured to the seat opposite her. "I'd offer you a drink, but these are Cyte's rooms, and I have no idea where to find anything."

"Thank you, but there's no need." Sothe walked to the table but remained standing, her lithe body preternaturally still. "You spoke to Marcus."

It wasn't a question. "I did. I don't think he took it well."

"Give him time. It's quite a shock we've given him."

"I suppose." Winter looked down at the table, which was covered with reports. The letters were blurred into incomprehensibility. "It just feels strange. It matters so much to him, and I . . . I don't even know what it *means* to be someone's sister."

"I am confident you will come to an understanding."

"Assuming any of us survive the next few days, you mean?"

"Yes. And that is why I have come." Sothe shifted, one hand on her hip. "You are looking for a host for the Caryatid, Feor's power, to help you find and destroy the Beast. I volunteer."

Winter stared at her. Of the hundred questions she had, she blurted out the first that came to mind. "How can you *know* that?"

"Deduction, for the most part. I have heard you tell your story of what happened in Elysium, and I knew of Bobby's unique condition. When you went to see Feor . . ." She shrugged. "Information is my stock-in-trade, after all."

"Then you know what we're asking," Winter said.

"You need someone to undergo the same ritual Bobby did."

"And there's no coming back. Bobby . . ." Winter hesitated. "When Bobby was transformed, she saved my life. By the time I woke up, she was . . . gone."

"I suspected as much," Sothe said, her face impassive. "I understand the risks."

"It's not a risk," Winter said. "It's a certainty."

"The certainties, then."

There was a pause. Sothe shifted slightly.

"Why?" Winter said.

"Because I am the logical choice," Sothe said. "I am highly skilled in combat, I do not have my own demon, and I hope that my loyalty is beyond question."

"What about Raesinia? Have you told her?" Winter watched Sothe's face and saw the tiniest flicker. "You haven't, have you?"

"She wouldn't understand," Sothe said. "She believes she cannot do without me."

"I've seen what you can do," Winter said. "Are you sure she's wrong?"

"*Yes.*"

The word was a hiss. Sothe retreated a step, her face shadowed.

"I'm sorry," Sothe said, into the silence that followed. "But you don't understand, either. Not really. You don't know what I've done."

"I've done things I regret," Winter said.

"But at the time, you believed they were necessary. Even if you turned out to be mistaken." Sothe shook her head. "I have no such defense."

Winter regarded the assassin curiously. "I didn't think you had pangs of conscience."

"I spent years rooting them out. When I left the Concordat and joined Raesinia, I . . . worried. She looked up to me. I didn't want her to become . . . like I was."

"She's not," Winter said. It was strange, hearing Sothe talk like this. She could feel the emotion in the words, trapped behind her flat affect and iron composure. "You know she's not."

"I know. Instead I have become more like her. Better. But it leaves me . . . torn. For a time I thought I could make amends."

"Like by finding me for Marcus?"

Sothe nodded. "But I was wrong. There are no amends, no cleaning of the slate. Only doing the most you can do, beginning now. And this is something I can do. If we win, Raesinia will not need me at her side any longer. And if we lose . . ." Another slight smile. "Then it won't matter."

"It doesn't have to be you," Winter said after another silence. "We could find—"

"Who? Some poor woman from the Girls' Own, who'd do it out of devotion to her general?"

Winter winced. "I didn't mean—"

"Someone who doesn't believe in magic?" Sothe went on inexorably. "Someone who might panic at the very idea of the Beast, let alone transforming herself into—"

"All right," Winter said. "I get it."

"Good." Sothe straightened. "I apologize again, for my . . . outburst."

"I suppose I never thought about things from your perspective," Winter said, scratching the back of her neck.

"I have never required sympathy," Sothe said. "Nor do I need it now." She paused. "But I do request one favor."

"Favor?"

"Do not tell Marcus."

"Why not?"

Sothe sighed. "Because he will convince himself my decision revolves around him and the debt between us. He will think he should have . . . *protected* me." She pronounced the word with distaste. "He is a good man, and he will do well by Raesinia's side. But some habits of mind are hard to break."

"I understand," Winter said.

"He is not angry with you, you know. Just working things out in his own mind. I meant what I said about giving him time."

"I know." Winter looked down at the papers. "To be perfectly honest, I'm still working it out myself."

When she looked up again, the slim shape of the assassin was gone.

As Marcus' assistant, Cyte had quarters in the palace proper, but the majority of the soldiers were camped a few minutes' ride to the north, where some of Ohnlei's lawns had been converted into a mustering ground during the revolution. Neat lines of weather-worn blue tents alternated with clear avenues, and in between regiments larger spaces had been left for drills and assembly. Muskets were stacked beside each tent, and jackets, shirts, and trousers dried in the breeze as the soldiers took the rare opportunity to launder their uniforms. At the intersections, big campfires blazed, heating the copper pots used to make the ubiquitous army soup. It was late afternoon, the golden light of the setting sun gleaming off buckles and bayonets. The soldiers sat in front of their tents, waiting for dinner, playing dice or cards or just telling tall tales in the oldest traditions of the army.

It was all so *familiar* that it brought an unexpected lump to Winter's throat. *This* was home, if anything was. A strange, transient kind of place, constructed every day and torn down every morning, lugged across the landscape in wagons and backpacks.

The sentries were the first to recognize her, snapping stiff salutes at the sight of her uniform, then drawing themselves up even further as they saw her face. She left her borrowed horse with a corporal, a young woman who looked like she was about to burst with pride. As Winter walked down the aisles of tents, she could almost feel the rumors running ahead of her, spreading with the lightning speed of gossip. Women in blue uniforms soon lined her path, coming to attention as she came abreast of them, a wave of salutes that seemed to go on forever.

The lump in Winter's throat got thicker. She felt like she should stop, say something, acknowledge the pride and relief she felt from every quarter. *But what the hell can I say to them?* She didn't trust her voice, in any event, so she merely nodded, and from the looks on the faces of the rankers, that seemed to be enough. After she passed, she could hear the storm of quiet chatter that followed in her wake.

The command tent was just where she remembered it, as though the camp had remained still while the world moved underneath it. Two guards came to stiff attention, and Winter stepped between them and scratched at the flap. At the barked acknowledgment, she ducked inside.

Abby sat at the map table, scowling at a sprawl of papers. At the sight of Winter she came to her feet, her salute precise. Winter waved it away.

"Started hearing rumors you were back," Abby said. She looked older than when Winter had last seen her, her freckled face pale and drawn. "It's good to see you, sir."

"You, too," Winter said. "I'm sorry it took me so long."

They looked at each other for a long moment. Winter was always a little uncertain around Abby. The girl had been Jane's lover after Winter had run off to Khandar, and though Jane had returned to Winter's bed when she'd come back, there had always been tension between them. Then Jane had betrayed them both, and neither Winter nor Abby had taken it well.

"Will you be assuming command?" Abby said. "I've been running the Second Division since Marcus took overall command, but I'm sure the soldiers would be happy to have you back." She gestured at the papers. "God knows I'd be happy to have someone to push this off on to."

"No," Winter said. "That's what I came to talk to you about."

"I should have known I wouldn't get off that easily." Abby gestured at the chair across from her. "Sit, if you like."

Winter cleared a stained tin plate out of the way and sat down. "There's an . . . assignment," she said carefully. "Something I need to do. It's important."

"Yours always are, sir," Abby said.

"I won't be back until after the battle," Winter said. "Assuming I make it back at all, of course. And—"

Abby sat back in her chair. "You've been talking with Marcus."

"I've been talking with Cyte," Winter said. "She's worried about you."

"And you're wondering whether you can trust me with the Second."

Winter closed her eyes for a moment. "When I left the division, in Murnsk, I would have trusted you in a heartbeat. I need to know if anything has changed."

"A lot of good men and women are dead," Abby said. "And Parker Erdine, too, I suppose. Does that count as a change?"

"You know what I mean."

Abby's freckled face colored slightly. "What do you want me to say? That it hasn't affected me? You know that's not true. We fought our way back from Murnsk, and then after Alves . . ." She shook her head. "Sometimes it feels like not going mad takes everything I have."

"I know," Winter said. "Believe me, I understand."

"When Parker died . . ." Abby swallowed. "Stupid, pretty boy. He didn't have any illusions about what we had. It was . . . just comfort. I wanted to feel something that wasn't fear or anger, that's all. And I couldn't even have that."

Winter's throat was thick. "I'm sorry," she said. "I should have been there."

"It's not your fault. It's nobody's fault but mine." Abby looked down at her hands. "I just started thinking . . . what am I even *doing* here? I joined up with Jane because . . . because I loved her, or thought I did. And when I realized she'd turned into someone I couldn't love anymore, I stayed because I felt like I had to keep her girls safe. That was all she ever wanted, really. She just lost sight of it sometimes."

"You've done a good job," Winter said.

"Have I?" Abby looked up. "How many of the old Leatherbacks are left? How many arms and legs are rotting away somewhere? Am I doing them a favor by leading them into the fight, or am I just lying to them to get them to make one more charge?" Her lips tightened. "I told Marcus we wanted to fight, you know. I was afraid he'd stick us off to the rear somewhere. The girls wanted me to do it, but if I hadn't said anything, some of the ones we buried might still be alive."

"And someone else would be dead," Winter said gently. "That's why they joined up. To take danger on themselves and away from others." She remembered Cyte's angry retort and found herself smiling. "Give them some credit, Abby."

Abby took a deep breath and blew it out in a rush. She nodded.

"I'm sorry," she said. "Cyte's right. I've been . . ."

"It's all right." Winter paused. "If you want, I'll find someone else to take command. There's no shame in it. You've given more than anyone could ask for."

"Don't even think about it," Abby said. "I've gotten the Girls' Own this far. I'm not going to abandon them now."

That felt more like the Abby who Winter remembered. She smiled.

"This really is the last time," Winter said. "I can't explain everything, so don't ask me. But if we win this time, the war will finally be over."

"There's never a last time," Abby said. "But at least we'll get a chance to rest."

CHAPTER TWENTY-NINE

MARCUS

Once again, the Army of the Republic was on the march.

The halt at the palace had given them a chance to rest and resupply, and consequently their appearance was much improved from the worn, bedraggled soldiers that had staggered down the Pale one step ahead of Janus' pursuing legions. Uniforms had been cleaned and stitched, cannon polished, horses groomed, and beards shaved. There were still the little touches that spoke of troops who'd been in combat—extra weapons tucked away, coats patched and repatched; here and there a shako, bicorn, or other souvenir taken from a luckless enemy on some distant battlefield.

Winter rode with the Second Division, at the head of the Girls' Own. She'd objected, since she wasn't going to be in command, but Marcus had insisted. Seeing her back at the head of her troops did wonders for morale, and it was visible in the bearing of the men and women who followed her, though Marcus did see a few curious glances at her new uniform. *They'll figure it out eventually.* Abby and Cyte both rode beside her.

The First Division, Fitz' men, were already on the road, forming the vanguard for the day's march. Light cavalry from Give-Em-Hell's command scouted the route ahead, while his cuirassiers brought up the rear. Vordan City had been scoured for cavalry remounts, every military stable emptied and civilian animals pressed into service. A joke said that the city cabbies were now running in the traces of their own carriages rather than give up fares; Marcus hadn't been back to the city to see if it was true. From the surrounding farms, more animals had been gathered, heavy draft and cart horses that were to pull the guns and caissons. Raesinia had promoted Archer to colonel and given him command of the artillery reserve, though the guns they'd pulled out of the arsenals and garrisons didn't come close to making up for those they'd lost at Alves.

In the center of the column, between the artillery and the cuirassiers, came the volunteers. They marched in a straggling mob rather than a formation, and they had nothing like a uniform. But there were thousands of them, men and women both. The first of them had started turning up at the gates of Ohnlei as soon as the army had returned, and as rumor got out about Janus' approach their numbers had grown greater and greater. Marcus was dubious of their combat value—for one thing, there weren't enough muskets to go around—but his plan called for a great deal of digging, and he'd told Raesinia he wasn't going to turn away anyone who could wield a shovel.

More civilians turned out to line the road as the long column wound away from Ohnlei. A few cheered, but most seemed content to watch, as though they wanted to be able to say they'd borne witness, one way or the other. It was nearly the same route the army had taken last time. *Some of us have marched a hell of a long way to end up back where we started.* This time, of course, they didn't have nearly as far to go. The enemy was coming to them.

As usual, Marcus spent the majority of his time riding up and down the column, straightening out snarls. As marches went, this one was easygoing, with the weather fair but cold and the road solid, well-packed earth. The new Third Division, formed from fresh recruits and the scrapings of the depots, caused the most trouble. The recruits had spent a few weeks parading around with their new muskets and uniforms, but hadn't yet been through a serious march, while the garrison troops had mostly never served together and were constantly getting in one another's way. Marcus had sorted out a half dozen arguments about seniority between prickly colonels. He'd promoted David Sevran, one of Winter's colonels, to command the new formation, and Marcus was determined to give him all the support he could manage.

They halted outside the village of Bellaia, a picturesque little place right out of a romantic landscape painting. A small cluster of houses huddled around a stone church, its double-circle spire gleaming as the sun set. The villagers made no appearance, and no wonder. Even reduced as it was, the army camp spread over a vast area, covering the fields outside of town like a horde of locusts. *At least the harvest will be in already.*

There'd be another half day's march tomorrow, to the spot Marcus had identified on the map. It had no official name, but the locals apparently called it Bear Ridge, a gradual rise in the ground to a rocky, wooded height that loomed in the distance. It wasn't as large or as steep as Marcus might have liked, but he'd judged it the best of his limited options.

The command tent was already assembled by the time he rode up, and light spilled out through the flap. Marcus handed the reins of his horse to the guard and ducked inside, finding himself the last to arrive.

Raesinia was there, of course. There had been no question of telling her she couldn't join the battle, not this time. She'd traded her somber dresses for riding leathers, without any ornamentation or jewels. Marcus guessed that most of the soldiers she passed had no idea they were within spitting distance of their monarch.

There was Fitz, imperturbable as always, and Winter, still looking less than comfortable in her new uniform, with Cyte at her side. The newly minted General Sevran looked more natural in his, the stars on his shoulders polished to a fine sheen. The quiet, competent Colonel Archer sat beside Give-Em-Hell, whose usual expansive mood had been checked by the presence of his queen.

As Marcus came in, there was a round of salutes from everyone but Raesinia. He nodded to the officers, bowed to the queen, and took his seat at the head of the table. A map was already laid out, annotated in pencil with the reports of the scouts who'd pushed ahead of the column. It showed Bear Ridge, roughly triangular in shape, with the longest side facing southwest. It rose from the plain between the rivers, only a few miles from the Marak to the west, considerably farther from the Vor in the other direction. The main road swung east to avoid it.

"Well," Marcus said, looking down at it. "Here we are."

Silent nods around the table.

"You all know what we're up against," Marcus said. "We'll do the best we can, but I'm not going to pretend these aren't long odds. When Janus comes against us, if we can hold until nightfall I'll consider that a victory."

"And after that?" Fitz said.

"There's a plan," Raesinia said. "You'll have to trust us on that."

Those who weren't in on Winter's part of the battle—Fitz, Sevran, and Archer—looked less than satisfied. Give-Em-Hell seemed oblivious.

"I must say," he ventured, "it doesn't seem very promising from the point of view of a cavalry charge."

"You'll get your chance," Marcus promised. "I have written orders for all of you, but let me give you the short version."

He picked up the leather bag containing the wooden counters, fumbled with the drawstring for a bit, then dumped them on the table. He picked out a few blue blocks and arranged them at the tip of Bear Ridge. One line stretched left, another right, so that the triangular shape of the ridge was extended into a V shape with the tip pointing northeast. The red markers he massed in that direction, where the main road came closest to the hill.

"Two refused flanks," Fitz said, raising an eyebrow. "Interesting."

"Like I said, it's the best I can come up with." He tapped the tip of the V. "This is the Second Division. We'll do most of our digging here, because that's where we'll catch the most hell. It'll be easiest for the enemy to focus their attack there, so we want them running uphill and into our breastworks. The volunteers will be there as well, and most of the artillery.

"This"—he tapped the right wing—"is the First Division. If Janus gets tired of trying to punch through the center, this is the way he'll probably swing. There's more room. The other wing is the Third, which will hopefully have the easiest time of it. But I'm going to take a few battalions from both of you and keep them in reserve here"—he tapped a point between the wings, inside the V—"along with the cavalry.

"The idea is that it's faster for us to move troops around inside the formation than it is for Janus to shift his reserves around the outside. Wherever he attacks, we can get there with the reserve quickly, and hopefully between that and our fortifications we'll be able to negate his numbers. Henry, your light cavalry will take the extreme right, down to the road, and make sure he doesn't try to slip anything behind us. The river should keep that from happening on the left."

"And if he refuses to engage?" Sevran said.

"If he tries to just move past, he's giving us a perfect shot at his flank and rear. If he sits tight, then we see who can wait the other out." Marcus shook his head. "But he'll attack. You saw the way he was in the Pale valley."

"Why station the volunteers at the point?" Fitz said. "That puts the least reliable troops in the most difficult position."

"It's also the position they're most likely to be able to hold," Marcus said. "Without training, they're not going to be much good in the open field, so I want them dug in. If they won't fight there, they won't fight anywhere." He looked around the table. "Any other questions?"

There were, of course. The queen excused herself early, but the officers stayed for another couple of hours, going over the details. By the time they were finished, the map was covered in fresh annotations, and Marcus had had to light several lanterns. One by one they departed, to return to their troops and pass along Marcus' orders. The plan would be hashed out around thousands of campfires, by everyone from officers down to rankers, and they would all doubtless form their own opinions. Marcus remembered second-guessing Janus with Adrecht, Val, and Mor, back in Khandar. *It's not so easy when you actually have to make the decision, is it?*

Winter was the last one remaining, studying the map intently. Marcus watched her for a moment, awkwardly, then cleared his throat. She looked up.

"Sorry," she said. "Just thinking about where the Beast might try to hide the core. Hopefully, it won't see us coming, or things could get very difficult."

"Ah." Marcus shook his head. "That's your department. I'm just here to handle the human side."

"I know."

She was so *serious*. It had seemed appropriate, for a general, but Ellie had always been wild and full of laughter. *She must still smile, sometimes.*

"You're . . . ah . . . getting along all right?" he said.

"I'm not getting enough sleep," Winter said. "But that's nothing new."

"I meant with respect to the other officers," Marcus said. "Since you . . . changed your uniform."

"Oh." Winter looked down at herself. "Most of them haven't mentioned it, to tell the truth. Some of them already knew, of course. And I wouldn't be surprised if some of the others suspected. I had gotten a bit . . . careless."

And only poor, stupid Marcus didn't catch on. He shook his head. *Enough. With the way you reacted, can you blame her?*

"I wanted to apologize," he said, drawing himself up. "For the way I behaved back at the palace."

"There's no need for that," Winter said. "I can't imagine how you must feel."

"Frankly, I'm a bit confused myself." Marcus scratched his beard. "But I was . . . reminded that I knew you as a soldier, and a good one, before . . . anything else." He took a deep breath and blew it out. "I hope it won't offend you if I continue to treat you like one."

"Of course not," Winter said.

She smiled, just slightly, and suddenly he could *see* Ellie in her face. The eyes were the same, the basic compassion he'd known from the little girl shining through the cynicism of the veteran soldier. He found himself momentarily unable to speak, and coughed to cover it.

"I ought to get back," Winter said, standing from the table. "Busy day tomorrow."

"Wait." Marcus fought to keep his tone level. "Winter. You *are* my sister."
Her face went guarded again. "I know."

"I . . . may not be entirely sure what that means. Not yet." He shook his
head. "But I would like the opportunity to find out. So . . ." He paused. "Be
careful, would you?"

That smile again, half sarcastic quirk of the lips and half good-natured grin.
"I'll do my best. I think I'd like that, too."

Bear Ridge was less impressive in person than on the map. Marcus hadn't been
expecting a craggy mountain, but the reality hardly deserved to be called a hill.
It was more like a patch of rough ground, sparsely wooded and overgrown with
bushes, that happened to rise slightly from the surrounding fields. Split-rail
fences divided up the land around it, more marker than obstacle. To the east,
the Marak was barely visible as a shimmering line, with the ground rising
sharply beyond it.

The cavalry had arrived at the ridge by midmorning, and the first of the
infantry trooped up in the early afternoon, advance parties dismantling the
fences in their path. The usual camp was laid out to the southwest of the ridge,
in what would become the rear if the enemy advanced from the expected direction. Instead of pitching their tents right away, however, officers told off
their companies to form work parties, and long lines of men slogged through
the rocks and undergrowth onto the hill. The sound of axes was soon everywhere, an irregular rhythm like rain on a slate roof.

By the time Marcus had sorted out the day's snags and made certain the
baggage train was going to the right place, the work was well along. He rode up
the hill on a track that the men had hacked through the thick bushes. At the top,
a ranker took his mount, and Marcus hiked on foot to the crook in the ridge
where the Girls' Own would be deployed.

The forest was thinning out quickly. There were stumps everywhere, and
stripped logs stacked beside the path, while the teams of axmen fanned out in
search of more prey. Marcus walked past the crest of the hill and stopped, taken
aback for a moment. The slope *writhed*, as though it were alive, like a patch of
dirt crawling with ants.

Here and there were groups of soldiers in uniform, officers directing the
work. The rankers carried shovels instead of muskets, and they were shifting
dirt with impressive speed, digging out pits and piling the earth in front of them
to make a rampart. They were far outnumbered, however, by the civilians, men

and women from the city who'd come out with nothing more than work clothes and tools. They were everywhere, burrowing through the hillside like moles. As he watched, a half dozen stout women in dockworkers' leathers roped themselves to a tree stump and yanked it out of the earth, clods of dirt clinging to the trailing roots. The rocks uncovered by the diggers were piled between the trenches and carried by relays of youths to be stacked down at the base of the hill, where they could be an obstacle.

"Enthusiastic, aren't they?"

Marcus turned to find Abby approaching. Winter's return had apparently done her a world of good. At the very least, the dead look had gone from her eyes, though she still had the thick, dark circles underneath.

"It's impressive," Marcus said. "Will it be ready by tomorrow?"

"More or less," Abby said. "We could do more, with more time. But with all the volunteers helping, we should have a triple breastwork across the whole front, assuming we have enough timber. I'd like to dig a second line, but this ground is full of rocks." She kicked the soil, as though it had personally offended her.

"We'll need space for the gun pits in front, remember," Marcus said.

"Don't worry," Abby said. "The Preacher and his hellion were marking out distances when we got here. And the girls are very eager to have some cannon around."

The Preacher's here? Marcus hadn't realized that. *I suppose I've been a bit preoccupied.* "Good. Anything you need from me?"

"If you have a moment, it would help if some of the ax companies cut more trails up and over the crest, then down to the cutters' stations. We don't want to be tripping over bushes when we're pulling casualties out of here."

"I'll see to it." Marcus smiled. "It's good to see you feeling better, Colonel."

"Well." Abby blushed. "I apologize for making you fret, sir."

Marcus walked back up the hill, satisfied that section of the work was well in hand. It was the most critical part, the tip of the V, where the heaviest attack could be expected to land. More trenches lined the flanks of the hill, petering out where it sloped down onto the flats. Here the line would have to be more mobile, and they didn't have the spare manpower to extend a full breastwork over such a distance. Still, men were digging gun pits, sloped at the back and deep enough to provide some shelter for the cannoneers. When a cannon fired, its recoil would drive it up the ramp, and then gravity would help run it back into position.

Just past the bottom of the slope was the boundary of the first plowed field, marked by a fieldstone wall that was already mostly dismantled. Immediately beyond it was the cutter's station for the Second Division, several large tents with their sides tied open, operating tables already set up inside. Around them, lower tents were ready to shelter the wounded, at least until the beds filled up.

Hannah Courvier, the Second's head cutter, was standing outside one of the tents, talking to a thin young man Marcus didn't recognize. To his surprise, Raesinia was with them, accompanied by her two Girls' Own bodyguards. Marcus went over in time to catch Hannah's frown.

"Well." She looked at the young man, then back to Raesinia. "I don't hold with foreign mumbo jumbo, but you come highly recommended. Can you do anything with a broken foot? We've got a light cavalry lieutenant who fell off his horse."

"I will do my best." The young man glanced at Marcus and nodded. "General."

Marcus nodded back. Hannah stomped away, and the young man followed. Raesinia looked up at Marcus. "How are the preparations going?"

"Well, for the moment. If they come tomorrow, we'll be ready. It would be better if we had one more day . . ."

"But you don't think he'll give us that," Raesinia said.

"I wouldn't," Marcus said simply.

"Winter says she's ready as well," Raesinia said. "But she doesn't know how long it will take, once the battle starts."

"I'm assuming we're going to have to hold out until dark," Marcus said. "After that, we should be able to break contact and retreat down the road to Vordan City."

"It won't come to that," Raesinia said.

"No harm in being prepared. We don't know exactly what will happen, even if Winter wins."

Raesinia nodded, her eyes distant, as though she were lost in thought.

There were more lines to inspect, more preparations to confirm. Marcus caught up with the Preacher as the sun was setting. Torches lit the way for the final preparations of the artillery.

"Oh, Almighty Karis, preserve us." The artilleryman's rasping voice was audible most of the way down the hill. "Captain! What kind of cannon is this?"

The answer was impossible to hear, but the Preacher's response was clear.

"Correct! And it fires twelve-pound balls, is that right?" Another pause, and then, "So what, *exactly*, were you planning to do with these boxes of *eight-pound* balls? Hurl them at the enemy with your bare hands? Do you think you might find somewhere they could be put to *slightly* better use?"

Marcus grinned as an anxious captain dashed past him. A moment later, he found the Preacher standing beside a cannon, running his fingers through his long gray beard.

"General!" The Preacher saluted.

"Colonel," Marcus said with a nod. "I didn't know you were here."

"Well." The Preacher rolled his shoulders with a sigh. "I said I was getting too old for this, but young Viera disagrees, and she's a hard one to argue with." He grinned crookedly. "Besides, your lads came to the school and hauled all the cannon away. I didn't have anything left to teach with. Or any students, for that matter."

"Sorry. Most of the artillery was captured at Alves. We need all the metal we can get."

The Preacher waved a hand, then patted the barrel of the gun next to him. "This is what they're for, not moldering away on a drill field." His face went dark. "I only wish it were infidels we were pointing them at, and not Vordanai."

"I think everyone here agrees with that," Marcus said. "Let's hope this will be the end of it." He frowned. "Do you want a command? I'm sure—"

The Preacher shook his head. "Colonel Archer offered, but I thought I could serve best as an aide. Dispensing my expertise, as it were." He glared at the errant boxes stacked nearby. "Ammunition is going to be a problem. Some of these guns are older than I am, and we've got balls in a half dozen obsolete sizes to deal with. We can't be spendthrift."

"You'll manage," Marcus said. "At least we've got decent ground."

"No complaints there." The Preacher looked out at the darkening horizon, where the flat fields stretched into the distance. "But ground isn't everything. I'm leading a service tonight, if you have time."

"I'll try to make it," Marcus said, though he knew he wouldn't, and suspected the Preacher did, too. It was an old dance between the two of them.

"Colonel!" Viera stalked up from farther down the hill, her blue uniform spotted and stained with mud. "Are you lazing about?"

"He's obliging the general," Marcus said.

Viera paused at the sight of him, saluted, and then turned on the Preacher.

"They're making a mess of things down at the third battery. When I pointed it out, one of them *patted me on the head*." She sniffed. "I considered tossing a torch into their caisson to administer a sharp lesson, but I didn't want to waste the ammunition."

"That was probably wise. Karis teaches us mercy, even for the lowest." The Preacher sighed. "Give me a moment."

He turned back to Marcus, who grinned. "Try not to let her blow anything up."

"Oh, I've given up on that. I just try to keep her pointed in the general direction of the enemy." His smiled faded. "I meant to ask you, when I got the chance. Do you know what happened to General Solwen?"

Val. He and his men had been taken by surprise before the Battle of Alves. Marcus shook his head. "Captured, I hope. I can't imagine Janus ordering a slaughter, and Val at least wouldn't fight against us." *Unless he's out there right now with glowing red eyes . . .*

"I will say a prayer for him," the Preacher said. He saluted again. "With your permission?"

"Of course. Good luck."

He walked off after Viera, whose Hamveltai-accented Vordanai was just as loud as her mentor's. *They're well matched, I suppose.*

Raesinia found him after another hour, back down among the Girls' Own trenches, inspecting the newly raised breastworks. The piles of earth in front of the trenches had been topped with logs, producing a makeshift fortification that would block a musket shot, if not a cannonball. Many of the soldiers hadn't stopped there, but had hacked gaps in the logs wide enough to lay a musket in, like the arrow slits of an ancient castle.

"General," Raesinia said, as Marcus bent to examine another trench. He heard the soldiers around him go quiet. "It's late. Don't you think you should get some rest?"

There were a few quiet chuckles. *I suppose everyone in the army knows about us now.*

"As you command, Your Highness." He straightened and looked out across the plain.

Tomorrow. The darkness of the fields was broken by tiny points of light, like a swarm of fireflies. The campfires of Janus' army, stretching as far as the eye could see.

PART FIVE

INTERLUDE

JANUS

He had almost begun to feel normal again when the touch of the Beast dragged him back into the whirlwind.

The campaign, Janus thought, was proceeding satisfactorily. His men had cleared the Illifen passes, diligently reducing the fortresses and accepting the surrenders of their garrisons. The tactics were sound and, more important, it took *time*. Time was what was needed, for all the moving pieces to fall into place. For Marcus to reach Vordan City, and for Winter to join him.

He'd sent them a final message when the Beast's core arrived. From then on, he'd guessed it would be too dangerous to communicate. The Beast's primary focus was no longer distracted by the pursuit of Winter. It watched his every move.

For a while, though, it had been content to observe, letting him inhabit his own body. He issued orders, studied maps, and received reports. He still let his mind slip free from time to time, of course, to look through the perspectives of other red-eyes. It was such a joy to be able to see what his scouts saw and not have to wait for a few hastily scrawled words.

Marcus' approach was not unexpected, though his dispositions showed more imagination than Janus had thought him capable of. *Perhaps I didn't give him enough credit. Or maybe it's the pressure of command that reveals new depths.* Either way, his old subordinate had set him an interesting problem to solve, and he had just been sitting down to figure it out when he felt the cold winds of the Beast at the back of his metaphorical neck. In an instant he found himself lifted from the realm of the physical, back to the mindscape of the Beast, where the dark, brutal winds of the core whistled terrifyingly close.

"What are you doing?" the Beast said, its voice like thunder.

"Planning for tomorrow's battle." Janus was unable to gesture, but he invited the Beast to survey the silver threads that led to its many bodies. "We will crush the Vordanai army, I guarantee. Losses will be minimal."

"Losses are irrelevant. Armies are irrelevant. I want the city, and I want the Thousand Names." The Beast drew even closer. "You have grown comfortable indeed in your . . . role."

"I wish only to serve as you have directed," Janus said. "Since, of course, you could dash me to pieces at once."

"Perhaps I should," the Beast said. "I have never seen a mind maintain itself so long. It is . . . unnatural."

"But useful," Janus said. "It allowed the campaign to proceed while you were busy hunting for Winter."

"Yes. But that hunt is on hold for the moment. So what further use are you?"

"When the Names are taken, Winter will be the only remaining threat to you," Janus said. "But sooner or later, your existence will become widely known. Hamvelt, Borel, and the other nations will come against you. I imagine you will want me close at hand to repel them while you pursue your primary purpose."

The Beast made a thunderous sound that might have been a chuckle. "You are very skilled at arguing for your continued existence, little figment of my imagination."

"As I said, I wish only to serve."

"Very well. But for now"—winds snatched at Janus, lifting him away from the silver threads that connected to the real world—"you will observe. I do not need you to fight my battles."

"Of course," Janus murmured.

CHAPTER THIRTY

WINTER

"Well," Winter said, doing up the last buttons of her coat. "I suppose it's time to go and save the world."

Cyte, still in just her uniform shirt, gave a quick nod, arms folded over her chest. Her face was tight.

"Be careful," she said. "Please."

"I'm not the only one who's going to be in danger, you know."

Winter leaned close and kissed her. Cyte hesitated at first, and then her lips parted, returning the kiss with desperate urgency.

"I'm serious," Winter said when she pulled away. "I'm coming back, and so are you."

Cyte nodded, blinking rapidly. Winter wanted to kiss her again, put her arms around her, crawl back into bed and never come out. Instead she slipped out of the tent, shivering at the sudden chill. The sun was only a suggestion of brightness at the horizon, and fall was slipping away quickly.

She walked up the hill, following the paths cut by companies of enthusiastic axmen the night before. At the back of the ridge, behind the artillery, a small copse of trees had been left untouched. Their leaves were fading to brown, but they still effectively concealed the small clearing at their center from prying eyes, and Winter had picked the spot for a meeting place. She pushed through bushes until she broke into the open, and she waited for the others to arrive.

In the center of the clearing, they'd made a pyre, a bed of firewood built on a layer of small sticks and kindling. Winter looked down at it and shivered, but not from the cold.

Alex and Abraham arrived next. Alex had trimmed her hair and traded her ragged traveling clothes for a tighter, darker outfit of leather and silk. Winter raised an eyebrow at her, and she shrugged, blushing slightly.

"I had this stashed in the city from the last time we came through," she said, looking down at herself. "I thought it was an appropriate costume for the world's greatest thief. This seemed like as good a time to pull it out as any."

"Having a fancy costume seems to defeat the purpose of being a thief," Abraham said, pulling his gray robe away from the bushes with some effort. "You're not supposed to let people see you."

"You clearly don't understand what it takes to be the world's *greatest* thief," Alex said. "You have to show off a little to build your reputation."

She grinned, but her smile was shaky. Winter did her best to project reassurance.

Sothe didn't so much arrive as materialize out of the shadows. She shot Alex a pointed look, then nodded to Winter.

"You're ready?" Winter said.

"Feor assures me the ritual was successful." Sothe looked down at herself. "I didn't feel different, at first. But I tested a cut on my arm last night." She held out her wrist. In a line across her old, fading scars, there was a stripe of flesh that had turned the color of marble. "It is . . . a strange sensation."

Winter blinked back a moment's tears, remembering Bobby coming to her when she'd first noticed the change Feor's magic was working. *How long could she have lived, if she hadn't followed me? Another year? Longer?* They'd never know now.

"If you'd like," Abraham said quietly, "I can send you into a deep sleep. I thought that might make the prospect . . . easier. Only with your permission, of course."

Sothe gave a small smile. "I consider myself as capable of bearing pain as anyone, but I must admit the prospect of being burned alive was unappealing. I think your way sounds better."

"Wait," Winter said. "What am I supposed to tell Raesinia? Assuming . . . things work out."

"She knows I intend to go with you," Sothe said. "Just not the details. Tell her I gave my life to stop the Beast."

The assassin nodded again politely. She dropped a small pack at Winter's feet, then lowered herself onto the pyre, taking care not to disturb the logs. Winter watched with a quiet awe at her self-control. *She's not even trembling.* When she was comfortable, Abraham stepped forward and put a hand on her shoulder.

"I don't blame you," Winter said abruptly. "For . . . what you did. And I think . . . maybe you *can* balance the scales."

Sothe only smiled. A moment later her eyes closed and her breaths became slow and deep.

Abraham stood up. "I should get back to the cutter's station," he said, looking from Alex to Winter. "If you need my help, you'll know where to find me."

"Thanks," Alex said. "Don't forget to keep your own head down."

He nodded gravely and left the clearing. Alex looked down at Sothe nervously, then raised her eyebrows at Winter. "So, now we just . . . light her on fire?"

"Not yet." The Steel Ghost's voice rang from nowhere. For a few seconds the air was full of flying sand, and then the robed, masked figure stood beside the pyre, looking down at Sothe. "This is a brave woman," he murmured.

"You have no idea," Winter said.

"I will start looking for the core," he said, straightening up. "Once I find it and the battle has begun, I will return here. The transformation will not take long."

"Good luck," Winter said. *We're all going to need it.*

The Ghost vanished into a tower of swirling sand, which rose out of the clearing in a rush of wind. Alex brushed a few errant grains out of her hair and sighed.

"I guess we wait here," she said.

"There's a lot of that in battles," Winter said.

"Do you get used to it?"

She reflected for a moment. "No. It's always the worst part."

Alex barked a laugh, then paused. "Can I ask you something?"

"Of course."

"The 'core' we keep talking about. The Beast's first body. It's Jane, right? Your old . . . friend?"

Winter nodded. "Ionkovo kidnapped her and took her to Elysium. The Priests of the Black forced her to read the name of the Beast."

"Are you sure you can do this?" Alex gestured at the pyre. "She's still . . . alive. Sort of. If we get there, you're not going to hesitate?"

There was a long silence. The sun, just emerging over the horizon, threw the shadows of the trees across the clearing.

"I loved Jane," Winter said. "But she . . . changed. She tried to kill me."

Winter smiled ruefully. "I don't pretend it's going to be easy. But it's not going to stop me."

Jane's face rose in her mind for a moment. Her mischievous grin, her flashing green eyes. *Take the knife . . .*

I will, Winter told herself firmly. *For Cyte, and Raesinia, and Marcus, and everyone else. This is what I want.*

Jane only laughed at her. In the depths of her soul, Infernivore stirred uneasily.

RAESINIA

The campfires went out as the sun came up. Through Marcus' spyglass, Raesinia could see men in blue uniforms forming up on the flats, looking for all the world like a military parade. She searched for Janus among the mounted officers, but couldn't make out faces.

They stood on a protruding rock just at the crest of Bear Ridge, above and behind the lines of trenches and the guns in their sloped pits. Straight ahead was the point of the ridge, facing northeast, directly toward Janus' army. The great V formation of the Army of the Republic stretched back and away from Raesinia on either side, like the wings of a bird. Most of it was beyond her view—the bulk of the hill and the remaining trees blocked her line of sight to the west and south, where the line dipped down onto the plain.

She handed the glass back to Marcus. A table had been set up at the base of the rock, and officers bustled about, delivering messages and plotting reports with a reassuring professionalism. For once, no one was suggesting that she shouldn't be there, or that she'd be safer farther to the rear. The men took their cues from Marcus, and she'd—at last—trained him out of such habits.

"Here they come." Marcus swung the glass back and forth. "He's not wasting any time."

"This is the attack?" Raesinia said. She squinted at the columns. "Already?"

"This is the beginning," Marcus said. "He doesn't know where we are, exactly, though his scouts have told him we've taken this hill. So he'll brush us, just to see what he's up against." He raised his voice, addressing one of the runners at the base of the boulder. "Message for Colonel Archer. Tell him to hold fire unless things get out of hand. No sense wasting ammunition and showing them our guns."

Whoever was in command of the artillery across the field had no such compunctions. Tiny puffs of smoke rose into the air, followed a few seconds later by the flat, drifting *booms* of the reports. Raesinia looked for the impacts, and saw only one, an explosion of dirt rising from the foot of the hill as a ball rebounded.

"Half a battery," Marcus said contemptuously. "He wants to scare us into opening fire."

Another half battery started shooting a few minutes later, at closer range. After the first few salvos, the balls started to land on the forward slope of the hill more often than not, but they still caused little damage. The Girls' Own and Second Division soldiers were huddled in their trenches, not formed up in easily visible ranks, and only a supremely lucky direct hit would prove deadly.

Meanwhile, the advancing columns got clearer. There were two of them, companies one behind the next, well spaced out. At two hundred yards from the base of the hill, still unmolested by any fire from the Army of the Republic, they deployed into a single long line, three ranks deep. Flags hung limp against their poles at regular intervals.

"Tell Colonel Cyte and Colonel Giforte to fire at will," Marcus directed a runner.

The line began its advance, men moving in unison to the beat of inaudible drums. For a few more minutes, nothing happened, except for the flash and boom of the distant gun batteries. Then, as the trench lines came into range of the oncoming formation, the Girls' Own began to fire. It wasn't a single volley, but spread down the line with a rolling crackle, a wave of light and smoke as the soldiers found their targets. Even at long range, some shots told, and bodies began to dribble out the back of the enemy line. They came on, steadily, as more and more fire rose from the trenches. Soon all that was visible on the slope of the hill was a roiling cloud of smoke, lit from within by muzzle flashes like fitful lightning.

The enemy halted, battalions shrinking toward their flags as they closed their ranks. They raised muskets to their shoulders, then fired, all at once. The flash of the volley was terrific, followed by a sound like a single clap of thunder, and a wave of smoke rose over them. Whether it had any effect on the women in the trenches was hard to say, but answering fire continued to rattle back. Marcus lowered his spyglass, looking satisfied.

"Just a probe," he said.

"They're still fighting." Raesinia found her eyes glued to the flashes.

"Not for long. Troops in the open are never going to be able to shoot it out with men behind breastworks. Janus will know that if he wants to take this hill, he's going to have to do it with bayonets." He looked over his shoulder. "He'll try the flanks first, though. I'm going to find Sevran. Where will you be?"

"Here, or at the cutter's station," Raesinia said. "Hannah said I might be useful for keeping morale up, if I don't get in the way. Marcus . . ."

"What?"

She wanted to kiss him, here in front of everyone, but couldn't quite nerve herself to do it. *It would only be a distraction.* But some part of her mind couldn't help asking, *But what if this is your last chance?*

"Be careful," she said, knowing how silly it sounded.

He nodded briskly. "If they start bombing the hill with howitzers, even the cutter's station will be in range. I know . . ." He lowered his voice. "I know I don't need to tell you to be careful. Just try not to get your head blown off where everyone can see it, all right?"

Raesinia laughed, and felt tears prick her eyes. "I'll do my best."

Sure enough, the fighting at the base of the hill soon died away, the enemy retreating out of the cloud of their own musket smoke. More units were maneuvering in the middle distance, and Raesinia could see cavalry on the move. At the base of the boulder, the young officers—she recognized a few from Alek Giforte's old staff—received a message from a rider or a runner every few minutes, and plotted small changes to their map.

I should find something useful to do. She felt *helpless*, the Queen of Vordan hesitant to interrupt her own men. *They know what they're doing. What do I have to add?* She was on the point of sliding down from the boulder when the flashes began in the fields below.

Guns. But more guns than before, more guns than she'd ever seen at once. There must have been a hundred muzzle flashes, so close together and nearly simultaneous that they had all died away into smoke before the first sound arrived. It was a bass rumble that grew and grew, rising to a crescendo that seemed to shake the very ground beneath them.

Then, all at once, solid shot was landing all around them. Geysers of dirt exploded upward from the face of the hill, spraying from where the balls buried themselves or bounced wildly into the air. One shot hit the log at the front of a breastwork and smashed it into a spray of flying splinters. Raesinia *saw* one of the balls as it ricocheted past, hanging at the peak of its trajectory for a moment before it crashed to the ground ten yards beyond her boulder.

"Your Highness!" one of the young officers shouted into the ringing silence that followed. He stood at the base of the boulder, holding out his hand. "Come down, please! It's not safe."

Raesinia wanted to scream. *Bad enough to feel useless without everyone telling you so.* But her eyes went to the huddle of staff, where one of the men was on the ground in a pool of blood, while two others struggled to remove a long wooden splinter from his side. She could see casualty teams moving on the slope of the hill, running to reach the injured.

They're risking their lives. Raesinia looked back at the smoking line of guns and felt like an impostor. *What am I risking?*

She slid down the boulder's face, letting the officer grab her hand and hustle her toward the cutter's station. Behind her, a second volley of cannon-fire began.

MARCUS

"Nothing serious," Fitz said. "A couple of regiments looking for a weak spot. We sent them about their business."

"That's more than a couple of regiments now," Marcus said, looking through the spyglass. Heavy columns of men were forming well beyond cannon-shot. Counting their flags, Marcus put them at at least two divisions, possibly more.

"He's not wasting time," Fitz said. "Now that he knows where we are, he intends to crush us."

"It's the same on the left," Marcus said. "A couple of divisions. It'll be a simultaneous attack from both sides."

"Is that what you would do, in his place?" Fitz said, with a slight smile.

"No. Converging attacks from multiple directions are hell to get timed right. That's the sort of thing *clever* officers come up with." He lowered the spyglass and looked at Fitz. "But it's what *Janus* would do."

"I agree," Fitz said.

"You know what I need you to do?"

"Take the reserve and advance. Defeat this wing. Then transfer the reserve back to the left in time to withstand the assault there." He looked over his shoulder at the hill. "Assuming the center can hold out, of course."

Marcus shook his head admiringly. "Why aren't you in command, Fitz?"

"Some days I ask myself the same question, sir."

"Do it. I'll ride back and start sending the reserve your way. Just don't take too long."

"Understood, sir."

In the distance the sound of cannon-fire went on and on like steady rain.

CHAPTER THIRTY-ONE

WINTER

Winter sat in the clearing, listening to the guns. She'd never heard so many at once. And they were all coming from the northeast, the face of Bear Ridge, where the Girls' Own were stationed. *Cyte. Abby.* They were likely crouching in a trench, hearing the balls zip overhead or plow into the earth. *Or find just the right target, where unyielding metal meets yielding flesh and turns my beautiful, brilliant girl into a mangled ruin—*

The urge to get up, to go to them, was almost overpowering. Winter fought it down, tasting bile at the back of her throat. *They've survived this long without me.* But it wasn't that she thought she could *help*, not really. It was a primal instinct to share their danger, as she had so often in the past, that tugged at her.

Something stung her eye, and she rubbed at it. Not tears, but flying grit. Sand. The wind rose, swirling into a funnel, and solidified into the masked shape of the Steel Ghost.

Alex jumped to her feet eagerly. Winter guessed the waiting hadn't been any easier on her. "You've found it?"

"I believe so," the Ghost said. "To the north, behind the enemy camp, there is a ruined castle. I sensed the presence of the Beast's core, and it did not appear to be moving. A large number of the creature's bodies waited nearby."

"That has to be it," Winter said. "Let's get started."

She looked down at Sothe, who was still sleeping peacefully on the pyre. Part of her, she had to admit, had been hoping they'd somehow manage to avoid this. *Let Sothe wake up tonight and find out we didn't need her after all.* But they'd never make it to this castle if they had to fight their way through half of Janus' army.

Slowly, she dug out her matches. Alex watched, silent, and the Ghost's masked face was as expressionless as always. Winter struck a match, held it for a moment, and looked down at Sothe.

"Thank you," she said, and touched the flame to the kindling.

The logs, soaked in oil, caught in moments, and the heat built rapidly. Winter had to take a step back, shielding her face, as flames leapt into the air, building into a column of smoke. She caught a whiff of burning flesh, unpleasantly like cooking meat, before it was thankfully buried under a rush of woodsmoke. Blinking, Winter backed away farther.

"How long does it take?" Alex said, eyes fixed on the flames.

"I wasn't in a position to count precisely last time," Winter said. "But—"

Deep in the heart of the fire, something went *crunch*. Logs shattered and split, the pyre breaking apart and spilling glowing sparks across the ground. At the center of the flames, a figure stirred, rising to its feet. Enormous dark shapes hung at her shoulders, the shadows of wings. The Ghost raised a hand, and sand rained down on the pyre, smothering the flames and embers. A moment later, the smoke cleared away.

The guardian resembled Sothe, but streamlined, inessential detail weathered away. Her lithe body was smooth and unlined, with skin the gleaming white of polished marble, shot through with darker veins. Her clothes were gone, though her naked form was as sexless as a mannequin. Her hair was gone, too, and her face was only a shadow of what it had been—two indentations for eyes, a slight bulge of a nose, and no mouth, as though a sculptor had wanted to give the suggestion of humanity without the substance. Her wings, rising up behind her, were not feathered but perfectly smooth, like a ship's sail in a strong wind.

"God Almighty," Alex said. "She's . . ."

Beautiful, Winter thought, *and monstrous.* When she moved, it was with the catlike grace Sothe had always displayed, but there was something deeply unnatural about watching a stone surface flex and bend. And when she was still, she was perfectly still, with no fidgeting or breath to disturb her, so that when she moved again it was like watching a statue spring to life.

"Sothe?" Winter said. Her voice came out in a whisper.

Sothe nodded.

"Are you . . . ?" She shook her head. She'd wanted to say "all right," but what was the point of that? Winter swallowed hard. "Can you carry me and Alex?"

Sothe flapped her wings once, producing a down rush of air that set sand and ash to swirling. Then she nodded again.

"I will lead the way," the Ghost said. If the sight of the guardian unnerved him, it was invisible behind his mask. He dissolved into a column of sand, rising in a swirling wind out of the clearing, remaining visible as a smudge overhead.

"How . . . ?" Alex said.

Sothe walked to Winter, bent over, and opened the small pack she'd left on the ground. It contained a number of leather straps, each laden with a complement of knives in various sizes. She put them on, her marble fingers dexterous as ever, buckling them around her stomach, her thighs, and her forearms. Then she gestured for Winter and Alex to come close.

They obliged, shuffling awkwardly together. Sothe walked behind them and slipped one arm around Winter's waist, then the other around Alex's. Sothe's skin was warm, but with the polished feel of stone, like a rock that had spent all day in the sun. Winter wriggled, trying to settle her weight more comfortably, the arm around her staying as steady as an iron bar. Sothe looked down at her and cocked her head.

"Alex?" Winter said. "Are you ready?"

"No," Alex said. "But I'm not likely to get any readier."

"Go ahead," Winter said to Sothe.

The great wings snapped out, gathering air beneath them, and Sothe rose from the ground. She moved slowly at first, wings beating steadily, hoisting them up to the treetops of the clearing and then beyond. Oddly, Winter felt no fear of falling. There was such a sense of *power* in Sothe's arm, in the wide sweep of her wings, that it seemed impossible.

If anyone down there is looking up, they're going to think they've gone mad. Fortunately, the soldiers below had plenty to distract them. From this vantage point, Winter could see Janus' troops massing to attack on the left flank, battalions marching in column to get into formation, teams of horses pulling cannon. In between friendly and enemy lines, light cavalry skirmished, horsemen riding back and forth and firing at one another with carbines. Each shot reached her as a single distinct sound, like a distant handclap, almost lost in the continuing rumble of gunfire from the north.

Saints and martyrs. What I would give to be able to command battles like this. It was the perspective every general dreamed of, hovering above the world like a god. The land unrolled like a living map, full of toy soldiers and cannon and towns. She glanced up at Sothe, to remind herself of what it had cost to gain this vantage. The guardian's nearly featureless face was set forward, her eyes on the smear of swirling sand that was the Steel Ghost.

A moment later they were picking up speed, the wind shrieking in Winter's face. The lines of blue-uniformed soldiers fell away, and then they were passing over more fields and villages. The twisted loops of the river Marak lay ahead, the ground rising to form a cliff face looking out over the water. Atop that cliff, some long-ago lord had raised a fortress, a rough half circle of wall that had once enclosed a few buildings. Now the wall was a tumbled ruin, and only fragments of structures remained, hard to identify from on high. But there were tents pitched within the circuit of the old walls. Down at the base of the cliff were many more, of all sizes and colors, arranged in perfect rows as neat as any Vordanai army camp.

Two groups of figures were on the move from the camp, not marching in column but *running* over the ground, like wolves in a pack. There had to be thousands of them, Winter guessed, a motley mob of uniforms and civilian clothes, with muskets, spears, and swords. One group was headed due south, directly toward Bear Ridge, while the other kept to the bank of the river and moved southwest.

"Red-eyes!" Winter shouted, struggling to make herself heard above the wind. "They're headed for the army!"

Alex nodded, her squinting eyes streaming tears.

"We have to warn them!" Winter said. "If we go back—"

"Marcus and Cyte know the red-eyes are out here," Alex shouted back. "They'll be ready. We have our own job to do!"

"And their departure makes that job easier," the Ghost said, out of thin air. "Only a small force remains to defend the core."

Winter looked down at the departing red-eyes, imagined the unstoppable tide of their charge crashing against the trenches the Girls' Own had dug. *Stay safe, Cyte*. She squeezed her eyes shut. *Please*.

"I will descend first," the Ghost said. "My winds will surround the castle and I will keep those outside from interfering as long as I can. Destroy the core and victory is ours."

The wind died away as Sothe came to a halt directly over the old walls. Looking down, Winter saw clouds of sand and dust rising, enclosing the ruined castle on all sides. They grew and grew, larger than anything she'd seen the

Ghost produce before, becoming a towering sandstorm whose eerie keening was audible even far above. In the center, the air was still clear, and small figures were emerging from their tents and running in all directions.

"Go!" Winter shouted.

Sothe dove, almost straight down. Winter nearly screamed, her throat frozen, all her previous calm ripped away in the terrifying descent. Alex was *laughing*, a mad cackle that blew away on the renewed wind. Just when Winter was certain nothing could arrest their fall, that they would plow into the earth like a spent cannonball in an explosion of stone and dirt, Sothe's wings snapped out. They were jerked upward with bruising force, came to a halt, and drifted down the last few yards at the speed of a falling leaf. Sothe's feet touched the ground gently, and she bent to deposit Alex and Winter on the rocky ground.

"You," Winter gasped, looking up at Sothe. "You're having *fun*, aren't you?"

Sothe shrugged, featureless face impassive. Winter had to imagine the slight quirk of the lip.

Alex sat up with a whoop, breathing hard. "Balls of the *Beast*. And I thought jumping off the cathedral tower was good."

"You're both mad." Winter caught movement out of the corner of her eye. "Here they come."

They'd landed near the ruined wall, which was less dilapidated than it had appeared from the air; it was still almost ten feet high and surrounded by chunks of broken stone. A collapsed gate led into a broad yard, with dusty ground studded with small rocks and tufts of grass. On the other side of it were two slate-roofed wooden structures. One of these had collapsed entirely, leaving little more than a pile of timber and broken tiles, while the other had lost one wall and most of its roof but still seemed intact on the far side. Beyond them was another yard, where the tents they'd seen from above were pitched. All around, enveloping the curtain wall, was the swirling, shrieking curtain of sand and wind called up by the Ghost.

A half dozen men and women ran into the yard through the gap between the two buildings. Two wore white Murnskai uniforms, stained with sweat and mud, while a third was in Vordanai blue. Another pair were women, in the long skirts Winter had seen north of the border, while the last was a boy of no more than twelve, shirtless and grubby, with long, ragged fingernails.

No matter who they'd been, Winter knew what they were now. Crimson light sprang to life in six sets of eyes, flaring bright for a moment, then dying away. Two of the soldiers still had muskets slung over their backs, but they hadn't made a move for them.

"Winter Ihernglass," one of the women said. "You're not supposed to be here. You're—"

Sothe drew a knife from one of her straps and flicked it at the red-eye. The assassin's accuracy had always been impressive, but now she had the inhuman strength of the Guardian as well. The woman's head disintegrated, a spray of blood and brain painting the rubble behind her as her body toppled.

"—supposed to be in Murnsk," the boy picked up without a pause. "What a slippery creature."

"We're here to put an end to you," Winter said.

"I gathered that, yes." The boy smiled, revealing stained, rotting teeth. "You're welcome to try."

The two soldiers went for their muskets. Alex raised a hand, and a lance of darkness speared one of them through the chest, withdrawing just as quickly and leaving him to stagger for a few moments before he collapsed. The other managed to get his weapon up and trained on Winter, but Sothe sidestepped between them as he pulled the trigger. The ball struck her in the shoulder and whined away, leaving only a tiny chip in her stony surface.

The remaining three charged, knives and clubs in their hands. Alex cut down the second woman with another bolt of shadow, and Sothe drew a knife as long as Winter's forearm and engaged the other two. The red-eyes were fast and moved with a coordination no human fighters could have matched, but even before her transformation Sothe had been death with a blade. Now she seemed unstoppable, weaving casually out of the way of a blow to crush a man's face with a punch, then drawing her knife across the boy and opening his guts in a spray of blood and bile.

Saints and martyrs, Winter thought. She hadn't even had time to reach for her own weapons. *Thank God Almighty she's on our side.* She shook her head and pointed to the tents.

"Come on! The Ghost won't be able to keep this up forever, and there may be a lot more of them outside."

Sothe nodded and jumped to the top of the pile of rubble in a single leap. Alex ran between the two ruined buildings, Winter following behind. Three large tents had been set up in what had been the castle's main courtyard, with another, larger pile of broken, rotting wood marking where a building had once stood. Red-eyes were pouring out of the tents. Soldiers, civilians, men and women, children and grandfathers. *We're all just fodder for the Beast.*

"Watch for Jane!" Winter shouted as they charged.

Sothe took the lead, another leap taking her into the middle of the red-eyes, and she almost absentmindedly flicked a blade out to slash a man's head from his shoulders. The nearest turned to engage her, but she was already moving, cutting a bloody swath through the press. It was like watching a master swordsman fight children, children made of soft dough who came apart at her slightest touch. Splashes of blood sprayed across Sothe, streaks of red dripping from her polished skin.

Winter drew her own saber as more of the red-eyes charged. Alex, just behind her, raised her hands and shot them down methodically, sending a single bolt of shadow through the head of each attacker. One woman ducked, avoiding the shot, and came at Winter with a short sword. The red-eye feinted left, and nearly got around Winter's parry. There was no time to pull away and riposte.

Instead, Winter let the woman's momentum carry her onward, and slapped her off hand against the red-eye's arm, unleashing Infernivore. The hungry demon surged into her opponent, and Winter felt the crimson thread of the Beast withdraw rather than face it, leaving the red-eye an empty shell. Winter stepped away and let her collapse just in time to see a young girl coming at her with a long kitchen knife, her blond hair spiky and crusted with blood and dirt. Winter thrust by instinct, and the girl willingly impaled herself, letting the saber sink into her belly as she thrust the knife at Winter's arm. Winter hastily grabbed her wrist before the blow could land; she once again called on her demon, and the girl's body slid limply off her sword as the Beast withdrew.

Up ahead, a half dozen red-eyes had thrown themselves at Sothe, ignoring her knives and trying to bear her to the ground by sheer weight. For a moment she staggered, even as she stabbed one opponent repeatedly. Then her white wings snapped out, throwing two enemies away from her, and she dropped her knife to put her hands around the necks of two more. She hurled them into the rumble with a *crunch* of rotten wood and shattering tile. She grabbed the last pair and slammed their heads together so hard that both skulls shattered, washing Sothe's hand in bloody fragments.

Really fucking glad she's on our side. The two red-eyes that had been knocked away were climbing to their feet only to be neatly speared by Alex. That left nothing moving in the courtyard aside from themselves, but there was still no sign of Jane.

Winter interrogated her senses, but Infernivore was so agitated by being denied its meals that it was hard to tell if it still felt another demon. "Alex! Can you feel it?"

Alex nodded, breathing hard. "It's definitely here." She frowned. "There's something—"

"The tents," Winter said. "She must be in there."

Sothe jumped again, landing in the center of the three tents and scattering the ashes of a dead campfire. She grabbed the fabric of one and pulled, tearing the pegs from the ground. The interior was empty, so she turned to the next.

Something happened to the air in front of the tent, something that hurt Winter's eyes even to look at. The air *twisted*, shimmering with iridescence like a raven's wing. Sothe was picked up and hurled backward with tremendous force, clipping the top of a ruined building in a spray of splinters before impacting with the outer wall. Stone *crunched*, and a whole section of curtain wall collapsed in a rising cloud of dust that was quickly sucked into the shrieking sandstorm.

The tent was hurled aside, and a black-clad figure rose slowly to its feet. It was a man, at least seven feet tall and almost skeletally thin. His clothes hung off him like funeral garb from a desiccated corpse, loops and folds of black fabric draped over him like a second skin. His face was invisible behind a dark mask made from tiny chips of obsidian. For a moment he looked in Sothe's direction; then he turned toward Winter and Alex.

"Penitent!" Alex hissed. She raised her hands, but before she could unleash her power, another weird ripple surrounded her with bands of color. There was the start of a scream, abruptly cut off, and then she was pinwheeling through the air, landing hard on the rocky ground of the courtyard.

"That's better." The third tent flap opened, and Jane emerged, followed by two hulking, leather-armored brutes with glowing red eyes. "As I was saying before we were so rudely interrupted, Winter, I thought I'd left you in Murnsk. Much against my will, I might add. Jane *so* wanted your company." The Beast tapped a finger against the side of its head. "But you had to be obstinate."

Saints and fucking *martyrs.* Winter raised her saber, not daring to look and see if Alex was all right. Jane hopped lightly up to a broken beam, spreading her arms for balance. Her hair had grown back, the long, silky red that Winter remembered. Her clothes were rags, her skin grimy, but she moved with such effortless grace that none of it seemed to matter. Even now, like this, Winter felt a twist in her chest at the sight of her.

"You're probably wondering," Jane went on, gesturing at the Penitent, "who this fellow is, since I don't allow interloping demons in my bodies. He's really a fascinating case. I found him in the dungeons under Elysium." The tall, skeletal figure in black turned to stare at her, and Jane shot him a smile. "He was locked away for heresy, you see. He'd come to believe that the Beast of Judgment *should* cleanse the world of humanity, since our sins are so very many. Because he attempted to free me, his fellow Priests of the Black had thrown him in their darkest hole to be tortured. They removed his tongue, lest he spread his blasphemy. Pity he was right and they were wrong!"

"Don't listen to her," Winter said in Murnskai. "The Beast isn't an answer for our sins. It's a demon. You should be trying to destroy it!"

"I wouldn't bother," Jane said. "What he wants more than anything in the world is to be a part of me. And I'll grant him that, in time. Once you are dead and the Thousand Names are mine, there will be nothing left in this world that can threaten me."

Winter felt a trickle of sweat run down her cheek. Jane and the Penitent were at least fifteen yards away, too far to cover in a quick dash. *And whatever his power is, it's* fast. She looked up at the whirlwind and wondered if the Steel Ghost could see what was happening. *I need some kind of distraction. As long as I can get to Jane, it doesn't matter what happens afterward . . .*

"No need to wait around all day," Jane said. "Kill her."

Helplessly, Winter raised her sword. As she moved, space twisted around her, a shimmering distortion forming at each of her wrists. The blade fell from numbed fingers as an unstoppable force lifted her into the air, her shoulders screaming as her feet left the ground.

The Penitent cocked his head curiously. He put Winter in mind of a child pulling the legs off a spider. He held up one hand, fingers spread, and the two twists in space started to drift apart, taking Winter's arms with them. It was a gentle, unstoppable movement, like the turning of a waterwheel. In a few seconds, Winter was stretched as if pinned to a rack. The force kept pulling, and she started to scream.

CHAPTER THIRTY-TWO

RAESINIA

"Another one!"

The cutter's tent was a concentrated mass of human suffering. The air was thick with smoke, shot through with the scent of blood and shit to form a concentrated miasma. The floor was awash in vileness, mixing with dirt to make a sticky mud that spattered everyone to the thighs. Raesinia's ears rang with screams, curses, and desperate pleading.

Hannah and her assistants strode through this morass like horrible angels, bone saws in hand. At the door, two men surveyed the incoming casualties and turned away both those who would live at least a few hours and those who would die for certain. The rejected were laid outside, where their howls added to the din. Those "lucky" enough to merit the cutter's attention were taken to one of the tables, strapped down, and given a wooden bit to put between their teeth.

That Hannah was an expert was apparent from how few strokes of the bone saw it took her to remove a limb. Razor-sharp teeth sliced through flesh with ease, and when they met bone they made the awful, almost musical sound that was capable of reducing any soldier to shudders. In no time at all, the ruined arm or leg tumbled to the ground and the cutter turned away, already moving on to the next victim. Her assistants tied off the stump, reducing the pumping blood to a trickle, and gathered up the discarded flesh to add to the pile outside. Transporting the patients afterward was a task for any able-bodied people who happened to be nearby. Which, in this case, included the Queen of Vordan.

You said you wanted to help, Raesinia told herself as she grabbed a lanky young man by the ankle. Another soldier took him under the armpits, and together they walked him out the tent flap, mud squelching underfoot. The hospital tents were long since full, and they were reduced to simply laying casualties in the dirt. They maneuvered the youth into an open space between an old man whose left leg ended just above the ankle and a volunteer woman whose colorful linen dress was splashed with blood.

The young man's breath rattled in his throat. Raesinia didn't think he'd live. Only half of those Hannah operated on did, she'd been told, and she was one of the best cutters. The old man was either swearing or praying, so quietly it was hard to tell which. The woman was still and silent. *Too* silent. Raesinia watched her a moment, then nudged her partner. He glanced at her, shook his head, and grabbed her by the ankles, dragging the corpse away. A moment later, two men set a mop-haired soldier with a splinted leg in the space thus vacated, deaf to his constant shrieks.

Underneath the screams and groans, the cannonade continued, a deep grumble like constant thunder. There was fighting on all sides of the hill now, and from the left and right came the occasional sounds of musketry. Closer, the Second Division and the volunteers had repelled three assaults, waves of Vordanai and Murnskai soldiers breaking against the breastworks like surf on a beach. Each time, after the enemy pulled back, the bombardment began again, the massive battery Janus had assembled pounding the hillside with solid shot. Howitzers joined in as well, less accurate but more deadly, throwing pot-shaped bombs that exploded into shards of spinning metal.

Raesinia looked up to find another casualty team approaching, two girls who couldn't be older than twelve or thirteen carrying an older woman on a stretcher. They left their burden at the tent flap and turned away. One of the pair, dark-haired and wide-eyed, was clutching her stomach, and her skin was pale as death under the blood and grime. Her companion had to support her through the mud. Raesinia got to her feet and stepped in front of them.

"You're hurt," she said, as the pair blinked at her. "You're not going to the cutter?"

The uninjured girl's lip twisted into a snarl, but her companion just shook her head. She tugged her shirt up a few inches to show a deep gash in her stomach, crudely stitched shut with twine.

"Gut wound," she said. "It'll fester by nightfall. Better they help those that might live."

"You don't—" the other girl said, then choked off in a sob.

Hannah would probably say the same thing. Raesinia looked around, satisfied herself that no one was paying attention to them, and put her arm on the girl's shoulder. "Come with me."

"I want to help," the injured girl said. "While I can."

"Just come here, all right?"

She didn't put up too much resistance as Raesinia walked her around the side of one of the hospital tents, her crying friend following behind. Away from the frantic movement at the entrance, flies covered the pools of blood and discarded limbs with a thick, living carpet. They rose in a buzzing, complaining cloud as Raesinia approached; then they settled again. Somewhere, crows were cawing.

Abraham sat on a stone at the rear of the tent, eyes closed, head lowered. Raesinia told the two girls to wait and knelt in front of him. She had to poke him before he responded with a low moan.

"Too many." His voice was breathy. "There's too many."

"I know."

Raesinia felt her heart twist. She didn't know Abraham well, but his compassion was obvious. Even a single person in pain made him want to help, let alone *this* nightmare. And while his gift was extraordinary, it wasn't without limits.

"Can you handle one more?" Raesinia said. "It's a small wound, but deep. A little girl."

"One more." Abraham opened his eyes. They were bloodshot, as though he'd been on a three-day bender. "I can . . . handle one more."

Raesinia beckoned the injured girl over. She hesitated at the sight of Abraham, but he mustered a smile, and she took a few stumbling steps closer. Raesinia caught her elbow and guided her forward, and Abraham put his hand against the skin of her stomach.

The wound, crusted with dried blood, closed as though it were being pulled together from underneath. The twine worked its way out, falling away. The girl gave a soft sigh, her eyes rolling up in her head, and Raesinia had to catch her under the arms before she fell. Her breathing was steady, and color was already returning to her cheeks.

"What happened?" Her friend hurried over, eyes wet with tears. "What did you do to her?"

"She's going to be okay," Raesinia said. "Find somewhere she can rest, and stay with her."

"I need to get permission." The girl was trembling. "From the lieutenant."

"You have *my* permission." Raesinia looked the girl in the eye and saw the moment recognition dawned.

"I—I didn't . . ." she stammered.

"It's fine." Raesinia transferred the unconscious girl to her friend. "Can you take her?"

The girl nodded. "Th-thank you. Your Highness."

Raesinia smiled, trying to ignore the screams and the boom of the guns. The two girls moved off, one carrying the other, and she looked back at Abraham. His eyes were still open, but he didn't seem to be looking at anything in particular. Raesinia frowned nervously.

"Abraham? Are you . . . ? Is this hurting you?"

"Hurting?" He blinked, focusing, and shook his head. "Just . . . tired. So tired."

"You should rest. At least for a few minutes." She felt suddenly guilty for bringing the girl over.

He snorted, rubbing his eyes with the heels of his palms. "A few minutes won't make any difference. A week wouldn't be enough." He looked up at her. "I will do what I can. It's just . . . worse than I ever imagined."

"I know," Raesinia said. "I'm sorry."

"You did not force me to come here," Abraham said. His hands tightened into fists. "Sometimes I wish I could fight like Alex. I could have gone with her and Winter."

"Sothe is with them," Racsinia said. "She'll keep everyone safe."

"I believe it," Abraham said solemnly. Then, abruptly, he held up a hand.

"What's wrong?"

"The guns have stopped."

It was true. There were still screams from the cutter's tent, and the more distant sounds of fighting on the other fronts, but the endless thunder of the cannonade had gone quiet. After a few moments, cannon picked up again, closer and louder. Those were Archer's guns, Raesinia knew. Marcus had ordered the gunners not to waste ammunition trying to knock out Janus' batteries, so if they were firing—

"They're coming," she said. "I have to go. Are you all right here for the moment?"

Abraham nodded, eyelids already drooping. Raesinia ran back around the cutter's tent and up the hill, following the tracks they'd cut this morning, now a churned mess of stones and mud. She detoured around the boulder and the command post and headed for another vantage she'd discovered, a stump at the top of the trench line, high enough above Archer's guns that she could see past the smoke.

Sure enough, down on the plain, tight-packed columns of infantry were moving in for the assault. Smaller guns accompanied them, their sharper reports like the yapping of excited dogs. Archer's batteries returned fire, solid shot arcing over the heads of the Second Division soldiers in the trenches to descend screaming on the plain, bouncing in wild, devastating arcs. The advancing troops were Murnskai, their white uniforms a vivid contrast with the dark earth. Whenever a ball struck, it mowed through the column, carrying away several men and leaving more broken bodies lying on a stretch of ground that was already littered with corpses.

As Marcus had said this morning, Janus was well aware that his attackers were never going to be able to win a firefight with defenders hunkered down behind breastworks. This time, four battalion columns came in at the double, breaking into a charge as soon as the first shots rang out from the trenches. They made no attempt to form into a line and maximize their firepower, but remained concentrated, relying on the momentum of thousands of bodies to carry them forward. The heads of the columns started to shrink, men falling faster and faster as they got closer to the trenches, but they kept coming. The neat formations, with one company behind the next, started to dissolve, producing a dense mass of men with bayonets fixed, huddling together against the deadly lead rain.

The Girls' Own, who held the first trench, didn't wait to receive them. They fired a last volley and ran, scrambling up onto the unprotected hillside. Volunteers farther up the hill continued to shoot, but the Murnskai could see their enemy fleeing and came on all the faster. Some of them stopped to fire, and blue-uniformed women tumbled and went down across the hill. The fastest crested the breastwork and jumped down into the trench their enemies had vacated.

Somewhere down below, Cyte gave the order with her customary good timing. Raesinia couldn't hear it, but she saw the effect. The Third Regiment, de Koste's troops, leapt up from their trenches farther up the hill and counter-charged, firing as they went. The Murnskai soldiers fired back, but soon discovered that the trenches, steep walled on the downhill side, were a gradual slope facing the other way and gave no protection at all from incoming fire. The men in white were no more eager to receive a bayonet charge than the women in blue had been, and they broke before contact, only a few stragglers being cut down with cold steel. De Koste's men continued to fire into the fleeing Murnskai, and Archer's guns thundered again, harassing them as they went.

Cyte had suggested the tactic, and they'd been using it all day, with the soldiers digging frantically to repair and extend their trenches even as the cannonballs fell like rain. Raesinia had watched it work three times now, smashing everything Janus had sent against them. But he seemed to have an endless supply of fresh troops to renew the struggle, while every time more of the defenders were hauled away to the horror of the cutter's station or the growing lines of corpses.

As though the thought had summoned them, Raesinia saw more enemy soldiers coming, a long line of them, pushing over the blue- and white-coated bodies that littered the plain. This new group was a motley bunch, with some representatives from both armies, but many in civilian clothes. Raesinia frowned at them. *Does Janus have his own volunteers?* Then, Winter's story running through her mind, she suddenly understood.

Red-eyes.

Raesinia jumped off the stump and started down the hill before she was quite aware of what she was doing. *I have to warn Cyte.* The bodies of the Beast were not like ordinary men and women—they knew no pain and showed no fear. They would never break, never run, only keep coming until they were dead. *And if they get too close, they can take our soldiers for their own.*

The regiments had been exchanging duties with each attack. The retreating Girls' Own had halted, now occupying the highest point on the hillside, just below the artillery. Someone recognized Raesinia despite her filthy state, and a cheer went up as she went by. It was passed on to the volunteers, in the center, men and women from the streets of Vordan without even uniform jackets to call their own. They'd started the day armed mostly with swords, spears, and a few shotguns and hunting pieces. Now most of them had muskets, looted from friendly and enemy dead. They shouted and *hurrah*ed as Raesinia ran, her legs feeling wobbly underneath her. *Would they still be cheering if their queen took a tumble and rolled down the hill?*

Fortunately, she managed to avoid that embarrassment, and arrived at the leading trenches, where the Second Regiment was lining the breastworks. Raesinia looked for the flag and ran toward it, dodging around bits of broken log, stones, and corpses. A woman, shot in the act of trying to run, lay half in and half out of the trench. Murnskai soldiers, huddled around wounds that turned their white uniforms pink. A teenage girl and a heavily bearded Murnskai lying in a heap, each with a hand still gripping the blade that had killed the other.

There was no sign of Cyte, but she found de Koste with one of his captains, calmly surveying the advance of this fresh batch of opponents. Archer's guns had shifted their fire from the fleeing Murnskai to the new threat, and the cannonballs were falling on the red-eyes. They kept no formation, which made the guns less effective.

De Koste's eyes went wide at the sight of Raesinia, but he calmed his features at once and made a deep bow, which was echoed by all the men around him.

"Your Highness," he said, "I, ah, didn't expect to see you here. You're not injured, I trust?"

"I was assisting at the cutter's station." Raesinia shook her head frantically. "The new attack—"

"Rabble," the captain said. "Half of them don't even have muskets. If this is all Janus has left, we can hold here until the Beast comes again."

It took Raesinia a moment to realize he was being figurative. "They're not just rabble; they're fanatics. Maniacs. They're not going to stop. You have to be ready."

"We'll stop them," de Koste said. "But please, Your Highness. For your own safety . . ."

Raesinia turned away, back to the oncoming red-eyes. They were still coming, thousands of them. Those in the lead spread out and came on a dead sprint.

"They're certainly bearing the cannon-fire well," de Koste muttered.

"We'll see how they like musketry," the captain said, voice full of confidence. "Fire at will!"

Sergeants passed the command up and down the trench. Moments later, muskets started to *crack*, the shots coming singly at first and then running together into a rolling, rattling crush of sound. Smoke billowed up around the trench, intermittently obscuring the view, but Raesinia could see red-eyes falling by the dozen, spinning or pitching forward as the musket balls struck them, while their comrades pressed on over their corpses.

They're not going to break. Marcus had told her once that a bayonet charge basically came down to a contest of nerves. If the defenders *really* believed the attackers would press the charge home, through the storm of shot, then they wouldn't stand to receive it. But if it was the attackers who lost their courage first, the charge would founder and break in blood. *But the red-eyes don't have any nerve to lose.*

"You're going to have to fight them hand-to-hand," she told de Koste urgently. "Warn your men—"

Too late, and in any event she wasn't sure he heard over the racket. The red-eyes took a last volley of fire at a range of only a dozen yards, and it inflicted horrific damage. A whole line of them went down, corpses falling among the dead soldiers already piling up at the base of the slope. But the charge rolled on, unstoppable, men and women leaping over the bodies and scrambling past the earth-and-log barrier. In a few moments, they were into the trench, and the world went mad.

Men were fighting everywhere, soldiers in blue against erstwhile comrades, or Murnskai in mud-stained white; or men, women, and children in civilian clothes. A Third Regiment soldier opened the throat of a Murnskai with his bayonet, nimbly sidestepping the dying man's riposte. The next red-eye was a young woman, ragged haired and dressed in rags, and he hesitated long enough for her to gut him with a skinning knife. Three children, in long formal dresses already torn and stained with blood, worked together to overwhelm another soldier, two grabbing his legs while the third pulled him to the floor of the trench and pressed her face close to his. A moment later he rose, a red glow in his eyes, and rammed his bayonet into the back of the man fighting beside him.

Raesinia saw the captain go down, shot at close range by a thick-bearded fisherman who held a pistol in his left hand, his right having been carried away by a cannon-shot. The stump drooled blood, but it didn't seem to impair him. De Koste drew his sword as an old woman, gray hair wild and filthy, scrambled over the trench wall. He ran her neatly through the stomach, then gaped as her clawlike hands grabbed the hilt of his sword and pulled him close. A young boy in the remnants of a smart page's uniform leapt from the breast-work and landed on de Koste's back, stabbing over and over with a long dirk.

The ferocity of the assault was too much. Some soldiers fought and were overwhelmed, torn to pieces or taken by the Beast and turned against their comrades. The rest scrambled up the slope, toward the second trench, trying to stay ahead of the wave of madness and death. One of them, thinking of his duty even in the midst of panic, grabbed Raesinia by the arm and dragged her along, stumbling up the rocky ground between the trenches to where the volunteers waited. Musket-fire was crackling again, balls zipping past despite the danger of hitting a friend.

"Charge!" someone was shouting. Raesinia caught a glimpse of a uniformed soldier standing beside a knot of volunteers who'd gathered around their makeshift flag, a Vordanai eagle sewn on a blue field by awkward, untrained hands. "We have to charge!"

No one was charging. The volunteers stood behind their breastwork, firing as fast as they could load, smoke billowing along the trench. Below, men were scrambling out of the way, but enough of the attackers wore blue uniforms that they were impossible to distinguish from those who'd taken flight. The terrified volunteers shot at anything that moved, cutting down Third Regiment men and red-eyes alike. Raesinia tumbled over the breastwork and lay for a moment in the bottom of the trench, half-stunned. She pulled herself to her feet just in time to see the next wave of red-eyes break from the smoke and come up the hillside at a dead sprint. There were screams and shots, and then the volunteers were running, throwing down their weapons and scrambling up the hill to stay ahead of their pursuers.

We have to stop them. Raesinia gritted her teeth and ran for the flag just as the man who held it tossed it aside and took to his heels. The officer who'd been leading the volunteers was long gone, and only a few men remained, frozen in place by terror. Raesinia grabbed the flagpole and brought it back up, the blue and silver now smeared with mud.

"Here!" she screamed, scraping her throat raw. "*Stand here!*"

Shots zipped past in both directions. Almost alone in the trench, Raesinia watched the shadows of the red-eyes approach through the smoke. *Very brave of me.* Her thoughts felt detached. *Or it would be, if I could die.* She wondered what would happen if the red-eyes ripped her to pieces. *Would I have to go find my arms and legs? Or would they grow back?*

Except. Winter had told her what had happened when the Beast had taken Elysium. The Penitent Damned, who'd had demons of their own, had been absorbed just like any of its other bodies. It had *banished* their demons, taken their minds.

For the first time since that awful night beneath the palace half a decade ago, Raesinia realized, she *was* in real danger. Not from a musket ball or a sword stroke, but from the horrible, annihilating light of those red eyes. If they caught her, she would *end*, cease to be once and for all. *Or else be stuck in some horrible half-life, like Janus.*

Her knees suddenly refused to hold her weight, and her bowels churned. She sat down heavily, barely keeping the flag upright.

What's wrong with me? It took a moment to figure it out. *Oh. I'm terrified. Is this how ordinary people feel all the time?*

The first red-eye—a lanky man with a fur cap and a hunter's look, a long knife in one hand—leapt into the trench. Raesinia screamed and swung the flagpole, the staff cracking him on the head and sending him stumbling sideways. She surged back to her feet, fighting the desperate urge to throw the stupid thing down and flee. *It's just a flag. Just cloth and thread. What the hell is it good for?*

"Stand here!" Her voice cracked. "Stand here!"

More red-eyes were crossing the breastwork, soldiers and civilians, some who'd been fighting for the other side minutes before. A Third Regiment soldier, eyes aglow, jumped down in front of Raesinia with bayonet raised, while the hunter came at her from the left. She managed to block the bayonet thrust with the flagpole, but the hunter grabbed her by the arm and collar, lifting her easily off the ground. She kicked him in the groin, hard, but he barely flinched, and pulled her close to his face.

"The queen!" someone was shouting in the distance. All of Raesinia's attention was on the hunter's eyes, the dark pupils replaced with a rising red glow, growing brighter and brighter until it filled the world.

"Rally to the queen!"

A bayonet entered the side of the hunter's head with such force that it embedded itself to the hilt in his skull. The red glow died, and the grip on Raesinia's collar slackened. The flagstaff fell from her numb fingers, but she saw it taken up again before it hit the ground, muddy banner waving.

"Your Highness!" A woman's voice. Raesinia looked at her. *Abby.* Her freckled face was splashed with gore. "Are you all right?"

All around her, women in blue uniforms were pouring into the trench. The volunteers were with them, too, rallied or shamed into courage. The fighting was desperate, hand-to-hand, but the numbers of red-eyes were finally thinning out. From the flanks, musket-fire cracked.

Did I just save the day? Raesinia thought. *Or nearly get myself killed for no reason?* At the moment she couldn't have said. She blinked at Abby and took a deep breath.

Sometimes it would be really nice to be able to faint.

MARCUS

Just hold out until the reserve gets back. Marcus sighed. *Why did I ever think things would be that simple?*

"General Warus reports that he's heavily engaged!" the young rider said.

His mount, drooping and exhausted, barely flicked an ear at the intermittent crash of cannon. "He's holding, but estimates at least four divisions to his front."

Which means he doesn't have anything to spare to send this way. Janus shouldn't *have* four divisions to use on the right without stripping the left bare. But Marcus had learned long ago not to question his former commander's ability to pull miracles out of his pocket.

"Tell him we're hard-pressed here," Marcus said, fighting to keep his tone professional. "As soon as he feels the pressure come off, we need anything he can send us. Especially cavalry."

"Understood, sir!" The boy kicked his mount in motion.

To the east, the drawn-out grumbling of guns continued, indicating that the enemy attack on the point of the V hadn't slackened. *He can't be strong ev-erywhere, damn it.* But here on the left, where Sevran's hastily assembled Third Division struggled to hold out, there had been no letup in the assaults. Three regiments stood in a long line, three ranks deep, while behind them the fourth waited to push forward to plug gaps. In front of them were the divisional guns, mostly small four- and six-pound pieces, silent for now to conserve their limited ammunition.

A heavy pall of smoke already hung over this part of the field, and the ground in front of the division was strewn with corpses, both human and equine. Janus' cavalry—mostly Murnskai dragoons and cuirassiers—was on the field in force, and the Third had already repelled two charges. At least one division of Murnskai infantry was out there, too, and one of Vordanai, re-forming for yet another assault. And, of course, the guns, which appeared to have a never-ending supply of solid shot. Muzzle flashes winked through the smoke, and while most of the balls over- or undershot the thin line, the occasional hit would sweep away all three men in a file together. In this brief lull in the fight-ing, casualty teams scurried back and forth, bearing screaming or limp figures to the rear.

Sevran was shouting to his runners, his brand-new general's uniform al-ready spattered with mud and gore. Marcus walked over to him and waited until he finished dictating an order, then cleared his throat.

"Word from Fitz?" Sevran said, without looking around. His eyes were fixed on the flashes from the enemy guns.

"He says he's got at least four divisions in front of him," Marcus said. "Ei-ther Janus has got two divisions we didn't know about, or he's pulled something out of his hat."

"Maybe he's split them," Sevran said. "Or he's marching them from one sector to another—"

"It scarcely matters," Marcus said. "Fitz can't send help. We have to hold here."

"How long?" Sevran said.

"Until dark," Marcus said. "Or until these stupid bastards give up."

He looked overhead, but the sun was invisible through the smoke. *Maybe that's the soldiers' hell,* he thought. *Died in battle without knowing it and now trapped waiting for a respite that never comes.* It certainly had the ring of the kind of ironic punishment that filled the *Wisdoms.*

"We're not going to make it that long," Sevran said. "These are good lads, but they can't keep this up all day. We need to retreat."

"We can't," Marcus said. "If we fall back, the left side of the hill is open, and the whole line comes to pieces."

"That's going to happen anyway if they break this division," Sevran said, frustrated. "And then there won't be anything left to form a new line. We're going to have to pull off the hill and fall back to the south."

"We won't get another chance at this," Marcus said. *Winter's already gone to fight the Beast. If we fold now, she'll lose her distraction.* But he couldn't tell Sevran that. "There's no ground on the road south better than this. If we don't stop them here, we'll be fighting in the streets of Vordan."

"We're not going to stop them here, damn it!" Sevran turned, his jaw set. "We're going to get cut to pieces in another hour. And if they get their coordination right, it won't even take that long."

Marcus was silent. It was true, of course. The only thing that had saved the raw recruits of the Third Division was that the enemy infantry and cavalry hadn't quite gotten their attacks timed right. It was a difficult trick, launching the cavalry assault to force the enemy into square just in time for the infantry to hammer them, but devastatingly effective. Watching the polyglot enemy force try to manage it made Marcus appreciate Give-Em-Hell, whose sense for that kind of timing was superb.

It also made him certain Janus wasn't on this part of the field in person. *He'd never tolerate that kind of bungling. Be thankful for small mercies.*

"We hold," Marcus said. "I told Fitz to send us cavalry when he can."

Sevran took a deep breath, fighting his emotions, and saluted. "That will help, sir. If they arrive soon."

Before Marcus could answer, drums thrilled all along the line, a quick

tattoo that every infantryman knew in his bones. *Emergency square.* The enemy
cavalry had returned.

To their credit, the scratch collection of recruits and garrison troops that
made up the Third Division responded quickly. *They've certainly had plenty of*
practice today. Each battalion folded in on itself by companies, transforming from
a long line into a roughly symmetrical diamond shape, with a point facing
toward the old front. The angle kept the sides of the adjacent squares from
facing one another, which helped cut down on friendly fire. Out ahead of them,
the cannoneers stayed by their guns, and the little cannon began firing. Canister flailed out blindly, storms of musket balls lashing through the smoke,
searching for an enemy barely glimpsed through the swirling mists.

Then they were there, shockingly close, a squadron of cuirassiers breaking
into view like a ship emerging from the fog. The closest gun let fly with a blast
of canister, and the front of the cavalry formation turned into a gory mess,
white-uniformed men toppling from their saddles even as their horses collapsed
in shrieking terror. The men behind came on, sabers drawn, shouting in
Murnskai as they rode toward the gunners. The cannoneers ran, not in panic
but in a planned retreat, leaving their guns and scurrying back to the cover of
the square. The fringe of massed bayonets parted to let them inside, then closed
again, presenting an unbroken wall of sharpened steel to the horsemen.

Marcus and Sevran also hurried to cover, taking shelter in one of the squares
of the reserve regiment. The cuirassiers split to flow around the squares, slashing
viciously at the bayonets as they passed but making little impression. A few fired
pistols into the mass of infantry, and some men fell, but the answering volleys
of musketry emptied many more saddles. The horsemen rode on, leaving dead
and dying men and animals in their wake, passing around the reserve squares as
well and receiving more punishment in their turn. They thundered by, wheel-
ing and re-forming.

It was too soon to see if they would try another assault. Marcus' eyes were
locked forward, in the direction of the enemy lines. Cannon were still firing,
the artillerists taking advantage of the better targets offered by the tight-packed
squares. *If they've got it right, this is when the infantry will attack, with the cuirassiers*
still hovering on our flank. He willed the smoke to stay empty just a little longer.
Come on . . .

Instead, a different kind of light emerged from the murk. Not the yellow-
white of a muzzle flash, or even the deeper yellow of lanterns, but a lurid,

sullen red. They pierced the smoke, two by two at first, then more and more. Hundreds of them. Thousands.

Red-eyes. The Beast's own bodies. Immune to pain, fear, and doubt.

Marcus looked around at the Third Division, all fresh-faced boys and old, tired garrison troops, fresh from civilian life or soft duty on the frontier. They had stood up to astonishing odds, done better than they had any right to. But he could feel them wavering, see it in the occasional glance backward or reluctance to put a musket to an already aching shoulder. Much more and they would break, just as Sevran had warned.

We're not going to make it. He glanced at the hill, where smoke continued to rise, and then farther north, toward where Winter had gone to make the gamble that would decide everything.

I'm sorry, Ellie. Marcus took a deep breath. *We'll fight as long as we can.*

"*Hold the line!*" he shouted as the first of the red-eyes loped out of the smoke.

CHAPTER THIRTY-THREE

WINTER

Winter felt something give in her right shoulder with an audible *pop*, sending bolts of agony through her body. She screamed, despite the pain it brought to her raw throat, her dangling feet kicking wildly.

Another sound, the harsh shriek of the desert wind, began down at the edge of hearing and rose to a rapid crescendo. The tall whirlwind of sand that surrounded the castle collapsed, the wind dying away and the flying grit falling to earth like dusty rain. A concentrated blast of the power of the Great Desol, a stream of wind and sand as dark and solid as mud, slammed directly into the face of the emaciated Penitent, sending him stumbling backward. He crossed his arms in front of his face, and distortion shimmered in the air, bending the wind around him.

At the same time, the force holding Winter up vanished. She fell in mid-kick, landing badly, and more pain flared in her ankle. Her shoulder was agony, her right arm hanging limp and useless, and she gasped raggedly for breath. On the pile of rubble, Jane grinned.

"You can't be everywhere at once; that's always the problem," she said, her smile growing wide. "Well, *you* can't."

As sand and dust filtered out of the air, dark figures became visible, climbing over the top of the ruined castle wall and pouring in through the gate. The Steel Ghost's whirlwind had held them back, but now that he was otherwise occupied, they came on at a run, red eyes glowing. One of the two big men who flanked Jane advanced on Winter, drawing his sword. Winter's own weapons were lying in the dust, somewhere nearby. She managed to pull herself to her feet, but even that took much of her remaining strength, and the thought of moving her right arm brought further stabs of agony. She held up her other hand, judging the distance to the brute.

If I can get to him with Infernivore before he cuts me in half, maybe . . .

It wasn't much of a chance. Much easier to surrender. Close her eyes. *Die. Then the pain will stop.*

I won't.

From the shadow of one of the ruined buildings, pure darkness slammed out, a finger-thin lance that drilled neatly through the big red-eye's head and out the other side. The man dropped in his tracks, sword skittering across the ground, and his equally large companion standing beside Jane just had time to look for the source of the attack before he, too, was scythed down.

Alex limped into view, one hand raised. Her hair was matted, and blood ran down her face. As Winter watched, she coughed, spilling more blood onto her chin. But she grinned defiantly, teeth stained red.

"Winter!" she shouted hoarsely. "Do it!"

"No," Jane snarled. "Westeb! Kill her!"

The tall Penitent lurched forward, his tongueless voice making a strange croaking sound. He pushed through the blast of the sandstorm and raised his hands, shimmering coronas dancing around them.

Like a hawk diving at a rabbit, Sothe came at him, wings folded, dropping out of the sky with shocking speed. The Penitent heard her coming just in time, and twisted aside as the marble assassin executed a neat somersault and landed on her feet, her arm coming around at throat height with blade in hand. His distortion shimmered around her wrist, but her strength was far more than human, pushing the blade forward in spite of the power of his magic. Across the bottom of his mask it left a long, ragged line that drooled blood, but Sothe hadn't had enough force left to sever the artery. The Penitent tightened his fist, and the rainbow colors around Sothe's arm redoubled, tightening their grip.

"Forget her!" Jane said, backing up along the ruined beam as Winter stumbled toward her. "Kill *Winter*. Kill her now!"

The Penitent kept one hand pointed at Sothe while the other swung toward Winter. Sothe jerked toward him, but the distortion held her arm fast now, keeping him just beyond her reach. The assassin paused, spread her wings, then *lunged*, throwing all her awesome strength into the leap. Her arm, pinned to the air, was wrenched backward, the elbow first bending the wrong way and then tearing free entirely in a spray of stone chips. The Penitent barely had time to turn back to Sothe before she landed on his chest with the weight of a falling statue, bearing him to the ground as distorted colors bloomed all around her.

The desert wind was blowing again, pushing and slashing at the approaching red-eyes, while Alex fired bolt after ebony bolt to bring down the closest. Jane had reached the end of the beam she was standing on, her eyes now locked on Winter, and her grin seemed forced.

"You don't want this," she said. "I know you don't."

Winter lunged with the last of her strength. Jane shifted backward another step, missed her footing and the pile of rubble, and went sprawling, rolling over to land faceup in the dirt. Before she could rise, Winter was on her, grabbing her wrist with her left hand.

Infernivore *raged*, as though it knew the scent of the prey it had once been denied. It roared through the spot where they touched, flowing from Winter's body into Jane's, wrapping itself around the great crimson form of the Beast. Jane snarled, and her other hand came up, grabbing Winter by the back of her neck. She forced her head down, as though for a kiss, and the red lights in her eyes flared until they obliterated the world.

Winter found herself standing . . . somewhere else.

There was nothing underfoot but a swirling dark whirlwind, stretching away endlessly in every direction. Overhead, banks of black cloud streamed past, as though driven by a hurricane. Two shapes slammed and grappled against each other, sending ripples through the sky. They were serpents of light, as big as worlds, glowing with brilliant energy as they thrashed and spun. One was a bright, vibrant green, the other a deep, sullen red. Lightning of both colors crackled between them. Each serpent had a hold of the other near the tail, locking them together, each devouring the other and being devoured in turn.

Just in front of her, staring up at the warring titans, was Jane. Her hair writhed around her, driven by the intangible wind, and her whole body was outlined in red light. Her eyes were pure crimson brilliance, from edge to edge.

The last time Infernivore and the Beast had done battle, it had been for only an instant, but it had been nothing like this. It must have shown on Winter's face, because Jane smiled, arcs of crimson lightning playing over her teeth.

"Not what you were expecting?" Her voice was shot through with a roar like thunder. "I have *grown* since we last met, Winter."

"Not enough," Winter said. "I will destroy you."

"Perhaps." Jane cocked her head. "But not before I destroy you as well. Is that really what you want?"

"It's not about what I want," Winter said. "It's about what needs to be done."

"What needs to be done." Jane strode closer, eyes flaring bright. When she spoke again, her voice sounded more like Jane's and less like a monster's. "That's what you care about, isn't it? Your precious duty."

"You never understood me," Winter said.

"Never understood you?" Jane's mouth twisted into a red-tinged snarl. "I *loved* you. Back at the Prison, I gave you my heart. I *forgave* you, even when you left me for that monster Ganhide. Do you know what he did to me? Shall I tell you about our *wedding night*?"

"I shouldn't have run." Winter's voice was quiet.

"I *forgave* you," Jane repeated. "And when you came back, it made everything worthwhile. Everything I'd gone through, every awful thing I'd endured, all the blood I'd spilled. All of it! I loved you, and I thought you loved me."

Winter shut her eyes for a moment. "I did love you, Jane."

"Liar!"

Overhead, the great serpents writhed. Red lightning slashed against green, bolts colliding and detonating in showers of sparks. The wind moaned like it was in agony.

"If you love someone, you don't abandon her," Jane said. "You don't choose your uniform and your *fucking* general over her."

"I did love you," Winter said. She felt oddly calm amid the thunderous crash of battling demons. *This*, at least, she understood. "But you're wrong. You don't give up your own mind just because you love someone. There was more to my life than you."

"*Fuck* that," Jane snarled. "You're a *fucking* traitor."

"I'm sorry you can't understand."

"You're sorry." Jane's snarl abruptly vanished. "It's all right. I forgive you. Again. All you have to do is give in, Winter. Just let go, and we can be together forever, here inside the Beast."

"What about the rest of the world?"

"*Fuck* the rest of the world. I don't care about it, and neither do you."

"You're wrong," Winter said.

"If you keep fighting, we'll both die," Jane said. "The demons will devour each other, and that will be the end of everything. Is that what you want?"

"No." Winter took a deep breath. "I want to live. I want to kiss Cyte, and help Raesinia, and get to know my brother. I want to see what happens next, once the wars are finally over."

"You don't need any of that," Jane said. "We'll have each other. When we were at the Prison, that was enough."

"It wasn't," Winter said. "We just didn't know any better."

"Please, Winter. Don't do this."

"I have to." Winter shook her head. "I really am sorry, Jane. I wish . . . things were different."

Jane threw back her head and screamed, a high, keening note. Lightning crackled from her in all directions, and overhead the red serpent surged forward. When she looked back at Winter, her eyes glowed so bright they were pure white, and her voice was thick with the thunder of the Beast.

"Then I will destroy you," she said. "I am stronger now. I will rend your mind asunder and scatter it to my winds, and your demon with it."

Then, like a distant echo, a tiny voice. "Please, Winter."

The Beast stepped forward, one hand raised. Crimson energy gathered in its palm. When it snapped out, Winter threw up her arms to defend herself, but the strobing bolt of lightning wrapped around her like a lasso. She felt its energy run through her body, thousands of silver needles tearing at her soul.

Overhead, Infernivore was falling back, pressed before the Beast. Winter was gripped by despair.

It's no good. The Beast is too strong. She'd waited too long, let it absorb too many minds. *I can't stop it. Nothing can stop it now.*

Once again they'd put their hopes in her. *The Eldest. Alex, Abraham, Sothe. Marcus, Raesinia. Everyone. And they're all going to die—*

No.

Winter gritted her teeth and pushed back. She put everything into it, her soul, her *self*, meeting the Beast head-on. For a moment she and Jane were face-to-face, power straining against power, mind pushing against mind. And then she saw—

—herself, as a girl. Awkward, uncertain kisses, hidden in a gap in the hedges. Days spent together, happiness bright even in darkness. Nights spent together, clandestine experiments, her own voice giving a soft moan.

Waiting in darkness. For her, for Winter to come to the rescue. As she'd promised.

Ganhide. Bruises, tears, cruel words, and rough hands. Pain, and the feel of the skin of his throat parting under the knife. The kiss of heat as his house took fire.

More images, faster and faster, Jane's life flowing between Winter's fingers. And her own, through Jane's. Winter felt Jane's spirit, pressed tight against her.

Oh, it said. *Oh.*

She saw herself seeing Jane, and Jane seeing her seeing Jane, and on and on, the hall of mirrors never-ending.

I didn't understand, Jane thought, as Winter's life flickered around her. *I couldn't see what I was doing to you.* Winter felt the brush of lips against her own. *I'm sorry. For everything.*

I forgive you, Winter answered.

They pulled apart. And there were three people on the cloud-swept plain. Jane had stepped *away* from the Beast, pulling free of the red light, leaving only a dark void surrounded by crimson radiance. She stood between the Beast and Winter, its lightning arcing into her body.

"No." The Beast's voice was totally inhuman now. "*This is not possible. You are a part of me.*"

"Maybe you don't know yourself as well as you think," Jane said. "Good-bye, Winter."

"Good-bye," Winter whispered.

The arc connecting Jane and the Beast flared even brighter, the power of the demon turned against itself. In the sky overhead, the red serpent fell back, and the green advanced, wrapping around and around its adversary. The Beast screamed, a wordless peal of rage and anguish, as Infernivore devoured its substance, drawing the cloudscape inward to a point. Out of the corner of her eye, Winter saw a single ring of swirling cloud spin away, as though flung outward from the vortex.

Then the red was fading away, and green filled the world. Winter felt Infernivore flowing back into her, returning to its lair in the pit of her soul, as sated as a snake that had devoured an elephant. A moment later a tide of oblivion, as dark and cold as the depths of the ocean, obliterated her.

CHAPTER THIRTY-FOUR

MARCUS

A few miles to the northeast of the grounds of Ohnlei Palace, the kings of Vordan had long maintained a hunting lodge. It was small, by royal standards, with only a dozen bedrooms for the king and his immediate circle, plus servants' quarters, stables, kennels, and everything else that a monarch might need when he wanted to ride out and kill hapless animals. It was called the Rose Lodge, in honor of the curling vines that crawled up and over trellises set into the walls, and which in the spring made the place a riot of red, white, and pink.

Now, of course, the colors were gone, the gardens ready to sleep away the winter. Leaves crunched underfoot as Marcus walked beside Raesinia down the path to the front door. Ahead of them, two sentries—one of the Girls' Own, another from the Grenadier Guards—saluted Marcus and then bowed deep to the queen.

They were only the innermost ring of a web of security that Vordan hadn't seen since Duke Orlanko had been toppled from the Concordat. Cavalry patrols rode through the woods, and an outer cordon of sentries—ignorant of what, exactly, they were protecting—challenged visitors before they even came in sight of the house. In addition to the guards at the doors and windows, there were sharpshooters on the roof, and no horses were allowed anywhere closer than the outer ring. Inside, a couple of longtime palace servants provided for the needs of the single occupant and kept surreptitious watch on his every move. And, unbeknownst to nearly everyone, Raesinia had asked the Steel Ghost to keep watch as well, to prevent any supernatural intervention.

There were moments when Marcus thought it was a bit paranoid. But given what the lodge's occupant had accomplished in the past, at least a *little* paranoia could be justified. Janus bet Vhalnich, commanding general, First Consul, and arch-traitor, had always been a hard man to pin down.

Raesinia's two bodyguards, Joanna and Barely, were back at her side after their departure to take part in the battle. Joanna had a bandage wrapped around her head, but otherwise the two seemed to have made it through the fighting unscathed. That was more than could be said for much of the Girls' Own, or indeed the whole of the Second Division. They'd borne the brunt of the enemy assault, and casualties had been high, among soldiers and volunteers alike. Marcus had heard the stories of Raesinia's rush forward, how she took the flag when the men started to flee the field. *Sometimes I don't know whether I want to kiss her or lock her in a cell for her own good.*

The guards opened the door, and they went inside. The lodge was decorated in a rustic style, heavy on preserved animal heads and ornaments made from antlers and bones. A silent servant directed them through the foyer and into a sitting room. Janus, dressed in a bathrobe, sat on a chaise with his feet propped up on a cushion. He was reading a book, turning the pages with his long, thin fingers. Already he looked improved from the skeletal figure Marcus had met back in the Pale valley; his face was filling out, the dark circles under his huge gray eyes receding.

He looked up as they came in, then carefully marked his place with a bookmark and set the volume aside.

"Your Highness," he said, inclining his head. "Marcus. I'm glad to finally see you."

The smile that crossed his face, there and gone again in a moment, was the old Janus to perfection. But there was something in his eyes that hadn't been there before, a distant pain that made the smile feel like more of a mask than it had been.

"We thought it best not to come until things were fully settled," Marcus said. "Alves surrendered yesterday, and with it the last of the rebel armies. The war is over."

Janus nodded. "And so passes away the dream of empire, to wait for another generation." He smiled again. "Or perhaps longer. We can always hope, eh?"

"We all know it was never *your* dream," Raesinia said. In her voice there was anger, kept carefully in check. "Why are you alive, Janus? All the others who were taken by the Beast just . . . collapsed."

In some cases that had been midcharge. Marcus' wavering men on the left flank had watched in stunned amazement as the mass of red-eyes coming at them simply dropped in their tracks, as though some cosmic puppeteer had abandoned his marionettes.

Janus' eyes were hooded. "I know what happened to me. As to *why*, I don't know that I'll ever be able to say. I kept my mind intact inside the Beast, which no one else seemed to manage for long. Perhaps I was simply fortunate." He shook his head. "Even so, it was a near thing, finding my way back to my body as it all collapsed around me. Would it have been easier for you if I hadn't?"

"Easier? Maybe." Raesinia shook her head. "I know you helped us. If not for you, Winter might never have reached Vordan City and Marcus might not have come back to meet her. But . . ."

"But you can hardly explain that to the public at large." Janus gave another summer-lightning smile. "I quite understand."

"They're going to want your head, Janus."

He looked up at her, unfazed. "Are you planning to give it to them?"

Raesinia glanced at Marcus. They'd been up late, trying to figure this out between them.

"I don't think that would be . . . just," Raesinia said slowly. "But at the same time, you'll be seen as a threat if you stay anywhere near Vordan. We thought—"

"Exile," Janus said. "Probably to the Southern Kingdoms. Perfectly appropriate, and probably better than I deserve."

He patted the book he'd been reading, which Marcus now saw was titled *Journeys Beyond the Great Desol and Through the Kingdoms of the South*. Marcus rolled his eyes and sighed.

"Do you ever get tired of doing parlor tricks?" he said.

"One takes one's amusement where one can," Janus said modestly.

"That's it?" Raesinia said. "I know it's unfair to you. I thought . . ."

"That I would fight?" Janus shrugged. "What would be the point? I know the position you're in, probably better than you do. If I were in your place, exile would be the best you could possibly hope for. Fairness doesn't come into it." He looked down at the book, his spidery fingers spread across the cover. "Besides. I'm . . . tired. A long trip will be just the thing."

"I'll make the arrangements, then," Raesinia said. "We'll keep it quiet until you've left port. No need to risk riots."

"Of course. Whatever you think best."

Raesinia looked up at Marcus again, questioning. Marcus nodded.

"Very well," the queen said. "I think that's all."

"Could we have a moment alone?" Marcus said.

Raesinia nodded slowly. "If you like. I'll be outside."

She left the sitting room, closing the door behind her. Marcus lowered himself into the chair opposite Janus, and there was a moment of silence.

"You saved us, again," Marcus said. "You saved everyone."

"An exaggeration," Janus said. "At best, I gave things a bit of a nudge when I found myself able. Winter saved us. And Sothe, and Alex, and you, and everyone who fought at Bear Ridge."

"Even so. You're just going to go off to exile?"

"Whatever my . . . contribution, my name—my *body*—were used to do terrible things." Janus shook his head. "I have had my chance at history, Marcus. The time has come for me to sink into well-deserved obscurity."

"And Mya?" Marcus said quietly. "Are you giving up?"

There was another pause.

"I used to believe in destiny," Janus said. "It was so obvious, when you looked at her. So *clear*. And then . . ."

"You've changed your mind?"

"Perhaps. Maybe things are only obvious in hindsight. When I think how much had to go just right in order for us to reach this moment—how easily it could have gone another way . . ." He smiled again. "Maybe there is no destiny. Maybe things just happen and nobody knows why and none of it means anything. Or maybe the pattern is more complicated than I understood. Either way, I don't think it needs my help."

"So what are you going to do?" Marcus said. "Find some king who needs a general?"

"I think not. I'm done with campaigns and armies, Marcus." Janus settled back in his chaise. "I'll write, I imagine. There are quite a few monographs I've composed over the years that need to be set down properly. And the wildlife of the Southern Kingdoms is vastly underexplored. A real gap in the literature. I'll be certain to send back my findings."

Was there a sardonic grin there, at the corner of Janus' lip? Marcus couldn't be sure. The big gray eyes seemed so open, but they never truly showed what thoughts lay beneath.

Slowly, Marcus got to his feet. He straightened up and saluted one last time.

"Thank you, sir. For everything." He paused. "It's been an honor."

"Likewise, Marcus," Janus said. "More than you can imagine."

RAESINIA

Raesinia found Winter on the roof walk that faced the front of the palace, looking south toward Vordan City. This would once have been the most magnificent view in Vordan, taking in the vast sweep of Ohnlei's gardens, the stately facades of the Ministry buildings, and the grand drive with its fountains. Now the fountains were turned off and the gardens were a torn-up mess, thanks to the army's long stay. The Ministry buildings still stood, except for the burned-out Cobweb, but though the sun had barely set, most of the windows were dark. It had been less than a week since the Battle of Bear Ridge, and the functionaries who made the wheels of bureaucracy turn were understandably still nervous.

Winter wore her uniform, stitched and cleaned, with her sword on her hip. She bore little resemblance to the dirty, gory mess cavalry patrols had brought in, covered in blood, one arm out of joint. Alex had been little better, one leg and several ribs broken, coughing blood. It had been Abraham who'd tended to them both, once he'd recovered enough of his own strength, and his power had once again worked miracles.

But not for Sothe. Raesinia swallowed. She didn't want to think about Sothe.

Winter, leaning on the wrought-iron railing, turned and bowed as Raesinia came in. Raesinia waved away the formality, slouching against the rail herself. She'd left her guards below, and the two of them were alone, far above the bustling life that was slowly returning to the palace. The sky was dark gray, shading to pink at the western horizon.

"How are you feeling?" Raesinia asked.

"All right," Winter said. She lifted her arm, as though marveling at the absence of pain. "Thank God for Abraham."

"He's good at putting people back together," Raesinia said. "But how are you *feeling*?"

"Like I'm waiting for the other shoe to drop," Winter said, turning back to the view over the palace grounds. "I know it's over, but somehow I can't make myself believe it."

"I know what you mean," Raesinia said. "Like any minute someone is going to ride in with news of the next war."

"We've fought the Khandarai, the Murnskai, the Borels, the League, and ourselves, twice," Winter said. "Who else is *left*? An invasion from the moon?"

Raesinia grinned, but Winter was shaking her head.

"The hell of it is," she went on, "all that and we're back where we started. What did we accomplish?"

"We stopped the Beast. *You* stopped the Beast. That has to count for something."

"We let it out in the first place, when we marched on Elysium." Winter waved south, toward the city. "For the people out there, what's changed? We didn't forge a new empire or build a utopia. We buried a lot of young men and women and wore out a lot of boot leather."

"It may not be a utopia," Raesinia said, "but I think Vordan is better off. We've got the Deputies-General—"

"—and what a great help they've been—" Winter muttered.

"—and we're rid of Orlanko. The Priests of the Black won't be meddling anymore, or snatching people off to the dungeons under Elysium." Raesinia looked south, too. The lights of the city were just about visible, a dim glow on the horizon. "And even if they don't know it, those people are living without a sword hanging over their heads. You did what *Karis* couldn't do, Winter."

"I had a lot of help," Winter said. She looked back at Raesinia. "I'm sorry about Sothe. She was a good woman."

"I know that," Raesinia said, her throat suddenly tight. "I just hope that *she* did, at the end."

For a moment they stood together in silence. Winter turned her back on the view, shaking her head, and leaned against the rail.

"So, did you just come up here to ask after my health, Your Highness?"

"No, as it happens," Raesinia said. "I wanted to talk to you. I've made my decision."

Another silence, this one darker and heavier.

"I'm going to marry Marcus," Raesinia said after a moment.

"Congratulations." Winter cocked her head. "Damn. That will make me your sister-in-law, won't it?"

"I suppose it will." Raesinia smiled. The revelation of Winter and Marcus being family definitely took getting used to. "We'll wait a while, after the

wedding. Six months, say. Long enough that people get used to the idea of
Marcus as king, and so that he and I can put some contingency plans into place.
After that . . ." Raesinia took a deep breath. "I want you to use Infernivore to
take my demon."

"You know that I have no idea what will happen if I do that," Winter said.
"You were nearly dead when you took it on. Removing it might kill you. Or
it might destroy your mind, like it did Jen Alhundt's."

"I know." Raesinia paused. "I talked to Ennika."

"Feor told me she woke up," Winter said. "She also told me that at first she
could barely speak."

"It did seem to inflict some . . . damage on her mind," Raesinia said. "But
it's healing. She's almost normal now."

"Still. There's no guarantee it would work the same way for you."

"I know."

"You're secure now, aren't you? Why take the risk?"

Raesinia's hands tightened on the iron rail, the rough metal digging into
her skin. "The people of Vordan would never tolerate a demon-host for a queen.
I don't look any older than the day I died for the first time. Sooner or later everyone will find out. I'll either have to flee the country or fake my death."

"Marcus could hide you."

"And then what? Watch him grow old without me?" Raesinia shook her
head. "There's also the matter of the succession. I want a normal life, Winter.
I never thought I could have that. You've given me a chance, and I want to
take it."

"And if things don't go . . . well?" Winter said.

"Then Marcus will be king. After a suitable period of mourning, he'll
marry again, and there'll be an heir. The kingdom will go on."

Winter sighed. "If it's what you really want, I can hardly say no. I'll talk
to Feor, and to Ennika once she's fully recovered. See if there's anything we
can do to make it . . . easier."

"Thank you," Raesinia said. "We'll have Abraham on hand as well." She
let out a long breath. "That's for the future. I've got a wedding to plan first."

"Good luck. I'd rather organize a battle."

"Have you given any thought to what you're going to do?" Raesinia said.

"A little," Winter said awkwardly. "Cyte thinks we should stay in the army.
I'm . . . not sure. She's only ever seen how things are when we're at war.

Peacetime . . ." Winter shrugged. "I may not be cut out for watching over parades and barracks politics."

"Can I offer another suggestion?" Raesinia said.

Winter looked at her cautiously. "Go ahead."

"The Black Priests are gone," Raesinia said. "I think we agree that's a good thing, on the whole. But they had a lot of demons locked away who are now free to come back into the world, and there's nobody watching for natural demon-hosts. In a few years there're going to be a *lot* of supernatural toddlers running around."

"People are going to have to learn to deal with it."

Raesinia nodded. "And we have the chance to help them. I want to start an organization to handle demon-hosts here in Vordan, and hopefully across the continent. We can work with the people at the Mountain, and—"

Winter held up a hand. "What do you mean, handle?"

"Not locking them up, like the Church did. But they're going to need to be guided, educated, protected. Everyone is going to have to learn that demons aren't always evil, and that's going to take time. And when a demon-host *does* use their powers to hurt people, someone is going to have to make sure they're apprehended and punished, as is appropriate under the law."

"Sort of an Armsmen for demons?" Winter smiled wryly. "I can see how that would be useful, I suppose. So you want me to help?"

"Actually," Raesinia said, "I was hoping that you would be the first captain. Or whatever we end up calling the top job."

Unexpectedly, Winter began to laugh, quietly at first and then so hard she doubled herself over. Raesinia watched her, concerned, as she finally subsided, wiping her eyes and gasping for breath.

"I didn't think the idea was *that* ridiculous," the queen muttered.

"It's a fine idea," Winter said. "But *why*?" She gestured down at herself. "What is it about me? Why does everyone seem to think I'm fit to be in charge of things?"

Raesinia cocked her head, puzzled. "Because you've been good at everything you've put your hand to, I imagine."

"I—" Winter paused, then shook her head. "Never mind."

"Will you do it?"

Winter let out a long breath, looking thoughtful. "I'll have to think about it."

Epilogue

WINTER
ONE YEAR LATER

It was the first time Winter had worn her new dress uniform. It was elegant, dove gray with blue piping, the two silver stars of the new rank of commander on each shoulder. It was also well tailored, unlike the old hand-me-down uniforms she'd been making do with while the new organization's look was finalized. This uniform actually fit, and the figure she saw looking back at her from the mirror was unsettlingly different.

"It looks good on you," Cyte said, coming in from the living room.

She wore a blue army uniform, her shoulders bearing the new General Staff insignia, but the tailoring was the same and Winter had to admit she liked the way it looked on her, too. Winter slid a finger into her collar and tugged, awkwardly, then ran a hand through her hair. She'd started cutting it when it reached her shoulders, but she was still getting used to the feel of it against the back of her neck.

"Thanks," Winter said. "Yours looks . . . um . . . good. Also."

"You need to relax." Cyte crossed the bedroom and put her arms around Winter's waist, drawing her close for a kiss. Winter closed her eyes as their lips met, letting the world melt away. "We're not exactly charging Borelgai lines tonight."

"It's worse than that," Winter muttered, reluctant to pull back. "It's a party."

The Great Hall of Ohnlei Palace lived up to its name. Possibly the largest room Winter had ever been in, it was tiered like an upside-down cake, with a dance floor in the center at the bottom and successive levels surrounding it, looking down. It had been designed to give maximum visibility to the royal family and whoever was lucky enough to receive an invitation to the bottom tier, and it certainly accomplished that task. To Winter, being there felt like being a lion on display in a menagerie.

Her arm through Cyte's, she fixed the smile on her face as she came in, passing from the relative darkness of the corridor into a brilliant explosion of light. Candles were everywhere, glowing from mirrored sconces and shining in their hundreds from the glittering chandelier overhead. Every surface seemed to be either gilded or polished to a fine sheen, and reflections of the thousands of tiny lights danced and spun in every direction.

The candlelight also reflected from the attire of the guests, who were dressed in their finest. Soldiers from the Girls' Own, now officially tasked with the security of the palace, stood at stiff attention in their dress uniforms, silver fittings gleaming bright. Winter felt her chest swell with pride at the sight of them, faces professionally blank, eyes alert.

As soon as they stepped out onto the floor, the hidden orchestra struck up a light, fast tune. Cyte spun in front of Winter, grinning devilishly, one hand extended.

"Now?" Winter said. "I don't get to . . . you know, get my bearings first?"

"You can get your bearings later," Cyte said. "When I need to catch my breath."

Winter had confessed, at an early point in their relationship, that she didn't know how to dance. It wasn't a skill that she'd ever had occasion to learn, and frankly, she'd been at peace with that, but Cyte had immediately proclaimed it unacceptable. Tutors were procured and quite a few ankles kicked. Ultimately, Winter found the movements less alien than she'd worried they might be, and once she'd gotten over her fear of embarrassing herself in public, she'd actually rather come to enjoy it. *Of course, I've never quite had the ability to embarrass myself in front of* this *many people.*

Fortunately, Cyte didn't give her a chance to overthink things. Her hands positioned Winter's firmly at her waist and shoulder, and they were off, executing a step whose name Winter had forgotten but whose motions her feet thankfully recalled.

The dance floor was full of couples whirling, colorful dresses and dark suits, uniforms and polished gems. Winter recognized a few of the inner circle. Second Prince Matthew, the ambassador from Borel, grinned as he partnered one court lady after another, under the watchful eye of one of his Life Guards. Alek

Giforte, in Armsmen green, danced with his daughter. Abby still wore a colonel's eagle; she'd refused promotion and stayed in command of the Girls' Own.

The Preacher danced with Viera, showing surprising grace. Given the thirty-year age difference, the announcement of their engagement had surprised everyone, but when Viera's father had objected she'd apparently threatened to blow the family home off the hillside with flash powder, and that had been the end of that.

After a few rounds, Winter managed to extricate herself, though a still-grinning Cyte insisted she'd be back for more. Winter made her way to the edge of the floor, where a few tables and chairs had been set up in front of the royal dais, laden with fruits, confections, and wine. Give-Em-Hell was holding court, telling stories from the Khandarai campaign to a collection of young officers, with Val sitting nearby offering pointed asides. Winter spotted Alex, who wore the same dove gray uniform she did, sitting beside a tray of chocolate-coated strawberries. She stood up as Winter approached, and they embraced warmly.

"I heard you were back," Winter said. "Sorry I haven't gotten the chance to stop by. You know how busy things are."

Alex rolled her eyes. "Believe me, I know. Where do you think all those reports you don't have time to read come from?"

"How are things going at the Mountain?"

"Slowly." Alex shook her head. "I can't believe I let you talk me into this liaison business."

"You were the best choice—"

"I know. I know." Alex sighed. "But you know how the Eldest loves to talk, and Feor's just as bad. I swear those two are up every night debating . . . ethics, or the nature of demons, or *something*. Trying to get them to actually agree to *do* anything means going down a hundred blind alleys."

"I'm glad they're getting along, at least."

Alex nodded. "Old metal-face is as grim as ever, though. You'd think he'd take the chance to let down his hair a little."

Winter grinned. It was hard to imagine the Steel Ghost ever relaxing. "When are you going back?"

"Another week." Alex yawned. "The Eldest said you should visit, too, when you get the chance."

"When I have the time."

It had become Winter's mantra. When she'd accepted Raesinia's offer to lead the new Ministry of the Occult, she'd had no idea that the work involved would dwarf even what she'd had to deal with as a division-general. *Fortunately, we've got a few more years to get things up and running before the demons* really *start popping up.*

"What about Abraham?" she said, as the orchestra wound down. The couples on the floor broke apart into a milling crowd, and the buzz of conversation rose. "Have you heard anything?"

"I got a note from him from Mohkba," Alex said. "He convinced the Church to let him go through their records—don't ask me how—and he thought he knew where he was going. He said he'd write again once he got there."

Winter nodded silently. *I hope he finds what he's looking for.*

"I should pay my respects," Winter said. "I'll find you later."

Alex lifted a strawberry in salute. Winter stood, pushing past the assembled grandees to the royal dais. It was flanked by a pair of statues, larger-than-life abstract female figures, carved from marble, with vast, curving wings. They mirrored a similar pair out on the grand drive, at the front of the palace. Raesinia had ordered them made not long after the battle. Winter looked at each of them in turn, then lowered her eyes.

Thank you.

When she looked up again, the king and queen were both watching her. Marcus sat awkwardly in his throne, less than comfortable in his court finery. He'd gained weight in the past year, and the streaks of gray in his hair had grown. When he caught her eye, though, he grinned and scratched his beard.

Raesinia, for her part, looked perfectly at ease in an elaborately frilled and bejeweled dress, which must have had to be resewn quite recently to accommodate the bulge of the royal belly. She was taller, too, and her shoulders were broader. Winter thought she looked radiant.

"Winter!" she said. "It's so good to see you."

"And you, Your Highness." Winter bowed to the couple.

"We were just talking about the new flik-flik lines," Raesinia said. "There are at least two commercial companies pushing to link Vordan City to Hamvelt, and competition is getting quite vicious. I was telling Marcus that we might have to put the whole affair under the purview of the Ministry of Finance. Surely having an efficient communications network is in the national interest. I'm sure Cora can work something out."

"And I was just telling Raesinia that she ought to stop working for the night," Marcus said. "How are you, Winter?"

"Good," Winter said. It still surprised her that she could say that and actually mean it. "It's still a mountain of work at the Ministry, but I think we're making progress." She hesitated. "I got a report yesterday that I thought you might want to know about."

Raesinia raised an eyebrow. "Something interesting?"

"In a way," Winter said. "There's a trader from Khandar in the city, and he's been talking to sailors from the south who stopped at Ashe-Katarion. Apparently there are . . . rumors."

Raesinia and Marcus looked at each other.

"What kind of rumors?" Marcus said slowly.

"A gray-eyed foreigner has led a great revolution," Winter said. "He's struck the chains from the slaves and helped the people defeat their cruel overlords. Now he's leading an army into the depths of the south, in search of the lost city of the gods."

There was a long moment of silence as the chatter of the court washed over them.

"I thought," Raesinia said, "he told you that he was done with campaigns and armies?"

"He lasted a year." Marcus sighed. "I suppose that's better than I expected."